THE
FAILURES

THE
FAILURES

—

BENJAMIN LIAR

DAW BOOKS
New York

Jacket design and illustration by *the*BookDesigners

Interior design by Fine Design
Edited by Betsy Wollheim

DAW Book Collectors No. 1963

DAW Books
An imprint of Astra Publishing House
dawbooks.com
DAW Books and its logo are registered trademarks of Astra Publishing House

Printed in the United States of America

Library of Congress Cataloging-in-Publication Data

Names: Liar, Benjamin, author.
Title: The failures / Benjamin Liar.
Description: First edition. | New York : DAW Books, 2024. |
Series: The Wanderlands ; [1]
Identifiers: LCCN 2024003323 (print) | LCCN 2024003324 (ebook) |
ISBN 9780756415273 (hardcover) | ISBN 9780756415280 (ebook)
Subjects: LCGFT: Apocalyptic fiction. | Fantasy fiction. | Novels.
Classification: LCC PS3612.I226 F35 2024 (print) |
LCC PS3612.I226 (ebook) | DDC 813/.6--dc23/eng/20240202
LC record available at https://lccn.loc.gov/2024003323
LC ebook record available at https://lccn.loc.gov/2024003324

First edition: July 2024
10 9 8 7 6 5 4 3 2 1

For the ones who never gave up

THE MOUNTAIN

A DIAGRAM OF THE END OF THE WORLD

by Bind e Reynald, Scholae First Mark

*for all those who wish to understand these terrible events
and their geography*

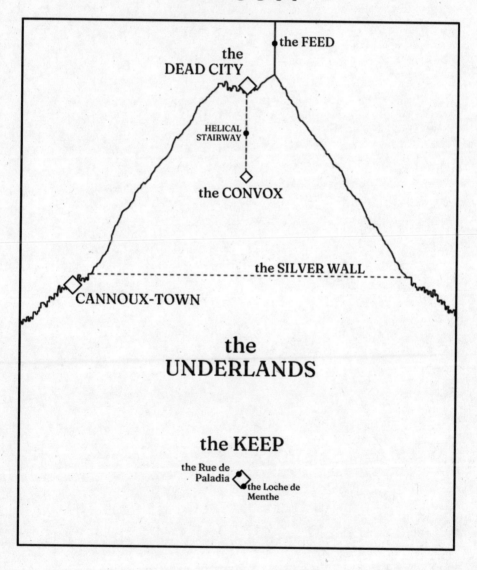

THE
FAILURES

PART I

THE CONVOX

The Utility of Fire

*"If we are truly just cogs, and part of some great machine,
then it must run poorly indeed."*

—ALVAREZ, 'ILLADIUM'

Something that is very much like a man makes his way down an old stone passageway, letting his fingers trail along the dusty wall. The thing that is not
quite a man is ruggedly handsome, with pale-gray eyes and laugh lines at their
corners. His clothes are travel-stained but of surpassingly fine make. His name—
at the moment—is West.

He wears a weapon at his hip that he does not need, but appearances must be
kept. There aren't too many creatures in these lost and broken days that can hurt
something like West, but his father had always said that something worth doing
is worth doing well. He wears the weapon with flair, a dashing jut of hip that
shows off the fine gold filigree and hand enameling.

West has been traveling for days through the darkness beneath the Mountain,
that monstrous edifice, so large that civilizations have risen and fallen on its
slopes. The Mountain is offensive to West; that something so magnificent, so
huge in history and legend should find itself so fallen, lost, and trivial. But then,
much the same thing could be said of the Wanderlands itself; much the same thing
could be said of *West*.

He does not often entertain such thoughts, and it is a testament to his dreary
surroundings that he is doing so now.

The worst thing about traveling to the Underlands is that there are no Doors
here, no easy way to step from somewhere to somewhere else, no quick way to
bypass the tedious business of walking. He had been forced to enter through the
rift that had opened untold ages ago in the side of the Mountain, exposing the
warren of long-black rooms and tunnels. Fortunately there was a backwater town
called Cannoux nearby, and there *had* been a Door there. He is annoyed at this
flagrant expense of his time, this pedestrian journeying, but an interesting invitation has been received.

And West is not the sort of creature who lets an interesting thing pass by.

Still, it is an unpleasant journey. He has the sense, and has had it for some days now, of descending into the black belly of a decaying beast. He has had the unclean sensation of climbing into a grave. West cannot in any sense be described as a sentimental person, but it is impossible to walk through these empty halls and passages without thinking about the thousands and millions of thinking beings that must have died here. Died huddled around failing lights, burning anything that would burn, praying to gods that didn't care for a salvation that wouldn't come.

West has been alive for a long time, but even he could not say how long the Underlands has been dead. Nor, even, how long it took to die. The Silver Age had been a finely crafted creature, and its corpse rotted slow.

There is a fire ahead; it is a thin flicker of light in a sea of shadows. A faint golden spark in a depthless black. West has sight beyond any mere man, however, and he perceives that the fire was built into a large open area and that the backdrop is a helical curve he cannot quite make out in the flickering light. He can see four figures at the fire, still little more than silhouettes. He makes sure his weapon is at the ready in case some braggadocio is required and, after some consideration, he adopts a jovial manner absorbed from a particularly charming acquaintance.

He scrapes his foot deliberately on the floor and sees one of the figures straighten to look at him. It is a clock-and-silver person, but this does not worry West. It takes all types, his father liked to say, especially in grim times.

"Hello, friends!" West calls, into the quiet of the firelit room. "Well met. And may I approach your fire?"

His voice echoes back from the gloom oddly, as if changed there, and the big room feels dusty and ancient. The space is bigger than he'd guessed; the fire is not bright enough to see how far it extends. There are vague silvery shapes scattered around, perhaps ancient sculptures or lightfixtures of some sort, but West ignores these. If there is any of the *Silver* here, the motive force that once powered these sculptures and gave the Underlands light, it is long gone now. These argent shapes describe a loose ring around a massive circular stairway that rises in a ponderous spiral up into the ceiling above. The fire is small against it, and the figures around the fire smaller still.

The tall mechanical figure stands and bows as West approaches and it, too, is bigger than he had thought, six span at least. It towers over the fire and the figures around it. The automata has a long flat-planed head and sharp, articulated joints. It is mostly white, a kind of glossy, flowing porcelain that gives the twin impressions of beauty and death. West recognizes the shape as that of a Jannissary, one of the old warmachines. The intelligence that lives in the body, however, is of another order. West knows this person, by reputation if not experience.

As West approaches the fire, the ancient automata nods its head, the language of its form conveying a sly smile.

"Hello, hello, and hello!" the automata says, giving West an ornate bow. Its voice is a reedy waver, a bellows-and-pump sound, rich and warm. "Welcome to our fire, my friend, and such comforts as it holds!"

West returns the bow, but much more shallowly. He looks around the others at the fire and judges them to be little threat at the moment. A young boy sits perched on chunk of stone to his left, and to his right is a large man reclining on a walking-couch. Next to him is a beautiful servant of no consequence. West returns his attention to the exquisite mechanical person. Fortunately, the proper mode of address is easy in this case. It is not always so with constructed creatures—or any folk for that matter. The tall machine is known to prefer a male honorific.

"Hello to you, Mr. Turpentine, it is an honor to finally make your acquaintance. I have heard much of your exploits down through the years, and it is rare that someone can match their own legend." West hides a sneer; if Mr. Turpentine matched his legend, he would be drenched in still-warm blood and the shattered teeth of children.

Mr. Turpentine flashes a knowing little smile—he clearly caught the jibe. West is not used to the company of those clever enough to attend his humor, and will have to be more careful. It would not do to make enemies just yet. Turpentine does not seem offended, however. He spreads his long, articulated limbs in a gesture of deference, itself only vaguely mocking.

"And you as well, the legendary Lourde—ah! Forgive me, but you go by *West*, just now, I had forgotten. To think I might gain the acquaintance of such a large figure of history! You will forgive me, of course, if I betray my delight overmuch. Please! Be welcome. A few of us have gathered, but our circle is not complete, so we may waste some pleasant time in frivolities. Care you for some *chûs*, as I make our introductions?"

"There should never be a walker of the Wanderlands," West agrees, "who turns away a cup of hospitable *chûs*. And especially not in such a dark and forbidding place."

The fat man on the walking-couch shifts, restless. West gets the idea that he is usually the center of the conversation, and is unused to being talked around. West then makes a point of giving the others around the fire a longer scrutiny. Advantage must be taken whenever possible—another of his father's truisms.

"Speaking of introductions, I fear to say the rest of our company are unknown to me." West gives those around the fire a general bow, appropriate for new colleagues of uncertain station and allegiance. "As our kind host says, my name is West, and I am in all ways at your service."

The man on the walking-couch clears his throat, unable to wait his turn.

"You can call me D'Alle," he says, turning to West and giving him no bow at all, but a mere inclination of his head. "I have the honor of traditionally being called 'Master,' but I suppose we can dispense with the bells and whistles for these proceedings."

His voice is rough but supercilious. He has dusty, almost blued skin that contrasts with his bright, garish robes and thick queue of raven hair. His eyes are of no particular color, but they glitter in the firelight. He accepts a small lozenge from the servant next to him and pops it expertly into his mouth. This is a man used to deference and accustomed to his comforts. West notes these things as a warrior might note lines of sight and good cover. He smiles and bows, far too deep. Giving them too much can be just as much of an insult as giving too little.

"D'Alle, then. It is a pleasure to make your acquaintance." West ignores the servant; it is plain that this person is so far beneath West's station as to make acknowledgment painful for them both. D'Alle's *cantrait*—the walking-couch—is a fine piece of work, a functioning remnant of the Silver Age, and he is amazed the man owns such a thing. It is a far more effective signal of his station than the ostentatious rings on his fingers.

"Master D'Alle," Mr. Turpentine says, fussing with an elegant ceramic pot at the fire, "hails from the grand empire of Cannoux, which resides on the lower slopes of the Mountain so far above us. Perhaps you noted its lights as you were making your way in."

"I did indeed," West agrees. "The fame of Cannoux spreads far, even in these sad days. It is said you are the prize jewel of the Mountain! It is an honor to meet a citizen of that great metropolis."

The ample man who likes to be called Master preens at this, and West conceals a smile. Cannoux is no grand empire; it is a twilight civilization at best, barely clinging to life on the very edge of the known world. West had never heard of it before he passed into the breach that led him here.

"And of course," Mr. Turpentine says, almost nonchalantly, "you would know the child, Gray."

The long blades of Turpentine's fingers uncurl toward the young boy who has been perched on a stone, looking into the flames. He is beautiful but motionless in a way that is very adult. West had paid him small attention other than to wonder what a child was doing in the company of Mr. Turpentine, but he looks closer now. The child has an odd coloration: almost pitch-black skin and bright golden eyes.

West frowns without knowing he does it; an unaccustomed slip. It takes all sorts, as they say, and in the Wanderlands it takes all shades and shapes. 'The Mother Spits Color,' as they say. The peoples of the Lands were made in every shape and combination of hue, and it is rarely a thing to notice or remark upon. But this *particular* combination . . . Or perhaps just those eyes.

West gets it, and feels himself pale.

"Not . . . that is not *Primary* Gray, of course?" West's adopted, cheerful persona takes a blow—he is genuinely surprised, an emotion rare for him. The child raises his head slightly, looking at West, and there is a silent thing that passes between them, a wordless thing that only the Wise ever need convey: *We are both old, but I am older.*

The boy returns his disconcerting golden eyes to the fire, dismissing West from his attention. West is too shocked to bristle at the slight. *Primary Gray!* He would have bet a great deal that this child had been dead for two—or maybe three—ages of the world.

Pretending that the boy isn't ignoring him, West gives him a careful and deferential bow. He fixes his smile as best he can and turns it upon Mr. Turpentine.

"I do remember the legendary Primary Gray, of course," West says, "though I met him long ago and Lands away. Still! Still. It is wonderful to meet you all, even under such conditions. Is our circle complete, then? I have a great desire to try your no-doubt excellent *chûs,* Mr. Turpentine. However, I know that to pour a session before all are present is, in some Lands, known as a bad omen."

West finds himself adopting some of Mr. Turpentine's flowery cadences of speech and decides that this is no bad thing. He has the sense that this meeting in darkness will require something of a melodramatic air, and even clock-and-silver folk are lulled by seeing themselves in a mirror.

"Alas," Mr. Turpentine says, pulling the pot from the fire, "our circle is not quite complete. Still, there is no need to go thirsty! I would never dream of pouring to a broken ring in normal times, but I daresay we will be safe in this case. Any bad luck we could earn has been long since paid for, and in the Underlands, there are only corpses to care."

Without waiting for either assent or dissent, Turpentine pours steaming liquid into cups as D'Alle coughs and the *cantrait* shuffles, restless. It forces the servant to move, startling West. He has forgotten they were there.

"While we wait," D'Alle fumbles at delicacy, "why don't we broach the topic of our meeting? I'll confess to ignorance, and I'll confess further that I don't care for that sensation."

"Information *is* the currency of the Wise," West agrees, accepting a cup. D'Alle nods, fatuously, in no way understanding that for him to be considered one of the Wise is ludicrous to the point of insult.

"It is indeed," Mr. Turpentine says, handing Gray a cup, which the boy sets aside. "And all thinking creatures should hew closely to that sort of wisdom. However, I fear that our true host is yet to arrive, and I daresay she would care little for my speaking out of turn."

D'Alle grunts at this and accepts a cup of *chûs* from Mr. Turpentine. He sips it and grimaces. He covers the reaction, but Turpentine sees and stiffens. It is a small reaction, but West revises D'Alle's life expectancy downward: *Not a good one to slight, my friend. Not if the reality matches the reputation—which is as considerable as it is dark.*

"As for who our host is, I confess to some curiosity myself," West says, sipping his drink. "Considering the august company already gathered around this fire, I'd hardly be surprised to find it was one of the Nine themselves!"

Mr. Turpentine laughs, a reedy whistle. "Oh, wonders await, my good West! Friends of friends, companions fresh and worn, delightful newcomers, and, dare I say, a surprise or two."

"Certainly no one more surprising than the legendary Mr. Turpentine," West says, "and the incomparable Primary Gray. Two persons who cast long shadows across the Lands."

"You set yourself too lowly, sir!" Mr. Turpentine cries, re-filling the pot and setting it back into the fire. "You are by no means an insignificant figure yourself."

West's smile grows easy. He can sense the faint hint of an insult here, perhaps more in the machine's tone than words. "You confuse me with my father, or perhaps my brothers and sisters. I myself am merely a servant of all, notorious only by proximity to greatness."

"I'm sure your siblings would say the same." Mr. Turpentine says, and for a moment, West's smile freezes. Is the thing taunting him? But no, this servile monster wouldn't dare, foul reputation or no. West chooses to laugh, a rumble that echoes around the room.

"My brothers and sisters have many fine qualities," West says, "but an over-burden of humility has never been one of them."

"Surely, the sons and daughters of Hunter Fine have no need for humility?"

The fucking thing *is* taunting him. West's fingers flex. He imagines that he sees a smile on the immortal Primary Gray's face, but—no. It is just firelight. And that's all right; West is just here to learn what the point of this invitation—this meeting—truly is. Once he does, perhaps he'll teach someone the dangers of sly manners.

"I'm sorry," D'Alle says, squinting at West, "but did someone say *Hunter Fine?*"

It is clear D'Alle does not know who West is, but he knows that name. Mr. Turpentine is known only in certain unpleasant circles, and Primary Gray is more a legend these days, but *Hunter Fine . . .*

West feels that old stew of conflicting feelings, half pride and half bitterness, bite at the back of his throat.

"He was my father," West says, reluctantly. "In a manner of speaking."

He hears a chuckle from the murk beyond the fire and the scrape of someone shuffling towards them. West's hand goes to his weapon, but Mr. Turpentine does not startle, nor seem alarmed. The voice—oddly familiar to West—chuckles again.

"I think what you mean," the voice says, still in gloom, "is that after he killed himself, he stuffed all his worst qualities into *you*."

West tenses, perhaps more than the insult itself calls for. There *is* something familiar in that voice, but he cannot immediately place it. In a life as long as his, this is a common sensation, but nevertheless alarm prickles his skin. A shambling figure enters the circle of firelight and falls into a seated position on one of the chunks of rock dragged there for that purpose. The voice belongs to a man, nothing more or less. He is *certainly* not one of the Wise.

He looks quite bad. His clothes are barely rags, and old savage scars the color of ash and mulberry spiral across what can be seen of his chest. His right leg seems to have been broken and badly set; it has been fixed at an angle that looks uncomfortable at best. He is wearing no shoes; his toes are mangled and poorly aligned. When he yawns, West can see that several of his teeth have been splintered and left uncared for, sharp shards still housed in blackening gums. He looks like a broken dog. When he stops rubbing his eyes, West can see something is unsettling about them, something wrong, but in the firelight he cannot tell exactly what. The ill-treated man heaves a sigh as deep as the gloom around them and straightens up a little. He looks first at D'Alle, then at West.

"Hullo, Lourde," he says, with an effort at cheer. "Or is it West, now? Hello, D'Alle! Fancy seeing you here. Mr. Turpentine, might I have some *chûs* before these two try to kill me?"

Mr. Turpentine titters, his long bladelike fingers covering his mouth. "Nothing like that will be permitted, Mr. Candle."

"Just plain 'Candle' is fine," the man says. "I lost my honorific years ago. Right around the same time I lost my honor. Eh, D'Alle?"

Suddenly the fat man on the walking-couch stiffens in recognition. Shock and rage crease his broad face, and a trembling finger raises. "*You!*"

"Me," the broken man agrees. "You've gotten fatter, D'Alle. You shouldn't let something else walk for you."

The *cantrait* dances on its slender clockwork legs, reflecting D'Alle's agitation. He is near apoplexy, his face red and flushed, his eyes staring.

"This . . . this is . . . Who allowed this *creature* into this meeting?"

"I will remind you all," Mr. Turpentine says, "that we are guests and under something of a flag of truce. Old enmities must be set aside, gentlemen, if only for the span of this meeting. As difficult as it may be."

West is still puzzled. There is something familiar about Candle.

Then he gets it. The face is the same, if bruised and broken, but the supreme arrogance that once animated it is gone. West should be happy about it, but he can't be. He had wanted to be the one to wipe Candle's arrogance away. He hasn't seen this man in years. He would have laid good coin on his being dead twice over.

Candle has been watching West's face, and now he grins. "*There* it is. Recognize me, eh? You might want to let your family know they can stop mourning."

West stares at the damaged man. "How are you here? We thought you were dead."

"Oh, I am. Dead as shit." Candle holds up his limp arms and waggles them. "Someone attached some strings and is dancing my corpse about."

"My brother," West says, "will have your head."

"He is welcome to it." Candle grins again, a ghastly sight. "If he can get it off my body."

D'Alle growls, interrupting. "I swore that if I ever saw you again—"

"Oh, hush." Candle waves his hand in a shooing gesture. "*Both* of you. Any revenge you ever wished upon me, consider it paid with interest. Even if you could get past Turpentine here, the worst you could do to me would be like gentle kisses compared to my morning routine. So calm down and enjoy the sight of me, brought so low. I'll even allow you to leer."

"This," West says, turning to Mr. Turpentine, "had better not be our host."

"Oh, no, dear West. I fear the days of Mr. Candle's making grand plans are quite firmly in the past."

Candle makes a face but doesn't disagree. He accepts a cup of *chûs* from Mr. Turpentine, blows on it, and sips.

"This man"—D'Alle is calmer now, but far from easy—"is more dangerous than you know, and if you think he is done with plots, you are very mistaken. I have experienced his plots firsthand."

Mr. Turpentine's only comment is another titter.

"Well *thank you*, Master D'Alle," Candle says, with mock courtesy. "I'm glad to have made such an impression. I'd nearly forgotten about you and your sad little Cannoux-Town. But Mr. Turpentine is all too correct—I am nothing but a tool these days, broken and re-broken until I fit the hand. I fear my days as a motive force in this world are done. I serve a new master now."

"And who *is* your new master?" D'Alle says, his voice tight. "What dark force do you follow?"

"Oh, the darkest, D'Alle. But you'll be re-acquainted soon enough. In the meantime, might I have more of this excellent *chûs*, Turpentine? I'm afraid I've quite drunk it up. This new master of mine isn't much for supplying creature comforts, and it's been a while since I've had anything sweet."

"Certainly, Mr. Candle!" Mr. Turpentine has reverted to the honorific. If stories are true, Turpentine delights in the strictures of polite society, nearly as much as he enjoys committing horrors upon it. He sets about fussing with his pots again. Candle, for his part, seems lost in his own thoughts for a while. Eventually he straightens himself, which appears to take some effort, and looks around the fire. His strange eyes flicker in the light. He adopts a faux-grand tone and spreads his arms, highlighting crooked fingers.

"So! Here we are. An idiot, a fool, a psychopath, and a child-god," Candle says. "I bet you wonder why."

"Our host wished—" Mr. Turpentine says, but Candle waves him off.

"I wasn't sent ahead for nothing, Turpentine. You know her; she wants us to get all the tedious exposition out of the way and not waste her precious time. Never fear that I betray our host, my friend. If you think my body is broken, just wait until you see my *spirit*."

He spits into the fire, looks at his dirty hands, and looks around again with his unusual eyes. His words have the flavor of a prepared speech, but not one that is eagerly given. West is again amazed to see him fallen so low; he cannot imagine what has happened since he knew him.

Candle clears his throat, a rough sound.

"In any case, what are we doing here? What a motley crew! What possible purpose could this convocation of personalities—this *Convox*, if you will—serve? What opportunity, in all the Wanderlands, could bring us to meet here in the darkness, out past the edge of the world and deep beneath the skin of the Mountain? What force could cause us to congregate in this dead grave of a buried civilization?"

"You haven't lost your flair for the dramatic," West says, a little sour.

"Well, I shouldn't." Candle jerks his head at D'Alle. "I learned it from him."

D'Alle shakes his head. "If I must listen to you speak, I'll listen to as little of it as possible. Say what you mean to, boy."

"You never were any fun, *Master* D'Alle," Candle says. He looks around the fire again, then up at the big circular helix of the stone stairway, rising into shadows above them. He seems tempted, for a moment, as if he could run for it and escape. But he sighs and returns his attention to the assembled worthies.

"We're here," Candle says, "because far below us, so far below our feet that it would beggar a man's imagination to consider, the most dangerous creature that ever existed lies bound, in the greatest prison built by the greatest magicians of the greatest age of the world. A demon that almost ended our world when it was full of light and life; one that, if it were to get free, would snuff out our existence as easily as I might snuff out a flame. I speak, of course, of the Giant, who lies even now restless beneath us."

West snorts, incredulous. What nonsense is this? He shakes his head. If this is what he has been dragged across most of the known world to hear, he has wasted a trip.

"The Giant is dead," he says, "and has been for a long time."

Candle smiles, a ghastly sight with his broken teeth. His peculiar eyes glitter. "I disagree."

West stands. He cannot believe that he has traveled so far for *this!* He decides to put an end to this nonsense.

"The Giant—and let me be clear, for those less informed of us, the Giant once named Kindaedystrin, the deadliest creation that the Mother ever cursed us with, yes, *that* one—is dead. He has been dead for two ages of the world. There is certainly a prison below our feet. My father helped build it. But I did not come all this way, under such conditions, to entertain nightmares and fairy-stories. I am in a position to know, perhaps better than any person living, and I assure you—the Giant is *long* dead."

Primary Gray, the ancient child, raises his golden eyes.

"No," the boy says, quietly, "he is not."

THE KILLERS

In The Beginning, An End

"A misspent youth can be recovered from.
A glorious one can never be."

—CORAZON LI, 'REVELIS'

S ophie Vesachai was burning butterflies again.

They weren't hard to catch. They swarmed around the balcony café where she stood smoking, leaning against the stone balustrade and watching the bustle of the Rue de Paladia below. The tiny mechanical creatures were attracted by the curls of smoke and scents that rose from the balcony café, the warm smells of roasted *chûs* and burning pepper. Sophie caught another, snapping her wrist in a practiced motion and snaring the small automata.

It fluttered in her hand, its tiny gears straining. It was a minute marvel, a miniature work of art. It had beautifully patterned wings and gearwork that was so fine and precise it could hardly be seen, even held up to the eye. Sophie drew a deep drag on her slot and blew smoke into the cage of her fingers, setting the little silver-made machine into frantic motion.

She wondered, idly, what purpose this little device had been made for. How old was it? How long had this device been fluttering around the Keep? She wondered, as she smoked and waited for the evening to come, if it had once been free in some other place and had, over the course of the slow millennia, found its way down through the endless leagues of rock and abandoned stone rooms above their heads, following the scent of *chûs* and burning pepper to find itself here.

Here, in a cage. Sophie considered this, studying the butterfly; but no. Not just any cage. It found itself in the grandest cage in the whole world. *The Keep.*

And the Rue de Paladia was the heart of the Keep, one of the biggest places in it. Though she would have resisted acknowledging such sentimentality, it was her favorite place in the whole world and had been since she was a little girl. The Rue was a winding boulevard paved with cunningly engraved stones that made intricate patterns when looked at from above. Long ago, someone had planted cherrywhistle and terra in huge pots along the center of the avenue, and when these bloomed, the Rue became a river of blue and orange fire. Flocking birds roosted everywhere in these tiny trees, and when one of the nearly-as-ubiquitous cats decided to pounce, the birds all took flight at once, filling the air above the Rue and scattering the butterflies.

It was a wide street, wider than most in the Keep, and whoever built it had expended unimaginable amounts of effort to make it lovely. Every surface was either patterned stone of nearly infinite variety, ancient woodwork delicately carved, or wrought metals the like of which no one living could still craft. It was a serpentine street, overlooked by stepped balconies that held cafés, restaurants, dancing parlors. There were even a few residences, high above and majestic, for those with the coin to afford them. The Rue was illuminated by huge columns of litstone, which glowed brightly during the day and dimmed down to a pleasing ember at night. Much more recently—but still a long time ago—huge, bronzed bowls of oil and char had been erected high above the street, and once the night-lights dimmed down, stilted technicians would make their way down the Rue, lighting the braziers and filling the street with a warm flickering fire-light.

Over all of this stood a sturdy ceiling of arched mosaic, tabs of colored glass that reflected the light in a shimmer during the daytime and sparkled at night— legend said that these were meant to evoke the long-forgotten sky, so far above. Sophie Vesachai wasn't sure that she believed in the sky, though she had seen it once in a dream. The Keep was an immense cylinder of stone, hollowed and tunneled through with too many rooms and halls and streets to count. But above it, past the Gap, was only more stone, and it, too, was tunneled and carved into long-dark rooms and halls and passageways; a whole vast dead civilization carved out of rock and hanging above their heads.

It might make a less jaded person shiver to think of, but just made Sophie flick ash from her slot onto the street below.

Sophie had been outside the walls of the Keep, which few could claim, and she'd seen for herself what lay above, past the Gap and beyond. It was easy to describe: Darkness. Past the bounds of the Keep there was little light, and if you pressed too far into the empty halls and rooms, you would find the true Dark, where the light failed.

And in that Dark, there were monsters.

Sophie shivered and scratched unconsciously at the scars on her arms. She examined the captive butterfly, still whirring against her fingers, and dragged on her slot. She was thinking about a certain young girl, a girl from a long time ago, who had no scars on her arms. A girl who used to dream of finding out where these butterflies came from, a girl who hadn't yet acquired a famous name and a tar-black heart. She brought the little captive creature close.

She took another deep drag on her slot, the ember at the tip flaring, and held it to the struggling thing's wings. The brightly stained paper caught fire, and she tossed the butterfly over the railing, watching it try to fly with burning wings. The flight traced a parabola of thin smoke in the still air above the Rue de Paladia, joining several others that were slowly unwinding in the quiet afternoon air. She watched it struggle, doomed to fail but too stupid to stop, until it landed on the street below. She heard a chuckle from behind her.

"My, my," Hunker John said. "The Capitana is feeling bloody!"

She turned and gave him a wink. Bear looked up from the book he was reading and grimaced at the new trail of smoke, joining several others. Bear hated it when Sophie burned the little creatures. "Yeah, no shit."

Hunker John did not have Bear's delicate disposition, and shrugged. He went back to paring his already perfect nails with an enameled knife.

Sophie stifled a yawn—it was the late hours of the afternoon, the slow time before the revelries of the night kicked in. She flicked the remainder of her slot down onto the street below. She pulled another, scraped the tip alight against the stone balustrade, and sucked in a heavy draw of smoke. She expelled this into the quiet air, causing more mechanical butterflies to swarm above the café.

Gods above, she felt tired. She tried to remember the last time she'd had a decent night's sleep, one not polished by drugs or drink or disposable love. A small scar cut across her lower lip and part of her chin, and it pulled when she took a drag on her slot.

She had other scars, too, a fine patterning that ran down her forearms. Nobody talked about those scars. If you knew what they were, you wouldn't dare, and if you didn't, she would have a fist in your mouth before you got the second word out.

Sophie Vesachai didn't think about those scars, much. The only consistent part of her look was the long-sleeved jackets that she used to hide them. She supposed she wasn't especially beautiful, at least by her standards of beauty, but some people would call her arresting. She had small, intense features, and the only concession towards ornament she ever made was a heavy dark paint around her eyes. These were a deep brown, almost black, and with the paint they gave the impression of a space into which everything fell and nothing returned. She wore her hair short, shapeless and dirty, and in her thirty-six years of banging around the Keep, had never had anybody complain.

She heard a viola tune-up, down-Rue, a sweet and lonesome sound that wound its way through the quiet bustle of the street below. It gave her a hollow feeling, adding a bleak undercurrent to her mood. If she had been a different sort of person, she could have looked inward and tried to discover the source of that feeling. But she wasn't, so she took a drag on her slot and watched the shopkeeps on the street below start closing up their carts for the day. With a lazy snap of her wrist, she caught another butterfly.

"Wish you wouldn't do that," Bear grumbled, then shifted in his leaned-back chair, as if already regretting speaking. Sophie glanced back, amused. It was curious that her chief enforcer, the cheerfully violent and quite large Bear, was so protective of small things.

"Oh yeah?"

"It's gonna bring the Practice up," Bear said. She lifted an eyebrow. He scratched big fingers through his close-cropped and tightly curly dark hair, peppered with gray. Bear was a big man with boyishly good looks and a smoothly dark olive complexion, but the gray hair marked him as the oldest of the Killers. Of course, no one knew exactly how old he was.

One of the few rules the Killers had was that they didn't talk about where they came from.

"The Practice Guard can suck a dick," Sophie said finally, blowing smoke at the new butterfly in the cage of her hand.

"Yeah, well." Bear settled back into his book. "*Some* of us have paper."

Sophie raised her eyebrow again. "Like I don't?"

Hunker John snorted, giving this comment the respect it deserved. Nobody in the Practice Guard was going to fuck with Sophie Vesachai and they all knew it. Every member of the Killers had lists of infractions as long as their arms, and Sophie's was as long as Hunker John's entire body. The truth of it, however, was that the unfortunate Practice Guard who tried to arrest Sophie Vesachai on anything but the Queen's own orders would end up in lock themselves.

She studied the trapped automata in her hand. Maybe she'd let it go; maybe she'd go home and get some sleep; maybe she'd turn over a new leaf, stop drinking so much, and get into charity work. Her mouth twisted.

She closed her fist, the frail creature snapping into shards against her palm. Bear winced.

"We all go into the dark," she told it. She brushed the still-twitching fragments over the side of the balustrade.

"Twins *damn*, Sophie." Bear said, alarmed. "You are bloody today, aren't you?"

"I'm something." Sophie scrubbed her face with her hands, trying to wake up. She turned fully and considered her friends with a frown. Their gang was understaffed at the moment. "Where the fuck is Trik, anyway? We've got business to be about. I got somebody to meet about a job."

"She's out running some grift." Hunker John yawned and tossed down his paring-knife. He sniffed at a half-warm cup of *chûs*, one of the many that littered their table, and instead popped a candied olive into his mouth. "Loves her grift, does our Trik."

"She is a hustler," Sophie allowed. She looked up at the mosaic arch overhead, thinking about old stone and inevitability.

Bear eyed her. "Speaking of grift—"

"Speaking of *debauchery*." Hunker John made a show of stretching. "We getting into any trouble tonight, Capitana?"

Sophie brought her attention down from the stone overhead. She watched her friend sniff a cold cup of *chûs* and discard it in favor of something stronger. As she did sometimes, she took in the spectacle of Hunker John; there was no one else quite like him.

Hunker John was small, slender, delicate in a way that begged exploration. He was a grandiose fop, a layabout, a degenerate. He had a long face and twinkling almond eyes that accepted all, forgave all, winked at all. His wavy and brightly colored hair might have been sculpted by a genius of the form, and he offset this majestic coif with a little fake goatee that made him look like a stage villain. He was one of those fortunate androgynous individuals who provided prospective lovers a fascinating puzzle as to what might lay hidden underneath his perfectly ornate tunic; from all the tales Sophie had heard, by the time the interested party found out, they no longer cared.

"Well, Capitana?" Hunker lifted an eyebrow.

"I started this night with some fun in mind," she said, finally, "and I mean to have my due."

Hunker clapped, delighted, and Bear stifled a groan. Bear was a good soldier, though, and would follow her into any fight—or wild debauch—with little hesitation. Sophie saw movement behind him, a tall girl winding her way through the sleepy café towards them. Bear straightened up.

"Triks!" he called, pointing at Sophie, like a child calling tattle-tale. "Capitana is feeling bloody!"

"Oh, *wonderful*," Trik growled, approaching the table. "I haven't stopped drinking in a fucking week."

Hunker John raised a glass of *chûs*. "Fasten your breeches up tight, dear Triks. We are in for a sinister road."

"Dunno when a girl is supposed to goddamn sleep." Trik made a great show of sighing, and settled herself carefully into a chair. She was tall and dark, with tattoos all over, and a great cloud of kinky black hair. A certain member of the Killers had confessed a desire to sink his hands into that hair, Sophie recalled. Bear still had all of his fingers, though, so presumably he had never attempted it. Trik didn't like being touched. She looked up at Sophie, eyebrow raised.

"Well? What lunacy comes, Capitana?"

"First we need to collect Ben." Sophie stifled a yawn, trying to rouse herself past her fatigue and into action. "And then I need to see a man about a job. And *then* . . . well, I propose we rampage through the Keep in a drug-and-booze-filled orgy of sex, violence, and madness until we find an answer for the unceasing and depthless darkness within."

"Great," Trik looked into a half-drunk cup and wrinkled her nose. "The usual, then?"

Bear tipped his chair back, getting into the spirit of the thing, and gave Sophie a passable grin. "Well? Killers Unite, I suppose."

Sophie grinned back, all teeth. "Just so, Bear. Killers fucking *Unite*."

———

The Killers made their way down the Rue de Paladia, preparing for revelry. Hunker John danced a little jig as he walked, excited about the prospect of debauchery, and upset the long walk of a Charm Chair. The graceful apparatus, more or less a loveseat on two long legs, picked itself delicately around John, endeavoring not to upset its rider.

It was late afternoon sloping off into the evening, and the Rue wasn't very busy. The bustle on the street was mostly the shopkeeps closing up their stores. Weaving in and out of the milling citizens and tall clockwork Charm Chairs were the Charboys high on their stilts, lighting the great bronze braziers above their heads.

One of the reasons Sophie liked the Rue de Paladia was that it put the variety and breadth of humankind on display as few other places in the Keep were able to. There were all sorts in the Underlands, it was said, and it was true. Light, dark, every shade between, every combination of eye and hair, every sex and variation thereof shopped and dined and drank and sang on the Rue de Paladia. And that was to say nothing of the clock-and-silver creatures; the Gallivants and Charm Chairs that made their way up and down the street, the spiderlike automata that maintained the mosaic far above, even the swarming clockwork butterflies.

One of the other reasons Sophie liked the Rue was that she came here enough that people knew to pretend they didn't recognize her. Even artificial anonymity was enough for her. There were always exceptions, though; she saw a particularly bold kid scowling at her. She was feeling bloody, so she scowled back.

"Hey!" the boy called as the Killers passed. "Ma says you Sophie Vesachai!"

His mother, a solid woman who reminded Sophie of one of her aunts, turned red and tried to shush him, but Sophie just gave him a rude gesture. "Get off, squib."

But the kid, belligerent, stuck out his jaw and shook his head. "Naw, you ain't Sophie anyways. Sophie ain't *old*!"

The child's mother tried to apologize, but Sophie waved her off. She felt that a certain amount of belligerence should be rewarded in the young. She hadn't had an over-helping of respect for her elders, either. "Yeah?" she said, stopping and fixing the kid with her best glare. "Don't think so, squib? Maybe I let my Killers have some fun with you, eh?"

Bear, getting into the spirit of the thing, loomed over Sophie's shoulder and put his hand on the hilt of his long knife. Hunker John did a passable imitation of a threatening leer. The child blinked, no doubt thinking of the darker parts of the stories he'd heard his whole young life, about Crazy Tom and Jubilee and Mad Vaas, of the long-gone Killers that figured so prominently in so many of those stories. Stories about a little girl named Sophie Vesachai and about how she had saved the world, a long time ago.

Sophie gave the kid a sharp grin. She didn't much like those stories, but she *did* like scaring children.

"Yeah, well." He screwed up his face. The kid had some spirit. "Yer still *old*."

Sophie laughed, straightened, and tossed him a lightweight coin. She ignored the mother's embarrassed thanks and pointed her finger at the boy. "You best spend that on something your Ma won't like, you hear me?"

The boy looked down at his newfound riches and nodded, eyes wide. Sophie turned to head back down-Rue, the Killers falling in line around her.

"You're so good with the little ones." Hunker John tipped an imaginary hat with his carved cane. "Surprised you don't have some of your own."

"Got too many kids already," Sophie said lightly. "Greedy little fuckers too, always drinking all my booze and doing all my drugs."

"Learned it from you, Capitana." Trik picked a cherrywhistle blossom and tucked it into her cloud of dark hair. It matched a flower tattoo on her wrist that was crowded with many other arcane designs, mottled over her dark skin. "Where are we going, anyway?"

"Gotta meet Ben, near the Guardians. Think he's bringing that new set of legs with him."

Trik groaned.

"Jealousy." Hunker John elbowed Bear.

"Fuck you, I'm not jealous," Trik said. "I'm *suspicious*. It's different."

"Why would anybody be suspicious of New Girl?" Bear looked confused. "She's sweet."

"Oh, *is she*, Bear?" Trik glared at him. Bear blinked and held his hands up. Trik sniffed and looked back at Sophie. "C'mon, are you gonna make me say it?"

Sophie, who was pretty sure she knew what Trik was going to say, held her peace.

"Nobody is at all skeptical," Trik said, in a lowered voice, "why a girl like that is hanging out with *Ben*?"

"Ahhh." Hunker John clapped his hands. "Well, you put it like that, I agree. There must be a sinister motive at work. What do we think; is she a spy? Deep-cover Lurk? *Assassin*?"

"I just figured he was blackmailing her." Bear tipped an imaginary hat at an elderly shopkeep who was sweeping her entryway. "Has her grandpa tied up in a storeroom somewhere."

"It's the only thing that makes sense." Hunker agreed.

"New Girl's not a spy, the Queen isn't that obvious," Sophie said. She saw the looming shapes of the Guardians up ahead. She paused, considering this, and laughed. "And who gives a shit if Ben's girl *is* a Lurk? Can you imagine the poor Ministry bastard who has to read *those* reports?"

"Scandalous reading, I would imagine." Bear said.

"A list of crimes committed," Hunker John intoned in an officious manner, pretending to read from a scroll. "Five derogatory terms used in conjunction of the Queen's good name. Ingestion of six unidentified substances—presumably highly illegal psychotropics. One fistfight with an enraged paramour. Another fistfight with said paramour's husband. Two hundred and seven slots smoked. Three counts of petty larceny, and one encounter of a sexual nature—the paramour's husband, under a bar-table."

Trik had to laugh. "And that was just Sophie."

"It was a slow night," Sophie said. She turned and fixed her Killers with a hard eye. "You lot leave New Girl alone; Ben never gets any legs like that wrapped around him, and you assholes do just fine. Let him have his fun."

"That apply to you as well, Capitana?" Hunker John asked, sly.

"Especially applies to me," Sophie said, and then grinned. "I always had a weakness for beauty. It's why I keep Bear around."

"Yeah!" Bear pumped his fist. "See?"

"I thought that's why you kept *me* around," Hunker John said, pouting.

Sophie frowned at him. "I keep you as a cautionary tale, Hunk. A reminder to look in the Twins-damned mirror before I leave the rack."

"*Thank* you. That's been driving me nuts all day." Trik turned to Hunker John. "What the fuck is that around your neck?"

"This," Hunker John said, patting an improbably folded and very colorful cravat, "is what you all will be wearing in a few months. Mark my words."

"Only if all the lights in the Keep go out." Trik squinted at an imagined glare from his neck.

Sophie chuckled and scraped another slot to life as her friends bickered and walked. Just another late afternoon on the Rue de Paladia; just another slow evening with her Killers. She tried to relax into it. She spotted a heap of half-destroyed machinery, all covered with flowers and drawings, left abandoned in the street. It was a memorial of the Hot Halls War; one of the invading mechanisms that had proved too heavy or too difficult to remove or dismantle. These were scattered all over the Keep; Sophie tended to avoid them. But she saw two figures standing near this one.

"Oiy! Hey!" A sandy-haired man with kind eyes was waving; this was Ben. He was next to a woman who was so lovely she was hard to look directly at, like a bright light in a dark room. Ben grinned as they approached. "Hoy there, gen-teels."

Ben was Sophie's oldest friend; the last of the original Killers. He had a soft face and a mild demeanor, but Ben had been with her through more trials and terrors than anyone else. He had followed Sophie into every dismal hell for twenty years now, though these days, the dismal hells were of the Killers' own making, and built of empty cups of booze.

Ben slapped Hunker John on the back and punched Bear on the arm; Trik got a respectful nod. She wasn't big on physical displays of affection. Or any sort of affection, Sophie supposed. Ben gestured at the girl next to him. "You reprobates remember Av—"

"We remember *New Girl*," Bear cut in, severely. "How are you doing, *New Girl*?"

New Girl tossed her long blonde hair. "I'm good, *Bear*. How you doing, *Trik*?"

Bear nodded, approving. The asinine but, at this point, hallowed protocols of Sophie's nicknames had been observed. Sophie let her eyes slide away from the girl; with those green eyes and that endless fall of light hair, she might have walked out of a broadly written fairy-story.

"Well?" Ben said, taking in Sophie's mood at a glance. He knew Sophie better than anyone else. "What's the plan, Capitana?"

"I'm thinking the Loche de Menthe."

Bear gave a low whistle. "The Loche! You *are* feeling bloody."

"I started this night with some fun in mind," Sophie said, giving New Girl a wink. "I may be full of shit, but I rarely lie."

———

The Guardians were huge, standing on low stone pedestals with their backs to each other, heads nearly scraping the mosaic arch far overhead. They were autom-ata, ancient clock-and-silver things, but they hadn't moved in a very long time. They could be mistaken for very complex, ornate statues, and Sophie supposed that's what they were these days. Legend had it they had once served as Domina-tors, and could control the peoples of the Keep by sending them into deep sleep or murderous rage, but Sophie had never believed it. It was too bad the Guardians no longer had any purpose; they would have been useful in the Hot Halls War.

The Hot Halls War. Gods, she didn't need to think about that tonight.

Sophie led her friends to the end of the Rue and the deplorable delights that lay in the direction of the Loche de Menthe. Her friends called her Capitana and followed her everywhere; it had been a long time since Sophie had bothered to wonder why. Perhaps it was her reputation, perhaps the role she had played in the Hot Halls War. Maybe she was just one of those poor bastards who were born to lead, and had nowhere to go. Her slot was down to the nub already—a sign of disquiet—and she flicked it with a trailing arc of smoke, a similar parabola to the ones the burning butterflies had left.

The Rue narrowed at this end, forming a big arch that was winged with massive semicircular doors. These doors could move, ostensibly, but if they could be closed, Sophie had never heard of its being done. Like many things in the Keep, the knowledge of how to make the doors work was long lost. Even her estranged family, the Vesachai, despite being a caste of techno-priests, knew barely enough to keep the lights going. The Vesachai were the only ones in the Keep with the ability, training, and discipline to manipulate the motive force of the Keep, the *Silver*. But Sophie knew firsthand that there was much more about the world— and the Keep—than her family knew.

She thought of her father, her eager little brother, her beloved uncle. Thoughts of her brother especially pained her. Her father and uncle were grown; they had made their own choices. Lee, however . . . Gods, Lee had worshipped his older sister. Followed her around everywhere. She remembered bringing him down to the Rue to get fairy-ice and foisting him off on a friendly shopkeep to go adventure with the Killers. She'd never been much of a sister to Lee, as she recalled, and then with everything that happened . . .

Well, it didn't matter. She was sure he was fine, a proper young Vesachai now, and she was sure he'd sneer at her just the same as the rest of them did. She pushed such thoughts away. Old news and old stories. They didn't matter. She had fun in mind . . . and she meant to have her due.

She scraped another slot to life on the rippled metal of the Right Guardian's foot as she passed it, resolving not to think about her fucking family tonight.

Bear, Trik, and Ben were arguing about which of the many illicit pleasures to be found in the Loche de Menthe they should start with, but she let them prattle. She looked New Girl over, partially because that was a pleasant thing to do and partially because of Trik's suspicions. She loved Ben, but his charms were not usually obvious to a girl like that.

New Girl caught her looking and gave her a quick little wink.

Careful there, Sophie warned herself. She hadn't been joking about that weakness for beauty, and she'd already stolen enough boys and girls from Ben. He was always cheerful about it, but Sophie intended he enjoy New Girl's company as long as both of them cared for it. She owed Ben that much, at least.

They passed through the big doors that capped this end of the Rue and into the more pedestrian byway that led into other parts of the Keep. The by-way was high-ceilinged and very wide, though nothing like the grand open space above the Rue de Paladia, and the Killers made their way against a light flow of citizens headed to the Rue. Behind them, the Rue was gearing up for nighttime, and indeed, Sophie saw the great columns of brightly lit stone dim to their night-hues. She sidestepped a big Gallivant carrying a full load of well-dressed passengers, excited to treat themselves to a dinner on the Rue. The Gallivant's big tea-cup silver eyes swiveled at her as she passed, and she could hear the faint sounds of rotting gearwork deep inside the thing. It made her sad; soon that rot would get bad enough that the thing would slow and stop, and the Keep would be graced with one more statue from another age littering its byways.

Mother above, she was melancholy tonight! She wondered for a moment where it was coming from, but self-reflection was for people who cared to improve. A Charm Chair was making its way toward them, carrying some rich fuck who could afford one. Sophie paid it little mind until it paused and swerved towards them.

She drew up short as the tall, spindly-legged construct slowed to a stop in front of her and knelt down. She heard the warm whirring of well-kept clock-and-silver machinery, and then a finely dressed aristocrat, saddled with a cravat almost as brightly colored as John's, came into view.

"Sophie Vesachai?" the fop asked, peering at her. He had a high, supercilious voice, and the kind of face that made you want to stick something sharp into it. He glanced at, and then dismissed, the rest of her friends. It didn't do much to endear him to Sophie. She took a moment, looking away, to drag on her slot. Eventually, she looked back at him.

"Yeah?"

"Ah! Well, just my luck," the fop said. He didn't actually say it with a sniff, but he might as well have. "Headed to dinner, and who do I stumble across? Two birds, one stone, and all that."

"What can I do for you?" Sophie asked evenly, because there was an outside chance that this rich idiot wanted to hire the Killers for something interesting.

"I," the aristocrat began, as if bestowing an extensive favor, "have a message for you. And considering the expense spared on it, I should think you'll listen!"

Sophie squinted off into the distance and took another drag. Plainly, the fop did not enjoy being marginalized, which was why she did it. She blew some smoke in his direction. "Okay."

He yawned, swaddled in the expensive fabrics that made up the comfortable seats of the Charm Chair. "Okay, well. Let me remember; I was to speak this verbatim. I had made a note, ah . . . and seem to have misplaced it. No matter."

Sophie looked over her shoulder at Trik, who made a cutting motion across her throat, and Sophie was inclined to agree. She raised an eyebrow at the rich bastard, giving him about ten seconds to say something interesting.

"I am to tell you, um. First, that 'nothing that is about to happen is what it seems.' And that you should not, ah . . . 'take the bait.' Forgive me, I have no idea what any of this means."

Sophie felt herself smiling. Take the bait? Nothing was as it seems? Ben looked as confused as she was. Was this a prank?

The fop found his note and his face cleared; he was happy now. "Ah! Yes. Second, I'm to tell you 'not to trust the man that you call Bear.' And, third—I must say that I truly don't know what this means—I . . ."

"Hold up." Sophie held up a hand, palm out. "Did you just say not to trust *Bear*?"

The fop frowned, looking up from his paper. "Ah, yes. Is that someone you know? Look, I'm just telling you what was told to me."

Sophie studied Bear for a long moment, who was looking earnestly puzzled. She returned her attention to the aristocrat in the lowered Charm Chair with an expression that would have sent a smarter man in the opposite direction as fast as was humanly and mechanically possible.

". . . some *bullshit*," Trik said from behind her. The fop was too absorbed to notice any of this, however, and squinted at his paper.

"The third thing," he said, plainly ready to be done with his errand, "is—"

"You know what? I don't think I care to know. How about this: Get the fuck out of here, and tell whoever paid you to fuck with me, be it the Queen Jane, or Lord Crowe, or my father, or who the fuck ever, go tell them to fuck the fuck *off*. Okay?"

"Yeah." Bear's voice was a low scour. He had dropped his cheerful demeanor in that way that tended to make the blood run cold. "Why don't you move out before you get hurt?"

The fop was clearly alarmed by their attitude, and the Charm Chair backed away a few span, responding to his alarm.

"Fine! Mother Above, fine. But I'm supposed to say—"

"I don't give a shit," Sophie said, flicking her slot into the man's face. He swatted it away.

"I'm supposed to say that 'the giant is still awake!'"

Sophie froze. The aristocrat rose up into the air, his cravat and alarmed expression disappearing from view with the graceful movement of the Charm Chair, and headed off towards the Rue de Paladia.

"A giant?" New Girl said, frowning. "What was that?"

"Some nonsense." Hunker John waved his hand airily. "I'm sure it's nothing to concern yourself with. Fools are always trying to pull our famous Capitana into their schemes."

Ben, however, set his hand on Sophie's arm. He knew those words as well as she did. Or, nearly those words. The way they had been spoken to Sophie, when they were children, went a little differently: *The Giant Lies Still Awake.*

"Ben," Sophie spoke through numb lips, watching the Charm Chair duck under the great arch that led into the Rue de Paladia. "Have we ever taught these kids how to take down a Charm Chair?"

Ben's face was pale, but he shook his head. "I don't think so, Capitana."

"We're doing what, now?" Trik said. Sophie got herself together.

"We're going to take down that Chair," she snapped. "C'mon."

She started moving, a slow lope that turned into a run. She heard Ben rallying the Killers behind her, explaining what they needed to do. Hunker John, sensing excitement coming, howled a war-cry into the evening air, and the Killers poured back down the passageway towards the Guardians.

As she ran, Sophie veered to her right and snatched up a short, dense piece of fakewood from a closing vendor stall, ignoring the woman's protests. She smacked it into her palm; it should work. She glanced over her shoulder to see if her Killers were following, but of course they were.

"When I tell you," Ben called loudly, "you have to haul *backward*. Got it?"

Bear, Trik, and Hunker ran ahead, catching up with the long-legged Charm Chair, matching its pace. Ben raced ahead and stopped, judging the distance, and gave Sophie a nod. She slowed a bit, eyes narrowed, trying to get the timing right, wondering how many years it had been since they'd pulled down one of these creatures. Ben dropped to one knee, making a cradle of his hands, and Sophie put on a burst of speed and stepped into it as the Charm Chair was passing. Ben heaved upwards, and Sophie bounded up into the air with just enough loft to jam the piece of fakewood into the backward-facing joint of the Charm Chair's leg.

"Now!" Ben called, as Sophie landed and rolled. The other Killers grabbed the opposite leg of the Charm Chair and hauled backward as hard as they could. The Chair, normally quite nimble, attempted to correct with its other leg but the fakewood caught in the joint and splintered. The Killers gave a last heave and the Chair went down.

It crashed into the middle of the Rue de Paladia with a terrible scream of surprise and pain. Sophie rolled to her feet and dove for the bleeding man still strapped into one of the seats.

He blinked, woozy, not understanding what was happening, and Sophie got a fistful of his bright cravat, hauling him out of the contraption. Bear joined her, his long knife out. The Charm Chair roared in anger and hurt, picked itself up, and staggered back toward its cradle for repair and comfort.

"All right," Sophie said, shaking the man to get his attention. They would only have a few minutes before the Practice Guard—or worse—showed up. "What the *fuck* do you mean about the Giant?"

"I don't know!" The aristocrat was trembling, terrified. His eyes rolled to Bear's wicked-looking knife. "I don't know! He just paid me to say it! I don't know!"

"Who?" Sophie said.

"I can't say—"

Bear made the tip of his knife slip up the man's jawline.

"How did you know where to find me?" Sophie said. The fop didn't answer, too focused on the knife-tip. Sophie slapped him. "How, man?"

"I didn't!" the fop squeaked. "I'm doing him a favor; there's a bunch of us looking for you! We all have the same message, I think, and I don't know what it means!"

Sophie heard the telltale whistle of the Practice Guard from down-Rue. She cursed silently and tightened her grip on the man's cravat.

"Who paid you? Who's fucking with me? Tell me, man, or you'll go missing a finger."

The fop wailed, trying to shy away from Bear's weapon. "The Consort! It was the *Consort!*"

This made Sophie drop her fist.

"The Consort? Of the *Queen?* The Beast's new paramour? Fuck off, man. What are you talking about?"

"I don't know." The man was crying, tears ruining his delicate makeup. She heard more whistles, closer now. They needed to get out of here soon. "I don't know, but it was him. It was him!"

"Sophie . . ." Trik said.

"I know." Sophie inspected the pale man trembling in her grip and swore. She looked up at the Killers. "All right. Run. We'll meet up in the place we agreed, yes?"

"Yes," Bear said, and the other Killers nodded. Ben took New Girl by the arm, and they ran back towards the Guardians, the fair-haired girl casting one anxious look back. As her friends dispersed Sophie straightened, looking down at the weeping, terrified aristocrat. She felt a strange sensation, as if tangible shadows were sweeping in and gathering themselves, unseen, spiraling tight around the scars on her arms.

The Giant Lies Still Awake.

The last time she heard those words—*gods.* The last time she'd heard them, she had been a little girl. They were one of the last things that Saint Station had said to her before it had opened its dripping blue teeth and torn her childhood away.

She touched the light scarring on her wrists, not wishing to remember. *The Giant Lies Still Awake, Sophie Vesachai*, the ancient monster had said, as if it were explaining why it was maiming her. She heard the whistles from the Practice Guard, closer now, but for a moment, she couldn't seem to move.

The last time Sophie Vesachai heard those words, she had been caught in events that nearly destroyed her, that nearly destroyed the Keep itself, that had turned her into a drunk and a reprobate.

The Giant Lies Still Awake, Sophie Vesachai.

Saint Station, and all of the other things that happened when she was a child—the magic Book and the Dream of Trees and the Hot Halls War—had stripped her childhood away as surely as those pearlescent teeth had stripped her skin away. Her bones had been wrapped in forbidden silver, and she'd earned a death-sentence from her family. Saint Station, that monster out in the deep Dark, had started something that ended with the Hot Halls War, the worst catastrophe that had ever befallen Sophie's home. And she had only been able to save it by sacrificing everything she had ever loved.

"The Giant Lies Still Awake, Sophie Vesachai," Saint Station had said, right before it had torn her arms open. *"And The World Needs Weapons."*

Sophie heard the shout of a Practice Guard, almost close enough to tangle with, and she turned to run.

THE MONSTERS

Welcome to the Wanderlands

"When we chose, we chose ruin."

—ANDERTON LOUIS, 'TWO FIGURES'

Once upon a time, there was a stairway that climbed from one world into another.

It was a very long stairway, but then, it would have to be. It had been built back in the dawn ages of the Wanderlands for a very specific purpose and was the only one of its kind. Climbing it would be the work of days, perhaps weeks; it was a slender helix of stairs supported by thin metal supports that seemed to climb forever up into the depthless stone above. But if you had the constitution, if you had the *will*, you could climb—in a few short days—up out of the Underlands, that dead civilization carved into the limitless rock beneath the Mountain, and into the world above.

The stairway—which resembled nothing so much as the rifling in a very long gun barrel—found its upper terminus in a large oval plaza set into the center of a very beautiful, very old, and very *dead* city.

This was a unique city in quite a few respects, and one of them was that it had been built into a shallow caldera atop the largest mountain in any world, in any universe, in any place or sense or time. It was *the* Mountain; there was none other like it in the Wanderlands, and that meant there was none like it anywhere at all. It was so big that empires rose and fell on its slopes, never knowing about each other, never climbing all the way to the top. It was so big that there was an entire civilization tunneled into the stone beneath it. It was so big that the dead city on top of it, grand and spectacular and acclaimed and large in history as it was, was barely a smudge of masonry and silver at the very top of the impossible peak.

And hanging over that lost city and the Mountain and the Lands beyond, like an ominous black blanket, stood the dead sky. It was featureless and dark—*no*. It wasn't just dark. It was the apotheosis of dark. It was the massive, utter, absolute weight of nothing, a heavy quilt of black that hung waiting, just overhead. It was as if someone had taken away—not just light—but the very hope of light. If you looked at that sky, you were looking at the impossibility of hope.

The sky was dead; heavy; dark. When you saw that sky, you understood why the word was said the way it was—not dark but *Dark*.

It wasn't just an absence; that could have been borne. It wasn't just a lack of light above; that could be rationalized. No, this was a burden of darkness overhead. It was a weighty, irrefutable cloak laid over the world. It had texture. It had heft.

The top of the Mountain seemed to scrape that oppressive black quilt; it was that big. The structure that could only be described with absolutes: the Mountain. There was only one Mountain; there was only one edifice in all of the Wanderlands so irresponsibly huge that it could earn such a simple name. There were other mountains in the Wanderlands.

But there was only one *Mountain*.

And, on the very peak of that Mountain, near the tall stretch of the Silver Feed that rose into the shadows above, there was some light. Just a little bit of light, and it shone on the streets of a very old, very famous, and very dead city built into the caldera at the very top of the Mountain. The light came from silver lightsculptures scattered through the highways and byways of the deserted metropolis. There was some litstone built into the buildings, shining on long-abandoned paving and cobbles. There were some remnants of the Silver Age, the age of light, of warmth, of legend and joy. But those remnants were failing; and whenever they failed, in crept the Dark.

The plaza in the center of the city was lined with silver columns, a sort of silver that was *more* than silver, a kind of silver that gave off delicious light and made one think of immense effort expended to achieve a very subtle effect. Like the Dark, it was unique enough for its own superlative: *Silver*. Most of these light sources still functioned, but like missing teeth in a wide smile there were several that no longer held light, and a few that were noticeably dimmer. To one side of this oval plaza, as noted, was a wide pit, lined with a delicate rifling stairway that led down into shadows—down into the Underlands.

On the other side was a round stone daïs.

The daïs—perhaps as wide across as a person striding twelve times—was plain but of quite fine make. It seemed somehow older—or perhaps more important— than the city around it. In the center of this circular disc, standing upright and unsupported, stood a door.

Now, it should be noted that this was not a normal door. It had a frame made of primordial gray wood and had a round silver handle set into the center. In those respects, it was similar to other doors in the dead city and indeed looked a bit like any typical door to be found in any city in this or any other world.

And yet, this door was quite different.

The most obvious and striking difference, of course, was the fact that *most* doors were by their nature openings, passageways, portals from one contiguous space to another. They were demarcations between states. They were slabs of material that said *this* space was outside and *this* space was in. But this particular door made no such demarcation; it stood alone in the center of the plaza. It was set into no wall and had no transitive property that could be easily discerned. There was nothing to indicate that, if the door was opened, it would provide any passage other than through an empty frame.

No one could look on this ancient and free-standing door and not imagine that something interesting indeed would happen if it were to be opened. Perhaps it was the incredibly fine engraving on the silver knob in the center of the thing. Perhaps it was the oddly technical runes arranged in concentric circles around the knob, which might put a clever creature in mind of coordinates.

It certainly put that in the minds of two creatures specifically, but as to their cleverness, we shall see. For in that dead city, at that particular time, lived two monsters.

Now, there are all sorts of monsters in the Wanderlands! There are ancient monsters made of silver and mindsprings, long gone mad in the deep Dark. There are new-made monsters, automata crafted with arcane energies by the Nine and the Deadsmith in the colossal redoubt of their White Tower. There are godlike monsters, one of them bound in torment far below the prodigious Mountain, the worst of them trapped in a circle of warding in a far-off land called Forest. And there are those everyday monsters in the shape of people, with no excuse other than greed or hubris.

These particular monsters aren't any of those.

These monsters were of the worst sort. These monsters were the kind of villains that wished well, and did badly. These monsters were of an order that had not been seen in the Wanderlands for many, many years.

These monsters were called Behemoth, and they were from another world.

———

Jackie and Gun didn't, at that time, know they were monsters. They did not yet know that they were villains. All they knew was that they were bored as *all holy fuck*. They were sitting on the edge of a bottomless pit, swinging their feet over infinity, doing what they usually did, which was waiting for something to happen. But nothing did. The last thing that had happened was when Jackie found the little floating silver ball that gave off light and followed her everywhere. And that had been months ago.

They didn't know if the pit was actually bottomless; the big circle in the big plaza in the middle of the big dead-ass city had a slender stairway that wound down along the inside edge, so presumably there was some kind of bottom to the thing. But the stairway disappeared into a rather sinister and inky gloom. They'd tried throwing chunks of rock and such down in there, and never heard them hit the bottom.

Gun sighed, looking down past his shoes at the shadows below. Occasionally a wind blew up out of that enormous hole—the only wind that blew in the dead city at all—and it always smelled like old dust, and gloom, and something that had rotted a long time ago. There was something almost mesmerizing about darkness that complete, and sometimes he imagined leaning forward and falling into the black, forever.

Better than being bored. He sighed again, louder this time. As he did more and more often when he was feeling some kind of way, he set his hand on the hilt of his ridiculous sword and felt a little lighter.

Jackie was whittling on her walking stick and ignoring Gun's moping as best she was able. She'd discovered a talent for it, both the whittling and the ignoring, and the small pocket knife that used to be attached to her keys was perfect for this kind of work. She kept the blade sharp with Gun's whetstone, which he hadn't yet used because it didn't appear that *anything* in this godforsaken place could dull his sword. She was, just then, adding a band of patterned lines around one end of the stick, cutting delicately into the wood with little flicks of her fingers, occasionally brushing the curls of wood off her lap and into the endless pit. Gun lifted his sword a delusory few inches and let it fall onto the ancient, meticulously crafted stone edge of the opening.

The blade sank about three inches into the stone with only the faintest cracking sound. Gun lifted it up and let it fall again, at an opposite angle, and smiled a little at the sound of stone breaking. He watched a triangle-shaped wedge, cut by his sword, slide free, down the blade, and into the blackness below.

There was no sound of its hitting anything at the bottom. Gun looked at his sword, bemused even after all these months, at the ease with which it cut things it should not be able to cut. The big oval edge of the staircase was littered with little notched 'v's, like a monstrous rat had been chewing at it.

"Okay," Jackie said, finally. *"What."*

"What do you mean, 'what'?" Gun cut another V-shaped wedge of stone.

"What the fuckin' what?" Jackie said. "What's your problem?"

"Nothing."

"Fuck off, you're on my tits with this morose bullshit. Cut it out."

Gun swung the sword too hard, cut too deep into the stone, and had to wrench it free. It annoyed him out of all proportion to the inconvenience.

"Sure," Jackie said and tossed her walking stick and knife aside. She put her elbows on her thighs and looked at her friend. "Well, what then?"

"What, nothing! I don't know."

"Gun. *Gunnar.* You're getting boring."

He flinched at the word. Boredom was ever the enemy, in the dead, museum-like city. They tried not to use it too much; it was too potent a descriptor. Too dangerous.

"Maybe," he said, "I want to be boring." Another chunk of stone cut free. It really was amazing how clean the cuts were. Practically polished.

"You sound like a man who wants to be thrown into that pit."

Gun leaned forward, looking down at the big murk below his feet. He shrugged.

"Go for it. Some change would do me good."

Gun tossed his sword aside. He looked up at the big gloom above, that somehow tangible and oppressive black sky. He looked over at Jackie, who was steadfastly whittling. She had some dust in her close-cropped cloud of ebony hair, and her hiking shirt was dirty, too. She had a bunch of random tattoos all down her arms and, presumably, other places. She had a pierced lip.

Jackie was *cool.* She was tall, dark, effortlessly badass. She looked like she belonged on an adventure. Gun, on the other hand, looked like what you would see in a dictionary, under the heading "nondescript male." He stretched.

"We're gonna have to do something soon," he said. "Maybe go see what those lights are, outside the city."

"Maybe," Jackie allowed. She set her walking stick across her knees. She'd found it in the woods, back in the other world, as they were hiking towards . . . well, they didn't like to think about that too much. It was slender, and about as long as her arms spread fingertip-to-fingertip. In the boredom of the dead city, Jackie had developed a borderline-frightening relationship with her stick. "That looks like a real long walk, in a big chunk of dark."

"I just wish we could tell how far away the lights are," Gun muttered. "They're so far below us. They could be a mile away or they could be . . . I don't know. Forever."

"We've got to be on top of a mountain," Jackie said, for about the millionth time, "but how could a mountain be *this* big?"

"I don't know," Gun said, testy, for about the millionth time. "How can a world exist with no sun, no daylight, no seasons, no wind, nothing living that we can see at all? We need some answers, Jacks!"

"*You* need answers. Because you're a *nerd.*"

Gun rolled his eyes. "You're so cool, Jackie Aimes."

"Thanks!"

"It wasn't a compliment. It was supposed to be like . . . what. An ironic insult."

Jackie sniffed. "Well, you're bad at insults. Like you're bad at cards, and fighting, and talking, and being a dude. And kissing."

Gun was affronted. "How would you know?"

Jackie grinned. "Your grandpa told me. Ah-ha! A smile! An actual smile, from the mope! I win."

"My grandfather," Gun said, nobly, "was a giant of a man and a patriarch entire. But he used too much tongue."

"Gah! Too far."

"You started it."

"I don't start things, I finish them. Anyways . . . damn. I wish there was some goddamn way to keep time here. I'm not tired yet."

"Me neither," Gun said, with a yawn.

"What do you want to do?" Jackie gave him a sidelong look. "We could go try some more combinations on that weird door."

Gun looked back over his shoulder at the freestanding door that stood on the other side of the plaza, in the center of the big stone daïs. "Man, I don't know. I've tried all the combinations I can think of. I don't think it works."

"It's gotta do *something*," Jackie said. "Bet it's like a magic portal or some shit. Like that one book, that . . . ah, shit."

Gun, in a rare fit of wisdom, didn't say anything. There had been many unpleasant things about the way they had come into this world, and they didn't like to talk about it much. They'd awakened to find themselves in a cave and did not know how they got there. Just outside it was a golden birdbath-looking thing. Gun, always the inquisitive one, had touched it and experienced an extraordinarily disagreeable sensation while an entirely new set of words, associations, language, and meaning had gotten shoved into his head.

This kind of learning was convenient, he supposed, for visitors from other worlds, but he couldn't help but resent the rather high-handed manner in which it was done. It had resulted in some odd memory loss, and they both, frequently, could not recall the names of things from their old world, or certain concepts that were common there.

Jackie hadn't taken to this unasked-for magic very well and had punched the golden birdbath to bits, and those bits into powder. Fortunately they had found some more of the birdbaths in the dead city—fortunate because they seemed to be the only source of food or drink in this entire godforsaken place. One of the other things the birdbaths did—other than replacing your native language—was to fill to the brim with a bronze-colored liquid metal kind of stuff, and when it subsided, packages of something like water and something like food were left behind. It was all *very* science fiction, which Gun approved of. They were also, Gun learned later, called *Wells*.

"I remember the book," Gun said, to distract her. "It does seem like the door should open up onto somewhere else, right?"

"Maybe somewhere with some actual people," Jackie said, looking around at the abandoned museum of a city. "Something to do."

"This adventure does seem to be getting off to a slow start," Gun allowed.

"Your adventure sucks. Sold a rotten bill of goods, Gunnar!"

"If I remember correctly, it was a certain over-excitable bartender that convinced *me* that she should come along on my adventure."

"You plied me with alcohol."

"*You* were the bartender!"

"Your excuses do you no credit," Jackie sniffed. "The truth is that you deceived me with fantasies of sexy elves and shit, and then you gave me *this*. No elves, nothing to do, *nothing to goddamn drink*."

"I never promised any sexy elves." Gun pointed out. "But this hasn't quite been the fun time I thought it would be. Before we grabbed that goddamn black pillar . . ."

"Careful," Jackie warned.

Gun shut up, wincing at the memory. That fucking octagonal, pitch-black pillar they'd found in the woods. He shuddered. It had stripped them down into what felt like the fundamental shreds of themselves, their component atoms, but it hadn't been fast, and it had been extraordinarily painful. And then they had been rebuilt—here.

But not rebuilt the same, *oh, no.* Gun grimaced and flexed his hand.

"I don't know," Jackie said, sounding defeated. "Maybe we should try to get to those lights. They can't be that far."

"Could go down the stairway." Gun watched her from the side of his eye. "I mean, the dream . . ."

"You know what? Fuck your dream. That stupid dream is why I'm not eating barbecue and drinking beer right now. If it weren't for your stupid dream, we could be sitting on a beach."

"If it weren't for the stupid dream," Gun pointed out, "we never would have met."

"Even better!" Jackie said. "Then I could be on a beach somewhere, *alone*."

Gun grinned, now trying to cheer *her* up. "C'mon. This is more fun than a beach! Hell, maybe there's some sun and sand through that door. If we can figure out the combination."

"Five rings with thirty symbols each, Gun. I'm not good enough at math to know how many possible combinations that is, but I'm good enough at puzzle games to know the odds ain't good."

"Yeah, yeah," Gun said, deflating. "We're gonna have to do something, though. Get this adventure started."

"Motherfucker, I know what you're going to say, and I don't want to hear it."

"I really feel like we got to go down there, Jacks." He looked down into the gloom below and shivered. He could understand Jackie's foreboding. There was something more dark than dark down there; he could feel it. And yet, the dream. That remarkable dream, of a giant and a silver sword; the dream that had yanked him out of his ordinary life like a champagne cork popping; the dream that made it so Gunnar could close his eyes and point, and he would know where he needed to go. Pointing led him to a black pillar tucked deep away in a lonesome forest.

Right now, if Gun closed his eyes and pointed, he would be pointing *down*.

"I don't want to go down there, Gun," Jackie said, and shivered. "I just don't like the smell of it."

"It just smells like dust. But I keep feeling like we're supposed to."

"Smells like old dust." Jackie wrinkled her nose. "And like, *darkness*."

"It is pretty dark. It kind of ominously disappears down into the depths, don't it?"

"Yes, it does. And I'm telling you, I hear sounds from down there."

"There ain't no sounds. Nothing's moved in this damn city but us for about a million years."

"You do take a girl to the nicest places," Jackie said.

"This wasn't supposed to be a date," Gun said, annoyed. "It was an *adventure*."

"You know, you use that word too much."

"It's from our last night! Remember the hotel rooftop, the tequila, toasting the morning sun? 'Here's to adventure!'"

"I *remember* what it's from, Gunnar," Jackie said, "but I'm putting a moratorium on that word until some actual *adventure* happens, all right?"

Gun blinked, surprised. "Who taught you how to use big words?"

"Motherfucker, I'll break you over my knee. Come on, Gun. *Come on.* Let's do something. I'm literally going to die of boredom."

"I don't think anything in this place can kill us, Jacks."

"Boredom will! And you better believe that if I'm gonna shove that sword in my guts, I'm gonna take you with me. Just for, like, justice."

Gun considered. "I don't know. Cards?"

"Fuck cards. All we do is play cards."

"Well I don't know!" Gun said. "Explore—"

"We've explored every inch of this goddamn city! How many of your stupid books have you found? Three?"

"I like those books."

"Because you're a nerd. And you like reading about robots and ancient civilizations and . . . oh! *Shit.*"

Gun startled. He didn't like the suddenly eager tone in Jackie's voice. "What?"

She was looking at him with an evil glint in her eye. "You reminded me. Cards. Remember? A few days ago? We made a bet."

Gun groaned. "No, Jacks, come on. I wasn't serious."

She pointed over his shoulder, at where a slender tower of stone stood, at the edge of the plaza. "A bet is a bet, Gunnar."

Gun turned. The tower was topped with a big silver sculpture, abstract, but with sharp bits. "No, you *psychopath!*"

"Come on, it will be fun."

"It will be fun for *you*," Gun said. "You just want to use my sword."

"The sword is incredibly badass. I'll admit it."

"Then you should have gotten one of your own!"

Jackie scowled at him. "They only had this one, because *you* just had to get the kind that had ripples in the steel. Besides, we didn't have time to steal two."

"I read in a book once that ripples in the steel mean it's very high quality. I can't help it if I'm smart. And I read. You'll have to make do with your walking stick."

"*Gunnnnn,*" she said, wheedling, "there's probably some of that silver stuff inside the tower. I'll need the sword to chop through it."

Gun groaned, theatrically. He looked at the tower again and then at Jackie. It *was* nice to see her animated, excited. And besides, it was something to do.

"Okay, fine," Gun said, handing the sword to her. "But if it kills me, you're going to be even more bored."

"Nah, I have some weird stuff I'm planning to do to your corpse."

Gun shook his head and looked heavenward. All he saw was the heavy black sky. "Of all the people to be trapped in a nightmare, shithole fantasyland with."

"Oh shut up, you love it," Jackie said, and dragged him upright.

———

In the plaza, Jackie had used the tip of Gun's sword to scratch a large 'X' into the big, fitted stones. It was better lit in this section of the city; more of the big silvery sculptures and pillars that provided light were still working. Jackie's silvery light-ball seemed to recognize when there was enough light and lowered its glow. If it ever needed to recharge, Gun had never seen it.

Gun had winced a little, watching her use his sword to scratch the mark into the paving stones. He liked to think that his sword was a noble weapon, brought to this world for some high-minded purpose, and Jackie's cavalier use of it annoyed him. Of course, he'd had no idea what the sword was going to be used for, when they'd bought it. He'd just known that he needed one. He'd been changed completely by the dream he'd had, back in his old world, that wild dream of a giant and a silver sword, the dream that had smashed him free from his old life like the swung hammer of a vengeful god, throwing him halfway across the country and into the unexpected embrace of Jackie Aimes. And sure, there had been a lot of other confusing stuff in the dream, stuff about an endless underground city and a giant with sad eyes, and inky black overtaking everything, but the sword had been the really prominent thing.

He didn't know much about this place, but he did know, quite surely, that whatever or whoever had sent him the dream of the giant and the silver sword hadn't meant it to be used for Jackie's brand of wholesale lunacy. Gun stepped onto the 'X,' though, because there are many rules and customs that change across the worlds, but a bet is still a bet.

"Ready?" Jackie called, from the base of the slender tower. Gun studied it; it was perhaps fifteen feet across, mostly very heavy-looking stone, and the sculpture looked heavier still.

"This won't hurt," Gun told himself. "I know it won't hurt."

"Ready?" Jackie called again, just *way* too excited, and raised the sword. Gun didn't bother answering. Oh, well. Jackie was right about one thing; it was better than being bored. He crossed his arms and waited, as resigned as he could be.

With a shout, Jackie attacked the base of the tower, hacking at it with his sword. The blade, changed the same way they had been, cut through stone with hardly any effort at all. She was right, though, and there were some threads of that silvery stuff in the stone, and those were harder to cut through. Jackie Aimes had the soul of a demolitions expert, though, and loved few things in this new life more than knocking down buildings.

Gun had tried to reprimand her about this, earlier in their days in the dead city, and she'd laughed. "Show me someone who will care," she'd said, "and I'll stop immediately."

With a creaking groan and the sounds of stone breaking and high-tension wires snapping, the tower began to keel over towards Gun. He was tempted to step aside, but a bet *was* a bet. And besides, it probably wouldn't hurt. Hadn't he jumped off one of the tallest buildings in the city, slamming into the stone below so hard it had made a fractured crater? If he was being honest with himself, he regretted the destruction of the beautiful old tower more than he worried about being hurt by it. He wanted to know more about this place, its history, its peoples, not destroy it.

He wanted to know why it was so goddamn *dark* in this world.

The tall tower shuddered and began to fall toward him. It smashed into Gunnar Anderson like a freight train, but didn't knock him down. To him, it felt mostly as if a very tall stack of floral foam blocks had been pushed over on top of him. He did, however, get clipped in the shoulder by the silvery statue on top of the tower, and it had enough weight to make him yelp.

When the dust cleared and Jackie stopped whooping, she helped him climb out of the rubble. She was grinning, and Gun acknowledged that it had been worth it just to see that genuine smile; they were becoming rarer and rarer.

"Fun?" Jackie said.

"You *are* a psychopath." Gun brushed himself off. He brightened, though. "Hey, look! That silver thing gave me a bruise!"

He pulled his shirt aside to show her; there was a faint purpling on his shoulder. She whistled; as far as they could remember the tower was the first thing they'd found—native to this world—that could hurt them at all.

He couldn't help but grin at Jackie, as the dust settled on yet another field of debris in the dead city. They were going to have to pick one of the two ways out of the city soon, or Jackie was going to demolish the entire place.

"I gotta say," he said, looking at his friend brandishing the sword, "you wear that thing well."

"It's because I'm completely awesome, in every way."

"See?" Gun shook his head. "You flew right by the compliment. Starting to hope we meet someone here who can take you down a peg or two."

"Good luck with that." Jackie expelled a big breath, looking around at the dead city, then up at the shadowed sky. Her chest rose and fell; they had been changed into nigh-indestructible badasses, but they still could run out of breath. She looked down at the rubble of the once-beautiful old tower, built in another age for purposes Gun could only guess at.

"Well," she said, brushing dust out of her hair, "what do you want to do now?"

THE CONVOX

The Utility of Giants

"Two meet; three plot."

—CORAZON LI, 'INVECT AL SARAMANTIC'

The man who calls himself West—first-made son of the legendary Hunter Fine, possessing all of his finest qualities and most important memories, not quite a man because he is quite a bit more than one—has done his best to explain to the five figures around the fire that the Giant Kindaedystrin, the greatest threat the world had ever faced, is unequivocally *dead*. West has some of Hunter Fine's memories, after all, memories of building the prison for that brute, building it leagues below their feet, and building it so that nothing could ever, *ever* escape.

Furthermore, Kindaedystrin was the greatest Returner—the greatest *Giant*—that the Mother had ever sent against her children, but he was still a Giant. When Giants lose hope, they turn to stone. Kindaedystrin has been bound in his prison below the Mountain for two ages of the world now. West *knows* that the Giant is long, long dead.

He knows it with all of his father's memories; he knows it with all of his long, considerable, hard-fought experience.

The beautiful, terrifying boy named Primary Gray, however, just looked at West—and fat D'Alle on his walking-couch, at the broken man, Candle, and the tall, menacing Mr. Turpentine—just looked at them with his disconcerting golden eyes and told them that the Giant still lives.

"The Giant is dead," West had pronounced; he was certain of it.

"No, he is not," Primary Gray had said.

Primary Gray is one of the Children, and he can never be mistaken and can never lie. The boy is, by some definitions of the term, a god. If Primary Gray says the Giant Kindaedystrin, the One Who Fell, the beast that had murdered the world—if Primary Gray says *that* ancient creature is still alive, then it is.

It isn't comforting news.

West doesn't care for that sort of news; no, not at all. But even if the Giant does lie awake, somehow, trapped for these long ages in his prison, West cannot imagine how it could have anything to do with him. His father helped build that prison, certainly. But the idea of anyone—especially this motley crew arrayed around this fire—tampering with the Giant or his prison is so ludicrous that West cannot countenance it.

So what is the true purpose of this convocation in the dark, this Convox?

Fucked if he knows. But he means to know. West did not come here just to leave. West gets himself together; it will not do to betray his emotions to these would-be allies. Not until he has leverage, not until they fear him more than they wonder.

Mr. Turpentine continues fussing with his beverages, not shocked at all by the proclamation, which tells West that the machine already knows this news. The broken man who calls himself Candle, too, shows no surprise; he sits with his own disquieting, off-putting eyes and stares into the fire like a beaten dog.

"Well," D'Alle says, clearing his throat and plainly not as overwhelmed with Gray's pronouncement as West was, "I guess I'm going to play the part of the *out-city bumpkin* here, who needs all manner of things explained. We were called—at a fair bit of trouble—into this black pit to discuss—what? A *Giant?* A fairy tale? Do you jest with me?"

Candle gives him a sour grin and sips his steaming cup of *chûs.* He looks up at the massive winding stairway, rising into the shadow of stone above. He adjusts his broken leg; it appears as if he needs help from his hands to do so.

"Master D'Alle, does your civilization not know the truth of this?" Mr. Turpentine says. "Say not so! Does Cannoux have no knowledge of what it was built upon? Have you no legends of the Giant Kindaedystrin?"

D'Alle snorts. "Of course we do. We drown in legends and improbable stories; who is to know what to believe? But you speak of some malevolent force, buried in another age. Come, friends. You try my patience."

"You always were a cocky prick," Candle observes, without looking at him. "Now you're a *fat* cocky prick."

"You'd do well not to antagonize your betters."

"But all folk are my betters, D'Alle! Who am I to antagonize, then?"

"You—"

"I fear," Mr. Turpentine says, breaking in, "and I fear indeed, that we discuss no fantasy, no safe stories, and no dead legends. Since dear Candle has taken it upon himself to broach the subject, I can assure you that wiser folk than I have convinced me that the Giant is all too real, that he is buried beneath our feet, and were he ever to escape his bonds, the world would lose whatever small amount of light it has left."

"That's one way to put it." Candle looks into the fire.

"I should assure my colleague that the Giant is indeed buried far beneath us." West rolls his cup between his palms. "Though it strains every scrap of credulity

I possess to imagine that he has survived these long years. Giants turn to stone when hope is lost, and certainly Kindaedystrin must have lost hope long ago."

Primary Gray raises his golden eyes to West's again, and West holds his hands out, palms up, placating. "Yes, yes. If Primary Gray says it, then it must be so. The Children do not lie, nor are they ever mistaken, but this is one time I wish they could be. The Giant Kindaedystrin was the greatest threat that ever faced us; it took the combined might of the Silver Age to put him down. I should know; binding him and building his prison was my father's last great work."

West allows a small amount of teeth into his smile as he looks around the fire. He's regaining some of his confidence, now. He winks at Turpentine. "Well. Last great work other than making *me*."

Candle snorts but doesn't comment. This is good; West has never liked the man and will not long resist the temptation to empty his weapon into his damned face. He sips his drink, feeling better and better. He is starting to understand this so-called Convox; and once he understands it fully, he will be able to control it. Neither West nor Primary Gray really lies, but truth can be disingenuous. The Giant . . . well, he certainly existed; he was perhaps the greatest villain in the history of the Wanderlands. And that history includes the Twins, so it is saying something.

It is even barely possible, West thinks, that the thing still lies awake, a hundred leagues below his feet, straining at bonds forged by his father and his peers. It is barely possible, but surely no more than a pretext; the idea that this small gathering could affect the Giant or its prison is so absurd as to be laughable. Surely, they are using this subject as a blind, to wow the unwitting.

Still, he will play along. There may yet be some advantage to be gained here.

"Forgive me," D'Alle was saying, "but I simply cannot entertain the spectre of a diabolic force buried in the heart of the world. It is preposterous—silly, even. You speak of fantasy and tales, but what is to be believed? That the Giant caused the Fall? That he broke the sky and caused the Dark to bleed into our world? That one soul—no matter how great—is the source of all this world's misery? It doesn't play, gentlemen, and I won't credit it."

"Master D'Alle!" Mr. Turpentine says, slyly. "Are you suggesting we should doubt that the Giant *punched the sky* and broke it? But I dearly love that tale!"

West, in the moment, decides he likes the idea of being the knowledgeable one. It will increase his standing in this group and make them dependent upon him. He clears his throat and adopts a bit of the manner of a distinguished lecturer his father had known, in another age.

"The Giant did not cause the Fall, nor did he bring the Dark." West leans forward, resting one elbow on a knee and gesturing with his free hand. "He is no fountain of destruction and evil; he is no supernatural being, and he is certainly no fairy-story. He is a *Returner*, one of the Mother's punishments upon our world, the greatest and most dangerous of them all. It took the combined might of the Silver Age at its peak to stop the swath of destruction he caused. And the greatest work of that civilization was the construction of his prison. I assure you that it is the greatest ever forged by men or gods, for I carry the memories of its making. Kindaedystrin was meant to die in that place, turned to stone in the manner of his kind. And if he somehow still lays awake after all these years, then I cannot but think that his bonds hold, and he should be left to suffer until this world ends."

"But what, my good West," Mr. Turpentine says, with a twinkle in his eye, "if those bonds weaken?"

West smiles. "If those bonds had weakened, Turpentine, we would all be dead. In the Silver Age, as they say, they did not fuck around. They built to last."

Candle chuckles but does not elaborate on his amusement. This is annoying, but West has decided that he will not let the broken man get to him; in fact, why should he care? West has never liked him, and he decides that this creature is beneath his notice. West sees Turpentine straighten, however, turn, and look out into the inky blackness beyond their fire.

"Ah!" he cries. "Finally, and none too soon! Our host arrives!"

A shape builds itself up out of firelight and gloom, coming towards them.

"I do indeed." A woman enters the circle of light, coming past the big dim bulk of the stairway that rises beyond. Her voice is rich and warm, a thrilling contralto. It makes West's neck prickle. His father remembered that voice well, and those memories make West's groin tighten. The woman looks around the fire, smiling. "Hello, my friends!"

"Dear Winter!" Mr. Turpentine says, and bows as formally as West has seen him do so far. "Welcome to our fire; as you can see, we are gathered and well lubricated by both wholesome drink and companionship."

"Excellent," the woman called Winter says. She is pleasant-featured, in a warm and comforting sort of way, and her eyes sparkle with firelight. She has long dark hair and quick, mischievous green eyes, and she sets her hand on Primary Gray's shoulder in greeting. The boy gives her a gentle nod of acknowledgment, which was more than he had given West.

"Master D'Alle!" Winter gives the reclining man a small bow. "It is good to see you again, my friend. In truth, I did not know if you would make the journey all the way from Cannoux."

D'Alle looks pleased; of course, he would be. A dog loves to be petted. He smooths his black queue of braided hair and preens. "I would not ignore such an invitation. I am glad to be among our number."

"And I am glad to count you." Winter casts a dazzling smile at him. She lays a hand on Candle's shoulder now, who reacts as if she were a spider of roughly equal size and shape.

"Hello, lover," she says, and Candle shudders. "Have you been a good boy?"

"*Fuck* you," the broken man says, but she laughs with delight, as if he'd whispered a poem. She turns her eyes across the fire, to West. He resists an urge to flinch from that direct gaze, from those powerful eyes. She glides across the space between them, skirting the fire, holding out her hand.

"And you, my old friend. You came! I was the most uncertain about you and the most hopeful."

"I came," West manages, and takes her hand after the slightest hesitation. She is dressed simply, in a textured gray tunic. It highlights her handsomeness without being ostentatious.

"Now, please tell me," she says, in a faintly admonishing air, "that bygones are bygones, Lourde. Or it is *West* now? Yes? You won't hold past difficulties against me? Business being business, and all that?"

"I do my best," he says, with a bit of difficulty, "to stay above the family squabbles."

"Of course you do." Winter's eyes crinkle at the corners. "And you, more than anyone, remember how close I was to your father."

West looks away. "I remember."

Winter's eyebrow quirks, just the tiniest bit, and she grasps his shoulder, letting her index finger trail along the bare skin of his neck. She turns back to the fire and accepts a steaming cup of *chûs* from Mr. Turpentine. West keeps his face impassive and ignores the leer that Candle is trying to throw at him. The man is beneath notice; West has decreed it.

Winter! So that's who their host is. West's mind is reeling with intrigue and memory. It is unexpected. Things have taken a turn, here in the dark. He sips at his now-cold *chûs* for something to do while his mind races. *Winter!*

"Now!" Winter says, brightly. "We are all arrived, and that is good and beyond good. I daresay you have an idea why I gathered us here?"

"There has been talk," D'Alle says, doubtful, "of a Giant."

Winter gives him a warm smile. "The Giant. Yes, and indeed yes. The big. Bad. *Giant.*"

"I am not sure I see how my humble services can play a part in such great events," D'Alle says, slowly.

"Not an insignificant part, I assure you!" Winter says. "Indeed, I have gathered you all, and you *alone*, to take advantage of certain interesting opportunities that are converging in unique ways. We stand at one of those rare moments, a fulcrum, when small actions can have great effects. Each of you has skills and resources that will be indispensable in exploiting this moment. And, as I hope we will discover, each of you has the motivation to do so, for I always prefer to work with folk who are attuned to their own self-interest. But first, I am afraid there is a small point of order to be disposed of. I truly hate to make a mountain from a pebble, but I know it was quite clear that the invitation extended was to each of you *alone*, am I correct?"

Winter looks around, smiling, and her eyes come to rest on D'Alle. He doesn't understand. And then he does, and blinks.

"Ah. But I am alone, essentially," he says. The servant next to him remains impassive. "Axeis, here, serves only to minister to my comforts. He has his hearing, for I do not maim my servants, but I promise you that he has been trained to remember nothing. You can consider him an extension of my person."

Winter smiles, a tacit apology. "As may be, my old friend, but I'm afraid what we discuss is for those invited members of our fellowship only."

D'Alle holds Winter's gaze for a moment, but only a moment. He drops his eyes, sighs heavily, and motions for the servant to come close. For a moment, Axeis is haloed in light; West sees a filigreed tattoo that curls up the side of his neck, black ink on parchment skin; for a moment the servant is beautiful enough to catch West's attention. The boy leans in to catch D'Alle's whisper. With a hard twist, D'Alle breaks his neck and lets his body fall to the ground. The *cantrait* dances away from the body as if offended by it.

"Excellent!" Winter says, clapping her hands again. "Now, to business."

Slowly, Primary Gray picks himself up off his perch, walks around the edge of the firelight, and crouches over the body. He looks into the dead servant's eyes. His hands gesture, as if casting spells, and Gray's eyes are bright and eager. West finds this is supremely unsettling, and turns his attention back to Winter and the strange Convox of personalities.

"To business!" Candle says, clapping his hands in a mockery of Winter's mannerism. He alone watches Primary Gray drag the dead servant away from the fire, and Candle's expression is complicated.

West has stopped paying attention; Primary Gray is a creature far beyond mortal comprehension. He is certainly no child.

"To business, indeed," Winter says. If she is annoyed by Candle's mockery, West cannot tell. "For we sit, all of us, at the barest edge of the Underlands, just beneath the skin of the Mountain. We sit inside the greatest and most spectacularly failed experiment in the history of this world, a utopia carved from stone and then left to die."

D'Alle shivers. His *cantrait* must have taken him through enough dim apartments, halls, and factories on the way to this meeting to make this idea potent. It is hard to forget the sheer number of people who must have died here.

"But the Underlands is not *entirely* dead," Winter says. "Master D'Alle, is it not true that your great empire has begun the process of exploring these dead halls, these catacombs?"

D'Alle shifts on his walking-couch, proud. "That is true. Part of the slope of the Mountain near Cannoux has collapsed and revealed a city underneath the city, part of which we now rest in. We have been making attempts to map this place, but those efforts have been only partially successful."

"An empire in stone," Winter muses, as if she'd only recently stumbled across the concept. "Hollowed from beneath the Mountain; long dead. And yet, Master D'Alle, there is still some life left here, is there not?"

D'Alle shrugs. "We have found some scraps, yes."

Winter becomes gently remonstrative. "Come, my friend. We are all entitled to our secrets, but for the purposes of this gathering certain secrets must be laid open. I vouchsafe these worthies; they will not betray you."

D'Alle looks around the fire, no-color eyes reflecting its gold, and sighs. "We have found remnants," he says. "Echoes of the civilization that filled these halls. Most mad, most broken, but . . . remnants. Places where there is still some light."

"And?" Winter prompts, with a warm smile.

"And we found something. A trove. A storing-house for rare machines."

"*War* machines," Winter explains, to the others.

"A Cache!" West is surprised, in spite of himself. "You've found a *Cache*?"

"We have been told that this is what we possess." Master D'Alle emphasizes the last word, uncomfortable. He twists a ring on his finger, fidgeting. West sits back, thinking. A *Cache*, and in the control of a backwater civilization like Cannoux? That would explain the walking-couch, at least. This is information his brother would well like to know. Come to think of it, his warmonger sister might be curious about a functional Cache as well. West wonders at Winter's confidence in letting him know this.

"That is portentous news, certainly," West murmurs, looking at Winter. She gives him a wink.

"So, one of the many reasons Master D'Alle is included in our august company is revealed," Winter says. "As is one of the opportunities that we are here to speak of. However, I bring it up to illustrate a point."

"May I posit—the point is that the Underlands," Mr. Turpentine continues her thought, "are far from dead."

"*Far* from dead," Winter says. "Beneath our feet, far beneath our feet, there are places where there is still light. There are twilight civilizations, there are old demons and ancient automata. There are other Caches. And below that, dug deep into the heart of the world, so deep that it has lost memory of the world above, lies a place where light still burns brightly, and people live out their mayfly existences, all unknowing that they huddle around the last embers of light in a place that would beggar their imaginations to consider. A place called—"

"*The Keep.*" Mr. Turpentine has a bit of an ominous note in his reedy, bellows-and-pump voice. He knows the place. Winter inclines her head to the old monster and gestures for him to continue.

"To the peoples of the Keep," Turpentine continues, "the wider world, the

Wanderlands, is as much of a fairy-story as most people consider the Giant and his prison. They think their light will never fail, that they alone in all the world are proof against the Fall. Their Silver technicians—the Vesachai—are a family of mystics who barely understand what it is they do. They are ruled by a dangerous madwoman who wishes to meddle in powers beyond her understanding. They believe the easy dream that what is will ever be, and what has been is of no consequence."

"That is a lovely speech," West says, frowning at Mr. Turpentine and wondering where this is all going. "But you could use the same words to describe a thousand twilight civilizations scattered through the Wanderlands. It is a sad story, true, but a common one."

"You are entirely correct, West." Winter smiles at him. "But this particular civilization, this Keep, and their power-hungry ruler have one characteristic that no other civilization can boast. No, not even mine."

West knows it's his cue to ask the question, but he refuses. He will not play the dog for this woman, no matter his father's complex relationship with her. D'Alle, ever the hound, gives her the cue instead.

"Which is?" He is plainly fascinated.

"This Keep," Turpentine supplies, "lies near the Giant's prison."

"Bullshit." West regrets saying it at once. He has decided to be *above* this, not *in* it, and he means to use profanity only inwardly. "Even in the madness of the Fall, no one would have dug that deep."

"Ah, but you forget that the Underlands was built by the Architects," Winter says, "and they went very mad indeed."

"Still," West says. "I refuse to believe even a madman—or madwoman—or mad *creature,* for that matter, would disturb the Giant's prison."

"They did not disturb it, dear West," Turpentine says. "The Keep itself is not truly part of the Underlands. It is something much older, something built as a way to keep watch on the Giant. In the Fall, it was repurposed. Those that live there know nothing of its original function, nor of their ancestors' duty. They are descendants of the Cold; but they have little of those magicians' craft."

"This is getting ridiculous," West mutters. "So, what? Are we worried this madwoman who rules the Keep will attempt to free the Giant? The idea is ludicrous."

Winter smiles at him, a slow, knowing smile.

"Is that the purpose of this cabal, then?" D'Alle furrows his brows. "To put a stop to this woman and her designs?" It is plain D'Alle feels this is none of his business and less of his concern.

"Master D'Alle!" Winter has a twinkle in her eye. "Have you no civic spirit? Still, I believe good deeds should be done by those who are properly motivated to do them, and I daresay we shall find something in this pot to tempt your co-operation. Yes, and you too, West. You shall not walk away with your pockets empty, I assure you."

Winter smiles at him and continues. "But that is getting the *come* quite ahead of the *kiss*, as they say, so let us be plain about our purpose. There is indeed a mad queen at the bottom of the world who has delusions of freeing the Giant and harnessing it for her purposes. She works even now to accomplish these goals—but I have never been one to attack the symptom of a problem, gentlemen. What I propose is that we form a Cabal, the purpose of which is to gather what resources we find necessary to infiltrate this madwoman's lair, this *Queen Jane Guin*. But my true intention is not to kill her."

West is confused. "Then what is your intention?"

"Come on, West," Candle says, tiredly, looking into the fire. "Think it through; it isn't that hard."

"My intention," Winter says with a bright smile, ignoring Candle, "is to do what my cousins and lovers, sisters and friends should have done a long time ago. What we should have done when the world was young and strong and full of magic. They imprisoned the Giant, leaving it as a problem for future generations to solve. But there are no more generations to come, and I would solve it now."

Winter looks around the fire, green eyes glittering. "I propose that we *kill* the fucking thing."

THE KILLERS

The Loche de Menthe

"Light is the endless issue of these times, so much so that it is taken universally for granted. We live by the cycles set in literal stone, the glowing rock that makes life possible in this vast warren. We think of Dim, we think of Dark, but these are things long ago and far away, out beyond the bounds of the known world. If the peoples of the Keep realized how close the Dim is, how easily the Dark can fall, they would tear themselves apart."

**—BIND E REYNALD, SCHOLAE FIRST MARK,
'THE FALL OF THE UNDERLANDS'**

Sophie found her friends easily enough; they all knew the way to the Loche de Menthe. It was good that she had a bit of time alone, though; the message from the terrified fop in the Charm Chair still clattered back and forth between her ears.

The Giant Lies Still Awake.

She was annoyed. Someone was trying to fuck with her, either for arcane political purposes or for some obscure revenge or, most likely, just to fuck with her. She had a famous name and had been stepping on toes for as long as she was alive; it wouldn't have been hard for someone to hire that idiot aristocrat and teach him some words out of an old story. All she had to do was ignore it.

All she had to do was *ignore it.*

By the time Sophie set her crooked smile on her face and gave Hunker John a wink from down the hall, she half believed it. The dead hands of the past had been clawing at her for years; she'd gotten good at ignoring them. And there was no better place to set about ignoring and forgetting than the Loche de Menthe.

No better place to forget about her childhood, and Giants lying awake, and dead friends, and that demon Saint Station. In the Loche de Menthe, Sophie need not worry about or remember her estranged family, or the death sentence that hung over her head, or even the melancholy that had chased her all evening. The Loche de Menthe would cure all ills.

It wasn't clear what the Loche had been, originally; some extensive audience hall or concert space, some open factory floor or unknowable section of the Keep used for arcane purposes back in the dawn ages of the world. It had been abandoned to the Dim far back in the Keep's history, longer than anyone could remember. It had a couple of virtues, however, that some enterprising citizens had exploited. One, it was adjacent to the Keep Proper. A little-used but well-lit passageway ran right above the Dim space that would become the Loche. And, two, some long-ago conflict or war had knocked a large hole in that passageway, allowing access down into that big space.

Whoever had started the Loche de Menthe—and legends varied—had built a makeshift staircase down into that great empty area and then started carting in lamps and liquor and whatever other illegal substances they could get their hands on. They cleaned it up, clearing rubble and old, half-mad machines and using the abandoned materials to form slapdash walls and partitions, dividing the huge space into a warren of small alleys, pubs, hovels, and bordellos. Eventually the wrong sort of people started to show up, cued by word of mouth, and the Loche de Menthe was born.

The original expediters were happy to encourage competition, and other bars, fight-clubs, and increasingly specialized bordellos opened up. They made ties with some of the more open-minded Houses Preator for supplies and got a pretty decent little vice empire going.

The Twinsmen, the pious religious bastards, were constantly trying to shut the place down, but the Loche occupied something of a unique niche in the Keep. Being in the Dim and having been officially abandoned, it was technically and psychologically not part of the Keep Proper and therefore not subject to the various Councils, Preators, Houses, Twinsmen, and Ministry oversight that it would normally have been. The Queen could have crushed it in a moment if she'd so wished, but she decided to wink at the place since it tended to congregate a fair percentage of the Keep's undesirable elements into one handy location.

So Queen Jane turned a blind eye to what happened there and kept the Practice Guard out of the place. In return and thanks, the Loche only killed and ate her more obvious and obnoxious agents. There were probably some Redarms wandering around, keeping their ears open, but no one had ever heard of those bastards actually showing their color down there.

It was assumed that there were occasionally some of the Lurk in the Loche, but nobody worried about that very much either. Jane's Espionage Corps were too secret and too frightening for normal people to fear very much. In any case, the Queen was too smart to use those bastards on low-level crime like drugs or sex trade.

The place was a shithole, Sophie liked to say, but it was a *grand* shithole. Any substance or act you'd be ashamed to tell your parents about could be found in ready supply. There was really no mystery at all to why the Killers spent so much of their time there; they probably would have lived in the Loche if it wasn't so damned inconvenient to get to.

Sophie's uncle, Liam, had explained it to her this way: If you imagine the Keep as a rather large and barrel-chested Giant, squatting on its haunches in the Dead Lake, with arms extended for the bridges and its hat the Attics, then most of the peoples of the Keep lived in its chest. The Ministry, by accident or design, occupied the place where its heart would be, and most of the working factories were scattered through its head and shoulders. The Rue de Paladia wound through part of its belly, Spake Field and the Blue Halls took a chunk of its abdomen, and its thighs and feet were long lost to the Dim and Dark.

People liked to claim that, in this model of the Keep, the Loche de Menthe was located precisely in the Giant's asshole. It certainly smelled the part. The Killers made their way down the rickety rope-and-slat stairway that was the entrance into the place, and it smelled of sex and old booze and half-covered shit; smoke and drug-effluence and sweat.

"C'mon, New Girl!" Sophie said, offering the girl an elbow. "That's the smell of *freedom*."

"Freedom's got a heady aroma." New Girl wrinkled her nose and picked her way carefully down the slats. She lost her balance on a loose slat and stumbled onto Sophie's shoulder, her long and very fine hair trickling along Sophie's neck.

Sophie recalled what she had said to Trik, about being susceptible to beauty. All too true. She steered the girl back at Ben.

The smells of the place intensified as they descended into the thick haze of smoke that hung in the great space. Sophie looked down into the warren of makeshift rooms below; many of them had strung fabrics or lanterns across the ceiling to obscure just such a view, but others were wide open. Sophie turned to the Killers.

"All right kids, I have some biz, someone to meet. Shouldn't take long. Why don't you lot get comfortable at the Merry Prick?"

"You need any company, Capitana?" Bear said, meaning, *Do you need anybody intimidated, scared, or hurt?*

"I do, but not you, Bear. I hear the man's skittish and I don't want you scaring him away." She grinned. "But if you want to help, why don't you buy Trik a drink and see if you two can get to the bottom of it without getting in an argument?"

Trik rolled her eyes, and Bear blushed a little. Bear and Trik had maintained their sexual tension for so long it had become utterly tiresome for everyone else. Sophie glanced at New Girl.

"Mind if I steal your boy? I want my Number One along for this ride."

"Of course not," New Girl said, tossing her long blonde hair and giving Ben a kiss on his cheek. "I'll try to keep Hunker John from drinking everything dry before you get back."

"Good luck." Ben took his time about watching her go.

Sophie rolled her eyes. "C'mon, old man. You'll see them legs again."

"You're staring as hard as I am, Capitana," Ben said, with a grin. "Let's get this biz out of the way."

If there was a main way in the Loche, it would be Beggar's Row, a kind of horrible inversion of the Rue de Paladia. It was narrow and cramped and lined with maimed and unfortunates and those who were pretending to be maimed and unfortunate. Sophie kicked at a couple of the more egregious of the pretenders and ignored the rest. One grizzled old beggar with a stone bowl and dirty bandages across his eyes pulled her attention, however.

"Hey there, old-timer," she said, stopping and crouching next to him. Ben slowed to wait; he knew Sophie had a soft spot for war dogs.

"A lightweight? Lady? For something to eat?" His voice was gruff and brusque. He plainly didn't like begging. Sophie laughed, a rich deep laugh that her friends didn't hear often.

"Piss on that," she said. "Light or heavy, I only give coin for drinkers."

The old man chuckled. Behind the dirty bandage, his face seemed to relax. "Truth, girl. Food is for the sober."

Sophie studied him a moment, the bandage across his missing eyes.

"Lost them in the Halls?" she said, referring to the Hot Halls War. It wasn't really a question.

"Lost for good," the man agreed, mouth twisting, but pride in his voice. "I led in the Fourth, though. Second through the walls and got 'em burned in the Bridges Brigades. End of the war, that was."

"Yes," Sophie said, "it was."

"Before your time, I'm sure," the old man said, his voice like old warm gravel.

Sophie shook her head; she had spent enough time wrapped in old memories tonight. She pressed a thick coin into the man's gnarled hand and stood up, but the old veteran caught her jacket.

"Too much, girl." He frowned, feeling the weight of the coin. "You'll drown me with this."

"Nah," Sophie said. "Old war-whores like you? You know how to float."

He laughed, rubbing the face of the heavy coin. "Aye, girl, that we do. That we certainly do."

———

Sophie and Ben were supposed to meet the contact at a bar called the Dead Sky, but they didn't see him at first. The Dead Sky was a small place, intimate. Most of the establishments in the Loche de Menthe were open to the high ceiling above and used the dim but still working lightsculptures hanging there for illumination. The owner of the Sky, however, had laid a heavy black velvet over the top of the space and then suspended small pots of burning oil on strings for light. Each pot was fitted with a clockwork mechanism that capped the light every few minutes, plunging the place into a deep gloom, echoing tales of the mythical dead black sky that lay far overhead. Sophie had entered when the lights were muted and the bar was unlit. When the mechanisms lifted and the flickering light returned, she saw a young man motioning to her from a deep alcove that held a table and two bench seats on either side.

All along the boundaries of the bar were tall cages filled with tiny flocking birds of many colors, glittering iridescent in the low light. Caging birds was a crime, and something you only saw in the Loche de Menthe. She knew that if you wanted to spend the coin to make it happen, they would release a cat into one of those cages. Depraved as she occasionally was, she didn't enjoy such displays and was glad nobody had spent for it just now.

She slid into the padded bench after Ben and accepted a set of drinks from the wait; they were known here. She used a slow sip to study the young man across the table from her.

There wasn't a whole lot to study; he was wearing a tangler, a not uncommon Silver-Age device that shrouded identity. In a place as insular and well-trod as the Keep, it was understood that sometimes folk needed a little anonymity. It was something like a semitransparent mask, a fine mesh laid over the face; it allowed expression to be read but kept Sophie from discerning any concrete details. She saw that he had sharp eyes, dark brows, and a thin face. She thought he might have been handsome, but with a tangler, it was difficult to tell. He had a little knowing smile that she didn't care for and wore a long-sleeved green brocade jacket that was quite ostentatious. Sophie set her drink down.

"Hi," she said, finally. "I'm Sophie. This is my lieutenant, goes by Ben."

"Hello to you both," the young man said. Something seemed to amuse him. "Why don't you call me Mr. March."

Sophie shrugged. Noms de plume—and tanglers—were a fairly regular part of her life. Hell, she didn't even know what *Trik's* real name was. And she'd forgotten Bear's. There were many legitimate reasons why you would want to hide your identity in a place like the Loche de Menthe. "As you like. You have a job for me?"

"I do." The little smile played around the edges of March's mouth, as if he knew something amusing and was only half trying to hide it. Sophie felt a sudden urge to stick her fist into that face, but she resisted. She meant to find out what was on offer, at least. She exchanged a glance with Ben, but her friend shrugged;

no read on the kid yet. The young man settled himself. "I have a job uniquely suited to your talents."

"You need a lord seduced then," Sophie said with a grin. "Or his wife? Both?"

"We're flexible," Ben offered.

Mr. March smiled faintly. "I've been informed that you and your group of friends have some talent at getting into places and taking things out of them. Yes?"

Sophie tapped the table, studying March. Something about the man disturbed her, but he didn't have the feel of a Queen's agent or anyone else that might be trying to set a trap. No, she was just still rattled by the Consort's cryptic message about the Giant.

The Giant Lies Still Awake, Sophie Vesachai.

Just then the caps covered the lights, plunging the bar into gloom. She pulled her attention back down to March as the lights returned.

"Sure," she said, finally. "We're decent safe-breakers if the price is right."

"It will be."

With a studied carelessness, he withdrew something from his carry and tossed it on the table. It was a slim package, wrapped in heavy blue paper and sealed. There was fine gold writing inscribed on the outside, but Sophie didn't need to read it to know what it was. Her eyes widened, impressed.

"Is that . . . ?" Ben said, leaning in. Mr. March nodded.

"Ansiotropic."

"Battle Drugs." Sophie let loose a low whistle and elevated her opinion of Mr. March by a few orders of magnitude. Jane Guin, the Queen herself, commanded the only supply of Ansiotropic, and she guarded both the formula and distribution of the drugs zealously. It was reserved for her crack troops, it was legendary, and it was extremely hard to get. Sophie picked up the drugs, looking for signs of subterfuge, but if this was fake, it was the best she'd ever seen. It was heavy for its size, too; it held an indefinable air of authenticity.

March's mouth twitched behind the silvery screen. "Ever try it?"

"Once," Sophie admitted, getting excited despite herself. "It's heady stuff."

"I agree." He seemed amused by her. "There's more where that came from."

Ben gave her a nudge under the table, but she didn't need it. *More?* She settled against the padded bench back. She handed the package to Ben, who inspected it. "How much more?"

"Were you to do this particular job for us, distribution wouldn't be out of the question."

"You can get a regular supply of *Ansiotropic*?" Ben asked, with a frown.

"Possibly," the young man said, "enough for both distribution and personal use. Could come in handy for a girl of your talents. And tastes."

He sneered when he said it, but Sophie was hardly listening. Handy, indeed. With a steady supply of Ansiotropic, she could . . .

It was tempting. She remembered the other thing the messenger fop had said before he'd mentioned the Giant. *Nothing that is about to happen is what it seems.* But Sophie didn't need that kind of warning—and hadn't, not since she was young. She brought all of her attention onto the young man across from her.

"Brass tacks time. Who is 'us'? And what's the job?"

"Us is myself and my partner," Mr. March said, "whom you do not need to concern yourself with. Suffice it to say we have secure access to Ansiotropic and are willing to share."

"Why don't you let us worry about what concerns us." Ben said, pleasant, but with a hint of menace. He wasn't usually good at menace, but he, like his Capitana, smelled something wrong with this deal.

Sophie gave it a breath. "What's the job?"

Mr. March studied her for a long moment, that sly smile playing around the corners of his mouth. Then he looked at Ben. "There is a silver vault," he said, "deep in Vesachai territory. A vault with a certain symbol on it, like a slash through a helix. A vault that my partner is confident you can open."

Sophie and Ben exchanged a long look, and she sat back. She took her time, considering replies, but finally just said, "I know that vault."

March grinned, quick. "I know you do. There is something inside that we want. What it is doesn't matter. Some bit of arcane frippery that interests us."

Sophie nodded. "That's some heist. Vesachai territory, and a Silver Age vault. I can see why you came to me."

"Great rewards require great risks." Mr. March gestured at the blue package on the table. "You could become the queen of the underworld with that."

"I sure could." Sophie picked up the package, turning it over in her hands. "I sure as fuck could. How does that sound, Ben? *Queen of the Underworld.*"

"Sounds pretty great, Capitana," Ben said. "Sounds like a good time."

"And all I have to do is unlock a vault, eh?" Sophie crossed her arms, watching March.

"That's all," he said.

Sophie laughed and tossed the package of drugs back at him, too hard. It hit him in the chest and he caught it, frowning. She gave him a grin. "The answer is no."

Mr. March smiled, as if he'd been half-expecting this. "No?"

"No."

"Can I ask why?"

Sophie studied him, crossing her arms across her chest. She considered several ways to respond and discarded them.

"Ben," she said, finally, "do you like this guy's fucking face?"

"No, Capitana, I can't say that I do."

"See? There you go. We don't like your fucking face."

March grinned. "You can't see my face."

"I see enough of it." Sophie shook her head. "No, I think you can fuck off, friend. If you know what that vault is, you know I'm not welcome in Vesachai territory. On pain of death, as it happens. And I won't be able to sell very much Ansiotropic when I'm dead. So, thank you, but no."

"Oh, come on." The young man's face twitched again in that unpleasant, knowing smile. "The great Sophie Vesachai, afraid of sneaking back home? I thought the Killers were an accomplished gang of sneakthieves; known far and wide for stealing from Lords and the rich. There would be no need for you to invoke the wrath of your family, unless you were careless."

Ben leaned forward, and there was real menace in his voice now. Ben could seem soft sometimes, but he had faced Outkeep invaders and he had killed Feral Children. He had fought in the Hot Halls War. "I'm starting to want to know your *real* name, friend."

Mr. March smiled widely. "Don't you know it?"

"Should I?"

He threw this away with a little gesture. "We've met, on occasion, but it is of no matter. One last chance, Sophie; yes or no?"

"No," Sophie said.

"*Fuck* no," Ben said.

Mr. March made a show of sighing. "I think you should reconsider. All present know that you and you alone can open that particular vault, Sophie; so pretending otherwise wastes all of our time. It is known, in certain circles, what you found in there when you were young. My partner is quite resourceful and quite *determined* to get inside that vault. He could make life very difficult for you."

Sophie smiled. "I'm sure he can. Behold my terrified expression."

"Difficult for you *and* your friends."

"What the fuck did you just say?"

"I said that a smart girl might want to take these very rare and enjoyable drugs, and open a vault, and get back to drinking. A smart girl might not want to lose any more friends to forces beyond her control."

Sophie had leaned across the table and gotten his brocade lapel in her fist before she even meant to move. She spit her words into his shifting tangler of a face.

"You threaten my friends one more time, you piece of shit, and I'll be digging you out of my fucking *teeth*."

The young man tsked, moved, and Sophie felt something hard against the side of her head. March must have had it ready and waiting. She didn't need to look to see it was a chutter, and it was best to assume it was geared and loaded. She didn't give a shit.

"I'm serious," she said, into the screen that shrouded his face. "You think the Hot Halls War was a mess? You fuck with my people and I'll bring this Keep down around your ears. Don't test me, you piece of shit."

"Sophie . . ." Ben's voice was worried, but she ignored him. She was aware of the bar security; they wouldn't get involved. Ben could be too cautious sometimes.

Mr. March, not visibly troubled by her threats, blew a low whistle and let his nasty smile show, full force. "Such devotion to your friends, Vesachai. If only you'd shown this same loyalty to your Queen, or your family."

"The fuck do *you* care about my family?" She let go of the asshole's coat and stood, brushing off her shirt. "And if I had? Shown that loyalty to my family?" She gave him a hard grin. "We'd all be dead."

———

Sophie and Ben made their way across the Loche de Menthe, pushing through a press of partygoers, where the rest of the Killers were waiting. Sophie paused at the entrance, looking up above the makeshift partitions that made the walls of the bars, at the high stone ceiling almost lost in the gloom overhead, at the scattered silver lightsculptures glowing dully there. Ben watched her face.

"Tonight's getting weird," Sophie said, finally.

"Yeah. The fop with the warning, and now this Mr. March. What's going on, Sophie?"

Sophie was still looking up at the dark stone, the dim sculptures. Her expression was distant, and a small frown creased her forehead. "I don't know, old man. Someone is stirring the pot again."

"Stirring hard, if they're trying to bribe you with Ansiotropic."

"Hard to believe they'd think I'd go for that."

Ben chuckled. "Sophie, we've spent the last twenty years convincing everybody we would indeed go for that."

Sophie gave him a quick grin. "True enough. Kept us out of trouble, mostly. But tonight . . ."

Ben made a small sound, frustration or anger, and shook his head. "I thought we were done with this shit. Usually they're trying to get the Book, though; the silver vault is a new angle. Do they think it's where you hid the Book?"

Sophie frowned. "I don't know. Maybe? I probably *should* have put the Book in there."

"What's in it?"

"I don't know," she said, remembering the strange man at the end of the Hot Halls War, handing her something silver. "Some necklace or something? Maybe some other old shit; I can't remember. It was twenty years ago. But I think it's a blind; I think this Mr. March does indeed want what every other one of these lousy fucks has wanted—"

"The Book," Ben finished, sourly. "The *fucking* Book."

"The fucking Book."

Ben took a breath. "Well? What are we going to do?"

Sophie laughed, a bleak sound. She clapped her oldest friend on his shoulder, and made herself grin. "What we always do. Say fuck it, and go get a drink."

Ben nodded, reluctant. "Yes, Capitana."

"Good man. We all go into the dark, right?"

"Sooner or later," he finished, and they ducked into the Merry Prick.

THE MONSTERS

The Great Enemy, Boredom

"It is not their strength that makes Behemoth so fearsome, or even their alien perspective. No, nor even the weapons they bring with them, transformed all out of reason; the thing to truly fear about Behemoth is their carelessness."

—JOHNSTON FLEIS, 'TAEN EIY'

Like any birth, Behemoth did not come into this world easily. The translation from their world to this had been a hard one, in which they had been stripped, still conscious, down to their component pieces and then re-assembled in what they could not help but feel was a rather slipshod manner.

Sure, something about that re-assembly had made them incredibly dense, incredibly strong, and very nearly indestructible, but god *damn* had it hurt. And for a long time after they arrived in the Wanderlands, waking up to their own moans of pain, they felt like their skin was not quite their own. They felt that their bones did not fit precisely, that their teeth were just a tiny bit too small, that their eyeballs were just a touch too big.

Gunnar, the one who actually *had* the magical dream that brought them to this place, took it in relative stride. He was on an adventure, and adventures required certain hardships. All the books and films on the subject that he'd ever read or seen—and he'd read and seen a *lot*—agreed on this principle.

Jackie took it a little bit less well. She hadn't had any dream at all, and until they found the black octagonal pillar floating a few inches above the forest floor, she hadn't really believed in Gunnar and his dream. It had just been a fun reason to ditch her job and go on a cross-country trip, the kind of spur-of-the-moment lark that she was known for.

But waking up into a different body—even a really badass one—and on a broken, dreary, and miserable shithole of a world wasn't in Jackie Aimes' weekend plans, and it took her a little while to regain her natural cheerfulness. Fortunately, the two new-made monsters had time to adjust.

The portal—the twin of the pillar that, when touched, had yanked them into this world—was located in a small defile high up above the dead city, a desolate cave that had only the faintest of light. Even if they had been disposed to treat their new circumstances charitably, there had been reasons to feel less than hope-ful about this new place. For one, the cave they found themselves in was plainly intended to be a cage; its only exit was blocked off by heavy bars of pure silver, like an expensive jail, and there were several makeshift tunnels that also ended in silver bars. However, someone—or *something*—had torn a serviceable hole in those bars, hammering them out of the way with significant force.

Later, Gun and Jackie would discover that they could have done this as well, and whatever those silver bars had been installed to keep in—or out—they were no match for Behemoth. In one of the books that Gun found, there had been a few limited references to Behemoth, and they were, to say the least, discomfort-ing. It appeared that there had been others that had come through the portal and been changed. Enough of them to have a name—*Behemoth*—and enough of them for Jackie and Gun to know that not all had been nice.

In fact, to Gun's consternation, one of the books seemed to indicate that Be-hemoth were, in fact, generally regarded as villains. But, as Jackie reminded him often, we all get to choose what we do, and neither Gun nor Jackie needed to be any more villainous than they wanted to be.

In any case, it took both of them a fair bit of time before they were accus-tomed to their new bodies and new circumstances, and that indeterminate span of time was, to say the least, *unpleasant*.

Gun wasn't proud of how many times they tried to go back through the oc-tagonal pillar during that time; how many times they tried to return to their mundane, comfortable lives. But the black pillar only worked in one direction; unless and until they could find one that went the other way, they were stuck in this miserable dark armpit of a world.

Which is all to say that once they found the willpower to go explore and found the heavy dead sky above them, with no sun, moon, or stars anywhere, and a clearly abandoned and dead city set into a caldera down below, they weren't in the best of moods. Eventually, they explored the city and even hiked up to the top of the mountain to look at the slender silvery tower—which Gun would later discover was called a *Feed*—that rose up into infinity there. They started playing their games and began to discover that these new, ill-fitting bodies were pretty useful, as long as you mostly just wanted to destroy shit.

They discovered the joys of punching down buildings. Once you figured out how easy and fun punching down a building was, it got hard to stop. And it was something to do! Gun and Jackie discovered that they had spent their entire lives swaddled in a civilization geared towards keeping them amused, in what-ever fashion possible, nearly every moment of every day. To say that it took some adjustment to get used to the unceasing, unchanging nature of the dead city, the one stripped of any possible amusement long ago, would be a grand under-statement.

Boredom became their enemy; and they knew it would be, until they forced themselves to act.

From his dream of the giant and the silver sword, Gun had a feeling that he knew where to go. It was a small but sure tugging in his chest. It had led him halfway across his homeland into a deep and wild forest, and led him to the floating pillar that had brought them here.

And now it was telling him that whatever they had come here to find or do, it lay far beneath their feet. But the only way down that they could see was the Stairway, and the Stairway was ominous. Their new bodies were quite heavy now, and the steps looked fragile. So they waffled, and fought boredom, and waffled some more.

But what they really, *really* hoped for was a visitor; someone cool and interesting and wise and perhaps with a gnarled old staff and frayed robes, to explain everything, show them how to work the weird freestanding door, and take them to *somewhere* and give them *something* to do. They waited; and they waited some more.

In one of the books that Gun had found, there had been much to say about the state of the new world they'd found themselves in, as well as the sorts of folk they might expect to encounter. The book had been so inaccurate about the world around them that it bordered on parody, but Gun was able to glean some small amounts of information from it.

The denizens of the Wanderlands (the slender book said) were wide, varied, and wonderful. There were all sorts of creatures in the length and breadth of the Lands, but for short-cutting purposes, they could be grouped into a few handy categories. The first category was Low-Order Automata, and Gun read between the lines to guess that this category seemed to include both natural animals and animal-analogs created by some *unexplained* but *fascinating* process.

This information was unhelpful, however. Neither Gun nor Jackie had seen so much as a roach in the dead city, much less a cat or a monkey. Gun still had visions of finding, like, a sweet-ass robot dog, though. He supposed that Jackie's floating little silver ball-light might be one of these 'Low-Order Automata.'

The other two categories seemed to be *people* (which the unhelpful volume didn't do anything to describe or quantify, and which set Gun's fevered imagination quite to buzzing) and High-Order Automata. These were people too, but *made* people. What? Made how? How in the hell was that possible, in a place that didn't seem to have any technology other than "slowly failing lights"? Gun had no idea, but he was pretty keen on meeting some of these robot people. In this, Jackie quite agreed—though her preference was for *sexy* robot people.

The book described a place and a world that was almost hilariously at odds with the dismal shit-hole Gun and Jackie had found themselves in, but they had hopes that there were still people somewhere. Made people, real people, at this point it almost didn't matter. They were so lonely they would have been happy with a mechanical bug if it could carry a conversation. Gun obsessively read the smattering of books he'd found, trying to get a clue about who and what they might meet.

But nothing in that welcoming volume, and certainly nothing in their previous lives, could have prepared them for the creatures that he and Jackie would come to know as the Feral Children.

———

"So what do you think these birdbath things are, anyways? Something like . . . I dunno. Vending machines, but with only two ingredients?"

"I don't know, Gun."

"I mean; I get it. There's no sun here, right? Or moon, obviously, or like, anything at all. That means you can't grow food. But if people here ate stuff, they'd have to get it from *somewhere*. So why not the golden birdbath things?"

"Oh, gosh. I'm sorry, Gun. I just said 'I don't know.' What I meant to say is *I don't care.*"

"But it's interesting, right? There must have been people here, at some point. Those might have been restaurants that we found, right? But where did they get their food? Must be from somewhere. I bet it was from these golden things."

"I don't care, Gun."

"Just doesn't make any sense, why the things won't give us anything other than these disgusting candy bars and this gross sports drink stuff. No way that's all people ate. Right?"

"You would need to invent, like, some kind of new scientific notation—and some new kind of computer to compute it—to arrive at the sum total of how much I *do not care, Gunnar!*"

"All right, all right. Here's your dinner."

"Fuck you very much. Tell that fucking birdbath if it puts another goddamn language in my head, I'll do it like I did its cousin."

"I think it heard you."

"And tell it to give me a goddamn beer, while you're at it."

"I asked nicely, and it gave me some more salty piss. Will that work?"

"Gross, Gun."

"I just want to know how this all works, you know?"

"That's because you are literally trying to kill me to death with boredom, and if you don't shut up about your stupid magic food wells and low-order *automatations* and the 'Wonders of the Silver Age' I am going to kill you to death, Gun, and no, I'm *not* joking, and I need you to shut the fucking fuck up before I murder both of us!"

"Whoa, hey. You all right?"

"Fuck off."

"You want some alone time?"

"Yes. *Fuck.* No. I don't know. I don't know, Gun! I can't be in this place anymore. I can't be in this goddamn city much longer."

"Maybe—"

"If you say something about that staircase—"

"No, maybe we should try for the lights. Seriously. We've got all the time in the world, I think. Why not? We can always hike back up here."

"What do you mean, all the time in the world?"

"Jacks, I've been thinking about it. No, wait! This isn't boring. Have you noticed our hair hasn't grown at all since we got here? Not even a little? I used to have to shave every other day at least, it was the only manly thing about me. Ha! There's a smile. But our hair hasn't grown at all, and we only need to eat what, once every few days? We don't need much water—or whatever this salty shit is."

"Gun, I don't like—"

"I don't know if we are aging the same. Maybe time works differently here, or maybe we . . . hell, I don't know. We're super dense now, right? Super goddamn heavy? Maybe it did something to our metabolism."

"Walking away, Gunnar."

"Okay, I'll stop! I know you don't like talking about this but my point is, maybe there isn't any rush. I *feel* like there is, because of the dream, but fuck the dream, right? Maybe we got all the time in the world. So let's load up your backpack with these shitty food bars and something to drink and take a hike. You found the little ball-light thing that follows you around, so it won't be totally dark. What do you say?"

"Shut up, Gun."

"C'mon, Jacks, I think we really are going crazy here. You don't want to go down the Stairway, well . . . No problem. Let's do something else. But let's do something."

"Shut *up*, Gun!"

"Listen, I just feel like we have to—"

"*I said shut the fuck up, Gun!*"

Jackie clapped her hand over Gun's mouth. Her eyes were wide, and when she spoke, it was in a whisper. "Do you hear that?"

Muffled by her hand, Gun said, "Hear what?"

She didn't reply, just waited. And then he heard it.

Echoing off the old buildings behind them came a distant sound, a nails-on-chalkboard sound, a raw scream of anger and fear, an awful, tearing loneliness. It was a glass splinter of a sound, and it seemed to drag a sharp steel talon up both of their spines.

They looked at each other, eyes wide. Jackie's hand fell away.

"Holy shit," Gun said.

"Holy *shit*," Jackie agreed. They heard it again, different but the same, a terrible sound like a distant air-raid siren. A joyful grin blossomed on Jackie's face.

"Something's happening," Gun said, feeling hot, grateful tears start up in his eyes.

"Finally," Jackie breathed. She gripped her walking stick in excitement.

Gun put his hand on the hilt of his sword. "Came from the center of the city. The Stairway, maybe." He nudged Jackie. "Race?"

She grinned back at him. *"Race."*

———

The two new Behemoth ran towards the half-mad screams, as excited as they'd ever been in their lives. They were so excited that even Jackie's little silver floating light-ball friend had a hard time keeping up as they ran through patches of thick gloom. Gun had his sword out and was running with it, the hilt held so tight in his grip it grew warm and damp. It was a pretty good sword, though. An antique, and the people that made it hadn't made it to hang on a wall or sit in a case— they'd made it with the purpose of opening holes in other people and letting their blood out. So the hilt was wound tightly with fine cord and didn't slip in Gun's sweaty grip.

The awful screams—which didn't seem to be screams of pain or even anger, just bone-scraping howls—led them into the center of the city, where the oldest buildings and the Stairway lay. They slowed as they entered that section, partly because the screams grew more sporadic and partly because certain concepts that they'd temporarily forgotten about, like mortality, re-occurred to them.

Communicating mostly via loaded glances, they made their way toward the Staircase in the big plaza. It was the obvious place for screaming people to be coming from. Unfortunately, the area surrounding the Staircase was where the most tempting towers were, and Jackie had knocked over most of them. The Behemoth had to navigate around a great deal of rubble.

They climbed over a big pile of wreckage, once a beautifully ornate tower. They kept their eyes on the open space where the pit that held the Stairway was. Jackie gasped and stopped.

"The *fuck*, Gun." She pointed. There was a shape standing near the edge of the Stairway, near one of the broken light-pillars. It was small, and hunched, and seemed to be holding onto the column with a thin limb. It was preternaturally still, and Gun was certain that it was looking at them. He had a vague sense of wide, round eyes.

They heard a strange, half-metallic scrabbling sound off to their left but saw nothing when they looked. When they turned back to the column, the critter was gone.

"All right," Gun said, "I'm a *little* bit less excited now."

"Don't be a baby," Jackie said quietly, but there was a shake in her voice.

They heard a sound, bizarre in the sudden quiet and stillness after the screams. It was the sound of metal scraping across stone. They turned.

Something—as in, some *thing*—was crouched on the big hexagonal flagstones of the courtyard. It had an over-large head and long thin limbs, and it was looking at them with big tea-cup silver eyes. It yawned, the entire top of its head hinging open like some great snake, and revealed several rows of oxide-black and wickedly sharp teeth.

"Holy shit," Gun said.

"That is so awesome," Jackie whispered. "It's a friggin' *robot*, Gun! You were right!"

And it *was* a made thing, but disturbingly so; it looked like something a demented child might make. Its skin looked like old dirty burlap, and even from where he stood Gun could hear half-rotten scrapings from inside it as it moved. It cocked its head again, staring at them.

"I call dibs," Jackie said. "That's mine now. Its name is Roger."

"Your new friend doesn't *seem* like it's gonna bite our faces off," Gun said, frowning at the thing, "so that's good."

"Roger does need a bath." Jackie inspected the dirty burlap skin. Even far away, there was a distinct sour odor coming from it, like rancid lemons. She glanced around but didn't see any more of the things. The weird automata looked back and forth between them, curiously, watching them talk. It moved to its right to get away from one of the working light-pillars; it seemed to not like the light.

"*Sssssissstersss?*" it asked, and its voice was an awful thing, reedy and sibilant, like a squeezebox left to rot and then played by a madman. "*Sssssissterrssss come?*"

Gun and Jackie exchanged a look.

"I've, uh . . . changed my mind," Jackie said. "That fucking thing is creepy as hell. You can have it."

"Hello?" Gun called to it, trying to keep his voice warm and even. He extended his hand as if to a dog. He took a step forward. "Are you—"

The creature examined Gun's advancing hand, threw back its hinged head, and screamed.

"*MOOOTHHHERRRSSSS!!!*" it cried, a towering belt of noise.

It was a massive sound, a world-ending sound. Gun and Jackie both fell back and clapped their hands over their ears. When they were able to straighten up, they saw another of the things, almost identical to the first, perched on the pile of rubble from the downed tower. It was studying them. Something about the shape of the dirty burlap face gave the impression of a half-mad grin.

"Okay," Jackie said. She had her walking stick lifted, and her knuckles were tight on it. "*Okay*. Starting to not like this."

"Agreed." Gun glanced over his shoulder and saw two more of the creatures. The first one they'd seen crept towards them. The rotten-machinery sound it made as it moved set Gun's teeth on edge. It yawned again, exposing its rows of black teeth, needle sharp and spinning, like tiny drills. He was just thinking that maybe he should get his sword between him and the thing, when it leaped for him so fast he could hardly see it move.

It piled into him like a bag of broken sticks, wicked-looking talons scrabbling at his face. It was a horrible sensation, like being embraced by a three-foot-high spider. He lurched back, instinctively, trying to push the thing away, but it was too quick and threw its big head forward, clamping its rows of spinning needle-teeth on his arm.

He yelped, more in surprise than pain, and tried to shake the thing off. Its talons scrabbled at his face again and he caught at them, trying to pull the thing away. He felt something thin and brittle break beneath its burlap skin, like foamed metal, and the limb was ripped free.

Gun dropped it in disgust and registered real pain from the teeth, twin lines of fire across his bicep and shoulder. Plunging into a full-on panic, Gun flailed at the thing's face. He connected with his fist and felt its head cave in, deforming under his blow with a sensation that sickened him. And yet the spinning teeth ground in deeper. It was making panting, demonic harmonica noises, and then Gun just kind of lost it.

He hammered at his own arm over and over, smashing in the thing's face, until it began to fall away, and then scraping with the flat of his hand along his bicep to dislodge the black teeth. He saw with dawning horror that there was something thick and green coming out of those teeth, some poison or ichor.

He kicked the pieces of the thing savagely, and only then thought to look around for Jackie.

She was faring better than he had and under worse odds; both of the other robot-things had attacked her. She'd demolished one already, and as he watched she whipped her stick around in a batter's arc and smashed the other's face in half. Horribly, the thing was still scrabbling at her, and she kicked it in its slender chest. It sailed up and out over the depths of the Stairway, falling down into that endless shadow, screaming with half a head.

Jackie looked at Gun, panting, a tight grimace on her face.

"You all right?" she asked.

"I don't know." Gun pulled up his sleeve and was looking at his bicep. "Fucker bit me."

"Well, that ain't good," Jackie said.

Gun prodded the triple line of pinpricks on his skin, tiny but painful. He flexed his arm experimentally, confirming what he suspected. He looked up at Jackie. "It's going numb. Kind of like that shit they put in your teeth before they drill."

"That *really* ain't good."

"It's my fuckin' sword arm, too," Gun muttered, flexing it again and studying the pinpricks.

"No," Jackie said, pointing. "*That* ain't good, Gunnar."

Gun looked up and saw she was aimed at the Stairway. But she wasn't talking about that, either.

She was talking about the twenty, maybe thirty of the awful, rotten-gearwork creatures that had come up out of it and were advancing on them. One of them threw its hinged head back, the dim lights of the dead city glinting off its black teeth, and screamed.

"*Ssssissstersss Come!*" it crowed.

Jackie met Gun's eye and shook her head.

"I think"—and she wasn't grinning now—"our adventure has arrived."

"I guess," Gun said, perhaps not as excited about it as he felt he should be, and got his sword ready. He tried not to think about the fact that the things could talk. "Careful what you fuckin' ask for, I guess."

THE KILLERS

The Merry Prick

*"Never trust any overwhelmingly good thing. New love,
excellent drugs, the euphoria of success. They are all chemical,
they are all liars, and they will all lead you to ruin."*

—CORAZON LI, 'AMBIGUATIONS'

The Merry Prick was a mongrel of an establishment, one of the bigger bars in the Loche de Menthe and sporting a fight-pit, several dedicated card tables, and some cages where paid professionals and eager volunteers performed improbable feats of sexual congress that were usually more *interesting* than they were *stimulating*. They didn't have a stage, but there was a concert hall next door and it was plenty loud enough to serve as music for the Prick.

Hunker John had found the Killers a table; they were already well lubricated by the time Sophie and Ben caught up with them. Ben, understanding that Sophie would want to put the discomfiting interview out of her head, ordered them a bottle of a rare brew that promised psychotropic properties but would probably not deliver; it didn't matter. It tasted good. Sophie climbed into the circle of her friends and let Hunker John pour a pot of strong into her mouth. There were different varieties of the drink called strong; each bar and establishment liked to have their own private tincture, but there was one commonality across all varieties: it was gonna *fuck you up*.

She wanted to get fucked up. Mr. March was after the Book; of course he was. The silver vault was just a ploy; of course it was. One more labyrinthine plot. Sophie and Ben had lived through every possible trick, hustle, grift, and maneuver to get them to betray the location of the Book; the Twins-Damned, fuck it into every cold hell, Mother-pissed *Book*. Queen Jane Guin, the Beast Herself, had probably been behind most of them. But it had been a long time, and the schemes had slowed to a stop over the last decades. Sophie supposed it was too much to ask that they were done for good.

She remembered the fop's warning: *nothing that is about to happen is what it seems*. Well, she didn't need *that* warning to see through Mr. March's little ploy. Though why the Consort would be involved . . . Gah!

She banished Mr. March and the Book and all of it down into the vault within, and focused on the noble task of getting drunk. New Girl contrived to slip onto the round bench next to Sophie and was distractingly animated, her thigh pressed up against Sophie in an unambiguous manner. Sophie recalled Trik's suspicion that New Girl was a spy, but Sophie was starting to think she knew the target of the girl's intrigues.

Poor Ben. She hoped he'd had fun while it lasted. She scooted herself away from the girl as gently as she could and turned to study the crowd. She waved down a pretty wait with an ugly mustache and ordered something heavy.

Bear and Trik had gotten into a predictable argument about their favorite traverse teams and *hadn't* gotten to the bottom of a drink; or at least Trik hadn't. Sophie wasn't surprised; the girl was a bit of a lightweight and tended to pace herself. Hunker found a tall, androgynous person with a shaved head and war paint who was succumbing to his charms, and Sophie was half-listening while Ben tried to entertain New Girl with a story that had only the most passing resemblance to the truth, about one of the Killers' illicit adventures.

". . . so after weeks of planning this heist, right, we all make it into Lord Vail's manse. All keyed up, because Sophie kept telling us how dangerous it was, how fucked we would be if we got caught, like she was trying to steal state secrets or something, right? And of course we all get busted, almost immediately. Nothing was where it was supposed to be, the guards were all in the wrong places. I almost shit myself! Vail is ranting and raving, talking about her connection with the Queen, how we were going to be locked up in the depths of the Ministry and made examples of. Only one of us that didn't get taken was Hunker John. But Sophie has some old secret to trade, some old bullshit from the war, and gets us all out of it. And then, turns out, when we meet up with Hunker John, he's got a couple bottles of the notorious Vail Brandy, right? She set the whole thing up as a distraction. Just to see the looks on our faces, and to get a sip of that spirit."

New Girl's eyes were wide. "Capitana! You didn't."

Sophie gave her a distracted grin. "What can I say? That was good brandy."

"You're awful!"

"I am indeed. But your boy here ain't no flushing innocent, either. Ask him about the Spake Field Incident sometime."

"That," Ben said, slipping his arm around the girl, "was wildly exaggerated . . ."

Sophie turned away, left them to it. She got to the bottom of another glass and found herself looking up into the murky depths above, the barely seen arches and cross-beams, the dim and ancient lightsculptures that gave this place what small amounts of dusty light it had. Despite her best efforts, her thoughts returned to the Book.

The fucking *Book*. Of all the things to be reminded of, on top of the fucking *Giant*, and fucking *Saint Station*.

It was hard not to think about old, lost friends. Maybe because she'd been thinking of him earlier, she was reminded of Lee. Her sweet, eager, foolish little brother, who had wanted to be part of those great events and had always just missed them. Her little brother, who Sophie had never had much time for, because she was busy saving the world.

One more casualty, her relationship with her brother; just one more body thrown onto the all-consuming fire of the Hot Halls War, just one more butterfly trying to fly with burning wings.

She thought, for a moment, as she did occasionally, of finding Lee, of seeing if he would speak with her, a doomed fantasy of reconciliation. But, no, he was a fully bonded Vesachai now and she was Proscribed. He wasn't even allowed to speak to her. And why would either of them want to dredge up the past?

She scratched at the old, pale scars on her arms, conscious of them in a way she hadn't been for a long time, aware of the way eyes cut to them once they were revealed from under her long sleeves. She wasn't a person to care much about her appearance, and it wasn't vanity that occasionally made her wish she had either a lighter or darker complexion; the mid-tone skin of her arms highlighted the scars. But worse, there was a fine, intricate patterning of silver beneath those scars, wrapped around her bones; laid there by Saint Station's teeth. *Forbidden* silver. The kind of forbidden technology that carried a death sentence.

"Sophie Vesachai?" A piping voice pulled her out of her reverie. Some sour-faced kid, fourteen maybe, was glaring at her from the end of the table.

Bear leaned in, putting his intimidation face on. "Yeah?"

The kid wasn't intimidated; he looked like he'd seen some shit. He repeated Sophie's name.

She felt a thick reluctance; she thought she might know what he had for her. "Yeah?"

"Message," he said, and tossed a small scrolled paper onto the table in front of her. He was gone before she could ask him who it was from; in any case she suspected she already knew. She cracked the seal and read it. It wasn't signed, but it was the same message as the fop had given her. Her eyes snagged on the line *'Don't trust the man you call Bear.'* She lifted her eyes to see the big man looking at her, frowning. She tossed the message to him.

"Sophie?" Trik said, worry in her voice. "You okay?"

"I'm great." Sophie looked at her half-finished glass, then at the message. Bear crumpled it. Suddenly Sophie wanted to hit something. Trik, guessing what she was up to, called after her, but Sophie paid her no mind. Trik was overprotective of Sophie to the point of psychosis, and Sophie wanted none of that tonight.

She shouldered her way out of the table and stalked toward the bar, hunting. She eyed up a short muscular girl with damaged hands, a tough but slumped drunk, and settled on a big man with a big beard who seemed like he'd seen some war.

He was talking to a beautiful boy with an extravagant haircut, leaning in and working his rough charm for all it was worth. His smile swiveled around when Sophie tapped him on his shoulder.

He looked her up and down, the smile slipping a bit. He had cold eyes; good.

"Yeah, girl?" he asked.

"I don't like your face." She punched him in it.

The big man staggered back under the blow, more surprised than hurt. Sophie had a decent hook, but the fucker had a face like a block of old stone. It had just been a jab, anyway. Playful-like. Pain burned across her knuckles, and she shook her hand, enjoying the ache.

She grinned at the big guy.

"You can hit me or you can kiss me." She bounced on her toes. "Your choice."

The man rubbed his jaw, considering.

"Like that, eh?" he asked.

"It's like that."

The big guy shrugged and tossed down the rest of his drink. The pretty kid with the extravagant hair pouted, but the big man ignored it.

"It ain't in my nature," he said, taking off his jacket, "to keep a lady from her sport."

He raised a fist, and the barkeep obligingly rang the bell. There were cheers and whistles, and people backed out of the big circle chalked on the floor near the bar. She backed into the circle, cracking her neck, thoughts of Giants and Books and old demons—for the moment—forgotten. The big guy followed her into the circle, putting up his fists and hunching.

She felt better. Normally it was Bear climbing into this circle; that son of a bitch loved a fight. But then, so did Sophie.

She smiled and blew the big man a kiss. He grunted and came in at her, but Sophie was quicker than she looked. She took a jab on the shoulder and pretended to go for the groin—the obvious move for a girl half the size of her opponent. He reached down to slap her knee away, and she gave him a nasty forehead to the face.

He fell back, his upper lip split and a trickle of blood cornering his mouth. He touched it, amused, and looked at Sophie.

"Oh, girl," he said. "Now there's gotta be blood for blood."

"What else?" Sophie asked, and they started tussling in earnest.

He was good; there was no chance whatsoever that she could actually take him down, but that wasn't the point. He got a couple of strong hits in early, just to establish his bona fides. One made her head ring and another split her eyebrow, but nobody was trying to do any real damage. It was all in good fun.

Sophie got in a few good blows and then got lucky; she slipped in close, tangled her leg in his, and was able to topple him and give him an elbow in the tender part of the ribs before he crossed her with his forearm.

She got some teeth into that and put some power down; he howled and threw her halfway across the ring. They both scrambled to their feet. Sophie was finally starting to feel a little better.

The man examined his arm, where there were some pretty accurate representations of Sophie's teeth. He glowered at her. "You fight dirty."

"I fuck dirty, too," Sophie grinned. "Too bad you'll never find out."

He shook his head, smiling just a little. "You're a piece of work, girl."

"I try." Sophie got ready to make another run at the big son-of-a-bitch. However, against all reason and protocol, Trik ran into the circle. Her eyes were wide.

"Sophie," she said, tension making her voice tight. Sophie goggled at her. "Trik, what the hell? Get the hell out!"

"Yeah," the big man said, "why don't you get the fuck out of—"

He grabbed Trik's shoulder, which was a mistake; Trik didn't like being touched. She did something to his hand, and he howled and dropped to his knees, cradling his hand. Trik turned, and the look on her face was so alarmed that Sophie's recriminations died on her lips.

"Sophie!" Trik pointed up over her head. *"Look!"*

"What?" Sophie asked, puzzled. She followed Trik's pointing finger, past the candles strung along the edges of the bar, into the big open space where the ancient lightsculptures hung above them all. They were glowing dimly. *Too* dimly.

"That." There was an edge of hysteria to her voice. As Sophie watched, one of the lightsculptures—one that had hung above the Loche de Menthe for millennia, never changing or stopping—sputtered and went out. And then, immediately, another. The Merry Prick grew noticeably dimmer.

Sophie looked into her friend's panicked eyes and felt that same panic grow in her. The lights were going out, which was . . . well, that was impossible.

As Sophie watched, another light went out, and then another. It was like watching the world end.

———

In all the long history of the Keep—or what of it was still remembered, anyways—illumination had only catastrophically failed two times before. Once was during the war with the infamous Outkeep King named William the Vast, who raised all of the rabble and old automata that he could. He attempted to take the Attics and hold the Bridges, thinking to set up a kingdom in the upper levels of the Keep. He was unsuccessful, but he was able to do so much damage to a few floorsections during the fight that the silver connections between them were severed, and three or four factory spaces lost their light, trapping the poor workers inside for almost two days.

They were rescued eventually, but the psychological damage of the Dark they'd endured broke many of their minds. It was regarded as one of the sobering tragedies in the history of the Keep and a reason why so many citizens distrusted the Outkeep. And this was even *before* the Hot Halls War. Before the warlord Gutcher, and his awful warmachines. And of course, once that section of the Keep had gone Dark, it was lost; cut off, anathema. No longer part of the Keep, by law, custom, and preference. That was how things worked, in the Underlands. The loss of light is a cataclysm that cannot be recovered from.

Until the tragedy that befell the Loche de Menthe, the only other time the lights had suddenly and mysteriously failed was in a small bedroom, deep in the heart of Vesachai territory, where such a thing should have been impossible. For what purpose did the Vesachai serve, if not to keep the lights on? The thirteen-year-old girl who was trapped in that room for a few hours did not go mad, for she had seen the Dark before, but it did pour plenty of fuel on the growing fire of her reputation.

That little girl's name, of course, was Sophie Vesachai.

As the Loche de Menthe descended into panic and screams around her, Sophie was thinking about that shocking and sudden childhood plunge into black. It had disconcerted her, surprised her, but it hadn't especially scared her. That little girl had experiences—well, *dreams*—that had widened her tolerance for frightening things quite a bit, and in any case she'd turned off those lights herself.

She had been learning to use the Book, the artifact she'd been led to by a dream. It had been powerful, that Book, and she wished she had it right now. Maybe she could fight this, if she had the Book.

The Giant Lies Still Awake. And The World Needs Weapons.

Sophie was breathing hard, though she wasn't moving. She looked up at the shadowed pillars above the Loche de Menthe, the hanging presence of the lightsculptures there. They were Dim, of course. They didn't give off as much light as the sculptures in the rest of the Keep. But it was the same amount of light as they had given for, perhaps, the last thousand years.

With an odd, crinkling sort of *pop*, another of them went out. She looked down at her hands and realized that she could barely make them out.

She heard wailing from everywhere in the Loche de Menthe. The haphazard bars and drug-dens and music stages were emptying. People who had come for pleasure rediscovered a fear that took place only in nightmares, in stories of the Fall, or beyond the edge of their world. Some were starting to run towards the narrow exit, crushing each other and screaming. They would riot soon. The denizens of the Keep were used to dim light; many parts of the Keep dimmed automatically to night-hues during the later hours, and most apartments had controls, so the lights could be reduced at will. But they never went *out*.

Watching light-sources that had never dimmed or failed in a thousand years suddenly go black was horrifyingly, viscerally awful, like the way some feel about spiders, or heights. It didn't go pitch black; there was still some light available, there were burning pots of oil and glowswick lanterns and other sources of illumination. It would get uncomfortably dim in here but people would be able to see.

Sophie was looking up at the near-black ceiling now, and as she watched, another of the lights went out with an audible click. Her eyes flickered in the torchlight, the oldest form of light but the easiest to quench. She felt a hand on her arm: Ben.

"Sophie," he said, his voice grave. She turned and saw the same look reflected back at her, knew what that look meant.

She nodded. "You know what this means."

"Yeah."

Their eyes returned to the lightsculptures; another one went dark. Light sources did not go out like this. Someone was deliberately killing the Loche de Menthe, and while Sophie was in it. She swallowed, her throat dry. She discovered that she needed a drink very badly.

"It's happening again." She looked down at her arms, as if she could see the forbidden magic that was wrapped around the bones there.

"What are we going to do?" Ben asked. The last of the lightsculptures went out with a wrenching, tearing sound. It was a good question, and if Sophie had truly been the childhood hero that people thought she was, she might have had a good answer for it. That young girl might have raised her scarred arms, pulled silver fire into them, and found a way to fight whoever was killing the Loche. She might have ridden to war, might have confronted whatever forces were gathering in the darkness tonight, trying to wake old monsters best left quiet. If Sophie Vesachai was still the girl she had been, she might have fought.

"Get the Killers." Her voice sounded tinny to her ears, as if the failing light were affecting her hearing. "We have to get the fuck out of here."

THE CONVOX

The Utility of Doors

"Tactically speaking, lies and truth are indistinguishable."

—DEVELMAN ADDINGS, 'THE FORFEITURE LESSONS'

West looks up at the slender helix of stone that rises into the heights above them, the base of the Stairway. He knows what lies atop that spiral of stairs; he has even been to that dead city above, when it was still inhabited by the ancient order of magicians called the Cold. He is taking advantage of Mr. Turpentine's fussing over the *chûs* pots, the lull in the conversation, to think. He needs to understand the plot that he is being enmeshed in. He tries not to let his thinking show on his handsome and almost human face.

Winter—which he still can hardly believe, *Winter! One of the Nine! His father's former lover, arguably the principal architect of the Silver Age itself*—sits composed and amused, waiting for the group around the fire to digest what she has just said.

She said she wants to kill the Giant; she wants to kill Kindaedystrin. The Giant Who Fell. The worst villain in the history of the Wanderlands; worse, even, than the Twins.

But it is madness, and foolish to boot. His father, Hunter Fine, hadn't been able to kill that creature, not with all the power of the Silver Age at its height. The man who calls himself Candle now looks at him with disquieting eyes, a sour smile on his face. No, no. Winter is playing at something; her true purpose is yet to be discovered. This is a ruse, a stalking horse. He knows how this woman operates.

So, he will play along until he discovers her purpose, and then turn it to his own aims. For he has many!

And Candle. The man who calls himself Candle. What a strange thing to find him here. West's brothers and sisters—especially Charts—will be livid. West knew Candle by another name, a long time ago. That man betrayed West's family, and while West has ambivalent feelings about it, family custom requires that he see Candle dead for it. It is difficult to believe Candle stands once again in the heart of great matters, but here he is. West knows he must not take his eyes off him; he is of low making but as cunning as anyone who ever lived.

D'Alle is not worth considering. He cannot imagine what made the Lady Winter invite him. Mr. Turpentine bears some place in the equation that is forming in West's mind; the creature is not one of the Wise, but his exploits have made rumors even in these catastrophic days. He is as dangerous as any around this fire, and West does not mean to forget that.

Slowly, reluctantly, West turns his consideration to Primary Gray.

Primary Gray. Even the Lady Winter is not as great a shock. He had not known that *any* of the Children, those ancient oracles, had survived the Fall. Primary Gray makes Winter look young; he would have made Hunter Fine look young. Primary Gray might be old enough to remember the building of the Wanderlands itself. He might be old enough to remember the *Builders!* What comprehensible goals could such a person have? How could advantage possibly be gained over someone like that?

West stills his mind. Primary Gray is a thinking thing, after all, and that means he has wants, desires. Weaknesses. West must hold close his own strengths and remember that he is his father's firstborn son. West knows that everyone around the fire is looking at him, waiting for his answer to Winter's proclamation, her casual admission that she means to kill the most dangerous creature ever birthed in the Wanderlands.

Winter's statement, so calmly proposed, that she means to kill the Giant Kindaedystrin. *Madness.*

"Well," West says, as if thinking it through, "killing the Giant is a noble plan, certainly, and should be no hard task for a company such as this."

Winter just waits, eyebrow lifted and a slight smile on her face. Her famously green eyes are brilliant, calm, and sure. West smiles back. He knows these sorts of games and is almost relieved. All Winter's talk of grand plans had disconcerted him, but now he is back on solid ground. The Wise play games, but only for their own benefit.

"From what I understand—and please correct me if I'm wrong—we need only pluck one of the Rings from the sky, tap it, and make a wish," West says. "I presume that is what our good Master D'Alle is here for; he seems quite full of grandiose wishes."

Mr. Turpentine chuckles and conveys the impression of a wink. "Dear West, you *are* incorrigible."

D'Alle shifts on his walking-couch; he seems to be adjusting to the loss of his servant with some difficulty. He has to retrieve his *own* lozenges now; it must be hell for him.

"I know nothing of Giants, nor of their prisons," D'Alle says, "but I cannot imagine how this would be a concern of mine. Or my city. How does this benefit Cannoux?"

"Were the Giant to escape . . ." Primary Gray says quietly.

But West becomes tired of this nonsense, even if it is Primary Gray speaking it. "The Giant cannot escape; if he could have, he would have—and long since. I still can barely credit that he *lives*. And I cannot credit that some queen buried beneath leagues of stone could raise him. I doubt Winter herself could manage that feat, even with the resources she commands."

"And surely," Turpentine shivers, "she would never *wish* to."

"My concern, as ever," Winter says, "is with the safety and well-being of all in the Wanderlands."

Candle doesn't even bother to snort at this. Everyone at this fire understands the humor in her statement. Winter turns her considerable regard to West.

"Come, my old friend, let us play this game. Indulge me, please, for the friendship I bore your father, and the world we built together! We all could use a reminder, perhaps, a primer on what truly lies at stake."

West raises his hands in surrender. "As you wish. Let us—by all means—cast our minds hence. Mine, however, will need lubrication; is there any more of this excellent *chûs* on order?"

"Certainly!" Turpentine cries, and leaps into action. He seems happiest when he is occupied. "Certainly, and there is no need to shift and grumble, my friends; more comes for all!"

"The Giant cannot get free, and cannot be raised," Winter continues, with a smile at West.

"No, it cannot," West agrees.

"Yet, what if it were to?" Winter asks. "Impossible as it may be, my friend, yet—play the game out. What if that old Returner got free?"

West sighs. "The end of everything, Winter. The end of everything."

"No," Primary Gray says, with that disconcerting gaze. "Not the end of everything. But the end of the Silver Age, yes."

West shakes his head. "The Silver Age ended long ago, Gray. Even by your standards."

"Did it?" Primary Gray asks, with a small smile, a faint glitter of his golden eyes. West wonders what it would feel like to snap that delicate little neck. He wonders if there is any force in the Wanderlands strong enough to do it.

"'The end of everything' is close enough for our purposes," Winter interjects. "There is nothing the Giant hates so much as the Silver. If he were to get free, he would pull down the Feeds and uproot every vestige of the civilization we spent so long building. He would likely attempt to convince his cousins in the Land of Forest to free the Twins, and we all know what *their* purpose is. Those two really *were* sent to put an end to everything."

Again, West cannot in any sense be described as a squeamish person, but he shivers. He'd almost rather have the Giant free than *those* two.

"Without the Silver," Winter continues, "without the Feeds . . ."

"Darkness," Mr. Turpentine says, grinding seeds for the *chûs*. "Darkness forevermore."

There is a moment, and they all look to the fire, unpleasantly aware of the thing that would come for them if the fire were to go out. *The Dark.*

West shifts on his seat. "But let us continue the mental gymnastics, then. If the Giant were to get free it would be catastrophic for the Mountain and the peoples that live beneath it, certainly. But I cannot imagine that the Nine would be powerless against that creature. Let us be frank, Winter; you have resources now that even the Silver Age did not. You rule the greatest empire in the Wanderlands. You stand at the top of the White Tower itself, you rule at the intersection of the Spoke Roads, you command the entirety of the Crater Valley of Traffing and the Empire of Light beyond. Do you not?"

Winter smiles in the firelight.

"It's possible that my Deadsmith could bring down Kindaedystrin," she said, shrugging. "But only *possible.* And at ruinous cost, for who knows how many Lands would fall all the way into devastation before he could be stopped? How many, dead? How many lives, destroyed?"

"Please, My Lady," West says, with a smile. "We are of the Wise, are we not? Let us not pretend to care overmuch about mayflies, or this Convox shall be comprised of nothing but winks and sly allusions."

Winter gives him a wink. "My charge is the whole world, West. Certainly, mayflies come and go, but I would not see the whole lot of them wiped away."

"What point in being a god if there's no one to worship you?" Candle asks with a humorless grin. Winter blows him a kiss; she seems to find his hatred endearing. D'Alle clears his throat and his *cantrait* dances sideways. West thinks D'Alle a bigger fool the more time he spends with him. What sort of intelligent creature enslaves himself to an appliance that displays his every mood? But perhaps the idiot is unaware of it.

"I do not mean to be callous," D'Alle says, looking at Winter with hooded eyes, "but having seen firsthand what care the Wise have for us mayflies, I still cannot see what this has to do with myself or my city. We have no Feed, and we thrive."

"Don't be a fool, D'Alle." Candle accepts another cup of *chûs* from a solicitous Mr. Turpentine. "You burn twist for light; how long do you think you can keep that up? Oh, your sad little town will survive for a time, perhaps long after you are dead. But Cannoux will go into the Dark. You don't have the strength to make your own way."

"I hope," D'Alle says, glaring at Candle, "that this *creature* is of some use to us. But I refuse to be badgered by such a person."

Candle laughs. "What amuses me, *Master* D'Alle, is that you concentrate your ire on me. You are as great a fool now as you ever were."

"Lover." Winter sets a hand on Candle's neck, half-possessive and half-threatening. "Be nice to my guests. And yes, Master D'Alle, I assure you that Candle is quite essential to our plans. It is, after all, the only reason he is allowed to continue drawing breath! But let me address your concerns with a question: is not your presence itself a bid to involve your city in the councils of the Wise? Do you not—and not for the first time!—take great risks to gain our companionship and succor? For what reason, if not to gain the benefits of the Empire of the Nine? If not to gain the friendship of the White Tower?"

D'Alle shifts in his walking-couch. "I mean only that I cannot imagine what part I can play in such great events."

"Oh," Winter says, eyes sparkling, "we will find a role for you, my old friend. There is none at this fire that we can do without; our goal will be quite impossible without all of us."

"We are far from reaching an agreement," West says, pretending to lightness, "on even the nature of the conversation. Are we done with fancies? I prefer to live in the world as it is."

Candle chuckles through his drink. "That might be the funniest thing I've ever heard you say, Lourde."

"Shut that man up," West finds forced affability, "or I will do it myself."

Winter sighs and leans over. She captures one of Candle's fingers as the man struggles to get away and snaps it expertly. His scream is very loud, echoing up the great shaft of the Stairway and back down again. Candle hunches over, his face tight, and cradles his newly broken finger.

"Thank you." West accepts a cup of *chûs* from Mr. Turpentine. He blows on it, looking around the fire, wondering when they will dispense with this stalking horse and reveal the true nature of the meeting. He had not spoken entirely in jest; you might as well speak of reaching through the Roof of the World, the impassable barrier in the sky, and plucking a Ring through it, as speak of killing or freeing the Giant that murdered the world. His father remembers Winter very well; she does nothing simply or openly.

"I must wonder, then," D'Alle says, cautious, probably wary of looking the fool he is, "why those worthy ancients did not kill the Giant when they caught him. If he could be killed."

"Because," West says, annoyed, "he *can't* be killed. If they could have, they would have. The only way to kill a Giant is for it to lose hope, or will, or whatever it is that animates those bastard things. I assumed Kindaedystrin lost hope and went to stone a thousand years ago or more; that was certainly the plan."

"I assure you," Winter smiles, "the Giant Kindaedystrin can be killed."

West frowned. "Perhaps, but then why this gathering in gloom, with so many old enemies? Why not take the Nine entire, gather all your Deadsmith, and go put an end to the dread thing?"

Winter's smile is slow; almost apologetic. "Because, my friends, I am not a representative of the Nine—not in this matter. In fact, eight have voted on it, and I am quite forbidden from any action regarding the Giant. I find myself, oddly enough, in the interesting position of having gone rogue, and it would be a mistake to think that any help will be coming to us from the Nine, the Deadsmith, or our Empire of Light. The White Tower will not assist us in this."

There is a shocked silence around the fire. Even Candle looks up from his pained broken finger with a sharp frown. Winter makes a dismissive throwing-away gesture.

"In any case, I harbor much doubt that even all of the Deadsmith together could kill that brute. There are never very many of those toys, and they are quite valuable. No, I think we have all the resources we need for our endeavor right here."

"That," West says, with an air of devastating understatement, "is a bit hard to see."

"Much will be made clear," Winter says. "Mr. Turpentine . . . ?"

"I must assure you," the old machine says, solemnly, "that there are attempts being made even now to wake the Giant. I have spent some time near its prison and have had much reason to know. Worse, the attempts may succeed. So it is time for those who see the problem to solve the problem. I quote, of course. Was this not one of your father's great sayings, West?"

"I am not my father."

"Well," Winter says, "that is not entirely true, is it? You are at least partly your father. The best part, if his plans went aright."

West tightens his jaw. He does not enjoy this topic.

"Did they, West?" Winter asks, smiling. "*Did* you get the best part of Hunter Fine, or did something go wrong? Your father meant *you* to be the leader of your family, first among the pieces of himself. Well, tell me, have I made a mistake? Should I be talking to your brother?"

"Charts is an up-jumped pissant," West snaps, "and nothing more than the dregs left over from Hunter Fine's *true* sons and daughters. And the best was, indeed, given to me."

"And yet," Winter says, "*you* serve *Charts*. Do you not?"

West forces himself to take a breath.

"I serve no man, no creature, cabal or *Convox*," West says. "But I am loyal to my family."

"Hunter was always very loyal," Winter cocks her head, looking at him. "But his first loyalty was to the Wanderlands as a whole."

"I remember." West stares into the fire. He shakes himself and puts on some confidence, a pose of surety. It galls him to borrow from Charts, but he channels some of his brother's grim certainty and settles it upon him like a cloak.

"None of this," he goes on, "addresses the fact that what you speak of is plainly impossible. Even if we could gain access to the Giant's Prison—which we cannot—there is nothing in the Wanderlands that can kill a Returner. I don't care what strange blasphemy you have cooked up in your Tower, what White-on-Black magic you have up your sleeve, the Giant cannot be killed. Not by anything in this world."

"I agree," Winter says, "that the Giant cannot be killed by anything in this world."

"Then what is the *true* purpose of this Convox?"

"Come on." Candle is still cradling his broken finger. "You're not this stupid, West. Think it through."

West wants to snarl at him, but something does connect up, some slight inflection in Winter's words. *Nothing in this world . . .*

"Do you claim to have some Behemoth weapon, then?" he asks, trying to figure it out. "Some ancient thing, brought from that peculiar and other world? I know much of Behemoth, Winter, and I assure you that there were never any weapons of such power brought here. Some small knives, perhaps. Once a kind of chutter, but it would not fire. No Behemoth has ever brought anything into this world that could kill a Giant."

"I mean, dear West, to use a sword."

West laughs, shaking his head. "There are no swords from that cursed world in the Wanderlands. We have never been that unlucky."

"There have never *been* any Black Portal-forged swords in the Wanderlands," Winter agrees, eyes crinkling in amusement. She glances upward, toward the endless stone spiral of the Stairway above them and the abandoned city atop the Mountain that it leads to. "But there is certainly one here *now.*"

THE MONSTERS

A Curious Sound in a Dead City

*"Look first to the teeth. You see everything you need of
a creature's nature in the teeth."*

—DEMINS, 'SCOTIO AND TREMBLAY'

Gun heard it first: a strange, hollow sound like a glass bird catching at wind. He looked across the fire at Jackie, but she was staring into the flames, and if she heard it, she wasn't reacting. For a few moments, he lost the sound and then caught it. It was a thinning, warbling sound that crept around the corners of the ancient buildings and puddled in the flickering light of the fire.

It was unusual to hear any sound at all in the dead city, even after those screaming, hideous mechanical monstrosities had tried to kill them.

The aftermath of the Behemoth's fight against those awful robots was not the celebration they might have expected. After so long being bored in the dead city, they had been excited for any kind of action, but those demon moppets were unpleasant. Their hinged jaws, those spinning black teeth with the weird numbing toxin. Those deafening screams. The rotten-squeezebox sound of their voices.

Unpleasant was an understatement.

They hadn't kept track of how many of the creatures they'd killed; somewhere between twenty and thirty. For a while, it seemed like the awful things just kept pouring up out of the Stairway, and for a few moments, Gun had wondered if they were in actual trouble.

But, no. Gun was starting to understand why those old books talked so much about the destruction Behemoth could cause; it was just good for this place that him and Jackie were so sweet-natured. Though he had to admit, Jackie's little silvery light-ball had helped. Those awful demon robots didn't seem to like light, and the floating ball of illumination had helped keep them scattered, and prevented them from swarming.

The two newly battle-tried Behemoth had been sitting around the fire for a while, not talking much. They'd gathered up all the remnants of the rough mechanical critters and put them in a big pile, and then set it on fire. The things burned disturbingly well, and the fire turned into a rather macabre campfire. Occasionally some of the oxide-black drill teeth would get hot enough to explode in a series of sharp pops that made Jackie and Gunnar jump.

The Behemoth were morose; the excitement and adrenaline of the fight had given way to the suspicion that they'd just murdered something like twenty or thirty sentient beings. For a while they'd been proud braggarts, replaying the fight and making extravagant claims about their prowess. But with the threat of the creatures gone, so went the fear; and the slowly charring bodies of their foes began to weigh on them.

Jackie didn't even whittle on her walking stick. After she'd cleaned off the green ichor those *things* had exuded through their teeth, she'd tossed it aside and didn't look at it again. At least the numbness that the toxin had induced faded away.

By the end of the fight, Gun had barely been able to use his arm, the bite marks from those awful things having rendered his muscles useless. He had cleaned his sword more carefully, in case the toxin that came out of their teeth could etch the steel, but when he finished, he leaned it against a rock and ignored it.

The hollow sound came again. In the dim light of the city, it was odd and out-of-place. Gun looked out into the shadows beyond their fire, looking for something he couldn't see. In the aftermath of the awful mechanical things, the city had taken on a sinister aspect.

"What is it?" Jackie asked.

"You hear that?"

She listened for a moment, then shook her head. "No," she said. "Wait. Yes."

Gun's hand groped behind him for his sword. Jackie moved to find her stick. Their eyes met, and Gun nodded. The sound curled around them again, made haunting by the echoes of the dead city.

"If it's more of those fucking *things* . . ." Jackie had her stick in her hands.

"I don't think it is." Gun was trying to listen. "They don't sound like that."

"Then it's probably something even worse."

"Don't see how it could be," Gun said. More of the drill-bit teeth exploded in the fire, making them jump. For a long moment, they couldn't hear anything, and then the sound came back. And it was much closer.

"Gun," Jackie asked, leaning forward, "is that *whistling?*"

Gun looked at her, eyes wide. He stood up, his sword in his hand and the blade bare. He couldn't remember actually taking the scabbard off. He nodded. "Yeah. You're right. Whistling."

"What the fuck do we do with *whistling?*" Jackie asked. She stood too, and they both scanned their murky surroundings. The whistling grew louder; it took the cadence of a merry melody.

And eventually, a shape formed itself out of the shadows, joining the refrain.

It was a tall shape with a wide smile. Its hands were spread, palms out, as if to show that it held no weapons.

It was a man.

"Hello!" the man said, stepping into the circle of their firelight. Echoes of his whistling melody wound back through the city faintly, underscoring his words. He was tall and good-looking, with clothes that looked a bit strange to them but were clearly well made. He had light eyes and black hair and a very inviting smile. "Hello there, travelers, and well met! Very well met indeed, here at the end of the world. Might I approach your fire? I do not mean to disturb you, but I have been in the Dark long and beyond long, and could do with some of its comforts. Oh, but listen to me! All talk and no hear, as my father would say, and no greetings to be had. Hello, my friends, *hello*, and be welcome to the Wanderlands!"

The man smiled, all easy charm, and performed a small bow for each of them in turn. "My name is Mr. Vutch, and I am *entirely* at your service."

THE KILLERS

A Story About a Girl

"To call the Vesachai mere technicians, shadows of the Silver Age wizards that once brought light to every dark corner of our world . . . well, that would only serve to diminish what absolute bastards they can be."

—BILLIE WEISS, 'THE KEEP AND THE QUEEN'

There is a story in the Keep—a pretty good one—and it goes a little something like this:

When she was about fourteen years old, Sophie Vesachai saved the world.

Now, of course, like any good story, it plays a bit loose with the facts. Even with a charitable eye, Sophie could only have been considered to save the *Keep*, which is a very small part of the Underlands, which is a small part of the Mountain, which is a *very* small part of the Wanderlands entire. Hardly the entire world! And yet, to those who lived in the Keep, an oasis of light surrounded by desolation and lightlessness on every side—including upwards—that light was their whole world. The Mountain, so far above, and the Wanderlands beyond that, were barely legends to those folk. To their knowledge, no one in the Keep had ever been all the way up to the Mountain or seen the dead sky; they may as well have been talking about the long lost Rings or the golden moon Lode as talk about the Mountain or the Wanderlands. To them, the Keep was the only light left in the whole world, and Sophie had, indeed, saved it.

Sophie Vesachai had saved *their* world, and that will work close enough for story purposes.

Most good stories are built atop other ones, and Sophie had already been cultivating stories even before the Hot Halls War, even before the invasion by the Outkeep King, Gutcher, and his monstrous warmachines. Even before the dream—the dream of trees and a Silver Book—there were stories about the precocious daughter of the First Vesachai and her wild ways. Her group of ragamuffin friends were charming terrors; no pastries or fairy-ice stalls were safe from their predations. The First Vesachai was busy trying to keep the Queen from swallowing the Vesachai whole, and didn't have much time for disciplining his daughter. And then there was the famously long list of failed tutors; Sophie seemed to delight in breaking their spirits. She was a hellion, sure, but a fun one, the kind that mothers and grandmothers tsk about, and secretly cherish.

But then came the Mother's Call, the vivid dreams that gripped the children of the Keep for a season, the dreams that showed them a strange land, a land of sunshine and trees and Giants—and clawing darkness, and world-eating terror. Dreams that told them they must find a Book, a Silver Book, without which the world would descend into a final, and utter, Dark. Nearly every child in the Keep got these dreams, and most of them set out trying to decode the odd clues and symbols held in them.

But only one of those children actually did it.

Few adults knew about the dreams at the time—one of the principal features of the dream was the urge towards secrecy—but children are notoriously bad at keeping secrets, and the Mother's Call became part of Sophie's story soon enough. In any case, the young child-hero had discovered her purpose and her weapon: the Book. She gathered the best of her friends and formed the Killers, a gang devoted to discovering the meaning and purpose behind the dream. The story diverges, here, depending on who tells it; some mention the arrival of Sophie's last tutor, the fascinating and quick-witted Denver Murkai; some skip over him as being of little consequence. In any case, either the Book itself or more dreams pushed Sophie out into the blackness beyond the bounds of the Keep, looking for something else, some potent weapon that she would need to drive the Dark back. With her friends'—and perhaps, her tutor's—help, she found it. It was called Saint Station.

The stories diverge in describing Saint Station; some call it a demon waiting in the gloom, some describe it as a beautiful silver angel, ready to bestow the Mother's gifts. In all of the stories, however, it imbued Sophie with wonderous, magical powers, powers that she could combine with the Book to drive the darkness back, to fulfill the promise of the dream and bring light back to the world. The romance of this tale was heightened, not diminished, by the fact that these powers gave her scarred arms and earned her the enmity of her family. Sophie was a child-hero indeed; she had made a selfless sacrifice for the peoples of the Keep.

And then . . . and then. The Hot Halls War.

The worst tragedy, the worst conflict, in living memory. The warlord Gutcher came swarming over the Bridges with his diabolic automata and his Outkeep warriors, hell-bent on destroying every last bit of light and life in the Keep. Even Queen Jane Guin was caught unawares, and even her Dark-hardened forces, her Lurk and Redarms and Practice Guard, were no match for the invaders and their Silver-Age weapons. The only force ready for the attack—so the stories go—was Sophie Vesachai and her Killers.

The children rode to war with Sophie at their head. Using her forbidden powers and her Book, she found weapons for them, weapons beyond anything the

Queen had at her disposal, and Sophie herself had her arms, wreathed in red scars and silver fire, and they fought the invaders ferociously. Everyone old enough to remember has a story of seeing the Killers ride to war—though of course only a fraction of the Keep could have possibly done so. Stories grow in the telling, after all, but that is part of their fun. Sophie used the Book to compel Gallivants and Charm Chairs to fight; she used the Book to wake slumbering automata and bid them to destroy the invaders.

It wasn't enough, though. The invading army numbered too many, and their own weaponry was fearsome. Many soldiers and citizens died, many were blinded, and the invaders inexorably pushed in further to the heart of the Keep. It wasn't hyperbole to say that all hope was lost; all that were alive at that time remembered the feeling of hopelessness, the dead neighbors and friends, the terror and despair of those dark days.

And then—the story goes—Sophie remembered, or found, an ancient cache of warmachines, deep beneath the Keep, left there in another age for a purpose only guessed at. Left slumbering for some great need. Sophie Vesachai used her Book, the magical artifact sent to her in a dream, and the wild powers given to her by Saint Station, and raised those Jannissaries. The effort burned her arms and burned the Book to ash, nearly killing her, but deep beneath the Keep, those tall white machines woke and, directed by Sophie, scoured the Keep of its invaders. The Jannissaries were the greatest of all the soldier-constructs made in the Silver Age, and they killed every last Outkeep and invading automata, destroying the warlord Gutcher's power forever.

Some stories say Sophie killed Gutcher herself, though most don't make that claim. In any case, the Jannissaries were all likewise destroyed in the conflict, and for all intents and purposes, Sophie Vesachai had fulfilled her dream, had been brave and true and good, and pushed the darkness back. She had saved the world.

It's a pretty good story.

And like any good story, most of it isn't true. Or—well, it tended to miss the point entirely. There were some who had lived through those days, even those who enjoyed the story and told it often in their cups, who had questions. Questions, like, say—

Where did the Jannissaries go? Surely they all couldn't have been destroyed. Had Sophie put them back to sleep? Sent them away? And that begs another question: *How?* If she controlled the Jannissaries using the Book, but the Book was burned to ash in raising them, how had she done it?

Interesting questions, but the young child-hero didn't seem interested in answering them. In fact, in the aftermath of the Hot Halls War, the young child-hero didn't seem much interested in being a *hero*. She got wrapped into the Queen's Court for a time, as a teenager, and there were rumors about an illicit affair with her one-time tutor, Denver Murkai, but those stories weren't as fun and weren't as widely told. After that, she just sort of . . . slipped into the shadows. She stepped off the world stage and into obscurity.

Still, some people had questions. They couldn't help but pick at cracks in the façade. Everyone knew about the Vesachai's Proscription; if you messed with forbidden technology, the Vesachai would put their silver knives in your heart. No exceptions. Yet *certainly* Sophie must have broken this Proscription in the Hot Halls War. Most people waved this away; her own father was the First Vesachai, after all, and she had broken the rules to save the world. Surely they allowed her some grace.

Those who knew the Vesachai better, however, knew that this could not be true. The Vesachai allowed no grace, not to anyone, not ever. So how was Sophie still alive?

And this begged more questions, for those in the know: What did this all have to do with the Queen taking direct control of the Vesachai, after hundreds and perhaps thousands of years of independence? And what, exactly, did Sophie's last tutor, Denver Murkai, have to do with any of this, seeing as how he became one of the Queen's most trusted and high-ranked advisors in the years after the Hot Halls War?

But the most common question was also the most inexplicable. Sophie Vesachai had saved the world; she was as great a hero as the Keep had ever had. She could have done anything, accomplished anything, been anything. So why had she surrounded herself with degenerate grifters, and was—to all outward appearances—trying to drink herself to death?

To get an answer to that, you would have to ask Sophie herself, and she had never answered it. It was easier just to tell the story again, to recall determined child-heroes and great sacrifices, to polish the bright parts of the tale brighter and let the murky parts fade to dim. It was easier to raise a glass to the young hero and ignore the inconvenient woman.

It was, after all, a pretty good story. Nobody wants to ruin a good story.

THE MONSTERS

The Charming Thing

"Most people, when confronted by their doom, reject it. They squint and squirm, looking for reasons to explain it away. It is a rare creature that can look at its situation and really, truly understand how fucked it is."

—AAI YA LEASON, 'GRACES ATONAL'

"**W**elcome and *welcome!*" Mr. Vutch cried, grandly, settling onto a chunk of broken masonry and crossing his legs, the very picture of comfortable elegance. "My friends, *indeed!* A thousand welcomes to you, and a thousand welcomes to you both. Welcome! Welcome!"

Gun and Jackie looked at each other.

It was a loaded look. It said many things. They had been alone in the dead city on top of the Mountain for, what, three months? Desperate and aching for something to happen, for *anything* to happen. And then it had.

Those awful, rotten-gearwork automata who kept wailing the word "sisters" at them and tried to chew their faces off. Fun! Gun and Jackie had gotten a crash course in how unbelievably badass they were, sure, and had gotten to use their sword and walking stick in battle, *finally*, but their amusement had come at some cost. Namely, what was starting to feel like the murder of some thirty-odd sentient creatures.

And then, only hours later—this very charming Mr. Vutch walked up to their fire, whistling. The fire, in fact, that they'd made out of the rotten burlap skin and foamy metal bones of those very same sentient creatures.

It was, to put a point on an understatement, *a lot to process.*

"Um . . ." Gun said.

"What an extraordinary occurrence!" Mr. Vutch flicked his hat back on his head and gave Jackie a wink. "What a grand meeting, here, beyond the very end of the world! I must confess, my new friends, I had not thought to meet travelers in this city, of *all places*, and certainly not such well-mannered and delightful travelers such as yourselves."

Jackie blinked. She couldn't seem to find any words at all.

"But you must think me awful! *Awfully* crude and simple besides. Even in the dark places of the world we must observe the protocols of rank and respect, must we not? So let me offer you, *this*. And you, *this,* a genuflection quite as deep as can be given to any in the length and breadth of the Wanderlands. Well met! And—well, I see that you are unaccustomed to the strictures of polite society, so if you will allow me to—yes! Just so, and yes, hands like so and bent at the waist. A little deeper, my new friend. There! That is perfectly correct. And now," he said, turning to Jackie, "having seen your companion's fine example, I am sure that you, my dear, will . . . well, that will do, I suppose. Wonderful! The niceties have been observed, and now we *may* be and *can* be relaxed and welcoming."

Gun and Jackie exchanged another look.

"Please! *Please!* Sit, my new friends, sit! There is no need to stand on ceremony, not in these black wastes. It is well to meet you, well and beyond well, for I can tell at a glance that you are visitors from a great distance away, and—dare I say it—perhaps even a bit *lost*. Never fear! Mr. Vutch is the very soul of solicitude and, indeed, I see a great deal of mutual benefit arising from this chance meeting!"

The man clasped his hands together and looked back and forth between the two of them brightly.

"Erm," Gun said, when he judged that the strange man had run out of breath. "Um . . . Hello! It's nice to meet you."

"Hi," Jackie said.

The man performed a delicate cough.

"It would be *customary* for you to provide your names?" Mr. Vutch asked. They had clearly just committed some major faux-pas that the gentleman was very determined not to make a big deal out of but equally determined to correct.

"Oh! Sorry. I'm Gun. Gunnar. Anderson."

"Lovely!" Mr. Vutch said. "Many welcomes to you, Gunnar Anderson." He cast his eyes over to Jackie.

"Jackie Aimes."

"It is *perfectly wonderful* to make your acquaintance," Mr. Vutch said. "Gunnar Anderson, Jackie Aimes, I welcome you again to the Wanderlands and wish you many happy returns here."

"Thank you," Gun said, carefully.

"Now!" Mr. Vutch looked back and forth between the two of them. "You are both interesting in the *extreme*, if you do not mind me saying it, and I cannot help but inquire after your disposition and fortunes. And is that, may I ask, a *sword?*"

Gun looked down at the weapon still clutched in his hand. He made himself relax his grip.

"Oh, yeah. It is."

"It looks like an *uncommonly* fine weapon!" Mr. Vutch said. "I will confess that swords and sword-crafting are rare enough in these lost and broken days, but it gladdens my heart to see such a fine weapon here in this dark place. Would you mind very much if I took a closer look?"

Another exchanged look, but Gun shrugged. "Nah, not at all." He lifted up the sword and held it out, hilt-first, to the eccentric man. "Feel free."

"Your kindness will become the *very stuff* of legends," Mr. Vutch said.

Gun placed the sword hilt in Vutch's hand. Gun let it go, and the point fell instantly to the stone, cracking the tile in the courtyard. It was plain that Mr. Vutch held onto the hilt only with the greatest of effort. He grabbed it with his other hand as well and could barely keep the hilt off the ground.

"A most uncommon weapon," Mr. Vutch said hoarsely, straining with the effort of keeping the thing upright. "Most uncommon indeed!"

His fingers gave way, and the sword fell with a clatter to the tile.

"Sorry." Gun retrieved the weapon while Mr. Vutch retreated to his perch, the chunk of broken masonry, and rubbed his long digits. "Sorry again," Gun said. "I thought that might happen. It's real heavy."

"Well!" Mr. Vutch said, breathing hard and doing his best to regain composure. "It is certainly plain that this is no ordinary weapon. And to wield it so easily, you are no ordinary travelers! No, and no ordinary travelers *indeed*. Such strength! If I might be so bold, I can quite think of only one sort of creature who possesses such strength, though I can hardly credit it!"

"Oh?" Gun asked. Jackie nudged him, and he made a quick shushing gesture. "I'm not sure what you mean."

"Why," Vutch dropped his voice, as if confessing some grand secret, "you must be those singular creatures that we in the Wanderlands call *Behemoth*. Do I miss my guess?"

"Um," Gun said.

"Behemoth?" Jackie pretended to cluelessness.

"*Behemoth*," Mr. Vutch said, with the air of one setting the scene in a stage-play. "World-walkers! The Unbroken Few! And a thousand other names besides, for the Behemoth that have come to this world have stood large in its history. Indeed, children in the Wanderlands know of nearly every Behemoth ever to come here! You are both *extraordinary*, Gunnar Anderson and Jackie Aimes! Destined for enormous things, grand events, and great feats. Truly, this is a landmark day, and what a fortuitous meeting!"

Mr. Vutch leaned forward, almost conspiratorially. "What a meeting *indeed*, my friends, and how fortunate that you should meet *me*, of all possible folk, in this black place. For I will tell you a secret known only to a select few. I will confess a truth held close and rarely shown in the light."

The man who called himself Mr. Vutch took a big moment here; he might have been on stage performing in the most revered play in the world. He looked back and forth from Gun to Jackie and waited until the suspense was unbearable.

"I," Mr. Vutch pitched his voice low, "am no ordinary traveler myself."

Gun and Jackie exchanged yet another look and then back at their visitor. They were wide-eyed.

"No ordinary traveler indeed!" Mr. Vutch cried, really building up a good head of steam now. "I am making my way through the Dark a-purpose, a quest to return myself to the position from which I am cruelly withheld. As you might have guessed already from my bearing, I am not merely a traveler in the Dim, but a prince-in-disguise, exiled from my rightful throne and usurped. So you see, my friends! This is well met indeed, and great purposes may find their undertakings here, at this fire, and among our own august company! We are truly well met, my friends!"

"Uh . . ." Jackie looked helplessly at Gun. He just shook his head again, a minute negation.

"It is extraordinary," Mr. Vutch said. "*Extraordinary* that the three of us— perhaps the three persons in all of the world who are best suited to help each other—would find ourselves here, of all possible places! We stand a bare span from the entrance to the greatest prison in the history of the world, my friends. We stand atop the *grave of the Giant.*"

"Excuse me?" Jackie asked, thrown. "Did you say Giant?"

Mr. Vutch drew up, looking back and forth between the two of them, aghast. "But you don't—you don't mean—my friends, the Giant is the demon that broke the sky! He is the architect of the shadow that coils around you! He is the source of all misery, my friends, all of the darkness in these end days of the world. He is the Final Returner; the One Who Fell. He is the Giant. His name is Kindaedystrin, and he *lies beneath our feet.*"

"Whoa." Jackie nodded, impressed.

"*Very* cool," Gun agreed, with a nod at Jackie. "So is he, like, breaking free? Or something?"

Mr. Vutch blinked. "*Breaking free?* My friend, no. Such a thought! He would extinguish what light is left in the world as easily as you might put out a candle-flame. Your world must be an appalling place indeed, for you to be so easy with such black thoughts!"

"Not really." Gun grinned at Jackie. "I just have a lively imagination."

"Or read too many books." Jackie rolled her eyes.

"Well, that may be as that may be." Mr. Vutch made a great show of shivering and drawing his cloak around himself. "Still, let us turn our thoughts to more pleasant topics. I wonder—"

"If you don't mind," Jackie interrupted, ignoring Gun's sharp look, "what can you tell us about the . . . things, I guess? That live here?"

For a moment, Mr. Vutch's face went still.

"Live here? You don't mean the Cold?"

"I don't know what they are called," Jackie said. "They were little things. Small fuckers with black teeth. Liked biting."

"A lot." Gun looked at the remains of rough jaws and drill-bit teeth charring slowly in the fire.

Outré horror flooded into Mr. Vutch's face, but both Gun and Jackie saw that it was accompanied by actual, and badly hidden, relief.

"Oh, say not *so,* my friends! You ran afoul of the Feral Children? Say not so, indeed!"

"That is an excellent name for those little sons-of-bitches," Jackie said. "But I'm, like, surprised you're surprised. You can see parts of 'em in the fire, right? There's like a ton of corpses here, man."

Mr. Vutch didn't look down, appeared not to notice she'd spoken. "Oh, my *friends,* my friends!" he lamented. "The *Feral Children,* of all evils to encounter! But it is plain that you prevailed."

Gun and Jackie exchanged wry looks.

"Yeah," Gun said. "We, uh . . . we prevailed."

"But yes, of course," Mr. Vutch said, fussing, "I must remember! You are Behemoth! You are not bound to the strictures and laws of this world, and not prey to its dangers. How extraordinary! If anything, however, this convinces me that our paths have crossed, not by mere chance, but by the noble hand of destiny itself. Great things are moving the Wanderlands, dear friends, great portents! And you stand at the very heart of it! Having defeated *Feral Children,* of all terrible things! Extraordinary! Just extraordinary!"

Gun and Jackie exchanged another look, this one fairly long and full of portent.

Early on in their explorations of the dead city, when they were still getting used to the unfamiliar language that had taken up residence in their heads, they'd gotten quite accomplished at nonverbal communication. They'd discovered that, despite the fact that they'd only been friends and associates for a short amount of time, they were quite adept and had very little problem communicating volumes of information with just the lift of an eyebrow or the curve of a lip. It was one of those odd talents that sometimes arise between two people, like the ability to harmonize vocals or know instinctively where the other is going to throw a ball. And the look that they just exchanged said, more or less, just what all of their other looks during this conversation had said:

This guy is one hundred percent full of shit, right?

But they turned back to the odd man and smiled at him. *Full of shit* didn't necessarily mean bad, after all. If Gun and Jackie hadn't been able to deal with folks that were full to the brim with shit, they'd never have survived a day in their old world. In fact, one could argue that they were fairly full of shit themselves.

"I wonder," Mr. Vutch said, as if he'd just thought of it, "if a demonstration might be in order."

"A demonstration?" Gun asked.

"Well," Mr. Vutch allowed his tone to become serious, "I am considering offering you my services and making you a proposal that might lead to unimaginable wonders, quite beyond anything you could be prepared for. But Behemoth are, as I said, quite rare; I doubt there has been a visitor come through the Black Portal in a thousand years. All of those creatures are writ large as legend, but you must be aware that legends tend to grow. If we are to partner—indeed, if we are to join our righteous causes and accomplish the great deeds that seem more and more destined, I would love to see some demonstration of your powers. Some material witness of your, ah . . . *puissance*."

"I don't know what that word means," Jackie said, "but do you mean something like *this*?"

She picked up a loose piece of stone from the ground and crushed it in her hand, pulverized rock spraying out of the sides of her fist. She grinned at the man called Mr. Vutch. "I feel like what you meant was, *can we break shit?* And the answer is very much *yes*."

"That is most impressive," Mr. Vutch said, a little faint. "But I wonder if I might see something in the way of, say, weapons?"

"Well," Jackie said, "do you see all of those knocked-down buildings?"

Mr. Vutch nodded, slowly. "I thought some dire cataclysm befell this place."

Jackie pointed to her walking stick.

Mr. Vutch paled a little more and looked from the stick to Jackie's smile. He may have shivered for real this time.

Gun cleared his throat, for he thought he understood what Mr. Vutch was asking about. "The sword, to be honest, isn't as good a weapon as the stick." He lifted the sword till it caught the firelight and then let it fall down in an arc that happened to swing through the same space occupied by a big chunk of stone. He barely felt a tug as the sword passed through it. The stone fell in two pieces with a small cough of dust.

"It cuts through everything so easily, it's not even fun," Gun said and shrugged. "And it's damned hard not to cut your own arm off, when the blade never gets stopped or slowed by anything." Casually, he flipped over one of the halves of the stone and sat on it.

"Extraordinary," Mr. Vutch said, voice breathy. His eyes were bright and tracked the movements of the sword closely. "Just *extraordinary*."

"Yeah." Jackie was amused. "You said that."

"So," Gun said, "would you mind if we asked you a few—"

"I think, my friends," Mr. Vutch said, his tone suddenly much more clipped and businesslike, "that the time has come for us to speak of serious matters. Yes, for light is short and spoils belong to the bold, do they not? So let us speak of the future."

Gun and Jackie, once again, exchanged a look.

"Um," Gun said. "Sure."

Mr. Vutch leaned forward, and his voice was pitched quite low now, almost as if he were afraid of being overheard. "As I have said, I am no ordinary traveler, just as you are no ordinary travelers. We can be of great service to one another, I think, but swift action will be necessary."

"Well," Jackie said, "that's—"

Mr. Vutch held up a hand, cutting her off. "Please. There will be time for all manner of questions, and answers, too. But we must needs leave this city, my friends, and quickly. There are those who come behind, and they wish neither of us any goodwill. They make the Feral Children seem a *comfort*."

He leaned even further forward, and his tone became conspiratorial. "You see, my new friends, you were uncommonly fortunate to encounter me. There are many people in this benighted place, and very few of them wish well, though they can seem to. There are those who would take advantage of you, lie to you in order to win you to their cause. I would not see you set in the path of these villains!"

"They're all liars but me, right?" Gun asked with a faint smile, and Jackie choked back a snicker.

Mr. Vutch looked back and forth between them, a small uncertain frown on his face. "I do not understand."

"Look," Gun said. "No offense, but . . . I mean, how do we know that *you're* not one of those people?"

"Oh, good, are we done?" Jackie heaved a relieved sigh. "Can we cut the bullshit now?"

Mr. Vutch jerked as if slapped, and for a second, the affable personality on that face slipped, and they were looking into eyes that were cold and calculating and unamused.

"I cannot imagine what you mean."

"Listen," Gun said, exchanging what felt like the millionth look with Jackie, "I'm sorry to be blunt. But we could use some straight answers."

"Do you know about those fuckin' children monster things?" Jackie asked. "Were they with you?"

"Jacks!" Gun scolded. "C'mon."

Mr. Vutch wasn't quite as charming as he had been. The jovial, welcoming expression that had been hanging on his face like a poorly fitting mask was gone now, and something much more complex was in its place.

"Look," Gun said, "you obviously already knew what we were, right? Behemoth. You know we've been in the city for a while. Right? Well, listen, we don't care if you've got an angle, you know? We get it. Honestly, at this point, we're so fuckin' bored we'd probably be up for anything—"

"Yeah, *agreed,*" Jackie said.

"—but we've kind of been kind of terrified out of our goddamn minds for a while now, so we just need you to be straight with us. About who you are and what you want."

"Yeah," Jackie said. She gave Mr. Vutch a warm smile. "It *is* nice to meet you, really. I just can't, with the whole song-and-dance. You know?"

Mr. Vutch was doing something perplexing while they talked. He seemed to somehow grow smaller and more dense with their every word, compressing himself down and getting more and more still, more and more intent and intense.

"You *dare,*" he said, and his voice was different now. It became aristocratic, imperious. "You dare accuse me? Of infidelity? You *dare?* I, who have broken kings? I, who have crushed—"

He broke off because Gun gave a sharp cry and half-fell from his seat. Jackie looked at him, concerned.

"Gun? You okay?"

Gun doubled over, his neck straining and his back bowed. He lurched back off the rock he was sitting on and groaned, loud in the dimness.

"What in the *fuck* . . . ?" he said through clenched teeth.

"Gun!" Jackie said. "What the hell, man, are you okay?"

Mr. Vutch had stood up and backed away and was staring at the two of them with a strange, almost pleading intensity. Gun looked up at him, his face a mask of agony. His right hand kept flexing.

"Are you doing this?" Gun asked. "Is this you? *Stop it.*"

"You must . . ." Mr. Vutch swallowed, looked back over his shoulder, and made his voice forceful. "You must submit!"

"Stop it!" Jackie yelled. "Gun, what's wrong?"

Gun's hand found his sword, and it came up and pointed at Mr. Vutch. Then, slowly, as if dragged by some inexorable force that Gun couldn't quite fight, the point swung to Jackie.

"Something," Gun said, fighting for each word, "Something is making me . . . want to fuckin' hurt you, Jacks. There's something *in my fucking head.* Get away from me!"

"What the *fuck?*" Jackie asked. "What are you talking about?" She stepped backward and tripped over her walking stick, stumbling.

"It's like some kind of mental thing." Gun bit out. "Mind control. Or some shit." He took a step towards Jackie, and for a moment rage crossed his features, disfiguring them into an expression she'd never seen on his face before.

"Gun!" she said, getting frightened. Gun howled, then his own face returned.

He hauled himself back away from her and fell to one knee. He looked at Mr. Vutch.

"Is this you?" he asked. "Are you doing this? *Stop!*"

"It is not me," Mr. Vutch said, and he was visibly trembling. He fought to keep his voice firm. "It is not me! But you must submit, Behemoth! Follow your urges and kill her!"

"Quit it!" Jackie yelled at Vutch. She had her walking stick in her hand, and her knuckles were white on it.

Gun groaned and the sword-point wavered back and forth between Jackie and the man called Mr. Vutch. "Get the fuck away from me, Jackie. I don't know how long I can hold this off."

"Fucking *stop it!*" Jackie stepped toward Mr. Vutch. In a quick, practiced motion, Mr. Vutch drew a weapon from underneath his cloak. He hesitated only a second before shooting Jackie in the face. For a moment, the air was filled with a coughing, whirring sound, and a thousand tiny projectiles hit Jackie in her eyes.

"Aigh!" Jackie stumbled back with her hands over her eyes. Mr. Vutch moved the weapon to point at Gun. The muzzle of the weapon wavered.

"Submit!" Mr. Vutch hissed, but Gun screamed and threw the sword out into the shadow beyond the fire. He fell to his knees, his hands clutching the sides of his head. Jackie scrabbled at the ground until she found her walking stick. She scrubbed her hands across her eyes, clearing them of the fine needles.

"Quit it," she said, squinting at Vutch, her voice an angry rasp. He pointed the weapon at her again. This was too much. The end of the walking stick swung up sharply and erased the weapon in a fine spray of silver-and-black fragments, as well as a portion of Mr. Vutch's hand. He emitted a sharp, surprised cry, but that was all he had the time to get out. Jackie reversed the stick in a flat arc that she'd practiced on half a hundred structures and trees and caught Mr. Vutch in the side of the head with it.

In her old world, it would have stunned him or maybe knocked him senseless for a few moments, and perhaps that's all she meant to happen. But in this world, where her walking stick was one of the most powerful weapons in it, the stick took off the top of his head from below his right ear on an upward angle towards his brow. The greater part of Mr. Vutch's handsome face disappeared in a spray of golden ichor. His body stayed upright for a long moment, swayed, and then toppled.

Jackie stumbled backward a step or two, the stick falling from her suddenly nerveless hands. One end of it was coated with a thick gold paste.

"Gun?" Her voice was small. "Gun, are you okay?"

"Yeah," he said, hoarsely. "It stopped. Is he . . . ?"

"Dead," Jackie said, looking at the gold blood seeping from the thing's head, the vastly complex mechanism there, now smashed to wreckage by her stick. "*It* is dead. Not he. It."

"Fuck," Gun said. He climbed to his feet and put his arms around Jackie, who was beginning to tremble. "*Fuck*."

The body of Mr. Vutch was sprawled across the chunk of masonry he'd been sitting on. Gun saw a spreading pool of gold, like blood but thicker. As he watched, it turned black in spots, rotting before his eyes.

"What in the *hell*, Gun?" Jackie asked, her voice trembling.

"I don't know, Jacks." Gun took a deep breath. "I don't know."

They stood by the fire for a long time, holding onto each other, and then gathered themselves. From somewhere across the city, they heard the plaintive scream of a Feral Child.

Jackie pressed first one eye and then another firmly into Gun's shoulder, drying them, the closest she would get to acknowledging tears, and then backed out of his hug. She looked down at the half-headed corpse, dark-eyed, and then back up at Gun.

"Fuck it. Tired of this fuckin' place, anyway."

Gun walked over to where he'd thrown his sword and leaned down to pick it up. He looked at it for a long moment. His hands were trembling.

"Yeah," he said. "Yeah, me too. I'm done with it."

Jackie looked back at the way they'd come, back to the break in the caldera walls. "The lights? Down the mountain?"

Gun glanced over his shoulder, and they heard another Feral Child scream, closer this time. He nodded.

"Yeah." He slid his sword into its scabbard. "Yeah, Jacks, let's get the fuck out of here."

THE KILLERS

A Bar Called A Dream of Trees

"The failure of light is tragedy beyond real understanding. Our light has been steady for so long that we forget the repercussions of its loss. Oh, light fades—but so slowly that even a lifetime is not enough to sense it. Were the lights to suddenly fail in any part of the Keep, it would be disaster. It would be like amputating a limb, or removing an organ. It's possible that the body could survive, but only as something irretrievably changed."

—ABLE BORIA, 'NOTES TO THE QUEEN'

"So, ah . . . Sophie?"

"Hm?"

"Do you, uh . . . want to explain why we're here?"

"Dunno what you mean, Triks."

"I mean, *here*. Why are we here?"

"Seems obvious. We needed drinks and this place serves 'em."

"Okay, sure, but why *here*?"

"Still not sure what you mean."

"All right. Okay. Why, *O Capitana*, did we come to the most remote, unkempt, far-from-everything bar in the entire Keep to do our drinking? If you absolutely insist on drinking right now, what with everything that's going on?"

Sophie grinned at Trik and pointed over the girl's shoulder. "I like the view."

Trik turned her head and craned her neck, making her cloud of black hair sway, and looked. One wall of the bar had, a long time ago, been painted with a bunch of vertical brown lines, with halfhearted green splotches thrown in. It was supposed to be trees. Trik made a face.

The Killers were in a bar, deep in the bowels of the Keep, deeper even than the Loche de Menthe, though in a more well-lit part of it. It was a dismal little shit-hole of a bar that faced on a seldom used thoroughfare. Sophie had been there a few times, but it wasn't known as one of the Killers' hangouts. It had three things going for it: it was the safest place Sophie could think of at the moment, it had decent booze, and it had a great name. The bar was called A Dream of Trees.

Hunker John returned from the barkeep, bearing a tray full of pots of strong.

He distributed these to the Killers, who accepted them with varying levels of grace. Ben barely noticed his, a troubled frown on his face, and New Girl took hers with a warm smile. Bear gave him a distracted nod, and Trik ignored hers, arms crossed tightly over her chest, expression thunderous. Hunker set a small pot in front of Sophie.

"I, for one, approve heartily," he said, "for tonight has been an interesting night, and interesting nights require interesting toasts."

"John," Trik said, "don't be an ass."

"John's right." Sophie lifted her cup. "What's the toast, Hunker?"

He considered, then lifted his own drink. "To the Loche de Menthe; may it live in our memory as it died, with beautiful people doing ugly things."

Trik looked away, but Sophie nodded. "To the Loche." She threw the strong back, relishing the burn at the back of her throat. Maybe she could drown the sight of those lightsculptures going dark. She set the cup down, making an effort to keep her hand from trembling.

Trik was still looking away, arms crossed. "You still haven't told us why we're *here*."

Sophie sighed. "Because this is where I want to be, Triks."

"Sure," Bear said.

"In the ass-end of nowhere," Trik said. "Convenient."

"Not really," Sophie said, humorlessly. "Get comfortable, kids, because I plan to sit here drinking until I can't remember your names."

"Killers, unite!" Hunker John lifted his glass.

"Shut up, Hunk," Trik said. "Sophie, you can't be serious. First the fop with the warning, and then someone murdered the Loche de Menthe! There has to be something we can do."

"Oh," Sophie let her eyes wander back to the mural of trees on the far wall, "there's plenty we can do. There's just nothing we're *going* to."

"Trik," Ben said, looking miserable but trying to keep it to himself, "let it be."

Trik crossed her arms and stewed, pointedly not drinking the pot of strong Hunker had put in front of her. Sophie twisted and waved to the barkeep, signaling for more drinks. She was going to need them. They had escaped from the Loche de Menthe via a long-abandoned tunnel Ben knew about, and then Sophie had brought them here. As Trik said, in the ass-end of nowhere. All because the Consort of the Queen had decided to fuck around with her, sending cryptic warnings. And then her suspicious interview with Mr. March, his offer of drugs, and what he'd wanted her to do. Open a Silver-Age vault that nobody else in the entire Keep—maybe in the entire world—could open.

And then . . . someone had murdered the Loche de Menthe. While she was in it. Someone had systematically broken the lightsculptures that had hung above the place for a millennia, taking it from Dim to Dark. There was no way the place could survive, now. No one would go there, the psychological resistance to the Dark too strong for any desire for debauchery to overcome. Breaking lightsculptures wasn't just frowned upon, it wasn't just a crime. It was unheard of. It was something very close to blasphemy. The Vesachai would kill whoever had done it.

Trik made an unhappy sound and looked at Sophie. "Come on, we're the Killers, right? Why don't we try to find this Mr. March, at least?"

Sophie made a show of stretching and a bigger show of being unconcerned. "Go for it, Triks. If you want to go kick over tables and break some faces, don't let me stop you."

"I'm not leaving you, Sophie," Trik said.

"And I'm not leaving *here*, so why don't you calm down and have a drink?"

"Yeah, Trik," Hunker John said, "you're being tiresome. A beverage would improve your disposition. And look! There's one *right in front of you.*"

"Shut the fuck up, Hunker." Trik crossed her arms, glaring at Sophie, who raised an eyebrow.

"You better watch that fucking eyeball you're putting on me, Trik."

"Sophie—" Ben said, but she cut him off with a gesture.

Trik leaned forward, aggressive. "I don't suppose we deserve an explanation, at least?"

"Not really."

"So you want us to just sit here, in this asshole bar, and drink."

"Sure," said Sophie. "Do what we do best. Killers unite."

"Sophie, something just *murdered the Loche de Menthe.* While you were there! Do you think that's a coincidence? You can't just not engage with this. Don't you care what's happening?"

"Trik!" Ben barked, angry now. "Cut it out." But Sophie stilled him with a look. Trik was fuming, and she understood why. Trik was always happiest going directly at a problem, and triply so when it involved any kind of threat to Sophie. The girl was overprotective to a fault. But Sophie wasn't about to explain a lifetime of halted momentum to someone who should know better. She looked away for a long moment, considering her words, long enough for the barkeep to put a glass of something sweet in front of her. She took a further moment, letting the liquor sting her lips, feeling the promise of oblivion on her tongue. New Girl leaned forward, lips parted, waiting.

"I care, Triks." Sophie took another sip, and then scraped a slot to life on the rough edge of the table. She leaned forward, took a drag, and picked up her half-full glass of liquor. She turned it in the light from the litstone columns outside the bar, catching rays in the depths of the amber liquid. "I care about *this.*"

She drained it in one long draught, her throat working, then set it down on the table with a sharp click. She grinned at Trik. "And I care about the next one;

and the one after that. I care about some good drugs, a good night, a good laugh. I care about rolling over someone pretty, about waking up and kicking them out and doing it all again. I care, Triks, about having some *fun* before the night falls. About having something sweet before we go into the dark—because we're all going into the fucking dark."

She smiled at the Killers, bleak, and pushed herself to her feet. "The rest can go fuck itself. I'm going to the bar."

———

Ben waited until Sophie had gone to the bar for another drink, then pitched his voice low. "Trik, you are really pissing me off."

"*Fuck* you," Trik said. "We're sitting here like assholes, man."

"Yeah?" Ben lifted his hands. "What else are we going to do?"

"*Something,*" Trik said. "Anything."

"Something does sound better than *this,*" Bear spoke in a low voice, looking at Sophie's back. Sophie was hunched over on a barstool, out of earshot, staring at the atrocious mural of trees. New Girl was watching her too, a troubled frown on her face.

Ben sighed and swirled the contents of his glass. He didn't seem much in the mood for drinking. "Look, kids, we need to settle down. Yeah, especially *you,* Trik. Tonight is more trouble than you know."

New Girl brought her frown around to focus on Ben. "Trouble? How? I know the lights going out is strange, but . . ."

Ben caught them up on Sophie's odd interview with Mr. March, and the implications of it. Bear listened intently, a line of worry creasing his brow. When Ben finished, Bear shook his head.

"That doesn't make much sense. If they want the Book, why are they asking about this silver vault? Did they really think Sophie would open it for some *drugs?*"

Hunker John had a different reaction. "*Ansiotropic?* Sophie passed up *Battle Drugs?* Do you know how much fun we could be having right now?"

"Shut up, Hunk," Trik said. Ben ignored him.

"I don't think it matters if they thought she'd take the deal or not. It was just the opening shot in a complicated play. This is how these fuckers do things. Plots within plots within fucking *plots.*"

"Ansiotropic," Hunker wailed, forlornly, to himself.

"Wait," New Girl said, confused. "Who? Who are 'these fuckers'?"

"The same fuckers that came for us when we were kids," Ben said, heavily. "Back then it was the Queen; it was Denver Murkai, and Damien Crowe, and who the fuck knows who else. They wanted that Book—no. They wanted to use

Sophie, beçause she *had* the Book. Denver Murkai, her tutor, *led her to Saint Station*. He fed her to that monster. And then when she came back, with her arms full of forbidden silver—the First Vesachai's own daughter, no less—Jane Guin used the scandal to break the Vesachai's power, to put them under her thumb after a thousand years of autonomy. Who knows what she was planning for Sophie next; that's when the Hot Halls War happened, and everybody's plans went to shit."

He grimaced, and took a drink. "Not that we knew any of that, back then. We were kids. We were on an adventure; we thought we were saving the world, and these fuckers used that against us. Twisted us and used us to change the world into a shape they liked better. No, it's not right to say 'us'—I was there, yeah, but wasn't really us. It was *Sophie*. They used her, they destroyed her life, and then they threw her away."

"We know a lot of that," Bear said, still hunched forward, "But we don't know what that has to do with tonight."

"Or why Sophie is so—well, whatever she is right now." Trik glanced at Sophie's back. "I always thought that if something like this ever happened, I don't know. She'd spring into action. Take no prisoners. You know! *Be the Capitana*."

Hunker John yawned again, for real this time. "I think you ask too much of our dear Sophie, Triks. She is not the girl she once was. And thank the Mother for that."

"Shut up, John," Trik said. Hunker blew her a kiss.

Ben sighed. "Hunker's not wrong. Neither of us are the kids we used to be; but I think you all are missing the point. We call ourselves the Killers. Look, no offence, but we're mostly drunks and layabouts these days. The original Killers were something else. Mad Vaas, Tom, Luet. God, Jubilee! We were tight, and we thought . . . I mean, we all had the dream, right? We all had the dream about the Giant, and the Silver Book. We all had the Dream of Trees. We thought we were saving the world."

A complicated expression twisted Ben's features, and New Girl laid a hand on his arm. He gave himself a moment, and when he continued, his voice was pitched low, to make sure Sophie couldn't hear.

"What you have to understand about Sophie is that she can handle all of that. She can handle being used, tricked into breaking her family's power, seduced into wrapping her bones with silver, all of that. She can even handle Proscription, losing her family, her father and brother and uncle. But she can't handle losing her friends. She can't deal with that. So she doesn't know what to do, and she's being a piece of shit about it. Because, I mean, have you ever *met* her? She's not exactly a paragon of self-reflection and healthy problem solving."

Trik frowned. "What do you mean, losing her friends? Us? We're not going anywhere, Ben. I'm sure as fuck not."

Ben shook his head, impatiently. "No, you don't understand. The last time this kind of thing started happening, the last time the great forces of the world started trying to push Sophie around, trying to wrap her in their plots, her friends . . ."

He broke off, and when he spoke there was old pain in his voice. He was talking about his friends too. "Well, most of her friends *died*."

———

Sophie rolled a glass between her palms and was busy thinking about old days when Bear sat down next to her. She ignored him; she knew what he was going to say.

She was thinking about times before the Hot Halls War; before even Saint Station or the Feral Children or Gutcher, the Outkeep King. Even before she got the dream. She was remembering being just a regular-type little girl.

There was this prank that she and Ben and Crazy Tom of the old Killers had pulled, something with flour and Swatterflowers, that sent the Keep into an uproar. She could barely remember what it was about now; some tutor who had annoyed her. There hadn't been any life-or-death dashes through the Dark then, hadn't been any scars on her arms or death sentences. She'd just been an asshole little kid with a talent for trouble.

Gods, she remembered how much trouble they'd gotten in! That was before Denver, too, if she remembered right. She remembered the lecture she and Ben and Tom had gotten from her father. And the punishments that had felt like the end of the world, to a thirteen-year-old hellion.

So simple, so fucking *innocent*.

She smiled now, still rolling her glass between her palms. Her punishment had been to go ask each of the shopkeeps in the Rue de Paladia for chores to do, and her father had set her goody-goody younger brother as her tormenter and mobile jailer. Lee had gotten a stick—he called it the 'Sophie Poker'—and he just had the time of his life. How she'd hated that! But Lee had been so happy; he finally got to hang out with his older sister. He probably hadn't even realized he was tormenting her, probably thought they were playing a game.

Twins *damn*. What Sophie wouldn't do to go back to those dirty storerooms, getting poked in the side by her laughing kid brother.

Twins damn, indeed.

Bear cleared his throat, reminding her of his presence. He leaned on the bar, setting his chin in his hand, and stared pointedly at the side of Sophie's face.

She glanced sideways, irritated. "That seat is reserved for drinkers."

Bear chuckled and motioned to the barkeep. He ordered them two pots of strong, the cheap but effective spirit he favored. He waited until the two small pots were poured and set in front of them. He lifted his.

Sophie considered the small volume of liquid in front of her. She had no doubt this was the precursor to some ploy from her meddling friends. Some call to action. But some rituals were compelling, and poured liquor was a sacred rite. She lifted hers.

"Killers, unite," Bear said, and they tossed back their drinks.

It burned down the back of her throat, and she hoped it would do its job, which was to both invite and repel the murk, to fuzz the edges, to make the unbearable taste sweet. She was getting there, but she had spent fifteen years building up a tolerance that could go toe-to-toe with just about anybody in the Keep. It took a lot of strong to fuzz *her* edges.

Bear set his pot down and resumed looking at the side of Sophie's face. She resumed ignoring him.

"You're full of shit, you know," he said, finally.

"You're just figuring this out?"

"That little speech. 'All I care about is this drink, and the next.' I call bullshit."

Sophie sighed, and looked at him. Bear had been with the Killers for a long time, maybe ten years now. He was a big, sweet man with a pitch-black core, hints of some tragic or gruesome past, and a very useful capacity for violence. But sometimes she felt more like his big sister than his friend, and right now she felt like he was poking her in the side with a stick. "If you're not getting another drink, I could use a few minutes alone."

Bear ignored this. "I know something you care about, Sophie, and it's the reason why we can't sit here and drink until the problems go away."

Sophie rubbed her eyes. "Oh, I can't wait to hear about this."

Bear grinned. "You try to act like some hard shit, Sophie Vesachai, but we all know better. Who got that medicine for Hunker John when he was having trouble breathing? Who went to the *Queen* for it?"

"You don't know that. It just showed up."

Bear made a derisive sound. "And who goes behind our backs and pays our bar debts? Who sorted Trik's thing with the Coins Preator when they were trying to throw her in lock? Who's hooked us up with ten thousand drinks in ten thousand bars? Who's up and awake whenever we need you? Who's the one who sorts everything out, all the time, and tries not to act like she's doing it?"

"Oh, *fuck you,*" Sophie said, annoyed.

"All right, I'll stop. But I know there's some shit you *do* care about, O Queen of Darkness and Despair, and Ben told us about the threat Mr. March made."

"What threat?"

"Us, Sophie. When you didn't take the drugs, he threatened *us.*"

Sophie's jaw worked for a moment. "Yeah, well. Price you pay for being my friend, I guess. You want an apology?"

Bear set his big hand on her shoulder, and waited until she looked at him. His eyes were full of compassion. "No, Sophie. Look. We don't talk about our pasts. And I sure as fuck ain't eager to dig up old lives. But I know a little bit about getting tangled in the plots and plans of the Wise, and I know us little people don't often come away from that without scars. I don't want that to happen to us any more than you do. But I don't think you're thinking very clearly, here."

Sophie frowned at him. This was as much as Bear had ever said about his past. "Why not?"

"They killed the Loche. While *you were in it*. That's not just a plot, or a trick, that's a fucking declaration of war. Come on, you *know* that. I know this bar is off the beaten path, but it's still public. If they want to find us, they'll find us."

"Yeah," Sophie shot back, losing her temper and knocking his hand off her shoulder, "and if they do, this is the best place . . ."

She bit off her words and looked away. The mural of trees kept catching her eye, almost mocking her. *The Dream of Trees.* Faugh! The dream was nothing but lies.

"Yeah? Come on, Sophie, there's a reason why we call you 'Capitana' and it ain't just because you can drink and fuck us all under the table. I know you have a plan. What is it?"

Sophie stewed. The barkeep set another pot of strong down and she slammed it, the rough burn waking her up. She pointed at the glowing arch at the end of the public way the bar faced on.

"*If* they come—IF, Bear—we have line-of-sight on both entrances. All right? And this shithole of a bar is close to five or six hidden passageways; no matter who or what comes, Ben can get us out of here. And if—IF—something more is happening tonight than the same old shit, there's a Gallivant stop just beyond that arch that can take us somewhere. I might have an old favor I can cash in. We can't go home, and I don't want to panic the rest of the Killers. And I am *far* from certain that this won't just blow over; me and Ben have weathered this kind of thing before. So until we know *what the fuck is up*, this is what we're doing. And this is where we're doing it."

Bear was nodding. "Waiting. To see if Mr. March and his Battle Drugs were the whole play, or . . ."

"Or," Sophie said, the words tasting bitter on her tongue, "Or if the fop in the Charm Chair was right, and nothing tonight is what it seems, and this Mr. Fucking March is the thin end of a large wedge. So have another drink, man, and pray to whatever gods you believe in that it's not. Because if you *have* gotten tangled in the plans of the Wise, you don't need me to tell you how fucked we'd be if that's happening again."

Bear considered this, his expression frank. He smiled, but with little joy. "No, you don't."

"Sophie!" It was Ben, and the tone of alarm in his voice jerked her head around. She knew to pay attention to that tone. Her oldest friend was standing, white-faced. She became aware of a low buzzing sound, a familiar one. Ben pointed, and Sophie saw some floating silver balls, about as big as two fists held together, drifting at the far end of the thoroughfare.

"Swatterflowers?" Bear asked, confused. "They're not doing Festival here, are they?"

"No." She felt a tingling all down her arms. Was this it? She squinted at the little silvery balls.

"Sophie!" Ben said, urgency in his voice. *"Red lights!"*

Sophie got it then. The Swatterflowers usually presented cool blue lights; these ones shone speckled with an angry red. She had only seen Swatterflowers shine red once before—when she and Ben and Crazy Tom had played that prank on her tutor. Red lights meant that Swatterflowers were in Battle-Mode. As one, the swarm seemed to notice her and oriented on the bar. With a high-pitched whine, they sped straight at them.

"Well," Sophie said. *"Shit."*

It looked like the Killers were fucked after all.

THE CONVOX

The Utility of Behemoth

"Any utopia founded on the assumption that people will suddenly stop being selfish, irrational monkeys is a fool's dream."

—BLUE REE MACREADY, 'CHASER'

"You mean," West says to Winter, slowly, trying to understand, "to traffic in Behemoth."

This is interesting.

This is very interesting! West *knows* Behemoth; he might know more about them than any other person in the Wanderlands. He finds himself leaning forward, excited, and tries to control his reaction. First, Winter says she wants to kill the unkillable Giant Kindaedystrin; now she says she means to use a Behemoth weapon to do it.

A portal-forged sword! A sword that has been brought through one of those dread entryways from another world, changed into something that could cut anything. Could, perhaps, even kill a god. This is news indeed. West starts to get an idea; he feels inspiration coming on. He regulates his features to give nothing away.

"Trafficking in Behemoth," he says, playing at skepticism, "is a dangerous game."

"I mean to use the sword they brought," Winter says. "I am somewhat disinclined to make use of them personally. My impression of them thus far has been dubious at best."

"I would rather see them *dead*." D'Alle gives her a sour look, but Winter laughs.

"Master D'Alle has had some, ah, firsthand experience with Behemoth, though not these particular ones, and is not overfond of them. Yes, they are difficult to kill, yet perhaps less difficult to control. We shall see."

"Well, then." West grins. "My utility in this matter has become obvious."

"There is very little of this which is obvious." D'Alle grips his queue of dark hair. It is plain that talk of Behemoth has unnerved him. "We speak of fairy stories and monsters, of swords and prisons. If this Convox is to be nothing but held secrets and cards close to the chest, I cannot support it. *This* one says the Giant cannot be killed; *that* one says the prison cannot be opened. My Lady assures us all that this is possible and even easy, as long as we have a sword. A sword? Faugh! None in my militia have bothered with sword-craft in a hundred years; it is an antique and useless weapon. I have never heard that being brought through a door—even one between worlds—gives an item any special utility, and I cannot imagine any magic strong enough to make a sword worth this sort of trouble. If we speak in metaphors, then I will accept the role of the bumpkin and ask you to speak plainly. For mayfly I may be, but neither am I a fool, and none of this is obvious to *me*."

Winter smiles an apology at West for the interruption, but he waves it away. His mind is racing. *Behemoth!* Yes, his utility has become quite obvious indeed, and something else is coming clearer as well—the very opportunity he had hoped to find, here in the depths beneath the Mountain. It gleams before him, golden light in the shadow, and he only needs to determine its edges and dimensions, so that he might grasp it.

"Master D'Alle," Winter says, "I must apologize. Actually, I must apologize to us all. I am eager to be concluded with our business, and so, assume much. All of us have questions and perhaps I can sketch the outlines of the problem and the solution, as I see it. And then we can discuss a way to *capitalize,* if you will, on this remarkable confluence of events. Now—and Master D'Alle, you may remember this, for they precipitated rather remarkable events in your own city a long time ago—some while past, the Mother began sending *dreams*."

D'Alle's eyes were hooded as he looked at Winter. "I'm not like to forget that."

"Now, the Mother—say what you will of her—has an interesting method of accomplishing things, and for whatever reason her wishes are heard in the dreams of fools, madmen, and children. And what she wished for—what she *called* for— were certain artifacts. She bade those who heard her to search for hidden things. Yes, and dangerous things. Things too dangerous for our sad and darkened world to comfortably hold any longer. Things that have been locked away, or lost."

West, in a fit of brilliance, says nothing.

"Now, I and others of the Wise became aware of these dreams—through one method or another—and experienced various degrees of disquiet. The Mother, of course, has seen better days, and her motives are—let us say, *suspect*. It is impossible to know all of the dreams sent, or all of her plans, but I do know of a few, and they bear quite heavily on the matter at hand, so I hope you will forgive my explaining."

"I, for one," Mr. Turpentine says, jovially, "am quite fascinated!"

"One of the artifacts that the Mother called for so eagerly," Winter continues, with a smile at Mr. Turpentine, "is a Cold-Key."

West knows this. He adopts the appearance of a fascinated student and thinks about how to wrest control of this Convox from the damnable woman opposite. She clearly does not understand the true nature of this challenge.

"I wish her luck, then," Mr. Turpentine says, with apparent regret. "The Cold scoured all of the Lands for a thousand years and more; there can't possibly be any of those weapons left."

"Not even around the necks of the Cold," Candle murmurs, still cradling his broken hand.

"Just so, my good Candle." Turpentine inclines his long white head. "But no one knows where those ancient wizards put them."

"True enough," Winter says. "Even I do not know where the long-lost Cold disappeared to. And yet, the Mother is cunning, and a Cold-Key *was* found. And, through a great many *misadventures*—some of which good Master D'Alle might be able to catch you up on—the Key has washed up in a very unlikely place."

She looked around the fire. "It has found itself in the hands of Jane Guin, the very same barbarian Queen we spoke so earnestly of earlier."

West *is* interested in this. "Ah."

"Just so, West." Winter smiles at him. "*Ah*. But let me add trouble to the pot, as it were; the Mother also called for another artifact, neither as immediately useful as a Cold-Key, nor as dangerous, but perhaps more significant. She sent dreams to children, bidding them find a Book."

D'Alle blinks. "A book? Of what sort?"

"I think she means," West says slowly, drawing on old memories from his father, "a schema-book, one of the master tools of the Cold."

"Yes," says Winter. "They put their plans in these Books, Master D'Alle, and with them you can manipulate a wide variety of Silver-Age mechanisms. There were only a few of them made, and these were heavily guarded; great trouble could be made with one of those artifacts. They can bypass most protections built into the dangerous things of the world, and manipulate the flow of Silver to an incredible degree."

"Ah," West says again. He is thinking furiously and trying to look like he isn't. He is barely paying attention to all of this. Yet. "I thought all of the Books were destroyed in the Fall."

"One—or more—must have survived," Winter says. "I will give you one chance to guess where it was found."

"Oh, dear," Mr. Turpentine murmurs. "Not the damned Keep, again?"

"The Keep," Winter's tone turns dour. "And it is not in safe hands, my friends! Not safe at all. But, still, a Key and a Book; dangerous things. Great harm could be wreaked but, yet, not catastrophic. It was the other dreams she sent that were more troublesome; dreams sent not to madmen and children in our own Lands but, by some impossible expenditure of strength, to another *world*."

She glances at her audience, one by one. "The Mother called through the portals that link our worlds, my friends, to whatever fools and children could hear in those astonishing places, and she called for a *sword*. And as I said, some fool has listened, and they have brought a sword through that portal and into our world. Even now this sword walks the Mountain, wielding the last puzzle-piece in our doom, all unknowing and possessed of unknown motives. The Mother has assembled the pieces she needs, my friends."

"Pieces she needs?" echoes D'Alle, still confused. "For what?"

"To open the Giant's prison," West says, finally getting it. "That's the punchline, yes?"

"Yes." Winter nods at West. "That's the punchline."

D'Alle shakes his head. "I am getting tired of asking for explanations. What does a key, some sword, and a book have to do with opening Kindaedystrin's prison?"

"Dear Master D'Alle, I am happy to explain." West flashes a sharp smile at the idiot; happy to finally understand their host's baroque designs. "My father built that prison. It was built and locked by the Cold themselves. Every bit of their craft went into building the protections and safeguards found there, including the greatest Domination mechanisms ever built. But what is *made* with Silver can be *unmade* with Silver."

West pauses for dramatic effect, which his audience does not seem to appreciate. "There were those," he continues, "who imagined disaster, who imagined scenarios in which fallible humans—even Cold—could be tricked or enticed into opening that prison. So they bound the Giant not only with Silver but with the Old Gold. There was never a Dirt-Magic wizard in the Wanderlands like my father, like Hunter Fine."

He stopped to sip some *chûs*, then cleared his throat. "I did not know about the sword. A portal-forged blade, brought from another world, swung by an arm strong enough to swing it, would be able to cut through *damn near anything*. This world was not made for such creatures, nor such artifacts. It appears as if Lady Winter is correct, and the Mother has indeed called to the Mountain such tools as she needs to release her ancient servant."

There is quiet around the fire for a while, the only sound the crackling of twist-shards, burning in the fire.

"It is never a pleasant thing when a god turns against you," Winter says, quietly. "But we must fight in what manner we may. I propose that we use the tools the Mother has gathered, my friends. I propose we depose this barbarian Queen at the bottom of the world and take her Book and her Key. I propose we befriend these Behemoth at the top of the Mountain and use their sword. I propose we journey to the very deepest depths of the Wanderlands, and pass that portal-forged sword through the Giant Kindaedystrin's *neck*."

She smiles at the listening faces around the fire, each withdrawn in their own way, thinking about her proposition. She gives a kind of knowing shrug, as appealing as any sort of poisonous plea could be. "And then, of course, we can set to the very pleasurable task of enjoying the spoils of that endeavor. What use saving the world if we find ourselves poorer for it?"

Yes, West thinks, with an inward smile, *and now I have you, Winter. I know what you want.*

West now knows just how he will turn this Convox to his own purposes. He begins to smile openly, and who cares? Let them plot; let them finagle and twist. Winter does not often make mistakes, but she just made one here.

She trusted *him*.

PART II

AN ASIDE: THE UNDERLANDS PROJECT

The Underlands Project was the last and—perhaps—the greatest work of the Silver Age civilization. Its scope was immense; to dig out an entire world from the stone beneath the colossal Mountain; to tunnel out a self-sustaining civilization from the implacable bedrock there. Its purpose was simple—to build a refuge for speaking things, a place to escape and survive the Fall. It was thought, then, that the Fall was a temporary aberration, a self-healing mistake. The masters of the Silver Age were not worried that people would survive.

People always survive.

No, what they wished to preserve was their civilization, the one that had done the impossible—conquered the Wanderlands.

The Silver Age produced some spectacular works: the Tower, the Doors, the Nine Judges. It had buried the Giant Kindaedystrin and trapped the Twins. It had joined and united a place that had been built to prevent joining and uniting. The Silver Age had built the Feeds and birthed the Cold. It was no stranger to extensive projects.

The Underlands Project dwarfed all of those. The Cold and the Judges beggared the remaining Lands to build it. Architects were grown, massive constructor-automata that hollowed an entire world out of the stone beneath the Mountain, and every care was taken to ensure that speaking creatures would have every comfort possible for the long years ahead.

It was craven, in a sense; it was an admission that they saw little hope for the world above. They intended to climb into their burrow and let the world above die. It was cowardly, but cowardly on a grand scale. The magicians of the Silver Age never lacked for hubris.

In another sense, the Underlands Project was a logical plan; the Wise of that age could make a safe haven for themselves and fill it with everything they needed. They brought great caches of the weapons they'd built to fight the malicious things of the world, in case fighting needed to be done, and they made sure every comfort possible was near at hand. They built massively, expecting people to propagate and wishing to preserve the largest possible sample of thinking folk. Atop the Mountain stood the Feed, the second greatest ever built, and it was inconceivable that it could ever be tapped out or fail. It was inconceivable that the lights would ever dim in the new utopia they were building.

In the end, they built too widely and too well; they tunneled too far. They unearthed the Keep, the watch-tower built in another age to maintain vigilance over the Giant's prison. They stopped digging then; even in their hubris and ambition, they would risk nothing when it came to that creature.

The Wise of the Silver Age knew their business; they knew that to keep the Underlands—and the Giant's Prison—safe, they must protect it from the sorts of things that could harm it. So they built the Wall, that band of silver that encircles the Mountain and was meant to keep any sort of artificial creature out. And the only entrance to the Underlands—at that time—was at the very top of the Mountain; if that had stayed true, we may well have avoided our bad end. But greed and hubris hold hands with desperation, and they ran out of room and dug too close to the skin of the Mountain, weakening the very structure that kept the Wanderlands out.

This gave us the Breach, that avalanche of stone near the city of Cannoux that has caused us so much misery, and the kind of things that the Wall had been built to keep out were able to creep in. Into that dark hole crawled awful things indeed; the demon Winter and Mr. Turpentine, the two cursed Behemoth, the Brothers D'Essan, and all of the terrible monsters that worked so hard to bring about the end of our world.

—*An excerpt from 'A Compendium: The Underlands,'*
by Bind e Reynald, Scholae First Mark.

THE LOST BOYS

On Uses of Twist

"From such humble beginnings comes such grand catastrophe."

—ELIUT JONAS, 'THE BOYS IN BLACK AND RED'

Night was falling in Cannoux-Town.

Cannoux was a city located about halfway up the side of the great Mountain, next to the silver wall that marked the end of all human endeavors on those slopes. Below the silver wall lay endless leagues of broken, dark, and empty cities, while above there was only darkness. Save for, of course, the dead city on top of the Mountain. The Cold City, where the magicians used to live.

Night fell only occasionally in that town, Cannoux, that city on the slopes of the Mountain. They burned twist for light there, a vast industry of grinding up stone and firing the twist they extracted from it, using the energy to power crude light-towers. Unlike the more refined light-bringing contrivances of litstone and the delicate lightsculptures of the Silver Age, these couldn't be modulated, so Cannoux was always lit brightly—save for at Nightfall.

Nightfall was a holiday, observed every few weeks, where the Lords of Cannoux caused the light-towers to stop, and all artificial sources of light were to be extinguished. For a time—a moment, never more than a few of them—Cannoux stood lightless, dark, and all in that place found their eyes looking skyward, at the heavy blank nothing that stood above their heads.

It was a good time for introspection. It was a good time to hold your loved ones close. It was a good time to feel grateful to the Lords, for supplying the light in the first place, and an even better time to overlook some of their more regrettable excesses and foibles. And, most of all, the darkness of Nightfall provided *excellent* cover for young boys to escape from certain awful, implacable enemies—like school, or brothers.

But night was *falling*, not fallen, and James D'Essan had not escaped yet. He was only eleven but he was wiry, strong for his age, and he could climb like anybody's business.

He ran upwards through the city, climbing the side-ways and byways of

Cannoux, the unofficial pathways that wound through the places where the new city met the old. He ran along a rope-bridge between two ancient monuments, walked an old creaking beam over a garden, jumped over a narrow alleyway from the roof of a Lord's house into the abandoned basement of some decayed museum. A flock of bright red birds leapt into the air ahead of him, likely thinking him a rather big and boorish cat. Ahead were flashes of ancient silver—he was headed for the Wall.

If James could reach the Wall before his Twins-damned brother caught him, he might stand a chance of escape. He might not have to do any schooling today at all!

James D'Essan was proud of the fact that he was the most incurious, bone-stubborn jerk in Cannoux and would have punched anyone who said different. He regarded any day in which he didn't learn one damned thing as a success, and some days he managed to forget some stuff, too.

Those were good days. But he heard a sound from behind him and despaired: a familiar hiss of frustration. His brother was coming. His damned *brother*. His brother loved learning things, loved it more than anything else in the world, and this made him James' natural enemy. Chris—and James could still hardly believe it was true—read books for *fun*.

That couldn't be forgiven, any more than it could be understood.

Cannoux-Town was a city built upon the bones of another; a pastoral empire resting on the crumbling remains of a much greater one. Wooden houses perched precariously on the sides of slender stone towers; gourds flourished brightly in old balconies; young boys herded sheep on the slopes of ziggurats. Through it all were threaded heavy, crude ropes of conductive twist, an ugly web of humming wire connecting the light-towers together. Soon, the towers would go dark along with the rest of Cannoux, and James meant to be on top of the Wall and headed for parts unknown when that happened.

Perhaps, he thought with a little thrill of excited fear, he'd head up the Mountain, into the inky wilds of the upper slopes. There were a few scattered, tantalizing lights up there, only able to be seen when Nightfall was in full effect. Uncle said there was a city up there, at the top of the Mountain, but James only believed about *this* much of what Uncle said.

Uncle was one of his tutors, after all, which put him barely below his brother on his natural enemies list. In fact, it was Uncle's lessons that he was currently trying to skip.

Getting up on the Wall was no mean feat; it rose above the city on the up-slope edge like a great gleaming bar. It marked the edge of the known world, and beyond it lay the forbidden upper slopes of the Mountain, with whatever blackness and monsters lay beyond. There were no convenient stairwells up to the top and no handy ropes. But there were ways, and James wasn't the only person who some-times needed to escape the close bustle of the city and look out into the Dark.

He scaled up a leafy corner where a new rough masonry wall tied in with a heavily carved ancient one. The deep relief patterns were a perfect climbing sur-face. He scaled it quickly; James could always climb well. He bet his stupid brother couldn't get up the wall that fast! At the top of the wall was an old trellis that spanned a deep garden, abandoned and left to go wild years ago. A death-defying jump onto a slender tower covered in thick vines, and then a quick climb, and he was on top of the Wall.

Or, almost. James felt a strong hand close around his ankle.

"Gotcha!" Chris yanked him back down. James kicked out frantically, desper-ately, and his free leg connected with something. There was a squawk of pain from below, and the tight grip on his ankle disappeared. Quick as a cat, James rolled up onto the top of the wall and started running.

The city fell away from him, down the slope of the Mountain. It all seemed small, light-pillars flaring cold and blue and the warmer sparks of cooking-fires and lamps. The light-towers were fading, and Nightfall would start any min-ute now.

"Hey!" He heard Chris call from behind him, exasperated. "Come on, Squib!"

James could see families gathering on balconies and rooftops in legally re-quired observance; he saw the tiny warm sparks of flame and lamps extinguished. It was a crime to leave a light burning during Nightfall.

If the dark would just *come*. Chris was too smart to run along a very tall and not-that-wide silver wall in pitch-black shadow, but James wasn't. James some-times wondered how he and his aggravatingly intelligent brother could even be related. They certainly didn't look much alike; James had a dusky complexion and was already showing signs of being big when he grew up, whereas Chris was slender, narrow, and amber. James was eleven, still a kid, while Chris was fifteen, practically an adult. They had nothing in common. James had even nursed a fan-tasy that he was some secret prince, like in a story, and that Chris wasn't his brother at all, but Uncle had disabused him of this notion. "The Mother spits color," Uncle said, and said it was common for brothers to look dissimilar. But Uncle didn't know *everything*, and James D'Essan would be only too happy to believe that his overly talented, supremely smart older brother was secretly some-body else's problem.

With a hard *whomp* of arms and knees, Chris piled into James and the two went down on the pitted silver surface. James twisted as soon as he was able, half-dazed from knocking his head on the metal, but Chris had three years and half a hundred pounds on him. Chris was slender but tall, and James never won any fights with his older brother. That didn't stop him from trying.

"Twins *damn*, squib!" Chris panted, pinning James' arms with his knees. "Just stop for a second!"

But James gave his best battle cry and spit in the general direction of his brother's face, which was getting hard to see because the lights were nearly out. James wrenched again, hard, trying to get a knee up into Chris' stones.

"Just friggin quit it, squib," Chris grunted, still trying to pin him, "and I won't have to keep friggin' hurting you!"

But James wasn't about to stop. He twisted his neck until it felt like his neckbones were going to pop out then got his face close enough to sink his teeth into Chris' arm.

Chris squealed and grabbed James' face and bounced his head off the metal surface of the wall a couple of times.

"Stop it, squib!" Chris said. "Just stop! I don't want to hurt you!"

James just laughed, tears running down his face, and tasted blood in his mouth. He felt groggy; the whole world seemed to be ringing. He grinned at his brother.

"*NO*." He kicked out as hard as he could. Which, at the moment, wasn't very hard, but neither was that the point.

Grim-faced, Chris drew his fist back, just as the very last light from Cannoux went out, and the two boys were plunged into the depthless, impenetrable shadow that always waited just outside the range of illumination.

It didn't stop Chris from socking him a good one, though. Chris D'Essan always did what he said he was going to do. And James had never been able to beat Chris at anything, not ever. But James wasn't as dumb as he looked; and forcing Chris to beat the living shit out of his brother when he didn't want to was about as much a victory as James would ever get in this life.

James laughed into the massive emptiness of Nightfall. And then he spit blood in the general direction of his brother's face; it would have to be revenge enough.

What he was getting revenge *for* was one of the complicated, fussy kinds of ideas that James D'Essan never spent much time thinking about. He cradled his revenge, laughing maniacally, while Chris pummeled away.

———

James spit a little more blood on old cracked cobblestones as they walked back down through Cannoux towards the day's apparently inescapable lesson. He was feeling much better. He wanted to whistle, but he had a big ol' fat lip now. He didn't mind! He loved a good tussle. Fighting was about the only damn thing he was any good at, as Uncle pointed out to him fairly often.

Chris walked beside him, eyeballing him sidelong. He would occasionally touch his forehead and wince; Chris hated any kind of pain. James didn't really mind it. He sometimes felt like he was being slowly suffocated, like there was a vicious shape inside him, all full of knives that were pressing in towards his heart, and a good fight made that feeling go away. A few bruises made him forget about the knives.

A little pain made him feel okay.

The artificial lack of light they called Nightfall was over and Cannoux-Town was likewise ebullient around them; the natural response to the Dark was a celebration of light. Every possible torch was burning, every possible twistlamp turned on, every possible sparker and lantern lighted. They were walking down through the low city, taking a shortcut to Uncle's for their lesson; because James had made them late, and Uncle was unlikely to be pleased.

James was mostly watching stone-colored cats chase bright birds; something about Nightfall threw the animals into frantic activity. Perhaps for them, too, it was a reminder that the true dark could fall at any time, and it was best to be about their lives while they could.

"Squib," Chris said after a while, in that stupid older brother voice he used sometimes, "you remember what we talked about the other day, yeah?"

"No," James said truthfully. Chris had almost as much to say about everything as his tutors did, and he did his best to ignore his brother with the same force he did his lessons. Chris sighed and poked at his forehead again. James noted with spare satisfaction that he was walking with a small limp.

"Dreams," Chris said. "You supposed to tell me if you start having any strange dreams."

"Dreams?" James scoffed. He remembered the conversation now, but it wasn't *worth* remembering, which is why he'd pushed it out of his brain in the first place. "I dunno why you'd care about some dumb dreams. I got tons of dreams."

"I mean *special* dreams." Chris sounded serious, even more serious than usual. "No playing, squib, you should tell me."

"Well," James said, making a show of thinking, "I guess . . . well, now you saying it, I guess I *did* have kind of a weird dream."

"Oh?" Chris asked, giving him a sidelong glance.

"I dunno, though." James kicked a rock and looked up through a trellis at the brightly lit city above. "It was *real* weird."

"That's okay. I won't make fun, squib. Promise."

"Well, you shouldn't make fun," James squinted up at Chris. "You was in it."

Chris stopped, startled, and recovered. He looked at James very intently. "Me?"

"Yeah," James said. He dropped his voice and looked around. "It was about how you had a . . . well, about how you got a . . . ."

"A what?" Chris leaned close, eyes bright and wide.

"A squirrel peener," James said, gravely. "You was all the same, except for your peener was a little squirrel one."

Chris blew out his breath. "I'm gonna kick your stones up into your guts, squib."

"Amarelle Jenkis said she liked it, though," James said, giggling. "I heard she likes little squirrel peeners."

"You don't know nothing about peeners," Chris said, giving James a sharp punch on the arm and starting to walk again. "Or about girls from uptown, neither."

"Uncle says that's because I'm a more evolved form of person," James said, smugly. "Uncle says I'm already about a hundred times more evolved than you, on account of me not liking girls. Uncle says that girls are the main source of frustration in a man's life, and if he can get by without 'em, he's got a leg up on the competition already."

"Oh, you'll get to like girls soon enough," Chris said. "Or boys. And then we'll talk about being 'evolved.'"

"Won't," James said, with the pure and simple confidence of a person with zero experience in the matter. Anyways, girls *really* made him feel like those knives in his chest were pressing in, and he felt even stupider and dumber around them than he did around even Uncle or Chris, so James figured that he was one of those fortunate individuals that never got to like them at all.

They were getting close to Uncle's now, and Chris started to slow down. Finally, he stopped.

"James," he said, and now he was using his full-on Chris-the-Adult voice, the one that made James want to put a fist through his teeth. "Kid, you *have* to stop running away from lessons."

James crossed his arms over his chest.

"You have to, squib," Chris said. "You're getting too old now; you can't keep acting like a child."

"I *am* a child!"

But Chris was shaking his head. "Maybe if you'd grown up with some Lord as a father, or if Ma had a good dowry. But we don't get to be kids long, squib, and Ma . . . well. Stuff like you been pulling don't make it easier on her."

James scowled, as hard as he could scowl. He looked up at Chris through low brows.

"Uncle don't care, really," Chris explained. "But the others—Master Jule and Amy Lei said they'll drop us *both*, kid. If you keep running off, fighting it every which way, they say it just ain't worth it. They're already doing Ma a favor by teaching us."

"I don't want to learn nothing!" James said desperately. "I don't care about no stupid lessons!"

But . . . Twins *damn* it.

He wasn't stupid. He knew what Chris was saying, what he was really saying, and he wrapped his arms around his chest. What his brother was *really* saying was that nobody cared that much if *James* learned anything. If it was just about *James*, he could just go walk out into the shadows and get eaten by monsters and no big loss to anybody. But it wasn't about *James'* education. Nobody cared if *James* got on a fast track to status and fortune. It was clear to everyone involved that *James* was qualified only to spend his life toiling in the local rock-mill, and probably break some jaws and take some fists along the way.

No, nobody was worried about James. They were worried about his brother. If James caused enough trouble, Chris wouldn't get his education. There were an awful lot of hopes and dreams being pinned on Chris D'Essan; even a younger brother who struggled to know as little as possible knew that.

"We gotta have lessons, kid," Chris said, almost gently. "We're nothing, we're *nobodies*. All we got is our heads and hands, you see that, right?"

James didn't reply, didn't look up at his brother. The black feeling in his chest was all pressing in. But then Chris played his prize coin, the unimpeachable argument.

"We're gonna have to take care of Ma before long, squib," Chris said. "Or we'll end up indentured. You don't want Ma to be a cull, right?"

"I don't care about no stupid lessons," James muttered, but Chris won like he always won. No, James didn't want Ma to be no friggin' slave. So he would go to his lessons, and then Chris would become some rich lord's prize viceroy and take care of Ma, and James would run away and go see what kind of monsters lived in the dead city on the top of the Mountain, and nobody would even know or care.

———

The man every kid in Cannoux knew as "Uncle" lived downslope almost to the far gate, in an old flat building that was low but very large, and his workshops and study were in the center. Surrounding these, filling up racks of rough-made shelving and supports, was the boneyard.

The boneyard was where Uncle kept all of his failed—or at least no longer useful—experiments. There were gadgets of every size and description; heavy things with thick gearwork, auto-plows and clock-axes, and small finely made things of which purpose only Uncle knew. James used to like wandering through the boneyard, imagining the stuff that these machines could do, but he'd outgrown that and now found the whole mess boring.

"Boy!" Uncle roared as they approached, picking their way through the old contraptions. "Prepare your tender butt-cheeks, for I am going to whale upon them with a great fury and even greater vengeance!"

"What?" James asked, surprised. "What did I do?"

Uncle tossed his rounding hammer into a vat of oil and brushed off his hands. There was some ridiculously complex bit of twistcraft in front of him, half-made.

"Other than skipping my last two lessons, boy?" Uncle asked. He was a big beast of a man, old but strong, bald as an egg but with a mustache about twice as thick as any James had ever seen. "Other than *that*, I suppose what you did is be an obstinate little troublemaker who causes his Ma no end of worry. Well, seeing as you wasted most of the lesson by being a son-of-a-bitch, I guess we'll skip right to the *test*."

"Aw, man!" James said, screwing up his face. Though he *did* prefer tests to having to actually learn things; if you looked at them a certain way, they were a form of combat. "Test on *what*?"

"Geography." Uncle took off his work apron and tossed it on the wide table where Chris was setting up some fabulously complex bit of twistcraft he was working on—the purpose of which James could not have hazarded a guess even if he had the least inclination to. Chris was staring at James with a hooded, inscrutable expression, and James was trying to decipher it when Uncle whirled on him.

"You," he roared at Chris, "mind your own Twins-damned business for once in your already-too-long life, boy. You try to give your brother any hints, and I'll set you to digging for twist with your damn teenaged *peener!*"

Chris held his hands up, placating, and focused on his work. Uncle turned back to James, eyes narrowed.

"Geography!" Uncle said. "No doubt you are just now thinking to yourself, 'Self, Uncle doesn't teach Geography! Ms. Vale teaches me that, the lovely soul, and I ignore every Twins-damned thing she says! What does old Uncle care about geography?'"

James couldn't help but grin. He had been thinking this very thing. Uncle tapped the table with one blunt finger.

"Don't worry, boy, like everything I do, it has a purpose. Where do you live?"

"Um. Cannoux?"

"If you didn't know that one, I'd drown you myself and save your Ma the trouble. Where is Cannoux?"

James blinked. "What do you mean?"

Uncle gave him an eyeball.

"Oh," James said. "On the Mountain."

"Spinward or lee? Between which cities?"

James screwed up his face, thinking. This actually wasn't as hard as some questions might have been. Since he planned on running away eventually, he had allowed *some* information about Cannoux's surroundings to percolate through his brain. "Um. Alast to the spinward, Delavain to the lee?"

Uncle sighed. "Reverse those, but that's close enough. Like Cannoux, what are both of those cities built right up against . . . ?"

"The . . . Mountain?"

He got the eyeball again.

"I don't know!" James said.

"Here's a hint. It's *silver.*"

"Oh! The Wall!"

"The silver wall. Does it go all the way around the Mountain?"

James frowned. "Um. Yes?"

"Wish you had more confidence in your voice, boy. And don't think I didn't see that, Chris! I'd like to see how clever you are with both your arms stuffed into your mouth. All right, James, tell me what the Wall is there for."

"No fair," James said, eagerly, always one for rules if they were in his favor. "That's History!"

Uncle crossed his arms, undeterred. *"Might be,"* he allowed. "I got a little surprise for you if you pass this test. If you make me happy, I got a present for you. *Might* be. Now, what's the Wall for?"

James screwed up his face. "I dunno! It protects the stuff up on top?"

"Which is?"

"The old Cold-City," James said, "where the magicians used to live."

"And?"

"And, I don't know!"

Uncle gave him a hard eye. "What's on top of the Mountain, James? Big fucker, goes all the way up to the sky? Where we used to get our light before it failed?"

"Oh!" James' face cleared. "The Feed."

"How does the Wall protect the Feed and Cold-City?"

Now James was at a loss. He wracked the intentionally small amounts of knowledge in his beleaguered brain and came up with nothing. He shook his head, miserable; usually, Uncle had good presents, and he hated to miss one. But Uncle smiled a little.

"There's few enough living that knows this one, lad, so I'll give it to you. But pay attention! It keeps *any kind of automata* out," Uncle said. "High-Order, Low-Order, anything. Any person with a mindspring, whether it's the Old Gold or Silver-Age work or even rough twist, can't get near that Wall. You know what happens if they try to go over it?"

James shrugged. Uncle waited for a minute and then turned to look over his shoulder at his prize student, who was working at the table behind them. He made a come-hither gesture.

"They die," Chris said, not looking up from his work.

"They die," Uncle agreed. He peered at James. "You understand?"

"I guess?" James said. There were only a few clock-and-twist creatures in Cannoux, and most of them had been made by Uncle. He wasn't sure what point the old man was making, but he was getting bored. Uncle barked a laugh and gave him a light punch on the shoulder that nearly knocked him over.

"Good enough, boy. Come with me."

"Where we going?" James asked, suspicious.

Chris hid a smile behind his gears and twist-wire.

"Come, boy!" Uncle roared, disappearing into the dim rooms that were half house and half laboratory. After a confused look at his brother, James followed.

"Here," Uncle said, when James came into his study, "hold this."

James took it by reflex, and then looked at it. It was a deeply golden scepter, about as thick around as James' wrist, and it glowed softly. It was beautifully made, the patterning on its surface hair-fine and as intricate as James had ever seen, even in Uncle's work. It was connected to a boxy bronze container via a finely braided twist-wire.

"What's this?" James asked.

"Stop being sullen at me," Uncle said. "And don't ask—you're about seventy years' experience and two extra brains away from being able to understand the *explanation*. Suffice it to say I'm trying to do something nice for you, boy, though the Mother herself only knows why."

"Something nice," James said, holding the rod. "Huh."

But Uncle just chuckled, fussing with his box. "Don't know why I'd start now, is that it?"

James just glowered. He wondered if the golden rod was going to wipe out his brain and replace it with a copy of Chris'. Maybe then he would be useful.

"Just so you know," Uncle said, "this is far too fine a present for such a little asshole as yourself. Don't get airs. I got a powerful appreciation for your Ma, is all, and I suppose some of that affection is spilling over onto you. I figure, *maybe*, if you got yourself a new friend, you'd stop being such a stubborn, sullen little son of a bitch all the time, and I could get some actual learning pried into your head."

"Good luck," James said, and then looked at the big man suspiciously. "What do you mean, *friend*?"

"I mean one of them things you ain't got." Uncle tapped on a piece of high-stage twistcraft that was hidden from James' sight with a hypnotic little pattern. "Because the only skill you ever bothered to develop was how to throw a punch and take a kick. Which ain't skills that will endear you to the delicate sensibilities of the children in this city."

"I got friends!"

"No, you don't." Uncle turned to look at him and frowned. "I said, hold that!"

James sighed and gripped the golden rod. Uncle studied him for a moment and then sighed himself. He turned and faced James.

"Listen, boy. No, look at me. I ain't in the habit of apologizing, especially to snot-nosed stubborn little sons-of-bitches, but I figure . . . well. I came down real hard on you, last lesson, maybe too hard. I get a mite passionate about the subject of twistcraft, and it is possible the example your brother sets leads a man to expect too much of a regular-type boy. I suppose it's going to be a problem you should just get used to; Chris' shadow is going to be a long one. But still, I roughed you up pretty good, more than you deserved, and I'm sorry."

"Oh, *that*," James said, looking away. "I don't care about *that*."

Uncle rolled his eyes and turned back to his work. "No? That had nothing to do with why you were trying to run away into the dark rather than take a lesson today? Well, suit yourself, boy. Personally, I'd prefer you'd lie to girls and not yourself, but your Ma pays me to teach you twistcraft and not social grace. There it is. Now—take a deep breath, then let it out."

James did, and the golden rod in his hand grew warm. He got very light-headed for a moment. There was a rushing sound, like a strong wind, and all the light in the world went away for a moment and then came flooding back, too bright.

"Ah!" Uncle said, satisfaction plain in his voice. "Success."

"What?" James blinked. He felt very strange, but not bad. "What happened?"

"As fine a piece of magic as you'll find in this world, boy. Now, let's see if you two take."

"Take?" James frowned. There was a slight rustling sound, the soft kind that terrifically crafted clockwork made, and a little creature climbed up on top of Uncle's shoulder and looked at James suspiciously with tiny little tea-cup golden eyes.

It was a miniature person, maybe a touch bigger than Uncle's hand, with long thin legs and arms and a cunningly segmented torso, all in vivid shades of copper and bronze. It was a tiny lady with a marvelously expressive face and big, beautifully patterned wings that gave off iridescent swirls of purple and gold when they caught the light.

"James," Uncle said, "meet Buckle."

"No!" The tiny lady said, scolding, and leaped out of sight.

James clapped in delight, forgetting for a moment to be a pain in everybody's ass. "What is it?"

"*She*," Uncle corrected. "She is something I made for a journey I was going to take. She's a tremendous explorer. But that journey's going to wait, and I think she'll do better bumming around Cannoux with you. She's being a little shy at the moment, but I have the feeling that you'll be fast friends soon enough."

James saw her minute head peek up over Uncle's other shoulder, grimace at him, and disappear.

"She's wonderful!" James said, his anger forgotten. "Her name is Buckle? Can I keep her?"

"You can't *keep* anything," Uncle said. "If she decides she wants to friend up with you, then you probably won't be able to get rid of her. But listen close, boy, and I mean this: she's just a little person, but she *is* a person. You need to trust me on this. If you mistreat her or allow her to come to harm, I'll know. I'm a Twins-damned *wizard*. And I promise, boy, I'll come for you and beat you until you crap out your bones. You get me?"

"I get you." James was barely listening. Buckle had fluttered up to one of Uncle's shelves and was peering down at him in suspicion. James stuck out his tongue at her and she gave a comically horrified expression and tumbled off the shelf. He laughed.

"Yeah, you two will do fine," Uncle said, and brushed his hands.

James looked at Uncle, suspicious. "Why you doing this, anyway? Do I gotta share her with Chris, or something? You don't even like me."

"Oh, you're breaking my heart, kid." Uncle sighed. He cuffed James lightly on the shoulder. "No, you don't have to share Buckle. I doubt she'll like Chris very much."

The big man peered down at James for a moment, thoughtfully, and then smoothed his big mustache.

"Your brother," Uncle said, scratching the back of his neck and seeming reluctant to talk about it, "is going to do some big things in this life, and you should get yourself used to that idea or you're in for a long road of heartache. Chris is going to put his mark on this world; he might do great things and he might do terrible things and he might do both. He's just that sort."

Uncle leaned forward and gripped James' shoulder, almost painfully, forcing him to look up into the old man's eyes.

"But that don't mean you're nothing, boy. It just means you ain't *him*. And if you keep trying to beat him at his own games, you're gonna be in for a real disappointing life. You get me?"

"Yeah, I get you," James said, though he didn't know what the hell Uncle was talking about. James didn't care about beating Chris; how could he ever beat Chris at anything? That was stupid.

"See, now he's scowling again," Uncle said to the small winged lady, who obligingly landed on James' shoulder and kicked him in the ear.

"Hey!" James was shocked, and Buckle giggled and flew up into the air, giving him a rude gesture. He couldn't help but laugh.

"All right," Uncle said. "Your Ma pays me for lessons, and we still have a bit of time, so I better try to cram some knowledge into that skull of yours. You remember the steps of Stage Two twistcraft, boy?"

"Nope." James was watching the little construct flit around the room.

"What a Twins-damned surprise." Uncle said. "Well, since this is going to be a trial for both of us, let's get it over quickly. Up, squib."

Uncle stood, and then remembered something.

"Listen, kid, and this is very important—don't *ever* try to take Buckle past the silver wall. Like we just talked about, yes? The Wall was built to keep folk like her *out*. You try to take her anywhere near that Wall . . . well, she won't survive. And I'll come for you, boy, you hear me? I got love for that little creature, more than I do for you, and if you put her in harm's way . . ."

"Yeah, yeah," James said, distracted. "I got no desire to crap out my own bones."

"Well," Uncle said, "looks like you learned *two* things today then. Must be a Twins-damned record."

THE KILLERS

Swatterflowers

"And then she used all of her powers, all at once, knowing that without them the Keep would fall. She made her greatest wish on the Book, writing and signing it in her own blood, and the Book burned to ash in her hands from that great surge of power. But her sacrifice worked, for far away and very deep beneath us, the Jannissaries began to wake."

—BIRTHAN, 'SOPHIE AND THE JANNISSARIES'

The angry, buzzing Swatterflowers swarmed towards the bar called A Dream of Trees, coming right towards Sophie, their red lights flashing. Sophie looked across the bar to where Ben stood, looking at her with hooded eyes; he knew as well as she did what the Swatterflowers meant—meant that here and now, in the most backwater corner of the Keep, she had been found.

Her enemies were making a move. Sophie would have loved to know who her fucking enemies were. She'd thought to hide out in this middle-of-nowhere bar, avoiding whoever the fuck was trying to do whatever the fuck they were trying to do to her, but it hadn't worked. Now, she just had to try to keep her Twins-damned friends alive long enough to get another drink with them.

"Killers!" Sophie barked, watching the Swatterflowers come, buzzing angrily red. She glanced around. "On my mark, we break left! Head for the arch!"

There was a tall arch of litstone that marked one of the exits from the cavern facing the bar; she saw her friends' heads swivel to mark it. *Good.* The Swatterflowers buzzed nearer; Sophie counted five of them.

"All right," she said, using the old battlefield voice, holding her fist up, waiting. And then she threw her hand to the left. *"Now!"*

The Killers broke to the left, towards the arch. Sophie feinted that way, and then swung herself around a wooden beam, slinging off in the opposite direction. She had no intention of going with the rest of the Killers; the Swatterflowers would be trying to kill *her,* and she meant to get them away from her friends. She vaulted over a low decorative barrier, feeling an unwelcome twinge from the muscles in her lower back. She rolled, sprinting towards the opposite end of the cavern, where she thought there might be an old passageway into another part of the

Keep. If she remembered right. And if she could draw the Swatterflowers away from the Killers, she might be able to lose them in the close confines of the passageways. And if not, there was always the silver in her arms.

"Sophie!" This was Bear, and his voice didn't sound far enough away. Sophie glanced over her shoulder and saw that she hadn't tricked *all* of her friends. Bear was right behind her, but he was pointing back the way they came. Sophie looked for the little floating silver balls and saw that they were not, in fact, following her.

They were chasing after the rest of the Killers. They were targeting her friends. Bear reversed his direction with a quick tumble-and-roll and was sprinting back towards the rest of the group, his long knife in his hand, before Sophie could even skid to a stop. She saw a jet of flame spurt from one of the silvery balls, and she felt cold ice run down through her veins—her own version of battle-mode.

Sophie hissed and ran. If she could get close enough, she could destroy all of these things at once. She didn't, at the moment, consider the consequences. Bear, having gotten a head start on her, had swept up a tablecloth from the bar and was wrapping it around his arm as he ran.

Near the lighted arch, she saw Trik glance around and realize that Sophie had tried to trick them. The tall girl skidded to a stop, dismayed. The Swatterflowers swarmed closer, and another let off a long jet of flame; too far away to hit anyone yet, but they were getting close. Trik saw a wooden table near the arch with some sort of cards and pamphlets arranged on it, and she kicked it over. In a moment she'd broken off a leg and held a piece of fakewood in her hand, her eyes tracking the Swatterflowers.

Ben had turned too and spun nearly as quickly as Trik. He was running back under the glowing arch towards the floating silver spheres, his face a mask of determination. Sophie tripped over something, rolled, and tried to regain her footing. She just needed to get close enough . . .

A jet of flame enveloped Trik, who somehow stood her ground and swung her piece of wood, timing the blow exactly. Sophie saw one of the silvery balls slam into the stone wall and drop to the ground, buzzing around drunkenly. Trik pounced on it, but then Bear, knife at the ready, having wrapped the tablecloth around his free arm, reached the mass of Swatterflowers and took a leap up into the air that Sophie could scarcely believe for a man his size. She heard a ringing *crack* of metal on silver, and another Swatterflower teetered in the air. But Bear, too, took a full jet of flame and was lost inside it for a moment.

Sophie was almost close enough, now; she just hoped her friends weren't hurt too badly. Even New Girl had turned and run back towards the fight. The only one of the Killers with any Twins-damned sense was Hunker John, who was making his way adroitly down the passageway.

Trik was obscured by a jet of flame, but somehow she dodged and took another swing at a different silvery ball. Bear had fallen, rolled, and his knife was a blur, smacking the swarming argent shapes away from him, catching jets of fire on the arm that was wrapped in the tablecloth. It, too, was on fire, but he hardly seemed to notice. Another Swatterflower went down, lights flickering, but the Killers were still outnumbered, and now Sophie was close enough. She tried to find the old Vesachai mind trick, setting herself *an-tet,* ready to pull silver flame up her arms, to channel the power that thrummed in fine silver wires through the stone all around her. Gods, it was hard! She hadn't done this in what? Twenty years? She closed her eyes and got ready to break Proscription.

But something hit her, a blow that knocked her back onto her side. Her eyes shot open; for a moment she was disoriented. What had hit her? A Swatterflower? No. *Ben.* Her oldest friend pinned her arms down and yelled in her face.

"*No, Sophie!* Don't. They've got this!"

She struggled but couldn't at first throw him off. Then she got an elbow into his gut and he went slack; she pushed him off and rolled to her knees in time to see New Girl pull a small and finely-made chutter out of her carry, track one of the two remaining Swatterflowers, and pull the trigger. The silver ball exploded in a shower of flame and silver shards.

Now there was only one, and Bear was fencing with it. He looked fierce and joyful, despite his right arm being on fire, and he slapped the thing back and forth, raising the burning tablecloth to block jets of flame.

"Bear!" Trik yelled, beating a still-struggling Swatterflower to death with her piece of wood. "Stop playing with it, you goon!"

Bear grinned, took a step back, and performed one of the most beautifully executed sideways thrusts Sophie had ever seen, skewering the Swatterflower on the tip of his knife for a moment before it fell off, dying and jittering, to the ground.

New Girl looked at the exploded remains of the Swatterflower she'd killed with a curious expression on her face, quite unlike the innocent girl Sophie knew, and then tucked her extremely expensive, very rare, and highly illegal chutter back into her carry. She flipped her hair back, and her face and demeanor found their normal wide-eyed innocence again.

"Goddamn it, Bear, you're on fucking *fire,*" Trik growled, and put her dying Swatterflower out of its misery. She dropped her shattered piece of wood and smacked at Bear's arm, trying to put out the fire, but he slid his knife down inside the tablecloth and cut the smoldering fabric away. Sophie could see that his arm had taken burns, livid red and already swelling. Trik made a little dismayed sound in the back of her throat, and Bear gave her a crooked grin.

Sophie heard a groan right next to her; Ben was holding his stomach and had tears standing in his eyes. She remembered she'd elbowed him in the ribs.

"Twins damn, Capitana," he managed.

"Yeah, well," Sophie said. "That's what you get for mutiny."

But she helped him up, then gripped the back of his neck while resting her forehead against his for a long moment. After a bit, he nodded, and she let him go. Like a good soldier, he pretended not to see the tears in his Capitana's eyes.

She wiped these away; Ben had saved her life once again. She wondered how many times this was.

She looked around at her Killers: Ben next to her, Bear and Trik a few paces away. How Trik had avoided getting burned, Sophie had no idea. Her tunic had some scorch marks, but she seemed unhurt. Past them, under the lighted arch, New Girl stood, once again as innocent and lovely as ever. Behind her, Hunker John was sheepishly returning to the group. Sophie shook her head and allowed herself the exquisite luxury of a deep breath.

"Well, you're getting your wish, Triks. Those Swatterflowers were coming for *you* lot, which means we're all in the fire now."

Hunker John squeaked in surprise. "Why would they be coming for *us*?"

Sophie dropped her voice, looking around. "Because they want the Book, John."

"So?"

"So," Bear elbowed John lightly, "they might think that one of *us* can tell them where it is."

Hunker John frowned, then his expression cleared and his eyes grew wide, remembering a certain night, a lot of alcohol, and an unusually loquacious Capitana. "Oh. *Oh!*"

Sophie gave Bear a severe look. "*Or* it just means they think they can capture you, torture you, fuck with you, and *I'll* tell them where it is. All of which adds up to it being time for drastic actions. I'm going to go try to cash in a very old debt from a very dangerous man."

Trik frowned. "Who?"

"Damien Crowe," Sophie said, and Trik's face grew dismayed. "The Queen's oldest advisor. The Lord of the Lurk."

"Oh," Hunker John said, looking a little green, "*yay.*"

THE LOST BOYS

A Dream Of Giants

"When the Mother calls, only fools and children hear."

—APOCRYPHAL

It is a relative truism that dreams are uninteresting to anyone other than the person having them. However, an argument to the contrary could be made in one specific case: the dream James D'Essan had the very night he met Buckle. She was resting in her fugue state on a little shelf above his bed as Chris snored softly across the room.

It was the most extraordinary dream that James had ever had, and when he awoke from it, nothing was ever the same again.

It went like this:

James is walking in a place completely unlike any he has ever seen before, a place so fantastic and alien that if he were not dreaming and therefore protected by the logic of dreams, he might have fallen to his knees, insensate from the impossible wonder of it. James D'Essan is walking through something he has heard bed-time stories of, but never thought to see with his own eyes: a *forest*.

This forest is filled with huge trunks of ancient trees and a green canopy of gently swaying leaves. Small shafts of sunlight spear down through gaps in the leaves, making slantwise columns of light that dust-motes sparkle in. It is so different from his city of old stone that it is hard to believe that such things can exist in the same world—and it *is* the same world. With the irrefutable logic of dreams, James is sure of this.

He is sure of something else, too; there is something that he needs to find. Something important. Something more important, maybe, than anything else in the world.

James sees a shape carved into the trunk of a nearby tree, and the cuts glimmer with silver. It is the shape of a key, and James' young little heart rings. *This is the shape he must find. This is what he is looking for.* A key!

No . . . no, he is looking for a *Silver* key. And when he finds it, all will be well. All will be well, *everywhere*. He knows this as surely as he knows his own name.

The forest is bewitching, entrancing. As he walks, he sees five doors standing in between the trees, each with a different symbol on it, but James is too focused on the small animals playing in the branches, and the hinting, tantalizing glimpses of the sky through the branches above to pay much attention.

Suddenly, the trees open out, thinning to nothing, and James is walking under an open sky. But this is nothing like the heavy blanket of shadow that James has always lived under—*no*. This sky is deep. It is immense. Even in his dream, James falls to his knees.

There is a thick hoop of incandescent fire spinning slowly in the sky. It is the *sun*. James can feel its warmth on his face, and in his dream he is crying and not ashamed of it. The sky is so *big*, and there are other rings spinning, some enormous and some tiny, silver rings with unusual and bewitching patterning on them. He sees, too, something else out of legend, out of stories: the golden moon Lode, where the Mother lives. It is small but impossibly detailed and beautiful; it is covered all over with graceful gold towers and slender bridges and stairs.

But now James gets a sense of wrongness, a hint of disfigurement in this wonderful place. He hears a loathsome noise, the worst noise he has ever heard, a deeply awful mechanical sound. When he turns to look, he sees a freestanding door that has a silver knob in the middle, and it is slowly opening.

This is one of the legendary Doors, James knows, and he watches it open. It opens on *darkness*.

James' heart claws up into his throat. That darkness is the most terrifying thing he has ever seen. It is far more than the shadow that surrounds Cannoux-Town or that hangs over their heads and calls itself the sky; this darkness is malevolent and thick. It isn't dark but *The Dark*.

James watches the Door open, and watches as a thick tendril of that darkness claws through the doorframe and sinks into the lovely loam of the forest floor. Where it touches, everything dies.

James knows that *this* is what he must fight; this is what the Silver Key will vanquish, and if he does not find it this clawing black will cover the entire world. He gets up and runs, runs away from the shadow and towards the Silver Key. He can sense it ahead, and he *runs*.

But ahead is a stone wall, and to escape the awful dark James darts into it, and finds himself in a maze. His heart is pounding; he is far more terrified now than he has ever been in his young life. There are curious symbols and schematics carved into the stone walls but James runs past them, hardly seeing, following that sense of the *Key* ahead of him, the Silver Key that will unlock everything, *everything*, that he can use to save everyone and drive the darkness back . . .

And he comes to another Door, but this one glimmers with light around its edges and James throws himself through it. He finds himself once again under some trees, and sees a glint of silver ahead—the *Key!*

As he runs he looks up, and quails. Far up in that gorgeous sky, a black mote appears, an ink-dark absence that looks like a wound. As he runs, he watches it blossom, sending tendrils of ink through the boundless expanse above. One of those black tendrils reaches one of the silvery rings. And begins to *eat it*.

It is horrifying, wrong, disgusting. It reminds James of the time he found a bird being devoured by maggots. The nasty mechanical sound behind him grows louder, and the ground shakes as if it is being torn apart just behind him.

James runs through a sunny meadow full of flowers and tall black rocks inscribed with mystifying diagrams and runes, many pictures of barred and locked doors, but he barely spares them a thought. The Silver Key is ahead, and it is the only thing that can drive this terrible darkness back through the Door. He sees the glint of silver ahead, atop a large, rocky hill, and he tries to run faster. The noise increases behind him, and it is the most appalling sound he has ever heard. It is like the sound of your favorite possession smashed on hard ground, or the sound of beloved animals dying in terrified pain. The ground shakes under him as he runs, as fast as he can, but it's not fast enough, and he feels a shocking icy burning in his calf and falls.

It is a tendril of pure, malevolent darkness that has speared through his leg, and as James looks back he sees that the Dark is clawing through everything behind him, tearing everything good apart, and over him the gloom claws through the sky, devouring the Rings and the moon and the beautiful wheel of the sun. James screams as he can feel the Dark working its way into his bones, wrenching them apart, tearing his leg to pieces.

He claws towards the silver glint ahead, and the whole world grows dark as the black tendrils eat the sun, and the silver glint is the only bright thing he can see. The pain is indescribable and the darkness is eating him alive, but he reaches out towards the silver glint ahead, still trying to crawl towards it, and it *pulses*, but golden somehow, each gold pulse a vision, and James sees—

—*A vast underground castle, full of insane mechanisms, left to chew on each other in darkness, and it is where he needs to go*—

—*A silver thread that hangs from the sky, and a blade swinging towards it*—

—*A great lock, somehow made of people, and a silver key turning its mechanism*—

And as the clawing dark rips James' legs and guts apart and the black overtakes him, he sees one last pulse. A huge shape, great head bowed, imprisoned with a thousand silver cables and bound with enormous golden shackles. Just before the black takes James, the head lifts and he looks into the great, terrifying, sad, and depthless eyes of a *Giant*.

THE MONSTERS

The Adventure Has Arrived, Goddamn It

"All tactics fail when Behemoth are involved.
The best stratagem is to deny them the fight."

—HUNTER FINE, 'ON TACTICS'

The monsters fled down through the darkness, and murder followed.
Murder being, in this particular case, the screams of the Feral Children and the half-headed corpse of Mr. Vutch that they'd left behind them, in the dead city on top of the mountain.

Gun and Jackie ran down the side of the mountain in a frantic rumble, a slow, motion and barely controlled descent. They ran through the inky shadow, surrounded by a hollow sphere of silvery light thrown by the floating ball that hovered over Jackie's shoulder. The lights of the dead city above and behind them were gone, and the distant lights below gave them no comfort. Sometimes it felt as if the world was being created just a few yards ahead of them and erased a few yards behind, as if the small circle that they could see was all there was to the world. Gun sometimes felt as if they were trapped in a snow globe, swinging slowly through a dark room, watched by something malevolent.

Gun and Jackie had been bored in the dead city. They could have said *dead* bored if they had wanted to make jokes, but there were times when they might have chosen any option other than the damnable boredom, the ever-unchanging nature of the city on top of the mountain. They had *craved* adventure. And now that it was here?

It was nothing but complaints.

Ever since Jackie had killed the damned Mr. Vutch, that handsome not-man with golden machinery where his brain should have been, they had been pursued through the gloom. They were hounded twice; first by the maddening cries of the Feral Children. They had apparently not killed them all. Sometimes it sounded like there were hundreds of them out there in the shadows, baying like strange mechanical hounds.

But they didn't really mind the Feral Children. It was the other thing that was hounding them, the *mental* shit. *That* was getting to them.

Gun and Jackie were indestructible badasses, but the mental shit was profoundly distasteful. Something was clawing at their minds. Something was climbing *into* their minds. They'd been doing their own thing in the dead city on top
of the mountain, perhaps knocking over a building or two (or ten) and then
they'd gotten attacked by nightmare monstrosities with rotten-squeezebox voices.

That was okay! That was part of the adventure. And then they'd met a *very*
amiable man called Mr. Vutch, who was completely full of shit but a great con-
versationalist, and they'd just started thinking that maybe this dead world might
have some fun—or at least drinks—in it, and then everything had gone to shit.
The mental attacks started, and Jackie had killed Mr. Vutch.

And now here they were, climbing down a seemingly eternal slope of desolate
and broken stone, the side of the mountain, which any asshole who had ever been
on a hike could tell you was even harder than walking *up* one. It was dark, it was
annoying, and the best part—the really *best* part—was the fact that the thing that
was clawing into their heads and tried to get them to murder each other had apparently not been coming from the charming Mr. Vutch. He was dead as shit, and
it was still happening.

So they traveled down the mountain towards the few lights they saw, trying
not to kill each other and trying not to get murdered by the creatures that Mr.
Vutch had called Feral Children.

Occasionally they heard the screams behind them, sometimes closer, sometimes
farther away. Those screams had been bad enough, close in the light of the city, but
in the inky wastes they were haunting and awful, like a man scrabbling at a chalk-
board as he choked to death. The howling of the Feral Children pursued them down
the perpetual slopes of the mountain, and they could get no respite from them.

Their adventure had indeed arrived, and Gun and Jackie were anything but
bored. They would have been amused at that irony, if they could stop trying to
kill each other.

———

Gun decided, between one step and the next, that Jackie had to die. It was the
kind of clarity he had always looked for, like a bright crystal light suffusing his
mind; the feeling that, once this small detail was accomplished, all would be right
in the world. It was hard to believe he had never seen it before.

Murdering Jackie Aimes was his final truth; it was the thing he had been
looking his whole life for. It was the clear and irrefutable purpose that made everything else seem easy and light. All he had to do was kill his best friend, and
Gunnar Anderson could become the best possible version of himself.

Jackie had been walking in silence for a while and had gotten complacent.

They'd learned not to walk too closely together, but she was only a few paces away, and it was the easiest thing in the world to pull his sword out with a smooth motion and bury the blade in the side of her neck.

Instead he gagged, twitched, and threw his sword out into the shadows. He was hardly able to believe he was doing it, groaning with the struggle of fighting the beautiful crystal truth in his mind. He told himself (this was his way of fighting the disturbing mental control) that the sword was too quick for *her*, that he was going to use his hands. Jackie heard the clatter of the sword and turned, just in time to see Gun advancing on her. Her little floating light-globe danced back out of his reach as fast as she did.

"You father-fucking whore!" he raged, his hands out. "You traitor *bitch!*"

It felt so good to say, so primal and true. He was finally speaking truth.

But he was fighting it. There was a part of Gun that was horrified at what had just come out of his mouth, already begging Jackie for forgiveness and understanding; a part of Gun that was struggling to slow his lifted hands, to drag his feet so that Jackie would have time to get her walking stick up.

She did, her face going grim, and she tried to fend him off with it. But he was full of crystal-pure rage; he was driven to kill. God, he *wanted* to kill. He hated her so much! Hated her height, her hair, her tattoos; he hated all of it. So he barreled right over her stick, reaching for her throat, clawing for her eyes. The other part of himself, though, the smaller part, left his stance as open as he could, and Jackie was able to get an elbow into his face.

His head rocked back, the clarity slipping for a tiny moment, and then it came back with double and treble force. He went for Jackie, and they crashed into the stone slope of the mountain. His hands again tried to find her throat, but Jackie had grown up with older brothers and she knew how to scrap. She got a knee into his balls and elbowed him so hard in the ribs he might have felt one snap.

He scrambled in the old dust, trying to get to her, but she rolled to her feet and got her stick. "Stay down, Gunnar," she said, the stick ready to take him in the side of the head if she had to. But all of a sudden, the clarity was gone. The crystal light winked out of his head, and he was just Gun, lying on the ground, clutching his ribs and thankful for the sickening pain in his genitals, because it meant that Jackie had survived yet another of these awful attacks.

"Holy hell," Gun said, when he could talk, and pushed himself up on one knee. "That was a bad one."

"No shit." Jackie was breathing hard and still wary.

Gun coughed, spat. He looked up at Jackie, a complicated expression on his face. "Sorry."

"You called me a father-fucking whore."

Gun frowned and examined his hands. The feeling was nearly gone now, leaving him exhausted and hollow. "Yeah. Sorry about that."

"It's okay," Jackie said. Her tone was light but she was still ready, her eyes tracking Gun's every movement. "I mean, I've fucked my share of dads."

Gun barked a rough laugh and shook his head.

"Well, I'm still sorry," he took a deep breath, "for insinuating you'd accept payment."

"Not until rent's due, anyways. You okay?"

"Yeah, it's gone. But shit. That was a bad one."

"Seemed like it." Jackie grounded the butt of her walking stick against the broken scree they were stumbling down. She scratched fingers through her hair and looked up their backtrail. She looked back at Gun, who was still breathing heavily, eyes hooded. She went to say something, thought the better of it, and didn't.

"Well," she said finally, "you done fuckin' around? We got some miles to go yet."

"Yeah." Gun's voice was clipped. He started to rise and hissed, clutching his side. Getting back up on his feet had become a major ordeal. He held out his hand. "Gimme a boost?"

Jackie hesitated, looking at the outstretched hand.

Gun grimaced at her expression. "Right. Yeah, sorry. Safety first."

"You're a big boy," Jackie said, keeping her distance. "You can get yourself up."

"Sure can," Gun grunted, and took a couple deep breaths. He stood up and did his best not to groan aloud. Jackie had either broken or severely bruised a few of his ribs the day before, and they'd yet to find a hospital in this black wilderness. He had to stand there for a bit, taking gulps of air, before he could straighten all the way up. Jackie watched with wary eyes and headed for where he'd thrown his sword. She moved slowly, so he could keep up.

They walked in silence. Gun made a little thin sound every time his bad leg came down, and his voice was a tight mask of pain.

"So, they say anything about *this* shit," Jackie asked, "in your goddamn dream?"

"About what? Being attacked by a relentless internal murder-compulsion while scrambling down a pitch-black mountain in a world full of screeching monsters?"

"Yeah."

"No."

"Heh," Jackie said. "Too bad."

"Would have been helpful information." They reached where Gun had thrown his sword, and Jackie scooped it up, not thinking. Gun eyed her, warily, but she took it by the scabbard and extended it to him, hilt-first. He took it, and they took several steps away from each other.

They'd learned early on not to get too close. There were usually pauses in between the attacks, but sometimes they were short. The only blessing they could find in all this was that only one of them was afflicted at a time. This led them to believe that there was only one of whatever—or whoever—that was doing this to them. And it led them to pleasant fantasies of revenge against this unseen assailant.

"Well," Jackie said, "at least we know it wasn't Mr. Fucking Vutch that was doing it."

"Not him, but maybe he had some friends. He was yelling at me to give into it. God, damn, Jacks. What the fuck is going on?"

"Who the hell knows." Jackie sighed. "Far as I'm concerned, it's us against the world, man."

"The world seems to be winning."

"Only for the moment." Jackie was clearly doing her best to be cheerful. "C'mon, son! Those lights don't seem to be getting closer as quick as I'd like."

In fact, they couldn't even see the lights below them, far down the slope of the mountain, most of the time. The side of the mountain was folded over into cliffs and chases and steep valleys littered with ancient-looking ruins that loomed up out of the shadows but held no comforts. It didn't worry them much; down was the operative direction, and they weren't likely to misplace that one. Even if they missed the lights, down had to stop at *some* point, right?

How big could this goddamn mountain be?

They made their way down a slope of tumbled scree, careful of their footing. It wasn't that they were afraid of falling, exactly; they'd already tumbled off a few cliffs in the dark and the worst they got was bruised up. It was more that slipping and tumbling down the mountain for who knows how long was tedious, annoying, and just generally a pain in the ass.

"I tell you what," Gun said, after they'd been moving for a while, "I sure as hell don't know what happened to this place, but I'm not sure how much I trust those books we found."

"You think?" Jackie said, scrambling for footing. "Got doubts that some jackass Giant broke the sky, or whatever the fuck?"

"Yeah. I mean, how would you break a *sky*?" Gun asked, and nearly slipped. "I mean, even for a weird fantasy world, this shit is messed up."

"Is it?" Jackie asked, determined to try for banter. "I was too busy getting laid in high school to read."

"Har har," Gun said, ignoring this. "I mean, obviously there used to be a sun and some shit, right, but it sounds like all kinds of nonsense happened. That one book talked about this place like it was a perfect utopia. I told you about that Reset thing, right? Like, you get reborn when you die? Or you used to, anyway. How sweet would that be?"

"Depends on how much you like living, I guess," Jackie said. "Look, man, maybe the books were, like, fairy-tales or something. I feel like if this was the kind of place where you got reborn into a new life when you die, there would be a lot more people around. Sounds like you were reading a . . . what did they used to call those? A paradise fable."

"Yeah," Gun said, glumly. "I guess."

"Every civilization's got one." Jackie yawned. "Learned that in civics. A golden age when the gods walked amongst us, and everything was wonderful, and there were blowjobs and rainbows on every corner. And nobody ever got old, and nobody ever died."

"And then some asshole came and fucked all the shit up." He gave Jackie a wink. "Usually a woman, right?"

"If I wasn't so tired, Gunnar, I'd kick you in the balls again."

"Hey, I didn't invent dudes. Or like . . . religion."

"Maybe the Giant is just a euphemism for original sin."

"Ugh. Maybe." He glanced around. "Or maybe not. I mean, *something* bad happened here. Forget about utopia; this shit isn't even livable."

"Well, we'll see," Jackie said. They were making their way down a crevasse, and she pointed to its end, where they were able to see some of the distant lights that floated in the shadows far below. "That's a lot of lights. Maybe there's *some* livin' going on."

"Where there's living, there's booze," Gun said, trying to be optimistic around the pain in his ribs. "That's just a fact."

"Unless it's all demonic robots. Creepy demonic robots from hell to breakfast."

"C'mon, Jacks. I thought we were at least pretending to be cheerful."

"Yeah, yeah." Jackie kicked a broken piece of rock and heard it tumble down the slope, out of the small circle of light thrown by the floating ball behind her. "Maybe I don't feel so cheerful."

"Yeah, well." Gun shrugged. "I guess that's fair."

"Ain't nothing fair about this situation, Gun. At least *you* asked for it."

Gun was silent for a moment. "I didn't force you to come, Jacks."

"No," Jackie sneered, "you just sold me a *shit* bill of sale. Adventure! Escape! A grand plan and the meaning of life, finally! Portentous dreams! *Fuck* your dreams."

She spat and kicked a fallen, long-dead tree. It splintered into fragments, shards flying far out into the dark.

"Jacks—"

"No, fuck you, Gunnar, don't call me *Jacks*. That's for my fucking *friends*, who I'm never going to *see again*. Okay? Or did you find out how to get home, in that precious book of yours? No?"

"Jackie," Gun said, anguished.

"Don't even call me that, you worthless *fuck*. You lied to me, Gun, you're a fucking *liar*. Adventure, you said. Big dreams, and now all I've got is dust! Fucking *darkness*, Gun, and it's all your motherfucking *fault!*"

She turned on him and saw that he had scrambled back away from her and unlimbered his sword, scabbard still on. He watched her hands closely, and his mouth grew grim when she whirled her walking stick up.

"You backstabbing *cocksucker!*" Jackie screamed and threw herself at him.

"Jackie!" Gun yelped. "It's an episode! It's not you!"

But it did no good. The stick met the scabbard with a heavy *thunk*, and Gun tried to dance back from the long weapon, the pain in his side temporarily forgotten.

"Fight it!" he yelled.

But Jackie's face was a writhing mask of rage. She came for him again. "This is all. Your. Fucking. Fault!" The walking stick whistled. Gun barely got the sword up in time, and the stick slammed into his shoulder, knocking him off balance. Jackie was much better at using her stick than he was at using his sword.

But Jackie *was* fighting the compulsion, or at least well enough to give him time to recover. He got his legs underneath him and re-gripped the sword hilt. He'd learned early on not to take it out of the scabbard; Jackie had a shallow but long cut along her bicep from before he'd figured that out.

"Jacks," he said, pitching his voice low and soothing. "C'mon, kid. Fight it."

"*Fuck* you." She spun the stick towards him. He deflected one blow, and then another, but the third was a short hard jab with the butt-end of the stick, and it spun him. Jackie barreled into him, knocking him to the ground, and for a few moments they careened down the slope, a tangled mass of arms and legs. They fetched up against a big chunk of rock and Jackie's shoulder happened to catch Gun right in the stomach, knocking the breath out of him.

Jackie scrambled to her feet while he wheezed. He was completely incapacitated. He couldn't move. She screamed an inarticulate howl of fear and rage as she swept the walking stick down in a cruel arc, just missing his head by inches. It pulverized the top of the boulder, sending a spray of bitter dust and chips into Gun's face. As he got his breath back, she did it again, just missing him, and this time he had the presence of mind and control enough to sweep her legs out from under her. He rolled and was able to swat the stick out of her hands.

She fought like a demon, punching him in his damaged ribs once, then twice, before he could twist away from her. He almost blacked out from the pain, but he kept his grip. He tried to use his weight to keep her arms pinned down and avoided several attempted knees to the groin.

"Jackie!" he yelled. "Fight it!"

"*Fuck you!*" she screamed into his face and tried to bite him. "*Fuck you*, you motherfucker, this is *all your fault!*"

"I know," Gun said, and did his best to hold her down. She did manage to get a good heavy knee into his crotch, and he rolled off her, the world going white for a moment. It gave her enough time to get her stick again, straddle him, and put in a really good attempt towards crushing his windpipe.

Jackie *was* fighting the compulsion, though, and she didn't lean as hard on the stick as she could have. Gun was able to hold her back, barely, enough to keep sucking some small amount of air into his lungs. And then it was a little easier to get air in, and a little easier still, and then she tossed the stick aside.

Gun drew great ragged gulps of air into his lungs. Jackie was still, her head hanging back, looking into the big dark above, her chest heaving with the effort of trying to both kill and not kill her friend.

She rolled off him and lay on her back, flat in the dust of the inky plain. They stayed like that for a while, getting their breath back. Eventually, Gun found the energy to look over at her. He swallowed a couple times, getting enough moisture into his throat to speak.

"You know, when you get mad, you say the word 'fuck' a lot."

Jackie snorted a sharp, short laugh, and looked back at him.

"I mean," he said, relishing the feeling of air in his lungs, "it's just an extravagant amount. I'm going to say it's too much. Too much with the swearing, Aimes."

"Fuck you." She spat some blood into the dirt.

"There's my girl." He started the laborious process of climbing to his feet. He discovered that their fight had carried them to the end of the crevasse, and they had a commanding view of the lights spread out below them. "Oh, shit, hey. Look at that!"

Jackie dusted herself off, found her walking stick, and joined him. She squinted at what he was pointing at.

"What in the hell is that?" It was a tight cluster of lights, off to their right and downslope a ways. It had either been hidden by the mountain before this or had blended in with the lights below, but it was much closer than those. Jackie gave Gun a considering look.

"Yes," Gun said. "Yeah. Just let me get my breath."

"Wimp." She was still panting herself. "Maybe they got beer there."

"Maybe," Gun said. They studied the lights, trying to see anything else about them, but there was nothing.

Jackie looked at Gun for a long moment. "It's not, you know."

He turned, frowning. "It's not what?"

"Your fault."

Gun looked back out into the shadows.

"Yeah, Jacks," he said, after a while. "It is."

THE KILLERS

Gallivants

*"A precocious child is like a loaded weapon—both are
more charming in the pages of a book."*

—SLOW MIKE, 'BAD PROVERBS'

The Killers made their way down the passageway, back towards the more
inhabited parts of the Keep. Sophie knew there was a Gallivant stop up
ahead; they had some distance to travel and Gallivants were a decently anony-
mous way to move.

Sophie was nervous, looking to all points for danger. She wasn't used to this
feeling, this knot of tension at the back of her mind, this anxious alertness. It had
been a long time since she'd had anything more dangerous than a bad cup of *chûs*
facing her. She'd been ready to get away from the bar called A Dream of Trees,
and the owner had been even more ready for them to leave. He'd had a bit of salve
and some cloth that worked for bandages, so Bear's arm was at least covered. If the
big man was bothered by the pain, Sophie couldn't tell.

"So," Sophie said, after taking a heavy pull from Hunker John's flask, recently
refilled, "does anybody want to talk about the suicidal display of reckless courage
we all just witnessed?"

"You mean," Trik said, "do we want to talk about how we saved the day and
shit?"

"I peed myself and ran away!" Hunker John said, helpfully.

"It was the course of valor." New Girl patted him on the shoulder.

"You assholes need to learn how to listen to orders," Sophie said.

But Trik just snorted. "Then start giving some good ones. Ones where you
don't throw your life away when you don't have to, maybe."

Sophie rubbed her eyes for a moment, realizing she was being a piece of shit.
She took a breath, and gave them a short bow. "You are all magnificent, and that
was amazing."

"*Thank* you," Trik said. She brushed a bit of char from her arm, as if annoyed
that it obscured her tattoos.

"—Especially Hunker John," Sophie continued, "because peeing yourself and running away was the correct thing to do."

"*Thank* you." Hunker John mimicked Trik's tone exactly. He snagged his flask from Sophie and lifted it. "Somebody had to think about the liquor!"

"You assholes could learn a lot from him," Sophie agreed, with a ghost of a smile. "Bear, are you *sure* you don't need a Medica?"

"Hmm?" Bear said, having been lost in thought. "Oh, no. That salve works a treat."

"I saw that arm, Bear," Sophie said, "those are some real burns."

Bear shrugged. "I don't mind a little pain. Sharpens the mind."

"Your mind could use as much sharpening as it can get," Trik said. Sophie spied a few Gallivants up ahead, milling around and waiting for passengers.

Sophie approached one of the Gallivants and held a thick coin up in front of its great head, its tea-cup silver eyes. It nodded ponderously, and she deposited the coin in a special pouch. Why those creatures cared about the coins, and what they did with them, Sophie had never bothered to learn. The Killers started to scramble up into the carry-harnesses, but Sophie shook her head.

"I think we'll split up. Take two. We don't want to overload the poor things."

Trik frowned. "I'm not riding. There's plenty of room, Capitana." Trik professed to hate Gallivants—and most forms of transportation—and would always jog alongside when the Killers used them. It was just one of those inscrutable 'Trik' things, like her dislike of being touched and her pathological obsession with protecting Sophie, and they had all long ago gotten used to it.

Sophie gave her a look and, for once, Trik actually shut the fuck up.

"Let's do two," Sophie said. Ben was looking at her with hooded eyes and wasn't surprised at what she said next. "I'll take the one back there. Bear, you want to ride with me? And you, New Girl?"

The beautiful girl frowned but turned it into a smile. "Of course, Capitana."

Hunker John, who was never one for subtext unless it was sexual in nature, looked confused. Trik gave him a quelling look, however, and he followed Ben up onto the first Gallivant without comment. Sophie slapped its segmented hindquarters, and with a rumble of old gears, the ancient machine trundled away. Sophie looked at Bear and New Girl.

"Well?" She smiled. "Shall we?"

She offered a coin to the next Gallivant, and the three of them climbed up on top of the swaying conveyance. Fortunately, at this time of the night, there wasn't much traffic, and the Gallivants were empty. They followed set routes through the Keep, color-coded, and Sophie knew this one would get them to Hunter's Hollow eventually. She knew they would have a bit of time to talk.

New Girl looked back and forth between Sophie and Bear. Bear gave her a big grin, pulled his knife out, and began polishing the blade. This captured New Girl's attention for a moment, and then she lifted her eyes up to Sophie's. Her demeanor changed, just slightly, became a tiny bit calculating. She lifted an eyebrow.

"So, Capitana? What's good?"

"Not fucking much." Sophie cracked her neck and rubbed her eyes again. Gods, she was tired! She realized it was still only late evening; on a normal night, she and the Killers would barely be getting the debauchery started. But still, she was tired down into her bones. She made herself focus on the girl opposite and ignored her compelling but irrelevant physical attributes. Sophie gave her a none-too-kindly grin. "I'm curious, New Girl, about your ordnance."

"Oh!" She flushed prettily. "Yeah, I thought you might wonder about that. It was a gift from a patron. A lord, if you must know. A girl that looks like me shouldn't wander around unarmed, he always said. And I'm glad I had it!"

Sophie smiled. "Those lords love their beautiful people, it's true. Still, that is a pretty rare and, if you don't mind me saying it, quite illegal chutter you were hauling. Nobody's ever given *me* one of those."

New Girl blushed. "I don't know what to say. He was protective."

"I like protection. Don't you, Bear?"

". . . Sure."

Sophie made a show of frowning. "What's the hesitation, Bear? I can hear it in your voice. Best to be open, on a night like tonight."

"It's just . . ."

"Spit it out, we're all friends here."

New Girl was looking back and forth between them, flushed. She really was remarkably beautiful. Sophie tried to ignore it.

Bear sighed. "It's just her *stance*."

"Yeah," Sophie said, snapping her fingers. "That stance. That's what I'm thinking about, too. Such a professional stance. Hardened, even. Didn't even flinch, when that Swatterflower was coming at her."

Grinning, Sophie focused all the weight of her years and experience on New Girl.

New Girl took a moment, looking at Sophie, and several emotions flitted across her face. But she dropped her head. Her shoulders shook, and for a moment Sophie thought she was weeping, but it was laughter. Rueful laughter. "Damn," she said, looking up at Sophie and shaking her head. "I knew you'd figure it out eventually, but . . . damn."

Sophie just waited, and Bear kept polishing the edge of his knife with a faint expression of curiosity on his face. New Girl threw her hands up, let them fall, a gesture of resignation.

"Who are you?" Sophie asked. "What are you?"

"Well," New Girl blushed again, "I work at one of the slateboards. Madrigals."

"You work *slate*?" Sophie asked. "A reporter?"

"Well," New Girl said, squirming. "Yeah. Kind of. Listen, it's embarrassing. I grew up on stories about you, Sophie, even though you're not that much older than me. You were my . . . well, you were my hero. I wanted to know everything about you and the old Killers, about how it all happened. I've been working on a book, the true story of the Hot Halls War. We go through some training, us undercover reporters, and we know how to get weapons."

Sophie looked at Bear, who lifted an eyebrow but made no comment. Sophie made a twirling gesture to New Girl, signaling her to continue.

New Girl sighed. Her bearing was different, just a little bolder and more sophisticated now. "Well, I kinda met Ben, and he was sweet, and it seemed like a really great way to learn some stuff. About you. And then we all became friends. And . . . here we are."

New Girl bit her lip, dazzlingly, and turned her big green eyes on Sophie. "I know it's maybe a little shitty to have used Ben that way, but I really do like him, you know, and . . ." She trailed off, looking down at her hands, a picture of contrition.

Bear made a tiny shake of his head. Sophie agreed. "That's good," she said, after a minute. "That's real good, actually! But let's try it just *one more time*."

Bear yawned and stretched, a motion that just so happened to put the edge of his knife about a finger-width from New Girl's neck. The Gallivant shifted and rolled as it walked, but the knife held steady. Good hands, that Bear.

The girl looked down cross-eyed at the blade, particularly the sharp bit on the edge, then back at Sophie. There was a long moment where they held each other's eyes, and Sophie got the sense of a great deal of intense shit happening inside New Girl's head.

Then the girl laughed, a new kind of laugh, deeper and older, somehow, and she looked away. "Well, shit."

Her expression shifted. Her face changed, relaxing in places and tightening up in others; her posture fell into a casual stance that Sophie recognized as a result of certain kinds of high-level arms training. She seemed to take on weight; she seemed to be filling up with something just a bit dangerous. She smiled, a wise little smile that pulled at one corner of her mouth, and that couldn't be more different than the wide-eyed innocent look she'd maintained for as long as Sophie had known her.

"Not to explain your business to you, Sophie," New Girl said, and even her voice was different; a bit lower, huskier. A no-nonsense voice. She pushed the blade of Bear's knife away from her neck with two slender fingers. "But using

Bear as a heavy only works on people that don't know him. He's too sweet to be an effective thug."

"Girl," Bear said, and his knife slid back alongside her long, graceful neck to rest against the underside of her chin, "you don't know me. And I clearly don't know *you*."

"Oooh." New Girl gave him an unimpressed look. "Now I stand both corrected *and* aroused."

"Who are you?" Sophie asked again. There was no playfulness in her voice now. She gave Bear a nod and he withdrew the blade.

"You sure you want to know?" New Girl said. "I've got some other stories you might like."

"Oh yeah?" Sophie watched the girl. "How many?"

New Girl shrugged. "Five or six that will stand up to scrutiny, like the Madrigals one. But I can spin you as many pleasant stories as you want; I can become anything you desire. It's a talent of mine."

"Tempting," Sophie said. "I'm guessing—Espionage Corps?"

Bear made a low whistle. "A fuckin' *Lurk*?"

New Girl laughed. "No, I'm not a Lurk. Or a Redarm, or Practice Guard, or any of Jane's other toys. I'm not a big fan of the Queen."

"That's bad news for you, then." Sophie considered her. "Because the only other option that makes sense is you being cozy with Mr. March."

"There are more than two options, Sophie."

"So tell me."

"I'm a free agent. I work for myself."

"Capitana." Bear was testing the edge of his knife with his thumb. "I'm smelling bullshit. Permission to start slitting throats and hiding bodies?"

"Denied," Sophie said. "For now. What's your real name?"

"Avie."

"How much does Ben know?"

"I fed him some crumbs towards the Madrigals story. I mean, c'mon. He knew something was up."

"And on a normal night, it might not have mattered if something was." Sophie looked at Bear, who shrugged. "So what the fuck do you want, *Avie*?"

Avie smiled. If Bear and his knife bothered her, there was no sign of it. She watched the ornate stonework of this section of the Keep pass for a moment, and when she looked back at Sophie there was amusement in her eyes.

"I want what everybody else wants. The Book."

Bear grunted and leaned forward, his knife centered on the girl. Sophie held out her hand, staying him. She frowned.

"So you *are* working with March. This mysterious partner of his . . . is that you?"

Avie tossed her hair, grimness in her expression. "No. I have nothing to do with that. I told you, I work for myself. I have my own interest in the Book, and what happens to it."

Bear's voice was flat, no trace of his usual humor there. "And what interest is that?"

Avie sighed, and set her hands in her lap. "You're not going to believe me, but you should have *one* person around you that's not lying to you or trying to manipulate you—"

"You're off to a bad start with that, then," Sophie said.

Avie nodded, conceding the point.

"It felt necessary, but I won't argue. I infiltrated your friends because I knew a little—not much, but a little—of what was being planned for tonight. And I don't want the Book to fall into the wrong hands."

"Whose are the wrong hands?" Sophie looked at the girl, eyes narrowed.

"The Queen's," Avie said. "Mr. March. His partner. Maybe yours—I'm not sure yet. I thought it would be a good idea to be close to the person who was most likely to find the damned thing."

Bear shifted on his seat and gave Sophie a guarded look. "Maybe you should give me some reasons not to break her neck and throw her overboard. We can't trust a thing she says."

"No, we can't," Sophie said, doubtfully. There was something about her smile, though, some hidden knowledge, some laughing truth. She could hardly believe this confident woman had been hiding inside the shell of New Girl.

Avie grinned, like she had a secret.

"I can give you a reason to keep me with you. I told you I work for myself, and that's true. But I serve a purpose, Sophie, one I think you might know something about."

"I doubt that," Sophie said.

"I don't want the Book so that I can trade it, or use it, or manipulate you, or any of this nonsense you deal with. I want the Book to stay out of the wrong hands because I want what you want, Sophie Vesachai." Avie leaned forward. "I want to bring the fucking *trees* back."

THE LOST BOYS

The Hero of Cannoux-Town

"Children require adventure; adults need only tales of it."

—DAME BRESIS TE, 'SON OF A BITCH'

James D'Essan was daydreaming about various things—Silver Keys, kindly Giants, saving the world—and so wasn't paying as close attention to his work as he might have. He swung his tuning-hammer a little too hard and just a *little* too much to the left and smashed the tip of his finger halfway off.

"Ow!" he yelled, and danced back from Uncle's worktable in pain, sucking on his abused fingertip. Uncle looked up from a book he was writing in, one bushy eyebrow raised, and Buckle made a great show of falling onto the table and rolling around in paroxysms of laughter. James glared at her, aggrieved—she was supposed to be on his side!

"Careful, squib," Chris said, not looking up from his work; and that was justification enough for James to throw a hammer at him. But of course, his too-competent older brother caught the tool, gave him a severe look, and set it aside. James didn't mind the pain so much, but he didn't need nobody *laughing* at him. He examined his finger; it was red but not bleeding. He supposed he would survive.

One of Uncle's cadre of half-feral cats nosed at his injury, its bronze eyes seeming to gloat, and James swept it off the table with an annoyed elbow.

Uncle's workshop was warm from his twistcraft forge, glowing with dull orange heat, and James' fingernails seemed to throb in time with it. He wondered if the injury was going to be enough to get him out of this lesson, so he could go explore Cannoux, like he had been doing the last few days, searching for a certain Silver Key that he'd been shown in a certain *dream*. James sucked on his finger, smiling to think of it.

"You gonna live?" Uncle set his book aside. "You seem a little distracted today, boy! I wonder what it could be?"

"Ain't nothing," James said, and stuck his tongue out at Buckle, who was still really, *really* amused at his misfortune.

"Probably a girl." Chris was hammering on his own piece of twist, a compli-cated tat-a-tat pattern that made James' head hurt. "Squib's got an awful preoc-cupation with girls these days."

James was outraged. "Ain't no girl! You're the one who likes *girls!*"

"Sounds like a girl, all right," Uncle agreed. "I thought better of you, lad. Thought you'd be one of the lucky ones."

James almost threw a hammer at Uncle, but there were no hammers handy. And it would probably just bounce off, since Uncle was old and tough like a damn stone-stump. And anyways, his finger was fine now; it hurt, but pain wasn't much of a bother to James. Sometimes it even felt good, in a weird way.

He looked forlornly at his sad piece of dim red twist, uncurling in the morn-ing light. Uncle leaned forward and prodded it with his big blunt finger. He raised an eyebrow at James.

"Even for you, this is sad work."

"I did all the stuff you said!"

Uncle sighed. "Boy, I been watching you with my own two eyes and you have *not* done all of the things I've said. If you did three of the things I said, I'll spin around like a top. I tell you, lad, I despair of you ever making it more'n a step down the Path."

"The Path." James blew air through his lips, derisive. Uncle was always talking about the damn *Path*. If it were a real path, James would run down it! He'd jump over all the obstacles and do it faster than anybody! He was good at *real* paths!

But this made him think about the great kindly Giant, and the Silver Key stuck in his palm, and the terrible clawing Dark that ate them both alive every night. James shivered, even though Uncle's workshop was warm from the twist-craft forge.

He had to find the Silver Key.

James looked down at his small hands, so inept at crafting twist, and thought about wrapping them around the Silver Key, driving the shadow back, and saving them all.

Saving the WORLD!

"Look at this boy," Uncle observed, nudging Chris, "grinning like a loon. Can't stop smiling all day long. Only one thing that can cause that sort of dumb bliss in a lad that age."

"Girls," Chris said wisely.

James watched as Buckle hissed at Chris and kicked a bit of charring sand at the mechanism he was working on. Good old Buckle! Maybe she did have his back, after all. Bucks knew he didn't like no *girls*. He glared and crossed his arms. He knew Uncle and Chris were just teasing him, but that didn't mean he had to like it. He wouldn't have time to be talking to girls, anyways.

There were Silver Keys to find. His Silver Key.

His.

"He's grinning again," Chris said.

"Adolescence," Uncle said. "Welcome to hell, kid."

"What do you know about it?" James let Buckle settle down onto his shoulder. "Bet you don't even remember being a kid, you're so old."

Uncle chuckled. "Well, that's true enough. I'm even older than you think. But I remember plenty, and I remember your Ma asked me to teach you twistcraft. What would your dear lovely Ma say, if she saw this sad piece of twist in front of you? She'd cry, like as not, and old Uncle would have to comfort her."

"Ew," James said. Buckle screwed up her little face and stuck a tiny bronze tongue out at Uncle.

"Yeah," Chris looked up from his mechanism, frowning. "Ew."

Uncle winked at James. "Boy, you got no idea at all of the world, and that world is going to come for you sooner than later. Do you even know what all this is for?"

"All what?" James asked, wondering how long the lesson would run. Because as soon as the lesson was over, he could go *save the world*.

Him—*not* Chris. *Him*.

"Boy!" Uncle snapped his fingers in front of his face. "Twistcraft! Dirt-Magic! The Old Gold! What's the point of it? Why in all the hells am I wasting my time teaching it to you?"

"I don't know!" James said, annoyed at getting pulled out of his reverie. "Ask Chris. He's about half in love with stupid *twist*."

"Better than red-haired girls of uncomfortable provenance," Uncle said slyly, and now it was Chris' turn to scowl. But Uncle fastened his gaze back on James soon enough, looked at him for a moment, then shook his head.

"Buckle," Uncle said, "I thought you'd be a good influence on this lad, but you're a sore disappointment in that regard."

Buckle threw Uncle a rude gesture that she'd learned from James. James gave her a grin. At least he had *one* friend.

Uncle crossed his thick arms, and studied James like he was a bug. His eyes were black and glittering, and when he looked at James like this, James felt like some sort of out-city insect that had wandered into one of Uncle's unfathomably complex mechanisms and gummed up the works.

"Why do they call it the Dirt-Magic, boy?" Uncle asked, eventually. "Are you listening at all?"

"Not really."

"Then you're going to die early, and hard," Uncle said, blunt. "Why do they call twistcraft *Dirt-Magic*?"

James sighed and exchanged a sad look with Buckle. He was going to have to *learn* something now, despite his best efforts. It was the only way they could escape and find his Silver Key. "I don't know. Because it comes from dirt."

"Because it comes from *dirt,*" Uncle said. "The other magic, the Silver, where does that come from?"

"I don't know!"

"What's the opposite of dirt?"

James screwed up his face, thinking, but he didn't know. Then he saw Chris pointing upwards surreptitiously, behind Uncle's back, and remembered other lessons. "Oh! The sky!"

"Through the Feeds," Chris said.

Uncle turned to give Chris a look. "If you don't stop helping your brother cheat, I'm going to smack you so hard your *dreams* will spit out teeth."

"Yes, sir. Sorry. Minding my own business, starting now."

Uncle harrumphed. He gave James a wink, though. James always liked it when he threatened Chris. James had never seen Uncle hit anybody, but threats were more fun than nothing.

"So," Uncle said. "The Silver comes from the Feeds."

"But Cannoux ain't got no Feed." James knew that much.

"No, they burn twist for light," Uncle said. "Like imbeciles, because they don't want to learn what I've got to teach them, because they've got no foresight or sense of . . . Gah! Never mind. Maybe their vaunted *Nine* will save them after all. But no, they do not have a Feed. Hey! Pay attention, boy!"

"I *am* paying attention!" James said, though he had started thinking about how he was going to go find the Silver Key, and drive the darkness back, and save Ma, and Chris, and even Uncle, and how maybe they'd make a statue of him that said 'Hero of Cannoux' or something. And Chris would have to look at it and hang his head on his way to whatever dumb job whatever dumb Lord had given him. James peered at Uncle suspiciously. "Why you trying so hard to teach me stuff this week? And why ain't you beating me bloody about that stupid twist I messed up?" James jerked his chin at the ruined piece of twist on the worktable, abandoned at the beginning of their conversation.

Uncle exchanged a long, exasperated look with Chris, and then studied James with a shrewd look that James didn't much care for. "You ain't as dumb as you look, boy. Suffice it to say that *all* the kids in Cannoux—that I teach, anyways—are getting a crash course in the true shape of the world. I have reason to think they'll need it soon, including you. So tell me, boy. Do you know the nature of the Wanderlands?"

"'Course I do."

"Nice try. I'll ask again, then: what is the Dirt-Magic *for*?"

"To make stupid machines that I can't do right is about all I can tell," James said.

"Oh? Is Buckle stupid?"

"Well, no. Oh, come on, Bucks! I didn't mean *you!*"

"The Dirt-Magic is the *Path*, boy. With the Old Gold, anybody anywhere in all of the Wanderlands can take a few shovelfuls of dirt and a bit of fire and make themselves the basic building block of all civilization."

"Twist," Chris said, from behind them, and then withered under Uncle's glare. But the old man nodded.

"Twist is the foundation of civilization," Uncle said. "Or it used to be. Now, is making twist easy?"

"No." James could say this with assurance. He had a bruised fingertip and a ruined experiment to prove it.

"And it ain't supposed to be, boy. It's *hard work*, and the higher stages require higher and higher levels of concentration and skill. A person could spend two lifetimes building the skill it would take to make something like that forge behind you, and four lifetimes more to make something like Buckle."

"Come on," James said. "You ain't that old."

"I'm even older." Uncle was impassive. "*Point being*, you little stubborn sumbitch, that you can take some dirt and you can make the most incredible things in the world, but it takes work. It takes sacrifice. It takes time, and it takes commitment. It takes wisdom."

"Sounds boring," James said, and Buckle hooted laughter, pointing at Uncle. James gave her a grin, and she grinned back. Bucks was the best. Between her and him soon finding the Silver Key and saving everybody, life was almost all right.

Uncle gave a heavy sigh and pinched the bridge of his nose. "Mother help us all if it's you, boy."

"If what's me?" James asked, confused.

"Never mind. Tell me what the difference is between the Dirt-Magic—the *Old Gold*—and Silver."

"I dunno," James said. "I mean, Silver is *real* magic. The Silver Age! The Cold, right? And the Giants, all them stories. Hunter Fine, and Winter, and . . . and all the best stories got Silver in 'em."

"True enough. Is the Silver hard to use?"

James knew this one. "Only the Cold can use Silver."

"Untrue, actually, but beside the point. The Nine use it often, and there is a family deep beneath your feet that has some skill as well. You are essentially right, though; only a few very highly trained people with very special and *very* rare tools can manipulate the Silver."

"That's why they're wizards!" James said, but he should have known better. Uncle's face grew thunderous.

"*I'm* a wizard, boy! The Cold are damned *technicians!*"

"Yeah, well."

"Wizards," Uncle said, muttering. "Huh."

Chris coughed, from behind them.

Something occurred to James. "How come you don't use Silver, if you're so wizened?"

Uncle opened his mouth to retort, then stopped and peered at James, as if he'd sprouted a third nose. "That was actually clever. Chris, is your brother getting clever?"

"Mother help us."

James didn't know what they hell they were talking about. Uncle shook his head and answered.

"The Old Gold and the Silver don't get along, boy. If you got some skill in Silver, it don't matter none; it won't affect twistcraft devices. And vice versa. And that right there is about half what's wrong with the world."

James, who had recently become quite enamored of *Silver devices*, decided not to comment. Once he found the Silver Key, Uncle would be impressed no matter what nonsense he spouted.

"All right," Uncle said. "Because this isn't pleasant for either of us, I want to drill one last point into that thick skull of yours and hope that you never need use it. So stop daydreaming about whatever you're daydreaming about, be it girls or weapons or a good fight, and pay attention to *me*, for just one Twins-damned minute. Buckle, can you help me out here?"

Buckle landed on James' shoulder and kicked him in the ear.

"Ow!" James glared at her.

She crossed her arms and made a face, then unfolded one arm to point at Uncle, telling James to listen. James tore his imagination away from saving the world. He focused it on the old wizard. "Fine! I'm listening! What?"

"Dirt-Magic is slow, boy," Uncle said. "It's slow, boring, and hard. But it's good, and it makes you better, the harder you work at it. It's generally not admired in the world, because it takes a very long time to get good at. Most people, they've never even seen a piece of twistcraft above stage three. That's about all most craftsmen can manage in one lifetime."

He sighed. "On the other hand, Silver is . . . Silver is tricky. It's not bad, on the face of it, but it's a lot easier to make things with. It's a lot easier to do good things with, and a lot easier to do bad. If you were ever to run afoul of any old Silver artifacts, boy, I hope you'll remember to be careful. I hope you'll remember that the Silver Age was a time of wonders and grand tales, of great deeds and tremendous events."

Uncle leaned down until he was looking James in the eye. He seemed very serious now.

"And I hope you'll remember, boy, that the Silver Age ended with the *sky going dark*."

———

Finally, after about half of *forever*, their stupid twistcraft lesson was over. Though how James had started the lesson trying to make a simple twist-spring and ended it with Uncle rambling on about fairy-tales and whatnot, James had no idea.

It didn't matter. He was free for the whole afternoon, free to go adventuring. Free to go save the world!

Chris was going to study in Lord D'Atail's public library, and James was well rid of *that*, so it was just him and Buckle and the depthless mysteries of Cannoux-Town.

James looked at Buckle, who fluttered in the air next to him. Buckle looked at James.

They nodded.

"No!" Buckle said, eager.

Buckle only ever said the word "No," but James found he had little trouble communicating with her. It was damn refreshing, actually; she wasn't constantly trying to tell him all the things he didn't know.

They made their way through Cannoux-Town, finding the low-ways and byways, the interstices between the city above and the city below, the old and the new. James knew, in his guts, that he wouldn't find the Silver Key in the new city. He would find it someplace old, someplace grand, someplace . . .

He didn't know. He had this strange, half-formed feeling deep down, but it was hard to follow. It felt like remembering a dream, which, he supposed, it was.

"No!" Buckle said, and threw a melon-seed at him. He grinned in spite of himself. The little automata had a refreshingly liberal view of work and responsibility. He took a break from searching and taught her how to steal jerky from a street-vendor.

Chewing on jerky, prowling old stone alleys and dim half-ways, with the city bustling above and Buckle flitting to and fro, examining cracks for potential hidden treasures, James felt that tightness in his chest loosen up a bit. It seemed like it was always there, nowadays, and when it got too tight, it felt like knives all pressing in on the center of him, and sometimes he had to go punch on something until it eased up.

But it had been easier since the dream. He felt grown-up now; he had responsibilities. He had a purpose. He had to save the world.

Buckle, annoyed at this seriousness, pretended to run into a wall full-speed and then staggered around in the air, feigning dizziness. It was silly, but it made James laugh. He felt like maybe he *would* find the Silver Key, and before it was too late. He'd save the world from that awful, tearing darkness in his dream, and then maybe people would look and talk about that young D'Essan boy, and how he sure was something special, and didn't he used to have a brother or something? What was his name again?

He followed the vague dream-feeling down into the old, crumbling under-city, leaving behind the bustle of the new city above. He liked it down there; it was a little scary and a little creepy. There were shadows from the twist-lights above, and the Silver Key could be anywhere.

Anywhere, sure, but he *did* feel like he was getting closer.

Wrapped in these warm thoughts, James didn't immediately realize he was being followed. It was Buckle that alerted him, landing on his shoulder and pulling on his ear until he turned to see a flash of red disappearing behind a wall.

"No," Buckle said firmly, and James nodded. He walked on, letting Buckle scout for him. He saw another flash of red—was that hair?—behind him, and then Buckle gave the signal. He darted into a dim alley, scrambled up a wall, and flipped up onto a ledge. He ran back the way he came, leapt over a trellis and broke his fall on a heavy ledge of gourds, and dropped back to the ground. Buckle squawked encouragement, and he crept up behind his pursuer, gathering up a short length of fakewood to use as a weapon.

He turned the corner, and his assailant turned.

It was a girl.

She had long, brilliantly red hair and blue eyes, and James supposed that some dumb person like his brother would think she was pretty, but now she just looked silly, mouth hanging open in surprise. He noticed the tendrils of a slave-mark on the side of her neck. She was indentured. Not that it mattered to him; he and Chris were only one step above that themselves. He frowned at the girl; he had been expecting to get jumped by an enemy.

"Who are *you*?" he asked. Her eyes flicked to the stick in his hand and then to Buckle, and then back up to his face. Her eyes narrowed.

"I'm Katherine," she said. "Who are *you*?"

"I'm James, and I don't care who you are, why you followin' me?"

"If you don't care, why did you ask?"

She had that infuriating smile that girls liked to use that made James want to punch holes in rocks. She sniffed. "And I wasn't following you. Maybe you were following *me*."

"I wouldn't be following no *girl*." James sneered and Buckle gave him a little indignant kick.

"Maybe you would," the girl said. "Maybe you're a little creep-boy."

James' face burned but he wouldn't dignify this with a response. Creep-boy! "Why you following me?"

The girl looked away for a moment. "I ain't *following* you. We're just both looking in the same place."

"You was following me," James said, "I saw you. Me and Buckle both."

"Is that her name?" Katherine said, forgetting for a second to be haughty, delighted by the little person. "She really is wonderful.".

"No!" Buckle gave the girl a midair bow.

"Traitor," James muttered. But the red-haired girl was biting her lip, looking at Buckle, and then she sighed.

"Okay, fine." She tossed her red hair. "I *was* following you, okay? You seemed like you know where you're going. You caught me! You don't have to act so smug about it."

The idea that it was *James* acting smug was staggering and served to illustrate the fact that whatever girls used for logic, it wasn't anything like what *real* people used. Buckle lost interest in the conversation and flew up some old stairs to reconnoiter. James could hardly think of what to even *say* to this monstrous, this beastly—this *girl*.

"I ain't goin' nowhere," James said. "There ain't nothing down here, anyways."

Now the haughty smile was back. "Oh, sure. Come on, kid, you ain't gotta tell me where you were looking, but you don't have to lie about it."

James felt a wave of boundless, overweening anger at being accused of lying— which he had been—but *she* didn't know that!

"I ain't got even half an idea what you're talking about," James said. "Just don't follow me, and I won't have to—"

The girl's lips—which were also red—quirked. She eyed his stick, held limply in his fist. "Have to do what?"

"I'll get Buckle to do stuff to you," James promised, trying to extemporize. "She's got powers. And stuff. She can do all kinds of things. You don't want to mess with her."

Buckle flitted back from the stairs, attentive to her name. She gave the girl a fierce look.

"I believe it." Katherine got smug again. "Too bad she can't lead you to the Key."

James started a retort, then paused. "What?"

The red-haired girl frowned at his expression. "The . . . the Key. The Silver Key? Why are you looking at me like that? The Key from the dream, kid. We're both looking for the same thing. You and me and every damn kid in Cannoux . . . Wait. *Wait.*"

Katherine put her hand over her mouth, whether in shock, amusement, or horror even she likely did not know.

"Oh, no," she said, her voice small. "Did you not know?"

James couldn't answer; his chest suddenly felt very tight, like there were knives all stuck into it and they were all pressing in. He wrapped his hands around himself and squeezed, trying to keep them out. He felt tears creep up in his eyes and hated them.

"Oh, kid"—and her eyes were full of a terrible kind of sympathy—"did you think you were the only one?"

THE KILLERS

The Lord of the Lurk

"There is no such thing as a favor; there are only transactions.
A favor is merely a transaction in which one pays with self-respect."

—JESUIS 'ROD-TITE' MCANDLESS, 'TOPSY'

Once upon a time, there was a girl named Sophie Vesachai, and she had a dream.

Now, this was long before she used her magic Book to call the Jannissaries, those ancient soldier-constructs; long before she used them to defeat the Outkeep invaders and save her home. This was long before she almost single-handedly ended the Hot Halls War, even before the horror of Saint Station and the more subtle horror of her Proscription. It was before the bad deaths of Luet and Mad Vaas; before she learned the true shape of the world.

It was before she found the Book, her famous *Book*; but all of those things came after the dream and all of those things happened because of it.

Now: it should be stated plainly that this was no ordinary dream. There were many interesting and compelling things in this dream, many things to catch a young person's attention. When a boy named James had this dream, long ago and far away, he would remember mostly the Silver Key and the gnawing shadows chasing him. When a red-haired girl named Katherine had the dream, she mostly remembered the sad, desperate look in the Giant's eye as it was devoured by the Dark.

When James' brother Chris had it—though for him it was faded and hard to recall, because he was very nearly too old to get the dreams at all—he was most caught by the vast expanse of the sky overhead, the Rings, and the clockwork precision he saw there.

All of those memories would stay with the children for the rest of their lives, and in certain ways informed the things they would do and the people they would become.

But Sophie, now—*Sophie* remembered the trees.

It should be said that there were trees in the Keep, even some living ones. It was hard to keep trees growing in the Underlands, but it could be done. There were the potted cherrywhistle and terra that gave the Rue de Paladia such color; the pearlescent mottled barks of the trees that made the Labyrinthine, and the big dead sycamores of the Ransom Parkway. Yet all such trees were cultivated, even the ones bred specially to look wild. And none grew very large. Sophie had seen many trees, yes, but she had never seen anything like the trees she saw in her dream. In that, she walked through something she had never dreamed of before, never even imagined:

A *forest*.

She would never be able to properly articulate how that stretch of living trees affected her. Though she knew many children who had the dream, and would meet more later in life, few seemed to share her profound feelings for those immense spreading conifers and the shafts of sunlight that speared down through the green canopy above. Most children—especially the ones called *James*—tended to focus on the saving-the-world aspects of the dream. Sophie thought that the trees were the reason why you would *want to*.

Somewhat interestingly, a man named Gunnar Anderson once had this dream in a world where forests—and sunshine—were plentiful enough to be an annoyance, and in *his* dream he found himself walking through an endless stone castle, filled with all manner of tantalizing secrets and old treasure. The Giant in Gunnar's dream was the same as in the other children's dreams and, clearly, there had been a Silver Sword in it—or else there wouldn't be a story here to tell. But it's curious that *his* dream was the only one fundamentally different than those had by the children of the Wanderlands.

For the rest of Sophie's young life, and all of the terrible and wonderful things that would happen in it, the truest and most real thing for her would always be those moments in the dream, walking under a canopy of living green through a far-flung forest of enormous old trees, listening to the wonderful, bustling quiet of a living world. She would never forget it, and she would never get over it; it was her first and truest love. She was never to put much stock in religion, at least not the tripe that the Twinsmen spit, but when true believers tried to describe their reverence, she thought of that canopy of trees.

And sometimes, in her lighter moments, she thought that such a thing as that forest must still exist, somewhere above her, in the world that lay atop the leagues of stone above her head. Somewhere in the Wanderlands, there must still be some light, some trees, perhaps even a forest. More often, she thought it was an idle fancy, a memory of a time that could never come again. When she was a child and still young enough, she imagined that the forests could return someday, and that perhaps, if she were very strong and brave, she could help that happen. Which just goes to prove the old adage, "When the Mother calls, only fools and children hear."

But sometimes, they can be both.

————

Sophie waited in the antechamber of Lord Crowe's study, trying not to fidget and wishing she had borrowed Hunker John's flask. She could use a steadying sip, just now. Damien Crowe was one of the Queen's closest—and most loyal—advisors. Coming here was a hard risk.

But she had to know. The Swatterflowers that had attacked them in the Dream of Trees bar had been aimed at her *friends*. And whoever was fucking with her— be it Mr. March, his mysterious partner, the Consort, the Queen, or even Damien Crowe, the Lord of the Lurk himself—had known exactly where to find them. They hadn't been in the bar drinking for long, maybe only a half hour or so. Far too quickly to have been found by conventional means.

Sophie realized her foot was tapping against the lushly patterned carpeting of the foyer and made herself stop. She twisted strands of her short dark hair, wishing again she had a drink. She'd lost an hour traveling here and then explaining what she needed the rest of the Killers to do, setting up contingencies, and *far* too long trying to explain why they shouldn't kill or otherwise disappear the lovely, intractable, troubling *New Girl*.

Avie, she said her name was. Avie, and her *trees*. Sophie's foot started tapping again, and she pushed it down with one hand. Ben had been less surprised than she supposed, but still not happy. It was inconceivable that the girl wasn't in league with one of the major players tonight. Wasn't it? Sophie couldn't afford to trust her.

And yet . . . the way she'd said it. The way she'd leaned forward, green eyes intense, locked on Sophie's. *I want what you want, Sophie Vesachai. I want to bring the fucking trees back.*

Bring the trees back. She said it like she believed it; she said it the same way Sophie had said it, when she was fourteen years old and an idiot. The dream had been a lie, the way Saint Station had been a lie, the way that Denver Murkai and all of Sophie's grand young plans had been a lie. She couldn't forget that. She couldn't forget what these fuckers had done, and why they'd done it.

The only reasons the powerful forces of the world did anything. Power, money, advantage, and sport. *Trees* never quite made the list.

Sophie heard a rustling from beyond the big double doors that led to Lord Crowe's study, and straightened herself. The blonde enigma would have to wait;

Sophie had told Avie where the Killers meant to rendezvous—if they made it back out of Crowe House at all—and that would be its own sort of test. But she'd told the girl nothing of what their plans were. Sophie closed her eyes for a moment, questioning if this risk was worth it.

But it was. She had to know. And if there was any safe harbor for the Killers, it would be wrapped in the debt that Damien Crowe owed her, and had owed her, for fifteen years now.

A small chime rang, and the footman opened the velvet-lined door. She took her time standing up; giving herself a moment to steady herself. The footman waited, then ushered her into Crowe's study, and she heard the door click behind her. Lord Crowe himself sat at the far end of the study, behind a large desk.

He was a harshly handsome man, black hair winged with gray at the temples. He'd served with actual distinction in the Hot Halls War and knew his shit. Word said that he, himself, killed the warlord king Gutcher, though Sophie knew that wasn't true. He was the rumored (and factual) architect of the Espionage Corps— sometimes called the Lurk—and it was privately implied that he ran many of the Queen's off-the-book operations out in the Dim. He was, perhaps, the second most dangerous person in the Keep. He steepled his long fingers together behind the big desk, leaned back in his chair, and watched her walk in.

Sophie took her time, looking around the huge study and affecting a casualness she did not feel. The study was as sumptuously ornate as any she'd ever seen, but it had a strong trace of the military in it. It had the flavor of its master, decadence wrapped around fine steel. Antique silver war-engines were highlighted in curved glass cases along the sides of the study; their brutal clockwork mechanisms a fine contrast to the soft luxury around them. Crowe kept his study dim, with muted accents glowing behind tapestries and sconces, the area around his desk the only place well-lit. It was a striking effect, but one Sophie had seen too many times to be much impressed by.

Damien Crowe stood as Sophie approached him. "Sophie Vesachai," Crowe said, studying her. "It's been a long time."

"It has. Too long, maybe," Sophie said and found herself smiling at him. She could never keep herself from liking Crowe, despite his closeness to the Queen. "How are you, Damien?"

"Older, but well."

He reached a hand across the desk and Sophie took it. He gripped hard, but not in an attempt to cow. It was an expression of how he did everything. This man had honor, once; Sophie prayed he'd kept some. He gave her a considering look, let her hand go, and sat back down behind the desk.

"What brings you to me, Vesachai? Tonight, with the Loche going Dark, and Swatterflowers running amok? It's hard to believe you're paying a social call. After all of these years."

"No," Sophie said shortly, and sat down. "I'm afraid I'm here to cash in a very old debt."

Crowe sighed but seemed resigned. "It had to come someday. Though you took your time about it."

"It seemed like a coin that should be spent carefully."

"I suppose that's true." He studied her. "So what's it to be? Half my kingdom? Do I need to curse Jane's name to her face?"

"Nothing so easy. I need some information and maybe a little protection. Safe passage, maybe."

"Hmm," Crowe said, giving away nothing. "Let's start with the information."

"I don't need you to betray any confidence," Sophie said, "or tell me any sensitive plans. I just need to know one thing."

He waited, his eyes steady.

Sophie took a breath. "Is she fucking with me?"

He was quiet for a long time, long enough for Sophie to register the deep quiet of his study, the subtle ticking of clockwork and gears from several different places.

"That's not a simple question," he said, finally. "But the simple answer is: yes."

She took a deep breath, and managed a tight smile. "Well, *shit.* Then it might be a good time to talk about safe passage."

Crowe looked pained. "It's not that simple, Sophie. There is a lot going on right now, and your troubles are just a small part of it."

"That's comforting," Sophie muttered.

"Jane is getting some bad advice. From the Consort, I think."

Sophie blinked and tried to be careful about what she said. "I didn't think the Consort was a player."

"Neither did I. But Jane is making some suspect decisions lately, and he is the most likely culprit."

"It's hard to believe the Beast would let her judgment be affected by a paramour."

"I'll not hear that slur from your lips, Vesachai," Crowe said sharply.

Sophie was reminded what an implacable enemy of her family this man was, and how much he hated her father. Her mouth twisted. "I apologize, Damien. I'm under some stress."

"I'll forgive it." He made a visible effort to relax. "Wherever Jane's suspect counsel is coming from, she is making moves. And some of those involve you."

"*Shit.*" Sophie slumped back in her chair. "I never thought she could do this kind of thing, Crowe. I mean, I know she's never been a fan of the Loche de Menthe, but—"

"Hold," Crowe said, holding up a finger to stop her. "I've heard of what happened in the Loche. That wasn't the Queen."

"I thought you said she was fucking with me?"

"She is. But can you imagine Jane Guin doing damage to her own Keep? Can you imagine her destroying lightfixtures, even Dim ones? No, Sophie. Jane is not the only one making moves tonight."

"Ah." Sophie tried to digest this. "Well, that's great."

The Giant Lies Still Awake, Sophie Vesachai.

She rubbed her temples. "So what you're saying is that I'm double-fucked."

"No," Crowe said, almost gently. "I'm saying you're triple-fucked, or more."

"Doubt that will be as fun as it usually is." Sophie sighed. "If she didn't send the Loche Dark, then . . . ?"

Crowe looked away for a moment. "Jane's plan was more direct. And she doesn't have an extremely high opinion of your intelligence, as you know. She directed me to release a small amount of Ansiotropic."

"Okay," Sophie said, getting it. "You gave March the Battle Drugs, then. He's working for you."

Crowe narrowed his eyes. "Do you know who Mr. March is?"

"Should I?"

Crowe hesitated and seemed to speak against his better judgment. "Mr. March has ties to the Vesachai."

Sophie sat forward, frowning. "Ties?"

Crowe shrugged uncomfortably. "More than ties. He is a fully trained and bonded Vesachai."

She felt her muscles go weak. "But that . . . This can't be a Vesachai play, can it? My father would never send a part of the Keep Dark. Not even the Loche de Menthe."

Crowe seemed to arrive at a decision. He looked genuinely pained, and Sophie knew the look. Someone had fucked up, and it didn't even matter if it was him. He would bear the responsibility—and the cost of cleaning it up. "March was working for us. Me and Jane."

"Was?"

"He has gone rogue," Crowe said. "We gave him the Battle Drugs, but we never sanctioned anything like his attack on the Loche de Menthe or this incident with the Swatterflowers. He clearly has his own agenda, and we are as in the dark with what that is as you are."

"I doubt that." Sophie hissed through her teeth. "Great, so March is a rogue Vesachai who seems to be trying to frame me in criminal acts of destruction against the Keep, or at least implicate me. The Loche, and then Swatterflowers? *Shit.*"

"You understand our concern."

"It didn't make much sense that Jane would attack her own Keep. It's nice to know she has such a low opinion of my character, though. I know I'm a degenerate, but I'm not going to take a dive for some *drugs*."

Crowe waved it away. "Clearly, that plan failed. I said it would, for whatever that's worth."

"Thanks. I've never known Jane to have only one plan in place, though."

Crowe smiled crookedly and watched her.

She watched him back. "So," she said. "What does she want?"

"If that's not obvious, then maybe her estimate of your intelligence is correct."

"March might be too dumb to know it, but Jane is too smart to ever think I'd risk Proscription to open that vault. I think she is finally making a play for the Book."

"Our Queen has never been simple," Crowe agreed. "She does, indeed, want the Book."

"What in the fuck does she want with that thing?" Sophie asked. "After all these years?"

"As I said, she's making moves. Big moves. Dangerous ones, perhaps. She's getting bad advice."

"I've never known Jane to listen to advice much."

"Ambition can cloud even *her* judgment."

"What *ambition*?" Sophie asked. "She won the Twins-damned Hot Halls War. She broke my family over her knee like a thin stick. With *help from both me and you*, I might add. She's basically an immortal god, Crowe. What could she possibly be ambitious for?"

Crowe studied her for a moment, fingers steepled again.

"You've never understood her. Jane Guin only cares about one thing, really: *light*."

Sophie rolled her eyes, but Crowe ignored it.

"You know better than almost anybody," he went on, "that we live in a decaying, dying place. Every day, there's a little bit less light to go around, a little less Silver in the system. Every day, the outlying parts of the Keep go a little more Dim. Our Queen has her faults, I won't argue it. But if there was ever a more steadfast warrior against the Dark, I don't know who it is."

He shook his head. "Someone is tempting her with a very lovely idea, Sophie. Too lovely, maybe. You know her nearly as well as I do; can you imagine anything she wouldn't do if she were able to bring light back to the Keep? If she were able to reverse the slide? Can you imagine the lengths she would go to, for *that* prize?"

Sophie could not. She resisted an urge to shiver.

The Giant Lies Still Awake, Sophie Vesachai. And the World Needs Weapons.

"And Queen Jane's plan," she said, "requires the Book."

"This plan requires the Book." Crowe leaned forward. "But nobody knows where the Book is, Sophie. Right?"

"I'm not going to tell *you*, Crowe. I'll do you the courtesy of not saying it burned to ash when I raised the Jannissaries, though."

"You don't have to tell me. I doubt I'd believe you if you did. But if you've told anyone, *anyone*, they're in play now. They're probably safe from Jane, for now, because she thinks she has some holds on you. But whoever else is making moves tonight . . ."

"I haven't told anyone," Sophie said, distracted. That wasn't quite true. There had been a night, a few years ago, when she'd gotten quite drunk with the Killers and . . . she shook her head and tried to focus on Crowe. She could trust her friends; they would never betray *that* secret.

Crowe watched her, his gaze shrewd. "Look, Jane tried to appeal to your mercenary nature and it didn't work. And she had other plans for you, true; she is not in the habit of being frustrated in her desires. But I promise you those plans were much more forthright than you might imagine. There are a lot of things she could offer you, and just as many she could threaten you with. She has no need for the kind of things that March is doing tonight."

"Well, you say that, Crowe," Sophie said. "And if I were anybody but me, I might believe it."

"The situation was different back then."

"Fuck off. I made my own decisions when I was a kid, but let's not act like Jane Guin didn't throw down plenty of breadcrumbs for me to follow. And she was anything but direct. I just need to know how to get out of this, Crowe—me and my friends. We want nothing to do with any of it."

"You might as well wish for the lost sun to rise over this desk, Sophie. You *do* know the location of the Book. You haven't even bothered to deny it. So now you have two very powerful and very motivated entities—Jane and March—who will, I can only imagine, stop at nothing to get you to reveal its location."

"Please," Sophie sighed, "stop trying to cheer me up."

"You came to me for payment on an old debt, Sophie. And I mean to honor my promise."

"Good," Sophie said. "I won't insult you by asking you to protect me and my friends; clearly you are involved up to your fucking eyeballs. But I know you, Crowe, and I know you have safe houses, out in the Dim and Dark. I'm calling in that favor, now, for safe passage . . ."

But she trailed off. Crowe was shaking his head.

"No, Sophie," he said quietly. "I can't get you out of the Keep."

"My friends, then."

"Your friends are the most valuable things *in* the Keep," he said with reluctance. "They are the only levers over you anyone can count on."

"Which is exactly why I want safe passage."

"And exactly why I cannot grant it," Crowe said.

"This is a debt, Crowe, that you swore you'd pay. Are you betraying your oath?"

He shook his head. "Honoring the spirit, if not the letter."

"*Fuck* you," Sophie spat. "And fuck your *spirit*."

"Sophie," Crowe said, "Jane has been betrayed. By bad counsel, by some of the old bad things of the world, maybe. But surely you understand that what she wants is, ultimately, good. She can be cruel; she can make hard decisions. But she wants to save the Keep, just like you once did. And you can help; you can be the Savior of the Keep again. All she needs is the Book."

Sophie closed her eyes for a long moment, trying not to laugh. She hadn't saved *shit*. But Crowe didn't stop talking.

"We know you hid it. Trust us, we have spent years looking for it. But things are happening now—right now—that require it. Tell us where it is, Sophie. And then there's no need for safe passage; your friends will be safe. *You* will be safe. There will be no need for you to take part in the great events of the world any longer. Just tell us where it is."

Sophie opened her eyes. Slowly, fumbling, she patted her pockets, looking for something, while she tried to think of a proper answer. The awful truth was that it was tempting. It was *so* tempting to tell him where the Book was and go get drunk. Let the world burn. It was burning anyway.

The Giant Lies Still Awake, Sophie Vesachai.

But inside her was still a tiny, tiny shred of the girl she'd once been, a girl who had loved a dream about trees. One who remembered the friends who had died so that she could keep her Silver Book.

She kept patting tunic pockets and pulled out a slot. She scraped the slot alight against the edge of Crowe's desk. He frowned but didn't object. She drew in a deep lungful of smoke, and wished she had some butterflies to burn. She found what she was looking for, a slender wooden tube, and let it rest in her free hand.

"Well," Sophie said at last, "I think I've eaten up enough of your time, especially if tonight is as fraught as you say."

Crowe just waited.

Sophie cocked an eyebrow. "I am free to go, yes?"

He shook his head; at least he had the grace to do it regretfully.

"This is just too important, Sophie. We'll round up your friends, I'm sure they're close. You'll be safe, I promise it, you and your friends both. But we need that Book."

"I invoke the debt, then. I'm calling in the favor, Crowe; just let me walk out of here."

"I cannot, Sophie."

Sophie nodded and felt the slender tube of fakewood she held, notched with three small openings. She said a brief prayer to gods that she did not believe in, raised it to her lips, and blew. A very high note sounded, almost inaudible, but one she knew would carry through walls and stone.

She spent an eternal moment waiting, a no-time where everything was possible and all of it bad. And then there was a sharp rap on the anteroom door, a staccato code.

She let herself breathe and looked up into Crowe's puzzled face.

"Truly, Crowe. I'm sorry about this." She raised her voice. "Bring him in!"

The door opened behind her. When Crowe saw who came through it, the color drained from his face. Sophie turned to see Bear pushing his way into the room, his knife at the back of a handsome but somewhat frail older gentleman, who had his hands tied behind his back with a length of recently torn bedsheet. Ben held the footman behind him, his hand tight over his mouth.

Sophie allowed herself a small moment of relief before she turned back to Crowe. All of the things that could go wrong had not gone wrong.

Well, except for all of the other things that had gone wrong on this lousy shit-kicker of a night; those had gone about as wrong as anything ever could. Sophie watched Crowe sink back down into his seat, a remarkable transformation happening; she was watching his eyes fill with bile and blood.

"Evan," he said, his voice dead calm. "Are you well?"

The older man jerked his head shortly. He had a cut on his chin, and blood trickled slowly down his neck.

"He put up quite a fight," Bear said. "Impressive, actually."

Crowe wrested his gaze away from his beloved husband and focused it formidably on Sophie.

"Tell your beast to let him go." He spoke very quietly and calmly. Very dangerously.

"Sorry. What was it you said? You were honoring the spirit of our debt but not the letter? Your honor is garbage, and I need to leave. Evan is our safe passage."

"I'm giving you one last chance." Crowe's manner was cold, all trace of warmth gone. "Any hope you have disappears at the end of this sentence. *Let him go.*"

Sophie met his gaze, understanding the enemy she was making here. So be it. "No."

There was a gasp behind them, and Sophie assumed Bear did something clever with his knife. Crowe sank back further into his chair. She saw tears at the corners of his eyes and hated herself a little. Well, a little more, anyway.

"You took him before you knew," Crowe said. "Before you even knew I would hold you, you decided to hurt him."

"I couldn't risk it, Crowe. And I was right."

He held her gaze for a long freezing moment. "You've made yourself a bad enemy tonight, Vesachai. If Evan suffers one whit more than he has already, I will hunt you until you are dead. Do you understand me?"

"I understand," Sophie said. "So you'll let us leave?"

Crowe barked a laugh, humorless. "What choice do I have?"

"Only a coward exploits a man's love," Evan said, his voice a little hoarse, from behind her.

Sophie turned and gave the older man a flat look, and then turned back and gave Crowe one even flatter. "You were ready to exploit mine. You were ready to hurt the people I love, to get what you want. No. Not even that. What your fucking *queen* wants."

"Fuck you, Vesachai," Crowe spit out, his eyes red.

Sophie shook her head. "I'm sorry, Crowe. I really am. I guess we both could have done the right thing tonight."

She gave him a last look. "But we didn't."

THE LOST BOYS

The Trouble With Girls

"A child should possess three qualities in abundance: Wonder, Curiosity, and Mischief. The child should pursue these qualities constantly, and for as long as they are able, for this is the purpose and sole responsibility of Childhood. When the child becomes an adult, of course, these qualities become the most dangerous sort of liability."

—JULE ANTONY, 'GROWING THINGS'

James D'Essan woke up from the dream of clawing shadow, gasping, not knowing at first what woke him. He had woken at the worst part of the dream, while the tendrils of mangling black were splitting apart his muscles and bones. He was still getting the dreams, the dreams of the Giant and the Silver Key, even though none of it mattered a damn anymore. For a moment after waking, he was caught in a different sort of darkness, disoriented and confused, and then Buckle hit him with a pebble.

"What the hell?" he asked, rubbing his forehead. Buckle was hovering by the window, her wings whirring, and hefted another pebble in her clever little hands. She jerked her head outside the window and grinned at him maliciously, and then James heard it.

"*Boy!*" A voice was hissing outside, trying to be quiet but not managing it. "James! Kid!"

James groaned and thought about burying himself in his blankets. He thought about throwing something at the girl—for he recognized the voice—and slamming the window shut. He thought about getting Buckle and running away into the dark, becoming an outlaw and brigand, where there were no older brothers and chores and red-haired orphan girls.

He remembered the loathsome girl's half-amused, half-horrified face, looming large in his imagination, her red hair a cloud of fire.

"Oh, kid, did you think you were the only one?"

He had. Discovering that every damn kid in Cannoux was having *his* dream, that they were all looking for the Silver Key, hadn't been the best thing he'd ever experienced. The knives in his chest had been pressing in, cutting him all up inside.

"*Kid!*" The damn girl called again, even louder. Buckle threw another pebble at him, and it glanced off his shoulder. James felt hugely put-upon, and he had no choice but to go to the window. Chris had been sleeping heavily these past few weeks, but even he would wake up soon, and the idea of getting teased for the next seventy years about a pretty girl throwing rocks at his window was too much to bear.

With a sigh as old and heavy as the stone foundations of Cannoux itself, James rolled out of bed. It was, indeed, the red-haired girl. James steadfastly refused to learn or remember her name.

"What," he said, in a strangled whisper, "do *you* want?"

She grinned at him and tossed her handful of pebbles aside. She must have been giving them to Buckle, who threw them at James' head. *Traitor.* Buckle thought the red-haired girl was *funny.*

"Come on." Katherine waved him out. "Let's go!"

James looked at her incredulously. "Go where? I ain't going nowhere with you!"

Katherine shook her long red hair. "Don't be silly. Haven't you been paying attention to the dreams? We're running out of time, kid."

"I ain't—" James said, fiercely, and then remembered he was trying to be quiet, "I ain't sharing my Key with *you.*"

"Well, I'm not exactly excited about it either!" Katherine hissed. She smoothed her plain tunic. "But I need help. And so do you."

"Go ask somebody else," James sneered. "All your *friends.*"

She blinked and looked up at him with eyes full of hurt.

"You don't have to be a jerk, D'Essan."

James felt obscurely guilty. He didn't know why what he'd said had hurt her feelings. *She* was the one who acted like every damn kid in the whole damn city was out holding hands and laughing and looking for *his* Silver Key. He felt his face flush and clenched his jaw because why should *he* be embarrassed? He checked to see if Chris was still snoring in his bunk, and he was. But even Ma would wake up if he kept shouting out the window like this.

Trapped like a damn *rat!*

"Fine," he said. "Hang on."

He skinned himself into some clothes and threadbare shoes and was out the window before Buckle even managed to give Katherine a kick on her outstretched hand—Buckle's version of a slapped palm. James was further outraged; Buckle was supposed to be *his* friend. Now she was consorting with the enemy? He scowled at the red-haired girl, his arms crossed tight over his chest.

"I ain't," James said, "helping you find *my* Key."

"It ain't," Katherine said, mimicking his tone, "*anybody's* Key. Until we find it. Which I am proposing to do, while all you propose to do is stand there looking stupid."

"*You* look stupid."

"I don't have half my hair standing up from the back of my head." James reviewed what he knew about the practicalities of kicking a girl, especially one bigger than him. He vaguely remembered Uncle saying something about waiting till one hit him first. He gritted his teeth; seemed like all he did around this damn girl was grit his teeth.

"Look, I say we make a deal," Katherine said. "Everybody else is helping each other, all the kids that ain't got caught looking in places they shouldn't, or gave up. But nobody can find it. The dream is just too friggin' vague. So I say we team up."

"I told you," James said, "go team up with all these other kids of yours."

"Jerk! I'm a friggin' cull. No high-city kids are gonna join up with me. And no other cull kids got the stones to sneak out and look."

James remembered her tattoo, the fine tracery curling up from her neck. It was hidden now, by shadow and her long red hair. He frowned. "What the hell does being indentured matter?"

Katherine laughed and looked away. When she looked back at him, her features were softer. "You got charm, kid, when you ain't trying. Come on, what do you say? What can it hurt?"

James considered. He hadn't been looking much, the past few days. And Bucks had been bugging him to go.

"And besides," Katherine's tone went grave, "it don't matter about us, really. Does it? The dreams are getting worse. Desperate. I can't help but feel like we're running out of time."

James shivered. "I don't want that dark to come. But it's dumb, ain't it? Why do we gotta find it? We're just kids."

"You're just a kid," Katherine said, haughty for a moment. But then she grinned to show she was joking. "I am a highly refined lady. *Obviously*. And anyways, ain't you ever heard that phrase, 'When the Mother calls, only fools and children hear'? I figure you're a damn long pour of both, so we should be able to find that thing quick."

Buckle tittered, her tiny musical laughter loud in the nighttime stillness. James turned his scowl on her, which somehow did not cause her to be immediately burnt to a crisp.

"Oh, come on, kid. I'm joking with you. I don't get to joke with nobody much. Lighten up."

"Yeah, well." James kicked at one of the dropped pebbles. He squinted up at a hanging twistcraft light, spitting its dull fire above them. He looked at the red-haired girl and, just for a moment, she wasn't trying to be all high and mighty and just looked like somebody around his age with a problem to solve.

He groaned and started walking. "Fine. Fine! It's *this* way, if you're coming. Yeah, you too, you little traitor!"

He pretended not to see it when Buckle gave Katherine another kick-five.

———

It became quite apparent, very quickly, that they both had drastically different ideas about how to search for the Silver Key. The dream was up to much interpretation and was not seen by everyone the same way. Katherine drove James half to distraction with questions about the specifics of the dream, the details of the passageways, and the Door with the symbols, and landmarks, trying to scour his dream for clues.

"Listen," he burst out, "I ain't my stupid brother, okay? I don't remember stuff like that. I don't know the dumb symbols or maps or any of that crap, so I dunno why the Mother ever even *sent* me the damn dream. Okay?"

He fumed for a minute, looking at the city above. They were in a dim passage, an old stone channel that was overgrown with wild gourds and seedgrass. Night would be over soon, and he was tired and annoyed and was going to get in trouble again for nothing.

Katherine, who was more than a little frustrated herself, visibly took a breath.

"Okay, James, you must be doing something right. If you can't remember details or make maps, how do you try to find it?"

James shrugged. She'd just make fun of him anyways. It didn't matter. But she caught his shoulder.

"Kid," she said, "c'mon, seriously. How are you doing it?"

"I dunno."

"Come on, kid."

"I don't *know!*" James punched the wall nearest him. He caught it good, too, and tore open two of his knuckles. Katherine took a step back, shocked.

But James' fists had always kind of soaked up his anger, and he was able to reply more calmly now. "I don't know. I just do it. I know it's out there, I kind of can *feel* it, and if I just sort of . . . don't think too much, and wander around, I get closer. Only it don't matter because it's locked off. Every time I get close, it's locked off."

"Locked off?" Katherine asked, looking at him closely. "What do you mean, kid?"

"Stop calling me kid," James said. Buckle landed on his shoulder and scolded him soundlessly for his knuckles, but they'd already stopped bleeding. It was like

James' body knew it was always going to have blood coming out of it, so it had learned to heal up quick. He gave the girl another dark look. "If you shut up for *five seconds*, maybe I can show you."

Katherine's mouth quirked. "Fine, *James*, show me."

And he did. It took a while because he knew she was following and probably smiling her little know-everything smile and thinking about what a little *kid* he was, but eventually he got to that place where he didn't really think about anything specific, the same place he got to when he was training swords and sticks with Sergeant Willet. Buckle helped, playing her goofy games, and for probably, like, the first time in her whole damn life, Katherine kept quiet.

And, like he usually did, he came to another damn blocked door.

"See?" he said, frustrated. He could feel the Key, out there, deep under the city, but anytime he got nearer, he ran into one of these old doors, banded in iron and rough twist, with no means of opening them that he could ever see. "I always run into these stupid things."

"There's a door in the dream," Katherine mumbled, kneeling down to examine the door. "But it didn't look like this."

"I *know*. And there ain't no symbols or nothing on them, I check."

"There's something about a door like this," Katherine murmured, thinking hard. "Somebody was talking about it. Mr. Swaim? No. *Master* maybe? Damn."

She shook her head. "These doors are all around the undercity, but I don't know much about them. I think they might be something like the Breach, you know, where the Mountain fell in downslope and they found that whole other city underneath?"

"Yeah, the Underlands, but that was forever ago." James frowned. "You don't think we gotta go out to the *Breach*?"

"Oh, Mother," Katherine said, with a shaky laugh. "I hope not. I don't even know where it is."

"Nobody does, what I heard. Lords' business."

"Well, I serve a Lord. And they don't know as much as you think."

"I dunno. Lords gotta know something, else why they in charge?"

"You'd be surprised," Katherine said. "And you better watch how you talk, boy, or you'll find yourself with a cull-mark to match mine."

"I talk how I want." James yawned. "Can't you just ask him about the blocked doors?"

"Maybe," Katherine said, chewing her lip. "Asking questions of Master D'Alle is dangerous. You always pay, one way or another."

James didn't know what that meant, but he didn't like it. Katherine was looking at him, though.

"What about Chris?" she asked. "Would he know?"

James' scowl took on legendary dimension. "You don't know my brother. I ain't asking *him*."

"Oh, I know your brother," Katherine said in an odd tone. James frowned at her.

"What? How do you know Chris?"

Katherine tossed her hair. "Oh, everybody knows Chris. He's already got Lords fighting over who gets to sinecure him. Even Master D'Alle thinks he's smart, and Master doesn't think much of anybody. You sure Chris wouldn't know about the doors? Okay, forget it! I can see from the murderous look on your face that you're not going to ask him. Fine. I'll just put my *very soul* in jeopardy and see if I can catch Master D'Alle in a good mood."

"Better than getting my stupid brother involved." James gave her an ominous look. "Because if *he* finds out about the Silver Key, ain't *neither* of us getting our hands on it."

"Well," Katherine said, "that's as may be, but—"

She cut off when Buckle leaped off James' shoulder.

"No!" Buckle said, alarmed. Several large boys strolled into the underway courtyard where she and James were sitting and stopped when they saw them. Slowly, some big stupid grins crawled over their big, stupid faces.

"Hello, Cull!" the leader shouted, stepping forward and grinning. "Master let you out, eh? Digging for twist?"

"My name," she said, edging sideways, "is Katherine. Not *Cull*. And I'm just spending time with my friend."

"Oh, that don't look like no friend," one of the other boys said. "Looks like a little cull-in-waiting."

"How about it, D'Essan?" the third said as they advanced. "Thinking about it? Hear your Ma's on hard times, maybe gotta sell off a kid or two. Sure won't be your brother, eh? Maybe we show you what it's like, being a cull. It ain't so bad, kid, I promise."

Buckle, ever the good soldier, had taken this opportunity to explore the battlefield and indicated the location of a very nasty little piece of broken wood. James grinned at the boys.

"James," Katherine warned in a low aside, "don't do anything stupid. I can handle these assholes."

And maybe that was true, James thought, as he dived for the piece of broken wood, coming up with it clenched in a tight fist, but he hadn't been in a good fight in ages.

And fighting, as even Uncle would have admitted, was the *one damn thing* he was good at in this world.

THE KILLERS

Friends Old And New

"Trouble comes in threes, but it generally just takes Disaster the once."

—SLOW MIKE, 'BAD PROVERBS'

"So, listen," Trik said as the Killers made their way up the Ransom Parkway, the quickest way out of Hunter's Hollow—and Lord Crowe's territory—that Sophie knew, "I'm starting to hate always being the tiresome asshole of the group, but are we sure we want to keep a known spy and infiltrator around? You know, since everything is about to go to as much shit as there is shit in the world?"

The Killers, having escaped Crowe House and released Damien's elderly husband once they'd reached a populated and busy thoroughfare, were making their way up the Ransom Parkway to the promised rendezvous with Avie.

"She claims she's with us." Sophie looked up at one of the large, long-dead sycamores that appeared periodically on the Parkway. "But you're not wrong, Trik."

The Ransom Parkway was a helical byway of the Keep, something halfway between a spiral highway and a park. It climbed up through the floors lazily, a wide thoroughfare with a gentle incline; all in all a pleasant walk. It was high enough that big sycamore trees had grown there, once upon a time, but these had long-since died and turned to stone. Smaller trees and lightsculptures littered the parkway, yet more cunning design intended to keep the peoples of the Underlands from going mad in their long exile from the world above.

"I'm not sure what the problem is," Hunker John said, taking another pull from his ever-present flask. "Since when do we care about pretty people having agendas? They all have agendas. I know I do! You can't trust us beautiful folk."

"Your only agenda is getting drunk." Sophie grinned at him. He tipped his flask at her. He was well on his way. "And in normal days, I could give a fuck about anybody's motivations, but tonight isn't normal days. Ben, what say you? We don't have to meet up with her."

Ben looked up, frowning. He had been withdrawn since Sophie and Bear had gotten Avie to admit she wasn't what she seemed. He shrugged, convulsively. "I don't know, Capitana. She might know something important. Or she might be working for the Queen. Or March. I don't know."

Sophie clapped him on the shoulder. He would beat himself up over this plenty. He shook his head.

"She's so *different*. I didn't know, Sophie."

"I know you didn't, old man. Me and Bear watched the transformation happen. It was . . . eerie."

"Very fucking eerie," Bear said. "It was like New Girl was a skin she was wearing. I don't know how we trust somebody like that. No matter what she might know. Even if she brought up the dream, and the trees."

"It's up to you, Ben," Sophie decided. "You say no, we skip her. Tonight's fucked enough without a wildcard in the mix."

Ben took a deep breath and shook his head. "It's not up to me; I can't be trusted on the subject. But she knows more than she's saying. What if she *is* on our side?"

"What if she's *not*?" Trik shot back.

Ben grimaced. "The problem is that we don't know who is fucking with us tonight, right? We don't know who Mr. March is, or who his partner is. Crowe says that Jane is involved, but not pulling the strings anymore. Someone is trying to get Sophie to betray the location of the Book, while trying to make it look like she's the one gone rogue. There's already too many uncertainties, and . . . Twins damn it, it couldn't all have been an act. She was our friend."

"Maybe." Trik looked unconvinced. She hesitated, and looked around to make sure nobody was within hearing distance. "Ben, there's . . . there's no chance that *she* knows where the Book is, right?"

Sophie swore. "Trik, *fuck you*. None of us would—"

Ben stopped her, pained. "It's a fair question." He dropped his own voice. He looked around at each of the Killers. "No, Trik. I would never have told anybody . . . that. I think we all know that for *any* of us to ever breathe a word of *that,* for any reason, would be the worst sort of betrayal. Right?"

"Right," Trik said, emphatically.

Bear gave them a curt nod of his head. "Yes. I've told no one. I never would."

Sophie put her hand on Ben's arm. "*However,* if anybody *had* told someone, in their cups or across a pillow, I would understand. I'm the one who burdened you all by telling you . . . I didn't think it mattered anymore. I would forgive you for feeling the same. So if *any* of us have told *anyone*, that's ok. But we really need to know that, now."

One by one, the Killers shook their heads. And, one by one, turned to look at Hunker John.

"Hey!" he said, offended. "That's rude."

Trik growled at the back of her throat. "Hunker . . ."

He held his hands up. "I haven't! I promise. I wouldn't betray Sophie like that!"

"Of course not, Hunk." Sophie shook her head. "Let's not let these fuckers get us at each other's throats. That's how they win. All right?"

She looked at the fossilized branches of an old dead tree as they walked past it, thinking. She came to a decision. "And Ben's right, about New Girl. Avie. She *was* our friend. I'm not saying I trust her, but . . . keep an eye on her for us, yeah, Triks? And if she steps a toe out of line—"

"I'll fold her up and stuff her in a fucking trash chute," Trik said. Then she sighed, and gave both Sophie and Ben a frank look. "Just . . . let's make sure that we're thinking with our brains here, eh? And not any other parts? I'd rather not wake up dead just because you two wanted to have some kind of weird kinky three-way or something."

"Now that is a compelling image!" Hunker John produced a leer. Even Ben chuckled a little.

"Twins *damn,*" he said, and then laughed. It was shaky but rueful. He gave Sophie a wan smile. "I mean, I kind of knew she was here for you, but, man. I thought she liked me a little."

Sophie opened her mouth, wanting to say something comforting, but didn't. Anything comforting would be false, and she couldn't do that to her oldest friend.

"Oh, *Ben,*" Trik said, sighing, "you're worth ten of that creature."

"Amen to that, old man." Bear clapped Ben on his shoulder.

"I'll drink to that one!" Hunker John lifted his flask again. Sophie nicked it out of his hand and took a draught herself, though she felt as far from actually drunk as someone could get. At this point in the night, if she stopped drinking she might just fall over and die.

"Well?" Ben asked, after he'd gotten a good pull off the flask and given the customary yelp as the bitter liquid hit his throat. "What's the plan, Capitana?"

"Fucked if I know," Sophie said. "I took the risk on Crowe, hoping he'd have good news for me, and I got nothing but bad. Not only is Jane Guin after us, but we have to deal with Mr. March, and whoever he's working for, as well. And who knows what this Consort is up to. We only have one lead, and *gods fuck* do I not want to go follow up on it."

"March being a Vesachai?" Bear guessed.

"March being a twins-damned *Vesachai,*" Sophie said. "A rogue one, apparently. But it's the only thing we know about him."

"So we're tracking him down now?" Trik sounded eager.

"I dunno what else to do, Trik," Sophie said. "I was hoping Crowe would . . . well, never mind. Our only chance right now is to find this fucker, squeeze him, and maybe use that as leverage with the Queen."

"Thin," Bear commented. "But it's something!"

"Have we considered the version of the plan," Hunker John said, slurring his words just slightly, "where we just, like . . . give the Book to the Queen? If that's all she wants? Wouldn't that kind of solve all of our problems?"

"John!" Trik said again, scandalized, but Sophie shook her head.

"I will if I have to, Hunk. But I don't think it will get us all the way out of this fire. They need someone to *use* the fucking thing, and I'm the only one qualified. It's not a free pass, and I don't think . . . well, it won't solve all our problems. And I just hate to give her the Book unless I know it's the only way out for us."

Hunker John groaned. And, worse, discovered his flask was empty.

"Damn!" He shook his fist at the far-off heavens. "One tribulation too many! Why have you forsaken me, O Mother Above!"

"At least the group still has its *clown*," Trik said.

"Somebody's gotta balance out all the *bitch*," Hunker said sweetly. Trik gave him a fearsome look.

"Enough," Sophie said, and then frowned. They were near the top of the Ransom Parkway, where it let out onto a wide passageway that branched off in several directions. Sophie saw somebody standing at the top, something about his manner catching her eye. He seemed to be waiting. She frowned.

The man stood easily at the top of the Parkway, his hands folded behind his back, and his smile grew as they drew closer. The smile was clear, despite the obscuring tangler across his face. His green brocade coat was as ostentatious as ever.

"Well, hello there, Sophie!" Mr. March said when she'd gotten close enough. "Now, I know you're easily distracted, but wasn't there something that you're supposed to be *doing*?"

———

"Hello, March," Sophie said, as the Killers fanned out around her. Bear and Trik exchanged a glance, and Bear's hand went up to his knife handle. Sophie noticed that Mr. March was not above giving Trik a leer.

Sophie held out her hand to keep Bear and Trik back. For now. There weren't many people around at this time of night, and a few passersby gave them odd looks. It appeared as if March had come alone. It seemed foolhardy in the extreme, so Sophie kept her eyes roving for anyone who looked like they were with him. He plucked at his brocade sleeves.

"The last time we talked, I seem to remember asking you to open a certain silver vault. The one marked with the slash through the helix? You remember. I can't help but guess, seeing you here, that it is not open."

"The last time we talked, I seem to remember telling you to fuck off."

"I do remember!" Mr. March said, flashing his nasty smile under his tangler. "I hoped you'd reconsidered. In fact, I'd hoped—Ah! One step closer, Bear, and several of you die. Yes?"

March had pulled an efficient and deadly looking chutter from behind his back and had it trained on Bear, who had his knife out and had been sidling closer. Bear looked back at Sophie, uncertainly. She gave him a quick shake of her head.

"In light of recent events," Mr. March said, chutter still aimed at Bear but his eyes on Sophie, "I thought perhaps you'd reconsidered. It's really such an easy little job. I still have the Battle Drugs. There's no reason our original deal can't hold."

"We never made a deal, fuckface."

His mouth quirked under the shifting mask. "Of course we did. We made an agreement that, as long as you opened a certain silver vault, all of your friends would stay alive."

"I think you're overestimating how much I like these pieces of shit."

"I think you're *under*estimating how easy we are to kill." Trik took a step forward. March's chutter swung towards her, but she didn't seem discomfited.

Sophie flung her hand out, warning the girl to stop. "Back up, Trik. I like you when you have your whole face on your skull."

"I can't stress enough how little I'm worried about that."

"Trik!"

March watched this exchange with a half-smile.

"Such a beautiful friendship you all have. I can see why you betrayed your family for it."

"Fuck my family," Sophie said, "and that means fuck you too, from what I hear. Do I know you, then? Were you some jealous little trainee, wishing my dad would smile at you? Some little Vesachai hopeful, who just *really* wanted to be me?"

Mr. March chuckled, but it sounded forced.

Got you, asshole, Sophie thought. Now she'd see if she could get him to show her his cards.

"And now you want to play games with the adults," Sophie continued, looking for flickers of expression beneath the tangler. "But I think you're in over your head, little man. They give you the last name when they give you a silver knife, but that don't mean you get to be *the* Vesachai."

Mr. March raised an eyebrow, conveying vast amusement. "*The* Vesachai? Do you mean *you*? I wonder how your father would feel about that description."

"I'll worry about what my father thinks when he can be bothered to speak to me," Sophie said. "So, what, then? You grow up wondering what's inside that silver vault, and you figure you're going to scare me into showing you? You real- ize I've told the *Queen* to go fuck herself to her face, right? I don't think you've thought through your plan."

Mr. March looked at her for a long moment, as if considering what to say. A grimace flashed across that obscured face, gone in an instant, but Sophie knew her barbs were striking closer to home than he would like to admit.

"Sophie," March said, with a rueful laugh, "you are something. Nobody ever claimed you lacked for genitals! I told my partner it would be pointless to bribe you, nearly as pointless as trying to reason with you. There's no working with the 'Savior of the Keep.'" His finger twitched on the weapon in his hand.

"March," Sophie said. "*Don't.*"

"Yeah, March," Trik took a step towards him, "don't."

The chutter swung back to aim at Trik's face, but she only grinned.

"Try it, motherfucker."

"Trik!" Sophie said. She focused on Mr. March and forced a careless laugh. "Come on. You want to dance, let's dance. You don't need to ruin everybody else's night. I know what you can do; I don't need a demonstration. Let's go meet this 'partner' of yours, and let's fuckin' *dance*. I'm about tired of my night being ruined by this bullshit. You want my pressure point? There it is, right there. You are way out of your depth here, kid."

March laughed, yet there was some desperation in his eyes. "Oh, Sophie! It's funny that you think *I'm* out of my depth. It's truly just fucking funny. I don't know if there's another person in the Keep who knows less about what's really going on tonight than you. Twins damn, Sophie, you don't even know who your *friends* are."

He grunted, and silver-white fire enveloped his forearms, blazing in intricate patterns of argent fire, almost too bright to look at for a moment. He dropped the chutter; he didn't need that now. His eyes blazed nearly as brightly as his arms. He grinned at Sophie, wild, victorious, and probably half mad.

"You never . . ." He winced, and recovered with a shaky laugh. "You never told me how much this *hurt*."

Mr. March had implanted silver; he had paid a visit to Saint Station. She'd suspected it, when she saw the lights go out in the Loche de Menthe, but it was still devastating news. It meant her enemies were willing to go much farther than she'd hoped. She knew better than anyone how dangerous someone could be, with that shit in their arms. She knew how much damage could be done. She tried to pitch her voice low, intimate.

"March, don't. *Don't.* You don't have to do this."

He ignored her. "I want to explain something to you, Sophie. I want to show you why you're in so far over your head you don't realize you're drowning. I want to show you the new shape of the world! I want to introduce you to some new friends of mine. Hah! Though, I think they're old friends of yours. They don't much like the light, though."

March grinned, his face maniacal even through the tangler, and he reached his clawed hand out towards the nearest lightsculpture, a meshwork of silver a few span away. There was a hideous rending sound, and the sculpture grew very bright for a moment, and then, with a snapping sound, went utterly black.

Both Trik and Bear went for him at once. He did something with his other hand, and they went flying back, Bear smacking into an old half-petrified tree. March reached his arm up toward where several lightsculptures hung. The top of the Ransom Parkway was already noticeably dimmer, and Sophie heard shouts of panic and consternation. The few people out at this time of night were frightened and panicking.

"Shit!" Sophie said, but March closed his fist and first one, then another and another lightfixture shattered and went out. The Ransom Parkway was plunged into a dim gloom. Sophie could see, but barely. March let the silver fire die from his arms, and Sophie was gathering herself to leap at him when he scooped up the chutter again. He aimed it straight at her. The perforated nozzle yawned almost pitch black in the dim light. March was breathing heavily, his arms livid and raw.

Implanted silver was powerful, but it cost. She remembered that very well. Behind her, Trik had rolled to her feet but was afraid to move, seeing the chutter aimed at Sophie. Bear was picking himself up painfully, holding his burned arm.

"See you around, Sophie," March said, voice hoarse with pain. "If I were you, I'd open that vault, but honestly, if you don't quite yet, that works for me too. It'll get opened, sooner or later."

"Fuck you." Sophie's jaw was tight. Mr. March had just excised the Ransom Parkway from the Keep, as surely as if he'd cut off a limb. She felt a dim, hateful bitterness at that. "*Fuck* you, man."

March laughed, and in the new Dim, it was loud. What crowds there had been were panicking and running for the exits, where the light was. March turned to go and then turned back as if he'd just thought of something. "Hey, Bear? You're calling yourself Bear these days, right?"

Bear cut his eyes to Sophie, frowning. "Yeah."

March smiled unpleasantly. "That's a good idea. You wouldn't want your friends to find out who you *really* are. Eh? In any case, I have a message for you from my partner."

"Who *is* your fucking partner?" Sophie interrupted.

March ignored her, looking like a little boy with a mean secret. "He says not to make the same mistake twice. Not sure what that means, but he seems to think you'll know."

"Why should I listen to anything you or your asshole partner says?" Bear said, frowning.

"Why?" March asked, delighted. "Because you know him! You might have called him something else, but I call him by his true name: *Candle.*"

Bear didn't move. He looked as if someone had driven a spike through the top of his head and into the floor.

Mr. March seemed pleased by the reaction, though he was still breathing hard through the pain from his arms. "Well! Enough catching up. My friends have arrived. Delightful conversationalists, but their table manners are appalling. If you'll take some advice, you might want to run."

A sound came then, a kind of rotten bellows-and-pump sound, oily and re-pulsive, like badly made clockwork. From the corner of her eyes, Sophie saw the man who called himself Mr. March jog away, but she couldn't spare much atten-tion for him. She knew those sounds. She felt ice fill her veins.

"Um . . ." Hunker John said. "Guys? Friends? What the fuck is that?"

From out of the shadows, Sophie saw a shape resolve, small and hunched, with a too-wide mouth and rows of wicked teeth. It cocked its head, looking at them with curious, tea-cup silver eyes.

"*Ssssisstersss?*" it inquired, in its hideous rotting squeezebox voice. "*Sisssterrsss come?*"

"Hey," Hunker John said, his voice rising in pitch until it was a scream. "What in the fuck is that? *What in the fucking fuck is that?*"

"It's one of the Feral Children," Sophie said, through suddenly numb lips, "and March is right. We need to run."

THE MONSTERS

The Obvious Door

"It's a nightmare, and it's a tumble-down."

—HANNAH D'COURTES, 'SONETTA AND CALVARY'

Jackie and Gun reached their destination in the nick of time. They reached the lights that they'd been falling towards for days, running down the side of the pitch-black mountain, hoping there would be some salvation there, but they just barely made it. They were getting ready to kill each other.

Well, they had *been* trying to kill each other, obviously, but those were isolated, artificial episodes. Whatever bizarre force was prying its way inside their heads and forcing them to feel things, they had developed strategies for dealing with it and found ways to resist. It got easier, if no more pleasant, and for a while now neither of them felt like they were in much danger of actually harming each other. The mental attacks became something like an annoying and persistent friend who liked to drop by unannounced and drink all of your gin while they talked about politics.

The Feral Children, too, had become more an annoyance than danger; they howled from the dark, harrying them, but they didn't attack. In the hours and days since they'd fled the dead city, far behind and above them, they'd been made to try to kill each other maybe fifteen or twenty times. By this time, both Gun and Jackie confidently felt that whoever—or whatever—was fucking with their brains and emotions was getting tired.

No, they weren't getting ready to kill each other because of some malicious external force; they were getting ready to kill each other because of the *boredom*, which had once again reared its ugly head and was starting to say a bit more about the two of them than their situation.

Jackie never could have guessed that being harried by rough-made horrors and psychopathic urges down a pitch-black mountainside on a dead world could get tedious, but *oh boy* was she wrong. She supposed any repetitive action could get dull, but an uncomfortable one doubly so. She wanted to sleep without worrying she'd wake up with Gun's hands around her throat; wanted to have a conversation without ending it trying to stick a knife in Gun's eye. There was no drama or suspense to it anymore; they knew they weren't going to actually kill each other.

They were just waiting for the other shoe to drop, and it was boring as shit.

Worse, Gun had taken to venting his uninformed opinions about the cosmological and ethical implications of persons that could force you to feel things you didn't want to feel. This did not interest Jackie; in her old life she had worked as a bartender and the idea of people trying to manipulate how she felt was as normal to her as the process of drinking itself. The subject didn't interest her, but it *did* annoy her.

That, and the dark. The fucking capital-D *Dark*. It wore on her. It wore on Gun, too, but he responded with mania and speculation where Jackie responded with depression. This Dark was like nothing she'd ever experienced, ever wanted to experience, ever dreamed could be possible. It was an endless strip of fine-grit sandpaper abrading her mind, wearing it inexorably down. Human beings needed light, and far more than the pale silvery glow her floating ball gave out.

It was all awful and uncomfortable and bad, but it was so much worse because it had become awful and uncomfortable and bad and *boring*.

They needed to take a moment, once they finally got to their destination— the set of lights they'd seen, much closer than the distant smattering far down near the bottom of the mountain—and just sort of let the despair sink in. Neither of them was in the best of moods, and it was possible that they had developed some *understandable* but not necessarily *practical* hopes for what they would find at those lights. And now they were looking at them.

"Well, shit," Jackie said, gazing up at the big structure that held the lights.

"Yeah," Gun said.

"I'm not going to cry, Gun," Jackie said, firmly. "I fucking refuse."

"Oh, me neither." A sour rasp was the best he could manage. He looked up at the big, shadowed, utterly dead structure that held a few shining lights near the top. "I wouldn't dream of it."

As if to agree, a Feral Child screamed in the upper darkness behind them. They'd been hearing the screams all around them the past couple of days. They had both convinced themselves that the little bastards were holding off; surely, if they'd wanted, the ill-made monsters could have overtaken them days ago.

Gun heaved a sigh he immediately regretted, clutching at his side. His broken ribs had not been given much of a chance to heal.

Jackie looked at him and considered several comments, eventually deciding on the least harsh one she could manage. "You gonna die?"

"No such luck." Gun examined their surroundings. "Might as well get this fuckin' over with, yeah?"

"I guess," Jackie said. The opening into the big building was dim and dismal. "Ain't like we got anywhere else to go."

"We could keep going down," Gun said, but this was an old fight and one he'd lost already.

"Fuck that. I don't care if they are herding us; I need a fuckin' break from this Dark."

"Yeah, yeah," Gun said. "Well, come on then."

He hobbled toward the structure, and Jackie looked over her shoulder into the shadows the way they came. There was no sign of the dead city far above them, only the thin pale thread of that absurd silver tower that stood atop the mountain and joined the sky. She shivered and followed Gun inside the structure.

It was tall, inexplicable, and dark. It was made of metal plates, or maybe some impressively large slabs of stone. It was forbidding and very old, tucked into a small and relatively flat valley, the kind that occurred between the cliffs and crevasses of the mountain.

The lights at the top, the ones that they'd chased here for days, were high up on the structure and served no purpose that Jackie could discern. They were just there. There seemed to be no other light in the building.

The doors had been broken off by some massive force what looked like a thousand years ago, and lay half-rotten by the sides of the building. This place seemed very different than the dead city on top of the mountain; that place had the air of an abandoned museum, and this had the air of a crypt that a giant rat had eaten. And then shit out.

They realized that the building had mostly caved in a long time ago; rubble lay everywhere. There was an antechamber of some sort, but it was impossible to tell what its purpose had been; it was so full of shattered rock and broken wood. The entrance chamber led to a partially blocked but impressive passageway covered in panels of that semi-translucent material that, in the dead city at least, had given off light. Whatever power those lights had required was long since gone.

They did see a glimpse of light, however, from down the passageway. It was shifting, dim, and silvery, the same kind of illumination that their floating ball gave off. Jackie gripped her walking stick and Gun put his hand on his sword hilt.

There were big rooms off the passageway, some fallen in and some not. Jackie's little light didn't really give off enough illumination to see these clearly, but it was enough to tantalize. In another situation, they would have explored the place, but the shifting light ahead of them and the sounds of the Feral Children encouraged them to keep moving.

In one room, they saw an enormous relief map of a mountain, twice as tall as they were, with a thin silver column climbing up, from the peak to the ceiling above, and a matching silver ring surrounding it, about a third of the way down. In another room, they saw the familiar golden birdbath shape of a Well.

Despite the sounds behind them, they stopped and refilled their supplies. They weren't excited about this; they were very tired of the salty-sweet Well-water and digestible but unexciting food bars that the thing spat out. Eventually they would find out that the Well could deliver a nearly infinite variety of drink and foodstuffs, if you knew how to ask it properly, and they would have a very ironic laugh about *that* one.

There was another scream from a Feral Child, echoing in the ruptured hallway. Gun and Jackie exchanged a look and continued on towards the pale, shifting light. It was partially blocked by big rough debris, but they weren't called Behemoth for nothing, and they quickly cleared enough of it to pass.

Beyond the blockage, they found a big room, roughly oval. The domed ceiling had long since fallen in, leaving rubble everywhere. There were several steps up to a daïs, however, and in the center of that wide space stood a freestanding door made of old gray wood, a twin of the one near the Stairway in the plaza, in the center of the dead city, far above and behind them.

Gun and Jackie exchanged yet another long look, because even from this far away they could see that something bright and silver was attached to the frame of the door with a piece of black tape.

———

Gun and Jackie walked over to the door, studied it for a moment, then exchanged another look. Gun shook his head, amused.

"Yeah," Jackie said.

"A bit obvious, don't you think?" Gun asked. He walked around the door, examining it. "Surprised there's not a goddamn *welcome mat*."

"Didn't want to overdo it, I suppose." Jackie pried up the silver object taped to the door. It was a heavy coin, beautiful and ornate. "What do you want to bet that this coin opens this thing?"

Gun studied the coin, flipping it over. "Wouldn't take that bet. You see that?"

The coin was inscribed on both sides, but on one of the sides there were three thin bars etched into the metal. One of them was glowing; two of them were not.

"Like an amusement park ride," Jackie said. "I'm going to make a crazy prediction here, and stop me when I get too wild—I'm going to say that this little token is good for, say, *three* trips through that door."

"And only one left." Gun looked at Jackie, lifting an eyebrow. "Convenient."

"Yep. Who are these people? And how dumb do they think we are?"

"I dunno." Gun bounced the coin on his hand, thinking. "Maybe they think it doesn't matter how dumb we are, because they've got us by the balls anyway."

"Well I don't like it, and I ain't got any balls," Jackie growled.

"Somebody sure went through some trouble to make sure we go through this door," Gun said. "It's pretty obvious that they herded us here, right?"

"I am a cat, Gunnar," Jackie warned. "I do not like being herded."

"I don't love it myself. So we're decided? Fuck them, fuck their plans, I'll chuck this coin down the mountain?"

"Obviously. Only thing to do," Jackie said. She pulled a face. "Come on, you know we're going to open it. I'm a cat, and cats are curious. Let's get it over with. I'm dying to see what these fuckin' things look like when they open, anyway."

"Okay," Gun said. "Well, here goes some magic. Or whatever."

He reached out for the deeply silver doorhandle, set into the center of the old gray wood. He gripped it, holding the coin, hesitated, and then turned.

The coin in his hand burned cold for a moment. The knob turned slowly, heavily, as if it were connected to a set of gears that turned a great weight. And then it clicked over, and there was a sensation deep in his chest like a thick glass rod snapping, and the door swung open.

Light streamed through the crack, dazzling them. They both stepped back, shielding their eyes against a relative extravagance of light. For a few moments they couldn't see clearly and had to look at the floor, blinking, while their eyes adjusted. And then, finally, Gun and Jackie looked through the door into *somewhere else*.

"Well, ok," Jackie said, after they'd looked for a few minutes. "That is pretty cool. But it's just another shithole."

"Yeah, but it's a bright shithole."

And it was; the door had opened on something that looked like a very dingy basement, albeit one with a glowing ceiling. There were piles of old rubble and trash swept up against the plain, utilitarian walls. Through another door—a normal door, half-open—they could see a passageway that was likewise trashed, dirty, and old. Two of the walls dripped with moisture, and there was a puddle of dank-looking water in the middle of the room. This was the first standing water they'd seen since they came to this world.

"You hear that?" Gun said, and Jackie nodded. Low, almost subsonic, but loud in the stillness of the mountain, came the sound of machinery.

They stood, thinking, and eventually Jackie shook her head.

"Don't like it. Got that strong sense of being herded again."

"Me too." Gun looked around. "Well, what do you want to do?"

"Visitors," she said, pointing. Atop an old, dead light-pillar across the room perched the awful shape of a Feral Child. It was grinning at them, and the pale silvery light from Jackie's floating ball caught its teeth and reflected them.

Gun groaned and unlimbered his sword. He kept the scabbard on; he'd discovered it made a more effective weapon that way, if unwieldy. Jackie got her walking stick ready.

The Feral Child screamed and drove their eardrums about nine inches into their skulls. When they straightened back up, the thing still hadn't moved, but it had been joined by two more.

"Come on," Gun said, tensely. "Get it over with."

But they didn't. Whether they were articulating some strategy of their own or obeying directions from some other, none of the creatures attacked. But they kept coming in, first five and ten and then twenty, thirty, fifty. They seemed to be waiting for something.

"I think the implication here," Jackie said sourly, "is that we should just go through the door."

"Oh, you think?"

Jackie shot him an offended look. "There's no need to be an asshole."

"I'm just saying," Gun said, taking note of the Feral Children amassing behind them, "that this much is obvious. *Why*, is an interesting question."

"I'll give you that." Jackie grunted as one of the awful mechanical robots broke ranks and leaped for her. She'd gotten good with her stick, however. She swung it and cut the thing's face in half, sending a spray of oxide-black teeth out into the crowd of waiting horrors. This seemed to break the logjam, and the fight began in earnest.

"I'm just saying," Gun yelled, swinging his sword through the torso of one of the things and smashing it back into a few of its brethren. "What else are we gonna do?"

"I don't know," Jackie said. "I don't know, Gun! Augh!"

One of the things had dropped, spiderlike, on her head, and started chewing on her face. Jackie didn't seem to care for this sort of greeting and crushed its skull into a handful of broken parts with her free hand. She kicked one of the others, tearing off its leg and sending it flying. A couple were on Gun, spinning teeth bearing down. But running the flat of his palm down his thigh made a ruin of them.

The creatures backed off again, a loose circle around Jackie, Gun, and the door. They hissed and yawned at them, rows of spinning teeth leaking green ichor.

Jackie glanced at Gun. "Just don't like being pushed, man. Whatever we find through that door probably ain't gonna be good."

"Agreed," Gun said, lashing out and catching a Feral Child that had gotten too close, tearing a scabbard-thick hole through its torso, making it scream and fall back. "Question, though."

"Yeah?" Jackie said as the things attacked again. She swung her stick in a wide arc, smashing through the things.

"Will it be better," Gun said, grabbing one of the things by its lower jaw and yanking, "or worse"—he threw the jaw at another of the things—"than this?"

"Point." Jackie got an armful of a few of the automata and squeezed, smashing them into misshapen, screaming pieces of dirty burlap and ratcheting limbs.

Suddenly, Gun was tired of it all.

"Oh, fuck this," he said, wearily, and dropped his sword. "*Fuck* this."

A massive, overwhelming pointlessness came over him. He looked around at the small sea of awful things, and what was even the point? One of them fastened its jaws on his leg, but it didn't matter. They were never going to stop coming. There wasn't any point in fighting.

"Gun!" Jackie hollered, seeing him slump.

"It doesn't matter, Jacks." He was so tired. He decided to just lay down for a bit. If these things wanted to chew on him for a while, then far be it from him to stop them. He crumpled to the floor, crushing a couple of the things, but he didn't much care about that either. What was the point? It would all end in darkness.

"Gun, you *motherfucker*, what are you doing?" Jackie yelled from some infinite distance away. Gun smiled a little. Good ol' Jackie. Always givin' a shit about things.

Distantly, he was aware of black drill teeth breaking his skin in half a hundred places, injecting that disgusting green ichor. He almost wished they would hurry up about it. Didn't that stuff make you numb? Numb sounded good just now. Numb sounded like peace.

A bunch of the Feral Children went away violently. Gun blinked up at Jackie, and she kicked another of the creatures away from him.

"Hey, Jacks," he said. He hoped she wasn't going to make him get up.

"Get the fuck *up,* Gun," she said, and then kicked him in his side to make her point. Gun rolled away from her kicks.

"Stop it!" he whined. "There's no point."

"Come on, man!" She kicked him again. "Fight it!"

And then she went down under a swarm of the awful mechanical things, and Gun felt teeth clamp down on him again. *Oh,* he thought, distantly. This was another of the goddamn *mental attacks.*

Gun heaved a long sigh and lay for a moment, contemplating the unfairness and pointlessness of it all. And then, despite there being absolutely no reason to do it, he worked himself up to one knee and began fumbling around for his sword, incidentally brushing off a few of the parasitic little bastards that were chewing on him.

"Yeah!" Jackie said from somewhere, having regained her feet. "Come on, man!"

"Whatever," Gun murmured and got his sword. He stood up and started swinging, listlessly, knocking aside Feral Children. He *guessed* he could keep going. If he had to.

And then he staggered; life and adrenaline and passion came flooding back into him. Whoever it was that was fucking with his brain, they had stopped.

"Dammit!" he said.

He saw Jackie grin at him, in between demolishing several demon-faces. "Welcome back."

"Thanks." He set about clearing a circle around himself and dislodging the rest of the goddamn spider-things that had fastened themselves to him. He could already feel his limbs going sluggish from the bite-marks; hopefully he hadn't absorbed too much of the poison. The Feral Children backed off again, hissing. There were still an ungodly amount of them left.

"What do you think?" Jackie asked, panting. "Through the door?"

"It's the smart move." He tried to ignore the pain in his side.

"Yeah," Jackie said. She looked back at the open rectangle, then at Gun. "But—"

"Got an option?" he asked.

She looked around and scratched at her neck, then grinned at him.

"We could go through that door, like they clearly want us to," she said, *"or* we could kill every last one of these fucking things, including whoever is fucking with our heads, and *then* decide whether to go through the goddamn door or not."

Gun smiled. He shook his sword hand out, trying to get rid of the numbness before the Feral Children attacked again.

"You know," he said, "I *do* like your style, Aimes."

THE KILLERS

Feral

"Is there any transaction so transparent, so banal, so easy to cheat at, and so rigged as love? It is the lowest-payout game in the system, it's got the worst odds on the table, and it's the most irresistible bet you can find."

—JAKOB 'SIX FINGERS' ADADE, 'NUMBERS GAME'

"We need to run," Sophie said again, looking at the monster that had climbed up out of the shadows, and her past, and her nightmares.

"Yes," Ben said, trembling. "*Right now.*"

"Holy shit, I don't like those things." Hunker John's voice was thin with fear. Another one of the Feral Children climbed atop a newly ruined lightsculpture and yawned, its head opening impossibly wide. What little light was left glinted off its spinning black teeth.

She shuddered hard, and the thing snapped its jaws closed. It seemed to grin at them.

"*Sssissstersss!*" it cried, and then let loose one of those eardrum-shattering, world-ending screams that Sophie remembered from her childhood. Sophie gave Hunker John a shove and grabbed the back of Trik's tunic. But the girl was immovable, looking at the monsters.

"Trik!" Sophie screamed in her ear. "*We have to go!*" Fortunately it broke whatever internal struggle Trik was having, and she turned to run with the rest of them.

And just in time; Sophie saw another Feral Child materialize out of shadow. Trik started into a shambling run. The Killers got up to the top of the Ransom Parkway, heading towards the faint light of a passageway. Trik brought up the rear, jogging half-backwards to keep her eyes on the awful things. Sophie, fleetingly, wondered what in the *hell* had gotten into Trik tonight; she seemed to have a death wish.

They cleared the top of the Parkway. Fortunately Mr. March's killing of the lights had already made people run. Sophie had seen before what these Feral Children could do to unarmed civilians and she had no interest in seeing it again.

"We just have to get to the light!" Sophie yelled, pointing ahead at the glowing mouth of a tunnel. "They don't like bright light!"

One of the things screamed again, the sound so loud it seemed to drive itself five span deep into Sophie's skull. Hunker John dropped to his knees, and Bear slowed to scoop him up. Sophie saw four figures burst out of the passageway, four figures that at any other time would have made her run the other way, but now made her sag in relief. They were Practice Guard, and they were armed with big, brutal chutters.

"Run, you idiots!" The leader motioned to them. Sophie looked behind and saw the Feral Children were right behind them. Trik had lagged so far behind that the leading creature was almost on top of her. One of the Practice Guard, an almost miraculously competent one, fired from the hip and the Feral Child behind Trik dropped back. Sophie and the Killers passed the line of Practice Guard, who all had their weapons up, getting ready to fire.

"Don't try to fight them," she yelled to the Practice Guard, panting as they passed. "Get to the light!"

But these Guard were young; they hadn't fought in the Hot Halls War. They didn't know these monstrosities. They held their ground, and Sophie shook her head, swearing. The Killers reached the mouth of the entrance, and Sophie couldn't help but stop and turn.

The Practice Guard all fired in unison, and one of the Feral Children jerked back with a screaming hiss, part of its right arm and torso erased in a hail of flechettes. But it was far from dead, Sophie knew, and there were two more. A lucky Practice Guard hit one of the others straight in the face, temporarily blinding it and shredding that awful burlap skin. And then the undamaged one reached the four soldiers.

"*Shit!*" Sophie cried, wishing they would have listened to her and unable to look away. The Feral Child, grinning, yawned its mouth open wide and came down on one of the Practice Guard's shoulders, sawing away most of the man's torso in a spray of blood and torn flesh. He barely had time to scream before the creature's talons found his face, squeezed, and smashed his head into four sections. Sophie felt strong hands grab her tunic and drag her: Trik.

"Come on, Capitana. I'm not letting you anywhere near Feral fucking Children."

Sophie saw the wounded Feral Child claw its way, almost joyfully, at a Practice Guard who was firing his chutter madly in its direction, too panicked to aim. As she watched, she saw the horrible thing get one of its silvery talons into the man's foot and pull him down. In half a second, he was a bloody ruin.

"They're already dead," Sophie said. She heard a long gurgling scream from behind her and didn't turn to look.

The passageway was bright after the artificial Dim of the Ransom Parkway.

Sophie looked over her shoulder and then slowed to a stop. One of the Feral Children hovered at the entrance, blinking, hissing in frustration. But it would not enter the light. It gave off an eardrum-ending scream and slunk away.

"Oh, Mother-fucking-the-Twins-*damn*," Hunker John moaned, panting. "Fuck, I really *did* piss myself now."

"Yeah, Hunk," Ben said, "me too."

"What in the *fuck!*" Trik said. "What in the fuck are fucking *Feral Children* doing in the Keep?"

Sophie sank down to her knees. She was trembling.

"I thought those things were all dead." Trik's voice was low and shaking. "I thought they were all fucking *dead*."

Sophie started to shake. Her fists were so tight two of her fingernails broke the skin of her palms.

"Is that the kind of thing you fought in the war?" Hunker John said, voice shaky, fumbling for his secondary flask. "Holy Mother, I'm a fool."

"I *hate* those goddamn things," Trik muttered. She was looking at the end of the tunnel, as if she could barely restrain herself from running back and tangling with them.

Sophie squeezed her eyes tight for a long moment, trying to shut out memories. She felt a hand on her shoulder, concern in the touch. It was Ben.

"Sophie? What's wrong?"

"What's wrong," Sophie took a deep, shaking breath, "is that March brought *Feral Children* into the Keep, for the first time since the Hot Halls War. And there's only one group of people equipped to fight *those* Twins-damned things, and I was already trying to find every last reason not to go talk to them."

She lifted her head and rubbed her eyes. They looked haunted. "I've got no choice, now, not with those things loose. I've got to go talk to my fucking family."

Nobody knew how to react to that, except for Hunker John, who silently extended her his backup flask.

She took it.

AN ASIDE: THE TWO POINTS

The Wanderlands, it is sometimes said, hangs swinging between two immovable points: the White Tower and the Mountain. Between the Nine and the Cold. Between the Silver and the Black-and-White.

That's true enough, at least in these lost and broken days.

There was a time when the Cold wizards traveled throughout the Wanderlands, working with the Nine to create wonders. A time when the leader of the Nine, the Lady Winter, and the creator of the Cold, Hunter Fine, were not only friends but lovers. Together they built the Silver Age. Together, the Nine and the Cold worked for the betterment of all.

No longer; alas, no longer. Both organizations underwent fundamental changes during the Fall, that terrible time when the skies above so many Lands cracked open and belched forth gloom. The two groups became estranged and then became enemies.

The Nine you will know more of: they flooded their great Tower-City with light, making it into the White Tower, and began building their empire of Doors and fear. They turned their backs on the Silver-magic and embraced the wild magic, the uncontrollable, the terrifying and wonderful Black-and-White. They became powerful and strange. They gathered their Deadsmith and discovered that cruelty is more effective than love, when the world is ending.

The Cold, in contrast, started to make a worship of Silver. Once a military organization of technicians, they became something more like priests. They withdrew from the Wanderlands save for extraordinary need, and gathered in their city atop the Mountain, protected by their silver wall. Emissaries of the Nine were dealt with cruelly, for to the Cold they had become blasphemers and abominations.

The Cold gathered all the powerful Silver-Age relics they could find and began to view these one-time tools as holy. Only persons of extraordinary gifts and dedication were permitted to wield them. Above all of these artifacts, they revered the Cold-Keys.

Over the course of many hundreds of years, the Cold scoured all known Cold-Keys from the Wanderlands and found a place to keep them that would be proof against any incursion from the Nine. Even the Cold themselves were no longer permitted to use these powerful tools. They dreamed that someday their faith and self-sacrifice would be rewarded by the Mother's Grace. For many hundreds of years, to be found with a Cold-Key, anywhere in the Wanderlands, would mean your death.

The Nine, meanwhile, with the help of their Deadsmith, grew their gossamer empire of Black-and-White in the shadows. The Cold were seen more and more rarely in the Wanderlands, and the world ground on implacably towards its end.

And then, not so long ago, all of the Cold disappeared. Their city on top of the Mountain was abandoned, cleaned of any artifacts or trace of their existence. The Nine reached claws towards the Mountain, one of the last places in the Wanderlands where they held no sway, claws that had always before been cut off.

There was no response; the Cold were gone. Where? No one knew. There was no hint of them, not in any Land, not in any corner of the Wanderlands. Some said they escaped to the Land of Forest, to be with the Giants, but this is ludicrous. The Giants hate nothing so much as the Cold. Still, people looked, and no one found anything. Nobody knew where the Cold went.

It might have been more productive to wonder about why they all disappeared. And how much their disappearance had to do with the sudden appearance in the Wanderlands, after so long, of the Mother's Call. You know what I speak of: the dreams of Giants, and Silver Artifacts, and the end of the world.

—*An excerpt from 'Two Points: The Mountain and the Tower,' by Bind e Reynald, Scholae First Mark.*

THE MONSTERS

In the Belly of Some Strange Beast

"Savor the sun, my froward one, savor the bright of the day."

—UDHAY KELLER, 'THE GOOD DEATH OF ST. MARIE'

Gun and Jackie went through the door, of course. What? Were they going to stay and make a fire among the hundreds of new corpses they'd made? Were they going to toast their victory with Well-water, surrounded by their massacre? That was impractical as well as silly. The monsters had proved to their own satisfaction that they wouldn't be shoved around. They were not going to be easily herded. They were masters of their own destiny!

. . . and all that.

But it had been a shit-kicker of a fight. The Feral Children had been seemingly inexhaustible, flooding out of the shadows in a never-ending wave. Both Gun and Jackie had gone down several times and been assaulted mentally a few more times, but even though the Feral Children had bitten them with those drill-teeth in half-a-hundred places, they couldn't bring them down entirely. The Behemoth lived up to their name, and they just killed the living shit out of the creatures. When they were done, there were literal piles—in some places waist-deep—of the fucking things.

The fact that they had just massacred piles and piles *and piles* of speaking things, mostly because they'd been feeling stubborn, was a thought that occurred to them but was quickly discarded. After the fight was over, it only took a few minutes for them to decide to go through the suspiciously convenient door.

Of the shadowy presence that was messing with their minds, they felt nothing. It was too bad; they would have killed whoever was doing *that* with no compunction whatsoever.

They were from a world where murder was extremely uncommon, and they still weren't sure that the Feral Children qualified for that heavy word, but *that* fucker? The fucker that was fucking with their heads? Gun was convinced he could do murder, for *that* fucker.

In any case, actually going through the door was something of an anticlimax; Gun at least had been expecting some viscous sensation of travel, an icy shiver down his spine or some such, but it had felt like walking through any other door. Of course, at this point they were both full of so much of that green ichor, the numbing toxin from the Feral Children's teeth, that they could very well have merely missed the sensation.

"Well," Jackie said. The door swung closed behind them, blocking off the sight of their massacre.

"Well," Gun said. He flipped the token they'd gotten from the door to Jackie, and she examined it. None of the bars were glowing now. She tried the handle, just for kicks, and it was as solidly closed as the one in the dead city had been. She shrugged and flipped it into the puddle of dank water.

"Another shithole." Jackie looked around. It was a big round room, with a ceiling of chipped rock; they were undoubtedly underground. It looked as if it may have been richly furnished at one time, but anything of value had been pried up or broken and carried away. It had the air of a long abandoned basement. There were three ways out, all doorways that led into other dingy rooms, not as well lit as this one.

"A shithole," Gun agreed, wry. "But at least the ambiance is nice."

"Yeah, that sound is going to get real old, real fast," Jackie said. The low rumble of machinery they'd heard through the door was much louder now, and unpleasant.

"What do you think it is?" Gun asked, examining the walls.

"Fucked if I know. Giant mechanical monster? Something drilling a hole into hell? The grandmother of those goddamn Feral Children?"

"Stop being so cheerful," Gun murmured. "Hey, come look at this."

Jackie limped over to him; her right leg was still completely numb. Gun was looking at a doorframe daubed with red paint, faded but unmistakable. They exchanged a look.

"Convenient," Jackie said.

"Yeah, maybe. It's old, though."

"Yeah, so?"

"So maybe it ain't part of whatever's going on with us."

"Maybe," Jackie said, doubtfully. She squinted into the gloom through the other two passageways. "What do you think?"

Gun shrugged. "Fucked if I know. Looks like a maze. I vote we follow the red."

"Ahhh, I don't like it, man."

"What about any of this is to *like*, Jacks?"

"Yeah." Jackie sighed. "All right."

"Okay?"

"Yeah, I just hope we ain't gotta murder no more motherfuckers," Jackie muttered.

"They're just robots, Jacks," Gun said, but they both knew that probably wasn't true. There really wasn't a whole lot else to say, however, so he limped his way through the red-daubed door frame. "And at least the mental attack shit has stopped."

"For now," Jackie said. "Till whoever the fuck was *doing* it comes through that goddamn door."

"Yeah," Gun said, looking around the dismal room they found themselves in, and seeing another old daub of red paint on the far exit. He stopped and looked at Jackie. She gave his sword a speculative look.

"Can't come through the door if the door doesn't work."

"Well, shit, Jacks," Gun said, catching her idea and brightening right up. "It *would* be nice to find something useful to do with this thing."

They retraced their steps and found the big freestanding door in the middle of the room. Gun drew his sword, looked critically at the structure, and adjusted his grip.

"I'd say maybe from the right side, down to the left?" Jackie said diplomatically.

"I know how to use my sword, Jacks."

Jackie hid a smile. "I'd do it soon, is all I'm saying. I don't want to meet whoever walks through that thing. Probably the asshole who was making us want to kill each other."

"Look, do you want to do it?" Gun asked, annoyed.

"Yes."

Gun blinked. "Well . . . you can't."

"You're such a fuckin' batch of limp genitals, Gunnar. Do it already!"

Disgruntled, Gun swung the sword at the side of the doorframe and probably harder than he needed to. The door did not care for this kind of treatment and responded with an explosive shockwave of energy that sent both of the monsters tumbling back through a series of old stone walls, throwing them around like leaves in a hurricane.

When Gun was able to pick himself up to his aching feet, his hand tried to stabilize some ribs that really, *really* needed to not get re-broken every few hours. Then he stumbled back towards the door.

Jackie was wrenching his sword from the foot-long furrow he'd cut into the thing. She turned, grinning, covered in dust. "Wimp. You do it like *this*."

"Jackie!" Gun yelled, but there were no more explosions. Whatever intrinsic force the door held was expended already. She swung the sword once, twice, and hacked the ancient door into pieces. When she'd finished, she laughed, a little wildly, and handed the sword back to Gun.

"I hope that cheered you up." He put the sword back in its scabbard.

"You know, it kind of did." Jackie wiped dust off her face. "I was starting to get down about the whole, *you know*. Murdering a couple hundred creatures just because we were feeling stubborn. But this made me feel a lot better. Thank you."

"Yeah, well. Anytime."

But Jackie saw that something else had fallen victim to the blast, and she picked the thing up gently. It was the little floating light-ball that had followed her so faithfully and provided illumination in such dim times. "Oh!" she said, frowning. It was half caved-in and would fly no more.

"Shit," Gun said. "Hope it don't get dark down here."

Jackie eyed him severely. "Show some respect. I liked this thing a lot more than I like you."

"Well that don't take much. Can we go? Or do we gotta have a funeral? Say some kind words for the poor dead glowing ball?"

Jackie glowered at him, but tossed the broken thing over her shoulder and followed. She wasn't about to stage a funeral for a *flashlight*.

———

They'd been walking for what felt like hours when Jackie suddenly stopped, causing Gun to run into her. He was holding his side, and the collision did him no favors. He spent a few moments trying not to scream.

"Gun," she said, hoarsely. He opened his eyes and looked.

Against the wall at the end of the long passageway was light. Bright light. Brighter than any they'd yet seen down here. Brighter even than any they'd seen in the dead city on top of the mountain. As they watched, something—*something*—threw a shadow across it as it passed.

"Oh, shit," Gun breathed. They exchanged a long look. The mechanical sound, almost inaudible after so long an exposure, seemed to grow loud. There was another sound too, tinny and echoing, an irregular rhythm that unnerved them greatly. It wasn't the same as the mechanical sound, which had grown so commonplace they hardly heard it now.

They exchanged a long look, and Jackie nodded.

"We got to. We have to see."

"I know," Gun said. He took a deep breath, gripped Jackie's shoulder for support, and they made their way down the long corridor.

They reached the bend, the corner where the light shone, and Jackie edged up to it. She sketched one eye past the edge, looked for a moment, and drew back.

"What?" Gun whispered.

She shook her head. "I don't know. It's too bright. I can't see."

"Let me try." Gun poked a sliver of his eye past the corner.

The passageway ran for maybe twenty feet and then opened out onto somewhere *bright*. Very bright, too bright. Even this far away it hurt Gun's eyes a little. He could see nothing, just an irregular patch of radiance, but as he watched, something crossed the opening. It was impossible to discern the shape of the thing, but it threw a shadow.

He drew back. He was breathing hard. The pain in his side was forgotten.

"Okay," Jackie said.

Gun nodded. "Yeah. We are indestructible badasses. We will survive. Whatever this is. Okay."

They edged around the corner and crept slowly towards the light.

Something crossed the rectangle of brilliance again, making them pause, but they forced themselves to start moving again. The odd, tinny sound grew more robust, more modulated, and it set their teeth on edge. Its irregular, staccato rhythm grew more pronounced.

After what seemed like hours but could have been barely minutes, they reached the opening. They had to shield their eyes against the light. Gun saw green, then, a too-bright green that reminded him fleetingly of the Feral Children's green poison ichor, but nothing attacked them. He blinked against the glare, and another shadow passed.

"Gun," Jackie said, and her voice was tight with some barely controlled emotion. "Gun. It's music."

For a moment Gun couldn't imagine what she was talking about, and then what he was hearing resolved itself. That maddening, staccato rhythm was just that; a staccato rhythm. Drums, of some sort, very muffled, but he could hear the hollow thump of bass and some ringing patterns played on wood-blocks, maybe, or even cymbals.

His eyes were adjusting to the glare now. He saw first a wall of dressed stone, fitted and mortared, across from them. The green he'd seen was delicate ivy, climbing all over it.

Growing ivy. *Alive*. It was the first green and growing thing they had seen since coming to this world.

"Gun . . ." Jackie sank to her knees. She was looking up, and Gun squinted past the glare to see what she was looking at. Another shadow passed and halted. He saw that the dressed stone formed a bridge, above them and to the left, which ran from a building into . . . somewhere. The shadow was thrown by a large, placid animal laden down with heavy bags of grains, squash, and foodstuffs. It was led by a *woman*, who had paused to admonish her child, a belligerent towheaded boy. She gave him a smack on his bottom and then a hug to soften it, and then they were on their way. All around them Gun could hear the rich, wonderful sounds of people talking, laughing, bartering, yelling. The unmistakable sounds of a living city.

"Well, *shit*," he said, his voice cracking, and he collapsed up against the wall, still inside the passageway, and put his head in his hands. His body shook, and whether he was laughing or crying Jackie didn't know and was too busy laughing or crying herself to ask.

THE KILLERS

Charm Chairs

"Family's just whoever is left once your friends have all fucked off."
—AVON HARRISON JR., 'ASPOLETH'

There wasn't much wind in the Keep, and very little in the way of cool breezes. The Keep was, for the most part, an enormous hunk of inert stone, tunneled through with passageways, boulevards, huge factory spaces, dining-halls, and apartments, but there were nothing like the circumstances that would create pressure systems or weather. Air circulated gently, only occasionally gathering enough force to blow some hair around.

It was one of the nice things about riding in a Charm Chair; they were one of the only conveyances in the Keep that moved quickly enough to make their riders feel a breeze. Sophie scratched her fingernails along her scalp, enjoying the sensation, and saw New Girl—*Avie*—next to her, doing the same. Sophie rested her arm on the ornately padded armrest that lined the ornate contraption and watched the Keep sway by below her. Normally only Lords and the rich rode in these conveyances, and it was easy to see why they did. There was something dreamlike about floating above the mass of humanity below, something slyly comfortable about slipping through the Keep's rarified air. Sophie had spent extravagantly for the privilege; after the Killers encounter with the Feral Children, she had no time to waste and Charm Chairs were the fastest way to get around. She had picked up Avie and was now on her way to the last place in the Keep she wanted to go.

She should be thinking about the coming interview; she should be thinking about a lot of things. She should be thinking about why, exactly, she had spent the time to go pick up the perplexing blonde next to her. She should be thinking about what kind of an opponent she had in Mr. March and his partner, this mysterious *Candle*. She should be trying to understand the kind of person who would bring Feral Children into the Keep.

Hell, she should be worrying about the Killers, and the bullshit errands she'd sent them on. She should be trying to make plans, trying to figure a way out of the trap that she could almost physically feel tightening around her and her friends.

Instead, she was thinking about a fire, and she was thinking about her Uncle Liam.

The fire had been way out, far beyond the bounds of the Keep, deep into the depthless black of the Underlands, the long-dead civilization that surrounded them. It wasn't the first time Sophie had been out in the Dark, for her and the Killers had been sneaking across the Bridges and poking around in the abandoned rooms near the Keep for years. But this was the last time, the bad time.

This was the time that Denver Murkai had taken her deep into the black, a long way out into the Underlands. Oh, she had wanted to go; she had been dreaming of exploring the Big Dark her whole young life, and the Dream of Trees had only sharpened this thirst. Denver had not had to drag her. At the time, it had seemed a grand adventure, a thrilling expedition. For the first time, Sophie got a sense of how big the Underlands was, how monumental the dead civilization that surrounded the Keep really was. There were open spaces that dwarfed any in the Keep; there were mechanisms and devices so large and inexplicable they staggered her imagination. There was even a little light left, here and there, old lightfixtures guttering dimly in the black, old machines muttering to themselves in the gloom. She had been transfixed; at this point, she had just recently found the Book and still had the memory of trees, sunshine, Giants, and silver bright in her mind. She dreamed of bringing light back to these abandoned halls. Of seeing what these great automata might do, if they woke up.

And then she got her answer; she met the silver angel that called itself Saint Station, with its blinded eyes and silver teeth, dripping blue antiseptic. That extraordinary construct, half building and half statue, waiting for long years in darkness.

The Giant Lies Still Awake, Sophie Vesachai, that immense creature had said, as it picked her up in its silver-taloned hands, *And the World Needs Weapons.*

But that's not what she was thinking about, riding in the Charm Chair, headed inexorably towards her original home, though she scratched unconsciously at the scars on her arms as she did. She wasn't thinking about those teeth—though they weren't teeth at all, no more than Saint Station was an angel—that had torn apart her arms and began the long, awful process of laying silver along her bones. She was thinking about later, about a fire, about Uncle Liam.

He had come out to save her. Denver Murkai, either losing his nerve or by design, had run from what was happening to Sophie. He always maintained that he'd been run off by the Feral Children that prowled around Saint Station, but in later years Sophie began to suspect this story. In any case Ben and Crazy Tom went to her Uncle Liam when they realized she was missing, and he had gone to find her erstwhile tutor. She'd never known what Liam did or said to Denver, but the young man had led the older one back out into the Dark, back to Saint Station, where they found Sophie unconscious, her arms stitched up but still weeping blood, moaning about Giants and weapons and dreams of Silver Books.

Liam had nursed her back to health. He'd found a Well, sent Denver back to the Keep, and spent long weeks in the Dark with Sophie as she convalesced. She remembered that fire, the slow returning back to herself, the nightmares of dripping blue teeth and agony. Always Uncle Liam was there, soothing her, holding her when she needed to be held. In the big, suddenly terrible darkness around them, they heard the lonesome screams of Feral Children. But those never attacked; they just circled.

They were saving their strength for the Hot Halls War.

But this was before all of that. Back then, there was just a fire, and Uncle Liam. Sophie remembered the bleak look in her Uncle's eyes, the long hours he spent looking into the fire. And she remembered, too, when he finally judged her fit to travel back to the Keep, and when he finally judged her strong enough to hear the truth.

Sophie would never be able to complete the training, he told her, never become a fully bonded Vesachai. She would never wield the Rapine, and she would never take her place in the ranks of her family. It was worse; though Liam had been careful to stress that it had been no fault of her own, Sophie had been implanted with a kind of technology that was forbidden by tradition, rule, and law. Sophie now bore, under her skin, the very thing that the Vesachai held as their entire duty to stamp out and prevent. She had been touched by the old, forbidden, powerful forces of the world.

Sophie was Proscribed.

Liam, thankfully, did not try to explain to Sophie the political ramifications of the First Vesachai's own daughter being Proscribed, nor the coup that was soon to happen when the Queen used the scandal to break the Vesachai's power and bring them fully under her control. No, she remembered her big, bluff Uncle Liam, holding her small hand in that firelight, tears standing in his eyes but never falling, explaining how Sophie's life would have to change.

She was under a death-sentence now, and nothing could be done about that. Proscription was, perhaps, the core tenet of the Vesachai's beliefs; all else was built on it. They considered themselves the guardians of the ancient magic, the true descendants of the Cold, the last barrier the world had to anarchy and ruin. They knew the damage that could be wrought by indiscriminate—even accidental— use of Silver. There was only one punishment for Proscription, for touching the forbidden: death.

But Uncle Liam had explained to Sophie that there was, *just maybe*, a loophole. He explained to Sophie that, because she had not chosen to be implanted with dangerous silver, she might survive. If she kept her arms covered, perhaps. If she never spoke of what happened, *perhaps*. And most importantly, imperatively, supremely: if she never, *ever* used the powers Saint Station had given her.

Never. Not once.

Liam had explained, jaw working, his big hand trembling, that if she ever used the silver wrapped around the bones of her arms, even once, for *any* reason, her family would have no choice but to pull their knives and come for her. Yes, even her father. Yes, even *him*. Sophie remembered the firelight wavering in his eyes, the compassion and fear there, trying to make his headstrong and precocious niece understand the danger she was in.

Sophie remembered, looked out of the side of the Charm Chair, the baroque stonework of this part of the Keep sliding past. She almost smiled.

She had understood the danger. She really had; she had taken it seriously. She had promised her Uncle, sworn on every god she could think of, that she would never use what Saint Station had given her. It had taken her almost three months to break that promise. And it wasn't even the Hot Halls War that had done it; it had just been a friend in trouble. Luet, when she had met her first Feral Child.

In the Charm Chair, Sophie yawned and patted her pockets. She found a slot, scraped it alight, and then found Hunker John's purloined flask. She examined it for a long moment, then took a draught. She held it out but New Girl—Avie— just gave it a look.

"Are you sure that's the best idea, right now?"

Sophie tucked the flask away, tasting the burn on her lips. "If I stop drinking at this point, I might die."

"If you keep drinking, you're definitely going to."

"What are you, my mom?" Sophie said, annoyed. "She died when I was two and I'm not looking for another. Anyways, why don't you figure out how you can help me? Since you don't appear to be ready to tell me anything."

"I've told you what I'm willing to," Avie said.

"Not very fucking much. A line about some trees isn't going to last you very long. Not tonight, anyways."

"I really don't know anything that can help you right now, Sophie. You know who's doing this; Mr. March and somebody named Candle. I've told you that I've heard of him, and that he's bad business. And no, *again,* I don't know who Mr. March is. That's it."

"Not fucking much," Sophie muttered again, trying to forget about Uncle Liam and the fire. It wasn't going to help. It just made her think of the shattered look on her brother's face when she'd told him what happened. Poor Lee, caught between idolizing his big sister and her sudden fall from grace.

Sophie shifted, restless, dreading the coming encounter. She looked at Avie, her finely sculpted profile, her long fair hair. "So what did you mean, 'bring the trees back'? Is that a metaphor or some shit?"

Avie smiled, faintly. "No. Not a metaphor. And it's not just trees that I want to bring back; I want to bring the sun back, the sky. All of it. Stop looking at me like that; I am not crazy. Well—not *entirely* crazy."

For a second Sophie could *see* it, the unbroken sky above the Wanderlands, in the vivacity of the dream. Her face twisted. "I hate to break it to you, New Girl, but that dream was a lie. Just a way for some powerful people to get some kids to find some shit for them. If there are any trees left in the world, they're dead and sitting under a black sky. There's no sun, no Giant. It's just assholes with agendas. Assholes with agendas, all the way down."

Avie turned to look at her, green eyes vivid. "My name is Avie. And I'm not talking about the dream."

"You said—"

"I never had the dream." Avie looked out over the edge of the Charm Chair, as if remembering something distasteful. "Never that lucky, I guess."

Sophie frowned. "Then why are you talking about trees? What the fuck is *your* agenda?"

"Just what I said it was. Look, I'm not going to explain right now. Maybe later. No offence, but I don't know if the Book is any safer in your hands than the Queen's. I'm going to hold some cards to my chest until I'm sure about you."

"Until *you're* sure about *me*," Sophie said, snorting. "That's rich. You infiltrated my gang, seduced my friend . . ."

Avie laughed. "Ben didn't take much seduction. And who says I didn't like Ben? He's sweet."

"You don't get to talk about Ben. He really liked you."

Avie gave her a level look. "How many lovers have you stolen from Ben? Are you saying you would have resisted, if I'd tried to seduce *you?* Come on. We're all adults here. Ben knew the score."

"Maybe I'm not so cavalier with other people's feelings."

"That might be the funniest thing I've ever heard you say."

"You know what? How about we go back to the thing where we sit in sullen silence, and I reminisce about something pleasant, like my fucking family."

Avie drummed her fingernails on the edge of the Charm Chair's padded rest. "How about you tell me why you really split the Killers up? It seems bad strategy, on a night like this. Since you know your enemies are gunning for them."

It was Sophie's turn to offer a level look. "I don't think explaining my intentions to *you* is sound strategy."

Inexplicably, Avie grinned, as if flattered. "Can I guess?"

Sophie gave her a shooing motion with her hand, which Avie took for assent. She bounced a little.

"I think," she said, "it's because Mr. March keeps finding you."

Sophie stiffened, just a little, but Avie saw it and nodded. "That's it! First in the Loche de Menthe, then in the Dream of Trees bar. They knew exactly where to find you. And then again, on the Ransom Parkway; March was waiting for you. You split the Killers up and kept me with you, because you think *I'm* the reason. That I've been signaling March, somehow."

Sophie sighed. "You're very clever. Bravo."

"But I'm *not* the reason. So, I hope the rest of the gang is safe."

"What do you care?" Sophie asked, rudely. Avie looked affronted.

"I've spent the last three months hanging out with you guys. It was fun, even if I had . . . an ulterior motive. I don't want anything to happen to the Killers, Sophie."

"Me neither." Sophie stifled a short yawn. "And anyways, I didn't scatter them just to test a theory. They're all trying to scrape up something—*anything*—that can help us get out of this mess. Which is the same thing that we are doing."

"Speaking of which," Avie said, with a touch of reluctance in her voice, "I may have something like that to offer. *If* I decide you can be trusted. If things go badly."

Sophie frowned. "What?"

"Not 'what,' 'who.'"

"Fine. Who?"

Avie looked at her, pensive for the first time since Sophie had unmasked her on the Gallivant. "A friend. He drinks a lot, unfortunately."

"I like him already. Could you stop being coy? Who is he and how can he help?"

"Well, he used to be . . . someone pretty important. He's old, very old, as old as the Queen maybe. Extremely capable, when he can be persuaded to be. If it comes down to a fight—and we can find him, and he's not too drunk—he could do a lot of damage. Maybe he could counter some of the forces against us. Well, against you. You know what I mean."

"Twins damn, I am getting tired of cryptic answers tonight."

"Everything about him is cryptic." Avie's green eyes were troubled. "He used to be one of those 'powerful forces' in the world you keep talking about. Those that you might call *The Wise*."

———

All of the Houses in the Keep were, to one degree or another, artificial constructs— a way to impose a warlord mentality on a place that was not in any way designed for it. The interior of the Keep, for as long as anyone could remember, was in a semi-constant state of flux as Lords gathered and lost power, privilege, and territory. Some of their borders were mostly theoretical and enforced lightly, and some were heavily barricaded and well-guarded.

Jane Guin, when she took bloody possession of the Keep and installed herself as its Queen, put a stop to a lot of the infighting, but it still happened from time to time. Sections of an area were annexed and makeshift walls were installed. Territory was reclaimed and passageways were un-blocked. Traditionally, however, there was one house that never gained or lost any territory, one house that never needed to defend itself: House Vesachai.

The section of the Keep where Sophie grew up may have been some sort of barracks or training grounds back in the dawn ages of the Keep; it was certainly austere and held an indefinable military air that the Vesachai took pains to reinforce. Sophie had liked it when she was a child; she'd been enamored of military things to the point of obsession. The austerity had made her feel that she and her family were fundamentally tougher and more competent in some essential way, with no need for soft pleasures.

Now that she was older and knew quite a bit more about the subject of soft pleasure, she thought that austerity could be just as much an affectation as luxury. Having plain walls isn't the same as hardship, and most Vesachai were just as soft as any Lord's valet. It was something to keep in mind as she put herself inside the jaws of the cat.

She called the Charm Chair to a halt in the large plaza just outside of the entrance to Vesachai House. The smooth contrivance knelt down to let her and Avie climb out, its long spindly legs grumbling a little. Sophie recalled the Charm Chair they'd toppled on the Rue de Paladia, back in the . . . was that only a handful of hours ago? Mother Above, it felt like days. This was already a long night.

The plaza outside of the large, well-lit entrance to Vesachai House contained a concert-space, a big teardrop-shaped arena with a stage at the bottom and tiered steps leading down to it. There was some sort of late-night jug-band playing for tips; at this distance the sound was muffled and staccato. The upper tier served as a curved boulevard of sorts, leading to other parts of the Keep.

It was strange, being back here. She had not been here in many, many years. The times she had walked across this plaza, with Ben and Tom in tow. The times she'd played on the steps of that amphitheater with her little brother Lee, always forcing the poor kid to be the Outkeep bandit in their games. For a moment, she saw a young man passing below with dark hair and her heart spasmed. *Lee?*

But, no. It was just a passerby, not even a Vesachai. Sophie thought she could face who she'd come here to see, but she prayed that she wouldn't encounter her brother. She'd abandoned him in this place, to these people, to her family. No, she didn't want to see her fucking brother just now. Not tonight.

Sophie took a deep breath, jerked her chin Avie's way. "Come on. Let's see if we survive this."

"Whatever you say, Capitana," Avie said. She hummed a little along with the band playing down below, as they walked toward the rectangle of litstone that marked Sophie's home. Sophie glanced at her sidelong, her strikingly blonde hair glowing against the stage lights behind her.

Trees. Huh.

They approached the entrance to Vesachai House, and the two young Vesachai that guarded it, as was custom. They were both male—though the Vesachai were, overall, largely female—and understandably paid more attention to Avie as the two of them approached. Sophie, however, had no intention of actually entering her home, at least not via the front entrance. She was self-destructive, but she wasn't suicidal.

"Hello, citizens," the shorter of the two guards said, pleasantly, his eyes mostly on Avie. He gave Sophie a quick once-over. And then his eyes cut to her scarred wrists, then back up to her face. It was somewhat gratifying to see the blood physically drain out of his face when he realized who she was.

"Hello, Trainee," Sophie said, dryly. "I'd like to speak to my Uncle Liam."

The shorter guard seemed to be strangling on his own tongue. His friend did better, but only just.

"Liam Vesachai is unlikely to be available at this time of night," he managed. His eyes returned to her arms, covered by her long-sleeved tunic, and her wrists, which were not. His eyes did their best not to bulge out of his head.

"He will be for me." Sophie faked a yawn. She looked through the softly glowing rectangle at the wide boulevard that she knew so well, the spare and utilitarian barracks and fronts. She raised an eyebrow, putting a snap in her voice. "Or do you want to explain to him why I was kept waiting?"

This was enough. The taller one took off at a run, after a nod from his partner. The shorter one had recovered himself and looked over Avie and Sophie more closely now. She saw some craftiness come into his expression.

"You might be more comfortable," he said, "if you waited inside? We have a room with refreshments, *chûs* . . ."

Sophie's sharp smile made him trail off.

"No, thank you, *Trainee*." She put a little emphasis on the title. "I think you probably know that I am not allowed on these grounds, on pain of re-activation of my Proscription and, very shortly thereafter, my painful *death*."

"Ah," he said. "Well."

"Nice," Avie observed, and the Trainee flushed scarlet.

"If I know my Uncle Liam," Sophie said, "your friend is likely to find him abed with someone too young for him, and it might take him a while. We'll be over there, enjoying the music. Yes?"

"Yes," the Trainee said, miserable.

"And if anyone *else* should come talk to us," Sophie said, "say, a Triad of Full Bonded, with their knives out, it's going to be *you* that explains to both my father and the Queen why a peace that has lasted for twenty years has been broken. Do you understand me?"

She watched him swallow, slowly and visibly. He nodded. Avie blew him a little kiss, and the two women found themselves a vacant step nearest the entrance, where they sat and pretended to watch the jug-band. Sophie discovered that, after the murky uncertainty of the last night, the open hostility and easily understood parameters of her family's antagonism were refreshing. Almost relaxing, even.

She cracked her neck. Avie looked at her sidelong, a small frown line between her eyes, as if *Sophie* were the puzzle that needed solving.

"You know," Avie said, after a while, "I'm starting to think you might not be this . . . thing. What you pretend to be."

"What's that?"

Avie appeared to consider several words, then settled on one. "Broken."

"Oh, fuck you," Sophie said. *"Broken."*

"Well, you sure as hell try to act like you are. All I'm saying."

"Why don't you stop trying to figure me out, and focus on how you're going to use your charms to help me here."

"If I can find out who March is, I will. I do have skills other than being attractive."

"I hadn't noticed," Sophie said, earning her a frown.

"You know, you don't always have to try so hard to be a piece of shit."

"Am I trying hard?" Sophie grinned. "Because it *feels* effortless."

Avie crossed her arms over her chest and went back to watching the music.

"Sophie?" The voice was from Sophie's past, as familiar as her favorite childhood blanket, though it was hard and forbidding now. She turned to see her Uncle Liam, older but still as bluff and formidable as ever, looking at her severely, and flanked by two hard-eyed Vesachai—one young, one older—with their Rapine at their waists. Sophie covered a nervous swallow by rising to her feet.

"Hello, Uncle," she said. He narrowed his eyes, glowering, but Sophie saw a glint there.

"You got some big, swollen old genitals, coming here," he said, impassive. "Especially tonight."

"At least mine still work," Sophie said. She saw a hint of a smile under his big mustache, now gone to gray but as formidable as ever.

"The years haven't taught you to respect your elders, I see. But then, I don't know that we ever earned much." He smiled. "Hello, little Soap-Stone. Come give your favorite uncle a hug."

Sophie found herself stepping up to him before she'd meant to. She hugged him tight for a moment, the big barrel chest feeling the same as it had in her childhood. For a moment, she was fourteen years old again, and he had just rescued her from the Dark. Then she let him go and stepped back. Then he saw Avie, and his eyes brightened in a way that Sophie remembered often from her youth.

"And who is this? I taught you better manners, I think?"

Sophie blushed, though it was funny to think of *Uncle Liam* teaching manners. "Sorry, Uncle. This is—um—" Frowning, she looked at the girl. "New Girl?"

"*Avie,*" she said, giving Sophie an annoyed look. She had a warm smile for Liam, though, and shook his rough hand. "It's nice to meet you, Liam Vesachai."

"And you." He gave her a small bow. "I wish it were under different circumstances, though. My niece always liked walking the thin edge."

Sophie watched the two Vesachai next to him, who were plainly horrified at his warm treatment of this rogue, this criminal, this *Proscribed*.

"You might be right about the thin edge," she said, "if you bastards are going around in Triads."

Liam's smile fell away. "Things are a little tense at the moment. But that's to the side; it's good to see you, girl."

"And you." Sophie discovered that it was true; she'd forgotten how much she missed this old son of a bitch. "So do I take it that I'm not under arrest?"

Liam lifted an eyebrow. "Well, that's an interesting question. Should you be?"

Sophie gave him a look and pulled up her sleeves. She twisted her arms so her scars caught the light, old and pale. Both the Vesachai behind him took sharp breaths, though only one of them hissed, *"Abomination!"*

Uncle Liam gave Sophie an apologetic look and turned. Almost casually, he backhanded the young man across his face, driving him to his knees. Liam extended one blunt finger at him. "That's my niece you're talking about, Garet. You want to repeat that?"

Garet poked at his lip, glowered at Sophie, but shook his head.

"Good," Liam said. "You start a war on your own fucking time. Get out of here, go. Both of you. I don't care, just get out of earshot and listen to the music. I want to talk to my niece in private."

The other Vesachai, an older woman, frowned but obeyed, helping young Garet up and going to sit a few span away.

"Mother above," Sophie said, amused, "is that what passes for Vesachai, these days? Dad must be letting things slip."

Liam turned his blunt finger on Sophie.

"You be polite yourself. You're still my niece, and I can still teach you manners at the end of a good ass-paddling; I don't care how famous you think you are."

Avie snorted a laugh and then bit it back at Sophie's expression. "I, ah, think I'll go see to your man's lip, there."

"Never found a cure for a sullen disposition as effective as young-and-pretty," Liam said, giving Avie a wink. "If you don't mind me saying so."

"I imagine you could get away with saying a great many things, Liam Vesachai." Avie grinned and went after the two Vesachai. Liam watched her go, taking his damn time about it, and then gestured toward a nearby bench. When they sat, his face lost some of its humor.

"It *is* good to see you, Sophie. But I wish it were under better circumstances. This would be a good night for a girl with a well-known name—and scarred arms—to stay home."

"Yeah, well," Sophie said. Liam's kindness made her feel obscurely guilty; she expected cold anger and hostility from her family and had forgotten how amiable Liam could be. "I'm not *allowed* to come home, remember?"

"Call me Uncle," he said, mildly, "or my feelings will be hurt. I think I've earned that?"

Sophie clenched her jaw for a moment. "Have you?" she said, bitterness flaring up in spite of her best intentions. "Family are those who act like it, seems to me."

Liam examined his blunt fingers. Sophie remembered him doing that in the light of that fire, out in the big Dark, long hours of looking at his hands and thinking.

"It's a hard situation," he said, finally, "and we all approach it in different ways. Maybe not always the best ways. But my door has always been open to you. You chose not to walk through it."

"I preferred not to be reminded that most of my cousins want their knives in my heart, Uncle."

"I could have reached out, it's true." He sounded sad. "And so could you. It was a hard thing, not knowing what to do, and I thought it best if you weren't reminded of the past. But I may have been wrong. This wasn't easy for anybody, Sophie."

Sophie's mouth twisted, and she watched the jug-band below for a little bit, trying to get her emotions under control. She'd forgotten that, while she intellectually understood the reasons behind her estrangement from her family, when they were right in front of her, she tended to lose her temper.

She shook her head. She thought about the fire, the Dark pressing in all around, with this man explaining why she could never truly be a Vesachai, that she would forever be an outcast, that her childhood, for all intents and purposes, was over. She tried to let her anger go; it wasn't helpful. "'There are strangers in the Keep,'" she said, quoting the old children's story. "'The old things are stirring. And they're trying to involve me.'"

"I've discovered as much, myself. Someone is working to keep your name on everyone's lips."

"Yeah," Sophie said. She watched her Uncle's craggy face. "A rogue Vesachai, from what I hear."

Liam twitched, but he didn't disagree. "Do you know who it is?"

"No," Sophie shook her head. "But I've met him. Calls himself 'Mr. March' and wears a tangler. I saw his arms."

Liam expelled a long breath.

Sophie looked up at him. "Who is he?"

But he shook his head. "It's not important. He's Proscribed, and every blade in our House will be hunting for his heart. You will not need to worry about this Mr. March for very long."

"I am Proscribed, too. You still have to worry about me."

"This man will not have the Queen's protection," Liam said, stiffly. "Nor your very good reasons to have done what you did. You saved the Keep when you raised those Jannissaries, Sophie. Not all Vesachai have forgotten that."

"Yeah, well," Sophie said, bitterness rising up again. Something about being so close to where she'd grown up, something about talking to Liam, was making her want to lash out. "Those reasons wouldn't have saved my life, would they? They wouldn't have kept your silver knives out of my heart."

Liam didn't bother to answer, just watched the jug-band for a little bit. The teardrop shaped amphitheater was tuned for music, and the lilting music was a counterpoint to their conversation. He turned to look at Sophie, and his eyes were shrewd.

"Well, Soap-Stone? Here we are. I am sorry that you've been dragged into this sorry business, but here we are. What can I do?"

"You can tell me how to find March. Or who he is, at any rate, so I can find him myself."

"I will not, Sophie. This is Vesachai business now."

"I'm a Vesachai."

Liam sighed. "You use the name, and your father never had the heart to forbid it. But you weren't trained, Sophie; you never passed the tests or took the oaths. You're no more a Vesachai than your pretty friend over there. I'm sorry to say it so baldly, but it's true. A Vesachai bears the Rapine, and you bear something else."

Sophie looked away, watched the jug band for a moment, getting her temper under control. When she turned back to her uncle, she did her best to be calm.

"I don't think you can handle March. Maybe I can."

Liam looked at her, surprised. "And use the silver wrapped around your bones? Don't be a fool, Sophie; then we would have two people to kill tonight."

"I won't need to do that. And he's the only way out of this trap, Uncle. The Queen—"

"The Queen is due a reckoning," Liam said. "And perhaps you should not worry overmuch about her, either. She has reached too far and grasped too much, and crossed some lines she should not have crossed. I'm telling you, niece, there is nothing better that you can do than go hide somewhere quiet for a few days. This will work itself out."

Sophie shook her head. "No, Uncle, I don't think it will. Maybe before, but not now. I have some bad news you might not know yet: there are Feral Children in the Keep."

Liam's mouth dropped, genuine shock on his face. His eyes grew sharp, as if trying to see how much he could trust what she was saying. *"Feral Children?"*

She nodded, curt. "I saw them with my own eyes. On the Ransom Parkway, which is Dim now. March has destroyed the lightfixtures there."

"Shit," Liam said. "Shit. And we're stretched thin already. Ala! Here!" He called the older woman over, and she leaned down. He spoke to her urgently, and she took off at a run. Liam looked off into the distance for a long moment then shook himself and turned back to Sophie. When he spoke, he was very serious.

"Listen to me, Sophie. I brought the two Vesachai I could trust most with me, and you saw how they looked at you. I can't guarantee that others won't be over-zealous. There is more going on than you know, and it won't help you to get mixed up in it."

"I'm already mixed up in it, Uncle," Sophie said, but Liam shook his head.

"You can't do anything but make things worse. If my word means anything to you, I give it. Go home; take that lovely girl and a bottle of wine and have yourself a night. But *keep your head down*. Please—if not for me, for your father."

Sophie barked a short laugh. "That man has earned no consideration from me."

Liam's face tightened. "The burden your father carries would break you three times, Sophie. I won't hear you speak ill of him. Spit whatever hostility you have at me, but he hasn't earned it."

Sophie didn't—maybe couldn't—reply.

"Go home," Liam repeated. "You can only make this worse, and in the worst case, you might be driven to use the abominable magic in your arms, Sophie. And I could not bear to take the news of your arms being newly scarred to your father. Whatever you think, he loves you dearly, and your breaking Proscription would break him. Just as it would break me to hunt you."

Sophie shook her head. "You didn't hurt me the first time, Uncle, and you won't hurt me now. Not you. Don't pretend you would."

"Oh, Sophie," Liam said, heavily. "Don't you ever believe that. If I see red on your arms, if I see evidence that you've used that forbidden filth wrapped around your bones, I will put my Rapine in your heart. I will hate it, but I will do it. And I will know I was *right* to do it. Do you understand?"

Sophie laughed, helplessly, and shook her head. "No, Uncle," she said and looked at him, eyes searching his lined face. "No, I've never understood that."

There didn't seem to be much to say, after that. Uncle Liam gave her another hug, this one a little awkward, and gathered his pet Vesachai, rushing off to—hopefully—fight some Feral Children. Sophie walked towards the thoroughfare, shoulders hunched. Avie hurried to catch up.

"Well?" Sophie said, trying to bite back the bitterness that kept trying to swamp her. "You any fucking use at all, *New Girl?* Were you able to find anything out? Did I just put myself through that for nothing?"

"Sophie," Avie said, with a strange reluctance.

Sophie gave her a dark look. "Well? What did you find out?"

Avie's eyes again held a terrible sympathy, and she was slow to answer.

"I found out who Mr. March is."

"Come on, spit it out. We don't have time to—"

"It's your brother, Sophie." Avie bit her lip. "It's your brother Lee."

THE LOST BOYS

Wanderlanding

"Is there any creature so both beloved and abhorred than a brother?"

—TOMAS AVOSS, 'NINE OF VERSE'

Three brave adventurers stood before a set of broken bars, a gateway to some unimaginable future. Well . . . *two* of them stood contemplating unimaginable futures. The third kind of flitted near the wrenched-apart portcullis disinterestedly, gave it a casual 'No!', and moved on.

James looked at Katherine. Katherine looked at James, her red hair bushy and unkempt from their long exploration. They both looked at the remains of a barrier, iron and twistcraft bars long ago pulled apart by some appalling force. Beyond lay a dimly lit passageway, the kind that James remembered from his dream.

They had found it! After all the wrong turns, dead ends, and fruitless searches, they had finally found it. They found the path to the Silver Key. James had followed the directions in his guts only to be stymied by half-a-hundred barred, gated doors, but now, *finally,* they faced one where the bars had been broken and bent out of the way, allowing them entry.

James had learned the shape of the city in the last few weeks, had learned to map it out in his head. Cannoux was a new city built on top of an ancient one, but parts of that ancient one had been blocked off long ago, for reasons no one knew. There was a whole part of the old city that they just *could not get to,* even though James could point at it and know the Silver Key lay inside there. Every time they thought they found a way in, they would turn a corner and find another barred entryway. Until now.

The Silver Key lay up ahead! James could feel it. It felt just like in the dream.

"How did you find this?" James asked. They were in a strange, deep part of the undercity of Cannoux, and he could barely follow how they had gotten here. Katherine hesitated before she answered.

"He showed me," she said. "Master D'Alle. We took a field trip. He does that with, um . . . some of his servants. Sometimes. Calls them 'walking instructions.' It doesn't matter. Can you *feel* it? The Silver Key?"

Slowly, James grinned at Katherine. "Yeah."

Katherine grinned back. "Good."

James felt something pulling at him from down that corridor, something bright and terrible and frightening and wonderful. *The Silver Key. HIS Silver Key!*

Well. James glanced at Katherine sideways. He supposed that maybe it wouldn't be so bad sharing the Key. It might not be so bad having a friend to save the world with.

"All right," Katherine said, and opened her pack. She pulled out a thick pot of red paint and a heavy artist-brush. James frowned at it.

"What's that?"

Katherine gestured through the door, into the dim passageway beyond. "If the dream holds true, kid, that's a damn maze in there. I'm hoping you can find your way through it because I'm sure all the maps I made of it are wrong. This paint is so we can find our way back out again. Or back in, if we need to."

"Oh." James nodded. "Pretty smart!"

"For a girl?" Katherine dug him in the shoulder with her elbow. It was playful, but it made him wince.

"Oh, sorry," she said, not sounding sorry, and dabbed some red paint on the buckled outer frame of the old door. "I forgot you're still healing up. From being a Twins-damned crazy person."

"I ain't no crazy person. And anyways, most girls would thank somebody for saving 'em from those uptown boys that was messing with you."

"Only thing you saved me from was having to do a little unpleasant flirting and make some false promises. I know how to handle boys like that."

"Well, whatever," James said, aggrieved. There *had* been three of them, but you'd never know it from how much thanks Katherine had given him. "I didn't mean like I saved your life or nothing."

Katherine grinned at him as they made their way down the long, dank passageway. The sounds of the city were mysterious here, muffled and somehow sinister. It felt as if they'd entered a whole new world.

"The way I remember it," she said, "I had to call the constables to keep you from getting your head kicked in. So I saved *you*. If we're counting it up."

"Yeah, well," James shrugged. "I woulda beat 'em down, eventually."

"You might have drowned 'em in your blood, sure."

They reached the end of the passageway, which opened on a low-ceilinged room with four exits. She raised an eyebrow. "You got any ideas, Mr. Hero Savior Boy?" She gave him an elbow in the shoulder again.

"I hate girls," James muttered, his warm feelings about friendship gone, and then he ducked a small piece of broken rock thrown at him by an indignant Buckle. "Well, not *you*, Bucks!"

He studied the exits. He studied each one. He didn't feel that pull towards any of the directions, because there was something that had been knocking around inside him ever since she said it, and it was knocking too loud to hear the call of the Key.

"What did you mean," he said, "*his* servants?"

"Hm?" Katherine looked up from some notes she had scrawled on loose pieces of paper.

"You said Master D'Alle takes 'his' servants out on trips. The way you said it was weird."

Katherine sighed. "Ah, man. Nothing. Don't worry about it. Let's just find this thing, okay?"

"You said it weird!"

Katherine looked at him, kind of like Ma looked when he asked about adult stuff or Uncle when he asked about high-order twist. Like he was too young and dumb to understand the answer. And he felt like he always did, the burning in his chest, only it was way worse because it was this stupid red-haired *girl* and she was only a couple years older than him and a cull besides.

"Kid . . ." she said. "Look, D'Alle's got two types of culls, all right? Until yesterday, I was one kind. Now I'm . . . another."

"What does *that* mean?"

"It's none of your business, is what it means," she snapped. Then shook her head. "Look, I told you asking Master questions was dangerous. You always pay, and well, in a few years, I'll have to pay. It's not what you're thinking; it might not even be bad. It's just a different kind of life, I guess. That's all."

She tossed her long red hair, dismissing Master D'Alle and an uncomfortable future.

"So come on," Katherine said, gesturing at the doors. "Let's find this thing, yeah? Make it all worth it."

But James thought of something that cheered him immeasurably. "Once we find the Key, I'll just kill him! Then you ain't gotta be nothing but what you want. Right?"

Katherine shook her head. "You're a bloody-minded little sumbitch, James D'Essan. But it's a sweet thought."

"You don't think I'll do it!" James accused, but Katherine laughed and gave him another chuck on the arm. He felt better, though. The problem of Master and his "servants" sufficiently settled in his mind—due to the certainty that James would just murder D'Alle once he got the Key—made him feel lighter. He pointed to where Buckle was floating, impatient, and he grinned. "That way."

"Some pieces of work, these D'Essan boys." Katherine murmured, daubing red paint on the doorframe.

"What?" James asked, frowning.

"Nothing, Hero Boy. Let's go find you a Key."

James glared at her; he'd almost prefer "kid." And Buckle's hysterical laughter didn't help at *all*.

———

They searched all day and didn't find the Key, but they found something.

"What is that?" James asked, exhausted, as Katherine splashed a long line of red paint on the inside of the doorway.

"It looks like a door." And it did. It did look like a big door, a little bigger than a normal sort of door, made of a sturdy, old-looking gray wood, set into a heavy looking frame. Only, it was standing in the middle of a big round room all by itself, unattached to any wall, and couldn't possibly lead anywhere.

"I know *that*," James said, sourly. Whatever meager friendship he and the red-haired girl had forged in the excitement of trying to find the Key was gone.

He had no idea what time it was, but it must be deep into the day by now. He felt like they had been wandering through this endless, musty maze of abandoned rooms for half their lives, and Katherine's know-it-all air had stopped being cute about ten minutes in. "I don't see no friggin' *Key*, is what I'm saying."

He was too tired to even be disappointed. He hadn't been sleeping well, what with the nightly dreams of the end of the world and late night exploring and all.

"There was a door in the dream," Katherine pointed out, finishing her paint job. At least they wouldn't die in here, he supposed; they'd be able to follow Katherine's marks back to the city. He wondered where they even were; maybe way beneath the skin of the Mountain. Maybe even beneath the silver wall. He remembered Uncle's warnings that no made creatures, no folk with mindsprings, could pass it. He looked anxiously at Buckle, but she seemed fine.

She should, the little jerk; she'd slept through half of this boring slog, snoozing on his shoulder.

"I know there was a door in the dream," James said in a nasty tone, because he wanted to vent his frustration, "but that one was *open*."

"Kid," Katherine said, "calm down. *This is it*. This is what we were looking for!"

James scowled, looking around the big, dim, dingy room. There was a puddle of water in the center, and it looked like somebody had long ago stripped this whole place of anything valuable. "Don't see how. Ain't nothing *here*."

"*Kid*," Katherine said, exasperated, and set her pack down. She pointed at the door, standing alone in the center of the room. "Ain't you never heard any stories? That's a Door. A *Silver Age* Door! What's wrong with you?"

"What's wrong with *you!*" James yelled. He closed his eyes for a second and realized he was holding his arms very tightly across his chest. Buckle lit on his shoulder, concerned, but he shook her off.

"I just wanted to find it. I really did."

"Yeah," Katherine said, awkwardly. She was examining the big Door. "I mean, me too. But—"

"I know about *Doors*. Uncle knows everything about the damn *Doors*. And they don't open, right? You can't use 'em unless you're a friggin' Cold Wizard. So unless the Key is *here*, on *this side* of the stupid Door, well? We're screwed, is what I figure."

"James," and Katherine had a condescending tone of voice that could be used as justification for murder. She was prying something off the back of the doorframe. "Where's your faith?"

"What's that?" James asked, anger forgotten, seeing a glint of silver in her hand.

"Somebody left it," she said, prying off some sticky fabric, "stuck to the back of the Door. What did your Uncle tell you was needed to open the Doors? What do the stories say?"

"A Key," James tried to remember, "a Rapine, or a Coin."

"Master D'Alle said the same thing. Only, he called this a token."

She flipped the silvery thing to James, and he caught it. It was small, surprisingly heavy, and made of some unusual silver that was more perfect and wonderful than anything he'd ever seen in his entire life. Except for maybe Buckle. On one side was a fluid, beautiful engraving of a tree, and on the other there was a peculiar triune pattern.

And one of the sections of the finely inscribed pattern was glowing with a soft radiance. James looked up at Katherine, eyes wide. Buckle flew near, a comical expression of amazement on her little face.

"A *Coin*." He felt like he was holding a fairy-story made suddenly solid.

"Yep," she said, and for once he didn't even mind her superior, know-it-all air. She grinned at him.

"So, we can open the Door!" James said. Buckle landed on his shoulder, excited. But Katherine bit her lip. She looked at James, and her face was withdrawn now, pensive. He hadn't seen that expression on her before, and he didn't like it much.

"I don't think we can." Her finger traced the concentric rings of symbols around the knob in the center of the Door. "Or I mean, maybe we can, but we shouldn't. Look at the symbols, James. Remember the dream? Those symbols are important. I think if we don't get them right, the Door doesn't take us to the right place. And if it don't take us to the right place . . ."

"We don't find the Key," James said. "Well, you remember the symbols. Right? With all your notes and whatnot?"

"Some of them," Katherine admitted, "but not their order. Or not enough to be sure. And we only get one shot at it, I think."

James made a frustrated sound. "C'mon. There's got to be some way, right?"

"Well, that's the thing." She looked very wary of him, almost scared. "I think there is. But you're not going to like it."

And she was right. He didn't. He really, *really* didn't.

———

James thought Katherine's red daubs of paint made a lot more sense now. The daubs weren't meant to lead James and Katherine back *out* but to lead someone else *in*. And that someone, of course, was James' older and much more talented brother.

Most of the time waiting for Chris to arrive passed in a somewhat uncomfortable silence. It wasn't uncomfortable because of James—James didn't care at *all*—but Katherine kept watching him like he was gonna all of a sudden bust out and kill somebody or scream or something. Girls, as he had said many times before, were *stupid*.

James wandered the room, waiting for Chris to show up, seeing what there was to see. It wasn't much, but he wandered. It was kind of nice, really, having all the pressure off him now. Chris would come, and he'd know the symbols, obviously. He'd work everything out *fine*. Of course he would! Chris D'Essan never failed at anything. James had done his part, so he guessed he could relax now.

So, apparently—and this was *so* wild—Katherine already knew his older brother! Knew him pretty damn well. Well enough to work out a plan together and keep it from dumb little James. But he didn't blame them, not really. They were saving the world, right? Can't let a stubborn *little kid* get in the way.

"James," Katherine said, "will you stop pacing? And talk to me?"

James laughed because he thought that was funny, but she acted like he was screaming in pain or something when he laughed. She was so *stupid*. He couldn't be bothered with any of it; even Buckle was acting like he was mad. He wasn't mad. He was just getting to know the room. He supposed once they got the Door open, he'd probably just stay back here while Katherine and his brother went to get the Silver Key and finish the adventure. It would be smart to leave someone behind. It made sense that it would be James; he wasn't really good for anything anyways. He had served his purpose. It was time for Chris to take over and get all the credit and praise and all that stuff that James didn't care about anyways, so this was probably good for everybody.

"James," Katherine said, anguished, "*stop*."

"You stop." He kept making his way around the room. So apparently, Chris wasn't such a deep sleeper after all. So apparently, he'd been having the dreams too. Of course he had. Why wouldn't he? Everyone had!

So what do you do, when you're insanely smart, extremely clever, and overwhelmingly driven, but can't find the Silver Key because you're too old to see the way clearly? You get your girlfriend—or *whatever* Katherine was to him, not that it mattered to James—to make friends with your little brother. Not *real* friends, obviously, but your little brother is pretty stupid, so it's easy to trick him.

James understood! It was a perfectly *Chris* thing to do. He just didn't know why Katherine kept acting like he was mad. He wasn't *mad*. If he was mad, it would just be at himself, for not remembering how good Chris is at everything. How silly to believe that it could have ever been James who saved the world. Silly James! Thinking that just because he could point to the Key, he was going to be something more than some stupid little kid. Silly. And so *stupid*.

"James," Katherine said again, and James thought that maybe, even though he really wasn't mad, if she kept saying his name like that, he was going to start screaming and not stop until he puked up blood. Now *that* would be funny!

He heard the sound of a foot scraping on stone and looked up; his brother stepped into the room warily, handsome and competent and older and better at everything.

"Hey look!" James said, very brightly. "Katherine! It's *Chris!* Chris is here, finally!"

Chris sighed and looked at Katherine. "You told him."

"What did you want me to do?" Katherine asked, angrily. "The poor kid—"

"I'm not a fucking *kid*." James meant to say it really calmly, like it didn't matter, just with that one swear word in there, but he heard it echo back from the empty rooms and he must have said it pretty loudly. Katherine had her hand over her mouth and her face was white. Chris shook his head.

"I was hoping you wouldn't take it like this, squib. We—"

"*We* what?" James asked, with a big smile for his handsome, charismatic older brother. So attractive! So charming! What girl wouldn't want to follow him around? Chris studied him for a minute. Then he shook his head, as if James were a puzzle with pieces missing that made it impossible to solve.

"I didn't think you'd help me, squib. You can be awful stubborn sometimes."

James crossed his arms. Help Chris? No, he wouldn't have helped *Chris*.

"If it makes you feel better," Chris said, "I needed you to find it. I think you're the only kid in Cannoux who could have found this thing. That's something, right?"

"Yeah!" James said, through a cheery smile full of teeth that all felt much too big. "I'm *so* proud of myself."

"Chris." Katherine spoke in a low voice. "Don't patronize him."

James flapped his hands at them. "Go on! You got this!" he said, still cheerful. "Me and Bucks will patrol the perimeter. Or something. I mean, I already did *my* job, right?"

Chris just shook his head, turned away, and studied the Door. Katherine kept looking at James, and he was really starting to wish she would just *stop*. He'd served his purpose; he'd done his job, and now Chris and Katherine could just go through the Door, get the Silver Key, and become the King and Queen of everything. How nice! He just wished they would get on with it, already. He was getting *bored*.

He held his arms tightly around his chest, so the knives didn't push too far in, and walked around the room, not looking at much. Buckle landed on his shoulder and gave him a hug on the ear, which was nice.

He felt like maybe if ol' Bucks hadn't been there, he would just let the knives press all the way in and see what happened. Maybe they would cut him all up inside, and then people wouldn't be able to fool you into thinking you were friends so easy.

Chris spun the five dials around the doorhandle through several rotations, lining up the symbols. Of course he remembered them perfectly; Chris D'Essan remembered everything perfectly. James felt only a vague curiosity about what lay beyond the Door; it all felt very distant and surreal.

Chris hesitated, then looked over his shoulder at James. "Squib, I think it should be you that opens it. Don't you think?"

James laughed; that was *funny*. He didn't reply, just laughed and laughed, and eventually Chris shook his head again and turned back to the Door. Chris gave Katherine a long look that was probably something about how super pretty she was. James wouldn't know because he didn't care, and Katherine gave Chris a look back that was probably about how great and smart and good-looking he was. And then Chris turned the handle.

And then?

Despite his decision to not even look at what the Door revealed, he couldn't help it.

And then . . . and *then*.

And then James D'Essan forgot all about his fierce determination to not care, and he forgot all about knives in his chest, and he forgot all about the pretty red-haired girl who had pretended to be his friend; forgot about his domineering older brother, and pretty much forgot about everything. With a sound and sensation like a broad stone wheel grinding an arc beneath them, the Door opened and something flooded out, something bright and warm and wonderful, and all of James' adolescent megrims were burned away in its beautiful light.

The Door swung open, and the three Cannoux-folk and a curious little automata looked in amazement through the open doorway into something that they had never seen before—indeed, that only a handful of people alive had ever seen:

The rich golden warmth of *sunshine*.

PART III

THE DEADSMITH

The Door Into Darkness

"Don't fuck with a Deadsmith."

—APOCRYPHAL

A spark floated in vast, empty darkness, a single star plucked from some better sky. The Deader walked toward it because there was nothing else to walk toward. It was the only light that could be seen anywhere. He could be walking through a field of silently waiting horrors and would never know.

For a while, the Deader had convinced himself that the spark ahead *was* a star, one of those legendary and long-lost treasures, and that he was walking endlessly through a bleak hell towards a light he could never reach. But this light was low and on his plane. It wasn't a star, and the Deader had been walking towards it too long for it to be a torch, campfire, or glowswick. That was litstone ahead, he was certain of it, and litstone required upkeep, power, people, and life.

The Dark! It spread everywhere before him. It was like wading through congealed blood. Occasionally, the Deader would step on some long-dead thing that would shatter to dust under his boots, and he wondered if it was a plant or stick or bone. A month now, with no light other than that faint flickering spark. A month was too long without light.

"Attar." His Fate whispered to him, with the faint scent of jasmine. *"Tystete."*

The Deader grunted; his Fate was near to useless in this black expanse. It had panicked days ago and driven him half-mad with scents and colors, gibbering in its nonsense language. Since then it had quieted but was still restless, feeding him pointless warnings of things it couldn't possibly know. It worried about traps, but what traps could be laid in this dark waste?

His Fate spoke in no language that he knew, but he always understood what it meant. How could he not? It had once been part of him. He endured its warnings.

The Deader was close to his Prey now. He could feel it.

He had been on the trail of his Prey for months. He wished for an end to the chase. He wished to return to his Lady's side. It was an ache, that separation, and the only salve for it would be the Prey's blood. The Deader trod the dust, eyes fixed on the spark of light, never slowing his pace. He tried to find joy in the hunt, for it had been many years since he'd been given a task like this. But he was unable. He just wanted it done.

He had walked the Wanderlands for years beyond count, had brought down people and things that speak as people and puissant demons from the deep dark. He had slain kings, broken empires, hunted magicians; he regularly slept in the bed of a god. He carried a Machine that was like none other; he had torn a piece of his own soul away and broke it to his council. He had ruled, he had been a slave, he had loved and lost and died. He had climbed to the top of the White Tower and looked upon the Roof of the World. He had stepped through Doors without count and walked the dust of a thousand dead Lands.

There was only one creature in all of the worlds that he could properly be said to fear, and he feared only her displeasure. She had pointed and bid him return with the Prey's blood on his teeth, and he had gone. From the moment her finger had extended, the Prey's fate was sealed. It was only a matter of time and distance now. The Deader had never failed his Lady, and he would not fail her here.

The Deader wondered what sort of Land this had been before the Dark had taken it. A flat one, thankfully. Had the terrain been varied or filled with obstacles, he would have had to risk a light. As it was, he could tell when an obstacle was approaching by the tiny spark's disappearance, occluded from his sight by the barrier ahead. It was usually a simple matter to move to one side until the spark re-appeared. The obstacles were mostly rocks, though once he'd dragged his hand across old timbers and planking; an abandoned building. His Fate warned him of smaller things, rocks to catch shins and holes to break feet. The Deader didn't need light to avoid these.

He heard music, a lilting song from another age, and realized he was whistling. He cut off with a jerk. A month was too long; he was losing control. He was fraying, attenuating into the Darkness. Soon the hallucinations would start, and the built-in protections in his mind would only stand for so long. If the Deader was not to lose his mind, he would need light soon, and not just a speck, floating on the horizon.

A wind blew up from over the plain, a dirty, choking wind. The Deader drew his hat down and covered his mouth and nose with a kerchief. The spark ahead wavered and died, occluded by the dust. The Deader shut his eyes and walked, trusting his Fate to lead him past any small obstacles.

The Deader thought of his Lady; he felt unaccountably weary. This hunt was too long, too long away from light, and civilization, and the White Tower. And *her*. He just wanted it done, and to lay in the bright stonelight of his Lady's chamber, wrapped in her arms, drifting from sex to sleep with no effort or intention to either.

The Deader opened his eyes. He realized that the wind had stopped blowing a long time ago, that he had been walking with his eyes closed, smiling beneath his kerchief, for hours. Or more. Time had slipped from him.

It frightened him, and he was a man unused to that sensation. He became aware that his Fate was chattering at him. There were washes of crimson at the edges of his vision.

"Dissidea!" It was crying. *"Irith!"*

His pace faltered, stopped. He swayed for a moment. He felt as if he had no limbs, that he had become an ink-black mote, a twinned and reversed copy of the bright star he'd been following. He was losing his mind to the Dark, and it was happening more quickly than it should.

He looked up and saw the star had grown, changed. It had taken the form of a city, with tall walls of litstone, shining in the shadow. His mouth tightened into a grim line; the hallucinations had started.

"Amaranth." His Fate sounded relieved and gave him the faint scent of honeysuckle. The Deader could not understand why—it should be gibbering in terror. And then the panic receded, he came back to himself, and he looked at the brightly shining city before him.

It was no hallucination. He had arrived.

———

The Deader saw that a man stood before the city gates, a small dim shape against the bright litstone. He was clearly waiting for the Deader, but the Deader had no intention of hurrying himself. He made himself sit for several minutes and stare at the city, letting his eyes acclimate to the light, burning the backs of his retinas until he could look at the hot walls without flinching. Presently, he was able to see other things, too.

The city wasn't huge, but it was large enough to sustain itself. The Deader had seen a thousand cities like this, the last embers of a dead civilization, able to find stability in the long Dark. They tended to be insular, monomaniacal, religious. He wondered if perhaps he'd found another apostate-city, a Land that had not yet become subject to the Nine. There were more of them out in the deep Dark than people would believe.

The gates were closed, and the Deader thought he could see folk on the ramparts, waiting. For him. There would be few visitors from this direction. He had been warned of the Prey's powers of rhetoric and glamour, but he had seen little evidence of those yet. He might discover them here.

Finally, he stood up, twisting his thumbs into his thighs to ease the cramps in them, and shaded his eyes to get a good look at the man. It wasn't the Prey; he was sure of that.

"*Callach,*" his Fate whispered. "*Callach an Merith!*" But the warning was unnecessary; he had no intention of being incautious. He walked toward the brilliant city, shading his eyes against the light.

The waiting man was old, dressed in a sort of tight wraparound blouse and a long pleated skirt that was tangled through with skeins of jewelry. He had beautiful white hair, tied at the back, and a proud face. The Deader saw no silver-work in his eyes or under his skin, which was good.

He saw the slender silvery thread of their Feed rising up into the sky from somewhere inside the city, but like many lost civilizations, they were unlikely to know how to utilize Silver's more dangerous uses. They undoubtedly used their Feed only for light, but the Deader tried to take as few chances as he could.

The man had a table beside him, laden with supplies. The Deader stopped about seven paces away, a polite circumference out of easy range of most mêlée weapons. He coughed, then spat dust out of his lungs.

The old man bowed, gravely, but the Deader did not return it.

He studied the old man. "They put you out here to meet me?" he asked finally. His voice was a croak. He had not used it in many weeks.

"I have been bid to greet you." The man bowed again and gestured to the table. "And offer you refreshment."

The Deader looked where he pointed, saw a plate of food and a jug of something to drink. He squinted up at the walls of the city, where indistinct shapes were looking down at them. He coughed more dust. He nodded at the man. "I'll take a drink." He almost hoped it was poisoned; that would be a quick way to judge the city's intentions. The old man made a ritual out of pouring from a clay pot and presenting a cup to the Deader. It was good; cold and spicy. His Fate detected no poison, which wasn't proof, but it was something.

The Deader sat down, cross-legged, in the dust before the bright city walls. He could tell that once this had been a paved road, though only gravel remained. He took another draught from the pot. After drinking only recycled water for weeks, this was heaven. He finished it and sighed. He yawned widely and looked up at the man.

"Your gates are closed," he said. The man nodded. He was brave; there was only the faintest tremor in the movement.

"I can offer you supplies and light, food and drink," the man said. "But we cannot admit you to the city."

The Deader laughed, a rasp in the dim illumination from the walls of the city. "You've had another visitor."

The man hesitated, then inclined his head. He was terrified but hiding it well.

"Bring him to me, and I will not need to enter your city." The Deader smiled, the best one he could manage, and held the cup out. The man swallowed and glanced up over his shoulder at the watching faces. The man tried to mask his fear by refilling the Deader's cup. When he set the pot down, it sloshed due to trembling hands. The Deader took another draught and waited.

"It will not be possible to bring anyone to you," the man said.

The Deader shook his head. "It is. It is by far the simplest thing for you to do."

"The man you seek is beyond your reach." Now the old man had grown a little spine. He straightened up and firmed his jaw. "We can offer you supplies, light—"

"Beyond my reach?" The Deader laughed. "An easy phrase. Does that mean he is not within? Or that he *is* within, but you think you can keep him from me?"

The old man made no response. The Deader took another sip of the drink. It really was extraordinarily refreshing.

"It is not too late," the Deader said, and he pitched his voice to be sympathetic, commiserating. One of a Deadsmith's many tasks was diplomacy, though his masters rarely used the Deader for such. "I just need this one man. I need not ask any other questions and need not pass your gates. My business is not with you."

"The man you seek is beyond your reach," the old man said again, more firmly this time. The Deader recognized someone who was preparing himself to die with dignity. He drained the last of the drink, sighed, and rubbed his eyes. Wearily, he climbed to his feet and looked up at the waiting faces on top of the wall.

"Do you know what I am?" the Deader asked, knowing the answer. The old man nodded. "Do they?"

Again, the old man nodded.

The Deader tried to think of a way out for these people, but they were subjects of the Nine. This city held the Watches and the Codes; the Deader could read the signs. There was nothing he could do. Refusing him entry was treason, and there was only one answer for treason.

"Are you sure," he said, "that you mean to deny a Deadsmith—*a servant of the Nine*—admittance to your city?"

"We mean no disrespect." The old man spoke with a funereal finality. "But you cannot enter."

The Deader nodded. It was out of his hands now. Refusing a Deadsmith was ultimately the same as attacking one.

"I am sorry," he said to the old man, who had been brave, "that I cannot make this painless."

The Deader's smoke-gray skin flared with black-and-white tracings, and shocking power flooded through him. While the faces atop the wall watched, he tore the old man into pieces.

———

Custom required a literal river of blood to flow in the city, but the definition of a "river" was open to interpretation, and the Deader contented himself with a bare trickle that ran down their law-house's steps. He was annoyed at the necessity of it, bothered by the waste.

They fought him hard and with the light of fanaticism in their eyes, but if the Prey thought suborning this city would be an effective trap, then he was too stupid to be alive. The Deader slaughtered the militia and any who raised a hand to him—he had no choice there. He hoped that once the way of it became clear, some of them would strip their weapons off and dress as civilians, and escape the death the Deader must deliver to those bearing arms.

The decimation of the rest of the city took a long while, and by the time the Deader was finished, he was sodden with blood and exhausted. He took no particular pains to root out every last citizen, and he hoped at least some of them had the sense to hide well. The leaders he garroted in the center of the city—for these, it was a pleasure. This was their fault; they had rebelled and their citizens had paid the price. The Deader spat in each of their faces as they died.

Worst was the growing knowledge that the old man had not lied to him; the Prey was no longer in the city. The Deader could taste disappointment at the back of his throat, blood-copper and bitter. He thought of another journey through shadow and was not eager. Who *was* this man who he chased? How had he bent an entire city to his will, to the point where they would risk standing against a Deadsmith?

And how had the Prey escaped?

The Deader found out soon enough. The city broke; once the horror grew too great, the will of the people shattered, and they became passive, letting him slaughter them with little resistance. They waited for it to be over, staring at him with dull and hunted eyes. It sickened him; he had never cared for this sort of work. Better one of his brothers or sisters more suited to it, but he was Deadsmith and had his duty. He had accepted it at the end of a silver knife and did not mean to set it down now.

He normally used his Machine for this sort of work; that's what it was for. But it had been too long without a kill, and the Deader feared it would run riot and butcher the city to its roots. He resolved to let it hunt more often.

He was led to the heart of the city by a hard-eyed old woman and a broken, sobbing priest. The priest couldn't speak and collapsed in a heap on the steps of the city's civic center.

"He went in there," the woman said. "He's not come out again."

"But he's gone." It wasn't a question. The Deader would be able to tell if the Prey was still in that building. And in any case, he sensed a Door.

"He's gone." The woman jerked her chin up; she was not easily cowed. "Him and you both, I figure."

"You figure right," the Deader said, and then studied her. "You have a message for me."

"I do," the old woman said. "He said exactly this: To give you his congratulations, that you have succeeded in annoying him. That the journey changes now, and for you to turn back before he is forced to harm you."

The Deader laughed, and why not? He had succeeded in *annoying* the Prey.

"He said to say that you have been warned, and you proceed at your peril, and that the roads you walk now will be more treacherous than you know."

"Very well," the Deader said. "I thank you for the message."

"Fuck that, and you too, I reckon." The old woman spat again, not quite at his feet, but almost.

"What will I find beyond this arch, old mother?" the Deader asked, ignoring her anger. The woman smiled mirthlessly.

"A sacrifice. To our new betrayer god."

The Deader looked at the arch. "Take this city in hand, mother. Help them remember their oaths. And to beware new gods."

"Oh, I'll do that," the old woman said.

The Deader nodded. "Do it well. The second time is much worse."

He walked up to the wide doors of the structure, leaving her behind. Whatever lay inside, she need have no part of it.

"*Carnivas,*" his Fate muttered at him. "*Dissidea.*"

"I know." He could feel the threat emanating from the place. Though it blazed brightly with pillars of glowing stone, it felt dark, malignant.

The Deader held out his hand and said a magic word, a White-on-Black word. The doors smashed open.

Inside was a wide, cool, and dim space. It was dominated by a single freestanding Door in the center, wide and tall and ancient, with a true-silver knob in the center. The Deader closed his eyes; it was as he suspected. The Prey was gone.

"*Que Haran.*" His Fate was panicky, darting smells and colors across his senses. It was convinced of a trap here, a mortal danger, but the Deader could see none. He did his best to quiet his companion and studied what the Prey had left for him.

Five rough columns of stone had been erected in a loose semi-circle around the Door, and five people were tied to them. They were dead.

The first was a big man, rough-featured and just starting to gray. He had been stabbed—a single knife thrust into his heart. The Deader looked closer and saw that his tongue had been cut out. The boy next to him was nearly a man, beefy and thick. He had the face of a natural sadist, but that face was purple now. He'd been choked to death.

The little girl next to him was hard to look at—the side of her head had been caved in, her long raven-black hair matted with blood. The Deader was not usually affected by trauma of any sort; he had caused too much of it to feel anything at the sight. But this one—this one was difficult.

"*Attar!*" His Fate sobbed, and the Deader tasted old blood and roses.

He wanted to look at the last two columns of stone, on the other side of the Door, even less than he wanted to look at the young girl. He felt strange, and he did not know why he should feel so. There was something about these figures, their arrangement, that disturbed him.

He made himself look at the raven-haired woman who was tied there. Her eyes were wide and staring at nothing, filmed with death. Her throat had been slit. There was something about these people, something half-remembered, something hidden. But he could not discern it. They weren't even related to each other; the Prey must have picked them at random. The Deader could not get a sense of this trap, yet his Fate wailed danger into every sense.

The last figure, hung by his hands on the rough stone column, was a slight boy with fair hair. He had a familiar look.

"*Genevive.*" His Fate sounded as if it were weeping. "*Anniver.*" The Deader smelled mown hay and rot. The boy raised his head weakly and coughed.

He was still alive.

"Please." The boy's voice was hoarse, helpless. "Please help me."

His hair was the color of straw, and the smallest finger on his right hand had been cut all around its circumference. It was still bleeding. The Deader looked over his shoulder, saw the old woman standing, looking through the door, hard-eyed. The Deader straightened and walked back to the other figures hanging from their stone posts, studying them. The cut finger was the clue. He rubbed slightly at the matching scar he bore on his own smallest finger.

The older man with the graying hair—yes. He bore no real physical resemblance to the Deader's father, but the wounds were the same. This man had been killed in the same manner his father had.

The boy next to him, with the sadist's face; that was meant to be his brother. The Deader remembered him dying as well, bravado turned to piss on his lips. He turned the boy's head this way and that. Not a perfect resemblance, but then the Deader could hardly remember his brother. He just remembered that he'd been choked to death, and he mostly remembered because he himself had done it.

He felt a strange reluctance to look at the small girl, with her caved-in head. Across the years, he could hear her, pleading and screaming.

And his mother—*ah*. The raven-haired woman, dead, was the closest likeness and she looked, in fact, a little like his Lady. The Deader felt the trap twitching, but could not quite see its jaw or feel the points of its teeth. He squatted before the still-alive young boy again. He rubbed the circular scar on his smallest finger and used his other hand to open the boy's tunic.

The Deader made a sour sound; it was as he suspected. The tattoo was there. It wasn't identical, of course, but it was similar enough. He bore one very much like it on his own chest and had since he was a boy. He rocked on his heels for a few long moments, thinking. The boy gasped again, tears leaking from his eyes.

"Please," he said, faintly. "Help me."

The Deader looked back at the entrance, but the old woman and the priest were gone. The meaning was clear; no one was going to help this lad. He was meant to be a sacrifice to the Prey, and he would die tied to this stone.

No one was going to come along and save him, the way someone had come along and saved the Deader, when *he* had been young and straw-haired, with a new cut on his finger.

Was this the trap, then? He didn't know how the Prey could have known about his family, so many years lost. But it didn't matter if he did. And it didn't matter if this was a trap.

He cut the boy down and gave him some water. The boy wept and thanked him. The Deader waited until he was done drinking, and knew a moment of comfort and hope, then pushed his knife through the back of his spine, into his brain, the quickest way of killing he knew. He stood and wiped his blade on his already blood-soaked clothes.

The Deader stepped over the body of the child and looked at the Door; the message written on it in blood. The hand it was written in was scrawling, looping, its import incomprehensible:

How do you make a machine?

The Deader considered the question and looked around once more at the dead simulacra of his family. He reached out and wiped a hand through the message, dried blood flaking away in a soft rain. His skin flared white-and-black as he prepared himself for whatever might come, and he turned the ancient, pure-silver knob.

The Deader threw open the Door onto sandy copse, dying scrub-trees littering the horizon. The sky was on fire, roiling. This was a dying land. Clearly, in the sand, were footsteps that led away from the Door.

Berenniast, his Fate whispered nonsense, a warning.

"I know," the Deader said, and walked through the Door.

THE KILLERS

Festival

"Sometimes the only play is the hand dealt."

—CORAZON LI, 'NINE TIMES SEVEN'

The highways and byways of the Blue Halls, the high-ceilinged park-district adjacent to Vesachai House, were ablaze with revelry. They were doing Festival here, and the broad hollows of sculpture and carefully tended trees were a riot of color and sound. False Twins with their long masks and garish warpaint stilted around, throwing candy and rocks together. Hawkers kept trying to pin flowers into Sophie's hair but she just pushed past.

"Sophie!" This came from behind her—the damned girl. Sophie stepped around a couple languorously kissing. They wore flamboyant masks pushed up on their foreheads. She felt a wave of unreality, of bitter weariness. She should be among them, succumbing to some flagrant drug or drink, fingers entwined in some pretty thing's hair.

Lee. Her fucking brother. Mr. March was *Lee* . . . ?

"Sophie!" It was New Girl again—or Avie, or whatever—trying to keep up in the crowd. Her extravagant beauty made it difficult; she was accosted by every hawker and drunk with a good line. Sophie elbowed aside a couple dressed in the typical style—the woman had one breast bared and painted, and the man's scrotum was displayed in a clever miniature diorama. They were painted in contrasting colors; her skin was naturally dark and his light, but they painted themselves to match.

There was so much beauty here, so much delicious flesh. Every type of person; every style, color, hue, combination, gender, or non. Sophie caught the eyes of a triplet: a hulking brute and two twee waifs. They gave her a wink. On another night . . . but, no. She had to deal with her *fucking brother.*

Overhead, Swatterflowers flitted, flashing festive blue lights, attacking nobody. Sophie hardly saw any of it.

Lee. There was a rage building inside her so deep she could barely sense its extents. Fucking Lee. Her tender, kindhearted younger brother, always tagging along, always wanting to be part of her "adventures," always singularly un-equipped for them. She remembered the mocking, nasty look on Mr. March's disguised face. That was Lee?

The last time she'd seen her brother he'd just been confirmed as a full Ve-sachai, and he'd been maybe fifteen years old. He'd tracked her down at one of her haunts and had delivered a half-accusatory, half tear-streaked speech that, frankly, she couldn't now remember. Betrayal was prominent; her once adoring little brother was not one of those Vesachai who understood why she had used her forbidden powers. He had become a true believer, as fundamental a Vesachai as there was. It was most of why she hadn't tried to keep in touch. He'd made it clear that familial gestures would be unwelcome.

And, in truth, it had been easier to just let the whole thing go. Easier to get drunk. Easier to say *fuck you* and look away, and let the past become the past.

Sophie pushed her way through the crowd. She didn't doubt that the sneering Mr. March was her brother; as soon as Avie said the name she knew it was true. She could hardly believe she hadn't seen it before; it had been years since she'd seen him, but . . . still. *Lee.*

"*Sophie!*" Avie yelled, and Sophie felt a hand catch at her wrist. She was pulled to a stop and found herself face to face with Avie, flushed and out of breath.

"You have to tell me what's going on." Avie's eyes were searching her face. "I can't help if I don't know what we're doing."

"I don't have to tell you shit."

Avie narrowed her eyes. Her hand tightened on Sophie's wrist, hard. "I'm not one of your little friends, *Capitana.* Don't treat me like one."

Avie was pressed close by the crowd and Sophie was seized, for a moment, with the nearly overwhelming urge to pull forward, to take the beautiful girl's lower lip between her teeth and bite, to let go and slide into that liquid gloaming that had taken her so many times before. It was a shocking sensation, perverse and dangerous, just the kind of self-destruction that Sophie liked best.

She jerked her hand out of Avie's grasp and gave her a small shove. "Fuck off." She pushed off through the crowd. Everywhere she looked, she was reminded of her little brother. Many people wore tanglers at Festival; it was kind of the tone of the thing. Obscured faces, displayed bodies. Tears threatened the corners of her eyes, and she refused them.

Lee. Fucking *Lee.*

Her memories of her brother were curiously thin. When she was young he had been an annoyance; too young to be useful and too old to be cute. Mostly she remembered trying to get out of watching him, trying to keep him from follow-ing her and the Killers around. His blind devotion had made her feel awkward; she preferred *informed* devotion.

And then . . . and then came Saint Station, and Mr. Turpentine, and the Hot

Halls War. There hadn't been any time to think about her little brother. She wondered, for possibly the first time, what it must have been like for him—wishing
so badly to be part of her group of friends, a group who became legends for saving
the Keep. Watching the Keep devolve into madness around him, with his big
sister at the heart of it, and him left only with fear and uncertainty.

Sophie shook her head and pushed through the crowd of revelers, shoving a
hawker who tried to set a crown of flowers on her head.

And then, in the aftermath, Lee had gotten sort of bundled up with the rest of
the Vesachai in her mind. They had passed the death sentence of Proscription on
her, and only the Queen's direct order kept them from carrying it out. Those had
been bad, bewildering days; she had just lost most of her friends to the Hot Halls;
she was a famous child-hero but spat upon by passing Vesachai. She had little time
or willingness to consider her little brother's feelings.

She had seen him a few times, growing up, first with a betrayed hurt in his
eyes and then a sullen indifference. This had matured, finally, into the cold-eyed
disapproval she got from most of the Vesachai. She tried to square that with Mr.
March's amused cruelty and couldn't. How could he have done it? What had they
offered him? Had they threatened him? She remembered the livid scars on his
arms.

"*Sophie!*" Avie dodged in front of her and ran her shoulder into Sophie's chest,
knocking her to a halt. "Fuckin' stop!" Avie grabbed her shoulders and shook her.
"I can't afford for you to go to pieces. Do I have to slap you?"

"Yes," Sophie said, so Avie did. She gave Sophie a full open-handed crack
across the side of the face.

"*Shit!*" Sophie's vision went white for a moment, and she prodded at her
cheek. She blinked. She did feel better. She looked at Avie and grinned. "Do it
again."

Avie gave her a look. "No."

"C'mon."

"We can wrestle later."

Sophie grinned, crooked. "That a promise?"

Avie shook her head, impatient. "Stop it. You don't look right, Sophie. Tell
me that you're not going to do anything stupid. I'm not letting go of you until
you do."

"That a promise?" Sophie said, faintly. She suddenly felt as if all her bones
were made of water, and the world seemed dimmer than it should. Avie steered
her back a few steps through the revelers to a park bench, and they sat down.
Sophie let her eyes close for a moment. Her pulse beat at the edges of her vision,
lines of faint fire. Now that she'd stopped moving, she felt the weight of all the
alcohol she drank earlier, the stimulants and low-grade hallucinogens they'd done
in the Loche, and Mother knows what else. She felt so tired.

Had she ever been so tired? She must have. Gods, only months ago she and Bear and Hunker John had done a three-day-long bender, each daring the other to quit first. How long had tonight been? The night-lights were still on, so it hadn't been that long. Why was she so tired?

"Here," Avie said, peremptorily, returning from a brief absence and pushing something into her hands. It was a heavy ceramic tankard. Sophie supposed she could use a drink. She raised it to her lips and sputtered.

"Water?"

"Drink that," Avie said.

"Don't tell me what to—"

"Idiot, you're about to pass out. Drink the Twins-damned water, please?"

Sophie tried to think of the last time she drank plain water. Last week sometime? She drank, grimacing at the clean, clear taste. Avie sat down on the bench next to her.

"All of it."

"I thought I gave the orders in this outfit."

Avie snorted and watched until the water was gone. Sophie handed the mug back and closed her eyes again. She did feel a little better.

"Tell me a story," Avie said.

Sophie opened her eyes, frowning.

Avie snapped her fingers in front of Sophie's eyes. "C'mon, tell me a story. Something true. Prove you're not dying on me. When was the last time you had food?"

Sophie shook her head. "Doesn't matter. And I'm not in the mood for fairy tales."

"I look like I want a fairy tale? Tell me about the Hot Halls, then. Or whatever," Avie said. "C'mon, focus. I want to make sure you're not going to pass out again."

"I didn't pass out," Sophie mumbled. "And I don't want to talk about the Hot Halls War."

Avie laughed. "All right. A story about you and Ben, then. Something nobody knows."

"Everybody knows all the stories," Sophie whispered, squeezing the heels of her hands into her eyes until she saw stars. She took a deep breath. They'd fed her Twins-damned *brother* to Saint Station . . .

"Sophie," Avie said, snapping her fingers again.

"You know why they call them the Hot Halls?" Sophie asked, still rubbing her eyes. It felt vaguely good.

"No, I wasn't around then."

"The bastards who were invading had found a bunch of old warmachines, out somewhere in the Dark. Somewhere, somehow. King Gutcher and his Outkeep assholes found soldier-automata and a bunch of old Silver-Age weapons. One of those was the flares."

She opened her eyes, looked down. Her hands were open too, the backs of them resting on her knees, her fingertips trembling and twitching. That wasn't good. Maybe she had been hitting the bottle a little too hard lately. Her tunic sleeves rode up slightly, and the edges of her scars were visible.

"The flares were—I dunno. Sort of like Swatterflowers, I guess. But they flashed light—very bright light. If they caught you close enough, they would burn the eyes right out of your head. Even if you had your eyes closed, sometimes. It's hard to fight, when you can't fucking see anything, right? So if you saw that flash of light, you probably only had a few more minutes of sightless terror before some old monster out of the deep Dark came and chewed you into pieces."

She laughed, humorlessly, and shook her head. "Funny thing was, the Twins-damned things flashed *cold*. Freezing, even. But anywhere they were swarming, the veterans called those the 'Hot Halls,' and . . . yeah."

"How did you fight that?" Avie's voice was soft.

"I had goggles, and the shit in my arms. I wasn't around for most of that, any-way. I was too busy, off playing at being a hero. Wasting my time, and getting my friends killed. But there was one time—we had to get all the way down-Keep, right? We had to get into the Dim, so I could get to where the Jannissaries were stored. And we had to pass through some pretty bad fighting."

Sophie was quiet for a long time, looking at her wrists. Her face twisted mo-mentarily, and then smoothed.

"Ben was never very strong. Never really brave, I guess. Not like Tom or Luet. And Mad Vaas *liked* it, liked the terror of war, that crazy fucker. But Ben wasn't built for that kind of thing. He spent all those months and years pretty much constantly afraid. I think sometimes that being my friend is the worst thing that ever happened to him."

"Sophie—"

"Anyway," Sophie continued, not wanting to hear it. "We got separated. The Killers, I mean. Those of us that were left. Ben thought I was trapped back behind the lines, but me and Jubilee had found another way out. So Ben, he climbs back into the battle, trying to get back to me, fighting off Tom, who was trying to drag him back. He was crying the whole time, pissed his pants because he was so scared, but he wouldn't leave me behind. Finally he got flashed, blew his eyes out for a while, and Tom was able to drag him away."

Sophie rubbed her eyes, and stifled a yawn.

"I wasn't even there for him to save. That's the funny part. The poor mother-fucker put himself through hell to save me, and I'd already left him behind."

She swallowed. "Because I had to go save the Keep, you see. Because I had to go raise the Jannissaries and be the fucking hero. I didn't even know Ben was still alive until after the war."

"Oh, Sophie," Avie said.

Sophie looked away, off into the milling crowd. It parted for a moment to reveal two bored-looking Practice Guard standing near the entrance.

"I can't let it happen again, you know?" Sophie said, barely audible. "I just . . . can't."

Sophie felt cold rage starting to slip in between the sinews of her arms, her fingers, into the bones, where it mixed with old forbidden silver. The shorter of the Practice Guard laughed at something, braying more noise into the revelry. Sophie felt her face twitch.

She looked up at Avie again. Her lovely green eyes were full of some complex emotion, sorrow or pity or some other nameless thing. Sophie shook her head. "My fuckin' brother, man." She had to laugh. "The entire Keep to pick from, and Jane Guin used *my brother*."

"Sophie . . ." Avie said, watching Sophie's face change.

Sophie stood. Suddenly, she was feeling a lot better.

"Sophie, what are you doing?"

Sophie grinned down at Avie. For the first time since she'd punched the guy in the Loche de Menthe, she felt clean and clear. "See you later, New Girl, I got something to do. I hope you turn out to . . . I don't know. Not be a piece of shit."

"Sophie!" But Sophie yanked her wrist free of Avie's grip and stalked off through the crowd. A kind of pure, perfectly distilled rage was filling up her mind, like argent light. It was a smile that would have made the Killers dive for cover. It grew on her face as she strode up to the two Practice Guard.

They barely had time to notice her, much less recognize her, before she kicked the woman on the left as hard as she could in the crotch.

"What in the . . . ?" The Guard grunted, and staggered back under the blow. The other guard spun towards her, outraged, and Sophie slapped him once across the face, smartly, and grabbed his lapels. She grinned into his confused face.

"Tell the Queen," she said, "that Sophie Vesachai wants to have a fucking word."

THE LOST BOYS

The Door Into Summer

"Life, it seems to me, is a slow process of learning the bland truths behind that which we once thought was magic. What reaction can a sane person have, I wonder, to experience that process in reverse?"

—DEMINS, 'MUSIC-BOX'

Four people stood in front of an absurd doorway, one that had opened onto somewhere that shouldn't exist, something out of a fairy tale and not a very realistic one. Four people—three medium-sized, one very small—looked through a freestanding doorway at a thing almost forgotten in their age of the world:

Sunshine.

It was so bright! It was so bright it hurt their eyes, but they didn't look away. It transformed them, it warmed their faces. For a long time none of them spoke; they just drank in the beautiful golden light of the sun. James stood poleaxed for a while, mouth open. Buckle stood on his shoulder, holding onto his ear, mimicking his expression.

Katherine's hair, always red, looked like a fire in the light of the sun, and even Chris couldn't keep from being wonderstruck. They were looking at sunshine. Big shafts of it, coming down through a green canopy of leaves. *Sunshine.*

It was incredibly beautiful. As vivid as the dream had been, it couldn't compare with the real thing. Nothing in their young lives could have prepared them for the real thing.

They didn't go through the Door for a long while; it was just too much. It was easier to see it as some sort of extremely vibrant painting stood up on its end, and never mind the clean, wonderful scent of living dirt and old forest that blew through it, tossing Katherine's long hair around. James smiled at her in wonder, her betrayal forgotten for now. For now, they were looking at sunshine.

"This must be Forest," Chris said, in a hoarse voice. "We opened a Door onto the Land of the Giants."

"That's impossible," Katherine whispered. "That's just a story. Right?"

"That's *sun*, Kat," Chris said, his analytical voice suffused with wonder. "And when we walk through and look up, I think we're going to see the rest of the sky."

They could see a sliver of it from their perspective, a deep cornflower blue through the trees. They could see that the trees opened out, maybe a couple hundred paces past the Door, and they could see a tantalizing glimpse of strange terrain past the woods.

"The sky." James remembered stories Ma had been telling him since he'd been little. "The Rings!"

"The Rings," Chris agreed, "and the golden moon, and . . ."

"And the sun," Katherine said.

"And the sun," Chris said, with perhaps the closest thing to reverence he would ever manage in his long, terrible life. If James had looked, he would have seen tears standing in his brother's eyes. But Buckle was restless, and that decided him.

"Okay," he said, breaking the spell the sunlight had cast on him. He looked at Chris and Katherine, and a hint of shadow entered his expression when he saw them standing together. But it still wasn't time for feeling that. The knives would have their time to press in, later. He shrugged awkwardly. "I'm going through."

Buckle jumped up off his shoulder and was the first of them to enter the Land of Forest, the first creature to do so, in truth, in a very long time. But she didn't know that and likely wouldn't have cared if she did. James followed, looking in wonder at the thick, hoary old trunks of trees.

He'd only seen cultivated trees, the kind that would grow in the balconies and small farms of Cannoux-Town. These were *something else*. These trunks were as big around as him and Chris together might be able to reach, and rose so high. And then the leaves, rustling slightly in a breeze—*a breeze!*

He felt something on his shoulder, a hand, gripping hard. Chris stood next to him, and for a moment, the brothers D'Essan were just that: brothers.

"Wow, squib," Chris said, wonder suffusing his voice.

"Yeah," James said.

"I feel like I'm in a dream." Katherine looked at Chris, excitement and wonder and happiness plain on her face and in her eyes, and James suddenly felt like he just wanted to push off his stupid brother's hand and go see what lay at the end of the path, that tantalizing glimpse of gray and green and sunlight, so he did.

"C'mon, Bucks," he said, roughly, and didn't wait to see if she'd follow. Maybe she would want to spend all of her time with Chris now too. It didn't take him long to reach the end of the path; the big trees opened out, and James was, once again, thunderstruck.

He was looking at a rocky place, all grays and greens, steep valleys that fell down into each other in ravines. From somewhere he heard the trickle of running water, and a warm breeze blew over his face, bringing exotic scents. It was the most wonderful thing he'd ever smelled in his life. Better than Ma's scrappling, or the distant memory of his Da's bristle-cream. Better than anything. He stepped out into a living world and slowly raised his eyes to the sky.

He let out a little inadvertent cry and fell to his knees. He didn't know what to expect; nothing in his life—or anyone's life—could have prepared him for the sight of the clean, healthy sky of the Wanderlands.

It was so impossibly beautiful that he squeezed his eyes shut for a while, because it was too big for them to contain, and then got it in little quick blinks, capturing one detail and then shutting it out again.

There—the massive silver curve of one of the Rings, spreading across half the sky, patterned in odd and wonderful whorls and lines that reminded him of Uncle's twistcraft. He had heard tales of the Rings, of course; in one of them, the Mother herself had taken the rings from her hands and thrown them up into the sky, where they stuck. But he hadn't ever imagined that some of them would be so *big!* And there—he could see the golden moon, Lode! It couldn't be anything else. It was small but distinct; irregular with cunning towers and endless stairs, spinning slowly above the mountains. There—three more Rings, scattered across the sky, from as big as James' hand held out in front of his face down to tiny, almost too small to see. They spun through a faint, silvery-sparkling haze of stars, visible even in daytime, and everything spun stately around the great lovely incandescent hoop of the sun.

James closed his eyes and let this great thing warm his face. He inhaled the scents of new trees and rich earth and free animals and falling water, and didn't know what he smelled. He only knew that he could never leave this place; that to leave it and return to the bleak gloom of Cannoux and the Mountain would break his heart far worse than even the way Katherine looked at his brother.

"Mother above," he heard Chris whisper, as all of them in their own way accustomed themselves to the unimaginable depth of the sky. James couldn't look at it too long; he felt as if he would suddenly break free from the ground and fall upwards, towards those great Rings, and burn up in the brilliant arc of the sun.

Finally, James got to his feet, because there was something pulling at him, something tugging insistently enough to overcome his awe. Something ahead.

The Silver Key. He felt a little thrill of excitement in his chest, stronger even than the joy of seeing the sky. *His Key.*

The land fell away from them, heading into a great ravine that led into a wide valley bounded by mountains and an enormous, irregularly shaped boulder at the foot of the valley. But James had eyes for something much closer to them. It was a vertical chunk of glassy black rock, unlike anything else in their field of view. And there was something *silver* hanging from its face. He got to his feet.

"James," Chris said. "Careful."

But James didn't want to listen to his brother anymore. He made his way down the loose trail to the black rock. Buckle left off sparring with some sort of big iridescent insect she'd found and alighted back on his shoulder. Behind him, he heard his brother and Katherine follow, but he had eyes only for the rock.

That was it. He could feel it. He had found the Silver Key.

But when he got close, he saw that the object was not in the shape of a key; in fact, it was a skeleton. All of its bones were wrapped in a fine whorling mesh of silver and held in place by a slender, long-bladed knife driven through its skull and into the black stone beneath. The knife was deeply *silver*. He reached up to touch the skeleton.

"James!" Chris said, sharply. "Be careful!"

But nothing happened. He thought for a minute that the silvery knife was the key from his dream. It was certainly silver—the same kind of deeply pure silver that James had seen on the doorknob of the Door behind them—but the knife wasn't the Key from the dream. He didn't know how he knew. He just knew.

"Holy shit," Chris said, in a strange voice, but James ignored him. He started looking around and saw a small glint of silver from the ground underneath the skeleton, right at the base of the black rock. He knelt, brow furrowing, and pushed aside the tall grass.

"James." Katherine's voice was sort of strangled and intense, but James was busy. He brushed aside the grass and saw a small arc of silver, half-buried in the rocky dirt.

"James!" Chris said, his voice frantic, but James had his fingers on the silvery thing and as soon as he touched it, he felt this kind of hollow pulling on his insides, and he knew that this little circle of silver was—*somehow*—the Silver Key from his dream. He smiled joyfully and his chest felt tight but not in the bad, knives-pressing-in way; in a good way, because now he was finally going to be able to save everybody, *everybody*, even his know-it-all older brother and girls who pretended to be his friend, and . . . He dug into the hard dirt, hooked two of them around the thing, and pulled it free.

He stood up, some colossal feeling unfolding in his chest, and brushed the dirt off the thing. It was about as big as his palm, extraordinarily crafted, and so *silver* it almost hurt his eyes. There was a finely woven silver cord looped through a small silver eyelet; it was an amulet.

"James!" Katherine's voice was half a scream, and finally James looked up, frowning, to see what was so all-fired important. He saw, and the amulet fell from suddenly nerveless fingers.

The huge, irregularly shaped boulder down at the base of the valley had lifted its head, turned it, and was peering up at them with immense, burnished golden eyes.

It was a *Giant*.

———

For a long time, nobody moved; the four companions looked down the valley at the distant Giant and the colossus looked back at them. There was no expression they could discern on its face; it was not a human face. It was as if someone had given the most talented sculptor in the Wanderlands the word "strength" and bid them carve. It looked as if it were made of living stone. It didn't look anything like the Giant in James' dream, but he knew unmistakably what it was.

Eventually, James recovered himself enough to realize he'd dropped the silver amulet—*the Silver Key*—and picked it back up. It was eerie, having the massive thing stare at them, unmoving. The close curve of the hill prevented James from seeing its entire body, however, and he took a few steps forward, bringing it into view.

As soon as he passed the glossy black stone, the Giant moved, pushing its great head forward slightly, as if to see better. It was as if James had broken some invisible barrier, alerting the enormous creature.

"James," Chris said, his voice sounding half-strangled, "maybe you better step back."

He pointed to the left, and then the right, and James saw other stones, set a few hundred span apart, making an unbroken line that ran down the valley. An unbroken line that James had crossed, and while carrying the amulet. The great thing, still sitting at the base of the valley, seemed to take on life and vitality and passion and started to move. Its eyes glinted golds and reds. It opened its mouth and roared.

Even at this long distance it was a massive sound, titanic; it swept up the valley toward them like a strong wind. James fell back and Chris caught him under his armpits, and held him up. He dragged James back across the line of stones, but it was too late. The Giant was climbing to its feet, still looking right at them, anger and rage clearly conveyed in its stance and expression.

"Holy crap," Katherine breathed. The thing was gigantic, as big as the Tower d'Atail in Cannoux maybe, or bigger. It churned its great legs, covering the steep ground between them in a stride that seemed caught in slow-motion and yet ate the distance with a terrifying speed.

"Run!" Chris yelled and yanked James backward. The ground shuddered beneath their feet with the Giant's footfalls, and its image grew in James' vision more quickly than could be believed. It looked to be covered in—or *made out of*—a kind of strangely patterned stone armor, with big thick three-fingered hands that seemed engineered to crush. It roared again, and James turned to run.

He seemed caught in that slow-motion movement of the Giant; it felt as if everything was happening far too slowly. Chris and Katherine ran ahead of him, Chris' eyes wide in fear and awe as he glanced back quickly. Buckle flitted ahead, faster than any of them. James ran as fast as his syrupy, caught-in-a-nightmare legs would let him.

The Giant roared again, much closer, which knocked James down onto his face. He rolled, and when he came up he saw the Giant was nearly at the black stone and seemed to blot out half the sky. It drew up, however, and roared again. James scrambled to his feet and ran.

He made it to the Door where Chris was fumbling, trying to get it open again.

"Chris!" Katherine said, looking behind them. James looked too, and his stomach dropped. The Giant seized a huge gray boulder, as big as James' and Chris' entire bedroom, and hurled it into the air. They watched, dumbfounded, as the stone flew in a widening arc, growing larger and larger, and then slammed into the ground a few hundred span to their left, splintering the trunk of a huge old tree.

"*TRESPASS!*" the Giant roared, its voice like great pieces of stone torn asunder. "*YOU CANNOT COME HERE! FORBIDDEN!*"

It leaned down to get another boulder and glared at them with its gigantic golden eyes. Its teeth were like pillars, gnashing together. James could feel the furnace-like exhalation of its breath, even at this distance. It got ready to throw, and Chris got the Door open. They fell through in a jumble, scrambling into the dim and dingy room, soaking their knees in the puddled water there. They saw the sky darken with the approach of the boulder from above, and Chris kicked the Door shut, closing it on the Giant, on the sunshine, on the trees, and on the Land called Forest.

THE MONSTERS

The City on the City

"Trust, unlike love, is a deliberate exercise of will. You can't help who you love. But you sure as hell can choose who you trust. Even if, as is sometimes the case, you happen to love them."

—HUNTER FINE, 'ON TACTICS'

Gun and Jackie walked the streets of a living city, drawing curious looks but not caring, pointing at the wondrous sights, delighting in being tourists. The sight of so much life was intoxicating. The sensation of so much light was heavenly. It made them giddy, as if they'd breathed too deeply of rarefied air.

The city was amazing; there was much to gawk at. It all fell away from them, for one thing; the whole city was built on the side of a steep slope, so you might walk through an archway at the base of a building and onto the roof of another. The lights of the city, arc-bright and hanging overhead in a rough tangle of wires, prevented them from seeing much of what lay beyond the city walls, but they could guess: *Darkness*. It didn't matter.

It was a city constructed on a much older city; a pastoral empire built on the crumbling remains of an ancient one. Wood-frame houses were wired together atop old palaces; people herded sheep on the balconies of ziggurats. Gourds grew atop ancient walls, and the whole place was linked together by a dizzying array of bridges and stitched with those roughly made twistwork wires that seemed to power the lights. If Gun and Jackie had been trying to get anywhere specific, they would have gotten hopelessly lost.

But they weren't trying to get anywhere specific. Their fatigue was washed away, the hurt in Gun's side had faded to almost nothing, his broken ribs didn't matter. There were *people* here! The city was alive, and so were they.

After the long boring time on top of the mountain, in the dead city, and then the brief and far-too exciting time of being harried down the side of the mountain, pursued by both the Feral Children and the artificial urges to kill each other, this city was indistinguishable from a paradise. They walked in open-mouthed wonder, tourists to their core.

The people of this place were a fascinating mixture of what Gun and Jackie might have once called cultures and ethnicities. They were varied, and lovely, and favored blues and grays and cool tones in their clothing. Many had a single splash of bright color somewhere, sometimes a sash and sometimes a piece of jewelry or a hat. Some men and women, invariably shaved bald, had facial tattoos on one side of their heads.

Many of the roofs of the old buildings had been converted into farms, and everywhere they looked they saw yellow wheat and climbing vines and gourds. The new structures were chaotic things—close, cramped, yet comfortable. Gun and Jackie realized where all of the ornament from the tunnels below had gone; these people were first-class repurposers. Old mosaic crusted roughly mortared walls; ancient metals had been beaten into shapes and polished, making sculptures and furniture.

There was evidence of war, too, or some disaster. It looked like something had demolished about a third of the city at some point. It was still rebuilding parts of itself. Jackie and Gun looked at this evidence of war, history, and renewal with wide eyes. *Exciting!*

Gun and Jackie drew attention in the way of wide eyes and hushed exclamations, but these seemed to be a polite people, or at least a culture that valued privacy, and no one accosted them. Gun figured that their clothes—which were still the ones they'd brought with them from their old world—probably looked pretty strange to these people. They'd discovered that these folk spoke the same language as the one that had been impressed upon them by the golden birdbath, though with their quick accent and obvious slang, it was difficult at first to understand what they were saying. People spoke rapidly, with a quick, biting accent that was full of fire and conflict. Jackie loved it.

The monsters didn't mind. Gun's cheeks were numb and burning from smiling so much. Jackie was agape; after so long in the dark and ruin, this place was overwhelming. So they wandered, exclaiming over the sights. The townsfolk didn't remark upon them, though they did get some odd looks.

"Why are they looking at us?" Jackie frowned at an old woman who cut her eyes away from them. "I got mud on my face or something?"

"No," Gun said, studying the people. They were just people, the same as Gun and Jackie; if someone had given them some matching clothes, they could have blended in quite well. It was a multicultural place; all sorts of skin tones and colorings were represented. Or, Gun mused to himself, perhaps his idea of 'multicultural' was useless in a place like this. Eventually, he shrugged. "They can tell we're from out-of-town, I think. Our clothes are weird. But they don't seem hostile."

"They better not." Jackie grinned and tapped her walking stick on the closely fitted paving stones of the street.

At some point they made it onto a major thoroughfare and joined hundreds of rapidly speaking natives, some of them leading the same large, weird cattle they'd seen earlier. They caught snatches of conversation:

—*The Lord won't see to that; you'll catch it*—

—*You didn't say that! She ain't never*—

—*Master will have your stones, you keep that language up!*—

And they had to grin at each other. *People.* There were people here.

The thoroughfare led past a large, open plaza, and Jackie and Gun wandered onto it. The light-pillars, newly made things that had the somewhat brutal, half-finished look of industrial design, hung high above it. There were several musicians playing, including the drums they'd heard in the tunnels below the city. They weren't so different from the instruments he'd seen people play in his old world; there were strings and wood, and an older lady was playing a sweet melody on something that looked almost exactly like a flute. Gun was examining the instruments, fascinated, when Jackie tugged on his sleeve.

"Yeah?" he responded, and she almost pulled him off his feet with her next tug. He turned and saw her pointing, open-mouthed, across the plaza. At first he didn't see what she was looking at. And then he most assuredly *did*.

It was a large, many-striped tent kind of thing, set up at one end of the big plaza, heavy fabric tied off to the old tower and spreading out to make a wide shaded area. People sat under the tent at long tables, laughing, drinking, and discussing, diverse mugs and jars in front of them. In the center, almost lost in dimness under the tent, was a high round bench behind which several people worked busily. It came into focus for Gun with an almost tangible *snap*.

"Holy shit," Gun said. "That's a bar."

"That's a fuckin' *bar*," Jackie said. They looked at each other.

"I might cry. Seriously, Jacks, I might start crying."

"Go ahead, you get a pass. This once."

Almost in a trance, the two made their way over to the tent. Its utility was even clearer the closer they got to it; it appeared that there were certain similarities to drinking establishments that transcended worlds and time. They ignored the sidelong glances they got; they had other priorities. They walked up to the bar like they were coming home after a long journey.

One of the barkeeps startled when he saw them. His eyes flicked over their clothes and then held, for a moment, on the hilt of Gun's sword. But he smiled and bowed, very quickly, quite unlike the elaborate and faintly insulting thing Mr. Vutch had done. He was pleasant-featured with deeply mahogany skin and a sharp little moustache. He was nearly as wide as he was tall, but his bow was graceful.

He made a quick hand gesture, beckoning them. "Welcome. Please, be welcome. Drink, yes? Two?"

Gun and Jackie exchanged a look. "Um," Gun said. "Yeah."

"Yes, please!" Jackie was almost dancing with excitement. The man performed the quick hand-signal again and turned to fill up two coppery looking mugs with something from a large barrel. It *foamed*.

"It's foaming!" Jackie whispered. Gun punched her in the arm, lightly, to shut her up.

The barkeep returned, and Gun realized there was a problem. "I'm sorry." He patted his pockets, knowing they were empty. He had seen something change hands, bronzed tabs that looked like matchsticks. But he obviously had none of those. "No, ah . . . no money."

But the barkeep was already shaking his head. He pushed the two mugs at them and backed away, giving them another quick, rapid-fire bow. "Welcome," he said, gesturing at the long tables where people were standing and drinking. "Drink and be welcome."

He turned to do something else behind the bar and steadfastly refused to look at them again. The other barkeeps tossed quick, furtive glances their way, as if afraid some secret ritual had not been properly performed, and the two strange, dirty people in strange, dirty clothes would not leave. But neither Jackie nor Gun were pikers. They didn't know much, but they knew how to drink in bars, and they sure as fuck knew how to appreciate a free beverage. They picked up their coppery mugs, tapped them together, and went to find a table.

"That bartender is the best person I've ever met," Jackie said, once they'd found a place to sit. Three friendly-looking people were sitting a few feet away; they nodded at Gun and Jackie politely and then took great pains not to make eye contact again.

"He," Gun began, lifting the mug to his nose and inhaling deeply, "is a prince and a lord amongst all folk."

"To him. The unnamed barkeep." Jackie took a slow, careful sip. She closed her eyes and shuddered.

"That good?" Gun asked, grinning. She made a sound that she certainly had never made when drinking Well-water. Gun inhaled again; it smelled faintly nutty and just slightly astringent, but in a pleasant way. *Very* pleasant. He took a sip and made something of a sound himself.

"It's not quite beer," Jackie said. "Not wine, either."

"I don't give a *shit*." Gun felt the small muscles all over his body unwinding and un-tensing for the first time in days. Maybe months. "I don't care what it is. It's the best thing I've ever had."

"Hands down," Jackie rolled her eyes into the back of her head, so lovely was the taste of the sweet, sweet booze. "Hands fuckin' down."

"And here," Gun said, through a heavy sigh of pleasure, "I'd thought my experience with *you* had ruined bartenders for me forever."

"I was the best bartender you ever had, you son of a bitch!"

"Well, until *that* guy." Gun gestured at their beloved barkeep.

"Okay, until that guy," Jackie amended. "And anyway, jerk, you should wake up every day praising the heavens that I even *deigned* to ask what you were writing in your dumb book. Being a fuckin' weirdo at my bar, huh."

"Oh, hush." Gun took a long sip, closing his eyes with pleasure. "Admit it—I had you hooked from the start."

"I am an easily amused person." Jackie sniffed. "And prone to all sorts of ill-advised behaviors."

"That is a damn understatement." Gun lifted his mug.

Jackie grinned at him and they toasted. "So I have an idea."

"Is it that we should drink about six more of these things?"

"No. But also, yes. Shut up. Here is my idea: *dinner.*"

Gun groaned. "Okay, you win. I *can* smell something cooking."

"I bet it's one of those cattle-things," Jackie said, inhaling. "I bet it's roasting."

"Right." Gun clapped his hands together a little too loudly. "Okay. How do we make this happen? We got no money."

"I dunno." Jackie shrugged and took another long draught. "Maybe they'll be feeling charitable again."

"Maybe," Gun said, doubtful. "I mean, I love having this problem but we're going to have to figure this money thing out at some point."

"True." Jackie snapped her fingers. "I've got an idea. We're these fuckin'—what did Mr. Vutch call us? Behemoth? We're these legendary *Behemoth* things, right? So we walk up to whoever runs this place, we say: Hey! We're indestructible badasses, and we can beat up anybody in the world. Give us some goddamn cash."

Gun was horrified. "You're going to *extort*—"

"No!" Jackie said. "I mean, like, *hire* us for something. Dude, we can punch buildings down. There's got to be a couple odd jobs a self-respecting mayor or king or whatever would have for us."

Gun considered this and nodded. "Makes sense. I could do the mercenary thing."

"Oooh!" Jackie snickered. "I like the sound of that. *Mercenaries.* That's badass."

"But I don't want to, like, hurt anyone, though," Gun said. And for a moment the two fell silent.

"Never happen," Jackie said, after a minute. "We won't have to. Right? I mean look, somebody walks up to us with a sword or a gun or something, we just delicately take it out of their hands, bend it into a cute shape, and hand it back. Who's gonna fuck with us then?"

"That's a point." Gun brightened up. "And maybe they'll just need some buildings knocked over. We've certainly been trained in *that.*"

"We got options, is the point!" Jackie said. She looked into her newly empty cup. "Whoosh! This stuff is hitting me already."

"Yawp." Gun giggled. "Either this business is stee-*rong* or my tolerance is for shit."

"Might be a little of both," Jackie said and grinned, a little goofy. "I do *not mind*."

They looked around at the bright lights beyond the tent, at the kindly-featured people, at the riot of life and color and sound all around them. Gun got to the end of his drink and set it down, his head enjoyably buzzing.

"Damn, Jacks," he said.

"I know."

"It's just—"

"I *know*. Let's just . . ." She shook her head, minutely. She looked off, into the city. Her eyes sobered for a minute, but when she brought them back to Gun, they crinkled at the corners. "Let's just have another fuckin' drink, yeah?"

"One of the things I like about you, Aimes?" Gun said, picking up his empty mug. "Top-notch goddamn plans."

"What can I say?" She was grinning ear to ear. "Got my skills."

But either the drink hit him harder than he thought or his wounded side betrayed him, because Gun lost his balance and fell backwards, arms flailing comically, into the table behind him. Fortunately it was an empty one, because he broke it all to shit. He felt the heavy wood give and snap under his considerable weight, and he went down to the ground in a pile of splinters and sharp wood. He hit hard enough to crack the big flagstone underneath him. He started laughing and couldn't stop.

"You dumbass!" Jackie said, shaking her head. Gun covered his face with his hands, laughing helplessly. It was just too funny. He didn't realize the entire bar had gone silent.

One of the polite people sitting near them, a big blond man with strong-looking hands and a manicured beard, got up and approached Gun. He looked wary but had a smile on his face.

"Are you well, friend?" he asked, and Gun couldn't reply for a moment, because he was caught in an almost hysterical laughing fit.

"He's okay," Jackie assured the man. "He's just an idiot."

"Well," the man said, with a smile, "let me give you a hand. That looked like a bad fall."

He reached out a big hand and Gun caught it gratefully and tried to pull himself up. In the relief of finding the city and in the muzziness of drink, he didn't think to be careful. He felt bones break under his grip and the man screamed.

It just happened too fast. Gun was still lying on his back, and he couldn't at first place what had happened. The man staggered back from him, cradling his hand, and stood looking at him with wide, horrified eyes. Jackie came over and now Gun realized that everyone in the bar was looking at them, and their expressions were no longer kind.

The man with the broken hand struggled to get a word out, and when he did it was pitched high with loathing and fear. *"Behemoth!"* he cried, staggering back. And again, his voice high with terror: *"Behemoth!"*

There was a rushing sound as people sucked in sharp breaths; and as Gun struggled to get to his feet, he heard the word again, repeated in the crowd, hysterical.

"Behemoth!"

AN ASIDE: WHEN THE
WANDERLANDS WORKED

So let's say that this is the way the world is supposed to work:

Let's say you're a rambunctious, aggressive civilization, you've quite dominated your Land, and you're feeling a little stifled by the Barrier Mountains and the general lack of empire-building options that any self-respecting tyrant would want out of his/her/its surroundings. You start thinking about the ripe, delicious civilizations just over those mountains, and how wonderful it would be if you were in charge of them, too. Maybe you lay on your back at night, looking up at the Skylands, and you think to yourself about how great it would be if you owned them.

Let's say you start getting ambitious.

Well, great! There's a lot of ways this can go. In a history as long as the Wanderlands', it's unlikely you'd try something that hasn't been tried before. But still, put a thinking creature in a box, and it will try to get out of it. There are technologies available, ruinously costly and legendarily forbidden but, really, who are you to listen to legends?

Certainly, the Wanderlands are full of legends, legends of what happens when a civilization gets too ambitious and starts messing with the forbidden. But it will be easy for you to discard these tales as nonsense.

Nonsense they must be, for who in living memory has heard the Call of the Mother? Who has ever seen a Returner—a Giant—with their own eyes? Sure, there are reborn cranks in every Land, on their fortieth or fiftieth life, but you can't believe every crazy story you have ever heard. *You* have an empire to build.

The most obvious barriers to your world-spanning plans of conquest are, ironically enough, the Barrier Mountains themselves. They surround every Land, they're impassable, and they strongly resist being tunneled through or climbed over. You *can* get over them, but not in the kind of numbers that will allow subjugation of whatever tempting and ready-to-be-plucked Land lies beyond.

So what's a self-respecting empire builder to do? Well, if you have any imagination at all, you look to the sky.

There are many legends surrounding the subjects of Flying Machines, and every civilization has tales of them. These tales seem to be universally sinister and end in tragedy, but you did not get to the pinnacle of your civilization by being put off by a few children's stories.

As soon as you've enslaved enough craftsmen, you'll discover that there's no scientific reason why flying devices should be impossible; the basics of the physics is clear. So? This becomes easy. You will build a fleet of sky-ships, and fly over the Barrier Mountains, and subjugate all in your path, and soon enough you will be the emperor of all the Wanderlands.

There is only one problem: the Barrier Mountains tend to hold storms, and those storms will absolutely wreck the shit out of your flying vehicles. Also they are *stupid* tall, and it takes some pretty impressive flying machines to even get near the top of them.

But you are a conscious being, and therefore, you spit in the face of limits. You build bigger and better flying devices. Ones that can fly higher and last longer than anything ever dreamed possible. You push the limits of twistcraft! And you discover something that many other civilizations have discovered before you—something you are just as unhappy about. You discover The Roof of the World.

There is something in the sky, something you cannot pass. There is an invisible thing high above you that cannot be pierced, not with all of your advanced technology. And cannot be breached, not with any means known to thinking folk.

Well, obviously this is intolerable.

Who knows what you do then? Mountains one cannot pass tend to be a breaking point for many would-be conquerors. Many civilizations have tried many things in the long history of the Wanderlands. If you are wise, you begin to look inward and hope to ease and better the lives of your citizens. You turn your ambition to the uplifting of all thinking creatures and seek to bring your civilization into harmony with the shape of the world.

This, clearly, is the weakling option, and not for a born conqueror like yourself.

If you are *not* wise, you begin to see the Mother—and the Roof of the World—as enemies and obstacles. And you begin to make plans.

Perhaps you raise an army, the like of which has never been seen in your Land before. Perhaps you enslave thousands of twist craftsmen, forcing them to build elaborate engines-of-war and flying machines. Or digging machines. Or both! In any case, you raise a fist at the sky, you curse the damned Mother, you will not be cowed, etc, etc.

And then, if you are supremely purposeful and effective at flouting the natural laws of the Wanderlands, if you force your civilization to go wrong in just the right kinds of ways, the Mother will take notice of you.

Perhaps you pricked her; perhaps you banged one too many flying contraptions against the Roof of the World. Perhaps you dug too deep under the Barrier Mountains, or perhaps you just messed with something that she didn't want you messing with. However you managed it, guess what?

Now you're fucked.

The Mother only has one real defense against the cunning and utility of thinking folk, but it's a good one. If you piss her off enough, she sends you a Returner.

Returners are conscious beings that wake in a strange land, full of anger and fear, overwhelmed with one motive: to destroy everything the Mother hates. Returners are enormous, are basically indestructible, and, in the first stage of their lives, utterly pitiless.

They're going to stomp on you. They're going to kick the shit out of your industry. They're going to—literally—punch your civilization back into the herding-sheep-and-writing-epic-ballads phase. You can't stop them; they are made out of something stronger than what makes your civilization work. They're going to destroy you.

And then? Well, then your story is over. Perhaps you get killed by the Returner, or you kill yourself, or your populace turns on you and kills you. You'll wake up, eventually, in a new body and in a new Land, with no power or influence or money or anything but your memories and dreams of empire. If you have any sense at all, you'll start to reconsider those dreams.

Your old Land, having been kicked back into the stone age, will hopefully find a more reasonable and boring leader. They will burn their flying machines and concentrate, at least for a while, on the business of fucking, drinking, working, and making some meaning out of life.

And, possibly, the experience will cause a few more to work their way down the Mother's ever-waiting way toward *true* power. Perhaps, out of all this ambition and bloodshed and hubris, some few will find The Path.

> —*An excerpt from 'The Path of the Mother,' attributed to Allanna Mardragal, well before the Fall, recovered from the Garden of Lode*

THE DEADSMITH

The Door Into Memory

*"You've been chasing this death through Land and Rill, over mountains
and streams and through rooms long dark and past obstacles
many and large. Do not run from it now."*

—APOCRYPHAL, 'THE TALE OF THE TIN-EYE AND THE JANNISSARY'

Night was falling in the Land of Elah, and violently.
The sky was both ashen and too bright, livid cracks of silver and gold
fighting with jagged spars of white and black. It hurt the eyes and made the teeth
ache; it made a man want to hide his face and pray. It was a storm of nothing, a
titanic battle with no purpose or effect, for the outcome was already assured.

It was always assured, in the end: Darkness. Darkness evermore, for the Land
of Elah.

The Deader pursued his Prey across that dying land, pausing only to kill those
who attacked him, stopping only to gather what meager amount of sleep and
sustenance his sort required. And from time to time, he would come across one
of the mechanisms that the Prey left for him.

"*Slaome,*" his Fate said, wary, when he came upon the first of them. But it was
just a small construct, a apparatus with one jerking leg that drove itself in circles.
It was roughly made, a Dirt-Magic thing, and it had nearly worn down by the
time he'd found it. He was reminded of the message on the Door in the city behind him.

How do you make a machine?

The Deader grunted and crushed the mechanism under his boot. This Prey
undoubtedly thought he was clever, but that was okay. The Deader had killed
many clever folk.

The Deader remembered the tableau of five dead that the Prey had left for
him, surrounding the cryptic question, written in blood on an ancient Door. The
Prey had set up representations of the Deader's family, depicting the way they had
died. His mother, his sister. The small boy with the cut around his finger, left
alive for the Deader to kill.

He remembered, too, the city that had fallen under the bizarre glamour of the

Prey, the fanatical light in their eyes, and the fact that he had been forced to decimate them. The Prey had turned an entire city against the Nine and had done it while the Deadsmith was on his trail.

Yes, the Prey thought himself clever indeed; perhaps he even thought he was powerful. But the Deader cared nothing for cleverness. And as for power . . .

The Deader put the Prey's traps and mechanisms out of his mind; they were of less import than the wind that blew across his face.

This land had been prosperous, once; a twilight civilization but a strong one. Their sky had gone Dim long ago, but they had adapted and been comfortable enough for many years. The twilight years were the times when a civilization should prepare for the coming Dark, but it was clear that this one had been foolish. They'd begun thinking that what is has ever been, and what would be was already written. It was the great failing of people and things that speak as people, and the Deader had watched this story play itself out more times than he cared to remember. These people had no Feed, they had no craft, and they had no foresight. They deserved their bad end.

The Deader was unsure how the Prey stayed ahead of him, yet he had. The occasional fires he found were cold, and the half-broken little contraptions left on his trail were mostly worn down. The Deader had to wind some of them to see what they were meant to do, his Fate whispering anxiously against the risk. But they were all inconsequential. Perhaps they were a game the Prey played with himself and had no meaning. Perhaps the Prey was mad.

How do you make a machine?

The words scrawled on the Door had taken up a kind of residence in the Deader's mind, cropping up in the middle of thoughts and reveries despite his desire to banish them. The question reinforced itself, setting up an echo that neither the Deader nor his Fate could quite still. He walked, inexorably, for if the Prey wished to play mind-games, the Deader wished him well at it. Games would not help the Prey and would not keep the Deader from returning to his Lady with the Prey's blood on his teeth.

The Land of Elah was mountains and rolling hills arranged around a spacious lake. What cities they had straddled the demarcation between hills and water, many of them thrust far out into the waves. The Deader tracked the Prey through these towns and coastal cities, all of them tearing themselves apart, and some of them starting to burn for light. The violent, shifting sky above transformed them from idyllic places to monstrous. Bands of new-made priests led new-made supplicants in bizarre rituals meant to call down favor from the Mother above, but there would be no comfort for them there. If there were gods, they had turned their eyes away from the Land of Elah.

The Deader felt an unusual kind of lassitude, a reluctance to consider the riddle posed to him by the Prey. He knew he should; the Prey knew things about the Deader that no one should know. Even his Lady did not know the story of the Deader's childhood. He should be worried about this. He should be considering the Prey's motives.

But it was difficult to care. He was a Deadsmith, and the Prey was a mortal man. What could a mortal man do to a thing like the Deader?

He came across another mechanism next to another cold camp. The mechanism, once activated, seemed to have no other purpose than to turn itself off. Like all the others, the Deader crushed it. After what the Prey had made him do to the boy, made him do to the city behind him, he even took pleasure in it. Sometimes he rubbed the small scar on his smallest finger, but he took care not to remember the day he got it. He guessed that this was the Prey's intent, that causing the Deader to remember the tableau would gain him some advantage, and the Deader was not in the habit of giving his enemies advantage.

Instead, he tried to imagine his Lady's smile, what she would say when he returned to her. For a moment he was seized with a longing so intense it nearly caused his pace to falter. He wondered what she was doing, where she was. It seemed very wrong that she should be without his protection and service.

But she would laugh at that, he knew, and clap her hands together. She would tell him not to be silly, that the only traps in our past are ones we built ourselves.

The Deader spat and shaded his eyes from the rent sky. Even darkness would be a relief after this. The Fall was never pleasant, not while it was happening.

How do you make a machine?

The Deader's pace slowed, his dusty boots coming to a stop. He looked down over the arc of burning cities spread across the long bay. He would not catch the Prey in this Land; he knew it.

Avalon, his Fate whispered, with the scent of honeysuckle. It agreed.

And his Lady would be right; he *was* being silly. It was time to take a rest, and remember. He gathered materials for a fire, enjoying the work of his hands, and made a light camp under the roiling sky. His Fate chattered at him, sending him scents and colors, but he ignored it. He prepared a little food and looked into the fire.

He still felt that lassitude, that reluctance to recall his youth, but he was Deadsmith. He would not fear the past. Had he not already survived it?

Loosening the bonds he had long ago strapped across his mind, the Deader remembered the sun.

———

The boy had grown up with some light. Not much, but some. Maybe one day out of every twelve, the sky cleared from the unpleasant Dim and let some brighter light through. It was still a flat sky, heavy overhead, but it glowed and was warm, and the boy loved those days. It allowed the boy's family to grow seed for selling to the nomads, and that was enough for them to live on.

They had built their farm around a Well and so never lacked for food, but life on the steppes was vulgar and hard, and the boy had worked ever since he could remember. Days when the sun came were his own, however, and he was able to escape his chores and his brother and wander.

His older brother hated him because the boy was strong and sure and talented. His older brother hated him because he was special and different. His older brother hated him because his mother loved him.

The boy exiled himself on the sun-days, ranging across the steppes and playing small, lonely games with himself. He was never comfortable, though, on these forays. When he left the farm, there was no one to protect his sister.

On this particular day, this day of light, the boy was mock-fighting with crooked sticks, pretending dead trees were nomads, but he was uneasy and felt guilty. He knew he should not have left the farm, but he could not bear to stay. His father grew wrathful on the sun-days, exposing some strange, twisted thing inside him, and often hit his mother if the boy wasn't there to stop him. The boy didn't know or understand how he'd become his mother's and sister's protector; he only knew that he was.

He was troubled as he smashed thin dead trees apart. Just the day before, he had come upon his brother in the curing shack. His sister was weeping, and his brother had fistfuls of her hair. The boy didn't wait to ask what was happening. He took a rake and beat his brother until the older boy wept and promised to change, promised that nothing would ever happen again. He'd said oddly pitiful things about being compelled, about being driven by forces outside himself. But the boy knew his brother's eyes. He should not have left the farm, not even on a sun-day.

Duty, his father said often, was a thing that only grew heavier when you set it down. The boy threw aside his crooked sticks and made his way back to the farm, his sister's tears running down the inside of his mind.

He saw the contrivances from far off, the tall spindly contrivances that the nomads rode in. He hurried, for while the nomads were generally peaceable, there were hard men and women among their number.

The boy ran as fast as he could when he saw what was happening. He tried. He was able to sneak up, to steal one of the men's weapons and kill him with it, but the others caught him and laughed and tied him up. They were the bad sort of nomads, and it appeared that the boy's father had been shorting them.

The leader was a man named Trail, and he had laughing eyes. He was amused by the boy's capacity for violence. He had one of the nomads stand next to the boy, and every time the boy closed his eyes, the nomad pushed a knife a little farther into the boy's side. So the boy watched what the nomads did to his mother. She begged the boy to save her, but he couldn't save her. Fortunately, she died quickly.

The boy's brother begged to join the nomads, and the leader with the laughing eyes allowed it. His brother proved his worth to the nomads with his sister, fists in her long black hair. The boy closed his eyes then, even though the knife went very far into his side. When he opened them, his sister was dead.

His father was weeping and begging. Trail explained how things would be from then on.

"It's the new law," he said, and laughed. He approached the boy and pulled the knife from his side. Trail told the boy he liked him, that he had fire. Trail said he would take pleasure in killing the man who the boy would become. He took the boy's smallest finger and cut, deeply, all the way around it. All of these nomads had the same mark.

"So you know how to find me," Trail had said, with his laughing eyes. The nomads took all of the stored seed and the boy's brother. They left the boy the knife.

When he had cut himself free, the nomads were long gone. The boy's father was still weeping. He said many erratic things the boy didn't listen to. The boy pushed the knife into his father's heart and left it there. The boy learned his first lesson: to hate weakness. After a while, he began digging graves.

Several sun-days came and passed when another visitor came to the farm, a hard woman with strange markings on her arms. She asked what had happened to his family, and the boy told her.

The woman asked him if he wanted justice, and the boy said yes.

THE KILLERS

A Heartwarming Reunion
With an Old Friend

*"Go ahead and burn those bridges, baby. But don't
complain to me about your wet feet."*

—ANNALEE X, 'SUMMONS'

Sophie was thrown in a jail cell that was comfortable, almost ridiculously so—
a posh drawing-room that just happened to be locked. Sophie supposed that
Jane had other cells, with fewer amenities, for guests without famous names.

Jane left her sitting for a while, which didn't surprise her. The woman was
unlikely to appreciate Sophie's method of getting an interview, but kicking a
Practice Guard in the tenders had been just too much of a temptation to resist.
They'd confiscated her slots, though, and she wished she had one now.

Or a *drink*. She'd just found out her brother was Mr. March; her cheerful little
kid brother had murdered the Loche, sent the Ransom Parkway Dim, and had
brought *Feral Children* into the Keep. She needed more than a drink. She needed
a fucking *bucket*.

She entertained herself while she was waiting by scratching pornographic
diagrams involving a woman with very long hair into the expensive wall-
covering. The Practice Guard hadn't found or confiscated her pen-knife, which
might have been a capital offense in any other monarchy, but the idea of Sophie
physically harming Jane Guin was so ludicrous it didn't bear consideration.

She heard someone come in behind her, the guards unlocking and re-locking
the door, but she didn't bother to turn. She knew from the cologne who it was,
though she hadn't seen him in a very long time. Funny, the way scent worked.

"Interesting composition," a voice said from behind her, "but I don't think
the Queen is quite that flexible."

"I don't know." Sophie finished her stick diagram with the pen-knife. "She's
managed to get her head up her own ass enough times."

"Very droll, but I'd get all of *that* out of your system before your audience."
He sounded amused. Sophie refused to turn around, working on her etching. She

heard him sit, heard the rustle of padded fabric behind her. He'd always been adept at making himself comfortable. "She's not in the best of moods tonight."

"Yeah, well," Sophie said. She took a last moment to steady herself, then snapped the pen-knife closed. She turned, preparing her best unconcerned grin for the man sitting across the room. "I'm not in the best mood myself. Hello, Denver."

"Hello, Sophie." He looked her over with his calm brown eyes. "You look good."

"Fuck you. I look like shit and you know it."

Denver smiled. "Well, it never hurts to be polite."

"Oh, it hurts," Sophie said, trying to keep her tone even, "plenty."

Denver had no reply. He looked her over again, with his keen and somewhat sad eyes.

She studied him for changes and found a few. Ten years had done him plenty of favors. His boyish, somehow unfinished face had strengthened and was now almost unbearably handsome. His dark hair had taken on a great deal of gray, but it suited him. His brown eyes held the same sharp intelligence they always had, even when he was a young man and Sophie's tutor. And they'd still held it some years later, when she'd become a young woman, and he became her lover. Some would call that adaptability, she supposed. She threw herself down into a chair. "Okay. What do you want?"

He lifted an eyebrow. "I thought it was *you* that wanted an audience, Sophie. Enough to kick some poor Practice Guard's genitals up into her ribcage, from what I hear."

Sophie smiled. "I asked to see the Queen. What do *you* want?"

"Perhaps I just wanted to see an old friend."

"We were never friends, Denver. You taught me to kill and then you taught me to fuck; that's about the extent of it."

Denver sighed, the sort of sigh one gives when confronted by a difficult child. Sophie remembered that sigh well.

"All right, then," he said, "perhaps I wanted to give you a warning."

"Denver, you can fucking *spare me*. I've gotten enough warnings tonight to last three lifetimes. Let me guess, was it going to be cryptic?"

A genuine smile came to his lips, and his eyes twinkled. "It was going to be a touch cryptic, yeah."

"So?" Sophie asked. "Any more arrows in that quiver? Want to try again?"

"Yes." He set the flats of his palms on his knees and leaned forward. His eyes lost some of their laughter. "The Queen needs your help."

"I find that difficult to believe, since I got myself arrested. But I'm a loyal Citizen; if the Queen calls, then I must answer."

His eyes narrowed. "An unexpectedly mature attitude."

"You of all people should know better than to trust my reputation," Sophie said, grinning. "So what can I help the Beast with? Does Jane need some drugs? Maybe some grift? A Lord's house broken into? Scandalous, but I'm not one to judge."

Denver sighed.

"Or maybe it's a personal problem?" Sophie continued. "I've heard about this Consort; are they having trouble in the bedroom? I can give her some tips. Or, hell, I'll join in if that's what we're talking about. Jane's not unattractive and, like I said, I'm a loyal Citizen."

"There's no need to be perverse, Sophie."

"Oh." Her demeanor went savage for a moment. "There's *every* reason to be perverse."

Denver pinched the bridge of his nose. "I told her this was a mistake. But she thought you might have some warm feelings left. From the old days."

"Oh, I have some warm feelings, Denver Murkai. Hot, even. Positively scorching."

His eyes crinkled in a smile. "I'm starting to worry about that pen-knife now."

"If I wanted to hurt you, I'd tell you about how many other tongues have been between my teeth, and how many sweeter than yours."

He had the grace to wince, at least. "No, thank you. I've heard the stories."

She sat back on the divan and crossed her arms. "If there's one thing I'm good at, it's *stories*."

"So time has not healed all wounds, I take it?"

"You can go to hell," Sophie said, evenly. "You and your Queen both."

He studied her for a while, then sighed. "All right, Sophie. The Queen isn't having a pleasant night; I would like to save you both some time if I can. I want to offer you a deal. I know you went to Crowe; I know you're trying to get your friends out of the fire."

She waited, legs crossed and arms along the back of the divan, a pose of casualness. "I'm breathless with anticipation."

"The Book."

"Imagine my surprise."

"It's all she wants from you, Sophie. I'll admit the little play with March and the Battle Drugs was inelegant; she doesn't always listen to my advice. Or have my high opinion of your character."

Sophie looked away, thinking. "Let me guess: if I give her the Book, she'll live and let live."

"If you give her the Book, you and your Killers can live out your lives in whatever way you choose."

"What about the silver vault?"

Denver shrugged. "She's not overly concerned with the vault. This Mr. March was trying to be clever; to kill two birds with one stone. She will be content with the Book."

"I bet she will be." Sophie chewed on her lower lip. "What the fuck does she even want with that thing? I've never known."

"Did you ever ask?" Denver grinned, crookedly. "I'm not authorized to tell you. But it's something grandly good, Sophie. I think if you knew, you would approve."

"But she never told me. She never just fucking *asked*." Sophie felt the old bitterness well up. "Neither of you did. You just tricked, manipulated, pushed. That's all you bastards have ever done. You never had the courage to just ask."

Denver chuckled. "Poor little Sophie Vesachai, is that it? An innocent little pawn? Give me a break."

He leaned forward. "Do you have any idea what a pain in the ass you were? Precocious doesn't cover the half of it. You want to know why we never told you our plans, Sophie? Because you're a fucking *maniac,* and you always have been."

He straightened. "Nobody can trust you, Sophie. You're not just a wildcard; you're a card lit on fire and tied to an angry cat. Of all the kids to find the Book, it had to be *you.* You want to know why we manipulated you? Why we tried to, tonight? Because you're too fucking crazy, too Twins-damned unpredictable to ever be relied upon! In all the versions and plans and scenarios of tonight, there wasn't a single one where we thought you would kick the shit out of a guard and then try to see the Queen. If I didn't know you, I wouldn't believe it."

"Now you're just trying to flatter me."

"Trust me, it's not a compliment. But I *am* trying to educate you; call it my last lesson."

Denver took a breath, composed himself. He put on an agreeable smile. "Well. All that to the side, I still want to help you. Do we have a deal?"

Sophie considered her old tutor, her head cocked. "No."

He sighed again. "Should I bother even asking why not?"

She smiled, slowly. "Because you could have chosen anyone, Denver. You had all of the Vesachai to choose from; hell, all you needed was somebody who can do the mind-trick. You could have sent anybody to Saint Station. And you fucks sent my *brother.*"

Denver winced. "Ah. It was inevitable you found out, I suppose."

"Yeah. It was."

He seemed to be weighing his responses. "We didn't have as many choices as you might think. Saint Station is . . . not biddable. She accepted Lee, but just barely. And we think—perhaps—that it was *because* he was your brother."

"Bullshit. Why would that demon care?"

"Don't ask me to explain that creature, Sophie." Denver met her eye. "If it helps, he was eager to go, Sophie. He was very motivated. Almost as motivated as you were."

Sophie snorted. "I wasn't motivated, Denver. You led me out to that monster, and then you fed me to it. You and your Queen both."

For some reason, this stopped Denver cold. He looked at her with an almost incredulous, unguarded expression. "That is a unique way of looking at it."

"Why deny it, at this point? You and your Queen needed someone with silver in their arms, and I already had the Book. She wanted to ruin my father, and she wanted a weapon under her thumb. Fuck, she didn't just kill *two* birds with one stone, she murdered a fucking *flock*."

But Denver was shaking his head. He laughed.

"Is that what you've been telling yourself all these years? Fucking hell, no wonder you hate us. Tell yourself a story long enough, and it becomes true."

"There isn't any point pretending—"

"No, Sophie. You think I fed you to Saint Station? You fed *yourself*. Have you been telling yourself, all these years, that I somehow tricked you into going out into the Dark, manipulated you into finding that monster? *You?*"

Denver looked at her, squarely. He seemed to have set aside some pose, or layer of polite dissembling. He looked at her the way he had when she was fourteen, and he'd offered to teach her how to kill—and won her young little heart. "Sophie, you were *obsessed* with finding that thing. It was those fucking dreams; you could feel it out there, waiting. I led you there, sure. I mean, you were *begging* me to. I helped you, and I did it on the Queen's orders. We knew where it was, and a little bit of *what* it was, from Jane's scouts. We took advantage of the situation—I won't deny that. Jane saw an opportunity and took it, and it paid off well for her. But you . . . Do you remember what you used to be like? There's not a force in the world that would have stopped you from finding your way to Saint Station. You want to blame me and Jane for a lot of things, sure. We fucked you up in a lot of ways, and if I could do things differently, I might have. But Saint Station?"

He laughed again, looking at her and shaking his head. "The lies we tell ourselves. We didn't trick you into putting silver in your arms, we just took advantage of it. *We* didn't feed you to that monster. The *Mother* did. The Mother, and her dreams. She told you, and all those other poor kids, that you were going to save the world. If anybody tricked you into those scars on your arms, Sophie, it was her."

Sophie felt cold. "That . . . no. Jane sent the dreams, she figured out some way of . . ."

Denver laughed, standing. "Listen to yourself, kid. Jane sent the dreams? You don't believe that. If *Jane Guin* had that kind of power, she wouldn't be fucking around with assholes like your brother, or trying to trick you with drugs. We ain't saints, Sophie. But there are more powerful forces in the world than *us*."

He went to the door and looked back over his shoulder at her. "I'll see if the Queen will see you. Maybe she'll explain. Or maybe not. But I would take that deal, kiddo. You are in way over your head."

"Fuck you," Sophie managed, through nearly numb lips. "You and your queen both."

"You told me," he said, grinning. "Now let's see if you got the genitals to tell *her*."

THE MONSTERS

Behemoth

"The best of intentions stacks up for shit against the weakest of needs."

—OVIA EST, 'CANDLEBOX'

A susurration of fear rose around the tables of the drinking tent. The man with the broken hand was stumbling back, away from them, eyes wide and terrified, as if he'd seen a horror beyond imagining. He stuttered, but he said it again, a cry of terror:

"Behemoth!"

"Gun . . ." There was a strange note of fear in Jackie's voice. There was panic in that exclamation, in that name, the panic of normal people faced with a weapon, or children faced with a monster. A circle opened around them and widened, people trying to get away from them, rushing towards the exits. Better to be crushed, it seemed, than to stand too near the monsters.

"What's going on?" Gun asked. He felt terribly confused. He could still feel the bones in the man's hand breaking, as if a small bird had been crushed. From somewhere, they heard the unmistakable sound of a siren wind up, a raw sound, a war sound. And people were still crying that word, as if they were saying something horrifying: *"Behemoth!"*

Jackie had taken up her stick, but her face was tight and hot and bewildered. Gun couldn't get his head around it; surely this was just a mistake? He hadn't meant to hurt the man!

The bar emptied, people fleeing across the plaza and, against that flow, other figures moved toward them, wearing what were plainly uniforms. These waved people away, encouraging them to run, to flee from the human-shaped monsters.

Suddenly Gun's side hurt again. He was aware of the weight of the sword on his back.

"It will be okay," he told Jackie. "I'll explain."

She shook her head. "I just wanted a drink." Her voice was small. Gun looked at the oncoming soldiers, looked at their faces. They looked like brave men determined to die well, and more than anything else it told him what he needed to know.

"I just wanted a fuckin' drink," Jackie said again.

"I know." Gun held his hands up towards the soldiers. He raised his voice. "It was an accident. We do not mean you any—"

If there was something more eloquent coming, it was cut off, because one of the soldiers panicked and fired his weapon at them.

Gun lurched back, an arm across his face. The weapon the soldier used threw something like heavy needles, and they peppered Gun's skin. They didn't break it, and Gun wasn't really harmed, but it *hurt*.

"Hey!" He held a hand up. "Stop! We don't mean you any harm!"

"Gun . . ." Jackie said from behind him.

"We don't want to hurt anybody!" Gun yelled, as loudly as he could. He spit out a black needle. "We just want—"

"Gun!" Jackie sounded frantic, and he looked over his shoulder at her. She jerked her head in the other direction, across the plaza. Gun looked, and paled.

There were things coming at them, big things. Mechanical things, heavy things. It took Gun a moment to realize there were men inside them.

The mechanisms were brutal, heavy-limbed, and had that same roughly industrial look that much of the new city bore. The mechanisms encased the men and moved with them; they had violent, heavy-looking weapons attached to the arms. What Gun could see of the men's faces was grim.

The soldiers backed away, their weapons trained on the Behemoth. Gun looked back at Jackie, helplessly.

"What do we do?" he asked. "Jacks? What do we do?"

"I don't know." Jackie had her stick in her hands, ready. Gun did not pull his sword free; he wanted no part of what *that* thing could do.

The men in the heavy mechanical suits drew closer, the sound of their footfalls sending heavy shudders through the plaza. Gun counted twelve of them but heard the sounds of more coming, echoing among the bridges of the city.

One of the contrivances, splashed in slashes of yellow paint, stepped forward. Gun could just make out the man's face, and he was old and grizzled and hard-eyed. He spoke in a loud voice, clear even among the sounds of fright and mechanical suits.

"Leave the city," he said, "and no harm will come to you."

Jackie laughed, a hopeless sound, a dark one. "Fuck *that*. We finally found some people, I'm not fucking leaving."

Gun held his hands up again, slowly. The soldiers in the mechanical suits closed, tightening a cordon around them.

"We don't mean any harm!" he yelled. He stepped forward. "We don't want to hurt anyone."

"Leave the city," the man repeated, with no change in his inflection, "and no harm will come to you."

"Listen," Gun said, sure that once he was able to make the soldiers understand, then everything would be all right. "We just wanted something to eat and . . . maybe a shower . . ."

"Leave the city and no harm will come to you," the man said again. The big mechanisms had closed a half-circle around them now. Gun took another step, trying to reason with the leader. His hands were still up; he was pleading.

"*Please,*" he said. "Please. We just want—"

"Supplies will be left outside the gates." As old and grizzled and hard as the man looked, he was sweating, and Gun saw fear in his eyes. "You must leave the city!"

"Fuck that," Jackie said again, low, behind him. Her voice was tight. "*Fuck that*, Gun."

"We're not leaving," Gun said. "Look, we're . . ."

"So be it." The man sounded grim. More quickly than Gun would have believed from the bulk of the mechanism, he raised the right arm of the big machine-suit and drove some heavy, brutal weapon at Gun's chest.

It was something like a pile-driver, a rod that shot out explosively and drove Gun back several steps. It hurt a bit, like being punched in the sternum.

"The *fuck* . . ." he gasped. He heard Jackie pick up one of the big heavy tables and throw it at the man. He knocked the table aside with one rough mechanical arm, but it staggered the thing back.

"Leave the city," the man shouted, glaringly loud in the confines of the tent, "and no harm will come to you!"

Gun saw the pile-driver coming for him again, and this time reached up to catch the mechanical arm. He heard machinery groaning, but Gun was pissed now and just reacting. He wrenched the arm down, hearing gears and metal tear and bend. The man in the suit screamed, his arm bent unnaturally with the broken mechanics, and Gun saw the sight of white bone through skin in his elbow. Gun stepped back, horrified.

He held up a hand, stopping Jackie. She had her walking stick up, getting ready to swing it.

"No!" he shouted. *"No!"*

She halted her swing and looked at him. He shook his head.

The other soldiers drew closer, pushing them from one side toward an opening in the tent. Gun, once again, had his hands up.

"We don't want to hurt anybody." His voice had lost all its power. "We just wanted . . ."

The men in the apparatus advanced, however, and the two of them backed away.

"What do we do, Gun?"

"I don't know, Jacks," Gun said, in a small voice. He was bewildered. He felt like a child who had accidentally broken something expensive in a store. The first soldier, white-faced, his arm a ruin, fell back from the lines, and Gun felt bile rise in his throat. He backed up another step. He couldn't bear to strike any of the soldiers. He could still feel the sickening sensation of tearing metal and gears and *flesh*. He had felt the bones in the poor man's hand splinter in his grip. He saw the sickly white of the soldier's torn arm.

The other soldiers advanced in their brutal mechanical suits, and the monsters retreated. More of the machine-suited soldiers joined them, forming a line that slowly but inexorably pushed them down a wide street where terrified soldiers cut off every exit. Jackie and Gun fell back before them, unwilling to hurt any more of them, bewildered and confused by how fast it all was happening.

They were herded back down the street that they'd walked up, and then down another. Gun and Jackie looked for escape, but everywhere they looked there was a metal-suited figure who they would have to destroy to get past. Nothing in their previous life could have prepared them for this.

For all of their games, all of their practice with their weapons, all of their playing at war, neither of them had ever intentionally hurt anyone before. Sure, Jackie had blacked a few eyes in middle-school, but that was mostly in self-defense and in the heat of the moment. The two Behemoth found that they were unable to hurt—and certainly not kill—these people just so they could . . . what? Have a drink?

So they backed up, driven as much by the awful anger and fear in the men and women's eyes as the threat they represented. Gun and Jackie were not the kind of people who enjoyed causing discomfort.

Before Gun could really get his head around it, they had been herded through a tall, heavy arch. It was dark out there, and tall walls rose to either side. Gun gradually realized that they had been pushed outside of the city, and the two of them stood watching as massive, banded bronze doors closed with a heavy, final sound. It echoed in the dark wastes outside the city, which was more dead and crumbling buildings, slowly decaying under a featureless black sky.

Once again Gun and Jackie stood in darkness.

Gun swallowed, hard, around a lump in his throat. He put his hand to his side and just stood for a while, his head down. He heard Jackie breathe raggedly next to him. After a while he looked up and saw lines of people atop the tall, heavy wall that encircled the city, all looking down at them with white faces and frightened eyes.

Jackie stood facing the gate, looking up at it, expressionless.

"I just wanted something to eat," Gun said. His voice felt small in the big emptiness outside the city walls.

"Yeah," Jackie said.

"It was an accident," Gun said. "It's not fucking *fair*."

Gun had grown up in the most prosperous nation in his world, as a member of what they called the middle class, and in that place and time, his race had the most advantages there. He was very, *very* unused to the concept of unfairness.

Jackie looked back over her shoulder at Gun for a long moment, and then out into the black beyond him. She shook her head. "No. It's not fair."

Gun found he was shaking, the adrenaline and fear and pure utter *unfairness* of it all catching up to him.

"I just wanted something to eat," Gun said, with a snarl. "You know?"

"I know."

He looked at her for a long time, then up at the gate.

Jackie turned as well. Into the quiet, Gun heard her say, low, "I had a fucking *drink* in my hand, man."

She looked up at the people high atop the wall, looking down at them, terrified. Something came over Jackie's face, then.

"And these fuckers *took it away*." She drew her fist back and slammed it into the gate. The gigantic door shuddered, heavily, and buckled where Jackie's fist connected. She looked at her hand for a moment, as if remembering what it was capable of, and then lashed out again, and then twice, buckling the big gate further and sending whispers of dust down from where the big hinges met the old stone of the wall. She drew back her fist again.

"No," Gun said, stopping her. He walked up to the gate and looked up at the terrified faces looking down at them. Suddenly, he didn't care; Jackie was right. He'd had a *drink in his hand*. He felt something hard and implacable come down over him. He reached behind him for the hilt of his sword.

"Let me."

THE DEADSMITH

The Door Into Confusion

"Light a candle, then blow it out. Now you know what you mean to the Wise."

—TECU SALAMAN IV, 'SPEECHES'

The Deader stepped through an open Door and his Fate wailed danger into his senses, a wash of chartreuse and the scent of old sand. His footsteps echoed, strangely, a confusing welter of soft noise.

He heard something and stiffened. It was laughter, and he couldn't tell where it was coming from. It seemed to come from everywhere and nowhere.

"Vaxis," his Fate said, and gave the Deader the scent of charred skin. The Deader agreed.

It was the Prey.

The Deader had found the end of the Land of Elah, with its broken sky and weeping people. He had followed the Prey's trail of peculiar, half-broken little machines. He had even weathered the memories of his youth, the cruel end of his mother and sister, the harsh tutelage of the Deadsmith. He had reached another freestanding Door, but this one held no message. The Prey hadn't even bothered to scramble that Door's coordinates; it made the Deader think the Prey *wanted* to be followed.

He was reminded of the old woman's message, back in the city that the Prey had glamoured against him:

The journey changes now.

Now the Deader stood in a narrow passage made of some crumbling, rough material that broke and shattered sound. The walls rose to perhaps twenty span and then opened out; there was no ceiling that he could see. The Deader could tell that there was something above him by the way the sound behaved; he guessed some mosaic dome or reflector.

"They call it the Whispers, Deadsmith!" A voice came, seemingly from everywhere. "Do you like it?"

"Dissidea!" his Fate said, tense. He let it do its work; it was much better at assessing threats than he was. Instead he knelt, pulling the oddly-shaped case from

his back and unlocking it. Inside lay the white-black beads of his Machine, and he assembled it quickly. The Prey laughed again, a curious sound caught partway between a giggle and a moan.

The Deader interlocked the pieces of his Machine, forming the thing into a low-slung shape with four limbs and a tail for counterbalance. It shivered, excited to be allowed freedom and eager to kill.

"I thought this would be a good place to talk!" The Prey let loose another half-mad giggle. "I wanted to have some words with you, you see. Maybe buy me some time. We wouldn't want this game over too soon, would we, Deadsmith?"

The Deader stood and bade his Machine hunt. It crept off, stealthily. The Prey's voice echoed for a while after he finished speaking. It was impossible to tell where the speech was coming from, but that knife cut both ways. The Deader began to move away from the Door.

"Show yourself," the Deader said, finally, "and I'll make my views clear."

The Prey laughed again. "I'm sure! I am certain you will, Deadsmith. Make your point at the point of the knife, as it were. Not that you need anything so common as a knife for your killing."

"I have my teeth," the Deader agreed, walking carefully along the passage. As he suspected, it ended in a branch; two identical ways.

He was in a maze.

"*Regis,*" his Fate whispered, with the scent of cinnamon. The Deader agreed and took the lefthand passage.

"Ah, Deadsmith," the Prey said. "What a wonder you are! What a prize. Did you enjoy my gift?" He was referring to the tableau of five bodies.

"No." The Deader was still trying to pinpoint the location of the voice. His Fate was quiet, its senses operating far beyond the Deader's own. "It cost too much to be enjoyed."

"Oh, my!" The sound of the Prey's amusement was starting to grate on the Deader's skin. It had a frantic quality he did not care for.

"You're a clever one," the Prey continued. "Do you speak, I wonder, of the cost to yourself, all those years ago? Or the cost to the city? Or perhaps you are tender—perhaps you mean the cost to the little boy."

"I'm not clever." The Deader reached another branching path. His Fate whispered, and he turned right this time. "And I am nowhere near tender; what is one boy when a tenth of a city falls?"

The Prey giggled again. "Tenth! I was afraid of that. A feel rather badly about it. This . . . *talent* that I stole from your Lady is a bit harder to control than I'd guessed it would be. Taking a little while to master it, you see! May have gone a little too strong. But I wanted to be sure you got my message."

"I got it," the Deader said, looking at everything, looking for any disturbance or marring of dust. Other than their voices, the place was very quiet. If the Prey was moving, he couldn't hear it. His own footsteps seemed loud. His Machine wasn't very smart, but it was very deadly, and as inexorable in its own way as he was himself. It was also very quiet, when it chose to be.

"Well," the Prey said, "I apologize for the rough nature of my plotting; I am normally a more exacting craftsman. I won't lie to you, Deadsmith, when I learned who it was that your Lady sent after me, I had a bad moment. In fact, I had a pretty bad day. It just goes to show that you can make all the plans in the world, Deadsmith, you really can, and one Twins-damned detail will throw them all in the wind."

"Perhaps if you return what you stole," the Deader said, watching for any hint of the Prey. "If you give Winter the Domination back, we can negotiate for your life."

But the Prey laughed at that, long and loud, the sound filling the big maze. "Oh, come now. You can do better than *that*. My life is done and we both know it, yet there are some things I wish to do. I don't like to set aside a goal once I've got it clear, you see? So you'll have to wait, Deadsmith. I would prefer you wait in the comfort of your White Tower, ministering to your Lady's vile needs. When my purpose is finished, I will come find you, and give myself up."

The Deader smiled, still moving. He entered a small chamber, open to the dome above. There was some small light, coming from ancient, flickering lit-stone. "Come on. You can do better than that."

"So, trust is a thing we have yet to find between us. Still, we have the time. There is a long road ahead, Deadsmith."

"If you say so." The Deader picked a path at random, since his Fate had no opinion.

"Your point is taken," the Prey said, almost sadly. "I am falling into old habits. Plots and plans mean little when the stakes loom so large. And who can say what tomorrow brings? Surely your life has taught you the same." This was delivered slyly.

The Deader ignored the implication. "My life has taught me," he said, sidling along a wall, "to serve my Lady."

"Oh, Deadsmith." The Prey sounded almost shocked with delight. "That is *exactly* what it has taught you! There may be hope for you yet. For me, very little hope indeed. I'll confess something to you, my new friend, I have worries. I worry that I've bitten off a little bit more than can be chewed. Oh, not with *you*—you are a problem that will either be solved or will choke me. As you say, only tomorrow will tell."

The Deader wondered how such an inconstant, half-mad creature managed to steal anything of worth from his Lady in the first place.

"No," the Prey went on. "I fear for my mind; it is quite eager to fail. This trinket, this trifle, this *thing* for which you are crossing so many long leagues—it may prove to be beyond me. Still, it is powerful, and power has its uses."

The Deader felt something change in the quality of the echoes; he thought he might be drawing closer to the Prey.

"Now." The Prey's voice had taken on a brisk, businesslike tone. "We have something to attend to, you and I; but since it appears you will not cry off, I would rather call you something other than 'Deadsmith.' Do you have a name? A thing you call yourself? Oh, not the one you were born with; I doubt you think with *that* name any longer. What is your true name, Deadsmith?"

"My name is my own," the Deader said, making a turn and trying to guess at the Prey's location. "And it is not for the likes of you."

"Oh?" The man sounded smug. "Very well, very well! I shall have to use the name your Lady uses; she calls you her *Deader*, does she not? When you lie in her bed, and she curls her fingers through your hair?"

The Deader froze. He felt something like ice crawl over his skin.

The Prey laughed, as if he knew the effect this had. "Fear not; I won't tell. But if you insist on following me, Deader, then I will call you by your true name. And you may call me by mine!"

"To me, you are just Prey."

"That," the voice said, chuckling, "is *hilarious*. But let us complete this ritual, for we are entering into something deep, and names are required. I have thought long about what name I should take; the one I was born with describes a man who no longer exists and the others I have had are too grand for the thing I've become. So I will call myself Candle, and be known to history as a thing that might be blown out with the least careless breath."

The Deader took a blind turn carefully, senses sharp. "Candle, you talk too much."

"You are not the first to make that observation!" The man who called himself Candle laughed again. It was a raw, grating sound, with almost no actual humor in it. "But it is astute. What a fine mechanism you are, Deader! How well constructed. Too well, in truth; something will have to be done about that. But I will say goodbye to you, for now it is time for *you* and *I* to have our conversation."

"We've been having a conversation," he said, "to no point that I can see."

The Deader felt maddeningly close to the Prey. He crept along a wall, trying to feel for him. There was something about the quality of the Prey's voice when he said '*you and I*' that the Deader did not like. His Fate was quiet, listening.

"Oh, no, Deader." The Prey laughed as if surprised. "I wasn't talking to *you*."

And then Candle began to speak. But not to the Deader, oh, no. His voice became everything, it became a titanic wall of irrevocable thunder, and the Deader knew what this man had stolen from his Lady.

Candle had stolen the power of *Domination*, and the Deader felt something very close to actual fear.

But the man who called himself Candle wasn't speaking to the Deader. If he had, his plots might have come to nothing, for the Deader had been hardened against such things. But the Prey was speaking to someone else.

"Anniver," the Prey thundered, in the voice of a mad god. *"Verimilise!"*

And his Fate started screaming.

THE LOST BOYS

Uncle Wizard

*"Anyone who has too much nostalgia about growing up
doesn't have a very good memory."*

—BENJI ELEV, 'CARRAL AND MORDACHAI'

Uncle was hammering on some incredibly complicated bit of twistcraft when
the boys arrived in his boneyard, shell-shocked. James and Chris reeled in,
still in a kind of hazy stupor from the sunlight, the Giant, and the trees. Chris had
made it clear, once they'd come back through that doorway, that the most important thing that they could do, maybe the most important thing *in the world*,
was to go see Uncle as soon as possible.

James was in, like, some whole *other* place. He had wobbled back through the
labyrinth below the city in a daze. It was possible that too much had happened in
too short a time, and his young brain had just shorted out. He wasn't even sure
why they were going to see Uncle: did they need to do a lesson? He didn't want
to do a lesson. Buckle flitted from one shoulder to another, scolding Chris with
sharp exclamations of "No!" whenever he tried to engage James in conversation.
Buckle had seen what James had seen; she'd seen a *Giant*. But she was handling it
better than he was.

James felt strongly that he was in a dream, some sort of awful-yet-beautiful
dream where all of your hopes came true and you watched them turn to dust in
your hands. At least they left the red-haired *girl* behind. James half-expected
Katherine and Chris to exchange a tender, loving kiss when they parted. Not that
he cared if they did! But they hadn't. Chris had just told Katherine to gather some
supplies and meet them back at a certain location.

For some reason, Chris didn't want Katherine to meet Uncle. James didn't
know why. He was too tired, too worn out to think.

He had seen a Giant.

He had seen trees, a living forest. He had seen the . . . he'd seen the *sky*.
The sun.

It was like the dream, but he could still feel the warmth of it on his face.

"Hush, squib," Chris said, holding out an arm to stop him from moving farther into Uncle's boneyard. "He's finishing up."

Uncle was indeed finishing something up on the workbench; some piece of indescribably high-stage twistcraft that fairly glowed with golden magic. It was only a few finger-lengths long and about as round as a slender branch, but even from where James was standing, he could see the intricate patterning, the wild confluence of hair-thin lines that were the telltales of high-stage twistcraft.

Uncle was hunched over in concentration, tapping on the thing with a small, very precise hammer. His rhythm was maddening, staccato, nothing that James could get a handle on, but still musical. It was like hearing one of the flutists uptown do a particularly hard solo, but more so. And the gold twistwork was responding to Uncle's concentration and rhythm; it pulsed in strange time with his blows. James felt a rare moment of introspection; that rhythm and pulsing gold from Uncle's table reminded him, oddly, of the forest and the trees and the enormous, terrifying, beautiful Giant. It made James feel like maybe Chris had done the right thing, bringing them across Cannoux with an impossible relic—*the Silver Key*—that he had found in a dream. And the beautiful magic Uncle was making told James that maybe the man he called Uncle *would* understand. Maybe he *could* help.

The tapping slowed, stopped. The big man with the big mustaches heaved, breathing heavily, as if he'd run a long race and finished slow. He lifted up the golden rod, examining it. For a moment, it glowed with its own inner light. James saw the slightest bit of smile from the side of Uncle's mouth; he was pleased. James thought, for a moment, that the rod looked a little like one of the common bolts you fed into a chutter but then dismissed the thought. He was just tired. And anyway, Uncle didn't make weapons.

Uncle admired his handiwork for what seemed to him like a long time, and then he set it down with a sigh. His big shaggy head turned towards them slightly.

"All right, boys," he said. "Come on in, if you're coming."

James felt a hand push him forward and found himself stumbling ahead. Uncle turned to look at them, a frown starting on his big bluff face.

"Well now, lads! Aren't you a pair. Scuffed from hell to breakfast. You been fighting with the ladies again?"

Chris swallowed, then swallowed again. He shook his head. "No, Uncle. We . . . need to talk."

Uncle narrowed his eyes and looked them both over more carefully.

"Talk, eh?" Uncle asked, pushing himself to a standing position with the short groan typical of any creature past their halfway point in life. "Well, it ain't time for your lesson and your Ma already turned me down for half a hundred by-your-leaves, so what makes you think I got things to discuss?"

He stood, tucking his thumbs into his belt. He regarded the boys with a strange look. Challenging-like. James felt a vague and unfocused belligerence well up; he felt like, in better days, he would try to throw something sharp at that look. But he didn't. He was so tired!

"Uncle," Chris said, his voice nervous but pitched low, "we have something to show you."

"Yeah?" Uncle had a slight smile on his face. "Is it better than the passable stage two work you've been shitting out? Or maybe you boys been building a sweet little fort out in the wilds, and want me to come see? No? Oh! Maybe the two of you have finally figured out how to *get along* and you want to sing me a fucking two-part-harmony."

James frowned, not understanding *any* of this, not the words or Uncle's odd tone, but Chris scowled. "No, *Alvarez,*" he said, in a tight voice. "Might be we got something to show you that will rock the world back on its damn foundations."

"*Ah.*" Uncle sighed. "One of those. Well, boys that will be boys no longer, come inside. Let's see what you found."

———

"I won't lie, gentlemen," Uncle said as he let the silvery medallion spin on its chain. The medallion looked small next to his big blunt-tipped fingers, "I'd rather you brought me a sweep-adder. Wrapped around your Ma's neck, maybe, or my own peener."

He pinned first Chris and then James with his flat, pale-blue gaze. "Do either of you know what this is?"

James tried to focus. Too much had happened in too short a time. First he'd found out that his friend Katherine—well, not his *friend,* it turned out—was in league with his brother. They'd tricked him, so that they could find the Silver Key from the dream. And then . . . they'd opened a magic Door. Into a place . . . There was sunshine. There were trees.

There was a *Giant.*

"I think it's a . . . Cold-Key." Chris said.

No. It was the *Silver Key.* And James needed it to save the world. He felt dizzy.

"Not bad," Uncle said, watching the thing spin.

His tone was odd; it was only later that James would realize he wasn't speaking to them as boys or students anymore.

"You're right, of course," Uncle continued. "It's a Cold-Key. Twins damn, if I had known the Mother was sending you kids out looking for *this* . . . Never mind. Where did you find it?"

"Under the city," Chris said quickly, but James frowned. He didn't understand why Chris was being so weird.

"There were trees, Uncle," he said, "and sun. And a *Giant*. It was like—was it a dream?"

Uncle leaned back, making his sturdy chair creak. He looked back and forth between Chris and James for what felt like a very long time.

"She sent you to Forest," Uncle said.

Reluctantly, Chris nodded. "If it's the Mother that sent the dreams, then . . . yes. I think it was the edge of Forest. There was a line of stones, black stones, and—"

Chris described their visit to that fantastic land: the sky, the trees, and the Giant that had attacked them.

When he was finished, Uncle looked away, and cursed under his breath. "Damned boys. I've never been lucky enough to see that for myself. You realize you two have seen something that only a handful of folk in the entire Wanderlands can claim to, yes?"

Chris nodded again. "I think I understand that."

"You went through a Door, I take it?"

"Yes."

"And you got the coordinates from the dream. This Mother of yours is really working hard to test my oaths, isn't she?"

Chris frowned. "What do you mean?"

Uncle sighed. "Never mind. Two idiot boys, and a secret that half the folk in the Wanderlands would kill the other half to possess. What are the coordinates?"

Chris looked reluctant, but picked up a piece of slate and chalk. Uncle slapped the slate out of Chris' hand, disgusted. Uncle pointed a blunt finger at Chris' face.

"Grow up, boy," he growled, "and sooner rather than later. Why would you give me that information? Information is a coin you can only spend once, and trust me, lad, you may have to spend it to keep yourself alive soon. You can't afford to be stupid anymore. Not you *or* your brother."

James couldn't follow half of what was going on, but this was too much. "We can trust you! Wait—why don't we take Uncle to the trees place? Can we go back?"

Uncle shook his head. "Don't tempt me, boy. If I find my way to Forest, it will be on my own power; I'll not take any Silver-be-damned *shortcut*. But I'm afraid that it's time for school, boys, time for one last lesson from old Uncle."

James scowled. "I don't want to learn no lessons." He wanted to go home, and hug his Ma, and eat something, and go to sleep. He yawned, hugely. Uncle shook his head, looking at James, half a smile on his broad face, and then turned his sharp gaze onto Chris. He dangled the silver amulet from one blunt finger.

"Let's play a game, boy, because I'm curious about just how smart you are. If you thought this even *might* be a Cold-Key, what in all the worlds makes you think I'll let you keep it? You know how valuable this thing is, correct? How dangerous?"

"Yes," Chris admitted. James frowned. Why would the Silver Key be dangerous?

Uncle sat back in his big heavy chair, making it creak, and set the silver medallion on his desk. He seemed caught somewhere between exasperated and amused. He studied Chris.

"I think," Chris said, "that you know a lot more than you act like you do, and *that's* why you'll let us keep it."

Uncle made the scrolling gesture with his finger that meant *go on.*

"I think you weren't real surprised to see this thing turn up because you knew about the dreams; hell, you were teaching half the kids in Cannoux how to find whatever the Mother was calling for. Wouldn't be surprised if that's why you showed me how to build a Silver-dowser. Or why you gave James Buckle."

Uncle did laugh now. "Too smart by half, boy. And stop scowling, James, let your brother show off. Looks like he's earned it."

"So I think maybe you wanted this Key found. So, to me, that means one of two things."

Uncle leaned back, narrowing his eyes.

"Please continue, my finest pupil. What are my two options?"

"One," Chris said, only a small amount of nervousness apparent in his voice, "you want the thing for yourself, but couldn't find it on your own. So you gave all the kids you were training clues, as much help as you could, so that they *would* find it. And bring it back to you."

Uncle's eyes glinted. "That's one option, yes."

"Second option is," Chris said, "you aren't completely full of shit, and you believe all of the things that you taught us."

Uncle raised an eyebrow.

"I'm betting on the fact that you're *good*," Chris said, earnest. "You serve the Path, and that means you serve the Mother. The Mother wanted us to find this thing; that's why she sent us the dreams. And so, you'll let us keep it. Maybe even help us."

"Your logic is shaky, but I'm intrigued," Uncle said, companionably. "But what makes you think I don't want it for myself? What makes you think I can't use it to serve the Mother in my own way?"

Chris shrugged. "I never seen you display much love of the Cold, nor the Silver-Age work. Seems like you get a bit sour on the subject, in fact."

Uncle laughed and clapped his knee, a merry sound. "That is true enough, boy."

"So I don't think that you want it for yourself, and I think maybe you'll live and let live where the Mother is concerned, and let us keep this thing even though it's about as dangerous to have as anything in the world." Chris hesitated and then plunged on. "But I could be wrong about all that. The real reason . . . well, if you know about the dreams, you know we have to do something important with that Key. I don't think you'll stand in our way, and I don't think you'll put yourself in the Mother's way. I know you, and I know you're good, even though you try not to act like it."

Uncle sat looking at Chris for a long moment and then smiled, but it wasn't totally a nice smile. It had teeth, and was maybe a little sad.

"Well reasoned, boy," he said. "And as it happens, more or less correct. But now I'm going to explain to you why you are a *damned fool*, and I'm ashamed to call you my student if this is all you've learned of the world."

Chris blinked.

"Hear me and hear me well, Chris D'Essan. Yes, and you might as well try listening for once too, James. What I'm about to say could be considered some pretty damn *sound life advice*, and from someone who's lived more than a few of them."

Uncle leaned forward, his voice grown serious. He put his big hands on his knees.

"First, I may be good or I may be bad, but I'm a lot more likely to be *both*. Like, for instance, every *single other creature that ever lived*. Thinking you know what someone will do just because you think they're 'good' or 'bad' is a quick way to lose at the game you're playing. Good people do appalling things for good reasons, and bad people do good things for selfish reasons and every combination between. I have a hundred—a *thousand*—good and unselfish reasons to kick you two out of here and never let you see this shortcut garbage Cold-Key again. You're smart as a whip, boy, but don't be blinded by that. A smart man can be twice the fool of anyone else, and it'll take him ten times longer to realize it."

Uncle took a deep breath, let it go. He shook his head.

"Second, there ain't no grand plan for you two boys. You don't know the first Twins-damn thing about the world or how it works. I happen to believe the Mother generally has the world's best interests in mind, though I differ in agreement on her methods. But the Mother ain't necessarily *good*, either, at least not the way you mean it, and she ain't to be trusted when it comes to personal safety. The Mother needs you, or needed you, but she don't care one whit for you personally, and trusting in her protection is a quick way to get yourself dead. Or worse."

Uncle looked from Chris to James, and then back. His eyes had grown serious, hard. He seemed very old and just a little bit frightening. He lifted the silver amulet and let it hang between them.

"And third, you are a *fucking idiot* if you think this thing is just 'dangerous.' Oh, it's dangerous enough to use; they weren't called 'The Cold' for nothing. But you two need to get it through your thick skulls that there is a *reason* why the Mother sent you through an ancient magic Door into a forbidden Land guarded by Twins-damned Giants to get this thing. Do you know why? Do you know why the Mother couldn't just send you down to the corner to *buy* one?"

Neither Chris nor James was stupid enough to answer this very rhetorical question.

"It's because those same Cold, those bastards that used to live on top of the Mountain, made it a point to scour every last one of those things from the face of the Wanderlands and kill the living shit out of anybody who knew about one, knew where to find one, or knew why they were doing it. And then they disappeared. Yes, boy, but you're a damned fool if you think they're *gone*. And even if they *were* gone, there are forces in the world that would dismember you by inches just to get a rumor of such a powerful device. They were the primary tools of the ancient Cold—the fuckers that *built* the Silver Age. The damage that could be done with one of those tools in these sad and broken days is incalculable. Do you understand me?"

Uncle grimaced and looked away.

"Hear me twice, now, and do not let sentiment cloud your ears. I *know this*, boys," he said, "because *I* am one of those forces in the world, and you got more lucky with me than you know. You should never have shown me this thing. You were counting on a goodness and largesse that I don't possess. The only thing— and I mean this, boys, I have affection for you both but not as much as you might think—the *only* thing keeping me from taking this thing from you and snapping your necks to keep the secret is the fact that I've sworn not to take part in these kinds of plots anymore. I leave the Mother to her work, I assist her when I can, and if she wants to drag two snot-nosed kids into her business, I am sworn by my word to leave her to it. Do you understand me?"

"Yes," Chris said. He was frowning, intently; Uncle's words were having an effect on him.

But James shook his head. "You wouldn't hurt us. C'mon."

Uncle looked at Chris, fixed him with one of his customary glares. "I wish you could have kept James out of this," he said, "but you will need to grow him up real quick now. Your childhood is done, both of you. It's a sad thing, but I've seen a long length of sad things in this life. I expect I will survive."

Chris hesitated. "I didn't find it, Uncle."

Uncle shook his head, impatient. "I'm not your tutor anymore, and you're no longer a boy. Call me by my published name, which is Alvarez. Which you already knew, *somehow*. What do you mean, you didn't find it?"

Chris glanced sideways at his brother. "James did."

Uncle turned his heavy gaze on James, who squirmed. Uncle just looked at him for a long moment. "Is that so?"

"Wasn't just me," James said. He glanced at his brother's shoulder, where Buckle was fidgeting. "We all—"

"James," Chris said, voice whip-sharp. "Shut up."

Uncle hung his head for a moment. "All?" He shook himself and looked up. "Tell me true. You're a man now, Chris D'Essan, and this could mean everything. Who else?"

Chris squirmed. "There was a . . . girl. She helped James find the Door."

"A red-haired girl, I'll wager. Where is she?" Uncle sounded tense.

"Hidden," Chris said. "Don't worry. She's waiting for us."

"Well," Uncle said, heavily. "If you'll take an additional piece of advice, don't involve *anyone* else. And this is going to be hard, lads, but you've been given a hard road: you tell your Ma about this and you'll sign her death warrant. She's a good woman, despite her resistance to my charms, and I'd rather not have her end be at the point of some Cold bastard's Rapine."

Chris shook his head. "We won't."

"You understand me? You understand what I mean?" Uncle said, looking hard at Chris, and the older boy nodded.

James frowned. "Understand what?"

"Nothing, squib," Chris said. "But Uncle . . . Alvarez . . . Listen, I came to you because we need your help. We need to know what to do next."

"Ha!" Uncle leaned back. "I would consult your dream, were I you. I helped you both along the road, I'll admit it, but now that I see what it was that the Mother was looking for, I'm more sure than ever that I must stay out. I told you I'd play no part, and that goes for the good as well as the bad. It's a hard road, sometimes, but I'm committed to it."

Chris shrugged. "The dream was unclear. There was something about a Giant. But not . . . not the one we saw through that Door. I know that, somehow."

"A *buried* Giant," James said. That part of the dream had been very clear—to him, anyway.

Uncle stiffened. "A buried Giant?" His entire demeanor changed. "No jokes now, boys; no old stories. Are you sure?"

James looked at Chris, uncertain. "I mean . . . yeah. He had great big chains on his wrists. And he was deep underneath a mountain. I think we have to . . . go there."

"Well *fuck me*," Uncle said, almost to himself. He rubbed his eyes again. "Fuck me! She's really working to test my oath, ain't she."

James frowned. "She?"

"The Twins-damned Mother," Uncle said. "Never mind. It makes no difference. Boys, I cannot help you, and if I could, I wouldn't. But neither will I stand in your way. If I had known the Mother was trying to uncover one of *these*"—his eyes shifted to the medallion—"well, I might not have tried to help the damned old crone. Ah! What's done is done. Take this damned Cold-Key and take my

best wishes, too. I taught you what I could, I suppose, though I never meant you
to put it to work for anything like what lies ahead of you."

"What lies ahead of us?" James asked, confused and—maybe—a little frightened by what Uncle was saying.

Uncle looked at James, right in the eye, like he was an adult. James straightened up.

"A hard road," Uncle said. "A lonely road. News will get out about that Key,
about the dreams, and if the Mother is trying to wake Kindaedystrin, then this is
world-shaking stuff, James. You will have powerful people trying to take that
thing from you. You will have the Wise trying to stop you from following the
Mother's plan. You will have ordinary people trying to kill you for no other reason
than greed or hubris or envy. It's a hard road, James, and you will have to grow up
very quickly now. I'm . . . well. I'm sorry I can't help more. But a vow is a vow."

"You sound," Chris said quietly, "like you're saying goodbye."

Uncle shrugged. "Life is long, and the plots of the Wise never cease. We may
meet again. And we may not."

"Is that it?" Chris accepted the medallion back from Uncle's big fist. "You're
just going to send us on our way?"

"Well," Uncle said, with a small chuckle, "the only thing harder than the road
you two are about to walk is my will, and I'd advise you not to get crushed between those two. No, I won't help, and I won't give you anything more than
well-wishes. Remember my counsel; leave your poor Ma out of this, and try to
do your best. That's all any of us can do."

Chris nodded, though he didn't seem to like it. "Okay."

"Wait," James said. "We're just leaving?"

Chris exchanged a long look with Uncle.

"Yeah, squib," he said, heavily. "We're leaving."

"Oh." James was so tired. In a distant kind of way, he felt huge, awful emotions lurking, but they seemed far away and unimportant. He yawned. "Well,
then . . . thanks, Uncle." He stuck out his hand to shake.

Uncle looked at it for a moment, and then his eyes crinkled. He shook James'
hand, his big hand dwarfing the boy's small one. "Take care of Buckle. You remember what I said now."

"Yeah," James said. "I let her get hurt and you'll come beat me till I crap out
my own bones."

"Yeah, goes for both of you. And yes, goodbye, you little scamp," he said to
Buckle. "I know better than to ask you to stay."

"No!" Buckle said, but flew to his shoulder and gave his ear an awkward hug.
Uncle endured it for a moment and then shooed her off. She flew to James' shoulder. They all looked at each other for a moment.

"Okay," Chris said. "Well."

And with no more ceremony than that, the Lost Boys bade the acclaimed Behemoth-Philosopher Alvarez goodbye. It wasn't the last time they saw him, but it was the last *good* time they saw him.

———

The streets of Cannoux were busy as the two boys walked, each lost in their own thoughts. Chris walked with his head down, thinking, and rebuffed James' questions. James yawned; he wanted to go to bed. The conversation and bizarre goodbye with the man he'd always called Uncle made him feel uncertain and shaky, and he just wanted to eat something and sleep. But he realized they weren't headed home.

"Hey," he stopped and pulled on Chris' sleeve, "home's that way."

"We're not going home, squib," Chris said, his voice distracted. "Not right now."

"What? Where are we going?"

But Chris didn't answer. That was okay. James figured they were going to pick up Katherine; surely Ma would be happy to feed the girl once they told her what happened. He felt odd in his guts, thinking about that. But they *couldn't* tell Ma what happened, could they? Wasn't that what Chris and Uncle had said?

It was funny; James had spent his whole young life wanting everything to be different, and now that it was, he only felt tired and kind of bad. He yawned again, feeling like his head was going to crack in half, and fingered the silvery amulet in his carry. He'd thought Chris would take it away from him, but his brother was too distracted. He was far gone into that deep thinking thing he did, so James just followed him. He got Buckle to steal a bit of jerky from a vendor, and that helped his hunger a little. The Cold-Key felt chilly on his fingertips.

Hey, he thought, *maybe that's why they called them Cold!*

See? Stupid *Chris* wasn't the only smart one. But he felt a strange sort of *pulling* from the amulet, a kind of sense of . . . *of something.* Of something that felt kind of like following the path in the dream. Kind of like following his guts through the maze underneath the city.

"Hey," he said, after a bit, looking around. "This isn't . . . We're not going home? Where are we going?"

"Katherine is getting us some food and supplies. I thought we might have to . . . never mind. Hush, now."

James followed his brother, grumbling and thinking about that weird feeling from the amulet. He was too tired to even care about *Chris* and *Katherine* making stupid plans about stuff together. His thoughts were all about the Key. The *Silver*

Key. How would this little necklace thing help cut the darkness apart? It didn't seem to do anything, though it did kind of tug at him, a little bit.

He felt like maybe he could reach *into* it, in a weird way, or reach *through* it. Every time he tried to think about what he was doing, the sensation slipped away. It was a sour, prickly feeling, but a tempting one.

"James!" Chris' voice sounded sharp, alarmed, and James looked up just in time to see a black-gloved hand clamp over his brother's mouth. Chris' eyes went wide, and James felt something catch at his sleeve. He threw himself to the side, instinctively. His sleeve tore, and as he fell, he saw a hard-faced man holding a scrap of fabric.

James realized a few things in rapid succession. They had passed into a dim part of Cannoux, and it was no longer crowded; the men accosting them had picked their spot well, and his older brother was being immobilized by his attacker. Buckle flew up above them, screeching. The man looked down at the sleeve in his hand and his face twisted.

"You little shit," he said and reached for James. Without thinking about it, James *reached through* the amulet he was clutching, kind of using his mind somehow, kind of like following the vague sensation through the tunnels that had led him to the Door and the Key.

James didn't think about what he was doing or how, he just reached. And it hurt; it felt like tiny hooks and cords were tied to all his bones, and somebody pulled on them hard, stretching him apart. He ignored the pain and *pushed* the man away. James was used to pain, but he wasn't used to what happened to the man.

Three shafts of something red-black and jagged flew from behind James and impaled the man, throwing him back against a nearby wall. The man looked astonished, and then blood bubbled up from his mouth and burst down his chin. James' head rang and the pain got so intense he could hardly stand it. He tried to let go of the amulet, but he couldn't feel his fingers; he barely felt it when another man grabbed him from behind. Everything started to get very dark, and James was distantly aware of a man's hand clamped over his mouth.

The last thing he heard was Buckle screaming above him, and then even that was swallowed by a rapidly growing dark.

THE KILLERS

The Queen and the Consort

"I've not, in my somewhat extensive experience,
found monarchs to be much appreciative of plain speaking.
The only thing they seem to like less is the word 'no.'"

—GENERAL ADAMI CUMBERLAND, 'THE OTHER SIDE OF WAR'

Jane Guin's throne room was huge and round, with an extensive dome overhead, painted to look like the long-lost sky. It was ostentatious and extravagant, and no expense had been spared to make it look like the gilded, sumptuous heart of the Keep. Everything in it was perfect and decadent and pointless. It was where the Queen of the Keep kept her prizes—the Lords and Ladies who thought they had something to do with the running of the last civilization left in the Underlands. Sophie wasn't sure whether it was a good omen or a bad one that Jane didn't choose to interview her there.

But she'd take any interview that didn't include Denver Murkai. The Queen's Guards—known as the Redarms due to the bright sashes tied on their biceps—led Sophie down the finely tiled hallway floor. She didn't feel ready to face the Queen, now; her head was pounding with a strange doubling of her memory, a confusion that was making her knees weak. Denver had told her that one of her core beliefs about herself was a lie; that instead of being manipulated and tricked into getting the forbidden silver wrapped around the bones of her arms, she had *begged* for it. Instead of being led into the Dark and fed to a monster, she had yearned to go.

She tried to clear her head, as the Redarms led her to the audience with the Queen—the audience that she'd kicked a Practice Guard in the crotch to get. It couldn't be true, what Denver said, and she had long ago promised herself to never believe another word of what he—or his queen—said. And . . . yet.

It was like thinking back on a fond childhood memory and discovering that there was a monster hidden inside it. Or the reverse. It had all been so confused, back then; all of the major events of Sophie's life had all happened in less than one year. She *knew* that Denver led her out to Saint Station on purpose. He even admitted as much.

But she *did* remember wanting to go. It wasn't that she'd forgotten, she'd just . . . she hadn't polished that part of the story very bright, and over the years it had gotten dimmer. Jane had tricked her, sent her the dreams, had ruined her life. Sophie had always been a pawn in her schemes. But what if . . .

No. She jerked her jaw up. There was no time for this now. She needed to save her friends, and she needed her revenge. The past could stay in the fucking *past*.

She squared her shoulders, and prepared herself to meet Jane Guin. She found the thread of rage that had been building in her, ever since Avie had told her who Mr. March was. She banked that fire, blew on it, brought internal bellows to bear. She started to feel it as the Redarms marched her through the Ministry, a tingling fire in her extremities. *Rage.* It pushed out confusing memories, and Sophie started to feel ready to face the Queen.

The Redarms brought her to Jane's war-room, a much more functional space than her Throne Room, filled with schematics, plans, formulae, and hard-faced people with hard-nosed attitudes. Publicly, Jane surrounded herself with so much soft decadence in the Lords and in the Royal Court that people found it easy to forget that the people she actually spent time with were all battle-hardened shit-kickers of the first order.

Jane was herself in battle mode, her knee-length blonde hair wrapped up in as severe a knot as that much hair could possibly manage. She wore a plain dark tunic with a red slash; she needed no other ornament. She was Jane Guin, and she'd ruled the Keep for something like eight hundred years, which tended to speak a lot louder than any medals.

Jane glanced up when Sophie was brought in. The chief Redarm spoke softly to her for a moment, and she nodded. The Queen's eyes were oval and dark, in contrast to her fair complexion and very long white-blonde hair. She was, Sophie supposed, beautiful, in the way a well-made weapon might be beautiful. Sophie maintained her squared shoulders and jutted jaw, a pose of belligerence, and waited for Jane to notice her.

Jane finished up whatever convoluted scheme she was currently working out with an advisor, set down some isometric maps, and motioned for Sophie to approach.

"Sophie." Jane didn't even have to be imperious; her imperial rights were accepted by all, down into their bones. But Sophie—especially tonight—wasn't going to be knocked over by a *tone*.

"Jane," Sophie said.

"You will keep a civil tongue in your head when you speak to me." It wasn't a threat or a question, just a statement. In any case, calling Jane names got you nowhere; names didn't touch the woman. It took the fun out of calling her "The Beast" to her face, which Sophie had learned many years ago. That didn't mean she wasn't going to try, though.

Jane went back to studying a large piece of paper that was marked off in re-
peating triangles; isometric graph. It was really the only way to make maps of a
place like the Keep, and even then, it was something of a labyrinthine nightmare.
It was better to just keep it all in your head, the way that Sophie did. But Jane had
never been good at that; it was one of the damned woman's few identifiable
weaknesses.

The Queen tossed down the map, cracked her neck, and focused on Sophie.

It was a considerable sensation, having this person focus their attention on
you. She had a way of making you feel every second of her eight hundred years,
had a way of pinning you with the weight of her office. It reminded you of certain
types of trivia, such as the fact that she openly encouraged assassination attempts
and only punished those who were inept or caused collateral damage. If they
were any good, she hired them.

Not for the first time, Sophie wondered what Jane *was*. She had every appearance of being human, but she had been alive almost a millennia now. Rumors
always swirled, some suggesting she was a Behemoth, some claiming she was a
daughter of Hunter Fine himself, some even hinting she might be an exiled
member of the Nine. Sophie didn't know; just now, she didn't care. She hadn't
come here to be cowed. So Sophie did her best to endure her gaze, refusing to
drop her eyes, and waited for the Beast to say something. She held tight to her
rage.

"You are to be fined and censured for assaulting one of my Practice Guard,"
Jane said, finally. "The purser will see to it. Do you have any objections?"

A *fine*. Less than a slap on the wrist. More than nearly anything else it told her
how unsettled Jane was tonight. Sophie noticed a medium-height, kindly-
featured man with sandy hair studying her thoughtfully from behind a planning
table. He looked vaguely familiar, but she couldn't place where from.

"All right," Jane said. "Let's get to it. The Keep requires your assistance, Vesachai."

"I'm sure it does." Sophie crossed her arms. "But that isn't why I came here."

Jane fixed her with a cool, somewhat amused eye. Sophie supposed there
weren't that many people who made a habit of talking back to the Queen. "You
are standing in front of me because I want to talk to you, Vesachai. If I didn't, I
would give you to my Practice Guard for their revenge. So I'll repeat myself, just
the once: the Keep requires your assistance."

Something about her tone suddenly *infuriated* Sophie. This woman had done
her best to fuck with Sophie's life, and now she was commanding her to help?
Fuck that. "The Keep can go fuck itself, and so can you. My brother? My fucking
brother?"

Jane raised a finger, an almost extravagant gesture of anger. "You will keep a
civil tongue, Vesachai."

Sophie lost her temper. It was like a bubble bursting; surprising, beautiful, dangerous to those nearby. It was an exorbitant, lovely sensation, like picking a fight with the big man in the Loche de Menthe, only more so. Like the dark urge to kiss Avie, to pull a viper into her chest just to see what the bite felt like.

"*Fuck you*, Jane!" Sophie said, channeling all of the rage and despair of this long night into a beautiful, white-hot stream of invective. "Fuck you, fuck your *plots* and *plans* and hidden agendas. Fuck you straight up your ancient asshole with your lying, snake-fucking *tongue*. Fuck your Keep, fuck your Ministry, fuck your stupid white-ass face with that ugly-ass mole growing out of the side of your mouth. Fuck that dumb *hair*, fuck that unamused *smile*, fuck that, and *fuck you*."

Sophie ran out of steam. She closed her eyes for a moment. Gods, that felt good. Twins damn, that felt good! She opened her eyes.

"Are you done?" Jane asked.

"I think so," Sophie said, and heaved a great cleansing sigh. "Wait, no—your voice sounds like a broken bucket leaking diseased piss into an open wound. Yes! I've been working on that line, I didn't want to forget it. And . . . I bet you look really stupid when you orgasm, right? Like, it's the only time an emotion ever shows on your face? I'm right, aren't I? And it's probably just *hilarious*, but nobody has ever had the balls to tell you."

The sandy-haired man coughed, red-faced, behind Jane; Sophie thought he might be swallowing his tongue to keep from laughing. Jane turned and fixed him with a look that half-froze Sophie's blood, and she was only catching a reflection of it. He got himself under control quickly, and Jane turned back to Sophie.

Sophie felt very calm. She almost giggled; she'd gotten part of what she came for. The only revenge she would get for what the Queen had done to her, and had done to her brother. Insulting Jane Guin to her face wasn't much, as revenge goes, but sometimes you just had to spit in god's eye. For a moment—for maybe the first time in this long night—she felt good.

Jane smiled, very slightly, and stepped around the table. She had a particular glint in her eye that Sophie didn't recognize. The Queen stepped close, looked her up and down, and then seized Sophie by the throat.

Her hand was strong, *strong*, infinitely strong. Sophie gasped and scrabbled at the Queen's hand and arm, but Jane's bones might as well have been old stone, her skin hardened leather. With no discernible effort, Jane picked Sophie up by her neck, still smiling, until Sophie's feet dangled two span off the ground. Jane's arm extended, fully, just to show that she could.

Sophie thought that she might, perhaps, have made a mistake here. Jane's fingers tightened inexorably and Sophie's air cut off. She felt caught in a piece of industrial equipment; all of her flailing didn't budge Jane Guin one whit. Nobody seriously thought that Jane Guin was human, but this confirmed it. The Queen's hand tightened.

The sandy-haired man stepped to the Queen's side and whispered in her ear, urgently, and Jane cocked her head to listen. Sophie was too busy struggling to suck air into her nearly crushed windpipe to hear what he said. Sophie tried to kick, but her foot connected with Jane's leg, and she might as well have kicked a post.

What a way to die, she thought. Through dimming vision, she saw Jane turn her face back to look at Sophie like she was a mildly interesting bug. Or a mechanical butterfly. The Queen's smile was sharp.

"So. Care to repeat any of that?"

Sophie somehow managed to indicate a negative. Still, Jane's hand held her aloft, and her vision went almost all the way to black. The fingers tightened one last tiny little bit, *right* to the edge of snapping her spine—just to demonstrate power and control—and then dropped her.

Jane went back to studying her isometric maps while Sophie coughed and sputtered on the floor. *Mother above!* Jane had certainly made a point. Finally Sophie pulled herself to her feet and eyed the Queen warily. Jane looked up, sighed in the manner of someone needing to confront a willful child during a busy day, and rubbed the bridge of her nose.

"All right, Vesachai. My instincts tell me that you are more trouble than you're worth, too broken a tool to be useful. My preference would be to round up your little group of friends and start doing awful things to them until you tell me where the Book is."

Sophie coughed and spat on the floor, half expecting to see blood. "Yeah?" she said, her voice hoarse and wavering. "But?"

Jane indicated the sandy-haired man with a small gesture. "My Consort is convinced that you can be useful. I certainly would rather *not* torture your friends to death, Sophie—that's not the sort of person I like to be, so I'm tempted to listen to him."

Sophie broke down in a coughing fit. "I came to make a deal. Okay? There's no need for any . . . I just really wanted to piss you off. I kind of needed to. All right? Seeing as how you've destroyed my life *several* times now?"

Sophie watched as Jane turned and exchanged a look with the sandy-haired man—the *Consort*, apparently the person who had sent the fop in the Charm Chair to warn her at the beginning of this very long night.

Then Jane turned back to Sophie. "A deal?" She sounded amused.

Sophie coughed a last time, and gathered herself.

"A truce. Somebody laid their plots inside your plans, and now you're *fucked.* Whoever is running my brother around, this Candle fucker, is ruining both of our nights. Right? So I say, truce. You don't fuck with me—or my friends—and I won't fuck with you. I'll be a good little citizen and keep my head down until this all blows over."

Jane watched her, steadily. Her expression was unreadable. "And the Book?"

"The Book is off the table. For now. Once the current crisis is dealt with, we can talk about that."

The corner of Jane's mouth twitched, just a little. A smile? "Tempting, but it's not clear what I get out of this arrangement."

This was the ace card. Sophie took a breath. "Sure you do. The famous Sophie Vesachai is about to become an ardent supporter of Jane Guin's plans. She'll tell everyone, far and wide, how important it is that we support the Queen in this trying time. Crowe told me you have big plans. I can help."

"And all I have to do is leave you and your little gang alone."

"That's why it's called a truce. Come on, Jane, you know we're at a stalemate. I'm not giving you the fucking Book, and you can't get it out of me. If I can get you off my back, maybe I can do something about Candle, and my brother . . . or maybe I'll stay out of your way while you do."

"Or," Jane tapped on one of the maps, as if considering, "I could just round up your little group of friends, and start pulling digits off until you give me what I want. Yes . . . yes. That seems easier."

Sophie gave her the best deadpan look she could manage, still barely able to hold her head up from having her neck half crushed. "Let's not play games. If you were going to do that, you would have done it a long time ago. Why be coy? You're afraid of the shit in my arms. And you *should be*. If you push me far enough, you know I'll say fuck it, break Proscription, and pull this Keep down around your head. Not to mention that if you did anything to me, half the Keep would rise up in popular revolt. They still think I'm a fucking hero."

Jane exchanged a glance with the Consort, who shrugged. She turned back to Sophie. She still seemed amused. "All right. Against my better judgment, I'm going to try something here, Sophie, because you labor under some misapprehensions. I can't trust you to make the choices you *should*, because you don't have all the facts. So? Let me enlighten you. Come walk with me."

What choice did she have? Sophie shot the Consort a puzzled glance, which he steadfastly ignored. She wished she could place where she knew him from, but it slid away from her, elusive. She reluctantly followed Jane, who walked across her war-room towards a heavy silver door. Hard-bitten military types watched them as they passed. Jane pushed the door open easily, though it must have weighed a thousand pounds, and Sophie followed her through.

And gasped, in spite of everything. The room beyond the door was huge, high-ceilinged, and utilitarian. Several pairs of silver discs dominated the room, one on the floor and one on the ceiling. Between the discs hung incredibly complex sculptures made of hair-thin strands of silver strung between them. There was a low hum of power here, and Sophie felt the forbidden tech in her arms tingle in response.

Jane walked over to the nearest set of silver discs, about four paces across, and indicated the sculpture hanging above and between them. "Recognize this?"

The sculpture was a dense field of thin silver wires strung vertically between the discs above and below. Via some Silver-Age magic, the width of parts of the wires had been increased and given color, allowing the creation of very detailed three-dimensional sculptures. Sophie stopped marveling, remembered the deadly danger she was in, and tried to *see*.

"That's the Dead Lake," she said. "And the edge of the Keep." It was a kind of three-dimensional map, and it was amazing. However, there were red and blue shaded sections that at first Sophie couldn't place. "Is that . . . an excavation?" she asked, pointing at a complex red-and-blue structure near the bottom of the Dead Lake.

"The reverse," Jane said. "We are building a kind of sideways caisson, in from the far side of the Gap, and pumping the water out."

Sophie tried to imagine the scale of such an undertaking, and her imagination failed. Nobody had attempted a construction project like that in . . . well, since the Underlands were built, probably. No wonder Jane's forces had seemed scattered lately. "Why?" she asked, but Jane moved on to the next wire-sculpture, the next set of silver discs. These depicted a rough cone, about twelve paces across at its base. The lower section of the cone was covered with what looked like tiny buildings, and there was a wandering silver line that ran around the circumference of the thing, about a third of the way up.

There was a small depression in the top of the cone, a kind of hollow, and there was the impression of more buildings in that. And from the top of the cone came a slender silver tube that rose all the way up to the silver daïs above.

"This," Jane said, "is what we think the top of the Mountain looks like."

Sophie's vision rippled and flexed in shock as she realized what she was looking at. "But that's just . . ."

"It's no legend, and it's so far above our heads that it might as well not exist. But do you see that silver column there, on the top?"

"Of course."

"That's something called a Feed, Sophie, and it's where all of our Silver comes from. It's where the motive force that gives us our *light* comes from."

"Holy shit," Sophie said, forgetting, for a moment, everything.

"Yes," Jane agreed. "Holy shit."

Jane walked over to another silver sculpture, this one immediately identifiable. It was the Keep, the massive squat structure surrounded by the Dead Lake, the five radial arms of the Bridges coming out from about three-quarters of the way up. But this model showed more of the base of it, and Sophie saw that there was more of the Keep *below* the Dead Lake than there was above it.

Sophie saw that the presence of illumination was shown with various colors;

heavy blue dominated the bottom of the Keep and several small locations scattered throughout it; a kind of lighter purple was much more prevalent through both the middle and all through the upper reaches as well. Yellow was by far the least used and congregated near the top. The dark blue represented the Dark, where the Silver and lights had failed. The purple was the Dim, places that still had a little light, but were lost to civilization.

"So little yellow," Jane murmured. "When you look at it like this, you really get a sense of how little light there is left. Do you not? And this is it, Sophie; all of the light in the entire expanse of the Underlands. As far as we know, it might well be all of the light left in the entire world."

"Fuck," Sophie said softly, looking at those small and scattered bits of yellow. Her whole world was contained in those patches of gold: the Rue de Paladia and Spake Field and Vesachai House. The yellow, where the Silver was still strong, and the Vesachai had been able to keep the lights on. The places that she—and all of the other peoples of the Keep—thought of as alive. She shivered. *"Fuck me."*

"Do you know why I want the Book, Sophie?" Jane asked.

Sophie swallowed again, painfully, and shook her head.

Jane gestured to the base of the Keep, solid blue. "Below us, below the Keep, lies a prison."

The Giant Lies Still Awake. Sophie shivered again.

"It's a large prison, from what legends tell us. Large enough to hold one of the fabled Returners. Yes, yes. It sounds ludicrous, doesn't it? Like something from a story. But you must believe me, Sophie, or at least you must at least believe that *I* believe it. There is a prison beneath our feet, one that the Feed atop the Mountain was built to power. Our whole civilization, Sophie, the entire Keep—hell, the entire *Underlands*—has been kept alive by a tiny fraction of the power that it takes to maintain that prison."

Sophie's imagination failed at even attempting to parse this.

Jane continued. "If that prison were decommissioned, say, and all of the Silver needed to maintain it were free for other uses . . ." Jane shook her head and pointed towards the sculpture. A technician fussed with the controls, cued by her Queen's gesture.

Yellow began to bloom all over the replica of the Keep, overtaking the purple and then even the blue, until the huge column glowed wonderfully, brightly. Sophie swallowed again, but for a different reason this time.

"Decommissioning this prison, however," Jane said, and now there was a little snap to her voice, "requires some extraordinary measures. It requires certain *tools*. Your Book is one. The underwater excavation in the Dead Lake is going to recover another. There are others that you need not worry about, but some that you do; some of those measures require someone trained as a Vesachai but implanted with a certain ancient Silver-Age technology." Jane smiled, looking down at

Sophie's arms. "Decommissioning that prison requires the Vesachai *themselves*—and fully under my control. It required breaking your father's power, because he would never have agreed to it. It required the forming of the Espionage Corps and a hundred other world-shaking things that you know nothing about. It will require far more, before it is all finished. It will require killing what lies inside the prison, for one."

"What?" Sophie's voice shook a little. "What's in there, a fucking *god*?"

Jane smiled, with teeth. "Oh, no. What lies bound in that prison is *the* Giant, Kindaedystrin. We are talking about killing a creature that has, itself, killed hundreds of gods."

Sophie felt dizzy; she felt like she wanted to sit down. She felt like she *really* needed a drink.

"So," Jane said, turning to her. "The curtain is pulled aside. The stakes are revealed." She gestured to the blazing yellow Keep. "The rewards are clear."

Sophie just shook her head; this was all way too much. Way too much. Her head pounded pulses of light and pain through her vision.

"So, in the face of such grand plans," Jane continued, her voice dropping down to a more intimate register, putting her head near Sophie's as if they were childhood friends telling secrets, "I want you to consider something. I want you to really ask yourself how much I give *one shit* about you. Or your friends. I want you to ask yourself, really ask yourself, if there's *anything* I wouldn't do to accomplish this work of bringing light back into the Keep, and restoring it to its glory. Ask yourself if there's *anything* I wouldn't do to destroy what gets in the way of that. And then, if you're able, I want you to wonder how *very fucking little* I care about your feelings, Sophie Vesachai. How infinitesimal my ability to give a shit about what you want must be, set against such goals."

There was a long moment where Sophie just looked at the bulk of the depicted Keep, brightly yellow. Light, brought back to the Underlands. She had never dreamed Jane had such ambition.

"We are not making a deal," Jane said, straightening. "You do not hold any cards; if the entire Keep rose up in revolt because I harmed the precious Savior of the Keep, it would be at the most, to me, a temporary annoyance. There will be no truce, no protection for your friends; there will be no consideration for you at all. I've had fifteen years to come up with ways to counter that very useful magic in your arms; it is no longer the strong card you seem to think it is. Are we clear?"

"Yeah," Sophie said, "we're clear."

"You understand your place, in my hierarchy of needs?"

"Yeah, I understand."

"Good." Jane's tone returned to its brisk and businesslike demeanor. "My Consort has convinced me that you still have use. So we will delay the pulling-off-fingers phase of this just a little longer. I will give you some time to think about what I've shown you. But Sophie, I would make very sure that *someone* knows where to find that Book. It's a dangerous night, and if that secret goes into the grave with you, everyone you ever loved will die."

"Yeah, yeah." Sophie closed her eyes. "Don't worry, Jane. I understand all of your threats."

"That last one was a threat, I'll give you that," Jane said with a small smile. "The rest were simple statements of fact."

————

She wasn't immediately dragged to the gates of the Ministry, as she'd expected, but she still didn't have time to collect her roiling thoughts. The Redarms threw her in another cell, only this one was plain and unadorned. She didn't have much time to think before there was a knock on the door.

The door opened, and she wasn't even surprised when she saw the sandy-haired Consort come through.

"Hello, Sophie." He gave her an odd, warning look, and Sophie understood that he would prefer if she didn't mention his having sent an army of aristocratic fops and children, earlier this evening, to give her cryptic warning messages. He turned to the Redarms who were flanking him, gave them a short nod, and they left the cell, shutting the door behind them.

"So," Sophie said. "You're the poor bastard who's fucking the Queen."

"I'm the Consort, yes. And I have some limited discretion with the Queen's troops. They'll follow my orders if they don't seem too stupid, I mean. I thought we could talk for a moment."

Sophie looked more closely at him. "No offense," she said, "but *you're* the Consort?"

He gave a mild shrug. He had an easy, disarming smile, but he wasn't particularly good-looking and had an oddly genial, almost goofy vibe that was very at odds with the poise Queen Jane usually prized in her confidants.

"No one is more surprised than me. It seems our Queen casts her affections where she will."

He twisted, awkwardly looking out of the small window set in the door, watching for something. He must have seen the nearest Redarm move out of hearing range, because when he turned back, his face was tight with anxiety and strain. "*Please*," he said in a strained whisper, "do not give Jane the Book!"

"You need to figure your shit out, man." All of a sudden, weariness gripped Sophie, the adrenaline of her audience with the Queen leaving her in a rush. "What the fuck are you doing? Are you working with my brother?"

"Oh god, no," the Consort said. He glanced over his shoulder, plainly nervous that the Redarms would return. Whatever he was doing, he didn't seem to want the Queen to know about it. "Your brother is working for a man named Candle."

"Yeah, he said as much. Who the fuck is he?"

The Consort looked pained. "Well, I told you not to trust Bear. Candle is . . . well, he's Bear's brother. I don't know if they're working together—maybe not. But they both have some fucking dark pasts, man."

Bear's *brother?* Sophie shook her head. This was all too much, too fast. "That doesn't make any sense. Why should I trust anything you—"

"*Shut up,*" the Consort said, tightly, with another look outside the window. "It doesn't matter, Sophie, not right now. There's no time, and if she finds out I'm talking to you . . . well. Nothing good will happen."

"I can't deal with this right now." Sophie put her head in her hands.

"Listen," the Consort said. "Listen to me. All you have to do is nothing. They're trying to force you to act, your brother and Candle. They're trying to push you into a corner, to hurt what you care about so that you'll lash out and do something stupid. They're trying to create situations where you won't be able to help but try to save lives—especially your friends. But nobody can force you to act, Sophie. Please! Listen: *all you have to do is nothing.* For just a little while longer. Don't let them force you into going for the Book. And don't let Jane trick you into giving it up; her speech about bringing light back to the Keep is not the whole story."

"But it doesn't make any sense," Sophie said. "If she needs the Book that badly, why would Jane let me go? If it's that important, why is she letting me walk out of here?"

The Consort hesitated, and when he spoke his voice was very low. "Bait. For your brother. He's striking with impunity, but he seems very focused on you. She thinks you'll flush him out. And she thinks . . . she thinks she can get the Book out of you anytime she wants. So she'd rather not risk you breaking Proscription, and . . . honestly, she doesn't like to be the kind of person who tortures people's friends. Not if she doesn't have to."

"Bait. This night just keeps getting better and better."

The Consort shook his head. "Don't give her the Book, Sophie. It is *literally* the most important thing in the world. No matter what she threatens, or what she showed you. I'll explain when I can. But right now there's no time."

Sophie groaned. "Fuck *off,* man. You and Jane both, I'm still too drunk to deal with this fate-of-the-world bullshit. Tell me how to find this 'Candle' fucker or get the fuck out."

"I can't do that. I'm sorry. You're not ready to face Candle. He's more dangerous than you know. Far more dangerous, in his own way, than the Queen could ever be." Frustrated, he combed his fingers through his hair. This gesture, maddeningly, made him almost swim into focus; *she knew this man.* Why couldn't she remember?

"Listen," he said, as Sophie heard footsteps in the hall, "you can trust your friend Trik, okay? But don't tell anyone else where the Book is."

"Fuck you. I trust my friends."

"Then you didn't learn much from the Hot Halls War."

"It's the only thing I *did* learn," Sophie said. "Where the fuck do I know you from, anyways?"

The Consort glanced out of the cell's little window again and grimaced. He looked back at Sophie. He looked pained. "It's not important right now. Just . . . please. Hold out a little longer. I'll explain everything I can. And I'm . . . I'm sorry. About all of this."

Sophie had to laugh; it was all too much. Too absurd. This earnest goofball, trying to meddle with great events. "You're not very good at this," she said. "You know that, right?"

"Oh," he said, eyes crinkling, "I know. But there doesn't seem to be anyone else willing to do it."

The door opened, and he was gone, and several guards with red sashes on their biceps came in and locked her in a secure grip. Sophie once again found herself in the ungentle embrace of the Redarms.

She wasn't surprised to discover that she really, *really* needed a fucking drink.

THE MONSTERS

A Feast Fit for Goddamn Kings

"I do everything I've done for wine, food, and sweet kisses. If pressed, however, I can usually manage without the food and lips."

—ERIC VARIS LEN, 'MORTAL COILS'

"Toast."

"Toast!"

"Hmm. What shall we toast to?"

"This one is all on you. Dazzle me."

"Well, I can but think of one toast appropriate for the occasion: Here's to *us.*"

"*Fuck* yes. Here's to us!"

"Supreme badasses."

"Supreme *motherfuckin'* badasses."

Thick glasses clinked, and the monsters drank.

"Ahhh," Jackie said. "Delicious."

"Good as it gets," Gun agreed.

"And how about this fuckin' steak?" Jackie leaned back in the sturdy chair—carefully—and sighed happily. She prodded the thick slab of meat with her knife. It was swimming in some sort of rich brown sauce, smothered in spicy peppers. "Shit is fuckin' dee-*vine.*"

"Couldn't agree more," Gun said, taking another bite. "Best goddamn steak—or whatever the fuck this is—I ever had."

"Agreed. You know? This is *nice.*"

"So nice."

"We should do this more often!"

"Why not?" Gun scooped up some of the spicy peppers on his knife and popped them into his mouth. "You are, and shall always be, a veritable fountain of good ideas."

"Well, now you're just flattering a girl." Jackie gave him a broad wink. She reached across the table and punched him in the arm. "I didn't say to stop!"

"Ho!"

"Ho boy! Comedy. At least *somebody* has a sense of humor around here, am I right?"

"There is a good chance," Gun pointed his knife at her, "that we are the two funniest people in this world. *Very* good chance."

"I think you're right, my man," Jackie said. She looked around and scooped up her tumbler. "Two funnier people have never goddamn lived."

They chewed companionably for a few minutes, being careful not to look around them too much.

". . . And charming," Gun said, around a mouthful of food.

"Hm?"

"Charming."

"And charming, clearly." Jackie poked at the remains of her steak with her knife, sliding it around in the brown sauce, which had begun to congeal.

They lapsed into silence. Gun sipped his drink and looked around the courtyard, trying not to notice the white-faced soldiers standing with their useless weapons, watching them eat. He took another sip and coughed.

"Erudite," he said.

"Hm?"

"We're also *erudite*," Gun said. "And good-looking."

"I assumed," Jackie said, "that those go without needing to be said."

"Ah, right. My apologies."

Jackie was looking at her now-empty glass, frowning. Suddenly she knocked, hard, on the table. Her knuckles left faint indentations in the heavy wood.

"Another!" she cried. She held up her glass and waggled it.

"Jacks . . ."

She ignored him. She waited, glass out, until their terrified and trembling waiter was shoved out of the restaurant's interior by someone. He made his way over to them like a man walking to the gallows. Gun shifted, crossed his arms, and pushed his steak—or whatever it was—away.

Jackie set her glass down and gave the terrified man a bright smile.

"Another," she said, with exaggerated politeness. "*Please.*"

The man nodded jerkily and fumbled up the glass. He almost dropped it, then recovered. He started backing away, shuffling, afraid to turn his back on them.

"Well, goddamn it, all right." Gun drained the last of his own beverage. He held it out. "Might as well make it two."

The server closed his eyes, and his lips moved in a small invocation to some unknown god. He took a step closer, reached out as far as he could, and snagged Gun's glass as if it were a live adder.

"Thank you." Gun gave him his warmest, friendliest smile.

Maybe it was too much teeth; the man appeared to just about die of fright, tip back slightly from the edge of death, and use the very last of his will and reason to scramble away from them and back into the relative safety of the restaurant.

"Top-notch service, this place." Jackie crossed her arms.

"Really is," Gun said, and couldn't think of anything else to say. His eyes tried to find somewhere to rest and skittered first over the terrified soldiers, then over a few smoking piles of wreckage that used to be mechanical war-suits, and then over what seemed like half the population of the city standing on balconies and down alleys, watching them eat with terrified and furious faces. At least they'd finally turned the goddamn *siren* off.

Dinner conversation had lapsed a bit. Arms crossed, Jackie stared at her half-eaten steak. She looked up at all of the soldiers and frightened people and grunted.

A stout woman, her mouth set into a grim line, brought out two more glasses of liquor. She set them down on the table and looked back and forth between the two. She had hard eyes. "After you finish," she said, "you have to go. No more." She turned swiftly, her courage having run out, and shuffled quickly back to the restaurant.

"We'll stay as long as we *want*," Jackie called after her.

Gun shook his head. "No premium on politeness in this town, I guess."

"I'm gonna go," Jackie pronounced, "when I'm good and fucking ready."

"Yeah." Gun concealed a sigh and lifted his glass. He hesitated. "Okay. Toast."

"Toast."

They held their glasses out for a while. Gun shook his head. "I dunno. I got nothing."

"Okay. How about . . . here's to us." Jackie lifted her glass.

"Here's to us," Gun said. They clinked, and Jackie held his eye and amended it. "Against the world."

They clinked. Jackie held his eye and amended the toast: "Against *them*."

"There you go, Jacks. Us against them. Whoever they may be."

The monsters drank.

"God damn," Jackie swore, looking into her glass. "Is there even any booze in this?"

"Dunno," Gun said. "Can't be much."

"Fuckers," Jackie muttered, but finished the drink anyway.

Gun looked at his steak. His appetite was gone. The clinking of his knife against the ceramic was very loud in the silence. The sounds of the city were gone; there were no voices of haggling people, no cattle moving through the streets or children playing. No music, just the clinking of Gun's knife and Jackie's breathing.

"All right, enough," Jackie said, finally. "This is bumming me the fuck out, man."

"Yeah." Gun pushed his plate away.

"Atmosphere in this joint is for shit."

"It's bad," Gun agreed. "You want to get out of here?"

"Fuck it," Jackie said. "Yeah."

Gun tossed his knife down and finished his weak drink. He fussed in his pack for a moment and came up with several coins, brought with them from their old world. He tossed them down onto the table, and they landed, heavily. Jackie watched this with a raised eyebrow.

"What?" Gun said. "Paying for dinner."

"With *those*?"

"I dunno. What else we got? And those are literally priceless, one-of-a-kind souvenirs."

"Somehow," Jackie said, "I don't think they'll acknowledge your largesse. Or be able to pick them up."

"Yeah, well." Gun strapped his sword over his shoulder and picked up his pack. He looked again at the ring of soldiers, all white-faced and prepared to die at the hands of the hideous monsters, the dread Behemoth. "I think our welcome is worn out, anyway."

"Whatever," Jackie said, gathering up her own pack. "Let's roll, I guess. Fuckin' tired of this place."

"Ain't the most hospitable," Gun said, and they made their way out of the courtyard, trying to ignore the terrified people who parted to let them through. The soldiers gripped their odd clockwork weapons, but they'd already been provided copious evidence that these armaments served only to annoy the monsters.

They made their way back down through the winding, makeshift streets. As layered and confusing as the city was, they had no trouble finding their way; they had only to follow the destruction they'd left coming in. They passed a pile of twisted wreckage that had once been a light-tower. Jackie had demolished it to demonstrate why the residents should stop shooting their dumb little weapons at her. Silent people lined the streets, watching them with hard, frightened eyes. The only sound was the click of Jackie's walking stick, the occasional whimpers of children, and the low hum of mechanics that pervaded the city.

Gun was glad to see they'd managed to free the soldiers from the wrecked mechanical war-suits. These were littered along the way, left to fall wherever Gun and Jackie had broken them.

They walked silently, heavily, their mouths set, and the city watched them go. Eventually they reached the buckled, wrenched-apart ruins of the city gates and climbed through. There was no sound as they left, only the waiting and watching eyes.

Jackie and Gun looked at each other for a long moment, standing before the gates.

"Well?" Gun said.

"Yeah," Jackie said, with a sigh. "Well."

The monsters turned and walked into the darkness.

THE DEADSMITH

The Door Into Desolation

"Do not think on beauty when preparing for war, and likewise never consider battles in the presence of love. Each can only poison the other."

—JAKE-JOHNSTON SAVALL, 'THE METEORE'

His Fate was still screaming.

The Deader lurched the last few span to the Door and held himself up with it. His Fate screamed mad nonsense into his head, and he could hardly see or think. His Fate was insensate and incoherent, a deafening scream of gibbering and of sick, gasping washes of color. The Deader gritted his teeth against the storm of queasy sensation and fumbled at the silver knob.

He had to try several times before his hand closed on it. His vision was doubled and trebled. The Prey had harmed him, hurt him badly. His Fate moaned in terror, remorse, and hunger.

The Whispers—the stone maze where the Prey had chosen to confront him—echoed strangely with the agonizing madness in his head. The Prey had spoken in that disturbing, overwhelming god-voice, speaking in the mystifying language his Fate spoke, a voice like mountains falling.

And his Fate was still screaming.

Whatever the Prey—the Deader refused to call him *Candle*—had done to his Fate had driven it insane, torn apart its fragile consciousness like so much wet paper. Concentrating hard and shutting off his Fate's bellowing of colors across his senses, the Deader was able to turn the silver knob in the center of the Door. It opened on roiling white, a blizzard. Snow whipped into the quiet maze; it was impossible to see more than a few span. But the Prey had gone into this storm, and so must the Deader.

He stood in blood, but not enough of it. His Machine had wounded the Prey, but not killed him. The Deader still had work to do, despite the wailing madness in his head. He staggered through the Door, throwing up an arm to protect himself from the whipping ice. His Machine ran into the storm, disappearing, eager for more of the Prey's blood. It was dark, too dark, so the Deader called forth a weirlight, and the snow seemed to freeze into a series of static images, a flickering roil of white specks. He told the light to expand as far as it would, and he gripped the free-standing doorframe just to stay upright. His Fate moaned in terror and confusion.

He didn't know how to judge threats properly without his Fate. He swept his hand across his eyes, trying to clear them of the colors his mad Fate sent washing across his vision, dire portents of things it couldn't possibly know.

The Deader went down on one knee, fighting against the sickening flood of emotions and colors and nonsense-words in his head. If he could have pulled his Fate free of himself and ended its misery, he would have. But while the Deader— and all Deadsmith—were triune beings, only he and his Fate lived inside his skull. His Machine, the third part of himself, was free of what the Prey had done to him.

The Deader pressed his fists against his temples as he fought against his Fate's hysteria. He couldn't think about how he would go on just now; he couldn't consider life without a third of himself. His instincts, his attention, his sense of self-preservation—all these had been cut away and given to his Fate. And now his Fate was destroyed, a hot welter of insanity in the back of his mind. Never in living memory had a Deadsmith been hurt so badly.

Finally, the Deader pushed himself up, forced himself to look around, to care about what he saw. He didn't see the Prey. The Door stood in the middle of an old stone daïs, as many of them did, but this one wasn't nearly as ornate or finely made as most of them were. It was a function-door, and it was one more thing that the damned Prey shouldn't have known about.

The Deader gritted his teeth against the weeping derangement in his head, tried to shut it out, erect barriers of will against it. But it was like trying to shut out your own thoughts. He did his best, however. There was a path forward, and he must take it. Cold creased his toughened skin; even he would need to find shelter.

He peered around, trying to see through the titanic walls of wind and snow that crashed into him. He was high in some mountains on an artificial flat space built into the shelter of two towering cliffs. The weirlight showed everything in sketches of gray, scribe-thin tracings like an awl dragged across old metal. He guessed he was high in the never-ending Barrier Mountains, which surrounded every Land in the Wanderlands. He could be anywhere; he felt lost. He didn't know how long he had lain in that whisper-maze, half-mad, his Fate's mind disintegrating, but it seemed a long while.

It did not matter. He reeled up the path, with no Fate to warn him of what might be ahead, no instincts to tell him where danger lay. He didn't know how to be wary; that was his Fate's domain, and now the Deader would have to learn how to be afraid again.

The Deader would rather have lost his hands. But nothing attacked him. The Prey's traps were a subtler sort.

The path wound up, steep, and led to a kind of cave or passage, farther into the depths of the rock. It wasn't ornamented but the floor was roughly flat and only small eddies of snow blew in here. There were the remnants of a fire in the center, and the Deader could sense some small heat still held in the coals. He swore, forcing the epithets out between clenched teeth. There was blood on the ground here, too, but not enough. The Prey had indeed survived whatever his Machine had done.

One end of the passageway had been caved in, and recently. The Deader could not manage to care very much about the blockage. When his Machine finished exploring, he would set it to clear the rocks. If the Prey thought such a simple maneuver would slow him, he was mistaken. The Deader clutched his fist, the patterns on his skin flaring white, and pulled twist from the surrounding rock. It formed rough red-black shards that he piled and lit. The Black-and-White magic was the master of all, and he was never above using twist when he needed to. The Nine's prohibition against Dirt-Magic was for the common folk, not the likes of Deadsmith. The shards would burn for hours. Long enough.

He unrolled his pack near the fire and sat wearily. Colors still washed across his vision, making his eyes hurt, but his Fate had reduced itself to a terrified, gibbering mutter. As the fire warmed him, he made himself think about the man who called himself Candle.

He understood now why he had been sent after the man. He knew what Candle—*the Prey,* damn it—had stolen. His Lady and a few of her cohorts in the Nine had been trying to perfect a certain technology for a long time; trying to find a host who would not burn out under the stress of it. They would not trust such a technology even to a Deadsmith.

It was a form of Domination—the old Cold-trick, the Far-Speaking. But it was a form in the way that the Deader's own Black-and-White magic was a form of the Silver. The way that Silver was a peculiar form of the Gold. They were similar in the way a pin-light was similar to a flare. The Black-and-White was the wild magic, the terrible and lovely master of all. There had never been a Silver technology—or for that matter, the Old Gold—that could prevail over the Black-and-White. Only the Deadsmith were permitted to use this wild Black-and-White magic, but not even the Deadsmith had been given *Domination.*

Domination. The Deader felt a strange sensation and realized it was fear. His Fate trembled, lost, a poor broken thing curled in the back of the Deader's mind. The Prey must have found a way to survive the implanting process. He had survived it and—against all reasonable odds—stolen it. From the Nine. From his Lady. He looked at the rough stone wall of the passage, lit by the shifting illumination of his fire.

The Prey had scrawled a message for him there, again in blood, and this time undoubtedly his own. It said only one word:

Tyrathect.

Another trap, he was sure, made of another memory. But the Deader didn't want to think about Tyrathect. His Fate moaned and snarled. The Prey shouldn't know about that place. But neither should he have been able to enter into the very chambers of the Nine and steal their secrets. He shouldn't have been able to destroy the Deader's *Fate*.

Tyrathect. The Deader spat and shook his head. His Fate was maddening him; it shouted garbled nonsense across his mind. He wondered if it would ever heal and suspected it would not. There was no way to remove it; it was as much a part of the Deader as his own hands and harder to cut away. He considered having a piece of himself, driven mad, trapped forever inside his own mind. It wasn't a comforting idea.

The Deader knew sleep would be long in coming, no matter how much his abused mind needed it. He withdrew a slim case from his pack; it held a hexagonal piece of ebon and diverse and finely made tools for shaping it. The top of it had taken a rough form; the approximation of a woman's torso, one hand lifted in the air.

The Deader blew on one of the delicate knives and began to carve. He prodded at that sensation in his chest, that ancient friend, *fear*. Distantly he heard his Machine knock some loose stones down the side of the mountain, but he ignored it. It was just hunting, just looking for something to kill, frustrated at having missed the Prey. He looked at the message in blood, written in the same rough hand as the one on the Door, back in the decimated city; the one that had scrawled that question.

How do you make a machine?

He felt weary, deeply weary. He wondered what his Lady was doing just then—entertaining or prosecuting art-politic among the Wise, playing her games of influence? Or on one of her frequent jaunts into the dark places of the world, hunting advantage and sport? He wondered if she had taken one of the other Deadsmith with her and felt a sour wash of jealousy. He flaked ebon away from the form, the small scratching of his knife the only sound in the cavern.

He felt a desperate longing for direction. He cradled the new fear that had flared to life in his chest, alongside the unaccustomed feeling of hate. And of course, he had truly learned the meaning of both in one place, a city called *Tyrathect*.

———

Tyrathect was a stone-city, and it sat at the bottom of a league-deep and league-wide cylinder that had been drilled into the Barrier Mountains. The city at the bottom of that well had been more prepared for the Fall than most Lands; it was so sunken into the mountains that it had never gotten much light in the first place.

It had a Feed and it had infrastructure, so it had survived the first end of the world. The Deadsmith that had saved him from the wreckage of his family, the Deadsmith that had promised him justice and then shown him how to do it, had taken him to Tyrathect.

The things he had learned and done under the Deadsmith's harsh tutelage had left him a shell, hollow of any kindness. With the Deadsmith's help, he had hunted down and killed the man called Trail, and all that bore the circle cut into their small fingers. He had tortured his own brother to death, using techniques taught him by the hard-eyed woman and justified by her brutal moral code. She had abandoned him in Tyrathect once his revenge was complete. The boy hadn't minded.

He felt no remorse about what they had done; he felt he had returned balance to the world, and there would be no more rapes and murders on the steppes of his homeland.

But Tyrathect was a curiously savage place. Curious because it was—on the surface—as civilized as anywhere in the Wanderlands. They held the Watches and Codes and were highly placed servants of the Empire of the Nine. But it was at the same time a charnel-house, a gigantic mechanism for turning children into warmachines.

There were many children in Tyrathect. The Nine were always looking for certain likely candidates, youth of extraordinary talent and resolve, damaged in just the right way. Few children were brought to Tyrathect by an actual Deadsmith, but many were brought there. The best of them had blue tattoos, a complex and painful patterning across their chest, all similar but none exactly alike. The hard-eyed Deadsmith herself had given the boy his tattoo. It was his reward for killing his own brother.

In the city of Tyrathect, if you bore that blue tattoo, you held no rights until you had earned them. There was only one way to earn rights in that sunken city, and that was in the School Inverse. If you had no rights, you had no home, and you had no food. You were hunted night and day by remorseless enforcers, hard-eyed and blue-tattooed, themselves survivors of the School.

The boy killed several of these enforcers, attempting to escape punishment for thieving food, but began to understand that he would be captured eventually. There were too many of them, too determined, and he was still more or less a child. But once he had killed the enforcers there were only two escapes for him: death, or the School Inverse. This was, of course, the point. Tyrathect existed because of the school and all of its systems pointed towards it. Still, he was too young to embrace the final dark; so he joined the School.

The School was monstrous in the ways of such institutions. Its only true purpose was to cull weakness and train strength. It was run by the hardest of the hard, blue-tattooed old men and women who had not only survived the school but surpassed it. The School built servants for the Nine, and the administrators of the School were those who had been brought back from posts within the Empire, those who had proven themselves to have no shred of human kindness and an utter devotion to the Nine's purposes.

As soon as he joined the School Inverse, every moment of the boy's life became a crucial test, and every fork in the road had death on one of the paths. It was the sort of place where you could earn an extra dessert by murdering a fellow student in a manner that pleased the teachers. It was the sort of place where the rules changed on the instant, and those who didn't learn quickly died. Many did die, but there were thousands of children with blue tattoos in Tyrathect, and there were always more coming behind them.

The boy survived the School; he learned. Instinct for survival and swift brutal reprisal became entwined through him, into his bones. He had learned that much from Trail, who had killed his mother and sister, and from the Deadsmith who brought him to Tyrathect. He progressed through arcane levels of skill and schooling, earning the ire and attention of the gray-haired masters. But he had learned well, on those steppes, at the point of Trail's knife, and learned even better under the hard hand of the Deadsmith. The School Inverse didn't break him, and it didn't end him. It did, however, make him cruel.

He grew older, surviving and even thriving in the School. His masters sought often to break him—or, more accurately, sought to break him if he showed even one moment of weakness—but they were unable. The boy became a fearsome brute.

However, he was still a boy, and even the School Inverse was not able to eradicate all of what that meant. He still lay awake long nights on his hard stone bed, listening for other children approaching in the dark with makeshift garrotes, and thought of his mother, his sister; of his life on the steppes of his homeland. He thought of the rare days when the sky was bright. He—very occasionally—dreamed of a different world, one where things like the School Inverse were not necessary.

He survived, and survived, and survived again. Eventually, he grew close to a girl, a girl with laughing green eyes and long dark hair who cleaned in the school. She bore no tattoo and had full rights in the city, but her family was poor and she was compelled to work for her place. She was fascinated by the School, as well as by those who survived it. She began to be fascinated by the boy. And the boy began to dream of her laughing eyes and her smile, and almost against his own will, began to take chances to see her.

In the School Inverse, *any* chances were dangerous ones.

He didn't know what love was, and if the sensation had been described to him, he might have laughed and struck anyone foolish enough to care for such a thing. He did not know that the girl reminded him a little of his sister and a little more of his mother. The girl's name was Anise, and one night she kissed him, softly, on the cheek.

The boy began to dream more often of other lives than this; he began to think about a life other than the School, and bitter strength, and brutal revenge. In the night, he permitted himself one moment of weakness: a small, secret smile, just for the girl with dark hair and laughing eyes.

But this was the School Inverse, and his masters were always watching. They saw that smile. They had been waiting for it.

The next morning, he woke to find her tied and bound on the floor of his room, a knife lying beside her. The intent was clear; the masters would tolerate no weakness in their weapons. This was the sort of object lesson that they loved, the kind you were forced to teach yourself.

But love, the boy discovered, was the weakness that bred strength. He took the knife, cut the girl free, and fought his way into the home of one of the gray-haired masters he suspected was responsible. He killed him—and many more besides—before he was subdued. He had been trained by a Deadsmith and was deadly. But even he could not prevail against the full might of the School Inverse, or of Tyrathect itself.

He was forced to watch the dark-haired girl die, cut to slow pieces in front of him as punishment for his hubris. They sentenced him to the Nine Days, a killing that took that long to finish. They flayed him open and salted the wounds, and the boy truly learned what it was to fear. He learned what it truly was to hate.

But on the seventh day, a woman named Winter, one of the Nine, appeared in the stone-city and looked down at the boy, near death. She must have liked what she saw because she commanded the blue-tattooed elders to tell her his story. When they did, she laughed. She bid the boy be cut down and healed.

And then she took him, but not to the White Tower, not yet. There was still a long road to walk before he found that particular home, and his place in his Lady Winter's heart and bed.

He still had much more to lose.

———

The fire had burned low, but his Fate still chortled and whimpered by turns, a fat knot of sickening emotion in the back of his head. He looked at the piece of ebon in his hands. Features were beginning to take shape. He never set out intending to carve her likeness, but always his knife uncovered her.

The Lady Winter. His god, his lover, his master. The Deader set the chunk of ebon aside and stared into the dying fire. Remembering Tyrathect had one beneficial effect; his Fate had quieted, and now just muttered and moaned to itself in the back of his head. It was profoundly unpleasant, but bearable.

Tomorrow, he would have to pick up the trail again; he would have to continue this long pursuit. His Lady had pointed and bid him return with blood on his teeth, and he would. He wondered idly what he would find beyond the collapsed tunnel but wasn't able to summon much care. He crossed his arms and looked into the fire for a long time, waiting for sleep to come.

Perhaps if his Fate had been whole, he would have been warier; he might have sensed something and taken precautions. But a third of himself had been torn away, and it was the part of him that was watchful of danger. The Deader just looked into the fire, trying to ignore the mad cackle in his head, and sensed nothing wrong until he heard a small crumpling explosion in the rock overhead.

He had time to look up, but no time for surprise, before the top of the mountain fell in on him. It killed him instantly.

He was not called a Deadsmith for nothing, however. It was far from the first time he had died.

THE LOST BOYS

The Man Called Master

"Only a fool fears change. And only a bigger fool seeks it."

—ALVAREZ, 'OBSERVATIONS'

In later years and darker times, the man that James would turn into would kill many people, and take the lives and futures from many men, and women, and thinking creatures of all sorts. None of those deaths stayed with him long, except for that first one, the man that tried to kidnap him. The sight of him impaled by jagged shards of something rough, the red-black spars throwing him back, already spitting out his life in a gout of red. The look of vast surprise on his face, as if looking into forever and seeing nothing but infinite reflections, folding back on themselves, fading away to nothing.

It would take James a long time to think of it that way; and for a while he hardly had time to think of it at all. And yet it was the first thing he saw, when he returned to consciousness—that surprised look on the man's face, and a feeling of shame.

It stayed with him longer than the memory of sunshine, of trees and living rock, of the Giant that had stood and roared. It stayed with him longer than the feeling of the knives pressing in when he'd found out that red-haired Katherine had tricked him and was really his *brother's* friend. It stayed with him longer than that feeling of chill, of bone-deep cold pain, when he'd reached through the Cold-Key that they'd brought through a Door from another world, reached through it and summoned up the shards of red-black twist he used to murder his assailant.

It would stay with him through long years in the dark, stay with him through the terrible things he and his brother would do under the Mountain in service of Chris' ambition; it would stay with him even through all of the tangled machinations of the Wise; through the part he would play in the Hot Halls War and all that would follow.

Yes, that first one stayed with him. His first killing. Of all the deaths that would come, that was the only one he'd really remember.

He lost consciousness after he'd killed the first man; less, he later reasoned, because of the murder and more an effect of using the Cold-Key. The Key hurt to use, and he'd lost his presence of mind for a while afterwards. When he started to come to, he discovered that he and his brother were being carried through the low-ways of Cannoux, but it was all very disorienting and vague. By the time he felt like he knew the inside of his head again, he and Chris had been deposited in a small, spare room inside some Lord's house.

His face burned when they pulled the hood off his head. He found himself on his knees, gasping, because the thug's rough shoulder had driven the wind from him.

"James," he heard Chris say. Chris was gasping too. "Don't say anything."

James saw a big shape approach, delicately somehow, as if dancing. It leaned down over him.

"Oh, James," the big shape said, sounding amused, "you'll say *plenty*."

James became aware of his surroundings by degrees, slowly expanding spheres of understanding. He was in a heavy, ill-featured room with no windows or furnishings. There were some men there, soldiers or thugs, and a couple of girls, one of whom was weeping and barely held up by the other. She had red hair—

James bolted upright, snarling, but was smacked to the ground almost immediately by someone behind him. His head rang and everything nearly went away again, but he scrabbled to hold onto consciousness.

"Tough little bastard, yes?" The amused voice spoke again, and James saw slippered feet pause on the floor next to his face. He pushed himself up from the stone floor with trembling arms. He felt like he'd gotten his face pushed into the back of his head.

"Fuckin' killed Donovan," one of the men who kidnapped them said. "Some fuckin' how." James felt a sharp pain in his leg; he assumed he'd just been kicked.

"Enough," the big man said. "Get up, boy."

James climbed gingerly to his feet, wiping blood from the corner of his mouth and spitting some more at the big man's feet. But the man, though he seemed fat, danced back; he was much more nimble than James would have guessed.

"What a rascal! Aren't you afraid of me, boy?"

James looked up into the man's face for the first time. He recognized him; it was Lord D'Alle, Katherine's Master. She was still weeping in the corner. Her face was badly bruised.

"Keep quiet, James." This was Chris, who was on his knees next to James. He had a seeping cut on one cheek. He sounded defeated, and it made James want to kick him.

"Say another word without me asking you, boy," D'Alle said to Chris, "and I'll have that tongue out."

"I ain't scared of *you*." James spit more blood. "I killed your man, and I'll kill you too, soon as I can be bothered to do it."

D'Alle smiled broadly. His dark hair was done in a long tight braid, and he whipped it forward around his shoulder. "Mr. Swaim, I like this one! Too stupid to breathe, but I like him."

A thin, severe man stepped forward and handed D'Alle the Cold-Key.

The man that Katherine called Master examined it for a long moment and shook his head. "Well you flat out *ruined* my red-haired girl, between the two of you. Had to beat her bloody to give you up. And then you kill one of my men! In addition to stealing an incredibly valuable and forbidden artifact from me. It's a long day's work, my young boys, and I won't pretend to not be impressed."

From the corner of his eye, James could see that Chris wanted to say something, and D'Alle turned his broad face to him, waiting, with a little half-smile. But Chris shut his mouth, struggling to do it. Katherine was looking at them now, tear-stained.

"I'm sorry!" she said. "I tried to—"

She was silenced with a vicious backhand that drove her to the floor, dripping blood. The assailant, a tall woman standing over her, smiled and licked her knuckles. James was up off his knees and going at the woman without thinking, but D'Alle was much faster than he looked. He caught James by the throat and slammed him down onto his back, driving the wind from him and nearly making him black out again. He discovered that he didn't much care for that feeling.

"I can see that you are a willful child with no sense of order." D'Alle's face was very close to James'. "And I've no patience with that. Do you hear me, boy? Defy me again, and I'll have *your* tongue out, and shoved someplace where you can taste what you're made of."

He let go of James' neck. James gasped, once, getting a little air. With a jerk of his abused neck, he spit a big mouthful of blood into D'Alle's face. He laughed, joyfully, painfully.

"James!" Chris cried.

D'Alle's face was savage for a moment, streaked with blood and spit, and he loomed over James like a mountain. James got ready to roll away, but instead D'Alle chuckled, a big booming sound. He visibly relaxed, holding out his hand so the thin man could put a kerchief into it. He wiped his face, patting at the thick skin, and the glittering in his eyes went from malevolent to amused.

"Learn this lesson, Ana," he said to the tall woman who had hit Katherine. "Don't make threats you aren't going to follow through on, because if your bluff is called, you look twice as foolish."

He laughed again and motioned to one of the kidnappers to get James up. The two boys were wrenched to their feet, their arms pinioned behind them. D'Alle was still holding the silver medallion, the *Cold-Key,* and James twisted against the thug's grip. If he could just get his hand on it . . .

But D'Alle smiled, seeming to know what James was thinking. "No, boy. I went through some trouble to get my hands on this, and I mean to have my due.

You two had quite the adventure, I hear, and it's more than most boys get. I hope that's a comfort to you."

He handed the silvery amulet back to the thin man and clapped his hands. "I'm late to Council," he said, "and must change my tunic. See these two lads to the basement storeroom, please, and if I hear even a whisper of their presence from anyone outside this house, I *will* have tongues out and fingers off. Good? Good! To it, then."

And the men dragged Chris and James away. The last thing James saw was Katherine's tear-streaked face, her lip bleeding, looking at them with some enormous, awful emotion in her eyes.

No, that wasn't right. She wasn't looking at *them*, not really. That would imply she was looking at *both* of them. No, she was looking at his brother Chris. She cared if *Chris* understood, if *he* forgave. And James discovered that this, for some stupid reason, hurt far worse than anything D'Alle's thugs had done to him.

THE KILLERS

Self Reflection is for Those
Who Care to Improve

"Only a fool steps over an unexpected weight of silver because they are hoping to find gold."

—SANDY LOXEN, 'DOUBLE THE DISTANCE'

Sophie stumbled back out into the Keep, the Redarms giving her an ungentle shove to help the transition. They released her at the gates of the Ministry facade and into the broad avenue that led away from it. Sophie didn't know how long she had been in the depths of the Ministry; it felt like half a lifetime. She almost expected the day-lights to be on, but it was still, somehow, night.

Sophie stood for a long moment, looking up at the folded series of softly glowing arches that made up the ceiling of the avenue. She saw some birds flitting between nests and envied them. She saw some beam-cats stalking the birds, and envied them too. She looked down the avenue and saw a small round structure, a fakewood-slat roof, and the unmistakable, telltale, rounded curve of a bar—and one that was still open.

"Well, thank the Mother," she said, and hauled herself over to it. She sank onto a stool gratefully, just sat there for a while, and then ordered a pot of strong from the barkeep.

"Say," she said as he was pouring, "any chance you have any slots you could part with?"

He grinned and pulled a can from beneath the counter. He opened it, pulled out two slots, and tossed them on the countertop. "On the house."

"Now *you're* a Twins-damned hero." Sophie slid some medium-weight coins across the bar. The barkeep laughed.

"High praise." He paused, considering. He leaned down on the bar, made eye contact. "Figured maybe you should know that your name is on a lot of lips, tonight. Not pretty words, either. Linking you to some of the bad shit that's been going down."

Sophie grimaced. "Yeah, I figured. You want me to clear out?"

The barkeep shook his head. "Nah. People are fools, and you deserve to enjoy your drink in peace. Just wanted to pass it along."

"I'll keep my head down," Sophie said. "Thanks."

The barkeep went back to chatting with some other patrons on the other side of the bar, and Sophie scraped the slot alight along the edge of her stool. She took a deep lungful of smoke in, held it, and coughed. She thought about an iron-strong fist clamped around her throat. She thought about Jane's cold blue eyes. She thought about that model of the Keep, blazing with golden light. She didn't know how to feel about that, about Jane's plan. It was a grand plan, ambitious, perhaps even—as Denver Murkai had said—'grandly good.' Could Jane really do it? Could she really bring light back into the Keep?

What *was* Sophie, in the face of that?

Sophie picked up the pot of strong, feeling strangely empty. She felt no real urge to drink it, to try to soften the edges or dive into the oblivion there. It was a dark liquid, almost black. She knew it must be nearly time for the Killers to rendezvous, to meet in the Rue de Paladia as they'd promised, but she felt no special urge to head there either. Jane Guin had stripped her gears, somehow, either with her grand plan or her threats.

Sophie yawned and rubbed her eyes. She had a lot to think about and no desire to think about any of it. This shadowy 'Candle' figure, March's partner, being Bear's *brother?* The mysterious Avie, and her trees? Jane, and the Book?

Nah. Didn't want to think about any of *that.* She looked at the strong in front of her again, black as pitch in the little ceramic cup. She could fall into it; just start drinking. That would solve problems, in a way. It always had before. She remembered her first taste of that solution, way back when; she supposed most true drinkers could. She couldn't remember her first kiss or even the first time she'd killed, but she could always remember the first time she'd really had a *drink.*

Her first had been at fourteen; she had just raised the Jannissaries. They had rampaged through the Keep, driving the invaders back out, destroying the awful soldier-automata and killing thousands of the Outkeep. She had been walking, she remembered, maybe crying. Stunned at the enormity of what she had done. Her arms had hurt; she remembered that clearly enough. The scars on them had been livid. She had been using her power profligately near the end of the fight.

She hadn't known, then, if any of her friends were still alive. She knew Luet was dead, of course, killed by the Feral Children. And Mad Vaas couldn't have survived. But Ben, Tom, Jubilee . . . she didn't know. She walked through smoking halls, still-twitching white forms of dead Jannissaries sometimes entwined with other warmachines, some silvery and some black, all painted with the bright colors of the invading army. All dead, or dying. So many dead, and even the soldiers that were still alive were wounded, blinded, burnt and burning. The Book was heavy in her carry, but she trudged on. She knew she had to hide it. Knowing now what it could do, she would have destroyed it—if that were even possible.

The memories were oddly both vague and sharply vivid; the emotions intense but the details fuzzed, blurred. It shouldn't be a surprise; Sophie had spent the last twenty years trying to drink them away. For instance, she couldn't remember quite how she'd come upon the odd man who'd given her the drink; if he'd been searching for and found her, if she happened upon him or he happened upon her. She didn't know if the meeting was an accident or one more layer of the darkly labyrinthine plotting she was just starting to see the first hints of back then. The details were lost but she remembered the horror in his eyes.

In the bar, Sophie rolled the pot of strong between her hands, looking into the depths. She didn't want to think about the end of the Hot Halls War. Why was she thinking about it?

The strange man had known her name; he recognized her somehow. At the time, it wasn't that surprising. She was already kind of famous, and she'd just saved the world. Only, it hadn't felt like she'd saved the world. It had felt, at the time, like she'd drowned it in blood.

"You're Sophie Vesachai," the man had said. "I've been looking for you."

Sophie had been too battle-weary to think much about this; she had been awake for several days now, and most of that had been spent in an adrenaline-fueled panic. She felt husked out, hollow, absorbing the carnage and the horror around her. She had lost her capacity for surprise.

"Okay," she said.

The man slumped down on a pile of broken masonry, the crumbled section of a wall destroyed by battling machines. He looked lost, broken, and overwhelmingly sad. He looked at her for a long moment, and she nearly left. She needed to get to the Library; she needed to hide the Book. She needed to find out if any of her friends were still alive.

"I'm sorry," he said, after that long look. He lifted a bottle of something and took a long drink, the muscles in his throat working. "For what it's worth, I'm just so goddamn sorry."

"Who are you?" Sophie asked. She kept her distance, inching her way around him.

He smiled, sadly. "It doesn't matter. I was wondering if you could do me a favor."

"I have to go."

"Please—" Something about his voice, some anguish or hurt, made her stop edging away. "Please. You're the only one I can trust. And it's not fair, you're just a fucking kid. It's not fair. But you're the only one clean in all this mess."

Sophie looked down at her hands, the livid scars on her wrists and arms, the burned sleeves of her jacket. She didn't have any physical blood on her hands, but she had just murdered thousands of folk, human and silver, by raising the Jannissaries. She had killed hundreds personally, with the silver fire in her hands. She felt like throwing up. *Clean?*

"What do you want?" she asked. The man took another drink from the bottle, and wiped his face. Some of the dried blood on his hands and arms flaked off. He felt around in his own jacket for something, and pulled it free. He looked down at it for a moment, mouth going grim, and then tossed it onto the floor at Sophie's feet. It clattered oddly, as if it were heavier than it should be. It was a small silver pendant with a silvery chain.

"Hide that somewhere safe," the man said. "Please."

Sophie didn't pick it up. The man started crying, an ugly, hiccupping sound, raw and unpleasant. It didn't seem strange, then, in that place, after the horrors that she'd just seen. She wished she could cry.

"I'm sorry." He tried to wipe his eyes. "I'm so sorry."

Reluctantly, Sophie knelt down and picked up the amulet. It was a Silver Age device, without question. She looked up at the man. "Why?"

"Why am I sorry? Oh—you mean why am I asking you to hide that. I don't know. I guess it's . . . it's the kind of thing that makes good people do bad things. And it's the kind of thing that makes powerful people do . . ."

He broke off, and then took another drink. When he spoke, it was barely a whisper, haunted and hoarse.

"They used us, Sophie; they *used* us. It was all a lie, every bit of it, every word. Just a way to get what they wanted." He wiped his eyes with the sleeves of his jacket, smearing them with dried flakes of blood, a macabre warpaint. He didn't seem aware.

These words hit Sophie with an almost physical blow. The Dream of Trees hadn't been so long ago, but she didn't see any sunshine around her. The dream had started to feel like a cruel joke; she had set out to bring the trees back and instead she had bathed the Keep in blood. She had gotten friends killed in the pursuit of that dream. She had lost her family. For all she knew, her own father would put his silver knife in her heart for what she had just done. The man looked at Sophie and something powerful passed between them, some shared sense of— what? Victimhood? No, that was too trite, too small, to encompass the feeling.

No, it was the knowledge, the bone-deep understanding, that for all of your hopes and dreams and sacrifices, you were nothing more than a cog in a machine, and that machine was being operated by someone who did not care about you. And it had been built for reasons that you might never comprehend, and used for purposes that you loathe.

Sophie put the amulet in her carry, where it sat next to the Book. She stood, awkwardly. She gestured at the bottle in the man's hand.

"Can I have some of that?"

He blinked, startled by the request, and she could tell that his first instinct was to say no, to tell her she was too young, to treat her like a child. But he reconsidered, and his mouth drew into something approaching a smile. He held the bottle out. "Why the fuck not?"

She approached, still wary, and took the bottle from him. It was about half-full, and even at fourteen, she knew enough to know it was a variation of strong. It wasn't the first drink she'd had, of course; she had been a rebellious and precocious child and had snuck nips of all kinds of drinks, just to say she had. But Sophie Vesachai had never understood the phrase 'I need a drink' until *that* moment. She gripped the neck of the bottle, just as the man had, and brought it to her lips.

It was bitter, and it burned on her tongue and against the back of her throat, and it felt like swallowing fire. But this is what adults did, and Sophie was a child no longer. She considered the sensation, decided that she liked it, and then took another pull.

"Okay," the man said, gently, and took the bottle back from her. The sadness had come back into his eyes.

"Who are you?" she asked again. He seemed to consider several replies.

"It doesn't matter. I doubt we will meet again, Sophie Vesachai. I hope . . . I hope you do well. You didn't deserve this. I hope you find a way to bring some light into the world."

He straightened, and looked down at the bottle in his hand. A savage expression came upon him and he hurled the bottle at the wall, where it smashed in a spray of dark liquid. A snarl marred his mild features, and he took a moment to get himself under control. He dragged his blood-flaked fingers through his sandy hair, and looked at Sophie one last time.

"I'm sorry," he said again, and walked away.

Sophie set the pot of strong down on the bar with an audible click, her eyes going wide.

The Consort.

That's why he seemed so familiar—and why Sophie couldn't place him. The last time she'd seen him was twenty years ago, and she had done her best to bury that memory along with all the others. The fucking Consort had given her that amulet—the same one she'd put in the silver vault twenty years ago, the one marked with the sign like a slash through a helix. It had been the safest place she could think of, in the aftermath of the Hot Halls War. It was the same one Mr. March had tried to bribe her with drugs to open earlier tonight.

What the *fuck* was going on?

Sophie felt a darkness yaw beneath her, all around her, glints of unseen meaning and half-hidden purpose, plots and plans and the dead hands of the past clawing for her. What in the literal fuck was going on?

She stared at the pot of strong. With a sudden jerk, she knocked it over, spilling its dark liquid across the bartop, echoing the splash of the bottle against the wall, so many years ago.

The Consort.

Sophie buried her face in her hands for a moment. Or maybe it was more than a moment. She felt a hand shake her shoulder, and jerked her head upright.

"Sophie?" It was Avie. "You all right?"

Sophie scrubbed her face in her hands. Had she fallen asleep? Everything seemed too bright. What had happened to her pot of strong?

"Yeah." She tried to get her head back together. "What's up, New Girl?"

"It's Avie. I'm fine; just looking for you."

Sophie looked around, and then frowned at Avie. "Sure. And you found me. That's . . . that's not suspicious *at all*."

"There's only two places the Redarms were likely to release you—if they released you at all. This is one, and my friend is watching the other."

"Lucky me," Sophie said, watching as Avie settled herself on the barstool next to her. "Is this your mysterious ancient friend, who's going to save us all, if you can be bothered to ask him?"

"Yes. Though he's not going to *save* . . . Listen. I just thought you should know he might be able to help. Maybe. He carries some . . . ah . . . heavy burdens."

"That's great," Sophie said. She lifted her hand to order another pot of strong; at some point the barkeep had cleaned up the one she'd spilled. She realized what an unconscious thing that was to do, how compelled she felt to do it, and put her hand back down. She tried to focus on Avie. "So what do you want?"

Avie blew out a breath. "The same thing I've wanted all along. What happened with the Queen? Why did she let you go?"

"Bait," Sophie said, but didn't elaborate. Avie frowned, looking at her. "What's wrong with you? You look terrible. What did Jane say to you?"

"She showed me the true shape of the world." Sophie laughed. "She wants to kill a Giant and bring light back to the Keep."

"Shit," Avie swore, softly. "And let me guess; she needs the Book to do that."

"You got it on the first try. You don't seem very surprised by that grandly ambitious plan, New Girl."

"*Avie.* And I'm not; it's not a new plan. It's a very old, very stupid plan. Sophie, I don't like the look in your eye. What are you planning on doing?"

Sophie crossed her arms, and considered this question. "I don't know. But . . ."

"But?"

"I'm tired. Too many surprises, too many revelations. Too much *past,* tonight. I'm tired, and mostly right now I'm thinking that Hunker John, bless his sweet little soul, might be right."

Avie looked wary. "About what?"

"If I give that Book to the Queen, all of our troubles are over."

Avie shook her head, emphatic. "You can't do that."

Sophie sighed and leaned her head back, looking up at the heavy stones that made up the high ceiling here. So much heavy rock above her head. Surely it was okay for her to feel so weighed down, with all that rock over her? "I can't do that? Why not, New Girl? Why *not?* Maybe Jane really does want to do some good with it. I certainly trust her with it more than my fucking *brother,* or this Candle son-of-a-bitch."

"You can't trust her—"

Sophie laughed. "Trust? *Trust?* Who the fuck can I trust? You? You haven't given me one reason to trust you, not one shred. Who should I trust? I just found out that Candle is *Bear's brother.* Can I still trust Bear, now? Can I trust the man who told me that? *Who the fuck can I trust?* And if I can't depend on any Twins-damned thing in my life—except for my friends—then why not pick one and trust Jane? Since that's the way I get my friends off the chopping block?"

Avie looked at her, worry strong in her expression. "You should trust the dream, Sophie."

Sophie laughed again, bitterness crackling through the sound. "The *dream?* I should trust the *dream.* The same one that got me into this fucking mess. For years I thought it was Jane that sent that dream, and now . . . now it doesn't matter if it was or wasn't. Trust the *dream.* Fuck you. I trusted in it once, I sacrificed *everything* for that dream. And for what? Do you see any fucking trees? Any sunshine, splashing through the branches? Do you feel any wind on your face?"

"Sophie—"

"No matter what I do, the lights are still going to fade a little bit. If I hand the Book to Jane, if I don't, if I paint myself like a minstrel and start dancing. The lights are still going out. The dream was a fucking *lie.*"

Sophie was shaking, and she turned away from Avie to get herself under control. The barkeep was looking at her, concerned, and she realized that she must have been shouting. She took a couple deep breaths, and the barkeep slid a tumbler full of water across the countertop in the universal, inarguable shorthand for 'you've had enough.' Well, maybe she had. Maybe enough *was* enough.

"Okay," Avie said, and an odd note in her voice caught at Sophie's attention. When the girl brought her green eyes up, they held something Sophie hadn't seen in them before. Pity? No . . . something else. Avie smiled, just a bit. "Okay, yeah. Trust does go both ways, doesn't it? And I haven't given you any reasons to trust me, you're right. I'm not much better than Mr. March, I suppose. Or Candle. I figured you wouldn't be able to resist a pretty face, and thought I could get by on that."

"It's like my uncle used to say; 'I'll be a fool for love, but not an idiot.'"

Avie chuckled. "It's easy to forget what you are, Sophie. You wear this thing around you like armor, all prickle and snark and the next drink, and you're good at it. It's easy to forget about the wounded girl inside."

"Oh, fuck *off*. If this is you trying to seduce me, New Girl, you picked a bad time for it."

"You are not that lucky. But I do need you to trust me—even if it's just a little. So . . . I'm going to show you a couple things that I've never shown anybody. Or not in a long time, anyway. Trust goes both ways, right?"

"Show me?" Sophie echoed, frowning. Avie's expression was oddly resigned. She looked around the bar, mostly deserted at this time of the morning, and checked for coming passersby. The barkeep had his back to them. Nobody was looking their way. She closed her eyes.

Avie frowned, shuddered as if in pain, and a faint silver fire began to play around her features. The skin of her cheeks tensed and bunched, the muscles beneath shifting. Silver glowed beneath her skin in faint but unmistakable patterns. Sophie stumbled back off her stool and watched this transformation with shock.

Avie opened eyes that were still as brilliantly green, just set into a different face. It was a plainer face, older, with more care and lines. The cheekbones weren't quite as high, the lips not quite as lush. Her eyebrows were a bit lower, her hairline a bit higher. She looked at Sophie. It was almost a challenge.

"Holy *shit*," Sophie said, looking at the faint scars on Avie's face, "you have implanted silver."

"I do." Avie said, simply.

"Well, shit." Sophie shook her head. It wasn't often she was rendered speechless. Finally she took hold of herself, found her seat again, and took a steadying drag on her slot, then examined Avie, at the new face with the familiar eyes.

"You're threatening to get interesting, New Girl," Sophie said. Sophie's eyes caught at those faint silver scars, at Avie's plainer, older, and infinitely more compelling face. She felt as if she were seeing her for the first time; and maybe she was.

"You're the first person in a very long time to see it," Avie said. "I can wear a lot of faces, and I do. But this is my true face."

"You have succeeded in arousing my attention. Among other things."

"Stop it. You know the risk in showing you this, right? The silver inside me isn't nearly as powerful as what is wrapped around your arms, but it won't stop your family from trying to kill me for it. This is the first thing I have to show you; I'm hoping it will be compelling enough for you to let me show you the other."

Sophie frowned. "The other?"

"The other one is much more important. Please, Sophie. I know you need to meet up with the Killers, but this is—perhaps—the most important thing in the world."

Avie reached out and gripped Sophie's hand where it lay on the bar counter, just for a moment, and something deep and unfathomable passed between the two of them, some understanding, the way it had passed between Sophie and the Consort when she had been young. Sophie felt as if she were on the edge of some precipice, and could choose whether or not to tumble off.

Implanted silver. Just like her.

"Sure," Sophie said, finding that her voice was a little hoarse. "Why not?"

———

Avie took her downfloor via the Slideways, polished tunnels that connected certain parts of the Keep. They were a quick and fun way to travel, if not the most graceful. Sophie had loved them when she was a little girl, back before all the dumb dreams and silly shenanigans. They went deep though, and were in a part of the Keep that was now rarely used.

She trailed her fingertips along a dusty wall, hardly able to remember herself as the little hellion who liked to cause trouble and fight fake wars with other child-gangs. She wondered, though, if she'd been spared the dreams—or if someone *else* had found the Book—maybe she might have been a better big sister. A better daughter, niece, friend.

Avie had slipped her into a *very* dim part of the Keep, one that Sophie wasn't familiar with. She smelled old dust and could easily believe that nobody had set foot in this passageway in five hundred years or so.

"So what's happening here, New Girl? You taking me somewhere Dark?"

"Dark enough," Avie said.

"Exciting. Is it going to be murder, then?"

Avie gave her a look. "You're not lucky enough for that, either. I told you, I need to show you something."

Sophie yawned. "Are we almost there?" She was on the edge of regretting this excursion. She was regretting not drinking that pot of strong when she had a chance.

"Yes," Avie said. "We're here, actually."

Sophie felt a hand take hers and then lead her into a dark side-passage; *very* dark. She bumped into an old stone wall and smelled ancient dust puff up. It was so dark Sophie could barely see the shape of Avie ahead of her, and trusted the girl to drag her along. She tried not to enjoy the feeling of strong fingers tight against her own. Avie pulled her into a wider space, so dark that Sophie could barely see. There was a tall, rectangular shape nearby, but the rest of the room was lost to obscurity.

"Where the fuck did you bring me?" Sophie asked, and coughed on old dust.

Avie stepped a bit closer, and Sophie was able to see her face.

"You said that Jane Guin showed you the true shape of the world. Remember?"

"I guess. What does that have to do—"

"She doesn't know the true shape of the world, Sophie. And neither do you. But you're about to."

Sophie frowned. Avie held her hand out to a tall dark rectangle near the center of the small room. Sophie squinted. There was a small gleam of silver near the center. Was that a knob? Sophie blinked, stepping closer. The shape was a door, and a doorframe, freestanding. Sophie's mouth went dry. "That's not . . ."

"It is," Avie said. She stepped around Sophie and set her hand on the silvery knob in the center of the door.

"There are none of those in the Underlands," Sophie said, faintly. "Everybody knows that. They were forbidden here; the Doors were only in the Wanderlands above."

"Well, there is at least *one* in the Underlands. We're standing next to it."

Sophie swallowed, her head reeling. A *Door?* Five minutes ago, she would have bet her life they were nothing more than a fairy story. But now she could sense the silverwork threaded all through the thing, more complex and denser than any she'd ever felt. The scars in her arms tingled with potential and power.

"Okay," Sophie said. "Okay, that's impressive, that's . . ."

"The Door is not what I wanted to show you." Avie turned the knob. "This is."

There was a tremendous sound, like millwork moving far beneath their feet, and Avie pushed open the Door. Sophie stumbled back, almost blinded with the brilliance. Rich light flooded out; brighter than any she had ever seen. She threw her arm up over her eyes against the glow. The light seemed *familiar* somehow. And then she saw it. She recognized it.

For the first time since she was a little girl, and even then only in a dream, Sophie Vesachai saw the golden light of the sun shining on the leaves of living trees.

THE LOST BOYS

Prisoners

"Is there any greater reason for kindness than cruelty? Any greater excuse for courage than the specter of threat? Is there any better answer for hunger than food?"

—TALL TOM, 'MARYWELL GOES UNDER'

The storeroom was a big, low-ceilinged space all dressed in heavy stone, with no windows, no gates, and only one massively banded door. It was a spidering confusion of a room, with alcoves and areas that twisted off into dimness, lit by twistwork lights roughly attached to the ceiling, but there were no escape possibilities or ways out. There was a big air-vent set into one wall, but James satisfied himself quickly that it was impassable; close-set metal bars as big around as his wrist blocked that way. He and Chris were in a prison by another name.

The man named Master D'Alle had thrown them there after taking James' *Silver Key.* The Cold-Key. James and Chris and Katherine had traveled to the Land of the Giants and brought back a priceless artifact, one that Uncle claimed was so rare that they might be killed just for *having* it. One of the legendary Cold-Keys! Like the Giants themselves, something out of a fairy story. And then the awful, thrice-damned fat man had taken it. He'd taken the Key, and humiliated James, and *beaten Katherine.*

He had beaten the red-haired girl, hurt her, and it didn't matter the way that she looked at his older brother. For hurting her, Master D'Alle would have to die.

He would have to die, James decided, with finality. He knew how to do it; he could still see those ragged red spars sticking out of the chest of the man he'd killed. He could do it again. D'Alle would die, yes, and just as soon as James could figure out how to get out of this prison.

James discovered very quickly that he did *not* enjoy being trapped, neither the concept nor experience. He had considered himself trapped into many things before: lessons, food that he did not like, having Chris for an older brother, even Cannoux-Town itself. He now realized how foolish he had been and how lucky. He could have left any and all of those things whenever he wanted—and often had! But *actual* prison was a whole other thing, and James resolved to get free of it as soon as possible.

Chris . . . Ah, *Chris*. Chris was no help. His vaunted, too-smart-for-this-world, ultra-competent older brother had gone catatonic. He had crumbled just when James actually *needed* him. He sat against the rough stone wall with his arms around his knees, staring off into space. He would barely speak at the best of times and couldn't be reached at all the rest.

"I'm sorry," is all he would say. If Chris meant this to be helpful, he was mistaken.

He spoke in a strangled, broken whisper and James couldn't think about it or deal with it so he left his stupid older brother—who was supposed to be taking care of *him*—alone and set about freeing them from the prison himself.

He hoped that Buckle was all right, that she had flown back to Uncle and was even now chattering at cats and birds and playing games, but he missed her terribly. He hadn't realized how quickly he'd gotten used to having her land on his shoulder and give him a companionable kick in the ear, until she wasn't there to do it.

But he tried not to think about Buckle too much. It made him feel all twisted up inside. It made the knives press in.

The lights that had been installed in the room didn't dim at night so James lost any sense of time. He prowled the room, taking inventory of whatever he could find, cataloging possible weapons and making outlandish plans. These involved escaping the room, killing everybody in the whole place, finding the Key, rescuing Katherine *and* his brother, and making their escape. He examined every span of the walls, looking for cracks or defects, and found none. He tried scraping at the mortar that held in the thick bars of the air-vent, taking half a day to drag over a heavy old dilapidated work-bench to stand on, but it was no good. He did everything he could possibly do so that he didn't have to think.

There were a lot of things to not think about; the surprised look on the face of the man he'd killed when those rough, jagged red shards had caught him in the chest; the way Katherine had pretended to be his friend; what Ma must be thinking and worrying about right now; the darkness that was spreading over the world because he wasn't there with the Key to stop it.

Sometimes James went into the very farthest corner of the room, out of sight and behind a big pile of old tools and refuse, and cried. He tried not to do that too much. It felt like there were a million tiny fishhooks caught all through his chest, and they were pulling at once. But he told himself it was like Uncle said—they weren't boys anymore. And *men* didn't break down crying, just because they were locked in a room. And they didn't sit there like a Twins-damned lump, staring off into nothing and saying 'I'm sorry,' neither, like his Twins-damned brother.

If Chris slept, James didn't see him do it. Every once in a while, one of the thugs or the cruel woman who had struck Katherine brought them food. James wanted to kill all of them but he never really got a chance; they had chutters and even James knew better than to rush one of those. Still, there had to be some way.

He found several old hammers and a thin-bladed saw, rusty with disuse; he figured this must have been a workshop once upon a time. He spent long hours scraping the rust off the saw, hoping he was sharpening it a little. He wanted to get it sharp enough to saw through Master D'Alle's neck, and figured he would get it there sooner or later. He thought a lot about that place where they'd gone through the Door, the place with the trees and the sunshine.

He thought about the Giant, that fearsome colossus that had thrown rocks at them. It seemed like a dream now, but thinking about it made him feel better. James was glad there was still something in the world that big, that powerful, that *vital*. Nobody could ever trap the Giant in a stupid storeroom with their stupid catatonic brother.

Thinking about anything else made him feel like his chest was too tight. When his chest got too tight, when those fishhooks pulled too hard, he wanted to go in the corner and cry, but he'd decided not to do that anymore. Instead, he just punched the wall until his knuckles got bloody, and eventually he felt better.

He caught Chris crying once, his head resting on his forearms, his whole body shaking with sobs. James didn't know what to do; it made him angry. James walked over to him and kicked him.

"Stop it," James said, feeling raw and savage. He didn't know why the sight of his brother crying made him so mad. He kicked him again and felt better. Chris curled himself away from the blows, weeping into the dirt on the floor. James kicked him again, savagely now, but it wasn't like punching a wall. It didn't make him feel better, and eventually, he went off to the other end of the prison and sharpened his saw-blade instead, loudly, so he couldn't hear Chris crying.

Later though, for some reason, when his hands were tight and sore from scraping, he found himself going over to Chris and leaning down awkwardly, wrapping his brother in an ineffectual hug. Chris didn't respond, but James didn't let go.

"Hey," James whispered, "we'll be okay. You're my brother. We'll be okay."

He didn't know why he said that, really, but it made him feel a little better inside, made the knives not press in so hard. Chris leaned his head against James' for a minute, but then he stiffened and pulled away, and James let him go. Chris resumed staring off into space, and James went back to prowling the room, looking for weaknesses that he wouldn't find and planning elaborate revenges he was unlikely to see. Later, on one of these circuits of the room, he saw that Chris had slumped over, asleep. He stood over him for a long time, looking down. He wanted to bash his stupid head in. He wanted to give him another hug. He didn't know what he wanted, or why.

Instead, he went and punched the wall until his fists were bloody and he was tired, and then he went to sleep too. For a while, the only sound in the storeroom was the brothers D'Essan, sleeping.

When James woke up, it was to Chris shaking him, gently, and then jumping back in alarm as James threw out fists and feet, thinking him one of the thugs.

"Twins damn, squib," Chris said. His voice sounded hoarse but the closest to his normal voice since they'd been thrown in here. "It's just me."

"Yeah, well." James rubbed his eyes and peered up suspiciously at his brother. "What, you actually moving around now?"

Chris looked down at his hands and sighed. "I know, squib. I'm sorry. I had a lot to think about."

"I don't care." James looked away. For some reason he saw Katherine's tear-streaked eyes, imploring, looking at Chris' back. "Do whatever you want."

"Listen," Chris said. "Squib, look at me. *James.* I'm sorry. I'm sorry I've been . . . but that's over. Okay? And I need your help now."

"Help?" James said, squinting at his brother. "Help with what?"

His brother smiled, a little grimly, and he looked a lot older than he had before they'd thrown him in this prison. He looked a little like the man he would become. He held out a hand for James to take, so he could pull him to his feet.

"I need your help," he said, his voice rusty with disuse, "getting us the *fuck* out of here."

THE DEADSMITH

The Door Into Yesterday

"What a savage monster, memory."

—ED LEE TIMBRALL, 'SWALLOWLAND SONNETTO'

The Deader stepped out of a Door into a city, dark and decrepit, and fell to one knee. He was still weak from his ordeal under the collapsed mountain; dying wasn't easy and it wasn't painless. The explosion that dropped the top of the mountain on him failed to cover the Door that had brought him. He was lucky. Without his Machine, he might still be trapped under that rockfall.

He stumbled through the ancient and crumbling city without much purpose other than the vague need to find the Prey. He had no sense of that man, however, and so the Deader just walked, wishing he was whole, the Black-and-White fibers woven through him struggling to repair his flesh. His Fate whispered tremulously, and he was able to ignore its mad rambling in the face of the greater pain of his healing.

He had died several times, under those tons of jagged stone, before his Machine had been able to dig him out. Dying was unpleasant but quick; it was returning to life that hurt. He lost sense of time in that gray fugue, and his Machine was of little help. It was made for killing, not for timekeeping. The Black-and-White fibers that wove through all of his flesh sought to heal him, but the Deader had endured a great deal of damage. He needed to rest, but he had no intention of giving in to such weakness.

This city where he found himself was nameless, at least to him, and he didn't care to discover it. It served the Nine and bustled, full of bright-eyed people who ignored the dull black of the sky above them and the decrepitude of the city around them. This time, the Prey hadn't turned the populace against the Deader, and he was dully thankful. He had no heart or strength to spend pacifying another civilization. He wanted to find the Prey, to tear his heart from his body, and to take it to his Lady.

And *then* he could heal. And then he could rest.

This had been a lovely place, once; a garden-city. What buildings and towers there were had once been slender, beautiful, and filigreed. Now they were ash-stained, burdened with rough lights, and fallen in on themselves. Gardens became tent-towns, refuse piled against sculptures, and brutal people held the peace through the long night by distasteful methods. It didn't matter.

The Dark reduced everything in the end. Their Feed was failing, the Deader could see that much, and the city was doomed. They would supplicate the Nine—what had they joined the empire for, if not light? But even the Nine no longer tried to repair a failing Feed.

Doom was coming for this nameless land, and the Deader was unable to care. He stumbled, his torn muscles and still-knitting bones screaming in protest, hunting for word of the Prey. He thought the Prey might be in the city, somewhere, but could not be sure. When his Fate was whole, it would have been listening to everything, taking in all, and then would whisper some strange word to the Deader, give him the scent of new leaves, and tell him where to go.

But now it only wailed, and the Deader had to find his own way. He was reluctant to disassemble his Machine and pack it away in its case, but it needed to recharge its own strength after the ordeal of digging the Deader free. And there were too many people around; he rarely let his Machine run free in cities. It liked killing too much.

He stumbled through the hovels and alleys of the city, asking for the man who had called himself Candle, but there was nothing.

Until there was something. An old man pointed at him and laughed.

"Yes," the man said, a certain kind of madness in his glistening eyes, "the Death-King! I smell them upon you, your crimes! They stink like justice, so all hail the Death-King!"

The Deader stopped short; he nearly killed the man for saying that name. He had heard that name before, oh, yes. In a sense, he wasn't surprised. The Prey meant to lead him down all of the paths of his memory, it seemed, and the Death King was a large part of it.

He looked the old man up and down. He was a beggar but clean enough, and missing one arm. His smile was ragged with broken teeth, and he had the Prey's glamour in his eyes. The Deader was sure that he would have the Prey's words on his lips, as well.

"Tell me what you mean to tell me," the Deader said. "I know my own story."

"Do you?" The old man cackled. And again: "Do you?"

The Deader again considered killing him. It would be satisfying, and he felt the urge to lash out. He considered torturing the old man to get answers, as a way to side-step whatever weary journey into the Deader's past the man called Candle had planned. But the old man winked at him.

"Walk with me, Death-King. Walk with me and let us speak of many things, and perhaps you shall find something of value."

The Deader considered this. He wished his Fate would tell him what to do, but it only moaned in cinnamon and washes of pale lavender.

"Walk, old man," he said. "If you lead me to danger, you will die before I do."

But the beggar just giggled. He had been formed into a specific shape by the Prey, his mind written over with the damned creature's script. He was, the Deader supposed, merely a more complex version of the ill-made machines the Prey had left littered across the Land of Elah, under that newly-broken sky. He remembered particularly the small contraption that hopped on one leg in never-ending circles.

The Deader tightened his fists and resolved to see this through; if it ended with the Prey's blood on his teeth, then it was endurable.

"This way, Death-King!" The beggar motioned toward a dank alley.

"If you call me that again," the Deader said, "I *will* kill you."

But it was an empty promise. The old man seemed amused by it.

"How do you make a machine?" He led the Deader into the dark alley. "Ah! I see you know the phrase! It is a question that my friend is consumed with; indeed, he thinks the world itself is a machine! For is it not broken? Has it not run down? And you are no different. Already he has removed an essential mainspring, already your parts flex and rub, already rot is creeping into the system. Do you not feel it?"

"No."

The old man led him through the alley and onto a close thoroughfare, busy with people.

"You sought to build a machine, once," the man said, slyly. "You made a mechanism of a nation, did you not? What a feat! What a noble goal! But thinking folk make notoriously bad cogs. Always slipping! Always with their *choice* and their *will!* Any machine built of people, Death-King, is bound to fail."

They turned off the thoroughfare into a residential district, relatively quiet. The Deader tried to be ready for attack, but it was hard without his Fate whole and sane. He wasn't used to having to pay attention.

"Did she know, do you wonder?" the old man asked, still sly, supercilious, reveling in his secret knowledge, or perhaps just formed that way by the Prey. "When your Lady took you to that place, that dying Land, did she know what you would attempt? It is hard to know, when considering the plans of the Wise. They do strange things for arcane reasons, and sometimes only history can see their plot entire."

"I was just a boy," the Deader said, "near death. She saved me on a whim; she dropped me where she would. She owed me nothing, and I owe her everything."

"How convenient for her!" the man said, and tittered. "But tell me, Death-King, why did you climb? Why the long years of murder and shambling art-politic, why the crusade? You could have found work, found a woman. Brought new life into the world. Instead, you brought death, in your pursuit of empire. Why?"

The Deader did not reply; he owed this man—or the Prey—no answer. They left the residential district, heading for the dim outskirts of the city.

"I think you had learned to hate disorder." The old man nodded to himself. "And I think you had learned what worship is. You saw your Lady, at the head of the greatest empire the world has ever known, the last bastion of light in a lightless world, the last order in an existence overrun by psychosis. Did you not? I think you saw disorder, and in your youth, you thought to copy your Lady Winter's designs. You sought to bring order to a place that needed it. You thought to yourself, if the Nine can bring order to a broken world, why not me?"

"Shut up," the Deader replied, but there was little heat in it. His Fate muttered wetly and sent him overlapping scents of rotten meat and sour lemon.

"But you were too ambitious to just copy, weren't you, Deadsmith? You wanted to build something *better*. You thought you could build a world without the School Inverse, without dead sisters and dead mothers. You thought you could build a world that was superior to the Nine's, didn't you? And so you built a machine of blood and bone, Death-King! You murdered your way to the top of it, and you forced it to run. You alone! By the force of your will, you made gearwork of a nation! Huzzah!"

By degrees, they left the city and entered the dusk, following no path that the Deader could see. He caused a weirlight to spring up, and the two walked through a long-dead countryside sketched in awl-thin slivers of gray.

"They called you the Death-King," the man continued, laughing, "and you earned the name, did you not? The blood you spilled, the bones you broke, the lives you crushed. All to keep your mechanism running."

"It was a dying land," the Deader said. "It needed . . . order. A strong hand. Justice. I was trying to save it. I was trying to make something good out of what I had become."

"Yes, certainly." The man nodded agreement. "Certainly you were. Great monsters must have great motives, must they not? And did you succeed, Death-King? Did your machine run well?"

The Deader did not reply. Still the man led them through darkness. Old dust puffed up from their steps, and the land rose. They were headed toward mountains.

"My friend prefers wood to bone," the old man said, looking out over the dark landscape. "Candle prefers metal and gear and mainspring. Minds are imprecise tools. He prefers to let people do what they do and involve them only when he must. They are such inconstant machines, Deadsmith. Well, most of them. Some machines are very constant indeed."

The old man bowed to the Deader, mockingly, and stopped.

"My friend went this way," he said, indicating the beginnings of an ancient path that led up into distantly sensed mountains. "If you wish to follow, this is your means. But he asks you not to. Bids you return to your Lady. He is growing desperate, my friend, and desperate creatures are dangerous creatures. He fears destroying you before he can make use of you."

"He won't be dangerous when he's dead, and I am not so easy to destroy."

The old man tittered, and once again the Deader considered killing him, purely for the satisfaction of it. But he would not kill a man for someone else's words.

"Are you done?" The Deader spat into the old dead dust. "Or does your friend have a parting barb?"

"No, Death-King." The man bowed again. "No barbs. He just wishes you to remember your making. He thinks it will be . . . instructive."

"I remember it well enough already." The Deader started walking up the dark trail into the mountains. Behind him, he could hear the Prey's half-mad cackle of laughter, spilling from the old man's lips.

THE KILLERS

A Land Called Forest

"Sweeter than sweet wine, baby. Sweeter than this tangle of limbs. Sweeter even than the kiss of the sun, and there shouldn't be anything sweeter than that."

—ELISE HUNTER, 'HOTHOUSE'

The two women sat at the edge of the trees, watching the sun go down over the Highlands of Forest. Sophie and Avie had walked, slowly, down the short path that led them to the edge of the trees and the vista before them. They didn't talk. They didn't need to. Behind them, back underneath the canopy of trees, the gray rectangle of the Door stood open, the red-gold sunshine making the dusty walls of the Keep inside it glow.

When they first entered this fantastic place, Sophie had touched the trunks of the trees in wonder, had inhaled their otherworldly fragrance. But she'd discovered that she really wanted to see the *sky*.

She looked at the gradually darkening expanse above her—whether by accident or design, Avie had brought her here just as the sun was setting—as the great incandescent hoop of the sun spun slowly up and away, becoming a ringlike ember. Sophie's eyes picked out five of the silver Rings, and a tiny golden dot she thought might be the moon.

It was indescribably beautiful. She breathed deep, inhaling the new, intoxicating scents of moss and living stone, running water and trees. A breeze pushed her short hair around, and the sensation was exquisite. She sat in the warm moss, with her scarred arms draped over her knees, just looking.

They sat on a chunk of rock at the edge of the forest; Avie warned her that they shouldn't pass a line of black stones a little ways ahead. Sophie didn't mind. This was plenty far enough into this impossible new world. She felt as if she might tumble upwards, fall up off the ground into that infinite sky. She had never in her life been anywhere that didn't have a ceiling, however cunningly disguised.

"Where are we?" she asked, when the sun had diminished into a tiny red halo, and the stars started sparkling in the indigo sky. Sophie's eyes found a big gray shape nestled down in the folded ravine below; was that a Stone Giant? She tried to convince herself it was a sculpture but was unable.

"The Land of Forest," Avie said, her voice quiet against the sounds of the forest around them. "Well, the Highlands. The real Forest—the place from the legends, where the Giants live—is down past those mountains."

Sophie shook her head. She listened to the gentle creaking of the trees behind her.

"How? How do you know about this? How did you know about the *Door?*"

"I can't tell you how. Not yet. I don't want to lie to you, but I can't tell you everything. But this place . . ." She sighed. "I was brought here when I was young. I have a lot of memories of it. That's all I can tell you right now."

Sophie tried to imagine waking up to this sky, every day. Smelling these smells, touching the rough bark of these trees. She couldn't. "Why . . ." Sophie fell silent. She didn't even know how to articulate it. Avie waited, and Sophie said, "Why doesn't everybody just live here?"

Avie was silent for a moment, looking out at the expanse of trees and rock laid out before them, slowly darkening. Finally she shrugged, a little convulsive gesture. "It's dying, too. It's just dying slower than everywhere else."

"But . . . why?"

Avie laughed. "That's the question, right? Why is everything failing, running down? Why did the Fall happen? Why does the sky go dark, why does it shatter and break, until there's only this one last place where you can see it? Ah, Sophie Vesachai . . . there might be people in the world who know the answers, but I'm not one of them."

She shook her head, looking at the silver Rings in the purpling sky. "The Giants have something to do with it. But even the Giants are dying off, going to stone, losing hope. And the Land of Forest isn't such a big place, really; it could never hold all the people in the Wanderlands, even if the Giants let them come."

"I'm just wondering if it could hold *some of* the people of the Keep," Sophie said, quietly.

Avie waited, as if knowing it was coming.

Sophie looked back out at the folded ravines, scattered with green and gray. She sighed. "Could I bring the Killers here? Could we escape?"

Avie shook her head, not without regret. "No, Sophie. It's hard to explain, but . . . this is a dangerous place. Not for us, not right now, but you couldn't live here. This is the most guarded, sought-after, legendary, and perilous place in all of the Wanderlands. Except for maybe the White Tower. There is a reason why there are no people anywhere. The Giants would never tolerate it."

"Hmm." Sophie was watching the sky deepen into purple-black. It was indescribably beautiful. It made her heart ache. The parts of her that she thought had been destroyed by booze and disposable sex and betrayal woke and stretched, and turned their faces up to the light.

"Is that what you want?" Avie asked.

"What?"

"To escape?"

Sophie shrugged, trying and failing to express something complex, but she didn't answer. Instead she looked at Avie, frankly, for a long moment. "Why did you leave?"

"Leave here?"

"Yeah."

Avie made an odd gesture, a kind of shooing-away thing with her fingers. "It's a long story," she said, eventually, "and mostly, an unpleasant one. But let's just say that I found something to believe in, and the path to it isn't here. It's in the Keep."

"Twins damn, if I get *one more* cryptic answer to a question tonight." Sophie shook her head, but it was hard to be annoyed when she was surrounded by living trees. She tried to remember that in the Keep, back through that Door, events were spinning out of control and she and her friends were in peril. She tried to focus. "Okay then, why did you bring *me* here?"

Avie considered for a while, and when she spoke, her voice was grave. "This is what the world is supposed to be, not that prison of rock you live in. Not the failing lights, not the Dark. *This.* This is what the Mother was trying to show you with the dream. This is what she was trying to get you to fight for."

Sophie shook her head again but didn't say anything. The Keep seemed very far away just now. Jane Guin, the Book, the bullshit she'd managed to get her friends into—all distant. None of it seemed real, not while she was watching the faint pinlights of stars wheel in the depths of the sky. The sky! It was so deep, so beautiful, scattered with silver Rings and the gleaming golden glow of the moon. She wished the moon was closer, so she could see if it really was covered in towers and stairways, the way it was in the stories.

Overhead the branches of living trees, ten times the size of any Sophie had ever seen, swayed gently in the wind.

"This is why the Book is so important," Avie said, her voice quiet, "why the dreams were so important. You have no idea the sacrifices that have been made, the lives twisted and shaped, the sheer effort spent to give the Mother what she needs. It's for this. The hope and dream of *this.*"

Sophie looked over at Avie and frowned. "What hope?"

"Why did you try to find the Book from your dream?" Avie asked, eyebrow raised.

Sophie scowled. "Because I was an idiot. Because I thought I was saving the world."

"Yeah, what an idiot."

"I don't know what you're trying to say."

Avie sighed, exasperated. "Look around you, Sophie! Is this a dream? This is real. The trees, the sky; that's the Twins-damned *Land of Forest* over there. That's a Stone Giant; do you need to see a live one to believe? Do you think it's *completely* impossible that the Mother knew what she was doing, when she sent you that dream? Do you think it's *utterly inconceivable* that the oldest, wisest creature in the entire Wanderlands might have had a *plan?* How much fucking *actual magic* do you need to personally experience before you'll let go of this goddamn cynical woe-is-me, my childhood-is-lost bullshit?" Avie took a breath, and then expelled it, slowly.

Sophie watched her, entranced by her intensity.

"I showed you this," Avie continued, "because you're about to give up on everything that matters. Because some two-bit queen in a little stone cave made some threats. You're *Sophie Vesachai.* When are you going to start acting like it?"

Sophie flinched, stung, and gave Avie a wounded, angry look. "I know the way the world works, Avie, I've—"

Avie cut her off. "Look around and then tell me which of the two of us knows more about the *way the world works.*"

Sophie opened her mouth, thought a moment, and closed it.

Avie shook her head, irritated. "I'm not a fool, nor a fanatic. I've seen shit that even *you* can't imagine, and I'm telling you, the Mother sent you that dream for a reason. She wanted that Book found for a reason. And, no, I don't know exactly what it is. Something to do with the Giant, something to do with . . . I don't know. I think she has a plan to reverse the Fall, somehow. You can't just give up, Sophie. You just . . . *can't.*"

Sophie considered this. She looked out into the depths of the sky and inhaled the unbelievable fragrance of the trees. Just now, Jane Guin's threats and promises did seem a little silly, and very far away.

"I can't get my friends killed, Avie," Sophie said, softly. "Not again."

"But . . ."

"I *hear you,* Avie. I do. I'm not blind." Sophie shook her head, and looked at the forlorn shape of the Stone Giant, mostly shadow in the slowly shifting silvery light from the Rings.

They sat for a bit.

"What are you going to do, Sophie?"

Sophie didn't answer; maybe she couldn't. She just sat for a little bit more, just a *little* bit more. Just a couple more moments of this. Not too much to ask after a lifetime underground, was it? A few more moments of . . . what? Was this *peace?* Was that what this was?

She'd had a dream, once, a dream of this place. And then Jane Guin, and Denver Murkai, and Saint Station, and the invaders that had started the Hot Halls War, they had torn it away. They had showed her that it had been a *childish* dream. They showed her that everything—*everything*—was subject to the whims of the powerful. The cruel plans of the Wise. She had found the Book, yes; but they had shown her that the Book was just a tool, useful only to achieve their ends. They'd shown her that *she* was just a tool.

But . . .

But she was looking at it. She was looking at living trees. She was looking at the clear, unbroken sky. She'd thought for so long that the dream had been just one more play, one more ploy to shove her around, to get her to do what the people running the machine wanted. Sophie closed her eyes, and let the last of the sun warm her skin.

But what if it wasn't? What if the dream had been true? What if she *had* given up? Abandoned her purpose?

It couldn't be. That's not the way the world worked. There was no truth, no clean and pure purpose, no real heroes. Sophie opened her eyes, caught between familiar despair and this new thing that was clanging around in her chest. It couldn't be hope. That would be lame as *fuck*. Sophie Vesachai was too jaded, too smart, too worldly-wise to believe in something so idiotic as hope.

"You all right?" Avie asked, bumping her elbow against Sophie's.

"I don't know." Sophie was unwilling to be cutting just then. She looked out at the darkening landscape. This couldn't all be real. It just couldn't.

Could it?

Something caught her eye then, moving erratically in the gentle dimness, sparkling a little in the light from the silver Rings overhead. It was small and seemed to dance around on invisible wind currents. Sophie frowned, looking at it, and it made its fluttering way over, nosing inquisitively at her, and then landed on the back of her hand.

It was a butterfly. Its finely gossamer wings opened and closed slowly. There was no gearwork, no silver, just the soft intricacy of a true born creature. Next to her, Avie watched to see what Sophie would do.

Sophie began to cry.

THE LOST BOYS

The Dirt Magic

"Judging by appearances is perfectly acceptable when you have very little time to make a considered evaluation, and your new companion is holding a weapon."

—COSMA ANDERSON, 'THE RIDERS THREE'

So here's how you make Stage One Twist, should you happen to be trapped in a windowless prison deep beneath a dread enemy's manor, left mostly alone with some crude tools, a lot of time, and a brief modicum of knowledge:

First, you need a few shovelfuls of dirt. Really! Any dirt—it doesn't matter. The elemental form of twist can be found anywhere, everywhere, in any base. Hell, you can even crush up a few cubic weight of stone, if you want. But dirt is best. Dirt is easiest to work.

That is, after all, why they call it *Dirt-Magic*.

Fortunately, someone has busted up some of the floor-slabs in your dreary prison a while back, and dirt isn't too hard to come by. You've got no shovel, of course, but there are some old tools that do almost as well. The earth is difficult and hard-packed, but that's no problem—you're young, and otherwise useless! What else do you have to do, other than wear yourself out digging?

So, first step accomplished; with a little bit of your easily coerced effort, you have an old rusty pan-full of dark dirt. The abandoning, useless old jerk you used to call Uncle would be proud. You remember, at this point, that the next step involves some of that most precious resource—*fire*—but there is none present in your dank basement prison. However, your extremely smart and competent older brother has been working on it. He sets you to breaking apart an old set of wooden chairs while he puts his great and powerful brain to work on the problem.

And of course, by the time you've done all your lowly grunt-work, your vastly intelligent and seemingly infallible brother—also handsome, don't forget that, just ask *Katherine*—has coaxed a flame onto some tinder. Somehow. From *somewhere*. But who cares, honestly? Because with this tinder, you set about making a fire.

The fire for Dirt-Magic is typically made out of good, well-dried hardwood— you remember that much from your dumb lessons with Uncle—but what you actually *have* is some old half-rotted furniture. It doesn't matter. Any fire will do for Stage One twistwork, as long as it gets nice and hot.

This fire also gets nice and *smoky*, and the overall quality-of-life in the under-ground prison/storeroom drops for a while. Fortunately the room is extensive and the guards only come once a day to bring food. And they don't seem to care *what* you do in here, as long as you don't actually die or escape. So you bake that dirt over the fire for a good while, until it's too hot to touch, and then you dump it all in some clean, clear water.

Aha! You might say—how in the world would two *prisoners* get enough water to dissolve a bunch of dirt in? Well, intrinsic to the plan is an old pipe in one corner of the storeroom that drips steadily. Filling up a tub requires just about all of the patience you have, but eventually it does fill, and your dazzlingly smart and good-looking older brother can get to work.

And now comes *another* job that you are qualified for! Amazing, the opportunities! You get to scrub the dirt in the water, scrub it and scrub it together, even the mud, until it is totally dissolved. No, no, it's *you* that has to do this boring, dirty work. Your important brother has *important* things to do.

Eventually, after what feels like years of scrubbing, you'll notice a reddish-black scrum accumulating on top of the water. That's good. That means the overall chances of you living to see your twelfth birthday have gone up slightly. And now you're allowed to take a nap. The Dirt-Magic needs time to do its work. When you come back, there's a bunch of silt at the bottom of the tub and a thick paste of red-black scrum floating on top of the water.

Now comes another boring part, and one you need to be reminded of by your know-it-all brother: you have to dry the scrum. You'll know when it's dry be-cause it's become a rough, hairy jet-black, with no red to be seen. Now you have to take part of it—*I know*, you'll say, *I remember this part*—and twist it up. As you do, it compresses down and a sticky fluid rises up from it—this is crim. Crim burns really well and will become very important soon; don't spill any. Dang it, you dumb little idiot, you spilled some! I just *bet* your brother is going to have a disappointed look when he sees that. But when you finally have it shaped into rough wet logs, get ready to make another fire.

This one has to be in a hash shape: two long and two set across and at least three high. Your brother will have saved some coals from the other fire because apparently there is nothing he will not remember and plan for—and he gets the fire going. This one burns *real* hot and without much smoke, which is good. You almost died from smoke inhalation during the last fire, and you cannot but think that this would throw some kind of wrench into the plans. Or maybe not; maybe all you're good for is digging dirt, and that part is over. But when the hash-shape is white-hot, almost too bright to look at, you can put the rest of the black scrum into the fire.

This will congeal and flow together, and eventually start glowing a burnt but livid orange, which takes a long time—actually *too* long. You run into a bit of difficulty in your manufacturing process. In ideal conditions it wouldn't matter, but just now it is catastrophic: *unwelcome outside attention.*

It appears your activities were given more attention than you'd like, and guards demand to see what you're doing. Now, you mostly useless younger brother, is *your* time to shine!

While they are distracted with listening to your brother make up convincing lies, you creep around behind them with your half-rusted sawblade. You don't manage to kill any of them, but there is a satisfying amount of blood, and they beat you half to death before the thin man that serves Master D'Alle comes and stops them. He seems amused by all of it; the bleeding guards and the bleeding you and the telltale crim-fire. He tells the guards not to enter the room again unless ordered, and not to interfere with you. This seems to confirm something for your older brother, though of course he doesn't bother *explaining* anything to his thick-headed little brother. Chris works much more openly now, though, and doesn't try to hide your industry much after that.

You win! It is of some comfort while your wounds heal. You refuse to wash the guard's blood off your face for a long time, though your faint-hearted big brother begs you to. This blood doesn't bother you like the first man's had, coming out of his mouth as those jagged red shards impaled him.

You'll discover, through your long and terrible life, that it was only that *first* gout of blood that really bothered you. This ability to not feel bad about killing may not say very good things about you as a person, but oh, boy! Will it ever come in handy.

Will it *ever.*

But back to Stage One Twist: while you convalesce, your brother works his magic. He uses the hammer you found, and the big heavy table, and he hammers on that mass of glassy, fused twist. This is the part that you were actually sort of good at, but there's no way you could lift a hammer right now, even once. The guards really did almost kill you.

It's all in the rhythm of the blows, Uncle used to say, all in the pattern. You don't need much craft to make Stage One, he said, but the better you start, the better you end, and your stupid brother sure is stupid, but he knows how to make twist. The glassy mass flows away from the blows, thinning and separating, striating along its length until cracks show. The best you had ever done was a long mess of something like red yarn, while your know-it-all brother ended up with a mass of something like superfine auburn hair. Almost like the hair of that dumb person you don't think about anymore—*her* hair. You are not going to think about her red hair, or about how she betrayed you and pretended to be your friend, or about how she looked at your stupid brother like he is the only thing that has ever existed.

At any rate, the superfine auburn strands that look a lot like Katherine's hair get soaked in water again and soak it up until they turns black. Then your brother knots one end to a heavy support beam, wraps the other around a broken axe-handle, and starts to twist it. At this point you start thinking about what your brother is going to *make*. A war-suit? A chutter? Something even more deadly?

You heal up as fast as you can, but those guards really did a number on you, and it takes a while. You pass the time daydreaming about running through the halls of the manor above while dripping red with blood, a war-suit wrapped around you. You feel bad about these daydreams sometimes, the sheer bloody-mindedness of them. But not much, and not for very long.

When the mass of fine red strands twists tight enough, they begin to fuse and turn black again. When that happens, you stick it back in the water until it swells up and becomes red; then you twist it again. Then the water, then twisting, then water, then twisting. Again and again, until you might as well be sitting through Uncle's dumb lessons again.

Dirt-Magic, Uncle once said, was not intended to be easy. He claimed that what made it magic, and not just technology, was that the harder you worked at it, the harder you concentrated, the finer the product would be. It was impossible to make a tool using Dirt-Magic that wasn't at least a little bit of *you*.

And you can say a great many things about your stupid brother, but he knows how to concentrate. By the time he is done, and as long as the twist doesn't take on any red color from the water, it ends as a glossy length of something that looks like intricately braided black rope. By now you have recovered enough from the guard's attentions to help your brother make another fire, the hottest yet, and he leaves the black rope in there until it glows white. When it cools, it is a deep red-bronze color. You know enough to know that this color means good news.

You help heat up a knife and cut the ends. You hold in your hands a length of Stage One Twist. The best Twist *you* had ever been able to make, even with Uncle's help, had been a dull and dusty red that only returned about three times the torque put into it. This is magnificently made Twist and will return twenty at least.

Your brother grins at you, and you can't help but grin back. You have, together, brought some magic back into the dying world, and you're still alive. For now.

———

You need a lot of Stage One Twist to make Stage Two, even more to make Stage Three, and so on. Stage One was also used—with some variations in the processing—to form struts, gears, sharp bits, do-hickeys, and whatnot; the need for raw twist was seemingly inexhaustible. James had no idea what his brother was trying to make, but he sure as hell knew it required a lot of *dirt*. Something was taking shape, its parts hidden in corners of the sprawling room in case D'Alle changed his mind and tried to stop what they were doing. James couldn't figure what it might be, and Chris wouldn't say.

"I don't know if they're listening," he'd said, once, when James pressed him. "But just trust me. I'll get us out of here."

However, it was going *slow*. Other than digging up dirt and helping make fire, James didn't have much to do, and there were only so many ways he could fantasize about dismembering Master D'Alle before he got bored with it. Chris was in some sort of frantic, intensely focused frenzy that meant he was about as talkative now as when he was catatonic. James threw rocks at the wall to improve his aim, now mostly healed from his encounter with the guards. He also dug dirt and tried not to think about Ma. Or Buckle. Or . . . anything else.

He didn't really worry about Buckle. Uncle was a jerk but he would take care of her. James didn't feel right without her, though. He felt hollow all the time and wished she was there to give him a little scowling face at Chris' back, to make him feel better. He threw rocks at a small circle he'd chalked on the opposite wall; he'd gotten pretty good at hitting it, and it made him feel a little better, but not as much as Buckle would have.

"Squib," Chris said from his spot at the table, where he tapped on a minute piece of twistcraft. "We'll need some more Stage One soon."

Which meant, of course, *I need you to dig more dirt*—since that was all James seemed to be good for. James threw another stone. Chris' light, rhythmic tapping faltered and stopped. James sensed more than saw his brother looking at him.

"James," Chris said, "I can't slow this down, right now. I need your help."

"No you *don't*." James felt tight in his chest again, the knives pressing in, and just wished Chris would shut up. He heard his brother sigh, and that made him madder than anything else. Like James was yet another burden Chris had to bear.

"C'mon, man." Chris' voice was falsely pleasant, wheedling. "I know this sucks, but I can't do this without you."

"Yes you *can!*" James yelled, suddenly. He was tired of playing along. "You can do *all of it*."

Chris' face darkened, the way it did when he thought James was being stubborn.

"You know what, squib? Grow up. We don't have time for—"

"We got *all* the time." James crossed his arms tightly across his chest. He knew he was being childish, and he didn't care. "What does it matter? You'll get yourself out and maybe I'll come too. And you'll get the Cold-Key and maybe I'll come too and you'll . . ." James shut himself up and looked away. *You'll get Katherine and maybe I'll come too*, is what he had been about to say, but that was stupid. He didn't need to say that.

"James." Chris sounded as if he were trying mightily to keep his temper. "We don't have time for this. We need to get out of here."

"You don't think I want to get out of here?" James asked, throwing another small rock at the circle. Just slightly left of dead center, that time.

Chris rubbed his temples. "I don't know what you want, squib. I never have. Hell, I doubt the Mother herself knows what goes on inside your head, and I ain't got room to think about it now. If you don't want to help, don't help, I guess. Only . . ."

James scowled and waited. He didn't want to hear it, whatever it was. He felt like if Chris said the right set of words, he would crack in half and fall to the ground in a bunch of shards, like a broke lamp, or a smashed gourd.

"Only," Chris said, "I don't see Master D'Alle letting us live. I think maybe he sent word to someone about the Cold-Key. Maybe the Cold themselves, maybe somebody else, maybe one of those "powers" that Uncle talked about."

"Alvarez. Said to call him Alvarez."

"Yeah, well, I'm still calling him Uncle, and if he's got a problem with it, he can come here and tell me. But he ain't coming, squib, and neither is Ma. I don't think anybody knows we're down here. And whoever it is that D'Alle is waiting on, I don't think we'll survive much past them arriving. I think once they get here, they'll beat on me till I give them that sequence for the Door, so they can find that place we went to. And then we're both dead."

James crossed his arms tighter. "I *know* all that. I ain't stupid."

"No," Chris said, with some snap to his voice, "you *ain't* stupid, squib, so I can't figure why you're willing to take on two hardened killers with an old bit of saw, but you act like the world's greatest martyr when I ask you to dig me a bit of Twins-damned *dirt*."

"That's cuz you *don't* figure me," James said, glowering. "At all."

"Well that's true enough." Chris shook his head. "Fine. Do as you like. You're right; I *can* do this myself. If I have to. But I damn sure wish I didn't have to."

James threw another stone at the circle on the wall, then another. He wished there were some more guards to fight. He wished their blood hadn't worn off his face. He wished . . . he wished. After a while he stopped wishing and went to dig more stupid *dirt*.

He was still digging, and so intent on it, he didn't hear when someone hissed his name. On maybe the third time, his head came up. Chris was at the other end of the room, hammering away. It took him a moment to realize that the door to the storeroom was open, and a red-haired girl was peeking through it, looking at him with anxious, wary eyes.

Katherine.

James' heart did something complicated and seemed to sprain itself; he scrambled out of the hole he'd been digging. "*You!*" he said, accusing. "What are you doing here?"

"Shh!" Katherine looked over her shoulder, into the hall outside. "The guards are close and I only have a few minutes."

"Are you . . . okay?" James looked at her. He had struggled with a lot of different feelings about Katherine. She had sold them out, but she got beaten for them. She probably liked his stupid brother, but he didn't care about that anyway. She was part of their little band now, like it or not, and he found himself admitting that he had been worried about her. More importantly, they had walked under the sun together and faced a Giant, and maybe he could forgive her, a little, for tricking him into thinking they were friends. He found himself breaking into a smile when he meant to scowl. "Are you okay?"

Katherine grimaced. "Better than you. But listen. I'm not much help. I can't help. It was all I could do to get here for five minutes. Master watches me like a hawk, all the damn time. He's waiting for something, and I don't know what. It's nothing good though. We're all in bad trouble."

"I'm sorry," James said, and she blinked.

"Don't be sorry," she said, "that's stupid. I'm the one who . . . Listen. I tried not to tell him about the Key. I did."

"Oh, *that.*" James brushed off her betrayal as if he hadn't thought of little else. Now that she was here, *right here,* it didn't seem to matter much. She'd done the best she could. "Who cares about that? You had to."

"Maybe," Chris said, coming up from behind him quietly and making him jump. "And maybe not. Hello, Kat."

Katherine swallowed and dropped her eyes. "I came to tell you that I can't help you. But . . . if you need a message taken out, I might be able to do that."

Chris watched her steadily.

James wanted to punch him; he was making her miserable.

"I don't think—" Chris said, finally, but James broke in.

"Idiot! She could tell Uncle where we are!"

Chris thought about this. When he looked at Katherine, his eyes were shrewd, and he nodded. "Okay. If you can. It won't do us harm if D'Alle finds that out . . . I don't think. But it's a long shot, James. Uncle said he wouldn't help."

"She could tell Ma!"

Some sharp emotion sprang up in Chris' face. His words were hard. "Do *not* tell our mother where we are, Katherine. No matter what. *Please.*"

She blinked. "No, I . . . Okay, I won't."

"Just . . ." Chris looked down, and his voice softened, "don't try to help otherwise. Keep safe. And if you . . . well. If it wasn't all an act, then I'm sorry. If you haven't been doing D'Alle's bidding this whole time."

Katherine's face flushed. Now she was angry. "An *act?*" She started to say something else but then turned at a noise from the passageway. She turned back to Chris. "I have to go. *Fuck* you, D'Essan. You could learn a thing or two from your brother. And you, James . . . Here. This was all I could do. Take care of her."

Katherine opened her cloak, letting something small and gold climb out and look up at James with little tea-cup eyes.

"No!" Buckle said, grinning at him, and flew up to his shoulder to give him a hug. James looked at Katherine, his eyes suddenly brimming, and she gave him a smile. She gave Chris a decidedly less warm look, then left, closing the door behind her. They heard the big bolts slide home.

"*Girls,*" Chris said, vexed, and for the first time in a long time, and for a reason he couldn't even begin to explain, James burst out laughing.

"No!" Buckle laughed too, a tiny sound like bells, and James felt okay for a few minutes. Just a few minutes, and just okay, but it was nice.

It had been awhile.

———

Maybe it was Buckle; maybe it was that Chris *actually* needed James' help in assembling the final version of his mechanical devices; maybe it was the way Katherine's last look at his brother had been decidedly less than warm—maybe it was all of them—but James found himself cheered in those last days of being trapped in the storeroom.

Chris worked feverishly, hardly eating, until the bones of his face stuck out and his eyes were sunken and dark. Something Katherine had told them worried him, that much was plain, but he didn't talk about it. In any case, the three of them—the two boys and Buckle—finalized their plans. The air in the storeroom took on an excited, charged quality. James often forgot to be surly when Chris asked him to do something menial.

There were even times when he was sort of proud of his older brother. A little. *Maybe.* Whatever he was helping Chris assemble was fearsomely complicated. He hadn't known Chris could do this kind of thing. He suspected that maybe Chris hadn't known he could do this kind of thing either. It was the kind of thing Uncle might have made, and then left hanging in his boneyard.

"Don't get too excited, squib," Chris said once, when James was admiring some particularly deadly bit of the contraption. "You won't like what this does."

"Then tell me what it does!"

"Then you *really* won't like it," Chris murmured. But he wouldn't explain. Still, it was a marvel, and it had been made with only some dirt and water. James, for the first time, thought he might actually see something of what Uncle and Ma and Chris had tried to tell him all this time. Might see some worth in this stuff. The Path, or whatever. Old Gold. *Dirt-Magic.*

Chris did say one thing that nagged at him, though. James had been wondering why the guards started leaving them alone, and even supplied them with plenty of water, and why Master D'Alle was too stupid to know what they were doing.

"Oh, he knows," Chris had said, distracted. James chewed on that, over and over, but he couldn't make it make sense. And anyways, it all started happening, and he didn't have much time to think.

They assembled one device in front of the door, a long-flanged thing almost like a vicious bird with three legs. The struts were heavy, red-black, and looked wicked. The spring that drove it was brutal, with heavy patterning and braid; it was as thick as James' fist. It took him and Chris both wrenching on a makeshift winding-wheel to torsion it.

"This one breaks down the door," Chris said, and would not show James how to activate it. James was too excited to even be offended. Things were happening, there was a possibility of violence, and that was enough for him.

He was able to help, however, by climbing up to the barred air grate and affixing a slender device, almost filigree and flexible, and wove it through the bars that covered it. He twisted the key until it was tight, and Chris nodded. The last device was a spiderlike thing, roughly made but heavy, with a mainspring so deeply copper and beautifully patterned it looked like Uncle's work. Chris had passed out for a while after he finished that one, frightening James because the construct jittered back and forth for a while until its limbs went slack. James gritted his teeth and helped Chris hoist the heavy thing up onto the table, under the grate.

"That one goes to find Uncle," Chris said, clapping James on his shoulder. "If . . . if he'll come. We can't count on that, James. You have to understand. We might be on our own."

James had nodded, excited. *Escape.*

The last device was slim, about half as long as James' arm, and incomprehensible. It was the thing Chris had worked on longest, and he couldn't imagine what it was for. Chris tucked it into his waistband and made sure it was secure there with a few rough-woven strands of twist.

"Okay," Chris said when everything was in place. His eyes were a little wild and had trouble resting on any one thing. He stood there for a long time, thinking, and James knew better than to interrupt even though he was about half-mad with excitement and impatience. Finally, Chris looked up at his brother. "Mother help me if I ever have to take a risk like this again."

He closed his eyes for a long moment, and when he opened them, they were harder, steadier. He looked at James, and his gaze was grave.

"Squib, if this doesn't work, we are probably going to die. And the only way it can work is if you help me with two things. Can you do that?"

"Yeah." James bounced on the balls of his feet. "Anything!"

"Don't promise too soon. One of the things I need you to do is send Buckle away."

"What?" James said. "No!"

"James," Chris said. "She's got to go. She can make it through that grate, now, before the . . . before it all starts. She has to warn *Kat*, James. You gotta tell her to find Katherine, and both of them have to *get out of here*. Whatever it takes. Do you understand?"

This last wasn't to James, but to Buckle, who was standing on James' shoulder and listening intently. The little person looked at James, who reluctantly nodded.

"No!" Buckle said, bravely.

"Will you go? Now?" Chris asked her.

Again she looked at James, and again, he nodded. "Be careful," he said softly, and gave her a little hug, careful not to squish her wings. She endured it for a moment and then kicked herself free, scowling at him. He grinned.

"No!" She gave him a companionable kick against his palm before she flitted up to the bars on the grate, slipped through them, and disappeared.

Chris heaved a sigh. "Okay. The next part is going to be even harder for you, squib—*James*. But I need you to promise me that you'll do as I say, no matter what. Just until we get out of here. You're not going to understand what's happening, and I'm sorry for that. I can't . . . I needed your help and I don't think you would have helped me, if you knew. You're not going to like it, but I need you to *do what I say*."

"Okay," James was barely listening, bouncing in excitement to fire up the weapons. "Fine! Whatever. I will."

"I need you to swear," Chris said. His voice was almost shaking. "Please, squib. Swear to me on Ma's name, swear to me on *Buckle* that you won't . . . that you'll do what I say. Until this is over."

James kicked some detritus on the floor. "Yeah. Yeah! I swear."

"On Buckle."

"On Buckle. I know . . . I'm not gonna be some stupid jerk, okay? I know this is dangerous. I'll do whatever we gotta do to get us out."

Chris studied him and eventually jerked his head in a nervous nod. "Okay." He took a deep breath and let it out. "Okay. Let's get this started, then. I need you by the cannon."

"Cannon?" James asked.

"The thing by the door. Get ready; this is going to happen fast."

"All right," James said, excitement spinning up in his chest. He took a position next to the bird-contraption, his heart beating hard.

Behind him, Chris climbed onto the table and hesitated. He met James' eyes for a second, and seemed to be whispering a prayer. Then he set the filigree device in motion, leaping back off the table as he did.

The lattice began to flex, tightening, and immediately the bars squealed and groaned, loud in the storeroom. The thin band of almost fabric-like twist pulled with incredible force, bending and twisting the bars until with a great scream of tortured metal and breaking stone, the air vent pulled itself out of the wall and fell to the ground, bouncing off the spider-like construct below.

Chris had managed to twist his ankle in jumping off the table, and he hobbled over to the spider-construct on the table. He was coughing in the dust that rose from the broken masonry. He turned a rough key on the spider-construct once, twice, three times, and James heard a smooth whirring start. The spider-thing twitched, extended one of its five legs, and then slammed it into the masonry wall. It was sharp, and swung itself up in a kind of swinging, stabbing pattern to climb the wall. It scrabbled through the new opening and disappeared into what-ever lay beyond.

James looked at it with wide eyes.

"Okay," Chris said, "the red switch! Now!"

James saw a roughly made red switch on the back of the big machine next to him. He threw it, and the big mainspring began to twist powerfully, sending half a hundred gears and springs spinning.

"Look away!" Chris yelled, but James wasn't about to do *that*. With an incredibly loud chattering sound, the device spat something at the door, something that made a sound like a Giant coughing blood, and then there was a slowly dissipating cloud of dust and fine rubble where the door—and part of the wall—used to be. But the thing wasn't done; it cycled up again and coughed, and the heavy stone wall that was exposed by the dissolution of the door likewise became dissolute.

Now *this* was more *like* it! James felt a strong hand grip his shoulder; he looked up into Chris' fevered eyes.

"That's *amazing*," James said, as the device coughed again, sending another spray of fine red flechettes into the dust, presumably to obliterate anything in its path. He realized there was nothing keeping them in the damned room anymore. "Let's go!"

But Chris' strong hand clamped onto his shoulder and kept him where he was.

"This is the part you're not going to like, squib," Chris said, with a distracted look.

"What do you mean?" James was unsuccessfully trying to squirm out from Chris' grip.

"I mean remember your promise," Chris hissed in his ear. "Do what I say. No matter what."

Something moved in the heavy dust that filled the corridor. Chris reached over and flipped the red switch, and the machine stopped spitting destruction. He waited, keeping a forceful grip on James' shoulder until one of the guards looked quickly around the edge of the chewed-up masonry.

"We're unarmed," Chris called. "And we don't want any more trouble. We just want to talk to D'Alle. We want to make a deal."

"*What?*" James gasped, but Chris clamped a hard hand over his mouth and didn't let it go until the guards tied him up and gagged him anyway.

THE DEADSMITH

The Door Into Death

"Having is good, getting is better. But wanting is best."

—STORMAND RAE, 'SMALL DILEMMAS'

The Deader stepped out of yet another Door into water, just high enough to cover his boots. The water was fetid and stank of rotten twist, with the bitterness of a sea that had not seen the sun in a long time. The sky here was mottled and bruised, not yet fallen completely Dark but gone far into the Dim. It gave off barely enough light to see by. It was an unpleasant place, he saw that immediately, but there were lights ahead.

They were all low and close to the water; the Deader saw doubles of each, one set muddled by the slight waves. He could not make out much detail but he guessed that this was what remained of an island civilization, whatever was left of shore-and-boat folk.

He heard faint sounds from over the water. His Fate was useless, no longer interfering with him but neither was it of any help. It curled in the back of his head, a tight welter of unhelpful emotion. The Deader kicked off his long boots and tied them to his pack. He would find the Prey, or whatever traps the Prey had prepared, up ahead.

The trail led on, seemingly endless. Always another Door into another Land. The crazy old beggar with the Prey's words in his mouth had pointed him towards this path, but where would it lead? Was he in some sort of hell, destined to trudge through death and darkness towards a man who receded infinitely ahead of him? Was he doomed to replay his entire hard life, from the murder of his mother and sister to the cruel training from the Deadsmith? From the brutal time in Tyrathect and the School Inverse to his failed turn as the Death-King? How many more innocent people would the Prey glamour with his Domination? How many more people would Candle force him to kill, all for some obscure lesson, some vague phrase?

How do you make a machine?

He had, for a short time, forgotten what his Lady looked like, as he followed

the Prey's trail through the mountains to the Door that waited. Could not, for
several days, remember the taste or sound of her. He needed to finish this. He
needed his Lady's touch, in a way he had not needed anything in a very long
time. Maybe since Tyrathect, and the girl called Anise. When he closed his eyes,
he could see her bad death, and he would wager he had not thought of her in
three lifetimes.

He sank into the black water, tasting the stale bitter sea on his lips, knowing
better than to drink. Living lakes survived in the Dim, occasionally, but not in
the Dark. He began to swim. He would have to remember to be careful, up
among those lights. That particular warm color of light meant Dirt-Magic, and
he had run afoul of high-stage Dirt-Magic before. True twistcraft—Old Gold—
was heavy magic, and it was good that there were almost no wizards left in the
world who had the grit to work it.

He swam steadily, conserving his strength, thinking of his Lady. He did not
wonder about what sort of arcane trap the Prey had set for him ahead; he did
not wonder what particular memory lane the damned Prey would try to force
him down next. It didn't matter. All traps would shatter their teeth on the Deader's skin, and then he would put an end to this wearisome task.

Without his Fate to warn him, the Deader stubbed his foot painfully on a
rock, and he put his feet down and rose up out of the water. It was a slimy shore,
and he climbed up it on hands and knees, wary of slipping. Stinking water cleared
from his ears, and he heard the sounds of muted revelry. It was coming from a
town up ahead, and the people there were caught up in a festival.

The Deader put his boots back on and climbed up the slope until he stood on
a gentle escarpment that overlooked the town. He breathed deep, trying to get a
sense of the place, trying to do the job of his lost Fate, trying to detect danger.

It was no good. He gave up trying and walked down into the town, feeling
dull and plodding. He considered assembling his Machine but was filled with a
curious lassitude, an uncaring recklessness. He had no fear of the past, nor the
Prey's obsession with mechanics. He could sense a Door ahead and despaired that
the Prey was no longer in this place.

He despaired that this hunt would never end.

As he walked down the slope, he traversed an island, and a modest one at that.
Other groupings of light on the horizon doubled, and he could tell they were
farther away. An archipelago, then a scattering of small islands connected by boats
or other watercraft. There might even be portions of the towns built out onto the
water; he had seen similar. Floating towns, sailing empires.

Music assailed him, drums and tambour. Most of the townspeople were congregated in a large, loose free space in the middle of the buildings; these were
short but well made in the manner of most water-borne civilizations. People were
dancing, singing, shouting along with the music, enjoying themselves in the ways

that common people did. The Deader did not fault them for it. There was a part
of him that was sorry to interrupt it. The last time he had danced and sung was
with his mother, once upon a time, chasing her dark braid as it flicked in time
with her movements.

He walked into the revelry, and it died where he touched it. Quiet spread out
from him like blood spreading in water. One by one the revelers slowed, turned,
and stopped. The quiet took the musicians, too, and the sounds of rhythm ceased.
The Deader walked into the crowd, letting it part around him.

He stopped in the center, turned slowly to look at everyone. He saw no obvious weapons. Their eyes were painted with livid colors, but now they were somber and afraid. These people did not know what he was, clearly, neither his
purpose nor his office, but they had been warned about him.

"I am looking for a man," the Deader said, as loud as he could with a throat
dusty from disuse. "A stranger to you. He would have come through here only
days ago."

Recognition. A slight rippling of sound, as people in the crowd murmured to
each other, but there was no answer. Then, suddenly, movement from the corner
of his eye, and he turned to meet it. He expected someone with gray in their hair
and the light of Candle's madness in their eyes, but it was not.

It was a girl, eleven years old, perhaps, with long dark hair. Her eyes were
curiously blank, unafraid. "Sir," she said, when she'd come right up to him. "Sir,
he said to ask you, sir—do you remember her?"

The Deader shook his head. As he'd thought, another memory-trap. He began to push his way through the crowd, heading toward the Door he sensed at the
edge of town. A woman, the girl's mother by the look of her, grabbed her daughter and snatched her back to safety.

"Sir!" someone said from behind him. Another girl. "Do you remember him?
And how he died?"

The Deader didn't turn. More girls pushed forward through the crowd, all
with dark hair, all young.

"Sir!" they cried. "Do you remember the bread merchant?" Or, "Can you see
her face? The broken queen?"

There were more. The Deader did his best to ignore them, did his best not to
call up the faces they spoke of. He would not play this game any longer. He
pushed his way through the crowd and to the edge of town, plagued by cries of
"Sir! Sir!"

The Door stood on a hill on the opposite side of town, out in the darkness.
The people of the town followed him, at a distance. It was likely that they had
only seen this Door open once before, and just a few days ago. When he reached
it, the Deader checked the dark wooden surface for messages, but there were

none. The crowd silently filled in behind, but he ignored them. He ignored, too, his roiling thoughts.

His Fate moaned in fear, washing his vision in sick-green, but he pushed it away. He set his hand on the silver knob, preparing to turn it, when something in him twitched.

It wasn't his Fate, but it was something, and the Deader listened.

He threw himself sideways as soon as it spoke. The first bolt smashed into the Door with a sound like shattering bone. He caught a glimpse of gold, from the corner of his eye, and despaired. The second whistled past his leg, and the third caught him in his pelvis, tearing his body around. He screamed a word, a Black-and-White word, and caught the other three bolts with his Black-and-White magic, freezing them in the air. As he fell, he propelled them far out into the dusk beyond the town. The townspeople had formed a half-circle behind him, and some of them had the light of murder—or the Prey—in their eyes.

The golden bolt exploded within him, and his body fought to reject it. His Fate screamed, a wordless howl, and he identified five other targets, closing in, weapons up. These were normal chutters, though. The Deader could ignore pedestrian weapons while he fought the war in his guts.

The golden bolt spun off filaments, thousands into thousands, clawing their way through his entrails, splitting and splitting into hair-fine threads and finer, rupturing bowels and organs. The Deader felt his liver perforate, sensed golden fibers hunting for his heart. Several men rushed at him, holding weapons up and screaming; the Deader reached out and caught one of them and ripped him in two. He could spare no attention for blocking the pain; it was overwhelming. The Deader's own magic kicked in hard, the Black-and-White, trying to combat the deadly gold that was hunting for his *true* death.

He felt chutter-bolts slam into him, one in his side and two a dull set of thumps that must have clattered off his Machine-case. He spared them no mind.

White mesh stuttered to life inside him, forming walls that the gold could not pass. Black pitch flooded his blood and where it touched the gold, the filaments died, withered, questing roots dipped in acid. The Deader felt an axe crash into his skull and rebound off the protections built into his bones. He grasped blindly, wildly, trying to keep the attackers at bay while the war raged in his chest. He captured another of his assailants, more by luck than skill, and caught him under the chin with hooked fingers. The Deader's hand flared white, and he ripped the man's jaw from his face and threw it into the crowd.

He grasped at what was left of the golden bolt—feeling it throw off fibers that clawed their way into the flesh and bones of his hand—and ripped it free of his guts. It took all of his will to do so; it felt as if he were ripping out his own kidneys. Another man swung an axe at him but the Deader could spare no attention.

He felt the blade sink deep into his shoulder and he bunched the muscles there, trapping the weapon. The man wrenched on it, trying to free it, but the Deader twisted and ripped the handle out of the man's hands.

Things reached a balance, a desperate delaying action, and then the tide turned. The golden threads, one by one, met the tar-black poison in his blood and died. The Deader felt a few of the filaments pierce his lungs and heart, and for a few long moments he could neither breathe nor feel his heart move. But he had died before, yes, and knew how to fight while dead. He pulled the axe from his shoulder, got up to one knee, and threw it. He did not make any sound; did not have the energy for it. You had only so much energy, once you were dead. He could waste none. The axe killed the man who'd attacked him, almost severing his top half from his bottom.

All of the Deader's skin flared white and black, now. Ice filled his chest and gray filled his eyes; his body was fighting the gold too hard to keep death from creeping over him. His limbs were sluggish, blood pooling in the low points, but the Deader forced movement from his muscles and whispered another darkling word, clutching his free hand. He was in no condition to be precise. His last assailant had withdrawn into the crowd, but the Deader knew approximately where he was. He clenched his fist, and maybe fifteen people were crushed into a ball of flesh and splintered bone five span wide. The assailant had been one of them.

The Deader fell back onto his side, seeing that the hand which had grabbed the bolt was now entirely covered in gold. He felt the bones of his hand being forced apart, golden fibers driving into the marrow and splintering them, and now he did scream with the pain of it. It didn't matter. He would survive; he could afford luxuries like screaming.

The golden threads slowly died in his chest; white mesh and ichor began to steal through his flesh, taking the place of the black, repairing his torn entrails, his lungs, his heart. When he could, he sent some black ichor into his hand; it was ripped apart up to his bicep now and was completely useless. It was terribly hard, directing his magic consciously like this. Before it had been maimed, his Fate would have handled all of this without his intervention.

His heart re-started with an awful jarring thud. For a few long moments it beat irregularly and sent his body into spasms. Dying was hard but resurrection was *torture*. After a little while, he was able to start breathing again.

There were no more attacks; the Deader had killed the primary antagonists, probably innocent townsfolk glamoured by the Prey. The Deader used the ancient gray wood of the Door to pull himself to his feet. His entrails painfully knitted themselves back together, and the black ichor went to war with the golden invasion that was eating his arm.

When he was able, he raised his eyes to the townspeople. Surprisingly, few of them had run, though they'd drawn back from the wet, bloody ball that sat like a mute challenge in the midst of them. The Deader didn't regret causing it. He spat blood, tried to speak, and was still unable. He waited a few more moments, and finally judged that he could block some of the pain without compromising his healing. He did so, and his disassembled arm went numb.

He coughed, spat more blood, and then spoke: "If I were one of my brothers or sisters," he said, biting off each word, "every last one of you would die."

The townspeople just stared at him, horror in their eyes. Whatever glamour the Prey had cast over them did not shield them from the shocking, monumental violence of the last few minutes. Somewhere in the middle of the crowd, a man started weeping.

The Deader tasted more blood in his mouth. He considered speaking again, making some other threat, warning them of their treason, but hadn't the care nor the strength. There would be only one death that would satisfy him now.

He opened the Door and saw the big, ghost-white trunks of long-dead trees, illuminated by the light from behind him. He stepped in front of the Door and cast a heavy shadow; the trees loomed like long, broken teeth in the darkness.

His Fate howled madness and terror into his mind.

"I know," the Deader muttered, and walked through the Door.

THE KILLERS

Reunions

"And so with a mighty sound the Jannissary drove his sword down through Tin-Eye's heart. And Tin-Eye went to the Rings knowing always that he had saved his home, and all it had cost was his life."

—APOCRYPHAL, 'THE TALE OF THE TIN-EYE AND THE JANNISSARY'

Oddly enough, the vision of the trees didn't fade on return to the Keep the way Sophie thought it might. Instead, as she and Avie walked through the Keep, it seemed the opposite: as if the stone around her, the ancient passageways and accumulated weight of millennia, the cares and worries of the thousands who lived in the barracks and apartments, the plots and plans of the Lords and Preators and, like a great spider hanging over them all, the Queen—as if all of these were the dream. And, worse, a bit of a silly one.

I'll show you the true shape of the world, Avie had said, and she had. Sophie walked through the Keep like a rung bell.

At some point while they had been sitting in the fragrant loam of another world, it had become morning. The day-lights were slowly cycling up, brightening out of their night-hues. Sophie blinked at them; even at their brightest, they were no match for the *sun.* She yawned; it was a long night. It didn't matter that the day-lights were on; it was still a long night. Sophie and Hunker John had established a rule years go; the night wasn't over until you went to sleep. They were the kind of degenerates that were just getting going with their evening when the day-lights came up. Sometimes they had 'nights' that were several days long, so it was easier just to call it one thing. She thought she might be putting that rule to good use, on *this* motherfucker of an evening.

They were approaching the Rue de Paladia, where the Killers had arranged—what felt like forever ago, but was only yesterday evening—to meet after splitting up. It was an almost suicidally reckless choice, now that Sophie knew what was truly going on, but there was no way to change it. They would just have to be careful.

"You okay?" Avie asked.

"I don't know," Sophie answered honestly. Avie had put her flawless, perfect face back on. Sophie studied it. "I like the other one better."

"Yeah, well." Avie blushed and ducked her chin. "Fuck off. If we live through this, maybe you'll get to see it again."

"Something to fight for, then."

Avie sighed. "I guess I should just be happy you're not catatonic. Or ready to hand the Book to Jane Guin. You're not, are you?"

Sophie frowned, thinking. Had the ceiling always been this low, in this part of the Keep? It felt awfully low. Stifling, even. Finally, she shook her head. "I don't know. I need to talk to my friends. But . . . I think that I'm not inclined to trust the Queen. She's got a big plan, but I don't think trees have any part in it."

Sophie could feel Avie relax, a little, and she liked that. She was annoyed that she cared. After their shared experience, she felt bound to Avie and resented it, a little. She didn't trust her yet, despite the sunlight that had just been warming her face. Despite what the beautiful girl had shown her.

Avie looked at her sidelong. "What are you going to do?"

"I don't know," Sophie snapped. "I just had everything I thought I knew about the world turned upside down, all right? Give me a Twins-damned minute."

Avie offered a paradoxical grin. "*There* you are. I was starting to think that butterfly broke you. Glad to know there's some asshole in you still."

"Yeah?" Sophie said, still feeling oppressed by the leagues of stone overhead. "Why's that?"

"Because you're going to need it."

———

They passed the great metal gates that marked the end of the Rue, and the potted trees that lined the street. Trees, hah! Sophie had just seen *real* trees. These were fucking *plants*. Even the enormous expanse of the arched dome far above, glistening with intricate tilework, felt close and mean in the face of the deep sky above the Highlands of Forest.

And she could taste the dust of this place, the bitter tang of ancient stone; she wondered how long it would take to get used to it again. She spat, trying to get rid of it and earned a glare from a nearby shopkeep. She flipped him a rude gesture and felt a little better. Something had gotten turned around inside her, in that fantastic *other place*. Something had broken free in her chest and was clanging around, causing who-knows-what damage, but Sophie was glad she could still be a prick. Avie was right. She didn't want to lose that.

She spied the big form of Bear ahead, leaning over one of the balconies, the spot where they'd agreed to meet. It wasn't their usual spot, that would be almost criminally foolish, but Sophie had the idea that nowhere in the Keep was going to be safe for them just now. Might as well stick to what they knew. Bear saw her first, and the obvious relief on his face did a lot to assuage some of the suspicion that had been accruing in the back of her head. He disappeared from the railing, no doubt to tell the rest of the Killers she had returned. She exchanged a glance with Avie, took a deep breath, and mounted the stairs up to the café.

Bear wrapped her in a tremendous hug that felt like it was going to snap her spine—but in a good way—and Trik buried her face in her hands for a long moment. When she was able to look up, her expression was shadowed, and she gave Sophie a tight nod. Ben clasped her forearm, and set his forehead against hers for a moment, the way they'd done when they were children. He was trembling, slightly.

"I'm okay," Sophie said. "I'm okay."

"We heard you were taken by the Queen," Trik said, in the kind of neutral voice you use when you're trying not to shout.

"She got *herself* taken by the Queen," Avie said from behind her, "because she's a fucking psychopath."

"Maybe you should watch your tone," Trik said, her voice heating up.

Sophie held out her hands. "Stop, stop. A lot has happened, Trik. I'll do my best to explain. But the subject of New Girl is more complicated than we thought. Okay? I'll . . . Wait. Where is Hunker John?"

Trik exchanged a look with Bear. "We were hoping he was with you."

"He's not. *Shit*."

Ben put his hand on her arm. "Hunk can take care of himself. And he's probably in some downfloor sit-em-up, drinking his face off. Which is where you want him, right? Come on, sit down. Tell us what happened."

Sophie sank into a seat and talked. Enduring several unflattering interjections from Avie, she explained her conversation with Uncle Liam and Avie's discovery that Mr. March was, in fact, her brother Lee.

Bear whistled low, and his eyes were humorless. "Brothers. Why does it always come back to *brothers*?"

Sophie gave him a sharp look, but didn't want to pursue that. Yet. *Candle was Bear's brother?*

"What about the Queen, Sophie?" Trik insisted.

She told them about her interview with the Queen, about the threats Jane had made. She told them about the odd conversation with the curiously inept Consort, and with the all-too-ept Denver Murkai. But she didn't bring up the Door yet. Or the trees, or sun. She wasn't quite ready to talk about that yet. She met Avie's eyes, and they were grave.

The Killers were all silent for a moment; perhaps they were digesting what they'd heard.

Sophie glanced over at the dim recesses of the balcony café. There weren't many customers at this time of the morning. A tough-looking man was slumped in the corner, nursing a drink, and once again her memory pricked at her, but she couldn't place it. Mother above, maybe she *should* take a break from the booze. She yawned; gods, she realized once again how tired she was. She realized she was delaying.

"Okay," she said to Bear, who had listened to all of this with a growing look of concern—or was that disgust?—on his face. "The Consort told me something about you and this Candle son-of-a-bitch."

An expression crossed Bear's face, like a bird sensing a cat. "He probably told you," the big man said, slowly, "that Candle is my brother."

Trik stiffened.

Bear kept his eyes on Sophie's. She looked for subterfuge, slyness, *something* that would allow her to distrust this man. She didn't think she found it.

"Okay," she said, "care to explain that?"

He barked a short, painful laugh. "Not really. I thought he was dead, Sophie. I thought he died in the Hot Halls War. I know you asked me to poke around my fight-club contacts, but I've spent most of the night trying to find him. I didn't."

"The Hot Halls War?" She lifted an eyebrow. "Did he die when you were a kid?"

"I'm older than I look."

Ben brought Sophie a cup of café and she accepted it. She looked across the rim at Bear as she sipped. He looked desperately uncomfortable, but not guilty.

He looked down at his big, almost brutal hands. "This is a mess, Sophie. If Chris is involved . . ."

"Chris?"

"Sorry, Candle. He took that name a long time ago, now. But old habits die hard, I suppose. I doubt he'll call me 'Bear.'"

Sophie gave him the ghost of a smile. "Why can't anybody just use one name anymore?"

Trik snorted. "Says the queen of nicknames. Is my name *Trik*?"

Sophie ignored this, stayed focused on Bear. "Is that why the Consort said not to trust you? Because Candle is your brother?"

Bear shrugged. "I don't know anything about the Consort. Maybe he has good reasons to distrust me, though; I don't know. I wasn't an angel before I met up with you, Sophie. I told you I have some dark shit in my past."

"And your brother is part of that."

Bear sighed, heavy. "Yeah. We did some awful things together. A long time ago. You've probably guessed that I'm not from the Keep; I grew up somewhere . . . different. But Chris—*Candle*—is the reason I came here. I came here to kill him, and instead I just ended up doing what he wanted. I would rather not go into the details. Not unless I have to."

"We don't talk about our pasts," Trik said, softly.

Bear shot her a grateful look at first, but then shook his head, reluctant. "That's a convenient fiction we maintain so that Sophie doesn't have to talk about painful shit," Bear said. "But it protects us too. Look. *Sophie.* I know you might already suspect some of this. But I had the dream too, when I was young. And I found my Silver Key—it was a Key, not a Book, in my dream. We found it, me and my brother and . . . someone else. I had the dream of the Giant, and so did my brother, and he's been chasing that dream his whole life. I'm here, in the Keep, because we found the Key, the thing the Mother was looking for. Because I think maybe she was trying to get us to *bring* it here. Only . . ."

Frowning, Sophie was watched him. He was struggling with his words.

"Only then the Twins-damned *Wise* got involved, you know? The Wise, and my brother. And everything got very, *very* fucked up. Like things are getting fucked up tonight. I don't know, I don't want to tell you the long sob story. There might be a time when I have to tell you all where I came from and how I got here, but . . . I would rather not do it just now. I fell in with you for no more sinister reason than you remember; we were drinking in the same place and you picked a fight with me."

"I remember." Sophie grinned. "That was a good fight."

She sighed, and combed her fingers through her short hair, looking at Bear. Finally she gave him a shrug.

"It's suspicious as hell, Bear. But so is everything tonight. You've been with me, what, ten years? If you say you haven't seen your brother, and don't know what he's doing, I believe you. You can't pick your family."

"Ha," Bear said. "Okay. But this is still a mess."

"Maybe more of a mess than we know," Avie said. "I never had the dream myself, but everything that's ever happened to me, happened to me because of it. And I don't think anything that's happening tonight is a coincidence. Not Bear, not his brother, not this Consort, not the fact that Jane is finally making her play for the Book after all these years. Nor, I think, that we find ourselves all together, here."

She looked around and shook her head. "Sophie. Maybe you should tell them."

Sophie was reluctant. It felt like telling someone the secret desire of her heart, but she thought Avie might be right. She took a draught of café, and told the Killers about walking through a Door into another world.

When she finished, Bear settled his big frame into his chair. He looked frankly at Avie, eyes narrowed, and then at Sophie. "This is getting weird," he said.

Sophie frowned. That wasn't the reaction she was expecting. "Why?"

"Because I've seen that sky. I've seen that Giant, though it wasn't stone when I saw it. That's where I found my Key. The thing that the Mother sent me the dreams about."

"Wait," Sophie said, struck with a sudden connection. "What did you call it? What does it look like?"

"It's called a Key. A Cold-Key, sometimes."

Sophie felt an icy chill all down her spine, and she remembered a small silver amulet, thrown on the floor in front of her. "Bear, what does it look like? Do you still have it?"

Bear laughed, bitterly. "Sophie, if I had that thing, we wouldn't have any problems tonight at all. If I still had my Key, I could tear this place down around Jane Guin's fucking *head*."

"What does it look like?"

It was Avie who answered. "It's a silver pendant. Very complex machinery in the center. A thick, braided silver chain."

Bear looked at Avie, agape. She shrugged. "I've seen one before."

"How?"

Avie considered her reply, and cut her eyes to Sophie. "There might be a time when we *all* need to tell our stories. But not right now."

Sophie felt a yawning, pitching sensation. This was too much. Too many surprises, all stacked up one after the other. "Bear," she said, voice faint, "I know where your Key is. It's in the silver vault, the one that Mr. March—*Lee*—has been trying to get me to open all Twins-damned night."

Bear's mouth hung open. "Sophie, that can't be. That *can't* be. How do you know that?"

Sophie offered a crooked little smile. "Because I'm the one that put it in there. Right after the Hot Halls War. When the fucking *Consort* gave it to me."

Bear put his head in his hands, but Sophie found herself watching Trik, who looked as if she had seen a demon, or ghost. Trik looked from Sophie to Avie and back. When she spoke, her voice was faint. "The Key is in the Keep? Both the Key and the Book are in the Keep? *Right now?*"

Sophie frowned. "Yes. If that silver pendant is the Key, then they have been. For twenty years at least."

Trik swallowed. "Then all they need is the Sword," she said. She rubbed her arms, as if cold, or to burnish the tattoos that covered them. "God, damn, no wonder. No wonder this is all going down at once. *All they need is the Sword!*"

"Trik," Sophie said, "what in the hell are you talking about?"

Trik laughed, a little hysterically. "The Key, the Book, and the Sword. The three artifacts that are needed to open the Giant's Prison, Sophie. No wonder they're trying to shove you around so hard. These fuckers almost have everything they need."

———

Sophie opened her mouth, not remotely sure what she was going to say; what the fuck did *Trik* know about any of this? And what *sword?* Who the hell used swords anymore? She started to speak, but then somebody called her name.

It wasn't anyone in the café. It came from the street below, and it was a playful voice, speaking in a sing-song. "Sophie Ve-*sach*-ai!"

Sophie looked over at Ben, who had been keeping watch at the railing, and who could see down into the street below. She felt cold, and knew instantly. "Does he have John?"

Ben nodded, the look on his face unpleasant. With the strange revelations about her friends momentarily forgotten, Sophie walked to the balcony.

Lee stood in the middle of the street, holding his wicked-looking chutter against the side of Hunker John's head. Lee smiled when he saw Sophie. His smile was too wide and too bright, even barely seen through the tangler he wore. She suspected he'd been dipping into that supply of Battle Drugs. He had his other hand on Hunker's slender throat.

Hunker didn't look hurt, but he did look scared. Sophie gave him a little nod, hopefully reassuring, and turned her attention to her brother.

"Hello, Lee," she called out. "Let him go."

"You know, that would negate the incredible amount of effort I spent getting him here!" Lee laughed. "Hello, sister! You figured out who I am. Took you long enough."

"I don't know who the fuck you are anymore, Lee, but you can take that tangler off now. And you can take that chutter out of my friend's face before I stomp on you for sticking it there."

"Threats?" Lee said, and ground his chutter into John's head. "Well, fine then, sister of mine, let's get right down to the *threats.*"

"He's going to kill me, Sophie!" Hunker cried, voice high and wavering. His eyes rolled in fear, and his left leg shook, almost uncontrollably. Sophie frowned.

"I could get to him," Trik said, voice tense.

Sophie half-turned. "Stay where you are! You'll get John killed."

She turned back to her brother, who had pulled the tangler off and tossed it in the street. His bright, manic grin was disturbing. She put her hands on the stone balustrade, where they could be seen from below, and leaned forward.

"What's the play here, Lee? I tell you where the Book is, or you kill my friend? You have to know that if you do that, we'll kill you. Are you making this all up as you go, or did you take too much of those drugs? Only an idiot gets himself into this kind of showdown, man. If you think this is the way to get the Book, you're—"

Lee's face was incredulous. "Book . . . ? Sophie. *Sophie.* I do not care about the Book. Not everything is about you and your fucking Book! Twins damn, the arrogance on you."

Sophie frowned again. Hunker John was white with fear, perspiring, eyes rolling, legs twitching. It was, oddly, almost comical. But John had never been good in tight situations. She tried to focus. Lee didn't want the *Book?*

"What the fuck do you want then, Lee?"

"Oh, so many things, sister of mine! *So many things.* I want to show the world what you are, to start, show them what a hollow drum you are. I want to do what you never could—I want to *actually* save the world. Not just this warren, this sad hunk of rock. You have no idea. They call you the Savior of the Keep! You don't know *anything.*"

"I know you better let my friend go," Sophie said, her eyes darting around for some way to fight. Charboys were capping the flames in the great braziers that lined the Rue, the last of the night coming to a close. Shopkeeps were opening their stores, and early shoppers were filling the broad way. Something about this just didn't make sense. Tactically speaking, this was the worst possible time and place for this kind of showdown; passersby were starting to notice the two figures in the middle of the street, one with an illegal weapon held to the head of another. Someone would call the Practice Guard soon, if they hadn't already.

Sophie saw a flicker of movement at the corner of her eye. Long blonde hair, ducking behind a blue-potted terra plant: *Avie.*

Lee wasn't finished, though. "If you think this is all about *you*, Sophie, you're the biggest fool of them all. I know it's probably hard to imagine that there are bigger things than the Savior of the Keep, but there are. I only need one thing from you, sister! It's all I've asked for, since the beginning of the night. *I want what's in that vault.*"

The Key. Bear's Key; the silver necklace handed to her by the Consort twenty years ago, with an entreaty to keep it safe. Trik's voice: *The Key, the Book, the Sword. These fuckers have almost everything they need.* Lee's bright, manic eyes; Hunker John's wildly tapping leg. The charboys, capping the braziers. The Swatter-flowers, finding the Killers in the bar called A Dream of Trees. A thousand clues, scattered through the night, and they all came together with a visceral *snap* in her chest.

Sophie looked away for a moment, and she felt something catch in her chest. *Oh, Hunker.*

She murmured, voice pitched low, to the Killers behind her. "Get ready." She took a breath and faced her brother. She made herself smile.

"Or what, Lee? What if I don't give you what's in that vault?"

Her brother grinned, and she saw his fingers tighten on Hunker John's throat. Lee shook Hunker, and her friend's eyes rolled in outré fear.

"Or you start losing friends, Sophie, starting with this one. I'm out of patience and you have two hours. I will trade you the Key for this degenerate piece of shit in Spake Field. In two hours."

"I heard you sent Spake Field Dark."

"Just Dim." Lee giggled. "Just Dim enough for Feral Children. You can't begrudge me *some* friends, can you?"

"You seem to be having your fun in places I'm known for," Sophie commented. She saw another flash of blonde, closer to the two in the street below; she was trying to get behind them. Sophie saw the silver of her expensive chutter in her hand.

She half-turned again, and hesitated. Lee's chutter was very real, and so was the power in his arms. Could she risk her friends? She felt cold. To stop what she suspected Lee was about to do; yes. "Rush them on my mark. Watch that chutter."

"But Hunker . . ." Trik said, anxious. Sophie stilled her with a look. When she spoke her voice was grim, and barely above a whisper.

"John sold us out. He's with Lee."

Sophie turned back to her brother, jerked her chin up. She wanted to keep him distracted, in case Avie was able to get the drop on him. "That right, Lee? You breaking all my favorite places?"

He laughed, a fever in his eyes. It was the drugs . . . or something else. "All part of the plan, Sophie Vesachai! Gotta keep people on their toes, for the next part of this. Can't have them rallying around a popular hero; can't have *that*."

Hunker John squeaked, his voice comically high and wavering, "He'll kill all of us, Sophie! They're crazy, him and Candle. Crazy!"

Hunker's left leg jumped, almost as if driven by a piston. Sophie remembered long nights of working with him on that; Hunker loved cards even more than she did, but he had a restless leg that was his tell. Besides, she'd seen Hunker scared and this wasn't that. This was Hunker *acting* scared, which she had seen far more of. This was how Lee had known how to find them all night; Hunker had let him know somehow. The only times Lee had found Sophie on this long night were either when Hunker had been with her, or here, the rendezvous she'd set up earlier in the night.

Hunker John, one of her Killers, one of her best and oldest friends, had sold her out. She felt a sour sadness; she hoped he'd gotten a good price for it, at least. Because Hunker John also knew something else, and it made a whole lot of things make a whole lot of sense: he knew where Sophie had hidden the Book. All the Killers did. She had trusted her friends.

Oh, well.

Avie moved again, behind Lee; she was getting close. Sophie again murmured to her Killers, "Get ready." She sensed Bear and Trik creeping down the stairs, hidden from Lee's view. Avie stepped within firing range, and Lee's expression brightened. Sophie's heart sank; he knew.

"Hello, beautiful!" Lee didn't look away from Sophie. "I really wouldn't; I've got a ready finger on this trigger."

Avie held her chutter steady on Lee's back. "Count of three. One."

Lee grinned up at Sophie, for a second almost looking like her eager little kid brother, always so excited to see his big sister. He called Avie's bluff. "*Two.*"

Silver fire enveloped his arms, burning the sleeves of his brocade jacket. It was dazzling, even in the well-lit Rue de Paladia, and Hunker John screamed in real fear and pain as Lee's fingers burned his neck. Lee clenched his free fist and Avie, understanding too late what he was doing, tried to throw her chutter away.

It exploded in a hail of violent silver shards and gears just as it was leaving her hand. Sophie saw a spray of blood and Avie fell backwards, behind a shopkeep's stall.

"Now!" Sophie cried, to the Killers. "Stop him!"

But it was too late. Lee raised his arms up, as if accepting some benediction from the Mother, lost and gone so far above them, and started to destroy the Rue. Silver fire arced out from his hands, his arms, and enveloped the huge litstone columns that lined the Rue and gave it its light. Bear and Trik rushed towards him but he repelled them again, throwing them back with a blast of force. Trik, however, recovered quickly and started to move towards him, as if climbing against a hard wind.

Sophie broke Proscription without even thinking about it; but she hadn't thought about it the first time, either, when Luet had been in the clutches of one of the Feral Children. She saw what Lee intended: to destroy the light in the Rue de Paladia, to stick a knife in the heart of the Keep. To plunge this enormous place into darkness, to strand all of the people in it in Dark. She reached for the silver fire instinctively.

But she was too late. It had been twenty years since she'd done this; twenty years of late nights and drinking and drugs and abusing her body and mind. It took her long seconds to find the right mindset, the Vesachai trick of *an-tet*, the centering stillness that let you work with Silver. It was maddeningly hard to do, and she hadn't tried it since she was a girl. Lee screamed, in triumph or pain or both, and the light in the Rue grew very bright, almost blinding.

Sophie found her stillness and reached down through the silver in her arms to something else, pulling power and vibrance and intention into herself. It *hurt*. Twins damn, it hurt! She felt her old scars sear, burning and healing the burns and burning again, a feedback loop of pain that was almost indescribable, cold and hot and glorious and terrible all at once. Below her, Trik was still fighting against the force Lee was throwing against her, clawing her way towards him—how? It didn't matter. With a roar, Sophie threw her power against her brother's, searching for his lines of force, trying to unravel what he was doing . . .

And she was too late. Too little. Lee had been profligate with his power all night; he was much more practiced with his magic. It took her long moments to even understand what he was doing, much less try to counter it, and then it was too late. He screamed, wrenching, pulling, all of the silver wirework around them glowing brighter and brighter, and Sophie scrabbled at those lines of force ineffectually, and she heard the rising groan of tortured lightfixtures.

With a huge rending sound, darkness came down on the Rue de Paladia like a great black hammer.

AN ASIDE: THE BARTENDER AND THE FOOL

Like all stories about the end of the world, it is hard to know where to start, and doubly so with stories about the Monsters. Do we start when Gun met Jackie? Or, perhaps, when they got the sword, the piece of dumb steel that would play such an oversized part in such great events? Do we instead travel back to when Gun first had the dream, the dream of darkness and a Giant, and of a shining, silvery sword?

Do we, perhaps, attempt to relate the unremarkable story of Gun's childhood, in an effort to tease out reasons behind what he did? Must we peer at the young face of Jackie Aimes to see if we can find the seed of the creature she would become?

No, I think these stories can lie still. The Monsters did what they did. Their childhoods would no doubt be as alien and incomprehensible to us as the birth of a mindspring automata would be to them.

Let me relate to you, however, one tale that may be instructive: the story of their meeting. It maybe be that in this account we can find some hints, some reasons, some genesis for all that came after. Certainly Gunnar himself would never have precipitated these great and catastrophic events without Jackie's influence. Certainly Jackie would have never found the Black Portal without Gunnar's dream.

And neither of them would have brought a sword into our world, not without the other. Their friendship is, in many respects, the story of the end of the world, so let us take a glimpse at the beginning of it.

Gun met Jackie in a bar, of course; could anything be more obvious? He was on a pilgrimage to find the place he had seen in a dream. For the time and place that he lived, this was a very strange thing to do, and it had required him to dig deep into whatever meager amounts of courage and resolve he had. He was an arrow that had launched itself into the unknown. But he was, at that time, a small man, a pedestrian man, shoved into a story for which he was unprepared.

In any case, Gunnar Anderson was weary in mind and spirit, and had run out of courage. He decided to stop at a drinking establishment to see if he could find more courage in the bottom of a glass, in the manner of all thinking folk in all the worlds. And there he sat, seeking clarity or at least oblivion, trying to articulate the images he had seen in his dream by way of a sketchbook.

His barkeep, that fateful night, was a woman named Jackie Aimes. Jackie was, in many ways, everything that Gun was not. She was quick-tempered, mercurial, and unhappy in an interesting way. She asked him why he was drawing pictures of swords in a book, and in that moment the most dangerous friendship in the history of our world was born.

Both Jackie Aimes and Gunnar Anderson shared a common trait that, it seems, they instantly sensed and clung to—they both wearied of the mundane character of their lives. There are always those who are surrounded by magic and refuse to see it, thinking that purpose lies over the next hill and past the next stream, and both Jackie and Gun were made from this particular and unhappy cloth. When Jackie—for no other reason than her bar was quiet and she was bored—was able to persuade Gun to tell her about his dream, she was caught.

There has been a great deal of speculation about whether the two Behemoth were lovers, but to that, I cannot speak. I can say only that they found something in each other. A call to adventure, perhaps, or a rejection of the mundane, the boring. In any case, and after many drinks, Gun found himself asking Jackie if she wanted to go with him; if she wanted to help him finish his quest and see what lay at the end of his dream.

The future of our world hung on her answer, but she hardly took a moment to decide. Jackie Aimes abandoned her life with a telltale lack of care, and the two Monsters made their way towards an uncertain—but certainly exciting—future.

We know what they found at the end of their dream-road, of course: the Black Portal. And still . . . and still. All might still have been well. The Wanderlands has weathered Behemoth before, even two at once. And even accounting for their restless boredom, they would have done relatively little damage. Certainly they would have found their way into the machinations of the Wise; Behemoth are too useful a tool to leave lying around long. There are always those who forget that Behemoth are dangerous tools to hold. But . . . all might have still been well.

It was Jackie Aimes, daughter of a preacher, occasional barkeep; it was Jackie who doomed us. Recalling Gun's book of drawings, she mentioned both the prevalence of *swords* in his dream and the fact that she knew of a weapons-shop nearby where her cousin worked.

We can imagine Gun smiling at the idea; a sword is a hero's weapon, after all, and while he may have been too intelligent to truly believe in heroes, that did not stop his wanting to be one. The Monsters got their sword, and took it to—and through—that gate between worlds, where it was changed from cheap steel into a thing that can cut what should not be cut.

This is a story about the end of the world; this is a story about monsters. From such small origins come such calamity; from such humble beginnings are born such dire endings. May the Mother have mercy on them for their innocence. And for what they did, for what they caused to happen, may the Twins rake the flesh from their bones until the end of all time.

    —An excerpt from 'The History of the End of the World, Vol. II,' by
    Bind e Reynald, Scholae First Mark

THE MONSTERS

Post-War

"Show me a happy creature, and I'll show you a good liar."

—ALLIE ELIE, 'MINOR KEY'

The monsters stared into the fire, occasionally pouring themselves cups of the strong drink the people of Cannoux-Town had left outside the gates. They were drunk and knew that once the barrel was empty it was empty for good, but they didn't care. They were all alone in a vast dark place, and what the fuck was the point of anything, anyway? In any case, the transformation that had been wrought on them by that octagonal pillar extended to their drinking; they appeared to be lightweights now. The barrel would last them for a while.

Gun and Jackie sat in the shadow of an old tower, in a small rubble-strewn courtyard that faced away from Cannoux-Town. They realized that they hadn't even escaped the Mountain when they took the magical door to the warren beneath the city; they'd merely taken a shortcut to a place lower on the slope.

They sat, now, with their backs to the city that had rejected them, ignoring it even as they used its overspill of light to make a camp.

They didn't talk about what had happened in Cannoux, didn't talk about the wrecked war-suits and wounded soldiers, didn't talk about the fear in the townspeople's eyes when they looked at Gun and Jackie. They didn't talk about how those townspeople hadn't seen them as people; they had seen only monsters. They didn't talk about what they might do next. They didn't talk about much. They just drank and watched the firelight dance and flicker.

They didn't even talk about the hundreds of Feral Children they'd killed; they didn't talk about the soldiers they'd wounded, the families they'd frightened. All because they'd wanted another drink.

Eventually, Jackie roused herself with a yawn. She blinked several times in the light from the fire. "Know who I miss?" she asked, after a while.

Gun returned from whatever sour reverie he'd been playing in and focused on her. "Hm?"

"I said, you know who I miss?"

"I heard you," Gun said. "Who?"

"That motherfucker," Jackie said. "Vutch."

Gun blinked at her and decided she was kidding. He shook his head. "I do *not* miss Mr. Vutch."

"Dunno. He was all right." Jackie gestured with her cup, sloshing a little. "Could carry a conversation."

"The conversation was tolerable. Yeah. The trying to kill us was the part I didn't like."

"Didn't say he was perfect." She considered. "Hell, every single person we've met in this goddamn place has tried to kill us, so maybe we shouldn't hold it against him."

"Ha." Gun crawled over to the barrel and re-filled his cup. The drink was more like wine than beer and tasted a little like old scotch. He didn't care very much. He was grateful that the people of Cannoux had left some booze outside the gates for them, even after they'd basically destroyed the town's entire military might. He knew it was more or less a bribe to stay away, but he didn't care much about that either. It was getting him drunk.

He went back to his spot, leaning against the moldering wall of an old building, painted with the light from their fire. "Maybe we shouldn't hold it against ol' Mr. Vutch, after all. *Does* seem like everybody we meet wants to kill us."

"Thing I liked about him," Jackie said, after some consideration, "was that he was refreshingly transparent."

"I will drink to that." Gun lifted his cup. "You certainly knew where you stood, with good old Mr. Vutch. I dunno; maybe they don't have subterfuge here. Or maybe they're all really bad at it?"

"He was like a salesman. A bad one. Though you did know where his priorities lay."

Gun chuckled, and sighed.

"Yeah," he said. "Something like that."

"Gimme another Mr. Vutch, I say," Jackie leaned her head back against the wall. "Why not?"

"Why not?" Gun agreed. He took another heavy sip of the drink and watched the world spin. They sat in silence for a long time.

Again it was Jackie who bestirred herself. "Hey, Gun."

"Yeah?"

"Can you remember it?" she asked. She lifted her head again and was rolling her cup between her palms. Her voice had the overt precision of someone trying not to slur her words. Her eyes were somber in the firelight.

"Remember what?" Gun finished his drink and shrugged. "Oh. Yeah, I guess. Some."

"Like what?"

"Jacks . . ." Gun said, reluctant.

"C'mon, man."

"I don't know. I remember everything, pretty much, it's just . . . distant. Like a dream. Or a story somebody told me once. But I remember the clearing pretty well. Those tall trees, and when we saw the black pillar thing. The portal. Just that feeling of it all being real, you know?"

Jackie shook her head. "I don't remember, really."

Gun looked at her, worried, and she shrugged. "I mean," she said, "I remember *doing* it. Falling into the darkness, putting our hands on the thing. But I can't remember what it looked like, really . . . What the trees looked like, or the sunshine. How it felt, you know? I can't . . . Whatever. It's gone."

Gun pulled his knees up to his chest and hugged them. "I remember. A little. The rays of sunshine, you know, that late afternoon stuff, the kind that holds the dust motes. Coming down through those big trees at an angle. And there were birds. You know. The wind. The sounds of the woods."

Jackie sighed, a low, plaintive sound. "Birds. I used to love camping."

"You told me."

"Did I? I don't remember. I'd go with my brothers. I was the littlest so they'd make me set the tents up and make fun of me if it took too long."

"They sound like real jerks." He smiled, faint.

"They were." Jackie smiled a little herself. "Yeah, they really were. I can't remember what they look like, now. Just that they were tall."

There seemed to be nothing to say to that, so Gun refilled their cups instead. He handed one to Jackie and returned to his spot. He wondered idly how long they'd been sitting there, staring at this fire. Drinking.

"I remember the sun," he said after a while. "The sunset over the mountains, the day we stole the sword."

Jackie laughed, in spite of herself, holding. "I *forgot* about that! That poor guy."

"It was your idea!" Gun said. "But yeah, that day . . . Damn. That day. I remember the sunset, just . . . all of those colors. Oranges and reds and purples just *smashed* across the sky. The clouds . . ."

"I remember the clouds. Yeah. I remember the road, disappearing into the mountains."

Gun laughed, without much amusement. "We had no idea where we were going."

"Yeah," Jackie said, and again, after a minute, "Yeah."

"And then we stopped at that shitty hotel. We got drunk, and went out onto the roof . . ."

"The *stars* . . ." Jackie said, and her voice was half-choked, and Gun pretended not to notice.

"And you made fun of me for bringing the sword everywhere," he said, smiling at the half-memory.

Jackie chuckled. "And we sat on the edge, right? That was the night we looked at the stars . . ."

". . . And said: Shit. What did we say? What do we say? Oh, right. 'Here's to adventure.'"

"Here's to adventure," Jackie said, raising her cup in an ironic echo of that toast, worlds away.

They were quiet for a while.

"Fucking idiots, man," she said.

"Yeah." All of a sudden Gun didn't want to drink anymore. He tossed his cup into the fire. "We were fucking idiots."

There wasn't much to say, after that, so they lapsed into silence. They watched the fire and listened to the low howl of dark wind through the dead buildings. Jackie's eyes grew gradually lost and distant. As distant as the lights atop the mountain. "What are we gonna do, man?" she asked quietly.

"I don't know, Jacks, I just . . . I don't know."

She fell back into silence, looking at the flames, and they wrapped themselves up in their own thoughts, their own memories. After a long time, when the fire had burned low, they heard the distant but unmistakable scream of a Feral Child, somewhere out in the darkness.

Jackie looked up from the fire, out into the dark, and then over at Gun. Their eyes met.

"Awesome," Jackie said. And then she laughed.

PART IV

THE CABAL

The Utility of West

"You want a story? Which story? Which lie shall I tell so you will have your fill? Understand that you do not truly want a story, children. You want ALL stories, the tale to tell that is all tales. You don't want truth. You want a pleasant fiction. Well I've a mind to give it to you, yes, and hope you choke."

—EMILY LIST IV, 'THE BALLAD OF THE HOT HALLS WAR'

The creature that is not quite a man, the remarkable firstborn son of Hunter Fine, the incomparable *West*, makes his way through more darkness, and on his way to yet another fire. He again walks alone, again he walks with a jaunty flair to his hips and his hand-enameled chutter reflects the small golden flickering of the fire ahead.

The last time he walked towards a fire, it was the fire beneath the helical Stairway, host to a six-span high killing machine that made excellent *chûs*. Where he had met the laughably named 'Master' D'Alle and his old enemy, who called himself Candle. Where he had discovered that Winter had a plot, a grand plan, and she had made the terrible mistake of putting *him* at the heart of it.

This was a different fire, burning in a different darkness. Things could not be more different this time. Everything is turning around West, and at long last things are turning his way.

He watches the still-distant spark of fire, through the dark remains of old buildings. There will be two figures waiting by that fire. They will be lost, they will be afraid, and they will be lonely.

They will be in dire need of a friend, and who better a friend than West? Winter had not dissembled when she said he knew Behemoth. Oh yes, he *knows* Behemoth.

The rest of the Convox—now rebranded as the 'Cabal,' since that implies action instead of conversation—waits in the gloom behind him. West has convinced them that their best chance of winning the Behemoth to their cause is to let him approach them, alone. Like all of the best lies, it is also true. It had taken some finesse to turn this Convox to his desires, to lay his plans inside of theirs.

But now he is in the position he'd been seeking for so long; this is his chance to turn everything his way.

Fat D'Alle, on his walking-couch, thinking to involve himself in the plans of the Wise! It is laughable. West almost feels sorry for the fool, and what West is about to do to him. But such people—"mayflies," Winter calls them—cannot be worried about overmuch.

He worries more about Candle, that preternaturally clever piece of *shit*. Candle has been trained by West's brother, Charts, and while West is no admirer of his brother, he is not foolish enough to say that Charts isn't good at training people. His brothers and sisters were all born of Hunter Fine, and only a fool underestimates even the least of them. Still, it will be good to throw Candle's betrayal in Chart's face, right before West cuts that face off.

The tall white mechanical demon, Mr. Turpentine, doesn't worry West a bit. That monster has comprehensible goals, no matter how disagreeable, and West knows how to counter that ancient automata's desires. Indeed, Mr. Turpentine might be something of an ally in the coming war. When West makes the Cabal his own, he may well include Turpentine and his very useful Feral Children in his plans.

West frowns, walking through the ancient and abandoned wreckage toward the fire ahead, thinking about Primary Gray. The godlike, golden-eyed boy disconcerts him, and he still doesn't have a good handle on what that creature wants. However, Gray has given every indication of being on a lark and has shown very little interest in any of the proceedings. West must, for the moment, trust that Primary Gray will accept a change in leadership of the Cabal, once the winds begin to blow that way.

West smiles to himself as he approaches the Behemoth around the fire. Oh, yes, there will be a change in leadership. Winter is about to learn the dangers of underestimating the firstborn son of Hunter Fine. And, perhaps, that sometimes the *son* can surpass the *father*.

Winter, for all her vaunted history and accomplishment, made two mistakes with West. He is no fool; he knows that she thinks him in thrall to Charts and therefore predictable. But West is the first son of Hunter Fine; into him was poured all of that great man's best qualities, and it is far past time to take his rightful place in history. West means to strike a bold course, one that no one—even the mighty Winter—could predict.

The Cabal thinks that he is going to approach these Behemoth and offer friendship, to seduce them with kindness and false promises, to win them and their amazing Black-Portal sword to the Cabal's side. The sword that had been brought through that gate between worlds, and had been changed into a weapon that could cut . . . well, anything. They *think* they will seduce them, that is. But Winter has made some mistakes. West grins in the darkness. Firelight reflects off his teeth.

Winter's second mistake is allowing West to approach the Behemoth alone.

But Winter has a fallacy, and like all fallacies of self-deception, this one is impossible to see in oneself. She is ancient and clever. She has been at the forefront of history for longer than history has been recorded, and directing the course of events comes more naturally to her than breathing. Her fallacy, however, is assuming that all thinking creatures are more or less the same, with the same faults, drives, and foibles. And this is more or less true, of *most* thinking creatures. But she does not know *Behemoth*.

When Winter thinks of Behemoth, she thinks of the great ones, the dangerous ones, the ones that stood large in history. She thinks of Alvarez, the legendary philosopher and wizard, she thinks of Indira Aviz who helped the Nine reach the sky. She thinks of Han Aki, who rained terror on countless lands before he was brought down, she thinks of Abayomi who set herself up as a god and very nearly became one. But West, in his study of Behemoth, knows something that Winter does not: *Behemoth are utter, utter fools.*

Oh, not later—not after they'd learned the ways and means of the Wanderlands and grown comfortable with their power and reputation. Mature Behemoth were *indeed* dangerous, and West would climb into the mouth of the Giant Kindaedystrin itself before he would challenge two of those. But new-made Behemoth are not the same as mature ones, in the same way that a mewling kitten is not the same as a mountain cat. Oh, indeed, not the same at all!

West doesn't quite know where these things come from, what sort of world it is. It seems a small place, backward and with none of the great technological magics of this one. It seems a grimy pastoral backwater, that place, with fire and legend their only true tools. They are a simple and ignorant people, credulous, ready to believe any story that helps them make sense of the strange new place where they've found themselves. They still believe in kings and gods in that place, and fortunately, West is just a little of both.

They are less than children, new Behemoth, and children love stories. West smiles to himself in the dark, making his way through the old buildings, watching the fire grow closer. Oh, West has a story for them; yes he does. But not one that Winter will care for.

West takes care, as he walks, not to grow over-confident. These two folk will certainly be innocent, unwise in the ways of the world and ready to trust a new friend, but he must not underestimate them. They have already provided ample proof of how much damage even new-made Behemoth can cause. West is under no illusions that he is a match for them if it should come to violence.

But it will not come to violence, of course. Is not West the most delightful of all creatures? Is not West the very soul of solicitude? Is he not the firstborn son of Hunter Fine? He will gather these poor lost persons into his hand like forest animals to food. He will wrap them tight with tales of wonder and daring. He will seduce them with the promise of glory and riches.

West knows the sorts of tales that seduce the weak-minded. He knows the stories beloved by the simple.

West flexes his fingers, flicking any anxiety away from him, and sets about adopting a manner. He has always been an excellent mimic, able to mix and match aspects of personality to meet his needs. He decides that the situation calls for warmth, for humor, for quicksilver wit. He thinks a little of Mr. Turpentine's loquacious speaking manner would serve quite well. It *is* charming, though made ridiculous by Turpentine's sly and supercilious affect.

Perhaps, too, a dash of Winter's warm command. Even as her enemy, West can recognize the implicit power in her form and voice. He straightens a little, adopting some of her regal bearing.

And just a modicum of danger, a twinkle of wildness behind the eyes, taken from his sister. It would not do for them to think him toothless.

Yes, he will win them. It is almost hard to credit that Winter has made such a fundamental mistake, to trust him for this work. But then, she thinks him small and able only to spit in his brother's eye. But when this bloody work is done, West means to do more than *spit* in his brother's eye. He plans to put it *out*.

West smiles now, wide. The fire has grown close, he can see two tiny figures outlined in it, sitting morose in the dark; it is time for the *chús* to meet the lips. It is time for the bold to drink deeply. He thinks of Winter's miscalculation and feels warm inside; it is on such small mistakes that empires rise and fall. West has no intention of helping Winter with her silly plans of killing the Giant; West has more immediate concerns. West has been waiting for something like this for all his long life, and now that the moment has arrived, he has no intention of fumbling it.

Winter's true mistake, and the one only West is clever enough to see, is a valuation of the wrong artifact. She sees only the *sword*, and how to procure it or manipulate the Behemoth into using it. But West knows there is a far more valuable artifact at that fire ahead—*love*. The love of these folk. Winter thinks of the weapon, and West thinks of the *arm that will wield it*. Who needs a sword when you have a friend with a sword?

And what friend will not fight to protect the ones he loves? West chuckles. Oh, *Winter*. So wise. So untouchable. Has she not thought that such a weapon, and a willing arm to wield it, can cut many things? The Old Gold, certainly, and maybe even the Giant's bonds, but West is thinking more along the lines of *necks*. Slender, ancient necks, topped with long dark hair and green eyes.

He can discern shapes around the fire, now. Two brooding shapes, staring silently into the flames, as well they might. They have just been through a harrowing experience. He knows that he must not surprise them; they are simple but still dangerous. No, he wants them to know he is friendly and welcoming from the very start. He begins to whistle into the darkness, a jaunty tune that will lift hearts and spirits.

There is one last question to be answered, one last thing he needs before he can take this first step towards reclaiming what is rightfully his. *A name.*

Names are important things, defining things; magical things. The man who currently calls himself West has had many names. They are like lenses through which he projects himself. There is power in names, power over hearts, channels for the mind. West cannot properly become the friend that these Behemoth need until he has the proper name.

He considers and discards several, too pompous, too whimsical, too obviously noble. He enjoys this, perhaps more than he enjoys any other thing. There is something intoxicating in taking a new personality; something powerful in taking a new name. He sees the two figures around the fire startle at the sound of his whistle, looking around for its source. West feels himself trembling on the edge of a precipice; the first step into the emptiness that is the beginning of flight.

His new aspect settles into him with a delicious, almost sexual feeling. He feels his face spread into a bright smile, a welcoming and broad-armed affectation.

Oh, yes. He will own these fools, these new-made monsters. He will win them and make them his. And then he will conquer this sad and broken world with them. A name comes to him, the way he knew it would, and it is good. It is perfect! He enters the circle of their firelight, letting them get a good look at him.

"Hello!" he says, grandly. Echoes of his whistling reverberate back through the city, underscoring his words. "Hello there, travelers, and well met! Very well met *indeed*, here at the end of the world. Might I approach your fire? I do not mean to disturb you, but I have been in the Dark long and beyond long, and could do with some of its comforts."

West sees the two Behemoth exchange a confused look, and he can see that they are every bit as weak, as lonely, as bewildered as he could have hoped. He tries to concentrate on the task at hand, but cannot help imagining the moment he will soon enjoy, the look on his brother's face when he tosses Winter's head at his feet, his two new Behemoth friends behind him. He looks from one monster to another and opens his arms in welcome.

"But listen to me! All talk and no hear, as my father would say, and no greetings to be had. Hello, my friends, hello, and be welcome to the Wanderlands."

West smiles at each of them in turn, and performs a small, precise bow for each. "I am Mr. Vutch, and I am *entirely* at your service."

THE KILLERS

The Big Dark

"If you're going to taunt a cat, pull its claws first."

—ALVAREZ, 'PRECIS'

The darkness was immense; monstrous. For a moment it was everything; a ravaging god that had swallowed the Rue de Paladia and all that lay within it. The Dark lay on Sophie like a blanket. A visceral terror stopped up her lungs, made it hard to breathe—or maybe that was the searing pain from her arms. And then she discovered that she could see. Faintly, so faintly as to be imperceptible, but she could see. She looked at her hands; she could barely make out individual digits. Near her, she saw a very faint impression of Bear's face. She turned.

Far down-Rue was a shifting golden glow: Some of the tall braziers that lined the long street were still lit. The char-boys on their stilts hadn't dampened all of them. Still, screams and wails of fear were rising all around them. Her brother had just murdered the Rue de Paladia. She reached out, through the magic in her arms, searching for motive force, for Silver, trying to find some way of bringing light back, but there was nothing. Lee had burned out the entire Rue; every lightfixture she could sense was a black ruin.

In the distance she heard the weighty sound of a Gallivant grind to a stop. And then, somewhere beyond that, the rising madness of a scream. It was an awful sound, a teeth-shattering sound. It held all of the mindless terror that was trying to claw at Sophie, and she felt something deep within her rise up in answer to it. The faint light wasn't enough, and it would fail soon. The *Dark* had come for the Keep.

It felt like the end of everything.

"Killers!" Bear's voice came out of the gloom. "To me!"

Sophie heard a sharp scraping sound, and then a small flickering light grew, illuminating Bear's face. He'd removed one of the bandages on his burned arm, and lit it somehow. Bear looked around, wrapped the burning bandage around his knife blade, and found Sophie.

Trik materialized in the weak glow. "We should see if Hunker is still down there."

Sophie shook her head. "He won't be. But Avie . . ."

"This way," Ben said, his voice wavering but clear. "Towards my voice, I'm near the stairway."

Sophie fumbled for her pack of slots, pulled one free, and scraped it to life. With the faint glow from Bear's makeshift torch, she ripped free a bit of tablecloth and dipped it into the remnants of a pot of strong on the nearby table. She held the lit end of the slot to the fabric and then wrapped it around a long table-knife. She had her own torch.

All around them, in the great darkness, she heard the growing sounds of people in terror. There were more screams, more weeping. Sophie moved forward, holding her torch out until she saw the place where her brother and Hunker had been; there was no sign of them now. Trik followed her lead. She broke off the leg of a chair and wrapped it in another long section of tablecloth, touching it to Sophie's fire.

Ben looked frightened, but he was holding it together. Sophie was reminded of when they were children, out in the Dark, as they raced to wake the Jannissaries; how terrified he had been. But he hadn't quit.

The Killers made their way down the narrow stairway and onto the main boulevard of the Rue; they could only see a few span of it around them and everything was bizarre and frightening in the wavering light of their torches. There was still no sign of Hunker John, but Sophie wasn't very surprised. Lee still needed him. She didn't have the space to think about Hunker right now.

She looked around, trying to orient herself. She saw a vague looming shape and thought it might be the abandoned shopkeep's stall.

"Sophie!" Trik yelled, behind her. "What are you . . . ?"

"Looking for Avie," Sophie said. She rounded the shopkeep's stall, trying to find where Avie would have fallen. Sophie was holding up the small flame on the knife, which was already starting to gutter. The sounds around them were growing ugly. She saw blood on the ground, but no Avie.

"Over here." Sophie heard a hoarse voice from the thick dark and turned to see Avie cradling one hand, a mess of blood. She had taken shrapnel to her face when Lee had exploded her chutter. She was cut up pretty badly. Even in the dim light from her torch, Sophie could see one eye filling with blood.

Avie grimaced and looked at Sophie with her good eye. "I tried."

"Yeah." Sophie examined her. "You're a fucking mess."

"Thanks."

The other Killers approached as Sophie examined Avie's wounded hand. She might lose some of those fingers, but she was controlling the pain well. Sophie shook her head. "Can you move?"

Avie nodded and held out her good hand, which Sophie used to help her up. They were surrounded by the big darkness, the desolate emptiness that used to be the Rue.

"Sophie," Bear said, his voice low, "we have to get out of here. These people are going to break."

"I know. We're close to the Guardians' entrance; there should be light there. It'll be rough, but people will find their way out. We need to go before they start rioting and it becomes a crush."

Trik agreed. "Yes, Capitana."

They made their way down a Rue de Paladia become sinister and hideous in the dark, a strange place where things leapt out at them. Bear was forced to shove a few people that rushed them, wanting their light. Up ahead, Sophie saw a faint pale illumination, so faint she worried she was imagining it; but she wasn't. There was light beyond the Guardians, beyond the ancient doors that marked the end of the Rue.

"Hold up," Bear said suddenly, holding out his arm and stopping Sophie. "What is that?"

Sophie didn't know what he was talking about at first; the whole world was only their small circle of light and the increasing sounds of people going dark-sick around her. But then she heard it, a slowly rising grinding sound, like an old Gallivant being dragged across stone. She looked at Bear, his frown a bare impression in the shadows.

"I don't . . ." she began, unable to place the sound, which was growing louder by the second, until she could. Her fingertips felt cold. "Oh, no."

"What?" Trik looked around, confused, as the grinding sound grew louder.

"He's closing the doors," Sophie said, unable to believe it. "Lee is locking us in."

As if to prove her point, the faint light ahead of them grew dimmer, and then disappeared just as a huge booming sound echoed through the Rue. After a few seconds, there was another sound from the opposite end of the long street, similar but distant. All of the noise in the Rue ceased, shocked into silence once again.

"*He locked us in,*" Sophie said again.

"This isn't good," Trik said. The darkness seemed mammoth, absolute. And then another sound came up out of it, but it wasn't the grinding of the doors closing or the mad echoes of people losing their minds in the dark. Winding up into the massive black, mournful and savage, came the unmistakable and unforgettable rotten-squeezebox scream of a Feral Child. It was quickly joined by two, and then three, then more.

Sophie's brother had brought Feral Children into the heart of the Keep.

THE LOST BOYS

Plots and Plans

"You kill a Cold, kiss a Queen, and calm a child all in the same way: carefully."
—GEORGES TAI, 'GENESIS LUX'

They dragged the brothers up through the labyrinthine depths of D'Alle's mansion to the same bare room he'd interviewed them in when he'd kidnapped them. James fought every inch of the way, despite his traitor brother's pleas to stop. Chris tried to remind James of his promise, to do what he said, but James didn't keep promises to *traitors*. And then the guards had thrown the two boys down in front of D'Alle.

He paced before the boys, not speaking, for long moments. His hand gripped his long braid tightly. James would have liked to spit on his shoes, but the thick gag stopped him. D'Alle was toying with something, smacking it into his palm. It was slender and elegant; it was the slim rod Chris had made and then tucked into the band of his trousers.

James felt very much like he would like to kill *all* of them, Master D'Alle and the thin-faced woman with the tattoos and his traitor brother, too. All those long weeks working on the strange devices with Chris, all of that tedious digging, all of the fear and waiting and wondering where Buckle was, and all for nothing.

All for nothing, because Chris—*after he'd given them a way to escape*—had surrendered to D'Alle instead, with only the slim bronze-red rod as a trophy. They all could have been miles away by now; they could have rescued Katherine and found Buckle; they could be in the *Land of the Giants*. He struggled and hurt his wrists on the cruel bonds they'd put on him. D'Alle's guards had learned to be wary of James, and James' teeth.

"All right." D'Alle sighed. He'd been examining the fine patterning and rich, deep color of the twistcraft object Chris had made. "My curiosity is aroused. What is this?"

He remembered that Chris couldn't answer him, and made a flicking motion to the guard—a man who had been none too gentle with James and had possibly broken one of his ribs. He loosened Chris' gag, and Chris spit, but not at D'Alle.

He worked his jaw for a moment and looked up at the broad man. When he spoke, his voice was steady.

"I have a proposition for you."

"Oh, wonderful." D'Alle sighed. "The child wants to *dicker*. I'm only going to ask you one more time: What *is* this, boy?"

"I think I've proved," Chris said, "that I'm no mere boy."

"All you've proved," D'Alle snapped, "is that you're a bigger fool than I thought. What is this?"

James tried to yell something through his gag, but it barely came out a squeak. He really was tied up tight; he could hardly breathe. He contented himself with sending D'Alle looks of such murderous intensity a lesser creature would have died from them. He hoped Buckle and Katherine had made their escape already, since his stupid brother didn't know what that word *meant*.

"I have a proposition." Chris' voice only trembled a little. "Part of it is telling you what that rod is, and what it does."

D'Alle hissed, his amused demeanor slipping for a moment, and pointed the bronze rod at Chris' face. "You think you're holding cards, boy, but you're in the wrong fucking *game*. Gods, the Twins-damned timing! It's almost hard to believe, as if you're cursed by the Mother herself. But very well; give me your terms, so I can tell you why they're *shit*."

Now Chris seemed uncertain. He cut his eyes to James and took a breath.

"You saw what I can do," Chris said, his voice steadying as he spoke, trusting in his plan, "locked in a basement with no tools. You need to think about what I could do with proper equipment. And in your service."

James yelled something else into his gag and struggled, but Chris ignored him. Master D'Alle laughed.

"Oh, I've thought of *that*. Why do you think I allowed you to keep working? You think I didn't know you were up to something down there? I'll even admit to being impressed—and not a little surprised. I wonder if you could have actually escaped if you'd wanted to. I had no idea that old man taught so well."

"I *learned* well," Chris said. "And I know some things he doesn't. I can cement your power in this city, D'Alle. *Master*."

D'Alle laughed again, unamused, and smacked the tube against his palm. "Oh, no, boy. You can twist some dirt, that's true enough, but this play isn't subtle at all. You still haven't told me what *this* is. I have artisans that could escape from that basement, but I don't have any that can make this. What manner of weapon is it?"

"It's not a weapon," Chris said. "It's a dowser."

D'Alle lifted an eyebrow. "A *dowser*? You grandly misstepped, boy, if you think I care about a dowser. The Wells give us all the water we need."

"This isn't a normal dowser," Chris said. "It dowses for *Silver*."

D'Alle stopped and looked at Chris for a long moment, then down at the slim rod.

"'There are old things in the hidden halls,'" Chris quoted, "'There are treasures in the deep.' I can think of uses for a Silver-dowser, in the Breach. In the *Underlands*. Imagine what could be found. What if you had ten of them? A hundred?"

"Stop." D'Alle sighed. He looked at the rod in his hands, almost longingly. "Your attempts at politic are like being groped by an eager child. But . . . the play is sound, boy. It won't do any harm to admit that. *Clever*. I suppose you were going to trade your indenture to me for your brother's life, yes? And your mother's?"

Chris opened his mouth; closed it. D'Alle's amused manner threw him off. "Yes," Chris said. "That's what I'm proposing."

D'Alle flipped the rod up, catching it with a smacking sound in the middle of his palm. "It's a good play. It truly is! I might have even gone for it. But, as I said, you got the game wrong."

Chris sounded plainly nervous now. "We don't need to . . ."

"Stop." D'Alle held up a hand. "As I said, your timing is execrable. Three weeks earlier or two weeks later and you might have had a deal. But you, boy, you *clever motherfucker*, had to stage your little demonstration while I have guests in the house. Guests from far away; guests whose curiosity has been aroused by all the racket, and guests it would be very dangerous to lie to."

D'Alle sighed again, and handed the rod to the thin woman standing behind him. He looked down at Chris and then, momentarily, James.

"You've tied both of our hands, boy. I was trying to thread the eye of a needle, and you just jogged my arm, so now we're both in the soup. You think you're clever, and maybe you are, but your *cleverness* just drew the eye of the Wise. And in that game, boy, you need to be a lot more than clever to survive."

THE KILLERS

The Dead Hands of the Past

"And I swear you had wings, wings like none I'd ever seen.
And I swear I saw you fly, boy, I'd swear those wings were humming."

—DAVID, 'TWO SONGS ABOUT THREE BOYS'

The Killers escaped the Rue de Paladia the same way they'd escaped the Loche de Menthe: by a small passageway tunneled through the rock of the Keep, one of the side-ways that Ben knew about. Once again Sophie was fleeing from a tragedy of her brother's making; once again she had no idea what to do or where to go. The tunnel was thin and dusty, rarely used, and lit with occasional slender chunks of litstone set into the ceiling.

"Sophie," Trik said, coughing in the dust they were stirring up. "Sophie! Stop for a second."

Sophie pulled up, looked around, and saw that she had been leaving the Killers behind, walking too fast for them to keep up. Avie was wounded, and was regarding her through one blood-filled eye. But she didn't *want* to stop; she felt a great desire to run, towards or away from something, to be anywhere but here. She made herself wait for her friends.

Trik coughed again. "What the fuck is going on? Where are we going?"

"I told you what's going on," Sophie said. "Hunker John is working with my brother, and this Candle asshole, who is somehow *Bear's* brother. No, I don't fucking know why. I don't fucking know very fucking much, okay?"

"Hey!" Bear said, a little sharply. "We're on your side, Sophie."

"Are you, Bear?" Sophie shot back. "You, Trik? I don't know *who* the fuck anybody is tonight."

"Sophie," Ben said, admonishing. "C'mon."

She closed her eyes for a moment. God, her arms hurt. She had forgotten how much this all *hurt*.

"I'm sorry," she said, and slumped against the rough stone wall. "I'm sorry. It's been a long fucking night. Avie, my brother, Hunker John . . . It's been a lot. Those poor motherfuckers back there, in the dark, waiting to get their faces chewed off by Feral Children. No, it's not a lot; it's *too much*."

Trik looked back over her shoulder the way they'd come, at the darkness and terror of the Rue de Paladia behind them. She swallowed. "I wish there was something we could do."

"Yeah," Bear said.

"I tried." Sophie looked at her burnt sleeves, the livid scars on her arms. Her mouth twisted. "As much good as it did."

Trik looked crestfallen. "Sophie, you—"

Sophie shook her head. "Don't."

Trik hugged her arms to herself, but didn't speak.

Avie let herself slide down the wall, mimicking Sophie, cradling her hurt hand. She studied Sophie. "Lee says he wants the Key. Do you think he'll kill Hunker John for it?"

"I don't know," Sophie muttered. "Maybe. I don't know what Hunker was to them, or what he did for them. I think maybe he was trying to warn me, with his shaking leg; it was really obvious."

"We can't give him the Key," Bear said. "Twins damn, Sophie. We need that Key."

"Why?"

He grimaced, and flexed his big fingers. "Because then I can help. I won't be helpless."

"What does it do?"

Bear frowned at her. "It's a Twins-damned Cold-Key. What can't it do? If I get my hands on that thing, I'll be a motherfucking Cold-Wizard out of motherfucking legend. I can take your brother—or the Queen—apart."

"We are really going to have to have a conversation about where you come from," Sophie said, "but not right now. Look, I don't know. I just don't know. Lee says he doesn't care about the Book, but that doesn't make sense to me. Yeah, yeah, I know 'everything is about me,' but that still doesn't track, right? Trik, you said something about them needing the Key and the Book, right? For whatever they're planning?"

Trik looked as if she were regretting that outburst, and she nodded reluctantly. "As far as I understand it. Yeah. They need all three things."

"We need to have a conversation about who 'they' are, and what they need this shit for, Trik." Sophie gave her friend a hard look. "And maybe about where you come from, too."

Trik looked down, but nodded again.

"I don't think we have time for all that just now," Ben said, crouching next to Sophie and putting a hand on her shoulder. "What do you want to do, Capitana?"

She choked out a harsh laugh, bitter and painful. "What do I want to do? Funny, old man. When have we gotten that choice?"

Avie shifted, and met Sophie's eyes from the opposite wall. "Bitter and bleak doesn't suit you, Sophie. Not when you can still feel the sun on your face."

Sophie winced and looked away. Her forearms were resting on her knees, and the sleeves of her jacket were in burned tatters. Ben's hand stayed steady on her shoulder, and she wanted to slap it off. She wished, for one infinitely painful moment, that Hunker John was here with his flask. He'd always known what she needed; another Twins-damned drink.

"I keep thinking about those butterflies," she said, finally, her hands raising in a twisting gesture, as if trying to shape the words. "Those poor Twins-damned butterflies. Trying to fly with burning wings."

She looked back at Avie, thinking of another butterfly, in another world. Sophie's mouth twisted. "These 'Wise' fuckers, lighting our wings on fire, watching us try to fly."

Trik frowned. "What are you saying, Sophie?"

Sophie shrugged, and rested her head on the stone behind her. "Shit, I don't know. I wish I had a slot. I guess I'm saying that I'm not much better, am I? All those poor fucking butterflies."

Ben's hand tightened on her shoulder, and she was suddenly glad she hadn't slapped his hand away. Her eyes filled with tears, and she blinked them away. Gods, what a long night. She was getting soft. She cleared her throat.

Ben asked again: "What do you want to do, Sophie?"

Trik leaned forward, dark eyes intense. "Yeah. What do you *want* to do, Capitana?"

Sophie laughed again, but it wasn't a short hard bark this time. She felt something loosen up in her chest. She put a hand over Ben's, tightening her grip, drawing power from the connection.

"I want to see those trees again," she said, around a sudden lump in her throat.

Avie's bloody green eye widened, across from her.

"What do I *want* to do?" Sophie echoed, taking in a deep breath. "That's easy, Trik. I want to stop my fucking brother from destroying my home inch by inch. I want to save those poor motherfuckers back there in the Rue from getting their faces eaten off by Feral Children. I want to stick a boot in Jane Guin's eye, and I want to have a real serious conversation with Bear's brother. I want to *stop running*. I want to stop the fucking *damage*."

She looked around at the Killers, her dark-eyed gaze intense.

"I want to go get my *fucking Book*."

THE DEADSMITH

The Door Into Loss

"The only way through is all the way through."

—MADDIS BEE, 'TOURNEQUIT'

The Deader stumbled on his way through the Door and went down on one knee. The Door closed behind him, shutting off the white-faced lake folk and the horror they'd wrought. The Deader fell to his side and lay there for a while, golden filaments disintegrating in his hand, flesh painfully re-knitting. He had never been so close to dying—to *truly* dying—as he had back on that archipelago, almost murdered by *twistcraft*. By fucking *Dirt-Magic*.

He was a Deadsmith; he regularly slept in the bed of a god. And someone, somewhere, had taken a few bucketfuls of dirt, had hammered away at it for a while, and had almost killed him. And not just a pedestrian death, soon recovered from, no. This was would have been the true death, the utter end.

The golden bolts, the ones that had very nearly destroyed him, were still wreaking damage through his body, and his own magic still struggled to fight them.

The Black-and-White was a powerful magic but a harsh one; it was not for the weak. Deadsmith alone were judged strong enough to bear it, but the Deader did not feel strong just now.

His Fate was still weeping in fear, but the Deader paid it no mind. When he could, he limped himself over to one of the big, stone-white and long-dead trees and sat there for a while. He unslung his pack and endured the agony of resurrection.

He had never encountered anything like those golden bolts. They were an order of the Old Gold so far beyond any he'd seen that he could hardly credit it. The Nine would need to be told. His Lady would need to be told. There was a twistcraft magician in the world who could harm *a Deadsmith!* He wondered, for a moment, what might have happened, had more of the bolts found their mark.

The Deader felt another frisson of that new/old emotion, *fear*. He could feel the Black-and-White magic inside him killing the last of the gold in the extremities of his hands, rooting out those malicious fibers with destructive black acid and healing white balm. If more of those bolts had struck him, he judged, he might well be dead now.

Truly dead.

He felt everything he knew of the world shift, just a little, under his feet. Who was this Prey, to possess such weapons? Was it possible that Candle himself had *made* them?

No. The Deader could not let himself fall into the other end of the trap. Underestimating this Prey was clearly dangerous, but he suspected overestimating would be just as harmful. From what the Deader knew of twistcraft, those bolts were stage five—or even *six*—work, and there had not been any creature in the Wanderlands capable of such advanced craft since the death of Hunter Fine. Perhaps that dirt-magic wizard in Cannoux—but no. He made clock-plows and simple gadgets. Such high stages would have taken many consecutive lifetimes of work—more, even. And there was no more Reset for the folk of the Wanderlands, no more rebirths and consecutive lives. They had only one life to learn in now.

The man who called himself Candle must have found the bolts; they must be leftovers from some other age. For a strange, cavernous moment, the Deader wondered if the golden bolts had been made by Hunter Fine *himself*.

But no. If they had been? He would have been destroyed. He could admit that. They say that in the Silver Age, they did not fuck around, but Hunter Fine had been a master of both the Golden Age *and* the Silver Age. If Hunter Fine made a weapon, it would kill.

The Deader bared his teeth into the darkness. The Prey had not lied; his road had indeed grown dark. He wondered if his Lady had known what the Prey was capable of. It was hard to believe there was anything his Lady did not know, but the Deader did not like to think she'd sent him only to be killed.

No, the Prey just had remarkable resources, ones that perhaps even the Lady Winter didn't know about. The Deader had grown lax and thought that memories and Domination were Candle's only weapons. The loss of his Fate had made him careless, and he could not afford to be careless, not if he wished to return to his Lady.

There could be no more mistakes; his Machine must always be mobile and ready to kill now. If his Machine had been mobile during the encounter at the edge of the lake town, it would have gone differently. He knelt and unslung the case in which he carried the black-and-white beads of his beloved Machine. He opened the case and discovered exactly how badly he had been hurt.

No, not just hurt. *Mutilated.* The case his Machine lived in bore tiny scars; the Deader remembered one of his assailants firing a chutter into his back. He hadn't thought anything of it at the time; a normal chutter could never hurt his Machine. But when he opened the case, he saw what manner of darts it had fired.

His Machine was frozen in a rictus of death; gold fibers had perforated its beads and mechanisms and ruptured them, spilling Black-and-White magic impotently, woven with vicious golden threads. The Machine had not been given a shape; it was sleeping when it was in the case. It had not been able to fight. The golden threads had killed it, a true death.

His Fate moaned, pointlessly, a howling scream, into the confines of his head. The Deader dropped the pack, spilling the dead remnants of his oldest companion across the ground. Threads of gold snaked into the bitter earth, returning to their home. This was another third of himself, destroyed.

How do you make a machine?

What was left of him, now?

He stared at the broken thing, his Machine, for a long time, struggling to name the thing that had just been born in him. No. Not born. Re-lit; it had been born in a farm-yard at the hands of a man named Trail, a long time ago. It was *rage*.

When the Deader had agreed to become Deadsmith, there had been many operations and ceremonies performed; his bones had been wrapped in Black-and-White and his flesh had been clawed through with stuttering white mesh and arcane black energies. He had been made into something far more than a man, and then made into less than one.

His mind had been ripped in three. His soul had been cleaved in pieces and apportioned out. He had become a triune being: his curiosity and instinct for self-preservation had become the seed of his Fate, his bloodlust and sex and violence had become his Machine. One third of himself was now dead, ruptured by golden threads. The other was a mad wreck inside his head, useless and clamoring. What was left?

The Deader sat looking at the destroyed remnants of his Machine, and wishing the part of him that was left was able to weep. He heard the words in an arcane whisper, and he didn't know if it was Candle's voice he heard, or his own.

How do you make a machine?

THE LOST BOYS

A Certain Unpleasant Narrowing of Choices

"Violence is a crude answer to a problem, and the enlightened find better ones. But sometimes, it's just the only answer that makes sense."

—SHEL ES VORSYTHE, 'SOLVING FOR X'

D'Alle's guest was a woman with long, raven-black hair and sparkling green eyes. She smiled warmly at the boys, and chided their captor.

"Oh, no, no! That won't do. Take their gags off, Master D'Alle, and free them! I deplore such . . . *obvious* mechanisms. We are all friends here. And these boys will not try to leave our company before we've had a chance to palaver; I am simply sure of it. Please! Please! Boys! Come. Have a seat. And a drink. I could almost wonder at the state of Master D'Alle's hospitality, given the state of you."

The woman was medium-height and she reminded James, oddly, of Uncle. He blinked at her, and then the rest of the room, as the guards untied him.

D'Alle rumbled with a light laugh, but James thought he sounded nervous. "Beware the young one, my Lady. He likes to bite."

"Oh," the woman said, and crouched in front of James, eyes twinkling. "I doubt this young man will bite *me*. Will you, my friend?"

James was discomfited by the woman's kindly, laughing manner. He had suffered too many shocks in too short a time, and the gearwork of his anger had slipped a cog. He shook his head.

"See?" the woman asked, beaming. She stood. "Friends."

"As you say, my Lady," D'Alle said.

"Master D'Alle, please. This is an informal company. Use my taken name."

"As you wish. Boys, this is the Lady Winter. I advise you toward whatever grace and manners you have. She is one of the Wise and, tales say, singular even among them."

Master D'Alle seemed nervous, though nothing about the woman's manner or bearing seemed to indicate he should be so. James looked at Chris, and Chris looked very, very scared. James, exasperated, gave up on trying to understand what was going on and settled into pleasant fantasies of murdering D'Alle.

The woman named Winter stopped in front of Chris, who had his head bowed. She lifted his face by hooking a finger under his chin, and her eyes sparkled merrily at the look she saw there. D'Alle settled near the center of the room, on a high couch. His thin servant wasn't there, and James supposed he was hiding Chris' dowsing rod somewhere safe.

James' eye was drawn by a man standing near the corner of the room, his hands at his sides, his face impassive. He seemed to not be interested in anything that was happening and yet aware of every movement and meaning in the room. James shivered; the man was frightening in a way that he viscerally understood. James wouldn't be spitting blood on *this* man's shoes.

Winter stepped back and leaned against the arm of a very tall-backed couch, fingers drumming against the rich fabric, looking at the two boys. Finally, she looked up at Master D'Alle and raised an eyebrow. "Well? Let's gather all the players, please."

D'Alle nodded, a little reluctantly, and waved a hand. Two guards brought in Katherine, and a cage that held Buckle. Katherine looked miserable, her hair disheveled. Buckle, for her part, was quite unamused at the situation. She squeaked and battered against the thin bars of her cage, and threw the woman Winter a rude gesture with her tiny hand.

"My, my!" Winter said, clapping her hands and walking over to the cage. The guard obligingly raised it to eye level. "Look at *you!* What a wonder, and in these lost and broken days. New-made, too, if I don't miss my guess, which is terribly interesting."

"No!" Buckle scowled at the woman. Winter smiled and gently drew the door of the cage open.

"Let's see who she belongs to, yes?" she asked, and Buckle flew like a dart to James' shoulder, holding his ear and trembling. Winter smiled. "Thought so."

She returned to her couch, and Katherine was brought to stand next to Chris. "I'm sorry," she whispered, but Chris shook his head, sharply.

"So!" Winter said. "This is the merry little crew that has caused such anxious trembling in the halls of the Wise, is it? And all because of such a little thing. Such a *trinket.*"

She picked up something that was lying on the tall couch, something silver, something that tugged at James' insides. It was the Cold-Key, the one he had brought back from the Land of the Giants. He twitched towards it.

"Don't," Chris breathed. Winter let it swing from her hand as if mesmerized by it.

"It's funny," she said, "these were never exactly plentiful, but I scarcely guessed

I'd chase halfway across the known world just on the *rumor* of one. If I'd known the damn things were going to cause so much trouble, I would have talked Hunter Fine out of inventing them."

She gave Master D'Alle a toothy smile and dropped the Cold-Key back on the couch. "As I said previously, and which certainly should be stressed, my fine new friend, you did well. Such a thing is too . . . too *pure* a device to be in this world any longer. In these lost days, especially! Such a device can catch an innocent man between forces best left alone."

D'Alle coughed. "Which is why I sought your council. Upon discovering it."

Winter smiled, puzzled. "But *you* did not discover it, Master D'Alle, did you? I thought it was these three children that found the thing."

"Of course. I meant only that I discovered it was within my city and took steps to contain the situation."

"And you did a marvelous job." Winter beamed. "It would not do for word to get out, eh? The dreams are bad enough. I don't think any of us want the Cold to come calling."

"The Cold are gone from the Mountain," D'Alle said, stiffly. "A long time now."

"Oh, not so long," Winter said. "At least, not in the way the Wise reckon things. Still, I feel safe enough! I commend you on a job well done. I could wish, of course, that you had seen fit to share *all* of the facts of the matter when we first arrived, but I'll not quibble. We are new allies! Trust must take time to develop, and I'm confident that all will be made known. And that it will be made known *now*."

There was an ominous note that arrived with that last word, and James felt Chris stiffen next to him. Winter looked between the three children, and her gaze settled on James. Her smile widened.

"And *you*," she said. "What is your name?"

James scowled, defiant. "James."

"Hello, James. Why don't you come a bit closer?"

James found himself taking a few steps closer. The green-eyed woman was strangely difficult to say no to. Buckle dug her little fingers into his hair but didn't leave his shoulder.

"Now, James," Winter said, "I want to ask you a few questions. I think that's okay, don't you?"

"I ain't sayin' *nothing*." James spat on the floor. He gave D'Alle a look, but the big man didn't react.

"I think you will," Winter said, still smiling. "We're all friends here, James! We just want to know how all of this happened. We know you had a dream, a dream with a Giant, yes? And it led you to *this*."

She patted the silver amulet lying next to her, the Cold-Key, and James for a moment thought about leaping for it, seeing if he could do that *pushing* thing again to this lady and D'Alle, the thing he'd done that had killed his first captor, that had pulled red-black jags of something and . . . But, no. She was too close to it, and something about her manner made James reconsider trying to out-maneuver her. There was something in her eyes that was old and hard and impla-cable. Again, he was reminded, a little, of Uncle.

"We just want to know how all of this happened," Winter said, reasonably. "That's all!"

"I ain't sayin' nothing," James said again, but less confident now. He looked back at his brother, who was looking at him with shadowed eyes but with no advice. James was bothered by the despair he saw there; it reminded him of when his brother had gone catatonic in the basement.

Winter was still smiling pleasantly. "Well, that's a shame. Do you see that man over there, James? Yes, the one with the dark hair. Do you know what that man is?"

James scowled. "No."

"Has your mother or father ever told you stories about the Deadsmith, James?"

The quality of the silence in the room changed. Everyone seemed to go very still. "That's just fairy-stories," James said. "Deadsmith ain't *real.*"

Winter smiled, fond. "Ah, but they are! And they're even worse than the sto-ries, I'm afraid. And my friend, there, he hasn't had a lot to say but he is *very inter-ested* in how you children found this Cold-Key. I would hate—I would *shudder,* in fact—to think of what he might do if any details are left out. I hate to think of what he might do to you; to your brother and your friend. I confess I'm afraid of what he might do to this *city.* Your mother lives here, does she not? And your friends? I really think it would be better for everybody if we all put our cards on the table, so to speak, so that we can wrap this nasty little business up all clean and tidy."

She smiled at him, reached out, and lifted his chin with her finger. He met her depthless green eyes.

"Don't you agree?" she asked, wearing that smile. James wasn't *stupid.* He knew she was threatening them. He knew, even, that she was threatening D'Alle too, and maybe everybody in the city. Suddenly Winter's eyes cut up, right as Buckle squawked. James turned, frowning, and saw Chris had moved; he'd slipped up behind him and snatched Buckle from James' shoulder. His throat was working, like he couldn't get the words out. Buckle squirmed in his grip, con-fused. Chris had never touched her before.

"Don't do that, boy," Winter said, warning, and her voice wasn't amused now.

"I'm sorry, squib," Chris said, his voice breaking. "I'm so sorry. But they're going to kill us."

He squeezed, twisting, and Buckle threw her tiny head back and screamed a long, thin wail as her beautiful wings and fine, delicate body were crushed in Chris' strong hands. His fingers found her slender mindspring, tiny and golden and perfect, and tore it apart.

Buckle's screams of pain cut off abruptly as she died, leaving the room in a shocked, appalling silence.

THE KILLERS

A Concurrence of Coincidence

"You can pour fact into ignorance, but there just ain't no cure for stupid."

—DWEMMER B, 'INROADS IN MINOR'

The Killers stuck to the side-ways as much as they could, testing even Ben's knowledge of the hidden passageways of the Keep. When they came to the lighted thoroughfares and the busy streets, the sense of fear was pervasive. Citizens walked furtively, hurrying from point to point, wondering if *this* section of the Keep would be the next to feel the cold fingers of the Dark and the sharp talons of the Feral Children.

The Queen's presence was oddly muted. Sophie would have expected to see Practice Guard, Lurk, and Redarms everywhere on a night like this, but she saw very few. Neither did they see Vesachai. With a grim kind of asperity, Sophie hoped that their absence had *better* be because they were busy prying their way into the Rue, and doing their best to fight the terrible creatures her brother had brought into the Keep. The fucking Feral Children.

Lee. Ah, Lee. She still couldn't reconcile the happy, bright boy she'd known with the villain that had killed the Rue. She just couldn't see how you could go from one to the other. But then, maybe people had similar trouble reconciling her with her past. It was a disconcerting thought.

Finally they could go no farther without parting, and Sophie slowed to a stop in a dim alcove near a main slideway that would take most of the Killers most of the way to the Library. Ben formed up smartly, old habits taking over. Old habits from when the Killers had been more than a degenerate group of safe-crackers and grifters and drunks. Old habits from when they'd fought in the Hot Halls War.

Sophie plucked at the sleeves of her new jacket; it didn't fit very well. Ben had offered a passerby several heavyweight coins for it while she remained hidden in a side-way; Sophie's own sleeve-burned jacket would be a signal flare for any Vesachai that saw it. It was bad enough that her livid red scars were plainly visible at her wrists. She had broken Proscription again and she had little doubt that her life was forfeit now, Queen's protection or no.

"What's the plan, Sophie?" Trik asked, scrubbing her fingertips through her halo of dark hair.

"Well, you're not going to like it, Trik, because we're going to need to split up again."

"As long as I'm with you, there's no problem."

"Well see, that's the thing." Sophie took a breath. "Listen, I think that Lee is on the way to get the Book. He says he doesn't care about it, but I just don't believe that. And Hunker's performance was so over-the-top that I have to assume Lee recognized it, too, and knows the game is up. I think he's going for the Book, now, while he still can."

"Wait." Bear frowned. "How would he know where it is? Isn't that the whole point? Nobody knows where it is?"

Trik cut her eyes to Sophie, and spoke almost out of the side of her mouth. "*Hunker* knows where it is. Remember?"

"Why would Hunker John know the location of the Book?" Avie asked, slowly. Her blood-filled eye gave her an ominous, macabre appearance.

"Because I told them," Sophie said, shortly. "And you can shut up with that look; it was years ago and I was very drunk and it felt good to trust my friends with that heavy fucking secret. Besides, with the amount I was drinking, I could have dropped dead any day. I figured somebody should know where it was."

Avie held her hands up. "It's your business, Sophie. I suppose it doesn't matter now, anyway."

"In any case," Sophie continued, "I think Lee—and Hunker—are either on their way to get the Book, or on their way to set up some kind of trap at the silver vault. I don't think we should let them do either one—and that means splitting up."

"I'm still going with you." Trik crossed her arms, grim. "I made a promise."

"Your pathological obsession with my well-being has been noted," Sophie said, dryly, "but I need Bear with me. I'm the only one that can open that vault, and he claims that if he gets his hands on a silver necklace, he gets to be some kind of wizard or something, and I want to see that."

"Sophie, I—"

"No, Trik! Capitana speaking now." Sophie gave her friend a look. "I don't know *what* you are, but I saw the way you fought through Lee's projection of force—the one that threw Bear around like a leaf in a wind. You don't like being touched, you won't ride Gallivants, and you are very careful when you sit on anything. Whatever you are and whatever you can do, *I need you and Ben to go protect the Book.* Understand? I left a . . . well, a trap. And a pretty nasty one. If Lee does go try to get it, he might be in some trouble. Him and Hunker both. I would rather not have killed my own brother tonight, Trik. Do you understand?"

Trik hung her head. When she spoke, her voice was muffled and thick. "Yes, Capitana."

"Good." She exhaled and looked at Ben. "Those of us that *don't* have some kind of mysterious pasts and wild powers might need something in the way of weapons; it would be good if I didn't burn through any more sleeves tonight. Do we have any stashed away between here and the Library that you can find?"

He nodded, shortly. "Yes, Capitana."

"And," Sophie said, turning to look at Avie, "speaking of mysterious pasts and wild powers . . ."

Avie sighed, as if expecting it. "You're talking about my friend."

"Time to fish or cut your line, New Girl. If you have a weapon we can use, now is the time for it."

Avie thought about it, a small frown-line forming between her eyes. Sophie wished she would wear her true face; it was plainer, but Sophie liked it better.

"Okay," Avie said. "I'll see if I can find him, and if he'll agree. He's . . . picky about what he'll fight for. But I think I can get him to help. If he's not too drunk."

"You are just *filling* me with confidence, New Girl."

"My name is *Avie*. You sure you want to piss me off, right now?"

Sophie grinned. "Oh, this is just how I flirt."

Ben cleared his throat behind her. "Time is running, Capitana."

Sophie blushed, and turned. "Ah . . . yeah. Sorry, old man."

"Let's see if we all live through the next few hours," Ben said, his tone quite dry and with a glance at Avie, "and *then* we'll worry about apologies and weird love triangles. Yeah?"

"I'm glad *you* said it," Trik muttered.

———

"*Shit,*" Bear said, finally. Sophie had been waiting for it. He had been quiet but withdrawn, and Sophie had fancied she could hear his teeth grind from several feet away. But he didn't slow down, and they had made quick progress.

They moved quickly, but they were wary. They were headed for the territory deep beneath Vesachai House, and while Sophie didn't expect to run into any of her Twins-damned family down there, it was a little too close for comfort. Jogging down a wide and very dim thoroughfare, littered with the long-dead carcasses of Gallivants, she gave Bear a sidelong look. "Yeah?" she asked.

"It's just too much, Sophie. This is all just too fucking much to be a coincidence."

"Tonight," she admitted, "is getting weird."

"Yeah. I mean . . . this is all getting ridiculous. This 'Mr. March' turning out to be *your* brother. And his partner turning out to be *mine*. That's not just coincidence, that's damn near criminal."

"Mother knows I don't like to pry, Bear, but who *is* your brother? What does he want with the Key, or the Book? I think I understand Jane's plans. But my brother, and this Candle . . ."

Bear was quiet for a moment. "I don't know much about 'Candle.' And I don't know much about a lot of long years. We separated when I was still a teenager, and didn't re-connect for a long time. Chris is . . . smart. Scary smart; maybe the smartest person I've ever met and I've met some *motherfuckers*. But the worst thing about him isn't how smart he is. It's that he's willing to do anything, anything at all, to get what he wants, to do what he thinks is right. I don't know how to describe it, Sophie. He'll use anyone, manipulate anyone, twist anyone. Kill anyone. Destroy *anyone*."

"He sounds like Jane."

Bear shook his head. "I don't think so. Chris . . . it would be easier if he just didn't *care*. If it didn't hurt him, to do what he does. But he does care, and it does hurt him, and he does it anyway. It's what makes him so fucking scary, because he knows what something is going to cost and then he just pays it. He did something when we were kids that . . . God, Sophie. I'll tell you someday. He *knows* how bad he's hurting you, he *feels* it, and he *does it anyway*."

"Now," Sophie murmured, "he's starting to sound like me."

Bear looked at her, sidelong, as they jogged. He seemed to be considering his words.

"Do you know why I call you Capitana, Sophie?"

Sophie laughed. "An honorary title, as far as I can tell."

"I have stood in the councils of the Wise," Bear said, in a somber sort of voice, "and I have crossed weapons with things that we might call gods. I've followed good people that have done terrible things and terrible people that accidentally did good. I sold my soul for Silver, and spent that coin doing more damage than you could believe, in the service of causes I hate to even remember. I follow, Sophie; no, don't shake your head, I know that much truth about myself. I follow."

"Ugh, Bear, don't make this weird." Sophie tried to lighten the tone. Protestations of fealty had always made her uncomfortable. Well—these days, anyway. Since the Hot Halls War.

Bear chuckled. "Sorry. But you're worth following, Capitana, even if it's just into another bar. Mostly because you *won't* pay that price. My brother would murder his own kin to preserve his life, because he thinks that he is the only one that can accomplish his great work. You—well, you were ready to throw your life away to protect your friends from a few flying silvery balls. And you can say whatever you want to about getting your Book, but I know you want to kill those Feral Children; I know you want to save those people on the Rue."

"If there's any of them left to be saved," Sophie said, and sighed. "I'm no fucking hero, Bear, but . . . I'm glad you're along, following or not. I hope I don't get you killed."

Paradoxically, Bear grinned. "No offence, Capitana, but things that you can't even imagine have been trying to kill me for longer than you've been alive. Maybe you should worry about *your* skinny ass."

"I'm worried plenty." Sophie thought about what he said, and then it was her turn to look sidelong at him. "You know why you're a Killer, Bear?"

Bear frowned. "Dunno. It's an honorary title, near as I can tell."

"Nice. But no. I've been thinking about it, a bit, wondering why all these secrets and hidden pasts aren't bothering me as much as they should. Hell, wondering why the *fuck* I'm still letting Avie hang around."

Bear cracked a smile. "She's cute, but I'll admit to wondering about that myself."

Sophie sighed. "I think she became a Killer, at some point, without me realizing it. Or maybe she managed it tonight, when she . . . I don't know. It's hard to describe. You've seen the people around me, right? The hangers-on, the barflies, the friends-for-a-day?"

"God, yes. Thick as rats, sometimes."

"Well, it's always been like that. Always people around, looking for something, basking in the reflected warmth from the spotlight, or some nonsense like that. I could give a shit; I'll drink anybody's booze. You want to fuck the famous Sophie Vesachai, or get fucked up with her? Why not, if you're interesting enough in the moment. It's all part of it, you know?"

Bear nodded. "I know. We all know. We don't hold it against you."

"I know you don't. But people have been pushing up against me as long as I can remember, Bear, and most of them want something. Once they get it, or once they figure out that they're not going to, they fade away. Friends for a drink, a day, a fortnight, and then they're gone."

Bear looked at her as they jogged. Her smile was crooked.

"The Killers are the ones who stuck around," Sophie said, after a while. "They're the ones who don't need me to be anything but me. They're the ones I couldn't drive away."

"Sounds like what family is supposed to be," Bear said.

"Yeah. Family. And family can do some shit and get away with it, you know? I ain't saying I'm happy about Avie, or you, or Trik. I'm sure as fuck not happy about Hunker. But you're Killers. And we'll work it out. Okay?"

Bear shook his head. "I tried to cheer *you* up, Capitana, and you're trying to reassure *me*. And you wonder why we follow you around."

"Hah. Let's see how many are left at the end of *this* shit." But Sophie was smiling. "Do you know what's up with Trik, by the way?"

Bear looked guarded. "Trik?"

"Yes, *Trik,* tall girl, dark hair, you've been in love with her for half of forever?"

"Oh. Yeah, I guess I know that one."

Sophie had to laugh. "Do you know anything about her? Before she joined up with us? Any clue why she's so determined to keep my ass out of the fire?"

Bear seemed reluctant to speak. "I don't know. Really, I don't. I think she has some secrets, but I don't know what they are. If she's another coincidence, then . . . I don't fucking know. I don't know why every Twins-damned thing in my life is all coming to a head tonight."

"*Your* life," Sophie said, and chucked him in the shoulder. "Huh."

"Hey." Bear grinned. "I'm the hero in *my* story. You're just gonna have to make room, Savior of the Keep."

Sophie grinned. "Glad to, Cold-Wizard."

And for a while, they jogged companionably through the dim and abandoned passageways, thinking about the nature of plots and brothers and threads coming together, twining around an uncertain future, when they rounded a corner and ran smack dab into a big posse of Vesachai, headed by none other than Sophie's dear Uncle Liam.

THE CABAL

The Utility of Candle

"Don't trust a man who never smiles, and don't trust a man who never stops."

—ALVAREZ, 'CREATURE COMFORTS'

Five surviving members of the Cabal find themselves in the dead city atop the Mountain, the ancient home of the Cold, abandoned for hundreds of years. Now it is littered with newly demolished buildings and more than a few corpses of Mr. Turpentine's children. But that is not what three of them are looking down at; they are looking at a recently made corpse of a quite different sort of thing. All of these corpses, however, were mementos of the brief time the monsters had stayed in this city, after coming through their portal from another world.

Such are the perils of dealing with *Behemoth*.

Winter, Candle, and D'Alle stand next to the ashes of the fire, looking down at the corpse of West. Or would it be 'Mr. Vutch'? Do you keep the name you died with? Even if it is ridiculous?

None present care enough to wonder about it for very long. They look down at the corpse of the firstborn son of Hunter Fine, killed by a *stick*.

He is half-headed, golden ichor splashed across several span of old stone. Behind Winter and the surviving members of the Cabal, Mr. Turpentine hisses in rage, examining the torn corpses of his Feral Children, his tall, bladed white form jerking with passion and violence. Primary Gray visits each corpse in turn, and where there is still some life left in the things, it leaves when the beautiful, ancient boy touches it.

It is unclear whether he is offering the foul things benediction, release, or if he just likes watching them die. The three others give West's corpse a moment of silence. Their Convox—now their *Cabal*—is down a member. None of the three seem particularly unhappy about it.

"What a fucking idiot." Candle sighs, after a while, through his broken teeth. "What a perfect, indescribable idiot."

Winter chuckles. She tosses her long black hair, and her green eyes sparkle. "To think that *this* was the son of Hunter Fine."

Candle shrugs. "We are all what we choose to be, eh? And West chose to be a fool."

"Just as his brother chooses to be a thorn in my side." Winter has a snap of asperity in her voice. "Well, I've relieved him of a burden, I think. I shall await his thanks."

"You're a fool, too, if you think Charts will thank you," Candle says. "You've likely just started a war."

Winter laughs, a sparkling sound. "Can a stone fight a war with a mountain? If it does, will the mountain notice?"

Candle grins humorlessly. "I think you're going to find out."

"I will deal with Charts when the time comes," Winter says. "Though I will admit to a certain *piquant* pleasure at this turn of events. If only as a probe, our West worked wonderfully well."

"Do you call this wonderful?" Candle gestures around. "Your probe got West and a bunch of Turpentine's . . . *children* killed, pissed off two Behemoth, and sent your sword running away down the Mountain."

Winter makes a light throwing-away gesture. "I never had much hope for plan A *or* B. *Adaptability* will be the watchword of this enterprise, and think of what we now know! Mr. Turpentine's Feral Children will be unlikely to incapacitate the Behemoth. However, from watching the fight, it was plain that these Behemoth, newly come to our world, are squeamish of the things. They can be used to effectively harry them. More importantly, we now know that these Behemoth are not unwise nor easily fooled. You saw yourself how quickly they saw through West's admittedly heavy-handed overtures of friendship. At the cost of a handful of rough automata and one colossal fool, our course is much plainer."

"Are you just listening to yourself talk?" Candle asks, sourly. "Or is this for D'Alle's edification?"

"I like to think aloud," Winter says, with a fond pat on Candle's head. "Though I am beginning to regret sending my Deadsmith away, it would be interesting to see how he'd handle two Behemoth at once. I never got to see him dismantle the last one. Oh—my dear. I forgot. You were there!"

"I remember," Candle says, still looking down at West's corpse.

Winter grins. "But still! I think we have resources a-plenty to pull down two new-made monsters."

"If you say so."

D'Alle clears his throat. He is still gazing at the smashed-apart face of West, where what is left of the man's mouth is drawn down in a rictus of horror and surprise.

"I am not sure that I approve," D'Alle says, his voice high and tight, "of the, ah . . . *careless* treatment of one of our own. It does not instill confidence in this

Cabal. And reminds me of previous encounters. I'll not have anything like *that* repeated, my Lady Winter."

To this, Candle just snorts and looks back down at West's corpse with his unusual, unsettling eyes.

"I see your concern." Winter lays a hand on D'Alle's shoulder. "But please, be soothed. Lourde—West—was an old enemy of mine, and I hope you will not begrudge me some small pleasure at his passing. Yet I included him in this Cabal in good faith! It was his choices that led to this bad end, not mine."

"He was trying to turn the Behemoth against us." Candle yawns. "He figured if he had some pet monsters, what does he need old enemies for?"

"Yes," D'Alle begins, eyes fixed on Candle, "but the . . . *what you did to them.* You meddled with the man's mind, made him want to kill the girl—and it very nearly worked. That was nothing I have seen or heard of. Was this the talent you spoke of possessing? Is this what Domination does?"

"Yes, Candle." Winter's tone turns flinty. "I'm reminded! I am reminded of *failure.* Let us speak of that."

"You know there's no guarantees. I've never tried to Dominate a *Behemoth* before. It wasn't as effective as I'd hoped."

"I have seen you overwhelm strong minds," Winter says. "I cannot believe you were unable to affect two scared, uncertain people, new-come to this world and never subjected to your charms before. You stole this power from *me*, remember. I developed it. I know what it can do."

Candle scowls. "I hit him as hard as I could. He's stronger than he seems."

"So you say."

"Yes, *so I say*. And you'll have to trust me when I say it, because I'm the only fucking person in the world who can *do it*. I'm the only one who can use your Domination, Winter."

"True," Winter says, with a light sigh. "Alas, true. Just let us not forget that this very same fact is the reason—and trust me, my love, the *only* reason—you are still drawing breath."

"I'm not likely to forget," Candle says. There is a moment of relative silence, with the three of them once again staring down at the dead form of the man once called West.

"So where does this leave us?" D'Alle asks. "Our Cabal is down one member already."

"Considerably more than *one*." Candle cracks, looking over his shoulder at where Turpentine is picking his way mournfully through the corpses of the Feral Children.

"Be nice, love," Winter admonishes. "And do not provoke Mr. Turpentine. We need him. *And* his children."

"Those things are abominations," Candle says. "The world will be better when all his children are removed from it."

Winter smiles and pitches her voice low. "And does it not seem that these Behemoth are uniquely suited to that task?"

Candle sighs and replies in that same low voice. "If you must have an audience, Winter, couldn't you focus on D'Alle? I'm sure your genius will amaze *him*."

"Poor Candle. Forever bored by the crawling pace of other's minds. Yet, I may surprise you."

"You surprised me once," Candle says, and looks down at his hands and fingers, most of them broken and re-broken. His mouth twists. "Once is all you'll ever get."

Winter laughs and turns, clapping her hands and raising her voice.

"We must not lose heart, my friends! These Behemoth delay us only a little and require from us some small additional labors. They head down the Mountain, and into the teeth of the Dark; I daresay they will not care for it. Where plans fail, knowledge grows!"

"Knowledge or not," D'Alle says, "your precious, vaunted *sword* seems to be taking off into the low slopes of the Mountain. And on the backs of some unstoppable monsters. Have you a plan to retrieve it? Wasn't a portal-forged sword the entire point of this enterprise? Do we remember this, that you wish to kill the Giant Kindaedystrin? I have to say, Winter, that I am losing confidence in your plan."

Winter wrinkles her nose. "I am not overfond of plans, good Master D'Alle. Plans can go awry. I much prefer to decide what I want, and then get it. And I *want that sword*. Mr. Turpentine!"

The old automata looks up from the corpses of his children, and for a moment he looks as savage and deadly as they all know he truly is.

"I must grieve," he growls like a broken harmonica, "for my sons. And for my daughters."

Winter's voice is firm. "You must grieve later. You have many other children, my old friend, and now is the time they are needed."

Mr. Turpentine hisses, mute violence in his posture and movement, and Winter holds up a warning finger.

"My dear," she says, "do not think I've forgotten the purpose for which you created these things. I know what sort of person they were meant to bring down. Be content that I allow them to exist at all."

Turpentine looks at Winter for a long moment, and then he pushes the violence carefully out of his limbs. He straightens, slowly, and bows. "Certainly." He forces a smile onto his long white face. "I forget both myself and our great purpose. Forgive me. I spent a great deal of time and care on these children, and perhaps I have grown over-fond."

"It is nothing," Winter says, lightly. "But we must seize this chance before the Behemoth get to the bottom of the Mountain. If they pass the silver wall, we will have great difficulty in finding them again."

"How are we to find them *now?*" D'Alle asks, with a sniff.

Winter smiles. "It is very dark, Master D'Alle, and they are accompanied by a light. I think we will manage."

Candle makes a derisive sound and holds his broken finger to his chest. Winter pats his head again, the same as she'd done when she broke it.

"They will be headed toward the lights of Cannoux, the closest of the cities below the silver wall, but they will discover that there are some lights much closer. I want you to harry them, Mr. Turpentine, you and your children. I want you to drive them toward those lights, and the Door that waits beneath there. And you, Candle—"

"I know what you want me to do." Candle sounds tired. "They will not enjoy their trip. And if I can get one to kill the other, I will. Don't worry, Winter. I don't have the will to cross you on this."

"Very well," Winter says. "Master D'Alle, you will come with me. Your walking-couch is not suited to this sort of chase, and in any case, we need to speak of certain ways you can better contribute to our grand cause."

D'Alle blinked, taken aback. "Where are we going?"

Winter pointed back, toward the center of the dead city atop the Mountain. "Through a Door, Master D'Alle, so that we may control where these Behemoth go. I have an idea, you see, but I warn you already that you are *not going to like it.*"

Winter laughs, merrily, and sends the Cabal off to do its messy work.

THE DEADSMITH

The Door Into Love

*"And with a great blow, the Giant Kindaedystrin drove his fist
against the Roof of the World, for he hated all of the good works of thinking folk.
And from that hate, from that blow, the darkness spread like ink
through the sky, and doom found us all."*

—TREMENS, 'STORIES OF THE FALL'

The Deader walked through the dark woods for a long time, his weirlight casting a long shadow ahead. It made the dead white trees look like silver sculptures.

He was not surprised to see the light of a campfire ahead, and he suspected it would not be the Prey. Nothing about this would be so easy. He did not particularly care to be careful, but he was a Deadsmith, even now, even a fragment of one, and he had a job to finish. Even despite the loss of his Fate, and then his Machine, he had a task to complete. He had blood that he must return to his Lady, on his teeth. He was debilitated, but he was still her Deader. He circled the camp twice, noting every detail, and sat for a long while in the murk, watching.

When he was satisfied, he stood, worked the kinks out of his muscles, and walked into the camp.

It was a well-lit camp, throwing warm light far out into the dark forest. There were three tents and the Deader saw they had made the camp around a Well, so they had all of the food and drink they needed. There was a fire going, but most of the light was provided by twist-lamps, glowing bronze rods of fine make. He saw no other Old Gold, no other weapons, but he still did not trust himself to see such things. That had ever been his Fate's job, and that useless third of him was wailing, impotent and terrified, in the back of his head.

He would have to do his best, on his own. He guessed it would be that way from now on, and he felt a faltering weight of sadness cloak itself around him. He guessed that sadness, too, would be there from now on.

There were three figures around the fire, and they watched him approach. They made no move toward weapons, and seemed to be holding none. A pot of *chûs* sat smoking on the fire, as if he'd been expected.

But, of course he had been.

He said nothing as he came up to the fire, and neither did the three women. The smallest, a girl of perhaps ten or twelve, fidgeted but did not speak. The Deader made sure there were no hidden caches of weapons near the fire and then sat, carefully, and placed his palms on his knees. He examined the women.

They were all fair, all dark-haired, all lovely. The youngest and oldest held the light of madness or glamour in their eyes, but the middle one looked at him, sober. She was just out of her youth, still young-looking, but the Deader saw a depth in her eyes that made her seem older. The oldest woman was just this side of middle age and looked so much like his Lady that he suspected surgery or magic had made her so. She smiled at him, lasciviously, her eyes clouded with the Prey's domination.

"He says," the middle one spoke, the sane one, "to say hello."

The Deader coughed into his hand, spat into the fire, and waited.

"Do you remember me?" the youngest asked, with a wide smile. She looked as if she were dreaming. "Do you remember?"

"I remember," the Deader said.

"Oh, *good*." The girl sighed. "He'll be pleased."

"How do you make a machine, Deadsmith?" the oldest woman asked. The Prey had somehow imbued her with some of his Lady's mannerisms. She giggled. "How do you *un*-make a machine?"

The Deader said nothing.

The young woman in the middle, the sane one, sighed and waited.

The older woman giggled again. "We are *all* made things, Deadsmith, casings that run mechanisms of thought. You are no different."

"Do you speak his words to me, woman?" the Deader asked. With her dark hair and green eyes, she was hard to look at. But the other two were hardly easier. The youngest grinned at him like a rabid thing.

"The thing is," the youngest said, "once you know how a machine is *made*, then you also know the secret of its *un*-making." She tittered, too. The sound was unsettling.

"He means to un-make *you*, Deadsmith." The older woman's smile was mad. "And yet it is *you* who pursues! If you merely stopped your pursuit, there would be no need for you to be pulled apart."

The Deader spat again, his comment on the quality of the discourse. He looked at the young woman in the center, the sane one. She had short-cropped hair, dark, and the Deader saw it had been dyed black. The better to fit the part, he supposed.

"I guess you have a message for me," he said finally.

The young woman's mouth twisted. "In a manner of speaking."

"Tell me. I grow weary of your companions."

Her mouth quirked. "As do I, Deadsmith. As do I. We have been waiting for you for a long time, and they do like to repeat themselves."

The young girl giggled. "A woman is a machine for making more women. And sometimes those women make men!"

"A man is a machine for making death!" the older woman crowed.

The Deader refused to look at her. He kept his gaze on the woman in the middle, the one with the clear eyes. "Tell me."

"There is a Door," she said, "a few leagues away. He has scrambled the co-ordinates. You will not be able to follow."

"I'll be able to follow."

But the young woman in the middle shook her head. "No, you will not. He has gone somewhere of which you know nothing. He has walked through a Door that is unknown to you and into a place beyond your reach. Unless I tell you the coordinates and their order, Deadsmith, you'll not catch his trail. You will never find him."

The Deader smiled, with no humor. "I will find him."

The sane girl smiled, conceding the point. "Well, perhaps. But not soon. And not until he leaves that place and concludes his business there. I will be long gone to gray before you find him again. This is truth."

The Deader shrugged. "Still."

"You are in pieces, Deadsmith!" the older woman pronounced, throwing her hands into the air. "They will be picked up as easily as stones to the hand!"

"Can you shut them up?" he asked, ignoring the older woman and the young girl, looking only at the young woman in the middle.

She shook her head. "They are here for a purpose, as am I."

"I may stop them myself."

"You are Deadsmith. That is your prerogative. It will serve his purposes as well."

The Deader smiled. It was ghastly. "He is a hard man, your master."

"He has great plans. He must be. And in any case, he is not my master."

"You serve him."

"I am doing him a favor," she said, and then sighed sharply. "Go on, make the threat so I can set it aside."

"I can get the coordinates from you," the Deader said.

The young woman cocked her head. "Can you? I wonder. But I would rather not find out how much human is left in you, Deadsmith. In any case, we each hold only a piece of that puzzle, and these will not give theirs up until I say."

"I can make you say."

The middle woman made a shooing gesture. "Enough. Do it or don't. I bar your way; find your path through me."

The Deader studied her for a long time, and she bore his scrutiny well. She was frightened, but she bore it.

"You love him," he said.

She smiled, and her relief was obvious. "Very good, Deadsmith! How can I not? He is the greatest man I have ever known."

"He is a dead man. You misplace your affections."

She offered a crooked smile. "Isn't that what affections are for? To be misplaced?"

The Deader considered his answer. "I would not know."

"Love," the young girl said, tittering, "is the greatest machine of all!"

"It builds itself unasked." The older woman leaned forward, as if confiding a great secret. "And destroys those who ride!"

"Come, Deadsmith," the middle woman said, extending her arms to include her companions. "You have known love. You know it still."

The Deader looked down and contemplated his hands. He looked back up at the young woman and hoped he would not have to kill her. "Tell me your test," he said.

She smiled. "You are in the midst of it."

"Why would the Prey allow me to continue this hunt?"

The young woman clapped a hand to her mouth, stifling a laugh. "The *Prey . . . ?* Is that how you see him? Deadsmith, you are a very great fool if you believe that."

"What does he want?" He was weary with speaking to these hauntings, these ghosts from another life.

"You, in his pocket!" the older woman cackled.

"An end to darkness!" the young girl wailed.

"He wants you off his trail," the young woman said evenly. "But if you will not leave him be, he will be satisfied with your destruction."

"I am not so easily destroyed."

She laughed again, incredulous, gesturing around at herself, her companions, the campsite. Her hand seemed to encompass the long trail behind the Deader, the madman cackling about the Death-King, the trap under the Barrier Mountains, the entire city glamoured against him. "Do you imagine that any of this was *easy?*"

The Deader had no answer for that.

She cocked her head again, looking at him. "I have a question. If you are willing to answer."

"Ask," the Deader said, "and I will decide."

"Who am I?" she asked, curious. She indicated the child, and then the older woman. "I know who that is—a simulacrum of your sister. And I certainly know that this is supposed to be your Lady. But I do not know who I am supposed to be."

The Deader looked at her for a long time and then looked down. Even as he answered, he did not know why. "The first girl I loved," he said, slowly. "Her name was Anise."

"Ah." She watched him, waiting until he raised his eyes to her. Then she lifted an eyebrow. "It's all a bit clumsy, don't you think?" she asked. "Manipulating a man by hurting the women around him? It's just so . . . *obvious*."

The Deader jerked. His mouth became hard. "Give me your test."

"But you have passed it," the young woman in the middle said, with a sigh. "There is still a man inside you, and so you will be permitted to try your teeth on the one I love."

The Deader narrowed his eyes. "He does not love you."

She laughed again, clapping her hand over her mouth, as if delighted by his folly. "Oh, Deadsmith! Of course not. For a ship steered wholly by love, you know very little of it."

"I have duty, not love." He stood. "Tell me the coordinates."

The older woman, the one who looked so like his Lady, cackled. "Lies are the greatest machinery of all! We build and build, until we are hollow!"

"Enough," the Deader said, and the young woman in the middle nodded. She told him a symbol and then touched the child's arm. She, in turn, gave him two, and then the older woman two more. The Deader committed them to memory.

"Well, Deadsmith," the young woman said, and the Deader saw real fear in her. "Will you kill us now?"

The Deader considered. He studied all three of the women: his sister, his lover, his Lady.

"I hope you live long lives," he said finally, "and never see me or the man that calls himself Candle ever again."

He walked into the forest, towards the Door that he could sense some leagues away. His Fate groaned and sent confusing scents and colors, but the Deader ignored it. When he came upon the Door, standing on its daïs in the middle of the dead forest, he did not hesitate. He used the coordinates given him by the three women and then opened the Door. For a long moment he stood, dumbfounded, something warm pressing against his face. The Door threw brilliance at him, washing the dead trees around him with warmth, for a moment resurrecting this forest into something alive. The Door seemed to tremble with the power of what shone through.

Sunshine, rich and golden and bright, flooded out of it.

———

It took a while for the Deader's eyes to adjust to the sun; it had been many lifetimes since he'd seen it. The great hoop was high in the sky, and the silver Rings shone brilliantly even in the deep blue of the unmarred, open expanse.

The Deader had forgotten how beautiful it was.

When his eyes adjusted and he could see, he stood before the Door—still had not stepped through, still in the dark woods—and examined the place where the Prey meant to lead him. He could see a bit of it, through the path in the trees. It was gray and green, rocky and vertiginous. The Door stood high in a folding ravine that fell away, littered with large tumbled rocks and falling water.

Down where the big ravine curved, or opened onto another, he saw the gray-green of steep hillside and a small valley. There was something in that valley, something white-gray, and the Deader set his hand on the doorframe and focused his remarkable eyes.

The white figure swam closer. It was sitting hunched over, head and back bowed, hands held before it in a pose of hopelessness and loss. Nearby trees gave the Deader a sense of scale; the figure was massive. It was a Giant, gone to stone, frozen in its last hopeless pose.

There was a flickering in the shadow of the Giant, a fire. The Deader focused as far as his eyes could and saw it was a campfire, and saw there was a man sitting at it. As if sensing the Deader's gaze, he looked up.

The Deader had the impression of a thin but commanding face, hard-used, and with strange eyes. It was the Prey. It was the man who called himself Candle. His hard slash of a mouth spread into the smeared impression of a grin, and he waved at the Deader.

The Deader took a step back from the Door, thinking, looking at the rectangle of beautiful light hanging in the dark wood. Candle was only a speck in that frame and yet somehow the Deader could see his smile, hear his laughter. Sense the trap that lay waiting.

How do you make a machine?

He closed the Door, shutting off the flood of bright sunlight. Shutting off the way to Forest. It was all right; he had the coordinates for it, now. He could find Forest, and the Prey, anytime he wanted, from any Door in the Wanderlands. But he didn't want to go to Forest just now.

He studied the Door, the gray wood. After the exposure to the sunshine, the dead forest seemed even darker to him. He nodded. No, he wasn't going to follow the Prey this time. Not quite yet. He needed to go somewhere else first.

He spun the concentric dials around the silver doorknob. He changed the coordinates to something familiar, a destination he knew well, and then he opened the Door again. A different kind of light shone out of it then, different but no less bright—the brilliance of the White Tower.

The Deader walked again through the Door, going home.

THE LOST BOYS

The Wizard Behemoth

"There are old things in the hidden halls, child. Strange things in the deep.
There are savage creatures in the far rooms, and some of them have claws.
But hold fast, and do not fear, for they deplore the taste of innocence."

—APOCRYPHAL, 'THE TALE OF THE TIN-EYE AND THE JANNISSARY'

Chris had killed Buckle. He had torn her slender golden mindspring apart with his fingers. Chris had killed Buckle, yet something was keeping James from killing his brother, something hard and immovable. Something that had him by the neck. He screamed, trying to get at Chris, and his whole world became a narrow tunnel of red with his brother's murdering hands at the other end of it.

His brother had killed his only friend.

The man that Winter had called a Deadsmith caught Chris from behind. Buckle's tiny, broken body fell from Chris' hands.

"I know you think that was clever, boy," the Deadsmith said in a flat voice, "but I've killed many clever men."

"Stop," Winter commanded, speaking to the Deadsmith, and James felt her hand on his neck tighten, and he couldn't move at all. He thought his neck might be breaking; the pain was overwhelming. He didn't care. "Don't kill him—yet. He did that for a reason, and I want to find out what it was. Was this your doing, D'Alle?"

"I swear not." Master D'Alle sounded terrified. "I know nothing about why he did that, or what purpose she served. I *swear*."

Winter eased up a tiny bit on James' neck. Her fingers were inhuman, far stronger than any steel James had ever felt. He gasped a little air into his lungs.

"As my Deadsmith says, I'm sure it was something clever." Winter looked at where Chris was dangling in the Deadsmith's grip. The corner of her mouth turned up. "Let him go. My gods, what an interesting lad we've found, and in this dreadful backwater! If you hadn't had the bad grace to get mixed up in Cold business, boy, I might have kept you for a pet. You are almost amusing."

Released by the dangerous-looking Deadsmith, Chris dropped to the ground.

But the Deadsmith stayed close. Chris shook his head, eyes brimming with tears. He reached for James.

"I'm sorry, James. It's all I could think to do."

James started scrabbling for his brother again, red rage thick in his throat, but Winter renewed her grip.

"And what *is* it that you did, boy?" Winter asked, looking at Chris curiously. Her easy, amused manner was back. But Chris didn't answer. Winter turned to D'Alle.

"Who made the automata? It is high-stage Dirt-Magic, and I'm getting curious about its provenance. No evasion, D'Alle, my patience with you has run out."

"I can't say for sure," D'Alle said, eyeing the Deadsmith, "but it was likely the dirt-wizard. He lives at the low-slope edge of the city and teaches the Doctrine of Dirt. He makes some constructs, and he tutors the boys."

"Well." Winter sighed. "I daresay we're about to meet this dirt-wizard; the better ones maintain a bond with their high-stage creations. As if we didn't have enough killing today. You know what we *are*, D'Alle, yes? You know that such . . . *transgressions* aren't tolerated by my organization? That the Dirt-Magic is forbidden?"

"Of course," D'Alle said, nervous. "We practice only so much twistcraft as we need to survive in this city, my Lady, and this man is an outlier, a harmless crank—"

"If he can make such constructs," Winter gestured toward the broken bronze and gold body of Buckle, "and if he can teach enough craft to help a *child* break out of your storeroom, then he's not a harmless crank."

D'Alle closed his mouth and nodded.

"Beware the council of the Wise," Winter quoted softly, "for they are quick to judge and uncaring of the cost."

She let James drop to the floor and pointed down at him. "If you move, boy, you'll die. Understood?"

But James was half paralyzed, and he could only lay on the floor for a minute, trying to feel his body. Buckle's little forlorn body lay a few span away, twisted and broken into a shape almost unrecognizable. James felt hot, shameful tears starting up in his eyes. Beyond the broken little body of his friend were the dark, guilty eyes of his brother.

There was a big sound, then, a massive sound like one of the great boulders thrown by the Giant slamming into the ground. The floor underneath James trembled.

"Oh, my!" Winter clapped her hands, surprised and delighted. "The plot thickens!"

There was another of those huge blows, and dust rained down from the high ceiling. There was a creaking, tearing sound, muffled but massive. D'Alle made a sharp gesture to the nearby guards, telling them to stay put. James was able to push himself up on one elbow and cough. He felt as if his neckbones had been ripped out and then replaced with crushed glass.

"James," Chris said in a hoarse whisper. "Get ready." But James only snarled in return. His brother had killed Buckle; he would never listen to anything he said, ever again. A heavy tread filled the hallway outside the chamber, and then something immensely strong ripped the heavy doors free and threw them to the side.

The man James had always called Uncle strode into the room, so furious that he was almost unrecognizable.

Winter's face was a study of surprise and pleasure, recognizing him immediately. "*Alvarez*! Can it be?"

But Uncle was in no mood for pleasantries. He pointed at Winter, one blunt finger stabbing at her face.

"I'll deal with *you* in a moment. Where is that Twins-damned boy?"

Uncle strode past the Deadsmith, barely acknowledging him, and stopped when he saw James and Chris, the broken body of Buckle laying between them. James looked up at Uncle, his eyes full of tears. He still couldn't seem to get strength into his legs, to stand up. Uncle's mouth was a thin grim line. He looked back and forth between James and Chris, understanding what had happened, and shook his head in disgust.

"Cousin," Winter said, amused, but Uncle turned and gave her the sternest look James had ever seen, and she held her hands up as if to say, 'Fine, fine; I'll wait.'

Uncle gathered up the tiny broken body gently, looked at Buckle for a long moment, and put her corpse away in his pack. He waited until Chris raised his dark eyes to his.

"You killed an innocent creature to save your life." Uncle's voice was very low and very grave. "Don't *ever* call it anything else."

Chris opened his mouth, but Uncle stuck his finger in Chris' face. Then Uncle's facial expression became savage. "One word of excuse out of you," he promised, "one word of justification, and I'll kill you myself, boy, right now. I swear it."

Chris swallowed and looked down. He nodded.

Uncle took in a deep breath and stood. He looked at James for a long moment, his face inscrutable, then shifted his gaze to Winter. "All right." His voice was rough, but with a trace of politeness now. "Hello, Winter. It's been a long time."

Winter smiled warmly. "It has been an *age*. How are you, Alvarez?"

"I've been better." He cracked his neck and sighed. "Seem to have half-adopted some boys with a strong talent for trouble."

"You always did collect that sort, if I remember rightly," Winter said. "I don't know that the word trouble quite covers what these boys have found, though."

"If you're involved, then no, I don't suppose it does." Uncle glanced down at

James again. "I'm guessing that you'll not trust me to deliver a stern lecture on the importance of keeping secret things secret, extract some promises, and leave it at that?"

"Oh, now," Winter said, drumming her fingers on the edge of the couch, "I can't see that resolving the issue. I'm surprised you'd even mention it!"

"I'm getting foolish in my old age."

"But I don't see any reason why we can't part friends," Winter said. "And I'll admit I had some ideas about putting a curb on your renegade religion while I was here. Master D'Alle referred to you as a harmless old crank—can you imagine? The most famous Behemoth in two ages of the Wanderlands, a *harmless old crank*. I suppose I can let those sleeping dogs lie around a bit longer."

Uncle smiled slightly. "You are too kind. I'll admit, I wish I was better known for my philosophy than my provenance; though I suppose none of us get to pick our reputation."

"Not even me." Winter smiled and showed her teeth. James was able to move his limbs now, for the most part. He worked himself up to one knee. He had one thought, now, and one goal: *the Cold-Key*. It was sitting right there, next to Winter. He felt calm. He just had to get his hands on the silver amulet, and then he would kill them all.

All of them. Maybe even Uncle, if he tried to stop him. James didn't care about anything anymore.

With another sigh, Uncle took something small and golden from his side-carry—a rod of patterned, high-stage twistcraft. "Still," he said, "the Mother calls, and her true servants must listen."

Winter laughed as Uncle tossed the golden device to Chris, but he fumbled and dropped it. It clattered on the fine porcelain tiles of Master's receiving-room, and Chris looked at it but didn't move. Winter crossed her arms, watching, a faint smile playing at the edges of her lips.

"If you touch that thing, boy," she said lightly, "we will hunt you through every Land that still bears light, and never stop until your blood is on our teeth. Do you understand? Touch it, and every hope you ever had is lost. We will put Deadsmith on your trail, and your life will be as worthless as the next gust of wind."

"Don't worry," Uncle said, "she's told me the same thing, and more than once. Take your brother and the girl, boy. Don't look back."

"I won't." Chris picked up the rod.

Winter chuckled as Uncle stepped toward her. He nudged James with his elbow, who had made his way unsteadily to his feet. "Get to your brother, lad."

But Chris came to James instead, and Katherine followed.

Winter picked up the amulet, the Cold-Key, and swung it coyly from her smallest finger.

Uncle held out his hand to her, palm up. "Much as I hate to be the easy way out for these little bastards," he said, "I'm going to need that. In for a shim, in for a heavy, and all that."

"Your 'Mother' is insane." Winter was still smiling. "And she is going to bury us all in darkness. You misplace your affections."

Uncle grunted. "Still, I like to stick to a plan of action once I've chosen it. It's this or a fight, I'm afraid."

Winter cocked her head, looking at him. "You've avoided that fight for two ages of the world, Alvarez. And you'd face me, now? Over two pissant boys?"

"I could give a slow shit about these two fucking boys. But the Mother is calling, Winter. You know what that means. And if she called these two, then I mean to let them follow."

"Even if it means an ignominious end to a very long life?"

"I don't think it'll come to that," Uncle said. "I don't think you'll kill me, and I don't think you could even if you tried."

"Oh," Winter said, with a quick little laugh, "I won't try. I tend to think I could . . . However, I might be wrong. And I am *not* ready for an ignominious end to a very long life, so I won't roll those particular dice today."

She let the Cold-Key drop into Uncle's big palm. She looked at the three children huddled together; Chris was gripping the golden thing Uncle had tossed to him.

"I will see you three again," she said. It was a promise and a threat from the woman who James would, in later years, come to understand was maybe the most powerful person in the entire world. She looked back up at Uncle. "But perhaps not you. Goodbye, Alvarez."

And she disappeared in a twisting shower of golden sparks. Uncle stood watching the place where she'd been for a long moment, and then turned. He, too, studied the three children, and the silver Cold-Key in his hand.

"I sure hope the Mother knows what she's doing," he muttered, and tossed the silver amulet to Katherine, who caught it with a startled yelp. He looked up at the Deadsmith with a crooked smile, and flexed his big hands. "So it's to be you and me, eh?"

"Looks like." The Deadsmith seemed calm.

"Always wondered if I could kill a Deadsmith," Uncle said. "Guess today's the day I find out. Chris, James. It's been nice knowing you. *Get the fuck out of here.*"

James opened his mouth to say something, but his brother grabbed his wrist, tight, and the world disappeared in another shower of golden sparks. James was picked up and thrown out of the world like a stone thrown by a Giant.

THE KILLERS

Conflict Resolution

"As long as there are people, lad, they will build and populate their own hells. And all the while sing of heaven."

—GEORGES TAI, 'THE COLD AND THE DEAD'

"Well *fuck me*," Sophie said, after skidding to a stop. She had to laugh. Of course. Of course she would run into her fucking family again tonight. Why not? For his part, Liam did not look surprised. It was plain he had posted himself and this gaggle of cousins here, just in case she tried something like this. There was no running, either; the Vesachai were waiting in a close passageway, closely-fitted stone veneer on both sides, and blocked the only way into where the vault was located.

"Sophie," Bear said in a low voice, "what's the play here?"

"Nothing. They will cut you into tiny pieces. Let me handle this."

Sophie approached Liam and the rest of the Vesachai, warily. They all looked tense, scared, ready for violence. Liam smoothed his expression with a visible effort and watched Sophie walk up. His eyes cut down to her wrists and she saw him wince. He knew what the livid scars there meant.

"Hello, Uncle," she said. She heard some grumbling from the Vesachai behind him, but he stilled them with a quick turn of his head and a sharp gesture. He turned back to Sophie. "Hello, Sophie," he said. "You didn't take my advice."

Sophie frowned. "Advice?"

"To go home."

Sophie sighed. "No, Uncle, I didn't. The night had other ideas."

"I'm sorry to hear that. What brings you here, Sophie?"

"I think you know."

"What an evil night." He closed his eyes. "Your poor father."

"That can wait. There's something you need to know."

"I know I see red on your arms, Sophie." Someone behind Liam whispered something, and he lifted a hand, calling for silence. He focused on his niece and took a moment to compose himself. He set his hand on the silvery Rapine at his belt. "I know your father will see both of his children die tonight."

"Uncle." Sophie tried to keep her voice steady. "There are more important things. Lee . . . he sent the Rue de Paladia dark. *Dark.* And he locked the doors at either end. He trapped hundreds of people in there."

"Sophie . . ."

"*He let the Feral Children in.* There is some light from the braziers, but they will only last so long, and then those things will own the Rue de Paladia. The heart of the Keep, overrun by monsters."

Liam took the shock well, but his face lost some color, and he closed his eyes again. "There are Feral Children in the Rue?" he asked, clearly pained.

"Yes," Sophie said. "Uncle, *please.* Before they scatter, before they find more places in the Keep and kill more Citizens, you could stop them."

His eyes opened then narrowed, meeting hers. The Vesachai behind him had their Rapine out and were looking at Sophie as if she were a Feral Child herself.

"You have twelve full Vesachai here," Sophie pleaded. "You—all together— could kill those things. You could save hundreds of lives."

Liam was shaking his head, but Sophie pressed on.

"You could put out a call, get more of the family, you could . . ."

Liam squared his shoulders. "No."

"Uncle," she tried, one last time, "you could save people!"

"No," he said. "No, Sophie. You cannot redeem yourself that way, and this is out of my hands. You must come with me, to stand trial before your father. Alive . . . or dead."

"Your duty is to the Keep. What are the Vesachai for, if not to protect it?"

"My duty is clear, and I have avoided it too long." Uncle Liam took a deep breath and pulled his Rapine free of his belt. "I am sorry, my niece."

She felt Bear reaching for his knife and threw out a hand to stop him.

"What duty?" Sophie cried. "What commands? To kill me, capture me? To kill my fucking brother? Kill us *later,* if we're not dead already. What the fuck does it matter? *There are thousands of people who will be hunted in the Dark.* The Vesachai are sworn to fight and protect!"

But instead of swaying him, her words were hardening him. He shook his head. "You do not understand our duty, Sophie. You never have. There are always those being hunted in the dark, there always have been. We must follow our code, and contain the greater threat. Which is *you,* Sophie, I am so sorry to say."

Sophie looked down at her hands, the scars at her wrists. They still hurt. She muttered something under her breath, something about inevitability.

"If you wish to say your last words," Liam said, with funereal finality, "you must say them louder. You might wish to say goodbye to your friend; of course we will not hurt him, unless he fights."

"Oh, he's gonna fight." Bear slid his long knife free.

"No, you're not," Sophie said. She looked up at her Uncle, the one who had nursed her back to health in the Dark when she had been a scared little girl, who had betrayed his oaths once already to protect her. Who was willing to order her death, for the crime of trying to fight for her home. She was done with this bullshit. A single sob escaped her, hard, painful, like coughing up a stone.

"*Fuck you*, then. You fucking *hypocrites*. You, my father, all of you. Hypocrites!"

She started rolling up her sleeves; no need to ruin a second jacket. She luxuriated in the anger; after the long night of fear and running, it felt good. The Vesachai behind Liam took a step back.

"To think I spent all of these years angry. Cowering. Ashamed. You weren't fucking *worth it*."

"Sophie . . ." Liam began, watching her roll up her sleeves, growing alarmed.

"Capitana," Bear said, putting his hand on her shoulder, "I don't think . . . Is there another way in, maybe?"

"I don't care. These motherfuckers have finally managed to *piss me off*." She met her uncle's eye. "Get the fuck out of my way, Liam."

He shook his head, his gray eyes filled with pain—whether for her or himself, it was hard to say. "Sophie. Please. Please don't do this."

"Last chance," Sophie said, looking at several Vesachai behind Liam. They looked frightened, but not frightened enough to run. Most of them were too young to remember the Hot Halls War. They didn't know what she could do. "Let us pass."

Liam's jaws tightened. "I will not."

"Then *fuck you*," Sophie said, setting her mind *an-tet*. It was easier, this time. She breathed in a certain way that she'd never been able to properly describe; then her arms flared alight with coruscating patterns of silver fire, brilliant and painful. The wirework that had been wrapped around her bones by Saint Station burned with a clean cold, so frigid it was hot. She clenched her fists, feeling the power flood through her, searing and delicious.

Her uncle, horrified, staggered back and was looking at her with wide eyes. Despite nursing her back to health, despite what he knew of the Hot Halls War, Liam had never seen this particular magic in action before. It said something about his biases and his bone-deep beliefs, that he reacted so badly to a bit of silver fire floating around her arms.

The Vesachai behind him were shocked as well, but they tightened their grips on their silver Rapine and rushed at her. Sophie, however, didn't need to fear anything made of *silver*.

She made a sideways, clutching gesture, and the long silver knives ripped themselves free of the Vesachai's hands and embedded themselves in the stone wall.

All except the one that was in Liam Vesachai's hand. Several of the Vesachai behind him cried out in surprise and pain—one had been cut on the hand and others had broken fingers. One of the ones nearest to the wall tried to pull the Rapine free, but it would take a lot more than strength. Sophie had fused the silver in them with the laid wirework inside the walls. They were effectively destroyed; but hadn't it always been easier to destroy than repair?

"All right, Uncle," Sophie said, holding up her hands, wreathed in silver fire. She had deliberately left Liam his Rapine. "Let's see how strong your duty is. If you truly believe I'm a *abomination*, then put your knife in my heart yourself."

"Sophie—" Bear said, but she cut him off.

"Interfere and I'll break your arm, Bear." She spoke without breaking eye contact with Liam. "I have nothing to fear from my uncle. He needs to discover that."

Liam's face was hideous to look at, but Sophie didn't drop her gaze.

"Well?" she asked softly. "Do you have the courage of your convictions, Uncle?"

Liam's face was momentarily savage, and he took two strides toward her. She held her hands out to keep Bear from protecting her. Liam held up his Rapine, activated and buzzing softly. His features were a rictus of pain. He raised the knife farther, and the tip began to tremble. Tears stood in his eyes.

Slowly, he lowered the knife. He laughed, like a broken instrument. He shook his shaggy head, and heaved a desolate sigh, looking at the silver knife in his hand. When he looked back at Sophie, his eyes were calmer but very sad.

"Ah, Soapy," he said, eyes crinkling a little. "Little Soap-Stone. You know me too well. No, I don't have the courage of my convictions. It was always my brother that had those. I'm just an old man, and he is full of regrets."

The silver knife fell from his hands, and he looked at her. "Will you kill us now?"

"Sure," Bear growled, but Sophie cut him off with a flat swipe of her hand. She looked up at her once-beloved Uncle. She shook her head, disgusted with them both.

"Will you kill us?" he repeated.

"Not if you're gone in ten seconds." She closed her eyes and let the last remnants of her family trickle past, disappearing by degrees into the dimness back the way she'd come.

God, her arms hurt. She'd forgotten how much this all *hurt*.

———

Bear did not seem to share Sophie's somber tone; he was effusive and animated. He had scooped up Liam's Rapine from where her uncle had dropped it and then bonded with the weapon in a way that was borderline terrifying.

"*This* thing," he said, slashing the air with it. "Holy shit! This thing is *great!*"

"It's just a knife, unless you've got the technique to use it properly," Sophie said, distracted.

Bear just grinned. "These things are wasted on your family. Watch *this*."

He activated the Rapine—which he should not have known how to do—and then used it in a way that Sophie had never seen anyone use it. It smeared trails of silver, and Bear flashed it in a blurring set of motions that cut deep, almost glassy scars in the stone around them. Sophie blinked; she had never seen anyone do *that* with a Rapine.

Bear laughed in satisfaction and flipped it around in a practiced smack against his palm. It went inert, just plain silver now. "Oh, yeah, my lovely little thing. We are going to have some fun together. Sophie, I never had any idea what these things could do! I would have stolen one years ago."

"Then the Vesachai would have hunted you down and killed you," she said. Her eyes were welling with tears, and she tried to push them away. The look on her uncle's face . . .

"Not if I had one of these. Twins damn! Even if you can't get that vault open, I'll be able to do some *damage* with this knife. It's going to break Trik's heart; I have a new love in my life."

"I'll be able to get the vault open," Sophie said. She tried to focus. "How do you know how to use that?"

"It's one of the tools of the Cold, right? The Key, the Rapine, and the Coin? Well, I trained with the Key for a long time. When I was a teenager. Some of the skills transfer, apparently. I mean, this thing is nowhere near as powerful as the Key, obviously, but still. I can fuck some motherfuckers *up*."

"Good."

They crawled through a long-ago-broken barrier of old metal panels and across the rubble of a partially collapsed stone wall; she vividly recalled climbing through it with Crazy Tom, Ben right behind her, so long ago. The barrier opened on a small alcove, and she remembered well that it would take a turn into the domed room that held the vault. She still remembered the code, the combination to the vault, the one that had been shown to her in a dream. She would have wagered strong money that she was the only person in the Keep who knew that code, which is why she'd hidden the Key there in the first place.

She saw it before Bear did, and stood there staring for long enough that he almost knocked her over as he climbed out of the ancient rubble. Even after a long night of impossible things, she genuinely could not believe what she was looking at.

"What the . . . ?"

Bear saw what she was looking at and he, too, fell silent. When he spoke, his voice was almost frightened. "Sophie, what in the fuck could have done *that*?"

It was a good question. Because the silver vault, a relic of the greatest age of the Wanderlands and absolutely impregnable by any force or weapon known to thinking creatures, had been ripped open. The silver it was made of stretched and battered, torn apart as if it had been made of shiny paper.

The Key, of course, was gone.

THE CABAL

The Utility of D'Alle

"I will confront the horrors of the Dark long before I face the horrors of the heart. All the Dark can do is kill me."

—TENDA ANTWE, 'SACRIFICIAL HANDS'

The Cabal is on hard times; their plans in disarray, thrown into chaos by two willful Behemoth. Now they stand at the gates of Cannoux, which have been demolished by those same Behemoth, apparently because they wanted *a meal*.

Master D'Alle cannot speak for long moments, staring at the wreckage of the city's gate, Cannoux's city gate, at the shattered pieces of the twistcraft war-suits beyond. Even Candle is quiet, looking at the broken beam and gates, span-thick and taller than five men.

Cannoux's war power had been gutted by the two Behemoth, its twistcraft strongsuits and mighty gates destroyed because the two monsters wanted a steak. If the Wanderlands ever needed another object lesson in the danger Behemoth posed, it had it.

The Cabal had reunited—or most of them had, anyway—outside of the ruined gates of Cannoux. Mr. Turpentine's Feral Children had harried the Behemoth down the slope of the Mountain, and Candle had harried their minds, herding them towards the Door that waited there. Winter and Master D'Alle had arrived there first, setting the coordinates of the Door to open on the catacombs deep beneath Cannoux, and leaving a helpful Coin to allow the Behemoth to gain passage.

The idea had been to trap them in those catacombs while Master D'Alle roused his city's military power and crushed them between the forces of Cannoux and the small army of Feral Children Mr. Turpentine had raised. In the close confines of the Catacombs, this plan might have had a chance. But then the two monsters had, on a whim, decided that instead of going through the Door, they would murder nearly all of the Feral Children. And then, after they'd gone through the Door anyway, they murdered the *Door*.

"These Behemoth," Winter says, with a light sigh, "are determined to be a trial, aren't they?"

D'Alle had accepted a report from a frightened soldier, whose eyes darted from Winter to Candle to D'Alle. Mr. Turpentine had been sent to gather more of his children, and so the gentle-souled inhabitants of dear Cannoux-Town would not have to be further discomfited by the sight of a six-span-high killing machine and his awful children.

"And the strongsuits?" Master D'Alle asks quietly, glancing at the wrecked harness of crude stage-two twistcraft that is lying against the door. Each of those destroyed strongsuits represented years and years of craft and work by a not-insignificant section of Cannoux's economy. The frightened soldier swallows, glances again at Winter and Candle, and shakes his head. D'Alle takes a moment to appreciate how badly he has been fucked by the two Behemoth and addresses the soldier.

"Very well," he says heavily, his *cantrait* dancing sideways, telegraphing his mood. "I am sure the Lords Council will wish to speak to me of this; have a session convened if one is not already gathered."

The soldier bows sharply at the waist, and gives Candle and Winter one last frightened, speculative look before he backs away through the wreckage of the gate. Primary Gray wanders around behind the three of them, looking at everything with his ancient, disinterested eyes. D'Alle seems to spend an inordinate amount of time collecting himself, or perhaps finding words and courage before he turns the *cantrait* towards Winter.

"I have the growing sense," he says, finally, "that neither myself nor my city will profit over-much from this *Cabal*."

"Profits," Winter flicks some dust from her sleeve, "come to those with patience. My friend! Do not lose heart, your city still has much to offer. For one, a way into the Underlands that bypasses that damnable silver wall. And this misadventure was not to any plan of mine, certainly! Who could have foreseen that the Behemoth would destroy a *Door*? Even now it is simply incredible to consider."

"You sent them into *my* city." D'Alle speaks through gritted teeth.

"Please." Winter seems amused. "I sent them to the warren *under* your city; if they had not destroyed that Door, we could have caught them between hammer and anvil. In any case I cannot imagine how they found their way out of that maze so quickly. Can you?"

D'Alle looks away. "I thought that path might be useful. I never intended . . . I should have scrubbed the damned red paint from the walls."

"You never thought something would come through that Door from the other way, I know," Winter says. "You forgot who left the paint there in the first place. Those troublesome children, so long ago, that gave us such an interesting afternoon. Though you certainly should have remembered—you're standing next to one of them."

Candle has no comment. If he is recalling that dreadful afternoon in D'Alle's parlor, when he murdered his brother's tiny friend to save his own life, it cannot be seen on his face. Perhaps he can no longer truly remember what it was like to be Chris D'Essan; perhaps by taking the name 'Candle,' he had wiped his early life away.

There is pain in his eyes, though. And certainly Master D'Alle remembers. His *cantrait* dances in agitation again. Due to what he remembers as Chris D'Essan's plots and plans, half of his city had been destroyed by the titanic battle between the Behemoth-Philosopher Alvarez and Winter's pet Deadsmith. He glares murder at the man who now calls himself Candle.

Winter pats D'Alle on his shoulder. "My point is that plans go awry as plans do, and we must all shoulder some small amount of blame. I shall certainly not underestimate these Behemoth again. They are proving excellent at being a pain in my ass."

"They seem to be the ruin of you," D'Alle says curtly, "as they are the ruin of *me*. How do you think to bring them down? They destroyed every warmachine in my city simply so they could *sit down to a meal*. Twice. First, when your pet Deadsmith and that damned Alvarez half-destroyed my city in their battle, and now with these Behemoth. *Twice* I sit at the heart of my city's desolation, and all due to your damnable plans."

"They were *our* plans, my friend. You entered into this endeavor with open eyes; I told you the way may grow difficult. And in any case these Behemoth have only tried their claws on rough twistcraft and ill-made Dirt-Magic. No offense to your strongsuits, but these monsters have succeeded in annoying me, and now I think we'll try some real war-weapons on them. So fortunate that you possess such!"

D'Alle dances his *cantrait* away, looking at the ruined gates of his city, remembering other destructions. Finally he looks back at Winter, and his face is a mask.

"It seems to me," D'Alle says, "that you ask me to hand over my last coin—no, my *city's* last coin. Our last thing of military value. Your plans did not go awry, Winter; they were demolished by those Behemoth. I cannot believe this new plan will be any different. If this is what alliance with the Nine means, well . . ."

He sniffs, and flexes his be-ringed hand, presumably studying his nails. He is doing his best to adopt a casual air. "Perhaps Cannoux can do well enough on its own."

Winter smiles, gently. "D'Alle," she says, "whoever spoke of alliance? Can the bird ally with the cat? Can a fish ally with the net? You wished to become part of the Nine, and now you are. Perhaps Candle, here, could explain to you what it means to become the property of my organization."

D'Alle's nostrils flare. "*Property?*" The walking-couch prances, agitated. "You—"

"Don't be a fool, D'Alle," Candle says wearily. "The White Tower doesn't do alliances. Many people have tried to tell you that, and you refused to listen. They accept your fealty, and that's about fucking it. You tried to buy your way in with *my* Cold-Key, a long time ago, and still somehow managed to avoid learning that lesson. One would think you would have, after the Deadsmith and Alvarez nearly destroyed your city. But you didn't. So here we are again, and all your chances are gone."

"Crudely put, love," Winter says, eyes glittering, hand caressing Candle's neck, "yet essentially correct. But here, look at us! Reduced to threats, our friendship splintering at the first hint of difficulty. To be honest, my dear Master D'Alle, I'd thought you made of sterner stuff. Still, all can be made well. If you wish no further part of our great task, so be it! I release you! You need bother yourself with these Behemoth no more. Indeed, as a member-city of the Nine, you can now apply for help from us, against them."

D'Alle looks as if he wants to spit, and spit blood. "I have only to release my Cache of warmachines to you, is that it? I have only to give you the only *defense . . .*" And here he looks back up at the splintered gate, the ruined war-suits scattered around. He shakes his head. He is bitter. But Candle steps in, and his voice is almost sad.

"You only found that Cache using the Silver-dowser I made for you, D'Alle. Easily gotten, easily lost. Let it go."

D'Alle is outraged. "Easily? It wasn't *easy,* boy. And now it is our last defense. We have ruled this slope of the Mountain for hundreds of years, and when Cannoux's enemies hear of this, they will come and we will be defenseless."

Winter just waits, head cocked to the side, looking at D'Alle as if he is an interesting insect.

"No," D'Alle says. "I will not give you our Cache. Not now, with our war-power destroyed. I must do what's best for my city."

Winter seems to consider several responses. A smile plays around her lips. "Do you mean to refuse me? To break a contract with my organization?"

Candle reaches up and sets a hand on D'Alle's arm. The *cantrait* dances away but Candle holds on, surprisingly strong for such a broken man. He forces D'Alle to meet his disquieting eyes. "Don't," he says.

D'Alle looks down at Candle with old hate and fear. His eyes flick towards Winter.

"D'Alle," Candle says, and again: "Don't."

D'Alle jerks away and spits again into the dust at Candle's feet. He looks up at the broken gates, the twisted heaps of twistcraft wreckage that were once the jewel of his militia. He looks back at Winter, and he composes himself as best he is able. "The only thing clear to me," he says, his voice high and tight, "is that this Cabal traffics chiefly in double-dealing and broken promises. I should have known it would as soon as I saw that *this* creature was involved."

He flings out his jewelry-laden hand at Candle, who sighs softly.

"I entered into it in good faith," D'Alle says, "but it is clear that it was a fool's bargain. I cannot—*cannot*—in good conscience—"

"Okay, yes, very well!" Winter claps her hands and cuts D'Alle off. "You've answered sufficiently; I have no need to hear the rest of the speech."

She curls her finger, and D'Alle's eyes widen in shock. His *cantrait* sidles toward her, plainly in defiance of his commands. It quickly closes the distance between him and Winter, and something in her eyes, perhaps, causes him to panic. But he has no time to scramble off the conveyance; Winter catches hold of him as easily as if he were a wayward cat and lifts him out of the *cantrait* with no more effort than a normal woman would lifting a child. She pulls his struggling, gasping face close, and smiles into it.

"Nothing personal, D'Alle," she says, "but the Wise have very little use for cowards."

She snaps his neck and lets him fall, using the same gesture he had used to kill his servant at the first meeting of the Convox. She then turns to give the watchers and soldiers on top of the wall a long, considering look. When they make no move she nods at them, a promise or warning of some sort, and turns away.

She steps lightly over the body of the dead man and kneels next to him, lifting one of his hands and studying the rings there. She brushes aside his dark queue where it had fallen across his arm; a dismissive gesture. She selects one, a plain silver band, and pulls it free. She looks up at Candle and smiles.

"Tiresome man," she says. "But I approve of his taste in jewelry."

Candle looks away.

"Oh, love! Was this some sort of respect-between-rivals kind of thing? Did you harbor warm feelings in your heart for our dear Master D'Alle?"

Candle looks up at the gates of Cannoux once again. He could be forgiven for some wistfulness; he had grown up there. Winter allows a smile to tug at her lips and slips the silver ring on. She admires it and waits for Candle to answer her. Behind her, Primary Gray kneels next to D'Alle's slumped body, whispering some curse or benediction.

"I never liked him much," Candle says after a while, "but I didn't think this would be his end. He lived a long life and this was a bad way to die."

"None of us get the end we wish, love. Are you done reminiscing? We have work to do."

"Behemoth to kill," Candle says, sarcastic. He turns away from D'Alle's body and the city, and faces the dark.

"Behemoth to kill, indeed." Winter admires the silver ring. She sighs, content, and then seems to remember something just slightly distasteful. Her hand comes down, as implacable as old stone, on Candle's shoulder.

"Things have slowed enough, I think, for us to address a certain matter."

Candle knows this tone of voice and tries to wrench himself away, but Winter's hand becomes a vise, clamping him in place.

She turns her hand and twists him so he is forced to look at her. Her smile grows sharp. "I don't mind the petty insults," she says. "I enjoy them, in fact. The *banter*, if you will. I know you're plotting, boy, and I know you'll turn this situation to your advantage if you can. Do you imagine that I don't know the extent of your powers? I know you're speaking to your little comrades, all over the place, using your little powers. I know you're trying to set your plots within my plans. I don't mind! I expect it, I look forward to the game. But from now on you *do as I tell you*, you fucking *worm*, and if I think you're holding back one whit, I will hurt you."

Candle manages a laugh and indicates his broken limbs, his scarred chest. "Hurt me more, Winter? How are you going to hurt me more, you awful fuck?"

She captures his hand deftly by the wrist and separates out his smallest finger, the one she broke around the fire. He grits his teeth—he has always hated pain.

She gives him a wide smile. "Lover, what has happened to you up until now was nothing. And neither is this." She pulls his hand to her mouth and chews off his finger with her perfect white teeth. His screams bounce off the ruined gates of the city behind them, but no one atop the walls comes to help. Even if they remember who he is, the city of Cannoux does not remember the name D'Essan fondly.

Winter spits his still-twitching finger into the dust and waits. From somewhere deep in the Dark, she can hear the heavy tread of soldier-constructs, the Cache coming for their new master. She smiles, paying little attention to the man weeping in the dust at her feet, clutching at his ruined hand.

She does, however, delicately wipe the blood off of her lips. It's no fun to be *too* obvious.

THE DEADSMITH

The Door Into Light

"And in the twinkling of an eye, he was somewhere else. He stepped from that world to this with no more trouble than you might take stepping across a threshold. But there were no watch-lights lit. There was no hearth and no home. He had stepped into a dark place, and he knew right away that he should have brought a lamp."

—EMILY LIST IV, 'THE TRAVELS OF PAUL THE ONION'

The Deader made his pilgrimage the old way, the way of salt and supplicant, of meditation and awe. He could have stepped straight through to the Door his Lady kept in her antechamber, but he needed time. He needed the old walk, the ancient ritual, before he faced her. The Deader decided to walk the Spoke Road Ethis, and climb the Tower as if he were a mystic in search of succor, or a peasant wishing a boon.

Perhaps he was a bit of both.

He had closed the Door on the Land of Forest; turned away from the Prey and whatever arcane trap was waiting for him. He had changed the coordinates, re-opening the Door on the White Tower, and the Spoke Roads, and the Crater Valley. He needed some walking time. The Prey would just have to wait, and the Deader supposed that he probably would. The trap was ready, after all; and the Deader would walk into it.

But not quite yet.

The words of the three women at the fire clanged in his ears, unpleasant and dissonant. His chest felt strange, too tight and too loose. His Fate, driven insane by the man Candle and the power of Domination he held, still gibbered in the back of his mind.

His Machine was dead, murdered by the Prey's golden bolts. No longer would the deadliest third of himself run ahead, protect him, be brutal when the Deader had no taste for it. He had been reduced to less than the boy he had been, watching bandits kill his family.

And then he had opened a Door onto something he never thought he'd see again—the unbroken sky. The clear sun, the whisper of living woods and tumbled stone. All this long chase in the dark, and the Prey had led the Deader to *Forest*.

Yes, the Deader needed some time to collect himself before he confronted his lover, his master, his god, his Lady. He was not the man he had been.

How do you make a machine? Perhaps the question should have been, *How do you break one?*

The Door he had come through was one of nine equilaterally spaced Doors, set high up at the end of the Spoke Roads, where they became only trails and the trails became mere paths up into the ring of Barrier Mountains that surrounded the Crater Valley. There were nine Spoke Roads, radiating outward from the central axis of the White Tower like, of course, spokes on a wheel. The edges of the crater were forbidding rock and old, dead vegetation, a wasteland. All of the light was ahead and down, growing toward the great spike of white in the center of the world.

The Deader began to walk the Spoke Road down into the Crater Valley towards the light in the center. The road was deserted here, and the Deader thought slowly, setting his thoughts down like heavy paving-stones, precisely, so that when he was finished there would be a straight and lasting path for him to return on.

When confronting a god, even one who took you to bed, it was best to have your thoughts in order and your heart at peace.

The Deader's heart was very far from at peace. He felt like one of the Prey's awful mechanisms, one-legged, driving itself in endless circles. When he blinked, he could see afterimages of the sun, that great glowing hoop of fire in the sky. He blinked them away, and blinked away the face of the man called Candle, the one he called Prey. The Deader recognized him; he had seen him before. A long time ago, and very far away, in a backwater called Cannoux. It was the same person. He had been just a boy then, barely in his middle years, but it was the same face. The Deader had many faults but his memory for names and faces was not one of them.

Chris D'Essan.

It was one more thing that he must ask his Lady. This puzzle, and its extents, had grown beyond him. He walked, reminded irrevocably of the first time he had made this walk, and wondered if the Prey—Candle—*Chris*—could be so omniscient. If, somehow, that damned creature could have known he would choose to do this, retrace the steps of his first pilgrimage.

He walked down the steep incline of the upper Crater Valley. Overhead, the sky was a roiling, lightless lightning, spewing out from the top of the White Tower in eternal waves. It comforted the Deader, however obnoxious. It was the sight of home.

The first time he had walked this way was after his Lady came for him the second time, the final time. She had rescued him once, from the dread city of Tyrathect, where he was being tortured to death for loving the girl Anise, with her dark hair and green eyes. And then, in the land that he had tried to lift up, to subjugate, to drag towards some better future, she had saved him again. Winter, with her long dark hair and green eyes, came to save him from another, slower death. She came to save him from himself.

She came for the man with the blue tattoo on his chest that his subjects called, fearfully, the Death-King, as he brooded upon his failed throne. She had laughed at him, just the same as she had when he was a boy and dying before her. She was the most beautiful, carefree, *competent* thing he had ever seen.

She asked him if he was tired of his throne and his broken kingdom. Tired of being the god and conscience of a people who he had to murder just to make obey. She asked him if he was tired of trying to wrench sense from a world long gone mad.

He was. Oh, he *was*. He offered her his service, knowing what it meant, and she accepted. He abandoned his throne with relief, and she had kissed him, laughing, for the first time. In that kiss was promise, strength, the assurance of order. It was the kiss of a woman who had forged an empire that lasted through the end of the world. It was the kiss of someone the boy with the tattoo could serve wholeheartedly. It dissolved the hard knots left by the deaths of his mother, his sister, the lovely girl Anise in Tyrathect, and countless others. She took his hand, and they disappeared in a shower of golden sparks.

They'd re-appeared here, at the edge of the Crater Valley.

Winter brought him to the head of the Spoke Road Ethis. She left him here. She bade him make the journey alone, on foot, and consider his life and the lessons learned. She would meet him high in the Tower if he still so wished, and his new life would begin.

He had. And now he did so again, walking past great trawling factories, feeding the ravenous industry in-land. He walked with groups of dirty miners, listened to their rough talk until they fell silent when they realized what he was. He walked into the far-flung shantytowns that ringed the Crater Valley far out, like the scum that accumulates on the edges of a pond.

The shantytowns gained dimension, becoming other sorts of factories and tall, slender buildings where the factory-workers lived. It grew louder, the hubbub of life almost painful, frantic. There began to be signs of affluence, buildings not covered in soot, clothes that were not stained with travel and work. He felt that lassitude again, that reluctance to continue, and he tried to let the growing light from the Tower burn it away.

He did not want to meet the Prey, not yet. He did not want to hear what that creature had to say. He thought of Candle waiting for him, when whatever arcane game he had planned finally reached its end. The Deader felt too weary to let the Prey's trap close on him. He needed to see his Lady first.

The Deader drew a tired hand across his eyes. He just needed to speak to Winter. He needed to know how this man had stolen what he had stolen. He needed to know why. He needed to know . . .

How do you make a machine?

The Spoke-Road Ethis gave way to the Bridge-City Ethis, cramped and narrow and tall and long. The Deader walked it, mostly unseeing, thinking about the Prey, and his Lady, and a small boy with a wound cut into the smallest finger of his right hand. He remembered the raider called Trail who had cut that wound into his finger. As he walked, the Deader rubbed absently at the old scar. Below him fisher-folk trawled the dark waters of the ring lake, shooting beams of silver light into the deep water to attract their prey.

The Ring-City started where the Bridge-City ended, and rose in front of the Deader like a mountain of light, one with a peak that sloped ever upward into infinity. The Tower rose before him now, monumental, inviolable, unanswerable. The Deader looked up, marking the spot a third of the way from the bottom where his Lady kept her apartments, and began to climb.

Here he broke from tradition; custom required following one of the spiral-roads that wound their way up through the city and, eventually, to the Tower. The Deader couldn't afford that extravagance of time; it could take a man weeks to climb the Tower that way. He knew, he had done it himself, that first time. But this time he took steps, and then risers, and then the slopeways that only a privileged few could ride. He watched the Crater Valley fall away beneath him as he rode up, thinking.

He reached the correct level and was passed through the gates by his Lady's guards. No one would stop a Deadsmith from going where they would; it was inconceivable that a Deadsmith would not be allowed wherever they wished to go. Still, the Deader paused on the threshold of his Lady's chambers.

He imagined his Fate whispering something arch here, and it would have been a comfort. Instead it only moaned, a cold wind of despair, and the Deader walked forward anyway.

———

For a moment the Deader stood with eyes closed, letting the stillness, the coolness, and the familiar scents of his Lady's apartments wash over him. And then he made himself open them, and walk forward. He left tracks of dust on the finely scribed tiles. He already knew his Lady was not there.

The apartments were empty; they were cold. The Deader walked through them, taking his time, looking carefully around. Robes were tossed over furniture, accouterments left carelessly. The Deader's Lady had never been one for tidiness, nor for servants meddling overmuch in her apartments. The Deader could feel her absence, a palpability, but he made a full circuit of the rooms anyway.

He lingered in her bedchamber, awash in sweet memories for a moment, hand hovering a mere span above the folded cloth, as if to feel residues of her heat. Then he grimaced and straightened. He surveyed the room. There was no hint as to where his Lady had gone, but she *was* gone. She had been gone for months. He inhaled deeply, trying to capture her scent, but there was very little left.

He closed his eyes again, trying to place her in the room, trying to remember the last time he had been here, on this bed, but he kept seeing dark, bloody hair, and the broken edges of his sister's skull. He kept seeing the mad eyes of the women at the fire. He left her bedchambers.

There was a man waiting at the entrance, small hands folded.

"Hello, my child," the man said, giving the Deader a nod. The Deader considered for a moment, and then returned it. There were those of the Nine that he would have gone to a knee for, but Diasz cared little for ceremony. It was one of the very few things the Deader liked about him.

"Hello, Diasz," the Deader said. "I am looking for Winter."

"That is clear. You miss her widely. She has been gone months or more."

The Deader nodded.

Diasz stepped into the apartments, looking around with bright interest. His quick eyes settled back on the Deader, however. His head cocked to the side. "Is there anything I can help you with, Deadsmith? We did not think to see you here."

The Deader grunted. He imagined that this was an understatement. "No," he said finally. "I had come for counsel."

Diasz lifted one perfect eyebrow. All of the Nine are perfect, in their own way. "Is that so? Well, I will offer what help I can."

"It is a matter for Winter."

Diasz's smile flickered. "Yet she is not here."

"If you tell me where she has gone," the Deader said, "I will find her there."

Diasz looked around the room again, and folded his hands. He looked at the Deader. His expression was inscrutable.

"She is beyond reach, I think. Prosecuting her aims in far corners of the empire, as is ever her way," Diasz said. "Come, now. Tell me your problem, and let's see if I can assist. I had *some* idea that the work you were sent on was vital."

"That may be." The Deader saw no way to put Diasz off; he served his Lady foremost, but he was a servant of all the Nine. He considered his words. "I have been sent to kill a man, but I think he may be no man, and there are implications that might trouble the White Tower."

Diasz's eyebrow lifted again. "No man? Implications? I had not known you to balk at challenges, my son. I rather thought it was why you had been chosen for this task particularly."

"This man can do things he should not be able to do, he knows things that he should not know."

"Ah, I see," Diasz said, smiling softly. "Forgive me, my son; I forget who I speak to. I thought you worried for your own life. But no—you wouldn't, would you? You worry that you tread on the plans of the Wise. That you interfere with great events."

The Deader looked away, thinking. Finally he shrugged, acquiescing the point.

Diasz stepped closer and laid a finely boned hand on the Deader's chest. It was an intimate gesture, and the Deader did his best not to recoil. Diasz smiled up at him. He smelled of lavender and anise.

"I assure you, Deadsmith," he said, "that there are only *nine* of the Wise that you need consider. If your mistress bade you return with this man's blood on your teeth, then you know all you need to."

The Deader considered Diasz. He would not go so far as to say he did not trust him, but it was foolish to think that the Nine were all of one mind. Plots were the favored drug of the Wise, or so it was said.

Diasz noted his hesitation and smiled. He pulled his hand away from the Deader's chest and tapped his lip, thoughtfully.

"Come with me, my son. Come! Spare a moment, and then you can return to your hunt. It may be I can offer you some help, after all."

Without waiting for assent, Diasz walked through Winter's apartments, to the wide balcony that looked out over the Crater Valley spread far below. After a moment, the Deader joined him.

"Beautiful, isn't it?" Diasz asked, looking down at the spreading web of light, spidering out from the solid column of brilliance that surrounded them. The Deader looked at the thick lines of radiance, the Spoke Roads that curved upwards into the obscure dusk of the Barrier Mountains.

The Deader made a noncommittal sound, and Diasz glanced at him, amused. "You don't agree? Perhaps you are not looking at the right things."

The Deader waited for the small man to get to the point.

Diasz gestured, a sweep of his arm. "I see beauty. I see light wrenched from a betrayer god; I see an empire in black and white. I see life where death was intended. Is that not beautiful? Can you not see the lights out there, far beyond sight, that all burn in the name of the Nine?"

"I've seen enough of them."

"Ah, but you must work to see their beauty. You see only the struggle and not the fruits. It was ever your problem, Deadsmith, but you should try. There is beauty there."

The Deader considered. "I have my Lady for beauty. All the rest is . . . ob-stacle."

Diasz laughed and clapped his hands. So like his Lady, when he did that. The Deader closed his eyes, letting the high wind blow across his face.

"Obstacle!" Diasz said. "You truly are singular, my son, even for a Deadsmith. That would be your lady's word, singular. I might use the term *broken*."

The Deader did not reply.

"Tell me," Diasz said, more severe now, "how does our empire function? How is the rule of the Nine prosecuted?"

The Deader spat over the balcony. "I need to return to my task."

"Humor me. How does our empire function?"

"I don't know what you mean."

"It's an empire of abstraction, isn't it? It's an empire built on gossamer webs of light, of distant rumor, of legend. So how can it possibly work? Most of our sub-jects, our allies and vassals, they exist to us only as a distant Door-coordinate. And we exist only to them as a once-in-a-generation visit from a functionary or—gods help them—a Deadsmith. So how do we maintain our empire? How do we keep control over a thousand—no, a thousand *thousand* lights, distant in the darkness?"

The Deader sighed again. "Fear."

Diasz shook his head. "You *are* broken, my son. Fear would not maintain it for more than a decade. No, it is love that keeps this empire strong."

The Deader laughed. "I recently pacified a city, Diasz. One in ten; the river of blood. It wasn't love I saw in their eyes. They do as we say because if they don't, somebody like *me* comes to see them."

Diasz watched him, his mouth a perfect, knowing smile. "Of course," he said, "but what makes *you* do it? What makes you spend months and years in the dark wastes, prosecuting aims of which you know little, killing and judging and main-taining order over places you may never see again, and can care almost nothing for?"

The Deader's looked away. "To serve the Nine."

"Come, Deadsmith!" Diasz said. "Don't be a fool. You do it for *love*. You love Winter. You love this White Tower. You love what we have built and what we have kept burning in the dark. Do you know why we stamp out the Dirt-Magic wherever we find it? Do you know why we crush the Old Gold whenever some poor fool re-discovers its use?"

The Deader shook his head; he could not imagine how this might help him.

"Because it *cannot save them*, Deadsmith," Diasz said. "It works; certainly. If you have the will and the time, you can make wonders. But it will not save them. Do you know why? Of course you do. Because it is a gift from the Mother, it is a thing from when the world was young and still had a purpose. But the Mother has turned on us, Deadsmith, and all of her gifts are poisoned. All of the old tools turn in the hand. We enslave the world so that we might save it."

"I am in no danger of losing my way. I will not betray the Nine. Nor my Lady."

"Yet you return with doubts." Diasz spoke softly. "You return with questions. You return with a heavy heart and wonder whether the man you were sent to kill truly needs to be killed—or maybe if he *can* be killed. You return with weakness in your bones and fear in your eyes. Do you cry off, Deadsmith? Do you wish one of your brothers or sisters to take up this task?"

The Deader spat again. "No."

"I wonder, my son." Diasz looked out over the great dark and the lights below.

"This man knows things," the Deader said, "that he cannot know."

Diasz laughed. "All things can be known, my son, if you have the force of will to discover them. Have you noticed a lack of will in the man you hunt?"

The Deader shook his head, reluctantly.

"So. I say to you what your Lady would say, should you have found her here." Diasz's voice grew stern: "You return with questions between your teeth when you were asked to return with blood on them. If you cannot—or *will* not—obey, we will find someone who can."

The Deader considered this. He held Diasz's eye for a long moment, but one does not cow any of the Nine. He nodded, accepting the rebuke, the finality of it. He walked back through his lady's apartments and out of them, to where the Door waited.

Diasz had followed him and stood near the entrance to Winter's apartments, hands folded. The Deader gave him a curt nod and dialed in the coordinates given to him by the three black-haired women at the fire; the women meant to represent his sister, his Lady, and his first love. The Door opened. Diasz watched.

Sunlight shone through, rich and gold. The greens and grays of the Highlands swam into focus. Almost casually, the Deader indicated the sunlight.

"I've found the Highlands. He's leading me into Forest. The Land of the Giants."

But if he was hoping for some reaction from Diasz, he was disappointed.

"Say hello to one for me, then," Diasz said, lightly. "It's been a long time since I've had the pleasure. Oh, and good hunting."

The Deader grunted, and stepped through the Door.

It closed behind him, and Diasz waited until it was fully closed before he laughed, and his lip curled into a sneer.

"Good hunting," he said. "You fucking *dog*."

THE KILLERS

Consorting With the Enemy

*"Take what you want and pay for it. If you don't want to pay the price,
don't take the thing. It doesn't matter if it's a coin, a kiss, or a life.
You'll pay for what you take; one way or another."*

—ALVAREZ, 'CONVERSATIONS II'

Sophie searched the mangled remains of the vault anyway. There was nothing
inside. Whoever had broken into it had taken the Key, and she and Bear had
just wasted precious time.

"What in the *fuck* could have done this?" Bear said, poking at the torn,
stretched, and violated metal. The vault had been made of pure silver, arguably
the strongest material known to thinking folk. One hair-thin strand of it could
suspend a boulder. "What in *all of the fucks* could have done this, Sophie?"

A voice came from behind them. "I think what you mean, Bear, is *who* the
fuck could have done this?"

They whirled, and Sophie saw someone familiar. Someone with sandy hair,
mild features, and a general air of being in over his head. The Twins-damned
Consort.

He was smiling at them and holding a silvery pendant in one hand. *The Key.*
Sophie remembered a similar gesture, when this man had thrown the silver necklace at her feet, but his demeanor was very different now. Bear surged towards it,
his Rapine activating, but the Consort held up his free hand, jerking the Key back
out of Bear's reach. "Calm down, Bear! Or you'll never see this thing again. Sophie? Please tell your dog to heel?"

"Calm down, Bear," Sophie said, softly. She focused on the Consort. "*You* did
this? You broke open this vault?"

The nondescript man shrugged, almost apologetically. "Yeah. Had to. I didn't
have the combination, and I didn't think you'd give it to me."

Sophie shook her head. "But why did you need it? *You* gave me the fucking
thing, told me to keep it safe! This was the safest place I could think of."

He grinned, disarming. "Ah! You remember me now. I was wondering if you
would."

"Yeah, motherfucker, I remember you."

The Consort looked around at the wreckage. "This was a good place to hide it, by the way. Better than I could have done, but still . . . not safe enough. Not when there are Behemoth around. Which, clearly, I am. And you'll be figuring out soon that Jane is one; not that it's ever been much of a secret."

Sophie shook her head. *Behemoth?* Well, it made sense. As much sense as anything had, on this long and brutal night. She remembered Jane's fingers, like an implacable steel vise, around her neck. Her hundreds of years ruling the Keep, the failed assassination attempts. "I still don't understand why you did this."

The Consort frowned, as if she were being dense. He held up the Key. "To protect *this* thing. Both your brothers have ruined half the Keep, trying to get at it, and if you think these are the only resources *Candle* has lined up, you're lying to yourself. Sophie, I thought you were smarter than this. Why are you here?"

"I'm trying to survive," Sophie snapped, "and that thing belongs to Bear."

"It used to belong to a boy named James D'Essan," the Consort said, slowly, "but ownership has changed hands quite a few times since then. If we're going by finders-keepers rules, possession is the ol' nine-tenths."

"Give that to me," Bear said, sounding hoarse, and again he seemed almost a child. "It's mine."

The Consort's face grew grave. "James," he said, but Bear hissed at the name. "Stop calling me that."

"I will," the Consort said, "when I think you've actually changed, actually left James D'Essan behind. There's no way in hell I'm trusting you with this Key otherwise. I know too much about you and your brother."

"Bear is my friend," Sophie said, "and you're not. So if we're talking about who to trust, well. I don't know you. Or what you want. As far as I'm concerned, you're just one more powerful bastard, trying to push us around to get what you want."

The sandy-haired man winced. "Ouch. But, fair. I hope I get to show you otherwise soon."

"Not as long as you're *literally* in bed with the Queen. Though if you're both Behemoth, at least your weird-ass relationship makes sense."

He gave her a wry smile. "Not a lot of romance options, when you can crush your partner with an accidental twitch. I honestly don't know if she likes me or just really needed to get laid."

"That's disgusting." Sophie made a face. "You're talking about the Beast."

"And you are talking about my girlfriend," he said sharply, then his face fell. "Though who knows? After tonight."

"Are you saying you're *not* working for her?"

"She's my girlfriend, not my boss. Still, I'm pretty sure she's going to take my actions tonight—when she learns about them—as the worst kind of betrayal.

Guys always used to say 'she's going to kill me' about this and that, but she might *literally* kill me."

Sophie couldn't help but be curious. This guy always disarmed her; he just seemed so out of his depth. "How could she kill someone who can do this?" She extended arm, indicating the demolished vault. "How could she kill a Behemoth?"

"Oh, killing a Behemoth is easy, when you're one yourself. Otherwise, I'll admit, it takes some doing. All right. As much as I'd like to pass a pleasant evening in conversation while your friend there tries to figure out how to murder me and get his toy back, we both have places to be. I assume you're going to go for the Book?"

"I'm not sure," she said, still feeling faint, "that telling you my plans is wise."

"Well, I can't blame you for that."

Sophie frowned. "I thought you wanted me to stay away from the Book. You sent out an army of fops and children, if I remember right, to send me the most cryptic warning in the whole world."

"It had to be cryptic, Sophie. I assumed some of my messengers would be intercepted. And I didn't want you to go get that Book, not if you were going to let Jane get her hands on it. But a lot has happened tonight, and we're running out of time. So I guess now is as good a time as any. It can't stay hidden forever."

"It would be a lot easier, if we had that Key." Sophie looked pointedly at the thing. The Consort grinned.

"It probably would be. *But I don't trust your friend there,* Sophie. Sorry. I have some good reasons. Maybe if he tells you his story, and you still trust him . . . I don't know. I don't know much, and I'm making most of this up as I go along. Sorry. Right now, the most important thing I can do is make sure Jane can't get her hands on either the Book *or* the Key." He sighed, then met Sophie's eyes. "Please remember: Jane *wants that Book.* Don't underestimate what she might be willing to do to get it. This Key she was less concerned with; she's known it was safe in this vault for years now. And she's known she could come get it any time she needed."

"Apparently not," Sophie said. The Consort's mouth twisted a little, and he shrugged.

"Love makes fools of us all." His eyes crinkled, and he looked at Bear. "I think you know something about that, James D'Essan."

"Stop calling him that," Sophie said, sharply. "He took the name Bear. That's who he is."

"I stand corrected, and I sincerely hope that your faith in this man is not misplaced. But I have to leave; in truth I did not expect to see you here. I only stayed because I was writing a letter for you and your friends. You might as well take it. And no, you don't need to read it right now. If you can survive the next few hours, you can read it at your leisure, and if not, well, it won't fucking matter much, will it? Do you remember the rest of my last message?"

Sophie remembered the fop in a downed Charm Chair. Terrified, he had squeaked at her: "The Giant Lies Still Awake." It felt like about ten years ago, but it was barely a day.

"And the world needs weapons," the Consort finished. "But I was talking about the other part, when I told you that nothing about to happen would be what it seemed. I wasn't kidding, Sophie Vesachai. Twenty years is all coming to a head tonight; twenty years and maybe longer. The Mother's Call is about to find its answer, for better or worse, here in the Keep. All of the pieces are in place, finally. The endgame can begin. The letter will explain a little more, but we don't have enough *time*. Twenty years of waiting, and now there's no time!"

He looked down at the silvery pendant in his hand, then back up at Sophie. He shook his head, and turned to go. Then he thought of something, and half-turned. "Oh, right. Can you give your friend Trik a message for me?"

Sophie blinked. *Trik?* "Yes?"

The Consort lifted an eyebrow. "Tell her to stop fucking around. Time for the gloves to come off. Tell her to remember her *promise*."

AN ASIDE: THE THREADS, THE LOOM, THE FABRIC

We know how the story ends.

We know what happened; we know who was there. History has already engraved their names on our tombstone. We know the villains; we know the failed heroes.

We know how the world died.

The end of the world is a loom that pulls threads from many times, from many places. Perhaps a more devoted historian could exhaustively detail each and every last story, tease out every connection and influence, laying bare the full breadth of the tapestry that led us all to this bad end.

But I am not a devoted historian; I am the least and last of my order and suffer from bouts of melancholy. I have neither the heart nor will to trace every thread back to its origin.

Weaving even the roughest fabric presents problems, however; do we start with Winter, her Cabal, and their role in the tragedy they caused, deep beneath the Mountain? But if so, where do I start? Winter's story is nearly as long as the Wanderlands itself, and the seeds of what she did were planted long before any of the players of this farce were born. And even Winter, huge figure in history as she was, played a role only in getting all of the players to the Giant's Gate, and perhaps not even the primary one.

Do we start with the Behemoth? Do I attempt to describe the remarkable world they hail from, so that you might better understand what they did? The fate of the world hinged on those two and their damnable sword, and yet they were only a small part of the tapestry.

No history of the Giant's Gate would be complete without a mention of Sophie Vesachai and her all-too-aptly named "Killers," of course, but then again, the threads get impossibly tangled. Do I tell her story from the beginning, from when she found her Book and raised the Jannissaries? Do I track her through the long years of dissolute depravity? If I only tell you what she and her friends did at the end, can you possibly understand *why* they did it?

And where should Bear's story start? With his induction in the Killers? Or must we travel back through long years of darkness to when he was a street urchin in Cannoux-Town?

And that is not even to mention his brother. Is there a figure who has played more roles in this farce than Chris D'Essan? Is there a name spoken more often in this appalling story than that of Candle? Has any one person, any one thinking creature, done more to bring about the end of the world?

Do we relate the long story of how Chris D'Essan stole the Domination from the Lady Winter, kicking off the long hunt of the Deader as Prey, or do we relate the awful aftermath? Is it more important to relate his and his brother James' harsh tutelage under the villain named Charts?

Or do we go further back, when the Brothers D'Essan were just two unextraordinary boys running around the streets of Cannoux-Town, avoiding lessons with the legendary Behemoth-Philosopher Alvarez?

Faugh! It is impossible.

I have not yet started and already I weary. I wish my brothers and sisters still functioned; they were more suited to this task than I. Even limiting my scope to those who were there at the end, even weaving the thickest of those threads that led them all there, the tale is maddeningly tangled. I am a small creature in a vast dark space, and my light illuminates only what is close to me. I cannot tell you why the world started to die, when the skies above the Lands began to fail and turn dark, why the Silver itself began to slow and stop. Why the Mother turned against us. What drove the Giant Kindaedystrin to drive a stake into our world's heart.

No, I know little of such things. But I do know what happened under the Mountain. I know the villains and their names. And I know something else:

At the start of every stitch, at the beginning of every thread, at the genesis of each section of tapestry, there is always one common instigator: the dream. The twice-and thrice-damned dream of a Giant, and of golden sun shining on living trees.

For the sake of nothing more than a dream, our world was murdered.

—'The End of History,' by Bind e Reynald, Scholae First Mark

THE LOST BOYS

Two Ways to Leave Cannoux-Town

"Think you this a children's tale? No, my friend, this is no children's tale. Those have happy endings."

—APOCRYPHAL, 'THE TALE OF THE TIN-EYE AND THE JANNISSARY'

The man named Alvarez reflected—as he was being torn apart by the Deadsmith—upon the nature of choices.

He had found, over the course of his long life, that choices tend to daisy-chain. One choice leads to another, which leads to another, all perfectly comprehensible, and then you find yourself doing something ludicrous like getting married, or learning to play the guitar. Or, in this particular case, having a fight to the death with a Deadsmith. Alvarez, instead of enjoying his customary cup of *chûs*, was lashed by arcane forces to a rough twistwork post as a demon tried to force his white-and-black glowing fingers into his heart. This was not, originally, going to be part of his morning! He had planned on doing some experiments and possibly flirting with the young grandmother that sold bakery across town.

He got his good hand free while he mused, managed to catch a hold of the Deadsmith's arm and crush the bones there into fine powder. That would buy him some time but would probably cause this vile creature to return the favor in a little bit.

See? It all came down to *choices*.

The man that Chris and James D'Essan liked to call Uncle hadn't meant, for instance, even to *become* a quasi-immortal, indestructible godling, trapped in a dying world with no way out or back. He had only meant to take a quiet walk and think about the choices that led him into a bad marriage and failing farm. But he had chosen to walk *this* way instead of *that*, had chosen this path over the other, and then had chosen to inspect the strange octagonal pillar he found half-hidden in the shade of the trees.

And such small choices—strung together on that daisy-chain—had ripped him free of his old world and life, remade him, and thrown him into the dark.

Here's another example: he had chosen to leave his home in Cannoux one morning without tucking away any of his more specialized and dangerous devices—devices he'd made for just this kind of eventuality. And now he was probably going to die. Sure, he hadn't exactly foreseen walking into a confrontation with a *Deadsmith*, but it was still a choice.

He managed to get himself free of the damnable thing's Machine; the Deadsmith had formed the thing into a kind of self-articulated whip-rope, one that climbed around him viciously, and wherever it touched, it bonded back on itself and did its best to chew through his skin. He had never experienced the Deadsmith's bizarre magic up close before, and found that he didn't much care for it. Whatever forces the Nine had harnessed in these brutes, they were no fucking joke.

He got a hold of the Deadsmith, the awful creature's ruined arm re-knitting before Alvarez's eyes, and threw him through some poor bastard's house. He pondered on whether he'd be able to make it to his workshop before the Deadsmith caught up with him, and guessed he couldn't. It was a shame; he had some trinkets there that could really ruin this son-of-a-bitch's day. Still, he'd try.

Alvarez considered the subject of choices, while he lumbered toward the workshop he would never reach, townspeople wailing and scattering out of his way. The daisy-chain of choices, starting long ago with his decision to discover the true nature of this world. His choice to reject the councils of the Wise; his choice to travel the Wanderlands and discover the truth that lay under the legends.

He could have made other choices, and then he wouldn't be dying, here, in this fuck-all end of nowhere. His choice to trust the Mother, as sad and broken as that old god was, as insane her methods might be.

Without *that* choice, he could have let Winter take the Cold-Key; he could have left the boys to their fate. He could have protected them earlier by taking the damned thing away in the first place. So many choices, all negated by that first one: to trust the Mother. And now he was going to die for it.

He allowed himself the luxury of a sigh, and heard the Deadsmith behind him, coming for him. He wouldn't make it to his workshop.

He didn't regret saving the kids; he'd long ago picked the side of the lost, bewildered, possibly insane god in the sky, and she had a use for those children. He wondered if he would have saved them anyway; wondered if he would have made that choice just because they were young and scared and didn't deserve the mess they'd created. He didn't know. A long life can make one callous, and an argument could be made that Alvarez's work was far more important than two snot-nosed kids.

But the man they called Uncle had never much cared for that kind of equation, and he liked those boys. He hoped they would be all right, though the chances of that were slim. He supposed that if he had to spend the coin of his life, it was good that he'd bought *something* with it.

Something slammed into his back, something that tore at his skin. That fucking Machine, glowing white with some awful power, dreadful enough to wound even a Behemoth. Alvarez stumbled and fell, demolishing a wide rope-bridge and stairway beneath. The two of them really were doing a number on Cannoux-Town, and he regretted that. It was his home these last years. But it couldn't be helped.

He crashed through layers of stone, hardly feeling it. The Machine clawed its way through the muscles on his back, ripping through skin that had not felt real pain in almost two thousand years.

The Behemoth chuckled to himself, the pain distant. There were a lot of choices made, in two thousand years. He felt ambivalent about them coming to an end. He would have liked to finish his work; he wished he had been able to convince more of his students to follow the Doctrine of Dirt. But it would be nice to rest, too.

The Deadsmith smashed into his back, his fingertips flaring white, dug them into the joint of his elbow, and tore one of Alvarez's arms off. He screamed, but the pain was oddly distant. He thought about that farm, back on that other world, so long ago, and that unhappy wife. He would be long dead by now if he hadn't chosen to touch that dark pillar he'd found in the woods that day.

His last thoughts, as the Deadsmith tore him to pieces, weren't about the boys D'Essan, or the Cold-Keys, or even the intractable problem of the Giant that lay so many leagues beneath his feet, the one he was here to study in the first place. He didn't think about the things that he'd spent so much of his long, long life obsessing about; he didn't think about his books or students or the nature of the Mother. He didn't think about the people he'd loved and lost.

He thought about the thing the damned boys had seen in the Land of Forest, the thing he had never seen, not in nearly two thousand years of walking the Wanderlands.

He thought about the *sun*. Alvarez had never seen the unbroken sky of this world, and he would have liked to. But he remembered another, very different sun, shining through leaves, a few hundred lifetimes ago and on another world.

The man the boys had called Uncle closed his eyes, feeling mostly the remembered warmth of golden sunlight on his face, and joined his friend Buckle—along with many others—in whatever mysterious lands lay beyond *these*.

———

James D'Essan, for his part, had very little time to think about the nature of choices, and even less inclination. His world was a rushing tangle, a confused welter of sensations, and then he was smashing through the city, him and Chris and Katherine, protected by the same force that was carrying them.

The gold thing Uncle had given Chris was transporting them—somehow—in a twisting shower of golden sparks, launching them across the city and protecting them at the same time. If James had been able to care about it at all, he would have wondered what impossibly high stage of twistcraft that golden thing was, and how long it had taken for Uncle to make it.

They crashed through an old tower crusted with hanging wall-gardens, slicing through an essential structural element and causing it to slowly topple onto a broadway below, thankfully clear of citizens. They plowed into another old building, out the other side, and finally ended in a furrow of old broken masonry, splintered bamboo, and stone. The gold sparks twisted themselves into nothing, leaving the three children gasping in the dust.

Before they could even stand, James scrambled, blind, eyes full of rage and tears, into his brother. He knocked him flat, swinging his fists wildly, rolling in the hot rubble and screaming.

"James!" Chris said, trying to deflect his brother's fists. "Stop it!"

"You killed her!" James screamed, trying to claw at Chris' eyes, skin, anything. "You *killed her!*"

"James!" He heard Katherine yelling, as if from far off. He got his teeth in Chris' shoulder and bit, getting a satisfying scream in return. Chris was never good with pain. But James was. James was fine with pain. Chris gave up on trying to pry him away and punched him, hard, in the side of the head. His vision exploded in hot agony.

"Squib," Chris grunted, punching him again and making him loose the grip with his teeth, "stop it! We don't have time for this. You have to *quit!*"

James didn't quit. He didn't know how to quit. There was a roaring redness inside his mind, those knives in his chest finally broken free, cutting up everything inside him, and this was the only answer he had for it. He drove his knee into Chris' stones, making his brother gasp and falter. Dimly, James felt the red-haired girl's hands scrabbling at his back, but he paid them no mind.

Another white explosion rocked his head; he felt his nose break and blood flow down his face. Chris had slammed his forehead into James', and for a moment the younger boy lost control of his limbs. Chris rolled off him and got a fist full of James' hair, while the other hand wrenched James' arm around, near to the point of breaking. By the time James was able to see again, Chris had him locked up. To James, his brother's forearm was a hot bar of pain across his throat; his arm was half-ripped out of his socket, and Chris' breath was hot in his ear.

"Stop it, squib," Chris said, breathing hard, his voice hoarse. "You have to quit."

James had started crying at some point, or maybe he had never stopped. Tears mixed with blood and ran down his face.

"You killed her." He tried to jerk backwards, to kick Chris in the stones again, but the older boy was much bigger and much stronger. Chris avoided the blow and tightened his hold on James' windpipe.

"I know, squib, I know. But you have to stop, we don't have the *time*."

James swallowed, past the twin pains of Chris' arm and the hard lump that had overtaken his throat. Suddenly, he went limp. "You *killed her*," he said again, and sobbed. Chris let him go, and got up to his feet. He looked down at James, who was bleeding, with tears running down his face. Chris glanced at Katherine, and she looked away.

"I couldn't think of anything else," Chris said, finally. "It was the only way to get Uncle to come. You know he said he would come, if Buckle ever got hurt. It was all I could think to do."

"Don't call me that." James' voice was almost a whisper. "You don't call me squib no more."

"James—"

"You *KILLED HER!*" James screamed and wrapped his arms around his chest. All the knives had pressed in now, all the way to the middle. Chris looked at his hands, and shook his head, his eyes dark.

"I had to." His voice was hoarse. "It saved our lives."

James was shaking, trying to hold his insides together. He looked up at his brother, smeary with tears, and shook his head. Chris was so *dumb*. "I *know that*. I know that. I ain't *stupid*."

Chris watched him, wearily and warily. "Then . . ."

"*Killing her—that* was your stupid plan?" Then he did a passable imitation of Chris: "'Don't worry, squib, just trust me, just do what I say, I got a plan.' You never talked to me about it! You—*you ain't always right!*"

Chris started to say something, and thought better of it. Maybe he was remembering what Uncle had said to him. Finally, he nodded.

"I'm sorry, squib."

"Don't call me that." James hugged his chest as tightly as he could, trying to keep all the pieces of himself together. He felt like everything was going to come apart inside. He swallowed. "She was my friend."

Chris looked away. He nodded, again.

"She was my *only* friend," James whispered. He saw, dimly, the blurry form of Katherine crouch down next to him. "Don't you get it, you . . . you *fuckers?* She was my only friend."

"No," Katherine said softly, "she wasn't."

James didn't want to look up at her face. He didn't want to see her dumb, stupid sad eyes, or her kind smile.

"I'm your friend," she said. James wanted to spit at her, to push her away, to scream in her face. But he didn't. She laid her hand on his shoulder, lightly. "We found the Door, man. Me and you. You ain't gotta be my friend if you don't want. But I'm yours."

James looked away. His mouth twisted. "No, you ain't." He felt like his words were stones that he was setting down, building a wall between him and her. "You needed me to get what you wanted. You both did, and maybe I don't blame you so much, but you ain't my friend. Don't say you are when you ain't."

He may as well have slapped her; she flinched back. She looked up at Chris, her eyes hurt.

Something was hardening in James' chest now, something solidifying around those broken shards, those knives. Not healing them, no, not even close, but hardening around them. James' insides were settling into a new shape. He guessed this is what it felt like to grow up.

"Kid," Katherine said, and her voice was raspy like she was crying, but that didn't make no sense. "It's not like that—"

"Don't call me a kid." James wiped his nose. But his voice was a little firmer now, and he was able to relax the arms holding his chest together. He looked at Katherine and managed a scowl. "Ain't none of us kids. Not no more."

"Yeah. That's true." Katherine took a deep breath and wiped her eyes. She looked over her shoulder at Chris as her voice steadied. "We need to get to the Door."

Chris didn't reply for a long moment but nodded. Katherine turned back to James and lifted the Cold-Key in her hands, then she fastened it around his neck. Chris started to say something, but she gave him a look that James couldn't see but felt sure must have been intense, because Chris bit off whatever he had been about to say. James didn't exactly feel *better* with the Cold-Key around his neck, but he felt steadier. Harder. *Colder,* maybe. He felt his narrow shoulders square against the weight of the thing.

From somewhere in the distance there was a massive crashing sound.

"That's Uncle," Chris said, looking back towards the city behind them. "We have to go."

"Are you okay?" Katherine asked James, ignoring Chris. Her hand was gentle on James' shoulder. "Can we go?"

"I'm okay," he said, but pushed her hand off. She smiled, not offended, and his insides settled a little more. He was able to breathe a little easier now. The knives were still there, pressed in, sharp and cold and painful, but James had never minded pain. And he discovered that he could breathe *around* them.

The Cold-Key was chill against his skin, but he didn't mind. He gave Katherine a nod. He looked at his brother, saw a flash of him tearing Buckle apart with his clever hands, and looked away. He didn't know if he'd ever be able to look at him and not see it. But he got to his feet, and his insides held together.

"Okay," he said, and wiped blood and tears from his face. "Let's go."

They stumbled their way through the maze of rooms under the city. Each was hurt in their own way. Chris' ankle had swollen, and he could hardly walk; he had nearly broken it when he jumped off the table. Katherine had been beaten by Master's goons, and she didn't complain, but it was hard for her to move easily. And James was nothing *but* pain. That was okay, though. It was almost comforting.

He was grateful for Katherine's daubs of red paint in the network of tunnels below the city. Without them, he wouldn't have been able to follow some half-hidden feelings sent by the Mother just now. He was barely able to follow his damned older brother.

And then Chris had stopped, bade them be quiet, and sworn violently under his breath.

"Somebody's following us," he said, simply, and they all started to go as fast as they could. Whoever it was, it couldn't be good. Distantly they heard the rumblings of great crashes and impacts as Uncle and the Deadsmith destroyed half the city in their titanic battle. Poor Uncle. James hoped he would win.

Still, they were able to find the Door. For a long moment all James could do was stare at it, dully. It seemed several lifetimes ago that they had all stood here and walked through it into a land of sunshine and Giants. Like some story he'd heard once, too silly to really be believed.

Katherine looked at Chris. "Where can we go? The Giant—"

"We can't go there," Chris said. "Not yet. Not now. Not with the Key."

"Then where?" Katherine despaired. "Do you know any other Door-codes?"

"No," Chris said, quietly. He examined the coordinate-rings around the doorknob and swore again. He glanced at Katherine. "Somebody changed this."

Katherine blinked. "What? That doesn't make any sense. Who?"

"I don't know," Chris said. "I just . . . *shit*. I don't know."

James felt very tired, suddenly, and was hardly even surprised when there was a sound from outside and the thin, sallow-faced slave of Master D'Alle stepped into the room, alongside a gentle-looking woman who sold candied gourds up on the Way. She didn't look gentle now, though. They both held long silver knives. The last time James had seen a knife like that was the one driven through the skull of the silver-wrapped skeleton, where they'd found the Key.

"Step away from the Door, children." The thin man, D'Alle's servant, said. They entered the room, but warily, spreading out along the walls. Their long knives were held back along their forearms, in the position that Sergeant Willet had taught James was the *convass*, or the close-fighting stance.

"James," Chris said, voice tense, "come here. We need the Key to open the Door."

James took a step backwards towards his brother and Katherine. The older woman shook her head.

"Don't, boy. We'll just follow you. And all we want is that Key. Such a thing is sacred, and not for the likes of you."

"You have no reason to let us live," Chris said. His voice was tight, agonized. "Come on, James, please."

But the thin man shook his head. "We're not what you think, boy. We serve none of the vile folk you imagine."

"I know what you are," Chris said. "They won't let us live, James. Please, trust me."

The thin man smiled, unamused, and glanced at his partner. "Everyone wonders where the Cold went," he said, sidling along the wall, knife still held ready, "but we didn't go anywhere."

The woman hissed. "Silence, Tomas." But the man grinned.

"Give us the Key, boy, and we'll let you go. We swear it by the Mother and the Silver itself."

"We swear it," the woman said. "We will even send you through the Door if you wish. But you must cease this blasphemy; you must give over the Key. It is not for you."

"They say that because they know they're going to kill us." Chris' voice was thick, pleading. "The third of them will be here soon; they go in threes. We have to *go*. *Please, James.* Come here!"

Chris was so *smart*. He never needed anything explained, not like James did. He remembered everything the first time, and he always figured everything out before someone could even ask the question. The two people were flanking them, moving toward them. James didn't know what Chris expected to find, on the other side of that Door, but he thought it was their only hope. Like killing Buckle had been their only hope.

"That's it, boy," the woman said softly. "Give over the Key, and you and your friends will go free. We have no wish to harm children."

Maybe that was true, James thought. Only, maybe it wasn't. He didn't know. Chris was the one who figured everything out. James would never be able to do that; he'd never be able to beat Chris at thinking. His older brother was always going to be better than him at everything, and James was tired of being mad about it. It all seemed sort of silly, now that Buckle was gone.

The Key was cold against his chest. James had never been much good at numbers, or twistcraft, or remembering the names of the Cities of the Mountain. James knew that he had been mostly a disappointment and a trial. But there *was* one thing that James D'Essan had always been good at. He found himself smiling, slowly, at the two Cold that were trying to flank him, their silver knives at the ready. Maybe there was *only* one thing that he was good at. But maybe that would be enough.

He reached *into* the Key, in a sideways sort of way, in that way he'd done before, only this time not in fear and anger. It hurt; gods, it *hurt!* It was like fish-hooks all through his body, and the harder he reached the more it hurt. He grinned at the two Cold, his smile bloody.

"*No,* boy," the man said, surging forward, knife slashing out, some species of panic crossing his face. But James pulled some red-black *something* from the stone around him and threw it at the man in jagged shards, tearing him nearly in half and pinning him in a bloody gasping mass to the far wall. James' vision went dark and pain crashed into him, a vast and unbearable pain, but he didn't let it stop him.

Maybe that's why they call them Cold, he thought. *You have to be cold-hearted to use this thing. You have to be hard.* The woman screamed and rushed at him, her silver knife flashing for his heart, but he drove a spike of raw twist as big as his thigh through the side of her face, and hot blood splashed across him. Katherine screamed, too, behind him, but that didn't matter. He went down to one knee, letting go of the Key's power, pain thundering in his head and body, nearly taking him down. But he had never given in to Chris' beatings and he didn't give into this.

He was only eleven, but he was a killer now. And he *liked* it. He wouldn't go down.

He gritted his teeth, ignoring Katherine's horrified tears and his brother's shock. He dragged himself to the Door, gripped the silver handle, and turned it.

The Door opened on darkness, and James fell into it.

THE KILLERS

Cold Comfort

*"You're born with nothing, son, and you'll return to it.
Don't get too caught up in the nonsense between."*

—AMIR VE, 'TINTRECT'

Trik and Ben were waiting for them at the entrance to the Library. Sophie had to laugh at the sprained expression on Trik's face. She couldn't tell if the girl was happier to see that Sophie was unhurt and alive—or Bear. She suspected that Trik didn't know, either. Ben gave Sophie a nod, clearly relieved. He looked jumpy, and held a military-grade chutter in his hands.

Sophie and Bear had rushed here after their confrontation with the Consort, taking a Charm Chair part of the way and running most of the rest. What might be happening in the Library was growing in her imagination; she didn't know if Lee or Candle had reinforcements, friends, armies, or *what the fuck,* but if they were going to deploy them, it would probably be here. Her instincts for battle were buried under twenty years of rust and soaked in booze, but they were telling her that this was the endgame.

The Library was where the Book had lay hidden for twenty years, and now Sophie feared that the shadows that had been swirling around her all night were going to converge here. *If* Lee had been lying when he said he didn't care about it. Sophie thought he had been, but this put them in a lot of danger for a hunch. She didn't trust the Queen, either; she didn't think Hunker or Lee would have told Jane where the Book was, but she couldn't be confident of anything on a night like this. She hoped she was wrong; that they would be able to duck in, dismantle the trap she'd set, gather up the Book, and find somewhere safe to figure out next steps. But Ben killed any such thoughts with a short shake of his head.

"We just got here," he said, once Sophie and Bear approached. "But we saw someone go in, Sophie. Three of them—and they looked like Vesachai. They had Rapine."

"Shit," Sophie swore. "How would Vesachai know about this place? It doesn't matter. Maybe I didn't keep the secret as well as I thought, when I was a kid."

"You hid the Book in a place called the *Library*," Trik said.

"Fourteen-year-old me thought it was very clever. The last place they'd look, right?" Sophie sighed. "Any sign of Avie or her friend?"

Ben shook his head again. "No. What happened at the vault? Did Bear get his magic necklace?"

Bear grunted, angry. "No. We ran into the *Consort*."

Quickly, Sophie caught them up on the encounter. Trik looked confused, brow furrowed.

"The Consort is a *Behemoth?*"

"Yeah." Sophie gave her a speculative look. "He has a message for you, too. Says to stop fucking around and take the gloves off, or something. And remember your promise."

Trik stiffened, eyes wide. Sophie watched her face.

"Trik . . . ?"

But Ben tapped Sophie on the shoulder, urgently. "Practice Guard!"

Sophie turned and saw two soldiers turn a corner and slow, looking at the Killers with growing expressions of puzzlement and surprise on their faces. Her luck! They were deep in the bowels of the Keep, in a nearly abandoned section of it. What the fuck were *Practice Guard* doing here?

Well. The answer was obvious: looking for *her*. And now they knew where she was.

"In. *Now*." Sophie shoved Trik, forgetting for a moment about the girl's dislike of being touched, and it was like shoving a brick wall. But Trik got going, and Sophie ducked in through the big reinforced doorway, into the cool dimness of the Library. She considered using the silver in her arms to override the big wardoor, to slam it shut and keep the Queen's forces out, but decided against it. The two Practice Guard kept walking, and it was *possible* that they weren't there to find her. If she flared her arms alight, there was no question that the Queen would have her forces here as soon as she could.

Sophie dragged the Killers into the depths of the Library, grim. Time was, indeed, running out.

———

It wasn't really a Library, of course; it was her and Ben's private name for the place. They had discovered it long ago, before they'd found the Book, even. Sophie had been a great explorer and Ben had an almost preternatural ability to remember the side-ways that wound through the Keep. The place that Sophie had dubbed 'The Library' was deep down in the Keep, more or less Dim, and far away from any of the inhabited areas. It had captured Sophie's imagination back then. Before the dreams had started her on the course that would lead her into Saint Station's jaws, she, Ben, and Tom had once spent many happy afternoons exploring here.

There was only one entrance—that Sophie knew of—and it was guarded by a war-door, a heavy silver frame and barrier that could be closed. If one knew how, and had the power. The actual Library was a bewildering series of octagonal rooms hollowed out of the raw rock, a sequence of small connected spaces that wasn't *quite* a maze, but came close.

The rooms were connected by passageways that twisted, turned, sloped up or down. There were sections of stairs, occasionally. The octagonal rooms ranged in size from twenty paces across to several hundred, but none were very large, and all had at least two entrances—many had three or four. All of them had shelves built into the crude rock walls, and each had several lightfixtures overhead, most of which still worked. None of them had high ceilings, and overall the effect was that of a labyrinth, and one full of old and moldering secrets. It goes without saying that Sophie had loved it when she was young. And it also went without saying that it was, tactically speaking, a *fucking nightmare.*

Wonders lay on those shelves—if anyone in the Keep had wit enough to know them—as well as a great deal of trash. There were long shelves filled with books and old maps and schema for silver-work creations that no one in the Keep knew how to make any longer. There were endless racks of old mechanisms made for no easily discernible purpose, and some of them still moved and jittered for their own reasons. Or perhaps, just out of ancient habit. Sophie tried to note concentrations of these devices; most of them had silver in them, and anything with silver in it, she could fuck with. The magic in her arms needed silver to work, and anything that had none of that was useless to her.

One of these, a kind of skeletal rat missing most of its lower framework, snapped at the Killers listlessly as they passed through the room that held it. Sophie rubbed at the scars on her arms, tense and looking down each hallway they passed. None of them were straight enough to see into the next room.

"Careful," Trik said, though it was unnecessary. All four of them were on high alert. Ben had brought Sophie a chutter, and she gripped the unfamiliar weapon with a sweaty palm. She didn't like it; she'd never really used them. Her eyes darted to shadowy corners, looking for Lee, or Vesachai, or something worse. Maybe Avie and her friend, only the mysterious girl had decided to betray them.

Sophie tried to concentrate on where they needed to go. It had been twenty years since she'd been here, and while she normally was pretty good with directions, she found herself pausing in rooms that had more than two exits and trying to remember. She had to hope that if Lee *was* here, he was still searching; though the place she'd hidden the Book was rather obvious. She would have done better to stick it under one of these random piles of junk. But she'd been fourteen, and romantic, and too clever for her own good. At that time, in the aftermath of the Hot Halls War, she had almost *wanted* somebody to try to find the Book. And find the trap she'd left for them.

They passed racks of old inscrutable weapons, and a few things that might have been an exotic type of chutter. One of the octagonal rooms had a Well in the center, the golden birdbath shape glowing dully in the overhead lights. She was half tempted to stop and order up some slots, but resisted. Piled in a corner against some shelving, she saw some things that she recognized from the Hot Halls War, and that disturbed her. Maybe this place wasn't as forgotten as she'd thought, if it was being used to store such things. She had little time to think about it, though; she turned a corner and nearly ran into three figures stalking the same direction they were.

The three figures were Vesachai, a Triad, and they set themselves quickly, taking guarded stances. They held their Rapines oddly though; blades back along their forearms. Sophie didn't recognize them but that didn't surprise her; she had a big family. And she'd been estranged for a long time. She didn't hesitate; she pulled silver fire into her arms and *pushed* their Rapine away, the same as she'd done to her Uncle and his people.

The Vesachai grinned, and hung onto their silver knives. The blades jerked in their hands, but did not fly towards the shelves on either side. Sophie goggled.

"Your tricks will not work on us, Abomination," one of them said, a pleasantly faced woman with a large scar on one cheek. "You stink of silver, and it is past time you were returned to the Mother."

Sophie felt a big shape step past her: Bear. He made a show of unlimbering his new best friend, his Rapine.

"Bear?" Sophie asked, and he answered without looking back at her. He bounced on the balls of his feet, getting ready for a fight.

"These are mine, Sophie. They're not Vesachai. I've run into these bastards before." Bear shook his head. "Never thought I'd see them again. They're fucking *Cold*."

"You just bought your death, apostate." The pleasant-faced woman smiled, the gesture pulling at her scar hideously.

"Maybe." Bear was doing an excellent pose of bravado, but Sophie could hear the tenseness in his voice and that, more than anything else, convinced her of the danger these three posed. *Cold . . . ?* That couldn't be. They had all disappeared, hundreds of years ago.

Sophie heard a cry, suddenly, a wail of pain from somewhere in the Library.

"It's Hunker," Ben said. Trik stepped past him, and set her hand on Sophie's shoulder, an extravagant gesture. Sophie couldn't remember a single other time Trik had touched her, voluntarily. Her hand felt very heavy, but somehow soft, too.

"Go get the Book," she said. "Save Hunker if you can. I'll help Bear."

"But—"

"*Sophie.* I've fucked with these bastards too, they're no joke. Go get the Book; I'll get to you as soon as I can."

Sophie opened her mouth, then looked at Bear, crouched and weaving his silver knife, ready to attack. Trik stepped past her, and nudged Bear with her elbow. He gave her a bright grin.

Sophie heard that wail of pain again, from behind them, and Ben tugged at her jacket.

"Out of our weight class," he said, simply, and Sophie saw a flurry of silver-on-silver blows as Bear tangled with one of the ancient Wizard-Priests. Trik roared and rushed in at them.

"Yeah," Sophie said, feeling cold, wondering who the fuck her friends were. Ben took off at a jog and Sophie followed him, leaving Trik and Bear to their fight.

———

She found her brother.

Lee was lying against some shelves, folded through, and perhaps inextricable from the dead, still-twitching form of a Jannissary. The porcelain-white form looked like beautiful death personified, even in its mangled condition. Lee had fought hard, and the long flat-planed head and bladed digits of the Jannissary were scorched and twisted. To Sophie's eye, her brother had nearly defeated the thing; but it had ripped him open in the attempt. When Sophie came out of the passageway and into the room where she had hidden the Book, he lifted his head drunkenly, trying to focus. When he saw who had joined him, he started to laugh. It was clearly painful to do so; he was near death, and his exhalation had blood in it. He laughed again, more blood running down his chin.

"Sophie, you *bitch*," he said, gasping out the words. "A trap? A fucking *Jannissary?*"

Sophie ignored him for the moment. Hunker was pinned against one of the shelves by a crude curl of silvery metal that had been wrapped around his wrist. It had broken the skin, and the small man was weeping. He looked up at Sophie, tear-streaked.

"I tried to warn you, Capitana."

She shook her head, a short jerk. "Don't call me that, Hunker."

She pulled silver fire into her arms, just a bit, and wrenched the makeshift handcuff away from his arm, freeing him. She looked to Ben and he nodded, hefting his chutter. He wouldn't let Hunker run, not until she knew what he had done. She realized she was putting off dealing with her brother.

She approached Lee, reluctantly, crouching down. He was on the floor, propped up against a shelf of books. She made herself study the wreckage of his body, and the wreckage of the long white-bladed form that he had killed, and had killed him in turn.

Lee was trying to laugh. "You fuckin' *killed me.*"

"Yeah, well. Sorry. I didn't think it would be my little brother who was trying to steal the Book, or I would have left a gentler trap."

"Always the problem. Never thought enough of me." He coughed more blood.

"Hah." Sophie squatted down near him. He was clutching a big, thick, ornate volume, traced in an complex lacework of silver. It had been rather prominently displayed on a fluted silver display stand, as befitted its station and pedigree. The display stand was destroyed, now, as were half the shelves in the room.

When Sophie was fourteen years old, in the aftermath of the Hot Halls War, when she was just beginning to understand how thoroughly she and her home had been fucked, she had decided to hide the Book here. She had set this trap, thinking at the time to catch some Outkeep villain, and then later hoping it would catch Denver or the Queen. Whomever tried to disturb the Book would wake the Jannissary she had hidden, which had been commanded by the Book to sleep until or unless it was disturbed.

"Well," she said, looking at her brother's bruised and battered face, "you took down a Jannissary, at least. How many people can say that?"

"Hah." He coughed a little. "Barely."

"Yeah," Sophie said, examining his wounds.

"You could have warned me."

"You didn't care about the Book. Remember?"

Lee looked a little lost. Whatever bright surety had filled him in the Rue was gone now. "Yeah . . . this all got out of hand. I didn't mean to let it get so out of hand."

For some reason, this sadly inadequate little apology made Sophie's eyes fill with tears. She wiped them away.

"*Sophie.*" Ben seemed tense. "Others will come. The Queen, or worse."

"Yeah," Sophie said.

Lee jerked, spastically, and Sophie realized he was trying to hand her the heavy book in his arms. She hung her head.

"Go on, then." Lee sighed. "Love to see how it works." He laughed, spraying tiny flecks of blood into the air. "I can't get it to do *shit.*"

"That is because your sister is a much bigger asshole than you ever imagined."

His eyes narrowed, confused, and then he got it. He closed his eyes. He smiled and relaxed, as if setting down some long-carried weight.

"Fuck me. It isn't real."

"No," Sophie said. "It's not the real Book."

"But you carried it everywhere. I saw you."

Sophie shrugged. "I was a suspicious kid. It seemed like a good idea to have a decoy."

Lee smiled, humorlessly, and rested his head back against the shelves. Sophie looked at his wounds and was amazed that he was still alive. But then that was the thing about Silver, wasn't it? Even regular Vesachai enjoyed longer lives from working with it. Having it twined around your bones made you pretty damn hard to kill. And it made a lot more people want to try.

She needed to get the real Book, hidden only a few span away, before others came; Practice Guard or more damned Cold or worse. But this was her brother, and he was dying. She looked for traces of the young boy he'd been and couldn't really find any. This man was a stranger and, with the Feral Children loose in the Rue, a mass murderer. So why did she want to cry?

"Sophie . . ." Ben said again.

"I know," she said. Lee opened his eyes. He watched her; he was fading in and out.

She finally just asked it. "Why, Lee?"

"Why what?"

"Did you hate me that much?" Sophie asked. "Why did you do this?"

Lee smiled again. She heard a guttural gasping sound, and for a moment she didn't think he was going to answer. But then he managed a shallow sigh.

"Nothing to do with you. Not everything is about you. Candle is in a war with the Queen, and you were in the way. It was about terror, Sophie. It was about *damage*. Destabilization. Bring the war into her fucking *house*."

"Those were your neighbors, Lee. Fellow citizens. How could you do it?"

Again, he looked a little lost, a little uncertain, as if some animating force had departed him. Maybe the Battle Drugs had worn off. Or maybe whatever influence Candle had over him had waned.

He closed his eyes for a moment. "It was necessary. You worry about a handful of people that are doomed anyways. You could never look up high enough to see it all. But Candle does. We're going to save more than a few people, Sophie. We're going to change the world."

A dreamy look came into his eyes then. "I'd do it all again. Even now. That's what you don't understand."

"I understand well enough."

"Don't make me laugh. It hurts. You don't understand *anything*. You don't know why we did this tonight. You don't even know who your fucking friends are. You're a joke."

Sophie looked back over her shoulder, where Hunker John was. He had pushed himself to his feet and had wrapped his wounded wrist in a torn piece of his shirt. His face was bone-white, and his fanciful hairdo was thoroughly wrecked.

She fixed Hunker with her gaze, and asked him the same question she'd asked Lee. "Why?"

He shrugged, a broken little half-gesture, favoring his arm. He had wiped the tears from his face and now seemed almost angry. "What do you mean, *why?* You knew I sold secrets to the Queen. You never cared before. I was just selling them to someone else, too. I didn't . . . *Shit.* I didn't know it was going to go down like this, Sophie. I didn't know what kind of shit they were planning. I promise you that, at least."

"Yeah," Sophie said, slowly, "that might be true. And I might have been able to forgive that. But the thing is, Hunk . . . once you did know, you kept helping them."

Hunker looked away. After a long moment, he nodded.

"So why?"

He laughed, "Why the fuck did we ever do anything, Sophie? *Money.* Money, and sex. I've never pretended to want anything else. Gods, I thought you would take the drugs. You could have taken the Battle Drugs, and we could have *ruled* the Loche de Menthe. I didn't know you were going to turn back into a fucking hero. Well, I'm no hero, Sophie. I never signed up for that. I'm a degenerate and a grifter. It's all I ever pretended to be."

He shook his head and looked at her with deep, wounded eyes. "I thought we were the same. I thought once I gave them the Book, once you opened the vault, we'd be out of it. We could go back to what we're *good at, Sophie.*"

Sophie nodded, and looked down at the angry red scars on her arms.

She looked back at Hunker. Behind him, Ben lifted an eyebrow, and she was chilled to know what he meant by it.

Hunker must have felt it too; he half turned to give Ben a considering look. "So, Capitana," he said, "you gonna kill me now?"

Sophie shook her head. "No, Hunk," she said. "I'm not gonna kill you. But you make me fucking sad, man."

This seemed to wound him far more than anything else had. He kept his head down for a long moment.

"Fuckin' *rat,*" Lee said. He seemed close to the end of his energy, only kept alive by the unnatural silver in his arms. When Hunker raised his eyes, they seemed calmer. He opened his mouth to speak, but Sophie never got to hear what he was about to say. She saw Ben stiffen behind him, and behind *that* she saw the

quite unwelcome sight of several Queen's Troops enter the shelving room, flanking the entirely unwelcome sight of her old lover, her old tutor, the one and only
Denver Murkai.

———

She hadn't even realized that her arms had flared alight until Denver yelled loudly,
holding up his strange-looking chutter. "Hey now! *Twistcraft* chutters, Sophie!
Dirt-Magic! No silver in these, okay? Nothing for your little arms to work on. So
let's all calm right down, okay? Weapons on the floor, everybody. Yes, even you,
Hunker John, you little traitor shit, down on the floor, very easy now."

He shoved Ben in the back of the head with his odd chutter, making him
stumble forwards. The guards fanned out, keeping all of the Killers within range.
Denver grinned at Sophie, and shoved Ben again. "Let it go, Sophie. Now."

She did. The silver fire—and the excruciating pain—fell away from her arms
and hands. She could sense that he was telling the truth, that there was no silver
in their chutters. She was helpless against them.

God, Jane must have been planning this for a long time. *Twistcraft?* Where had
they found a Dirt-Magic wizard—in the Keep?

Lee spoke, a ghastly whisper. "Hi, Denver. Thought you might show up."

"You can shut your fucking mouth, Lee Vesachai," Denver said. "I've heard
enough out of you for *five* lifetimes."

Denver stepped around Ben, approaching the trio of Sophie, Lee, and Hunker
John. He looked between the three of them and clucked, chiding. He tsked,
seemed amused. He tapped his large, wicked-looking chutter against his thigh.

"Sophie, Sophie, Sophie," he said. "Made a mess of this night, haven't you?"

"I do try."

He looked around. "Where's your big friend? And the tattooed one, with the
hair?"

"They're off fighting some legendary Cold Wizards that just showed up."

He grinned. "For the life of me, I can't tell if you're kidding. Never mind; the
rest of my troops will round them up. Now, I should warn you, Sophie Vesachai,
that both me and my Queen are *entirely* out of fucking patience with you. So
here's what's going to happen: you're going to give me the Book, right now. And
then I'll take all of you to the Queen, whereupon she will decide how each of you
can best assist her going forward. Sound good? Yes?"

Sophie made a show of slumping her shoulders. She forced herself not to look
at the shelf that held the *real* Book. She made herself not look at Ben. There still
might be a way out of this. "It's right there. Covered in my brother's blood."

Denver glanced at it. "*That's* the Book?"

"That's the Book."

Denver shook his head, sorrowfully.

"Try again, kid." He lifted his chutter, so confident of his aim that he didn't even take his eyes away from hers, and blew off the top of Hunker John's head.

Sophie saw a look of surprise, infinite and forever, on John's face, and then it disappeared in a spray of red gore. His slight frame, still immaculately dressed even after this long night, stood for a long moment, swaying. His mouth was slightly open, as if ready to deliver one last cutting quip or bon mot. And then his body keeled over, falling to the floor.

Sophie felt very cold, the way she always had once the battle had started. Everything seemed to start happening very slowly and very precisely. She watched blood pool out from Hunker's head, a crimson she couldn't pull her eyes from, but Denver snapped his fingers in front of her eyes.

"Sophie? Here, Sophie. Steady! Eyes up here."

She dragged her eyes up to his. His smile was calm, reassuring, like it had been when she was a child. Like it had been when he'd taken her to Saint Station. They crinkled a little at the corners when he smiled.

"The Book, Sophie," he said. "You have another friend here. And I'd rather not kill him. *Ben* isn't a traitor. And little Hunker John most definitely was. So, how about you give me the real Book, and then Ben, here, doesn't have to lose *his* head?"

He had his brutal chutter aimed at her oldest friend. One of his soldiers took a step to the side, getting out of the cone of needle-spray from the weapon. Sophie's eyes found Hunker John's corpse again, the spray of viscera where his face used to be.

"Give me the Book, Sophie. I'm almost out of patience."

Ben's eyes darted, looking for a way out. But the guards had them all covered. "Don't do it, Sophie," he said. His hand twitched towards his carry, where she knew he kept a small knife. She couldn't let him do that.

"It was always going to come to this, Ben," Sophie said. "And I've always known what the answer had to be."

She walked over to a nearby shelf and let her fingertips trail across the old, dusty books until they rested on a slim, unadorned volume. Her senses could tell, though. It *blazed* with silver. She pulled it out, looked at it for a moment, and held it out to Denver. But she heard a noise from the opposite entrance to the room, and turned to look.

"No, Sophie." It was Trik; panting, looking at her with wide eyes. Trik took in the scene; Denver with his chutter trained on Ben's head, Lee a bloody ruin on the floor, the half-headed form of Hunker John. Her eyes filled with tears, and she shook her head. "Don't give that to him."

"I won't let Ben get killed."

But Trik shook her head again, sending her dark cloud of hair waving. She walked, slowly, over to where Ben was standing, her hands raised. She placed herself between him and Denver's chutter, blocking the line of fire. Denver watched this play out, head cocked, bemused. Trik smiled, and it wasn't a nice smile.

"Trik!" Sophie said, sharply.

"Trust me, Capitana," Trik said, not taking her eyes off Denver.

"Trik!" Sophie felt panic rise up, because she knew the look on Denver's face. He was getting ready to *teach somebody a lesson*. He was smiling, too. She tried to catch his eye, to distract him. "Here's the Book, Denver! It's right here. I'm giving it up. Nobody needs to get hurt."

"Shut up, Capitana, and hold onto that Book." Trik focused on Denver. "How about it, big man? You want to take a shot at *me?*"

Denver laughed. "If you think I've got a problem killing a woman, *Trik*, you are sadly mistaken. And if you want to die in place of Ben, well? By all means. I always liked Ben."

"Everybody likes Ben," Trik said. "It's goddamn annoying."

"You best calm right the fuck down," Denver promised, stepping closer to Trik and focusing his chutter on her face, "or I'll take your head off just to prove a point."

"Shoot, motherfucker," she said, holding up her hand in front of the muzzle. He did.

Sophie flinched, expecting a spray of gore and fingers and brains, but nothing like that happened. The brutal spray of chutter-needles, which should have taken off her hand, arm, shoulder, *and* head, merely bounced off her palm. All she did was wiggle her hand, shaking it from the wrist. She blew on it. "Shit! I forgot that actually *hurts*. Been a while, since anything hurt."

"Trik . . ." Sophie breathed, unable to believe what she'd just seen. The guards were shocked as well, but Denver recovered faster than anybody. With a snarl, he centered the chutter on Trik again and tried to fire, but he was too late. Trik grabbed the chutter, squeezed, and the weapon crumpled into a ball of shattered gearwork, taking a few of Denver's fingers with it. He screamed and dropped to his knees. Trik looked down at him, a vengeful look on her face. She didn't look up when she spoke.

"*Run, Sophie!*"

Then, ignoring the chutter fire as the other guards opened up on her, she punched Sophie's old tutor in the face. Only, her fist didn't rebound; she didn't break his nose. Her fist went through the front of his face, and the sound of shattering bone was sickeningly loud in the close confines of the room.

Sophie ran.

THE DEADSMITH

The Door Into Deception

"Don't threaten a strong man with a weak stick."

—CORAZON LI, 'IV'

The Deader stepped through the Door into heavy sunlight, and for a moment held his face up to that ancient wonder, feeling it burn on his skin. The Door closed behind him, the Tower—and one of the Nine, Diasz—disappeared. The Deader held the last small bit of his Lady's scent deep within him until he could hold it no more, and then breathed her out—into the fragrant air of the Highlands of Forest.

The Deader wasn't made for wonder; such subtle emotions had been burned out of him long ago, by the ministrations of a man named Trail and the harsh tutelage of the city Tyrathect. And, perhaps, by countless years prosecuting the Nine's obscure aims out in the Dark; aims that, more often than not, required blood rather than subtlety. But even he felt a little wonder, looking around at the thick forest of living trees, the grays and greens of the Highlands sloping down before him. He looked, again, through the opening in the trees, past the slab of glassy black rock with the corpse with the silver knife driven into it, and saw the hunched shape of the Stone Giant down in the valley. He saw the flickering of fire on its rocky face. He knew the Prey was waiting.

His Fate, mercifully, was quiet. The Deader looked at his hands for a moment, curled them into fists, and let them go. He stood there for awhile, almost at peace, and then went to meet the Prey.

How do you make a machine? The Deader supposed he was about to find out. And then he would kill the Prey anyway.

If Diasz wanted blood on his teeth, he would bring it. He realized with a small modicum of surprise that he hated Diasz; he always had. He hated most of the Nine. He had never thought of it before. It had never mattered before.

He paused at the silver-wrapped skeleton of some nameless Cold, pinned to the black rock with a Rapine through its silver-wrapped skull. He felt the ward that exuded from the stone, but he was able to pass. He held no silver beneath his skin. His power was of another sort. He stepped past the stone and down onto the rocky slope, shielding his eyes from the incandescent wheel of the sun.

He felt as if he were walking into legend, and perhaps he was. Most folk in the Wanderlands thought that this place was more fantasy than the Twins themselves, than even the Giant, Kindaedystrin. He felt warm breeze on his face, fragrant with the incomprehensible smells of a living Land. He saw a tiny figure below him, sitting in the lee of the bowed Stone Giant, looking into the fire.

But this figure wasn't the Prey. It was too small. A child? The Deader made his way down the rocky slope toward the fire, circumnavigating big spars of dark-gray rock. When he got closer, he saw that the figure waiting for him was a young girl, dark-haired, and when he got closer still, he discovered she was rolling something small and golden between the palms of her hands.

He wished he had his Fate to warn him of the dangers. He was as careful as he could be, but the part of him that was instinct had been smashed like a bone-china plate. He wished he had his Machine to reconnoiter, but the hunter part of him now lay beneath the long-dead dirt of a long-dead forest. There was only *him* left now, and he wasn't sure what or who that was.

He tried to be wary, but this was just another little girl who looked a lot like his sister, just another arcane trap. Still, he thought the Prey might be near. This had the air of a tableau. A finality suffused the warm air.

The Deader approached the fire, shadowed in the sadly stooped gaze of the Stone Giant. The girl was maybe six or seven years old, with a scowl on her face. Looking more closely, the Deader saw that her hair had been dyed black. She had exactly Winter's brilliant green eyes. She looked like Winter; she looked like his long-lost sister; she looked like Anise, the girl from Tyrathect.

Her angry scowl made all of the women in his life live in her face.

The Deader looked around the campsite. The girl was dirty and her hair unkempt. He wondered how long she had been traveling with the Prey. He watched the glint of gold in her hands, something like a ball, and it rolled between her palms. She looked at him with undisguised hate. He judged the distances; no matter how fast she threw that thing, he could avoid it. He felt that lassitude, once again; what did it matter? Let the Prey do what he would. He wanted this *done*. He took another step towards the girl, and his Fate screamed in a wordless, directionless howl. But the warning was too late.

A circle of golden fire rose around him, perhaps ten paces across, a shifting wall of copper-bronze force, a prison of gold. The Deader snarled a word, a White-on-Black word, but it did nothing. His skin flared white, he made a grasping gesture, he tore at the gold fire with every trick he knew.

Perhaps his Fate could have helped him. Perhaps he could have fashioned his Machine into something to help him escape. But there was only him, and he could not. He was trapped in a column of golden fire. Eventually he stopped trying, and waited in the columnar prison, secured by the thin circle of gold that had been buried in the dirt in front of the girl. Eventually, a man walked down from the foothills, approaching the fire. He was thin, with exhausted, darkened eyes and hollow cheeks. He walked with a limp. The Deader supposed his Machine had left its mark on this creature. The man smiled, though, studying the Deader for a few long moments before speaking.

"Hello, Deadsmith," the Prey said.

No, the Deader thought, *no*. Though he must, he did not want to do this. He did not want to find out what this man had planned for him. He felt weary and wanted to sit down. There was a chunk of stone inside the golden circle, and so he did. The Deader looked up at the man, who he judged had earned his name. "Hello, Candle. *Chris*. I know you."

The man grinned. "I wondered if you'd remember. The last time we met, I had to lose my brother and my home to escape you. I wonder what I'll lose this time?"

"Your life." The Deader spat. The spittle was able to pass the golden walls of thin fire. The girl stared at him, savagely.

Candle laughed at the threat. He held something small in his hands, a simple chutter. The Deader saw a golden bolt chambered, and the man kept the weapon in between them. He sounded more tired than the last time they'd spoken, in the whisper-maze. He sounded more sane.

"My life," he said, finally, "has been lost for a while now. Ever since your Twins-damned Lady set you on my trail, to be honest. I had counted on her embarrassment, you see; I thought she would let me escape and keep the Domination that I stole from her. That will teach me to try to game with the Wise. What is embarrassment to a creature like Winter?"

"Tell me what you mean to tell me," the Deader said, "and let's be done."

But Candle just looked at him. His eyes were strange, disquieting. Something unpleasant moved in them. "You think I fear for my life, but you are wrong." His eyes slid to the girl, who still hadn't spoken, and he laughed, shortly. "My life isn't so much, and it would be fair payment for the things I have done. Only, I have things to accomplish yet, Deader, before you can claim me. I had hoped to cry you off, to kill you if possible or damage you enough to escape. But I'll admit to another purpose, a kind of last resort. A sort of gamble."

He laughed again, and this time he sounded half-mad once more. He gestured up at the blank, sorrowful gaze of the Stone Giant above them, and sighed.

"I have been avoiding this place my whole life," Candle said, "ever since I saw it as a boy. Have you ever seen a living Giant? No? They are terrifying. They are a whole *other thing*, Deadsmith. And I mean to enter their home. I cannot have you on my trail, not for that. But you will not quit, will you? So once again my choices come down to no choice at all. I must break you or I must kill you."

He looked at the weapon in his hands and then at the Deader. The Deader waited, feeling that thick lassitude in his limbs, wondering what the man's true weapon was. He was wearily sure he wouldn't have to wait long. This was the end of the hunt, one way or another. He didn't need his Fate to know that.

"You misplace your loyalty, Deadsmith," Candle said after a moment, with the air of starting a sermon. "You serve monsters."

The Deader snorted a brief bark of laughter. "It is a time for monsters."

Candle smiled. "That is certainly true. But do you know what sort of monsters you serve, Deadsmith? I am a monster, too, but an honest one. I know what you hunger for; you are a machine driven by a mainspring, but it is not the one you think. You gave up your purpose to serve another, and one not deserving of it. I would give you your purpose back, Deadsmith! I would show you a purpose beyond the maintenance of a cruel kingdom, an empire of fear."

The man's voice grew eager and impassioned, his hands making small gestures, shaping the air. His speaking patterns and cadence told the Deader that these words had been often repeated, shaped, and practiced. The weapon that held the deadly golden bolt wavered.

"You were made to hunger for order, for truth, for purpose. You have settled for the cold comfort of the Nine, but look around you, Deadsmith. Look! Don't you see? *Look* at what this world once was. It surrounds you. Taste the air, feel the sun on your face. Tell me that your Nine can give you this. Tell me that your Lady provides it."

The Deader studied Candle and his passion. He shook his head. "You are a fool."

Candle's eyes narrowed slightly, and then he made himself laugh. "That," he said, "is certain. And yet I would rather be a fool with the Mother's sun on my face than one of the Wise in the dark. And speaking of fools, Deadsmith, are you quite sure you know the nature of those you serve? Are you sure you have not been made a fool, yes, even by your *Lady?*"

"I would not speak ill of her, if I were you."

Candle smiled. "Oh, but my friend, the only reason I am here is to speak ill of your fucking *Lady*. Fucking *Winter*. And you will hear it, Deadsmith. You will hear it, and then we will be done. One way or another."

The Deader sighed. "Speak, then. I wish an end to this."

Candle laughed, a sharp and bitter sound.

"Very well, Deadsmith. Very well. I have done what I could, and so starts my last desperate play. I have shown you the core of you. Let us see if you can see the true shape of yourself."

The Deader spat into the dust again and waited for the Prey, finally, at long last, to spring his trap.

THE CABAL

The Utility of Winter

"Do not think to know her. Love her, worship her, fear her, or oppose her. But never make the mistake of thinking you know her. Every single person who has believed that has been destroyed."

—HUNTER FINE, 'OLD LOVERS AND NEW FOES'

"These fuckers," Winter says, delighting in the profanity, "are *certainly* hard to kill, aren't they?"

"Please." Candle's teeth are clenched tight in pain. His face is pale with blood loss, and he stumbles as he walks. "You want the Behemoth dead even less than you want the fucking *Giant* dead."

"What I really want," Winter admits, "is some new friends. And who is more ready for a friend than two outcast monsters, shunned by machine and man alike, harried through the darkness by all manner of awful circumstance, merely for the want of a meal?"

The Behemoth are certainly being harried now. Winter has summoned the Cache of departed Master D'Alle's warmachines, and together with the remaining Feral Children, they are doing their best to kill the two creatures from another world. *If* they can be killed. The battle rages in the dark outside Cannoux, and Winter and Candle follow the swath of destruction.

Candle walks, head down, his breath coming in hitching gasps. Winter frowns and prods him with an elbow. He grunts, shuddering, cradling his bandaged hand and missing finger. The one that Winter had chewed off, and spit in the dust outside of Cannoux.

"Must I?"

"Dance for me, boy!" Winter says, amused. "What fun is all this if I can't brag about it? Come, now, your finger can't hurt *that* much. I believe I was speaking about making new friends . . . ?"

"We'll see." Candle grunts. "They may see through your ploy. I would. And then what will you do?"

"Improvise." Winter examines her new silver ring.

They hear the sounds of an enormous battle, up ahead, a titanic struggle. They pass still-twitching soldier-constructs, great crablike things of silver, hardened porcelain, and unbelievable strength. They have been caved in, ripped apart, demolished. Some of them have been cut in pieces, clean cuts that seem almost polished. Winter's confidence in the sword is renewed.

"Come now," she says, remonstrating. "Where is your faith? It will work, one way or another. And in the process—"

"And in the process you managed to kill an old enemy, Lourde. West. *Mr. Vutch.*" Candle grunts, giving her what she wants, which is an audience. "*In the process,* you managed to destroy most of Mr. Turpentine's Feral Children, test my powers, and add Cannoux to your empire."

Winter made a twirling gesture with her finger: *go on.*

"Not to mention," Candle continues, "stick a thumb in West's brother's and my old master's eye. I'm sure you've been wanting to put a boot on Charts' neck for a while, haven't you? And, of course, you got to settle an old score with D'Alle. Who, from what I remember, only committed the great crime of annoying you once, a long time ago. You need someone else to gloat to, Winter; it just bores me."

"Don't forget this fine opportunity to test the warmachines!" Winter is clearly charmed with herself. "I really am quite good at this."

"We'll see. Don't try to pretend *now* that you planned it all in advance. And I think you're overestimating Mr. Turpentine's ability to be ingratiating to the people who are killing all his children."

"Candle! I'm disappointed," Winter ruffles his hair. "Don't you know anything about that old monster? The more he hates you, the more polite and charming he gets. Right up until he chews your face off."

"Well, he must hate you considerably, then."

"Oh, yes," Winter says, nodding. "I can't imagine anyone that evil bastard hates more. But in any case, don't overestimate his attachment to these Feral Children. Nothing about that creature is as simple as it seems."

Candle looks at her, sidelong, profiled in the light from the city. Behind them, he hears the distant but heavy tread of more of the soldier-constructs of the Cache, marching to meet their doom at the hands of the Behemoth.

"I like you, Candle," Winter says lightly, looking down at the carnage, mostly obscured by the gloom. "I always have, from that first moment I met you, so long ago, in Master D'Alle's study. You and your brother, with such bad luck and timing. You have always had an ability to fuck with my plans in interesting ways."

"Only you would enjoy that."

"Well, and why not?" she asks. "Games get boring when you always win."

"Let's not pretend that we're equals, all right? My missing finger still hurts too much for *banter.*"

"Oh, we're nothing like equals," Winter says, amused. "And yet I know you make your plans. I know that even now you move hidden pieces on the board. You do an excellent pose of helplessness, but it does not entirely suit you."

Candle is quiet for a moment, looking at his captor. "Why allow it, then? Why allow me to maneuver, to shuffle my pieces, if the game is for such high stakes?"

Winter rolls her eyes and makes a little throwing-away gesture. "Stakes are subjective. And even the highest of stakes can become pedestrian to someone like me. You don't mind if I add a little salt to my meal, do you? It *so* enhances the taste."

"You do like to take chances," Candle says. His face is ash-gray, the color of the old broken stone around them.

Winter smiles at him, showing teeth. "One must do what one can in these lost and broken days to keep oneself amused. Ah! And *look at this*."

She has seen something glint, on the edges of the light, and Candle shuffles after her, profoundly spent from his efforts harrying the Behemoth down the Mountain. He sees Primary Gray moving to the half-destroyed warmachines, and where he touches them, they stop moving. Winter is looking down at something long and steel-gray, lying on the ground at her feet.

"All this trouble," Candle says, finally, "over a cheap weapon no bladesmith in their right mind would admit to making."

"Amusing, isn't it?" Winter asks.

The Black-Portal sword is lying in the rubble of the fight. The Behemoth must have dropped it. It isn't long, and as Candle said, it isn't particularly well made or fine. It is just a sword, with a slight curve and one sharp edge, chisel-tipped, and with a crooked maker-stamp in the blade.

Candle cradles his wounded hand and looks at his captor. "Well? I sure as hell know *I'm* not going to be able to pick it up."

"There are few folk who could," Winter says softly, crouching down. Her fingers brush over the blade, the cheaply made hilt.

"And what if you can?" Candle says. "Do you still take the risk of befriending Behemoth? Or will you use it to kill them?"

"I'm not sure." Her hand touches the hilt, and wraps around it. "We'll play that one by ear. As I said before, they have succeeded in annoying me, and if I can swing this thing, perhaps I will swing it through their necks."

"You're too predictable, Winter. It's going to get you killed someday."

"Perhaps," Winter says. "But you won't be there to see it. You'll live as long as you amuse me, so I would concentrate on being amusing."

"Fuck you," Candle says. "Pick it up or don't. I have no intention of being *amusing*. I know what you need me for, so let's not play games with each other. I will live long enough to see the Mother herself, I think. And after that? Who knows? Who knows for *any* of us, if you get your way."

"Indeed!" Winter picks up the Black-Portal sword, admiring it. Muscles strain in her forearm, but she picks it up. "Who knows for any of us—*if I get my way*. But I tell you one thing," she says, ancient eyes twinkling, "my way won't be boring."

THE KILLERS

The War for the Book

"Cleaner to fall upon a sword than try to bargain with the Wise."
—CORAZON LI, 'ANALECTS'

Sophie was fourteen, running desperately through the Keep, trying to get to where the Jannissaries were stored, her Book clutched to her chest, her arms aching with burns from the silver fire. She was thirty-four, running through the passageways of the Library, trying to find a safe place where she could use the Book, where she could *fight*. When she was fourteen, and when she was thirty-four, chaos seemed to be blossoming around her like a demented flower.

Sophie and Ben ran from the room where her brother and Hunker John died and straight into a contingent of the Queen's troops, four soldiers equipped with those odd Dirt-Magic chutters. Ben dove to the side, firing his chutter and taking out one of them, and Sophie dove the other way. She wasn't able to affect the actual soldiers, but that didn't mean she was powerless. She just had to get creative. Her arms flared alight with coruscating patterns of silver fire and she reached out to any silver around her she could find.

There were some old constructs, Silver-made, on the shelves behind the guards and Sophie pulled Silver from the wirework in the walls and *jerked* the constructs towards it. It was an imprecise way to fight, but two of the devices—perhaps the size of cats—caught one guard in the shoulder and the other in the back of the head, killing her instantly. The injured guard spun around, shoulder smashed, and the two remaining troops were stunned for a moment. But only a moment, and then they snarled and brought their chutters up. Ben had to scramble one way; Sophie scrambled another, and ran.

The past always comes back to haunt, she knew. Once again she was running, trying to avoid a fight, trying to get to a place where she could use her Book and save her friends. Once again she didn't know if those friends were still alive. Could Trik—who must be a Behemoth, as reluctant as Sophie was to admit it—survive all of the Queen's troops? Could Bear survive the Cold? Could poor Ben survive, with only his chutter?

When Sophie was fourteen, she had saved the world, but most of her friends had died in the process. Now she just wanted to save her friends. She ran from room to octagonal room, hunting for somewhere safe, because she would be defenseless while she used the Book. But there was nowhere safe; the warren of the Library seemed to have filled up with small bands of the Queen's soldiers, and it was everything Sophie could do to avoid them. She heard a muted crashing sound; what was *that*? She stepped into a room where one of those Vesachai-like Cold was dancing around several of the soldiers, silver knife flashing—were the Cold fighting the soldiers . . . ? She ducked back the way she'd come before they could see her, and before she understood what was happening.

The structure of the Library made this kind of fighting bewildering, strange, almost hypnotic. The octagonal pattern of the rooms and oddly serpentine passageways made for sudden turnings of corners and unwelcome surprises. Sophie ran, ducking out of the way of more of Jane's troops; she must have sent half an army down here.

Sophie was trying to make her way to the outer edges of the maze; if she could find a room with only one entrance, she could barricade it and—perhaps—buy herself ten minutes with the Book. But she was all mixed around; she didn't know where the outer edge of this place might be.

When she was fourteen, that part had been easier. She knew where she was going; she knew where the Jannissaries lay waiting, in their sterile crypt, sleeping until it was time for some unimaginable war. The hard part, back then, was getting there. The hard part was knowing she had gotten hundreds—maybe thousands—killed because she was too fucking *stupid* to remember the Jannissaries, too young and dumb and stupid to put it all together and realize what the Book was *for*. Later she would realize that most of her friends were dead because she hadn't figured out the secret right in front of her face.

And now, maybe her friends were going to die because she couldn't find a *safe place to hide*. Well . . . her remaining friends. She tried not to remember that look of infinite surprise on Hunker's face, right before it was erased in a spray of gore. She almost hoped that Avie had betrayed her or abandoned her, recognized a lost cause and cut her losses; then she might survive.

Sophie rounded a corner out of a passageway and into one of the bigger rooms, its floor littered with old detritus, and collided with someone who was also running; a slim man with a broad face. Sophie caught a glimpse of silver at his waist before she piled into him.

He recovered quickly, more quickly than she did, and spun into a crouched, waiting stance, his Rapine held back along his forearm in that unusual pose like the Cold ones Bear fought. He smiled, slowly, and his eyes dropped down to the Book in Sophie's hand.

"Such a thing is not for the likes of you," he said, his voice high and firm. "Best to hand it over."

Sophie glanced over her shoulder, seeing if she could run, but she had seen Vesachai throw Rapine with deadly accuracy and knew she wouldn't be able to dodge. She took in the man's stance. He was a trained fighter, maybe even better trained than regular Vesachai. If Bear could be believed, this was one of the Cold.

It just figured that tonight, of all nights, would be when those ancient bastards decided to reveal themselves. One more coincidence? Or was nothing coincidental on this absolute clusterfuck of a night?

"Give me that artifact," the Cold said, again, eyes fixed on the Book. "Such a thing belongs with us."

"Afraid I can't do that." Her arms flared alight with that excruciatingly painful burn. She didn't try to rip his Rapine away; his friends had already shown her the Cold could resist that maneuver. She tried the *pushing* move her brother had used on Bear and Trik. The Cold should have been thrown back against the shelving behind him, but he only grunted and slipped back a little.

"The Cold *built* the thing that gave you those powers," he said. "You think we can't counter something we ourselves made? Hand over the schema-book, and you may survive this."

Sophie laughed. "I gave up on *surviving* it a ways back." And she charged him.

She didn't have a weapon, but she'd been brawling for the last fifteen years, and she'd fought more than one trained fighter. The thing about trained fighters was they tended to expect *you* to be trained too, to make moves that they could counter, so they could figure out your patterns and styles and defeat them. But Sophie didn't have any patterns or style. She threw strategy aside and put all of her concentration into using her magic to slow down that silver blade. She dropped the Book; if she survived this, she could pick it up; if she didn't, *fuck it.*

He tried to swing it up into her path, but she was able use her silver fire to push it aside just enough for her to dodge. He'd been expecting some move or feint, and it took him a crucial second to realize that Sophie was just going to barrel straight the fuck into him. She hit him hard, got hit hard, grabbed something that felt like an ear, and pulled.

The Cold twisted under her grip, and she dug a knee into the general region where his groin should be. She missed the good bits, but it gave her leverage to get a solid elbow into his face.

Her arms were still flared alight, and she reached out with her heightened senses, hoping to find anything with silver in it. There was something on a nearby shelf—a broken mechanism. She used the silver fire wreathing her arms to rip it free and smashed it into the man's face, but he got his hand up in time and deflected some of the blow. He twisted powerfully, throwing her off, but she contrived to plant a knee on his knife hand, hard enough to feel bones crack.

He inhaled sharply, but if he was a fucking *Cold*, he would be used to pain. Sophie was gratified and surprised to find she wasn't dead yet. Here she was, punching up on a mythical, legendary warrior-priest, and was kind of winning. He didn't let go of his Rapine, but because he was addled enough from Sophie's blow to the head, she took a risk. With a groan of power that felt as if it were splintering her bones longways, she *pushed* the Rapine away again, and felt it tear out of his grip.

Good. Now she could tussle. After this long, paranoid, surprise-filled night, it felt good to just let it all go and fight.

She slammed her face into the Cold's, breaking both their noses, and felt, for a moment, clear and clean and amazing. He got a strong-fingered hand into her side and clutched, maybe breaking a rib or two. He tried to throw her off, and she locked her legs around him and wrenched, taking back a few broken ribs.

He lashed out somehow and caught her in the ear, mashing it and making her head ring, but she kept squeezing with her legs and felt a few more things give. He gasped. Her hand pointed, wreathed in silver fire, at where the Cold's knife lay on the ground. She pulled the Rapine to her. Too late, he realized what she was doing and gasped, "No!" but then the knife was in her hand. And then it was in his skull.

She breathed for a few moments, feeling the man die underneath her, not a totally undesirable feeling. She had just killed a fucking *Cold*. Four hours ago, she hadn't known they still existed, and now one was dead beneath her. She laughed, but then she heard a noise behind her. She twisted to see.

A woman, soft-faced with hard eyes, a silver knife at her belt, crouched down and holding something in her hands. She was looking at Sophie, her eyes black pinholes.

"Marten was a good warrior," the woman said, tucking the Book into her carry, "and you'll die for that. But not now."

She stood, swiftly, gave Sophie one last death-black look, and ran away. Sophie saw another silver-knifed woman join her, and they disappeared into the complex space between the shelves.

The Book was gone.

————

Sophie stumbled through the maze of the Library. She was bleeding from somewhere. Her side? *Somewhere.* It didn't matter. She stumbled over a dead body and tried to focus on the face. She felt a vague relief; it wasn't one of her friends.

Sophie had killed how many, now? How many of Jane's soldiers? Seven? Eight? But she'd taken wounds doing it. She had to pull Silver from devices on shelves around her, attack the soldiers and their twistcraft chutters with whatever she could, and it wasn't always effective. Fortunately, she hadn't run into any more of those fucking *Cold* bastards. She was exhausted, and wounded in a few places. She'd taken a few stray chutter-needles in her left calf, but they'd gone clean through. She was still alive. Somehow.

She heard a sound from behind her and whirled, painful silver fire enveloping her arms—but it wasn't one of Jane's soldiers or one of the Twins-damned Cold. It was Avie.

"Hey, Sophie," Avie said.

There was blood on Sophie's hand, from something. Oh, right—she'd broken her nose. She looked up, and Avie was still there. "Hey," Sophie said.

"Ran into a couple tough motherfuckers," Avie commented and pulled something out from behind her back. "Made the mistake of attacking my friend. He's hunting them down as we speak. But they had this."

Sophie laughed, helpless not to. Avie held the Book in her hand. "Yeah?" Sophie said, finally.

Avie looked down at the Book, turning it over in her hands. Sophie noticed that she wasn't wearing her perfect—and to Sophie, somewhat boring—face. She wore her old scars and the new ones, from when Lee had exploded her chutter. Sophie tried to focus. She was having a little trouble staying upright. And staying, like . . . conscious.

"So?" Sophie asked, again, looking at the Book in Avie's hands. She couldn't help but notice that Avie hadn't handed it over yet. "You decide I can be trusted with this, New Girl?"

"My name," she said severely, "is *Avie.*"

But she held the Book out for Sophie to take.

"Thank you." Sophie tried not to sag with relief. "I just need five minutes with this thing, but I'll be helpless during it."

Avie nodded, and looked over her shoulder. "This way." She grabbed Sophie's hand and pulled her along, back the way Sophie had come. Sophie went, deciding on trust. Avie took a different exit from the room Sophie had just been through, though, and pulled her up a winding passageway, and into a dead-end room, small, filled with what looked like old clothes. Avie hefted one of the strange-looking twistcraft chutters out of her carry, clearly plundered from a dead soldier. She took up a defensive position near the single entrance and looked back at Sophie. Her one eye was still severely bloodshot, making the green iris fairly glow.

"Well? I've been hearing about this 'Book' all night. Let's see what you can do, Vesachai."

"Thanks, Avie," Sophie said, opening the Book. She heard the reply, spoken softly, but didn't look up.

"No problem, Sophie."

She didn't have time to feel a little warm glow at the way Avie had said her name, nor examine the quite complicated bullshit that would go along with acknowledging that feeling. She settled herself into a cross-legged stance, set the slim Book on her lap, and opened it.

When she was fourteen, she had done this too.

Most of the pages were blank, except for small, carefully lettered designations on the lower left corner of each page. She flipped through these—most of them still made no sense to her—until she found the one that meant "Keep." There was a black, irregular dot in the center of that page. She took a deep breath and set her mind *an-tet,* the Vesachai mind-trick.

It was hard; she was out of practice. Fifteen years of misanthropy didn't do much for your concentration. She heard the vague sounds of fighting nearby, but she had to trust Avie. She tried to concentrate.

The dot expanded and then frayed. She focused, trying to see both past and in front of the dot; she tried to hold her mind in a cold, clear state. It was maddeningly hard to do, especially after the night she'd had, but she had always been good at this. After a few moments, the black dot rushed towards her, expanding up beyond the bounds of the paper, a kind of optical illusion that gave the sense of three dimensional space where there was none.

She took a few moments to orient herself; it had been a long time since she'd done it. Silver lines formed a grid around her. She struggled to remember the old commands. She pulled her point of view back, and it started to make sense. She saw the laid silver in the walls and columns of the Library, tiny symbols denoting the lights, switching mechanisms, and some that she didn't know.

There were many invisible mysteries all around them, hidden in the stone walls of the Keep. Even Sophie only knew a handful of them.

The first thing she did was find the entrance to the Library, a symbol like a rotating cube, and sort of *pulled* on it in a certain way. Distantly, back in the real world, she heard an echoing boom.

Now they were locked in; Jane couldn't get any more troops in here. It was debatable strategy; that meant that Sophie would have to kill all of the ones that were *in* here, but it was the best she could do just now. Tomorrow's problems tomorrow. Sophie wiped her brow and concentrated.

There were no Jannissaries left in the Library, unfortunately, but there were many ancient things with some life left in them. And Silver was plentiful here; it was easy to pull from the heavy wirework in the walls and ceiling to activate old devices. The Book showed her, in curious symbols, what some of these did, and she worked feverishly.

She inhaled in that special way, her arms flaring alight, and the Book opened up in a manner that it had never been meant to. She was able to give commands that its makers had never intended; able to coerce and control devices that were never meant to be coerced and controlled.

The last time Sophie had done this, she awoke an entire cache of Jannissaries and commanded them to save the Keep. Now she activated old broken castoffs and commanded them to save her friends.

Far away, on a twist-work shelf, was a silvery rat-thing with half of its body missing. It stirred, filled with new power and new purpose. It saw a shape that it had been told was bad—the Queen's troops, and anything that looked like a Cold—and launched itself at it, clawing and snarling.

Somewhere else, a tall folding-construct awoke, snapped its fabric-bending arms into position, and went to find some soldiers to fold. Elsewhere a whole set of discarded chutters armed themselves and waited for a certain sort of person to walk by.

There was grunting nearby, wet sounds, and something splashed across Sophie's face. She had no time for it; she supposed it was just blood. She had work to do. She endured the exquisite pain from her arms and looked for more make-shift soldiers.

She found some heavy mechanisms that might have been meant to drill stone, back in the early days of the Underlands, and set them to work. She found a store-house of crude flying things, long inert, and filled them with Silver and the desire to find soldiers' eyes and claw at them.

She heard screams of pain rise, distantly, echoing. *Good.* Well, the easy part was done, then. She pulled her view back from the Library, grid zooming back, finding her way around. Finding the Rue de Paladia. She didn't know it, but she was biting her lip so hard it bled, a trickle of crimson down the side of her mouth. For a moment she felt a doubling; for a moment she was fourteen years old again, sitting cross-legged in the middle of the Hot Halls War, searching for the weapons she needed. Just like now.

She had used this Book, and the silver fire in her arms, to raise a Cache of Jannissaries, ancient warmachines that, for some unknown reason, were left sleeping in the Keep, in the dawn ages of the world. She had shown those Jannissaries the enemies that were killing her friends, invading her home, and she had set them loose.

Some people supposed that they had all been destroyed in the ensuing battle. And many of them were. But not all. And Sophie, with the last of her fourteen-year-old willpower, had told the remnants to hide, all through the Keep, and wait. Wait for another war, maybe. She didn't know what, back then. But she knew now.

One by one she found the sleeping Jannissaries, and used the Book to send them commands. Just like she had when she was young, she told them *there are strangers in the Keep*, showed them what Feral Children looked like, and told them where to find and hunt. In the Rue de Paladia, in the Ransom Parkway, in all of the dim and dark places of the Keep. She told them to hunt, find, and kill.

She clenched her teeth so hard that she later discovered she cracked one, and drew enough silver fire through her arms to kill a small god. She heard an immense, distant roaring, focused light blazing, and once again raised the Jannissaries to save the Keep.

Everything went into a white scream of pain and silver fire. On the very edges of her consciousness, she felt the Jannissaries wake, dust themselves off, and go hunting.

The Book fell from nerveless fingers, and Sophie came back to herself slowly. She felt hollowed out, rung like a great bell. Her vision seemed to be going in and out. She felt like she might be dying, just a little bit.

Her face was sticky. She prodded at it and saw that she was covered in blood. She blinked, looking around; the hallway outside the room was full of bodies, Queen's troops, dead. Something had fallen half across her; she'd been so deep in the Book she hadn't noticed. She frowned, trying to bring it into focus.

It was a long leg, streaked with blood. It was Avie's leg, still attached to the rest of her, thank the Mother; she had fallen half-across Sophie.

"No," Sophie said. "No."

Avie still clutched her chutter, her hand locked around its handle. Her hands twitched and she was trying to take a breath, but her chest was a red mess. Across the hallway, one of Jane Guin's soldiers clawed at the ruin that had been his face and died messily. Sophie scrambled out from under Avie and looked her over, frantic.

The damage was very bad. Avie's right arm had been almost completely erased by a hail of flechettes, and she had taken grievous wounds to her chest as well. Blood, rich and red, bubbled from her lips, and her green eyes found Sophie's.

"No," Sophie said, and gripped Avie's good hand, pushing aside the chutter. Avie tried to say something but was unable, and tears pricked at Sophie's eyes. She heard a massive sound, a rending sound, getting closer and closer, and then was thrown back by Avie's frightening friend bursting through the wall and shelves, scattering debris everywhere. His hands were wreathed in eye-watering patterns of black and white fire, like nothing Sophie had ever seen. The man skidded to his knees in front of Avie, his pale eyes taking in the damage and his already set mouth drawing down even further.

"*No,*" the man said, echoing Sophie and reached out towards Avie. The White-and-Black magic enveloped his arms up to his shoulders. Strange and terrifying energies flowed into Avie's wounds. Sophie watched, wide-eyed, as a white mesh

tried to stitch her flesh together raggedly, and black tendrils destroyed the flechettes that pierced her.

The remarkable man set his jaw, clearly struggling, and Sophie had to look
away and cover her eyes, so bright and terrible was the Black-and-White magic.
When it had waned enough, Sophie looked to see the man dropping his hands,
and shaking his head.

Avie's left arm was missing from below the bicep, but the stump was crudely
healed and only trickling blood. Her chest was somewhat healed, as well, but still
misshapen and leaking blood and bile from a dozen places. She was unconscious,
and Sophie could hear the sickening, labored sound of lungs that were barely able
to draw breath.

The man looked at Sophie. "That is all I can do. The Black-and-White was
only meant to heal me. She is still dying."

"Can we get her to a Medica?"

But he shook his head again. "This is beyond your people's craft. She has
many darts in her lungs, a few in her heart. I cannot remove them without killing
her, and her silver-work fights my magic."

Silver-work. Sophie felt her heart clench, looking at Avie's pained and blood-
spattered face. She saw the faint scars on her face, where the silver lay beneath. She
looked up at the man and recognized him. He had been in the balcony café, right
before Lee attacked them in the Rue de Paladia. But she had seen him before that,
too. He had been the tough-looking drunk she'd passed over in the Loche de
Menthe when she was looking for a fight. Forever ago. This was Avie's mysterious
and powerful "friend." She swallowed, her vision going in and out of focus.

"I know something that can heal silver-work," Sophie said. "A Silver-Age
Medica construct. Do you know such?"

The man's eyes blazed. "Yes."

"It is called Saint Station. You know of it?"

"*Yes.*"

"Can you find it, if I give you directions?"

The man shook his head. "There is no need. I can sense such things. You are
right; it is the best hope."

He picked Avie up effortlessly, as if she weighed no more than a blanket, but
Sophie caught his arm. He looked at her, his strangely no-color eyes bleary, but
impatient.

"Who are you?" Sophie asked. "Will you be able to coerce Saint Station into
healing her?"

"I am a Deadsmith," the man said, after considering his answer for a moment.
"I am her friend. Do not worry about your Station—such exist to serve such as
me. I'll save her, if she can be saved."

A *Deadsmith . . . ?* Sophie let his arm go. "Then save her. I owe her a drink. And you, too."

There was the barest ghost of a smile on that hard face. "I'll take you up on that."

And then they were both gone, and the great Library was, for a moment, as quiet as a grave. Sophie looked at the place where the Deadsmith and the unconscious Avie had been and discovered that all of the lights in the Library were slowly going out, fading to dark in a tunneling effect. She felt a small moment of panic, wondering what she'd done, when she realized with vast relief that she was merely passing out, her abused body and mind finally giving up the ghost on this long, long, *long* night.

THE LOST BOYS

A Final Flame in the Dark

"Few creatures are unlucky enough to know the exact hour that their childhood ended. Even fewer remember it fondly."

—EMIL-LEE CHEZCTH, 'FESTIVAL TALES'

A spark floated in darkness, a thin flickering of flame in a dark place. It was a fire, and it was up ahead. Chris and James and Katherine walked toward it because there was nothing else to walk towards. They had shut the Door behind them and Chris had changed the coordinates, hoping to keep the third Cold from following them.

He carried his brother; James was still unconscious. Chris' strange, preternatural, grasping mind tried to plan for whatever they found at the fire, tried to find options and the best course of action, but there was no data to be found. There was only dark, and there was only a fire. His options had closed down to one.

He hated that. He didn't know if he had ever hated anything as much as that feeling, the feeling that things were out of his control. When that happened, bad things came. When that happened, he had been forced to murder his brother's friend to save their lives. Or build a machine made of . . . of fucking *people*, who never played their parts right, to escape that damned basement. A machine that had exploded in his hand, and probably killed the wizard and mentor he called Uncle.

He looked down at his brother. James' face was just a faint impression in the distant light from the fire. Chris wasn't sure that he felt love like other people did, but the sight of his brother's face wrenched at him. Chris was a mechanist, a work-smith, a builder. He thought he could fix anything, given enough time and the right tools. He was starting to suspect that he could even fix the world, if he lived long enough. But he didn't think he would be able to fix what he'd done to James.

He felt Katherine looking at him but did not return her glance. She, too, was a problem for another time, a variable that had no possible solution at the moment. He wondered if Uncle was still alive; Chris very much doubted it. He had learned what he could of both Behemoth and Deadsmith years ago, and knew which one of them was more deadly.

But he hoped Uncle lived. He hoped the old man hadn't given his life for them, the way Buckle had. He hoped he'd see him again someday.

His brother was terribly heavy, dead weight, but Chris didn't falter. He did his best to ignore the pain in his ankle. It was irrelevant. He had always hated pain; it interfered with the fine gearwork of his mind. Made it hard to *think*, and that was almost worse than death. All he had was his mind, and he hated anything that troubled it—like Katherine, like his stubborn, brave, destructive brother. He also hated feeling as if he might start to cry. That, too, made it hard to think.

The fire grew closer, and Chris saw a figure beside it, waiting. Friend? Foe? His mind cast about for data and found none; this starvation of input and choice was a pain worse than even his ankle.

He didn't worry about leaving his mother behind, really; he supposed he loved her, but he had always had trouble with that particular habit of mind. She would be all right, or she wouldn't; he had no control over that any more. He would send word to her if he was ever able. In a certain way she had already ceased to exist for him. He supposed that made him some sort of monster, but he had no control over that either.

Chris D'Essan did what he could for the people close to him. But he had seen the sunshine on new trees, and he had seen the Rings spinning in the sky. He had seen a Giant. He supposed he loved his mother, yes. But he had *work* to do now.

They approached the fire, and Chris set James down. There was a man there, seated, waiting silently for them to approach. Katherine glanced at Chris nervously, but he knew it was more important to read the man in the wavering firelight. Chris wished he had a weapon; he wished he knew how to use the Key. But he didn't, and so he waited to see what would happen, and hoped new choices opened up.

The man's face seemed to jump and shiver in the firelight, though it didn't move at all. He was medium-sized, with dark hair and nondescript gray eyes. There was nothing remarkable about him at all, and yet he gave the impression of a storm barely contained in a fragile pot. If you looked away from him, you would swear he was twitching, shaking, paroxysms of extreme emotion nearly tearing him apart. But nothing in his face or eyes moved.

"Hello," the man said, his tone grave. He looked at Chris for a long moment, and Chris couldn't think of what to say. The man set his hands on his knees and studied all three of them. "You came."

Chris warned Katherine, with a look, not to speak. He had to hope she obeyed.

"We came," Chris said. "Did you set these coordinates for the Door in Cannoux?"

"That was me," the man said. "I've been waiting for you."

Chris nodded. He took in the tent at the outskirts of the fire, and the Well that had served to keep this man in food and drink while he waited. That was clearly why he had camped so far from the Door. He saw the man carried no obvious weapons, other than the unseen maelstrom of emotion inside.

Chris considered and discarded several responses. "How did you know we would come?" he asked, finally.

The man snorted, as if the question was beneath them both. "You had to come, if you weren't caught or killed. You had the dream."

"We were very nearly both," Chris said. "What do you know of the dream?"

Katherine started to say something, and Chris stopped her with a hand on her wrist. She trembled at his touch, and that data, too, became grist for the mill.

The man just looked at him, his eyes flat. But it seemed possible that at any moment he could scream invective, or attack them, or batter at himself. Chris had never seen anything like it. "I know a great deal about the dream," the man said. "And I know even more about what you found at the end of it."

Chris felt Katherine stiffen next to him.

"We won't give it up." Katherine's voice was small in the vast darkness. The strange man's mouth twitched, just the corner, as good as a laughing fit.

"I don't want you to." He stood up, and while he was nearly the same height as Chris, he seemed to tower over them. "I want you to learn how to use it."

He stuck out a rough, calloused hand. "My name is Charts."

THE DEADSMITH

The Door Into Truth

"You told me to start; now, tell me when you wish you hadn't."

—DRAFTER, 'SONG FOR MONA'

The Deader waited in his prison of golden fire for the Prey to spring his final trap. Over all three of them—him, the Prey, and the small girl with the bright green eyes—hunched the Stone Giant. If there was a symbol for the loss of hope and acceptance of inevitability, that was it. Finally, at a gesture from the man called Candle, the girl spoke.

"Deadsmith," she said, her voice tight with sullen hatred, "how do you make a machine?"

The Deader did not look at her. "I will not help you play your games."

Candle giggled, a hint of his old hysteria. "I have developed something of a flair for the dramatic, haven't I? I think it's this thing that I stole. This Domination dominates *me*, too. I am changed. Oh well! Let us cast our mind's eye over your long and suspiciously extravagant life, shall we? No, don't sigh! It is such an *extraordinary* life, Deadsmith, why would you not revel in it? It is the very stuff of epic yarns, the pure perfection of a cruel bedtime story: a boy, marked with a strange tattoo, his beloved—and dark-haired—sister and mother brutalized in front of him, murdered cruelly by a man who leaves the boy improbably alive. This is the perfect beginning to a bloody revenge tale. I could not write one better, Deader, I certainly could not. And then to be found by a Deadsmith, that hard-eyed woman who taught you so much. How perfect! How improbable—but how *perfect*.

"Not to mention the extravagance of your tutelage at the School Inverse—and what a place that was. The ideal—and I do mean *ideal*—crucible to melt you into the pure steel, Deadsmith. And, of all those blue-tattooed boys and girls, who prevailed? Who was so perfectly strong, vicious, and yet still *human* enough to try to overthrow the school when they threatened your lover? Who was so desperately deadly and yet still able to find love in that hard place? Only you, Deadsmith.

"Oh, and then that awful murder, that slow disassembling of the dark-haired girl, your love, and right before your eyes. How much you must have burned for revenge, for hate, for a world in which such things did not happen. How perfectly your passions must have flared, Deadsmith, etching the lines of your soul deeply, channels that passion would run through for the rest of your life. How perfect! How extraordinary.

"And what did that salvation feel like, I wonder? Of all people, a beautiful goddess comes with long, gorgeous raven hair, saving you at the last moment. Another version of your mother, saving you in the way your own mother never could. It was *perfect!* I couldn't have written it better myself."

The Deader looked away, but Candle was bright, now, incandescent with his tale.

"And then your time as the Death-King of that poor dying land; the sickening things you learned to do for a greater good. How well it taught you futility. How deeply it made you yearn for order and strength. How easily you chose to serve when the beautiful dark-haired goddess returned. How easily you chose to *love,* when she pressed her lips to yours. How easily you walked the Spoke Road, climbed to the top of the White Tower, and had your mind ripped in three. How easily you died at the point of Winter's silver knife; how welcome you were to the dark magics in which they wrapped your bones. How happy you were to rise again, one of the vaunted few, the knights-errant whom the Empire of the Nine rest upon—those unspeakable creatures whispered of in fear and longing the Wanderlands over:

"A *Deadsmith.*"

"All Deadsmith," the Deader said, as evenly as he could, through the haze of golden fire that demarcated his prison, "have had extraordinary lives. Else they would not be Deadsmith."

Candle clapped and laughed. "Oh, how much truer than you know, Deadsmith! And yet, yours is remarkable. Don't you wonder how I know so much about it?"

"I don't care." The Deader shook his head. "I am tired of your theatrics. Tell me or don't."

"I would be weary of theatrics as well, were I you," Candle said. "Your life has been nothing but. Still, one last bit of theater, since I spent so much work on it—look to the girl. Who is she? Ah, but I see the answer on your face; she is very nearly the spitting image of your long-lost sister, is she not?" Candle smiled.

The Deader hoped he was enjoying this; he would be dead soon.

"And yet," Candle continued, "I have not the least idea what your sister looked like, Deadsmith. How, in all the worlds, could I?"

The Deader jerked, and looked at him. Candle wasn't smiling, now.

"No," Candle said, "but I know what your *Lady* looks like, Deadsmith. So

many fair-featured women in your life, with dark hair and light eyes. All met
with terrible ends, all except one. Your Lady. *Winter.* No, I did not know every
detail of your life in particular. But I know how the Deadsmith are made."

The Deader felt his hands tingle; a kind of liquid weakness filled his joints. He
could only listen, each word building upon the last, thundering through him,
leaving cracks. But the Prey wasn't using his power. He was only using truth.

"*How do you make a machine?* How do you create a perfect warrior, intelligent
and hard and wise and compassionate enough to rest an empire on? How do you
build a knight-errant strong enough to be worthy of the Black-and-White, and
yet loyal enough to trust with such power?"

"No," the Deader said, softly.

"Oh, yes, Deadsmith. You are a mechanism made for a purpose, a tool crafted
to fit a particular hand. Even now, I tell you, there is a boy out there, in some
failing land, bearing a blue tattoo and with a lovely younger sister and a sadistic
older brother. Or perhaps the reverse; there are female Deadsmith and the same
equation works, does it not? There are many such families. What is the cost to the
Nine to gather such? What cost to compel raiders to play a part?"

"No," the Deader said.

"Even now Tyrathect chews through those, a vast machine for sorting children, a vicious sieve that polishes the silver. Even now that murderous city waits
for the next child who will dominate it; who will display enough strength and yet
be capable of love. Enough strength, and enough love, to try to destroy the School
Inverse and its perversions of justice. And that child will be rescued, Deadsmith,
perhaps by Diasz or Terrace or Ana-Fossoway. And that child will be taken to a
failing land, where they can learn futility, and start to worship order. You of all
people know how many dying lands wait out there in the Dark."

Candle looked down at his hands, and shook his head.

"It is a machine, Deadsmith, a vast mechanism, and like any machine that
runs on people, it runs badly. Thousands of blue-tattooed little boys and girls
die or wash out or are lost along the way. Thousands upon thousands, for every
Deadsmith made. How do you make a machine? You make it with *misery.*" He
paused. He seemed almost kind. "That is who you serve; that is who you *love,*
who you were *engineered* to love. Who you were *created* to serve."

"No," the Deader said, closing his eyes.

"Yes." And Candle sounded pitying. "Your life is a lie, told to you by a vicious
woman who needed a new lap-dog. Do you still think that she—that *they*—are
worthy of your service?" And then he was done.

The Prey had sprung his trap at last. The teeth closed on the Deader's flesh,
rending it, seizing him in their grip. He felt them close around the very essence
of what he was. For he knew that it was no trap, not really; the trap was merely

the truth. There was no questioning it; he knew it was true as soon as it was spoken.

For a long moment the two men sat, looking at each other across a dying ring of golden fire, in the shadow of a Stone Giant, while a young girl looked at them, confused at their silence. The sun was fading; it would be dark soon. Candle looked closely at the Deader, waiting.

The Deader began to laugh.

It started deep, far down in his twisted insides, in the place where his Fate used to be. He didn't mean to; it came from somewhere of which he knew nothing. Laughter—*true* laughter—came bubbling up out of him and spilled over, a light sensation like froth spilling from a heady beer.

The man Candle—the *Prey,* someone the Deader had once met, long ago, under the name Chris D'Essan—blinked, disconcerted.

The Deader couldn't help it; he felt great peals of laughter gripping him, a kind of madness. "That . . ." he managed to say, tears beginning to well up, doubled over, wracked with enormous sobbing pearls of laughter, "*that* is it?"

Candle's eyes widened. He was uneasy, surprised.

The Deader, in between gasps of manic laughter, clenched his fist. He whispered a word, a White-on-Black word, and made a sharp, clenching gesture. The golden prison, which had been weakening steadily all the time Candle talked, tore apart like so much wet paper. It tore the same way his Fate had torn, under the Prey's Domination. Candle tried to speak and tried to bring his weapon up, but the Deader, still laughing, swept the claw of his hand sideways and the weapon was torn from the Prey's fingers, breaking several of them in the process. The Deader slammed a wedge of White-and-Black force into the man's mouth, shattering his teeth and throwing his head back. Candle's eyes filled with terror and blood.

The Deader walked through the fire, kicking aside the girl who scampered away fearfully. He gripped the Prey by the throat, and with his free hand wiped his face of tears. He was still laughing but it felt like madness.

"Oh, you fucking idiot," he said into the Prey's purpling face. "You wagered your life on *this?*"

Candle tried to gasp, but the Deader tightened his fist. He felt the bones of the man's neck creak under his grip, felt the larynx beneath his palm verge on collapse. "I'm sure you're right," the Deader said, tears still rolling down his cheeks, still unable to stop laughing, his words escaping between gasps of dark mirth. "I'm *sure* you're right. I'm a made thing. You don't lie, that is clear. I'm sure you're right."

The Prey managed to gasp out a few words. "She made you—"

The Deader shook his head. Something moved in his chest, some looseness.

The Prey *had* broken him, he knew. Something fundamental in him was shattered. Candle had done that much. But the man was still a fool.

"You're a *fool*," the Deader whispered, tears falling unfelt. "Did you think this would make me stop *loving* her?" He looked away for a moment, the enormity of the Prey's folly heavy on him. He laughed, again, and tightened his grip. "You idiot. That's not how love *works*."

And he started to break Chris D'Essan, systematically gripping his Prey's body, bones splintering beneath white-flared hands, laughing—and crying—all the while.

———

The Deader stared into the fire for a long time, looking for portents in the flames. His Fate at turns moaned and cackled, jubilant, but he ignored it. It was a madman's glass-shard exhumation of pain and anguish, and the Deader would listen to its counsel no more.

He had found a flask in the Prey's pack, a spirit perhaps meant for twistcraft or maybe consumption. It tasted like flames, but the Deader drank it anyway. He had not ingested spirits since he had joined Winter and walked the Spoke Road for the first time. It tasted like Tyrathect, possibly, or the court of the Death-King.

From time to time, as the night slowly fell and the great Rings spun into prominence in the vast night sky, he looked through the flames at the mass of gasping, weeping flesh that had once been the Prey. Near him was the girl, dark-haired and green-eyed and full of hate, who hugged her arms to herself and stared at him. The Deader ignored her. Over them all, the Stone Giant hunched, staring its sad, lost gaze endlessly into its cupped hands.

The Deader's own hands trembled as he raised the flask to his lips and watched the fire. The broken thing that had once been the Prey, that had once been a man called Candle, that had once been a clever boy named Chris, gurgled on its own blood. The Deader wondered, idly, when he would die. It didn't seem to matter.

While the Deader was breaking him, he had forced Candle to reveal his plans, tell him of his grand designs. Candle told him why he had stolen the Domination from Winter, why he had taken the hideous risk of trying to suborn the Deader. Why he was heading into the Land of the Giants.

The Deader grimaced, looking into the fire, and shook his head.

The man was a fool, but he had no lack of ambition. He wanted to raise the Giant, but he didn't just want to *free* it; Candle wanted to *control* Kindaedystrin. He wondered, without much passion, what his Lady would think of that. He couldn't imagine her reaction, somehow, and in any case Winter did as she pleased for reasons that only she knew. But he thought she might have been impressed.

He wished she were here. He wished she would lay her hand on his shoulder and whisper against his neck. Instead, wind that smelled of wet dirt and new leaves blew across his face. The temperature was falling, too, a thing he was unused to, and he shivered. The temperature was always the same in the fallen Lands. He found that he enjoyed this chill.

He wondered where his Lady was, if he would have to wait for her return, to show her the blood on his teeth. The thought made him feel very tired. He looked at the broken thing that had once been a man, struggling weakly to breathe, the wet sounds of its respiration a counterpoint to the crackling of the fire.

The thing that used to be a man wanted to *control* the Giant Kindaedystrin. It was such absurdity that the Deader almost admired it. The creature, that sallow *mortal man*, that *nobody*, that *mayfly*, wanted to bring the sun back to the Wanderlands. He meant to travel into the Land of the Giants, forbidden for three ages of the world, to do it. He meant to confront what waited there, the monstrosities that would extinguish the peoples of the Wanderlands the moment they got free. The Deader shook his head and drank some more from the flask.

The man wanted to confront the *Twins*. Not only confront them, but to wrest information from them. Even the Deader was shocked by this ambition. It wasn't hubris, it was grand delirium. It was inconceivable. Candle was just a man.

The Deader looked up into the sky, tracked the slow movement of the golden moon, covered all over with tiny towers and stairways, an enigmatic mystery for all save those who'd contrived to visit it.

The Prey was just a man, but the Deader wasn't. The Deader didn't know what he was anymore. A machine, maybe, one-legged, hopping endlessly in a futile circle. He wondered where his Lady was, and guessed that she would be okay without him for a little while.

He stood, massaging the ache out of his thighs, and kicked dirt over the fire. The girl looked at him, a snarl on her face. He kept thinking of her by his sister's name. He sighed and tucked the flask of spirits away. He used his magic to heal the worst of Candle's wounds, but the Black-and-White was meant for him, and barely kept the man alive. The Deader picked him up and slung him over his shoulder. He could always kill him again, later.

He looked over his shoulder, up the ravine, at where the Door waited. Behind that Door waited his Lady, waited the Tower, waited Diasz and the Nine, and a vast empire of light held together with love and despair. He turned away and looked down-slope, to where big trees gathered, ominous and heavy with mystery. When was the last time someone had actually entered the Land of Forest, had faced the Giants? He shivered in the chill and looked at the girl.

"What's your name?" the Deader asked, expecting to hear her say his sister's name. But she frowned, and her green eyes were terrified and savage and brilliant. She spat in the dirt.

"Avie," she said, and the Deader nodded.

"Well, Avie?" he asked, taking another long drag of the spirits, feeling the burn down his throat. "Come, if you're coming."

He walked down toward the waiting forest, toward the Land of the Giants, carrying his Prey over his shoulder.

After a while, the girl followed.

THE MONSTERS

The Sword in the Darkness

"It's easy to say they were pawns, easier to say they were demons. Horror on the scale that they precipitated almost requires a reduction to stereotype. But the truth is both simpler and more complex than that; it is difficult to believe that they walked their path with eyes open and yet were not monstrous, but it seems to be the case. Or, rather, they were indeed monsters; but by all accounts rather nice ones."

—AVES IST SIERRO, 'THE SWORD AND THE GIANT'

Gun and his *goddamned sword*, Jackie thought bitterly, as she took another blow to the side of the head from a metal claw about as big as a beer-barrel. It fucking *hurt*, and she wanted it to stop. However, goddamned Feral Children and their numbing green ichor and drill teeth had worked a number on her right arm, and she'd lost her walking stick about forever ago.

Oh, she'd laughed when she'd heard that Feral Child scream, in the darkness outside of Cannoux. When her and Gun had been trying to get drunk and maudlin. She'd laughed; but she wasn't laughing now. The Feral Children had brought some friends with them, and their friends were *not fucking around*. Their friends were giant silver-and-black crab-things with small brutal faces and big brutal articulated fists on the ends of enormous arms, and they just loved to punch Jackie Aimes in the face with them.

"Fuck you," she grunted, and when the big metal fist came back around, trying to take her head off, she lunged into it, swinging her forehead into the oncoming blow. She head-butted it, felt the silver claw deform and buckle around her face, and through the bright light and ringing in her head, she felt savage satisfaction.

The monstrous thing reeled back. It looked like an upright crab some bad-tempered demigod had made for the purpose of killing everybody in the whole world. But Jackie *Fucking* Aimes had left half a hundred of these miserable things in piles of smoking rubble, and she'd leave this one too.

Only, another of the goddamn sons-of-bitching motherfuckers came barreling out of the dark and crashed into her, doing its best to twist the top half of her body off the lower half while it smashed her through what felt like about ten feet of solid steel.

Scrabbling for purchase, she got her left hand on what passed for its face, and felt her fingers catch against whatever served for the thing's mouth. Good enough. She closed her fist, felt her fingernails dig in, and yanked. The machine howled in pain, a sound like a murdered harpsichord. She brought her good leg up, used her knee to cave in its carapace, and hoped to do enough damage to its internal workings to slow it.

Fucking Gun and his *goddamned* sword. This had all been a lot easier before he'd dropped the fucking thing. Fortunately these bastards didn't seem to understand much about strategy or tactics and tended to attack singly or in pairs. Still, she was tired. Fuck that, she was *exhausted*. She heard the scream of a Feral Child and wondered with a kind of fatigued detachment if another wave of *those* goddamn things would be arriving soon. From somewhere off to her left, she heard Gun cry out in pain, and then some sort of titanic crash, and she vaguely hoped he wasn't, like, dead or anything.

She succeeded in crushing in one of the crab-things' chest-plates, and it roared and tried to roll back. But Jackie's last remaining hand was digging through the thing's face, tearing out gears and eyes and silvery strands of something that she didn't really give a fuck about. She felt the telltale oily sensation of a Feral Child landing on her head, and the icy points of its spinning black teeth closed around the side of her neck. She yanked the big apparatus towards her in a squeal of damaged gearwork, and smashed the Feral Child to bits against the bigger machine's carapace.

She finally got her fist far enough into the crab-thing, and her hand closed around the knotted length of heavy, writhing silver that seemed to make these things go. She grinned, bloody, and ripped its brain out through its *fucking face*.

She rolled to her feet; nothing was currently attacking her, and she looked around the dim scene for something to kill. She saw vague shapes moving off to her left. She grimaced and started limping towards them.

Another of the goddamn crab-death things rose up out of the gloom, turning toward her, and she wished for about the two hundredth time she hadn't lost her stick. These fuckers were practically *easy* when you had a working arm and a good walking stick. Didn't matter; she'd kill this one, too. She stalked toward the crablike monster, ready to do some murder. Only, something else got there first.

Something dropped down onto the crab-thing, something white and lethal that moved almost too fast to see. The silver device roared and threw itself backwards, but the white thing was too fast for it. It slashed with arms that looked like knives, and chunks of the crab robot flew.

Jackie blinked, and saw something else moving in the dark battle; was that a woman? And a *child*?

The woman looked relatively normal, but she did something with her hands and another of the crab-things, the one that was half-devouring Gun, threw its head back and screamed. All of a sudden another one of them hit Jackie from behind, and then she mostly concentrated on not getting her neck broken. When she eventually put paid to the thing, ripping its head from its carapace and throwing it out into the dark, the battle was all but over.

The white mantis-creature, having cut the other crab into pieces, spun those wicked-looking blade-arms, killing more of the automata with an ease and carelessness that Jackie admired in a very profound way. The Feral Children seemed terrified of it and ran away into the dark. Its expression was fearsome, but it made no move to attack Jackie, so she assumed that she'd found a new best friend.

She saw the woman, who was statuesque, handsome, and powerful-looking, crush several Feral Children from several yards away, and Jackie supposed she'd have to walk back a lot of her skepticism about magic because *that shit* sure looked like it. A small boy with bright golden eyes was looking around, seemingly bored, and Jackie's heart leapt into her mouth when the last of the crab things made a dash for him. But before Jackie could more than jerk toward him, the child turned and looked at the onrushing monster, and it fell down dead.

She saw Gun stagger to his feet, holding his side. She breathed a heavy, thick sigh of relief. Such a fuckin' bag of limp genitals, that guy! He gave her a half-hearted grin, and something that might have intended to be a thumbs up.

What a fucker. She gave him a thumbs up, too, with the arm that still worked. She turned her attention back to the newcomers. Who, *so far*, had made no attempt to attack them.

She looked around; it seemed like all of the crab-things were dead. The tall, thin white person with the bladed fingers finished massacring the last of the warmachines, and the statuesque woman walked towards her, a smile on her face and her palms out. Jackie bumped elbows companionably with Gun, who had hobbled up next to her.

The woman was wearing something like a long dress wrapped around her, but Jackie saw some leggings underneath. The small boy ignored everybody and, instead, seemed very interested in the dead or dying automata, making his slow way around to each and studying them, carefully. Jackie saw someone else, too, approach from behind the woman. Her first instinct was to look away; this person looked real bad. He looked as if he'd spent a couple years banging around the bottom of the barrel. He looked as if that barrel had been kicked down several long stairways. He had a bandage wrapped around one hand and it was red with blood. But his eyes were bright, and intelligent, and strange. They looked into and through Jackie, and she shivered. Gun bumped his elbow into Jackie's, a measured gesture of excitement.

"Hello, Behemoth," the woman said. Her voice was low and warm, a delicious contralto. She didn't say the word like the people in the town had said it, with fear and loathing. She said it like it meant "friend." She smiled, looking back and forth between them. "It is wonderful to meet you."

She reached around to take something behind her, and brought it around, slowly, holding it up. It was Gun's sword, rescued from the dark. She held it out, gesturing, and Gun stepped forward to take it. But he saw her hands trembling, and the point of the sword wavered drunkenly. It took her a great deal of effort to keep the weapon upright. He took it, nodding wary thanks.

The woman's smile grew, laugh lines crinkling at the corners of her eyes.

"We," she said, gesturing to her companions, "have been looking for you for a long time."

———

More quickly than could be believed, their new friends set up a fire-site. The tall white death-machine turned out to be named Mr. Turpentine, and a nicer tall white death-machine could not be imagined. It—*he?*—bustled about, getting the fire burning merrily and producing, from seemingly nowhere, some pots and apparatus. He soon had something that smelled absolutely wonderful bubbling along.

Gun and Jackie helped by hauling big chunks of masonry and stone over to the fire, so people had a place to sit. The woman named Winter directed them, somehow making it seem like the efforts were *their* idea and complimenting them on their prowess in carrying and placing the chunks of stone. Whoever this off-beat band of people were, they weren't overly impressed by—nor scared of—Gun and Jackie.

In short, they didn't treat them like monsters, which went a long way towards endearing them to the Behemoth. They were further endeared when the small, odd little boy led Jackie to where her beloved walking stick lay, shoved through two of the crab-things. Reunited with their weapons, Gun and Jackie were yet more disposed to look favorably upon their rescuers.

The badly disheveled and seemingly broken man—introduced as Candle—sat and watched them with his unusual eyes and didn't say much, but neither Gunnar nor Jackie got a sense of hostility from him. It appeared that he had been wounded in the fighting; he was cradling a hand to his chest, recently bandaged, and it looked like something had cut one of his fingers off. The small boy with the striking eyes more or less ignored everybody and wandered around in the dimness beyond the fire, presumably performing some sort of last rites for the dead and dying machines.

It was all too weird to even parse, so they just kind of went with it. They tried not to be overjoyed by the simple fact that there was *somebody to talk to*. Winter kept up a small patter of simple conversation, as if it were the most normal thing in the world to happen upon two invincible monsters battling a whole army of mechanical demons. Before they knew it, they were sitting at a happily crackling fire, and Mr. Turpentine was handing them small delicate cups filled with something deeply rich and *violently* delicious. Even the boy joined the fire, perching up on a big chunk of rock. He spent a few moments studying Gun and Jackie, and then, improbably, smiled.

Jackie found herself smiling back, so innocent and open was the expression. The small boy held it for a little while, his golden eyes glittering, and then turned to the fire. She and Gun exchanged a guarded look, and sipped their steaming beverage.

"*Chûs*," Mr. Turpentine said, after everyone was served a cup, "is the drink of commonality, of truce, of wayfarers meeting in the dark. The *finely* made *chûs*, as I confess this is, we refer to as *graveled*, and at risk of poisoning a new friendship with hubris, I can claim this is quite the most finely graveled *chûs* you are like to have in these lost and broken days."

The dangerous-looking but warm-sounding automata gave a half-modest tip of an imaginary hat. "In these dark wastes, at least."

"Mr. Turpentine is too modest," Winter said, smiling. "This is indeed one of the best cups you can find anywhere in the Wanderlands. I am glad you agreed to share it with us."

"Well sure," Jackie said, and held her cup up, a silent toast. "We, uh . . . thank you."

"Yes," Gun said. "Thank you. And thank you for your help, as well."

Winter made a little wave with her free hand. "As I said, we were looking for you, and we thought some trouble might find you before we did. In truth, you would have put an end to these ignoble creatures in any case! But I am glad we were able to help a little."

"More than a little," Gun said, holding his hand to his side, where his ribs had been broken again. "But, thanks. Thank you."

"It is nothing," Winter said. "I am only happy to find you relatively unharmed. I do not know if *you know* what these things are? No? I thought not. Well, there will be plenty of time to learn, and suffice it to say we are confident that our mission in finding you was a good one. If you can defeat so many of the War-Dogs, the Runnerkin, then you are well qualified to hear our proposal."

Gun and Jackie exchanged a look.

"Runnerkin?" Jackie asked.

"Proposal?" Gun asked, cautiously, and then shook his head. "Wait, *War-Dogs?* That's awesome as hell."

"That's cool." Jackie whistled. "Almost regret killing so many of them."

"Please," Winter said, putting a hand up and looking pained. "Forgive my eagerness. We truly have been looking for you a long time, and through many dangerous places. Our business can wait as long as you like. Please! Enjoy your drink, and indeed our dear Mr. Turpentine tells me he found a Well back a ways, and will soon have us something to eat. I will be pleased to explain our business whenever it is you are most comfortable hearing it."

Gun cleared his throat. "We'd be quite interested in hearing your proposal. But first, maybe you could set our minds at ease about a couple of things?"

"Of course!" Winter said.

The hunched-over man next to her shifted, restless, but sipped his drink and didn't say anything.

"Please, Gunnar and Jackie," she continued. "I will help in any way that I can."

"Okay," Gun said. He glanced at Jackie, and she gave him a short nod. "Well, I guess we . . ." He stopped, started again. "There's been something or someone following us."

A twitch at the corners of Winter's smile, and she glanced at some of the destroyed soldier-constructs on the edges of the firelight. "This, I can see."

Gun grinned, in spite of himself. "Yes, these crab-soldier things. And the things you call Feral Children."

Mr. Turpentine froze at the name, going still, and something dangerous and predatory shivered across his form before he began moving again.

"Terrible creatures." Winter sighed. "I know of them, of course."

"And," Gun began, "and something *else*."

Winter lifted an eyebrow and took a delicate sip of the *chûs*. Steam from the cup curled around her handsome features. "Something else?"

"Something . . ." Gun exchanged another glance with Jackie. "Something that was attacking our minds. Fucking with the way we feel. Making us want to kill each other, and shit like that."

Winter went still, looking back and forth between the two of them, and then shook her head. "Ah," she said, "I feared this, my friends. I hoped it was not the case, but I feared it. We hoped to find you first, you see, but alas. I daresay self-recriminations are not the most pressing matter just now. You wish to know who, or what, was attacking you?"

"Yes," Jackie said, firmly. "And how to make it *stop*."

"There is," Winter said, heavily, "a sort of organization—a *cabal*, if you will, that is dedicated to a certain end that, I assure you, we will speak more of later. This cabal wished to make you its tools, and especially that blade you carry. They learned of your coming the same way I did, though they command greater resources than we do and were plainly able to find you first. One of their agents is a man named Mr. Vutch, and you—"

"Oh, we fuckin' *met* Mr. Vutch," Jackie said.

Winter inclined her head. "Just so. We found his corpse as we were following your trail. Perhaps you do not know what a service you did this world, in ridding it of such a villain. A more vile and despicable agent I cannot describe. I do not know why you chose to resist him, but you did well in doing so."

"Well," Gun said, with a small smile, "he was more or less full of shit."

"As good a reason as any," Winter said, firmly.

Candle stirred, and fixed them with his odd eyes. "You claim these attacks happened *before* that person was ended? And continued after he died?"

"We didn't," Jackie said, slowly, "but yes, they did."

"Then my fears are confirmed." Winter sighed, giving Candle a sharp look. "Ah, what evil luck! I had thought Mr. Vutch might have been working on his own. Loyalty was not a quality of his, but it appears his full organization—this Cabal—is working against you. The attacks you experienced come from something called a Dominator, a rare brute—fortunately for all of us! They are capable of overwhelming the will and sense of most thinking creatures, and forcing them into a kind of mental and emotional slavery. It says much about your mental fortitude that you were able to resist."

Gun and Jackie exchanged a glance at this.

"Well," Gun said, "so there's this . . . Dominator out there? How can we make it stop?"

"Well," Winter said, "*should* you choose to accept our proposal and travel some ways with us, I believe there is something we can do to mitigate the effects. Candle, here, is our magician, and he is so ill-seeming because the last few weeks have been especially hard on him. It is by his utility that we were able to follow your trail, and locate you in so much darkness. Do you think we can do something for our new friends, Candle? Can you shield them from this mental *Domination*?"

Candle, the broken man, looked up at the woman, and there was sour twist to his mouth; then he looked back at Gun and Jackie. He shrugged. "I think so." Candle said. "I can stop most of it, at least. I'll do what I can. That's all I can do."

"That is very kind," Gun said, carefully. "We would appreciate it very much."

The man lifted his cup of half-drunk *chûs* to the two Behemoth, almost sarcastically, and drank. Gun looked at Jackie, who shrugged.

"Well," Gun said, "so you say you knew we were coming? And so did they?"

Winter met his eye. "The arrival of Behemoth to our world is a rare enough event that those who pay attention will, sooner or later, know of your coming. Still, yours is a special case. From what I understand, most of the Behemoth from your world come here because they accidentally stumble upon that portal between worlds. But that is not the case with you, is it?"

Gun and Jackie exchanged a look. "No," Gun said. "It's not. We didn't stumble on it."

"I daresay," Winter said, her face grave. She took a sip of *chûs*. "I daresay that you had a *dream*. A special dream. A dream of darkness."

Gun's half-drunk cup of *chûs* fell from suddenly nerveless hands, splashing on the ground.

"Shit!" he said. "Shit, I'm sorry."

Mr. Turpentine was around the fire in a flash, scooping up Gun's ceramic cup.

"Be patient just *one* moment," Turpentine said with a jaunty smile, "and you shall have a fresh cup, Mr. Gunnar."

"Sorry," Gun said again, feeling a bit lame. He looked back at Winter.

"A dream?" she prodded.

Gun nodded. "How do you know that?"

"I was made aware of the dreams," Winter said. She seemed to be picking her words carefully. "As were others. We knew someone was calling Behemoth to the Wanderlands. Such a thing had never been done, to my knowledge, but it was *possible*. And so those with an interest in such things began to watch the Black Portals that we know of. And wait."

"Do you—" Gun swallowed. "Do you know what the dreams mean?"

Winter smiled. "They were not for us. I cannot tell you what the dreams meant. Perhaps later, if I can hear them fully from you, I can be of some use. I am sorry."

"Oh, it's okay," Gun said. He exchanged a look with Jackie, who was biting her lip. Finally, she nodded and looked to Winter. "Okay. What's the proposal?"

Winter offered a charming smile. "I shall wait until we are all re-served. Yes, thank you, Mr. Turpentine, for this proposal is both meat and mead and I do not mind allowing from the first that a great deal hinges upon your answer. Nor do I mind admitting that we are doing everything in our power to charm you towards the answer we'd like."

She gave them a wink.

Gun grinned, and Jackie rolled her eyes but was amused. They accepted fresh cups of the deliciously hot beverage from the bladed digits of Mr. Turpentine. Winter accepted her own, crossed her legging-wrapped legs, and looked at them for a long moment.

"You are Behemoth," she said. "I think by now you have some idea of what that means."

"Well," Gun said.

And Jackie finished his thought: "Some."

"It means," Winter said, holding out her hands palms up, as if weighing scales, "that you have the power and ability to do as you like, here in our sad dark little world, and there is nobody to gainsay you. I do not know what you were, in your old world, but here you are like *gods*. There are things that can hurt you, and there are things that can kill you, but it is a ruinous effort and would require the cooperation of the great forces of the world. In short, and within certain limits, you have the ability to do whatever it is that you want."

Gun and Jackie blinked at each other. They looked back at Winter.

"This, meaning," Winter said, leaning forward, "that you have the power to cause great harm. I think you saw that, in Cannoux. And I think you see that you have the power to do great good, as well—all of these dead monsters and broken warmachines can attest to that. What we would like to propose, my new friends, is that you use this power, this great motive force, to help us accomplish a monumental *good* in the world.

"You can see that this world is a broken thing, with light its most precious resource and its most quickly fading dream. Yet there *is* light left. You have seen Cannoux, have you not? Yet I tell you that there are cities that *burn* with light, cities that could swallow Cannoux ten times over and never notice the difference. There is a great deal of beauty left in the world, but we ride the knife's edge. We walk always along the precipice. This is an old place, and it is full of old things. Many of those old things are wonderful, like the Doors, like the old lit stone, like our dear Mr. Turpentine here. But some of those old things were born or made for *old* purposes. Great purposes, grand purposes even, but ones that are too large for this small, sad world to contain any longer.

"Gunnar, do you remember the image of an eye, opening in darkness? Yes, from your dream—and I can see that you do. There is a great eye truly opened in the dark, my friends. It is open, and it is restless. It belongs to one of the old things of the Wanderlands, one of the things that is too large and dangerous for this world. It is a colossus we call a *Giant*, but do not let fairy-tale stories deceive you here. This is a soul born to destroy, and if it were to get loose of its bonds, it would snuff out the remaining light in the world as easily as you or I would snuff out a candle-wick.

"For longer than you can imagine, this creature, this *Giant*, has lain waiting, unable to escape its bonds. But there are those—and your Mr. Vutch was only one of them—who wish to free it. They think to loose this monstrous thing, this impossible danger, and they think to *harness* it. Madness! My friends, it *is* madness, but nevertheless that is what they wish to do. It is my life's stated purpose to stop them in this, both mine and that of my friends. I will do anything and make any sacrifice to end this threat.

"You, my two new friends, you who are *Behemoth* and therefore able to do as you like, good or ill, can decide this matter. My enemies made the mistake of trying to kill you or dominate you. They tried to take your blade by force or make you their slave. They wish you to take that portal-forged sword and use both it and your formidable strength to cut bonds that no one in this world has the means to cut. They meant to *use you* to free this Giant, and they foolishly believe they can control it once they have. Foolish, because it took the might of the dead civilization you see all around you, the same civilization that built the Doors and this endless city and the great towers and all of the magic in the world—it took *all* of that civilization's power to defeat this creature in the first place. And these fools mean to *release* him. Rank madness! But that is what we have come to, in these lost end days.

"I know, I know, I do go on. Passion will run away with my words! My friends, I do not ask you to fight any war for reasons you do not understand, as many Behemoth have been asked to. I do not ask you to take this side or that side, to choose this, to choose that. My proposal is just this:

"I propose that we travel together, through the dark wastes, and assemble what like-minded friends we can find; that we journey down into the heart of darkness, and we take your sword and pass it through the Giant Kindaedystrin's neck. And maybe, *just maybe*, with this evil gone from the world, we can start working towards bringing some light back into it as well."

Gun and Jackie exchanged a *very* long look indeed.

THE KILLERS

All Them Lost Children,
All Together at Last

"May your love, and all that you love, be reborn in light, remade in golden sun."

—ALI LONG, 'HYMN'

Sophie was getting slapped in the face, and it wasn't the playful, sexy kind of slap she liked. These hurt, and they were accompanied by somewhat familiar voices full of tedious, boring emotions, like urgency, and concern, and fear.

"Sophie!" someone yelled, and she got slapped again. "Sophie, are you okay?"

She tried to blink and discovered that it was not an idle undertaking. Blinking, just now, seemed to require the same amount of effort as, say, hoisting your own weight in gravel.

"Fuck," somebody said, relief evident in the voice. "She blinked! Sophie!"

She one-upped them; she managed to shake her head. A little.

"Oh, god, Sophie," another voice said.

"She's coming around. Mother *fuck*."

It was hard to imagine that anybody cared this much about anything. But still, Sophie fought up towards the wavering light that was the world, still half wondering why she was doing it. When that bright place came into focus, she saw some things she didn't expect.

She saw shelves, raw rock beyond—she was still in the Library. She felt blood on her hands—Avie's blood. She felt something lying against her arm—the fucking Book. Memory returned in reverse; the flash of light as she sent the Jannissaries once again to do her bloody bidding. The man with the curious markings that called himself a Deadsmith, carrying Avie off to see if he could save her life. Avie, giving her a smile and telling Sophie she wanted to see what she could do. The Cold, dying underneath her with his own Rapine driven into his skull. Trik's fist, going through Denver Murkai's skull. Hunker John, falling, half-headed. Her brother . . .

"Sophie? Are we losing her again?" Trik's voice. Somebody slapped her again, and she opened her eyes.

Trik's face was closest, huge in Sophie's view and anguished—not to mention streaked with blood. Next to her was Bear, an uncharacteristic look of concern on his face. His hand was raised, and Sophie realized who had been slapping her.

"Stop it, Bear," she said, her mouth feeling gummy. "Buy a girl a drink, first."

Trik sighed in relief. Sophie tried to focus on both of them.

"You both," she licked dry lips, wishing she had some water, "are still alive."

Bear glanced at Trik, who shrugged. "We're more worried about you, Capitana."

Sophie grimaced, and let Bear help her struggle up to a sitting position. "Just 'Sophie,' for now. Okay?" God, she hurt. Hurt *everywhere.* She raised a trembling hand to her temple, seeing the livid red scars on her wrist, and closed her eyes. She wanted them closed while she asked.

She swallowed. "Ben?"

"Here, Sophie," her oldest friend said, and she felt such an overwhelming rush of relief and sadness and fatigue and joy that she almost passed out again. She kept her eyes closed, and felt Ben grip her hand, tightly.

"Hey, old man." She opened her eyes when she was able. Ben was smiling at her. He didn't seem to be hurt.

"Hey there."

"Sorry for leaving you," Sophie said. "Said I wasn't going to do that again."

Ben's smile crinkled. "You never leave me for long, Capitana. I mostly ran and hid, anyways. Until you woke every Twins-damned thing in this place, like some kind of avenging god. That was a sight to behold."

"It was," Trik said. "It was spectacular, Capitana."

Sophie pushed herself a little more upright, wincing. "Is there anybody left alive in here? I shut the war-door. We should be safe for a little while, before Jane finds another way in."

Bear grinned. "Well, between Trik here being an unfathomable badass and that crazy stunt you pulled, Sophie, I think we're the last ones standing."

Trik sniffed. "Yeah? How many notches do *you* have on that new silver knife of yours? You psychopath!"

Bear was untroubled, and shrugged modestly.

"Okay, okay," Sophie said. She looked around for something to drink.

Trik hesitated, then asked, "The Rue?"

Sophie managed a faint smile. Her vision was steadying, which she supposed was good. "There were still some Jannissaries left after the Hot Halls War. I woke them up and told them to hunt Feral Children. The Rue is still Dark, but with those braziers lit, and the Feral Children gone, whoever survived should be able to make it out through the side-ways."

"Well that's something," Trik muttered. "What happened to New Girl? And her scary friend? I saw that fucker kill about twenty soldiers in twenty seconds. I don't know what the fuck he was, man, but I don't want to go up against him. And that's saying something."

"Yeah," Sophie said, remembering her fist going straight through Denver's face.

"So they showed up?" Bear said. "I never saw them."

"Avie . . ." Sophie shook her head. "She got hurt really bad. *Defending me*, Trik, while I used the Book, so you can put that expression away. Her friend seemed to think he could save her life, so he took her off to try."

"Huh." Trik sniffed. "Suspicious."

"Oh yeah, *Trik?*" Sophie said, with a wince at her bruises. "We gonna talk about *suspicious* now?"

Trik looked down. "I suppose I probably need to explain some things."

"I bet. But not right now." Sophie rubbed her eyes. "Lee?"

Ben replied, "I don't know, Capitana. We haven't been back to that room."

Sophie nodded. She looked down at her hands, her raw, silver-burned arms. It seemed impossible that they were all still alive. Well, not *all*. She needed . . . what did she need? Something to drink. A fucking *slot*. Denver, Lee, and Hunker; it had all happened too fast, and didn't feel real. She needed to see them.

With Ben's help, she struggled up to her feet, and discovered that they were steadier than she'd thought. She picked up the Book, splashed with Avie's blood, and tucked it into her carry. It was too light to have caused all this blood. It should be heavier. She stood, swaying, and rubbed her eyes with her palms. She grinned at the remaining Killers, knowing she must look ghastly.

"Come on, fuckers," she said. "Let's go look at the damage."

They made their way through the rooms and serpentine passageways, many of them littered with the aftermath of the battle. They passed a few soldiers, dead, killed by the Silver-Age devices that Sophie had activated. They passed a couple of dead Cold, their fists still tight on their Rapines. It wasn't always clear what had killed them, but Sophie suspected it was the long silver knife at Bear's hip. There were a few that looked as if they had been mangled by industrial equipment. She wished she could think of them as bad guys; but she had probably fought beside some of these soldiers in the Hot Halls War. She wished she could be as unconcerned with the dead as Bear seemed to be.

"Hey," she said to Trik, who was walking with her eyes downcast. Trik looked at her, and Sophie smiled. "Thanks for saving my ass back there. I'm glad you . . . I don't know. Decided to help."

Trik shrugged, awkwardly. "I made a promise to protect you. A long time ago. But it was hard to . . . I couldn't risk you guys to knowing what I was."

"Apologies can come later, Trik."

The tall girl nodded, and tried to wipe some of the drying blood off her hands. She looked as if she were regretting how easy it had been for her to kill.

Sophie knew that feeling pretty well. Close by was a young soldier, maybe only twenty or so, lovely and with long dark hair, her throat chewed out by a still-twitching clockwork rat. They all had a lot of blood on their hands tonight.

But no one had more blood on his hands—figuratively and literally—than her own brother. When they found the room where the Book had been stored, Sophie could see immediately that Lee was dead. It was about as sad as anything had been, tonight, that he had died unremarked and unnoted, a footnote. Nobody had even noticed his passing.

She pressed her fingers to her lips, and then to Lee's forehead. He looked peaceful in death, with a little half-smile on his face. He looked like her little brother. Before the tears came, while she still had some control, she straightened and joined Trik and Ben who were standing over Hunker's body.

His delicate, fine form was slumped inelegantly, face-down, a wide slick of blood surrounding his head. Sophie was glad she couldn't see his face, see that look of surprise permanently etched on it.

"He didn't deserve *this,*" Ben said. He shook his head, and Sophie saw that he was fighting tears. "He did what he did, but he didn't deserve this."

"Nobody ever does, Ben." Sophie shook her head, then turned away from the sad remains. No more long nights of drinking; no more making a game of seducing the same girl or boy; no more drug-fueled laughter in the wee hours of the morning. He *had* betrayed her. But then, maybe she had betrayed him. She wasn't able to hate John for selling her out. She had been selling herself out for years.

But she was able to feel angry, a little, for the harm he had done. She drew her arm across her eyes; Twins damn, she was tired. She straightened, and stepped over to another corpse. Denver *fucking* Murkai. Sophie looked down at her old tutor, her old lover. The man who had fed her to Saint Station, and taught her to kiss, and then to come. Who was still her first, and best, betrayer.

She looked up at the remaining Killers—at Bear and Trik and Ben. She grinned, with no humor in it.

"I need a drink," she said, and returned to Hunker John's corpse, knelt beside it, and fished around in his jacket for his flask. Good, there was a little left. She pressed her fingers to her lips, as she had with Lee, and pressed them to Hunker's cheek. "I assume you approve," she said softly.

"He probably would," Bear said.

Sophie straightened. "Let's go that way," she said. "There's a Well, and I wouldn't mind washing some of this fucking blood off my hands."

———

The room in the Library that held the golden Well was blessedly free of bodies, blood, viscera, or memories. Sophie pulled some packages of water from the golden bowl, and the Killers used these to wash themselves as best they could. Then she ordered up some slots, and some little paper cups. Marvelous things, Wells, when you knew how to ask them for what you want.

Trik looked better after she'd washed, but just as worried. "What are we going to do, Capitana?"

Sophie shook her head. "Not yet, Trik. I need a few minutes. Okay? I locked us in here, so even if the Queen has more troops to send at us, they can't get in. And they're going to be tied up with Jannissaries for a bit. I didn't tell them to attack anybody but Feral Children, but if the Practice Guard get in their way . . ." She shrugged.

Sophie lowered herself, gingerly, to the stone floor, and leaned back against some shelves. God, *everything* hurt. But she felt a kind of peacefulness, too.

She'd done the best she could. That was an odd feeling.

She scraped a slot to life and took a deep drag. *Ah.* That was nice. She hadn't had a slot since the bar, after she'd seen the Queen. Before Avie had shown her another world. Before Lee had killed the Rue, before she'd lost Bear's Key to the Consort. Twins damn, what a long night. She hadn't slept yet, so it was still the same night. Hunker John's rules. She felt a lump in her throat.

That reminded her. Something about the Consort.

"Hey," she said, patting her carry, "I just remembered."

She shook out the letter he had written to her. He'd told her to read it when she had a minute, right? She waved it at Trik.

"What's that?" Trik was rubbing at her tattoos, and frowned at the letter.

"A letter from your friend," Sophie said. Then, when Trik continued frowning, she added, "The Consort."

"What does it say, Capitana?" Ben asked, leaning in to look. She shrugged.

"I don't know. Never had a chance to read it."

Ben raised his eyebrows. "Well? Wasn't it him that kicked this whole thing off? With the message from the fop in the Charm Chair?"

"Shit," Trik swore. "*That's right.* Well, kicked it off for us, at least."

"He had his hand in every pie, tonight," Bear said. "And he gave us precious few answers when we saw him."

Trik was looking at the letter like it was a poisonous snake. Sophie shook it at her. "Up to you, Triks. You seem to know him. Should we read it?"

Trik swallowed, and met her eyes. "I guess you have to."

"I don't *have* to do anything," Sophie said, "but I'm curious. Aren't you curious?"

"I'm *suspicious*," Trik said, and then sighed. "And pretty fucking curious, too. Read it."

"Yeah, read it, Capitana," Ben said. "Maybe he knows something we need to."

"Or maybe," Sophie said, "it'll just be more cryptic bullshit."

But she straightened the paper, and started reading.

———

"Dear Sophie," she read aloud. She had to wipe a little blood off it, to make the writing legible. Then she continued, taking occasional drags from her slot.

Dear Sophie,

What a long night, huh? It's just crazy that this is all happening at once and yet, there are good reasons for it. There's a reason I tried to warn you, yesterday; a reason why your brother and Candle chose THIS night to make their play. A reason why the Queen decided tonight was the night to put the pressure on.

It's because of the Sword, Sophie. The fucking SWORD. The three things they need to open the Giant's Prison—the Key, the Book, and the Sword. They have the Sword now. I have the Key, and you (hopefully) have the Book . . . but that means we are now in their endgame.

In THEIR endgame, yes. But it's not OUR endgame, Sophie. I'm sorry to be familiar, but I do think we're on the same side. I had the dream too, you see; I had a dream about a Giant, and a Sword. All of the people around you have either had that dream, or had their lives shaped by it. We all had a dream of trees. We all tried to save the world. And we all failed.

It must stretch your credulity, realizing that those who have spent so many years at your side have deep—and suspicious—pasts, and are not exactly who they have said they were. It must be difficult to have to come to terms with all of this, and all so suddenly. Gods know I've wanted to tell you more, but I just couldn't trust you not to start a fight you couldn't win, to push away the very people you needed by your side, or to do something even I can't imagine. But I'm telling you, Sophie, that everyone is, finally, in their places. After all these long years, all of the Children of the Dream are here in the Keep, with the weapons the Mother gave us to change the world.

Jane, as she told you, wants to kill the Giant, and Candle wants to enslave it. But that's not what I want, Sophie, and I don't think that's what you want either. I want something better. I want to trust in the dream. I want to trust in the people I care about. I want to believe that the sun can shine again, that this world is more than just a failing machine. I want to believe that the Wise can be fought; maybe even defeated. I want to believe that everything we've gone through hasn't been for nothing.

I know you don't trust me—yet. Perhaps your friend Trik can help with that, if she can bear to tell you our story. I think she has probably figured out who I am by now, and I hope she can forgive me for not dropping by and saying hello. Bear, too, should tell you how he found himself in the Keep and, perhaps, you should tell them about the Hot Halls War, and all that you experienced in it. We are all here for a reason, Sophie, but until we all know each other, know each other TRULY, and know how we got here, we'll never be able to do what the Mother needs us to do.

There's no more time for secrets, or false names, or subterfuge. It's time that we know each other's stories; the long and painful and uncomfortable stories of how we ended up in the Keep, here at the end—and beginning—of everything.

This is all I have time for. I hope you survived, and I hope that, somehow, you survived it with your friends and your spirit intact. I am sorry I was not able to help more. This has been the longest night of MY life, too—and it's not over yet.

You need to find the Giant's Prison, Sophie, and I have some reason to believe that you—and only you—can do that. Or, at least, that you can find it before any of the rest of these bastard motherfuckers can. That's what I have to hope, anyway.

It's kind of nice, having some hope after so long without it. I hope you have found some, too.

Well, I have to go. If my girlfriend doesn't murder me for all this, I'll see you soon.

And then we'll see if we can't, finally, do some actual fucking good.

———

Sophie slowed to a stop, and raised her eyes. Trik's brown ones met hers.

"He signed his name." She handed the letter to Trik, whose dark eyes searched the bottom of the letter. Then she slumped, seeing the signature. A complicated expression crossed her face, and then she laughed. "Fuckin' goddamn," Trik said. "I should have known."

"So you know the Consort?" Sophie said, picking up the flask. Trik laughed again, helplessly.

"Yeah, I know that son of a bitch."

"He seems to think there's some hope," Sophie observed. "Seems to think that maybe everything isn't a waste. That maybe we're not as useless as we seem. Reminds me of someone else, actually; blonde girl. Fetching scars. Hope she's still alive." Sophie blew out a breath, and focused on Trik. "So." She lifted an eyebrow. "Can we trust him?"

Trik nodded, slowly. She met Sophie's eye. "If you can trust me, Sophie, I think you can trust him."

Sophie considered for a long moment, and then the corners of her eyes crinkled. She gestured with Hunker John's flask, and the surviving Killers held their little paper cups out. She poured the remaining spirit into them; a finger's width. It didn't matter; she wasn't trying to get drunk. It's just that some rituals were strong. Some rituals were important.

"Well, the thing is," she said, finally, "I do trust you, Trik. And you, Bear.

Maybe I shouldn't, after tonight. I don't know. Maybe we need to tell each other some stories. I don't know about that, either. But I trust you. I just can't help it."

"Sophie is a lot of things," Ben said, sniffing at his little cup and wincing at the odor, "but an inconstant friend ain't one of them."

Sophie grinned at him. "Learned it from you, motherfucker."

Ben grinned back. For this short moment, all of the hurts and betrayal and pain and losses of this long night were forgotten. For one moment, Sophie had a drink in her hand, and her friends by her side. The rest could wait. Slowly, she lifted her cup, and they followed suit.

She met each of their eyes. "It doesn't feel right, for anyone other than Hunker John to say it. But maybe . . . let's drink to him. The little fucker; I don't care what he did right now. I'm going to miss him. No matter what happens after this, no matter what we do, I'm going to miss him."

"Me too," Bear said. He lifted his cup a little higher. "But we know what he would say, right?"

"Of course," Trik said, wiping a tear from her eye. She looked around the little circle, and then at Sophie. She grinned.

"Killers, unite!"

THE CONSORT

In the End, a Beginning

"If you have fallen in love with the question, beware: The answer will be its death."

—CORAZON LI, 'THE FUNDAMENTAL SORCERIES'

He walked through an abandoned part of the Keep, whistling. He couldn't have said why, really; he just felt free. Felt freer than he had in years, in fact! Freer than he had in goddamn *years*. He felt free like the fuckin' . . . *Shit*. Whatever the things were called. Long ago and worlds away, those little creatures that had flitted around in the sky.

In the *sunshine*. Something he hadn't seen in a real long time now, but he remembered. Oh, he remembered!

In any case, he felt *free*.

He didn't know why. He wasn't really introspective in that way. Perhaps it was simply because, after so many years of subterfuge, of cross-purposes, of trying to learn the true shape of things, it was all too late. Everything was in motion, now. He had played his cards; he'd done his best. The chips, as they used to say back in his old world, would fall where they may.

Would Jane kiss him and forgive him, when she saw him next? Or would she run three feet of watered steel through his guts? Who knew? It was too late; she had already been betrayed. The deed was done. His girlfriend was not a famously forgiving type of person.

Oh well. The pain would come later; just now, he was whistling.

He wondered if Sophie had read his letter; he was already a little embarrassed about it. So pretentious, so maudlin! He knew that one of the Killers, at least, would be rolling her eyes halfway to heaven once she read it. He smiled, a little, thinking of her expression. God, he missed her. It had been so hard, staying out of her way, not letting her catch sight of him, not letting her suspect that he was back in the Keep. It had been hard, but necessary.

He understood her desire to take a new name, but why *Trik?* It was an odd choice. "Bear" he understood—James D'Essan was a big man, and vicious when cornered. But why his old friend had taken the name "Trik" still mystified him. Maybe Sophie had given it to her, and she liked it. But to him, forever and always, she would only be Jackie Aimes.

Surely she must know who he was by now. He wondered if she was angry at him. He couldn't blame her if she was. When they'd parted ways, twenty years ago, he hadn't known if he would ever see her again. When he'd thrown his sword into the depths of the Dead Lake at the end of the Hot Halls War, and she'd cast her bloody walking stick away.

"It all got fucked up, Gun," she'd said, tears in her eyes and blood on her hands. *"It all got so fucked up. And we have to make it good."*

And they had, he thought. Or tried to. Each in their own ways. Jackie, by promising to protect the young hero named Sophie Vesachai. First, from afar, and then as one of her gang, one of her *Killers.* Him, by walking into the big dark, alone, and looking for answers. Well, he'd found some. Oh, he had *found some,* all right!

Jackie's walking stick clicked on the old stone as he made his way down the seldom-used passageway in a seldom-used part of the Keep. It had taken him a long time to find the walking stick, but he had, eventually. He was looking forward to giving it back to her. She'd never finished carving it. And it was time to finish things.

Gun and Jackie had a lot of things to finish. And finally, after twenty years of waiting, of preparation, it was time to finish them.

He stopped whistling; he was getting close to his destination. There was still so much to do! But it felt good, after so much planning, for the pieces to be in place. The parts to be in motion. He remembered the sight—was it only yesterday?—of Jane Guin lifting his sword up over her head, smiling one of her rare, genuine smiles.

He remembered the sight of his girlfriend's long fingers wrapped around the corded hilt of the sword. *His* sword.

He didn't know how long it had taken her to excavate the damn thing, to dig it up from the bottom of the Dead Lake, to pump all that water out. Hell, he didn't even know how she'd known it was down there. But now she had it, and all of the forces that had been waiting, biding their time, laying their plans and preparing for that moment, all kicked into gear at once.

The Sword—*Gun's* sword, that piece of cheap steel that had been brought through a Black Portal and turned into something that could destroy—or save— a world. The one thing the Mother needed above all else. The thing that she had called across worlds; hell, had called into Gun's *dreams,* to get.

He hadn't lied, in that letter to Sophie. This was the endgame. Everything was finally here, all the threads converged, all the stories reached the same place. Where finally—*finally*—the fate of the Wanderlands could be decided.

And Gun wanted the one who decided to be Sophie Vesachai, that young hero who had her victory twisted so cruelly from her, that damaged woman who had somehow still held on to a tiny sliver of the girl she had been, and the dream she had once had.

He thought that *she* should be the one to decide it. She was the only one, out of all of the Children of the Dream, who hadn't compromised themselves, who hadn't betrayed themselves—and the dream—too deeply to be trusted with the decision. Gods, he hoped she survived this long night. He hoped that, somehow, once she knew the truth about her friends, and how they had all ended up in the Keep, she could still trust them, and rely on them, and command them.

The world needs weapons, indeed. And Gun hoped, in a humble sort of way, that it still needed him. But he knew for fuck's *sure* sake that it needed Sophie.

He had reached his destination. He paused for a moment before going in; he would need his wits for this one. Of all the tasks Gunnar Anderson had tried to accomplish on this long night, this one might be the most important. And the most difficult.

He cracked his neck and gripped his borrowed walking stick tighter. But weapons wouldn't help him, here. He shook his head, stopped sandbagging, and walked into the room.

It was a prison cell; half of the room was separated from the other half by thick silver bars. Those wouldn't stop someone like Gun, but they were plenty strong enough to keep the person inside contained.

He wasn't chained, but then he didn't really need to be. He wasn't strong, or at least not like Gun was. He stood, though, hands clasped behind his back, and watched Gun with an almost insectile intensity. His eyes were strange. His body bore the scars of severe trauma, and he was missing the smallest finger of one hand. Gun set the walking stick aside. He made himself meet the man's eyes.

He lifted up the silvery pendant, the Key, that this man—and his little protégé, Lee Vesachai—had tried so hard to procure tonight. The man's bizarre eyes fastened onto it like a viper tracking prey.

"Hello, Candle," Gun said. "I think it's time we talked, don't you?"

Candle smiled, very slowly. A coughing, clacking sound came from his throat, and he opened his mouth. Gun knew what to expect, but it was still a gruesome sight.

Chris D'Essan's tongue had been roughly cut out a long time ago. Just about twenty years ago, in fact, near the end of the Hot Halls War. The clacking sound was the man laughing. But Gun felt words form in his head, like distant thunder, with an oppressive weight like the coming of a storm. It was the same kind of weight that had once driven him to try to kill his best friend Jackie, on a pitch-black mountain, so long ago.

<Yes, Gunnar Anderson? What do we need to talk about?>

Gun gave him a look. "You know what *about*, asshole. We need to talk about what we did, twenty years ago. You and me, and all the rest of our bloody Cabal. We need to talk about what happened to *Winter*."

THE MONSTERS

A Grand Adventure Awaits Those Brave Enough to Sign on the Dotted Line

"If you ask me why I did it, if you just absolutely need a reason, well then I only have one answer—and I think it's the best reason. I was fucking bored."

—ALYS, 'A CONFESSION'

"Damn," Jackie said, looking out into the big darkness that lay beyond Cannoux-Town, the lower slopes of the mountain.

"Yeah," Gun said, expelling a large breath. He was studying Jackie. "*Damn.* What do you think?"

Jackie waffled. "It was a pretty good speech. That Winter lady knows how to talk, that's for sure."

"Yeah, but what do you *think?*"

Jackie grinned. "I think it sounds pretty fuckin' sweet, Gunnar."

They had begged the imposing woman with the dark hair for a moment to discuss between themselves, and then they retired to the gloom beyond the fire, leaving behind the merry band of new friends: Candle and Primary Gray and Mr. Turpentine and Winter. They found a balcony that overlooked the lights of Cannoux-Town, well out of earshot, to have their conversation.

"It does sound pretty sweet," Gun admitted. "Fuckin . . . Giants? C'mon. That's awesome."

"It's *totally* awesome," Jackie said. "And these fuckers make good drinks, too."

"God, yes. *Chûs*, or whatever? Gimme a *bucketful.*"

"And I gotta say, it might be nice to have a little company. We spent a fair bit of time alone, and some new friends . . ."

"Preaching to the choir, Aimes." Gun considered. "That lady ain't half bad-looking, neither."

"Hey yo!" Jackie chucked him in the shoulder. "You *dog.* I thought I saw you glancing."

"Can't keep looking at your skinny ass," Gun said, grinning. "So . . . I mean, are we gonna do it? Are we gonna go with them, join their little 'Cabal'?"

"I dunno, man." Jackie sighed. "What do you think? I'm powerful tempted, I'm not gonna lie. I'm tired of this fuckin' dark."

"Me too," Gun said. For a moment the two just looked out into the night, contemplating having new friends, especially friends who could make good drinks. But finally Gun shuffled and looked at Jackie sidelong, and cleared his throat.

"I mean . . . I'm almost embarrassed to have to say it out loud, but . . ."

Jackie made a shooing, get-it-over-with gesture. "Go on."

"Just so we're on the same page, I mean," Gun said, "I—"

"Spit it out, Gunnar!"

"These people are completely full of shit, right?"

"Of course," Jackie said. *"Completely."*

"Like," Gun went on, "they're definitely the same people that have been attacking us this whole time. With the Feral Children and the mental shit. And they obviously sent those metal crab things at us."

"Clearly," Jackie said. "I mean even the timing is just bonkers. I'd be offended that they think we're so stupid, but . . ."

"But," Gun made a weighing motion with his palms out, as if judging between two similarly weighted options, "on the other hand, *good drinks.*"

"Good drinks." Jackie laughed, an easy sound. "Hell, man, I don't know. It's something to fucking *do*, right?"

"It's something to do," Gun agreed. He nudged her. "Besides, that one dude is pretty cute, right? The magic man with the weird eyes?"

"Oh, stop." Jackie grinned. "But I do tend to like the damaged ones."

"Sleeping with the enemy! I'll take the robot guy."

"Pfsh," Jackie said. "You're gonna bang Ms. Leader Lady so hard."

"She is flirty! Got the sparkle in her eye." They watched the lights of Cannoux twinkle in the darkness. Gun grimaced. "But really. Are we really gonna go with them? It ain't smart. They tried to kill us. Several times now."

"Yeah," Jackie said, sobering. "I know."

They were quiet, frowning into the darkness for a minute.

Gun lifted a finger. "*Failed*, though."

"Couldn't do it!" Jackie snapped her fingers. "I think they threw everything they had at us, and we still shrugged it off."

"I didn't exactly shrug it off." Gun rubbed his bruised ribs. "But I know what you're saying. Couldn't kill us no matter how hard they tried. That's something, right?"

"Maybe we got one of those 'if you can't beat 'em, join 'em' situations going on," Jackie agreed.

"Yeah," Gun said. "But—"

"Yeah, I know. I don't exactly think these are the good guys, right?" Jackie asked, looking back over her shoulder at the group of strange folk around the fire. "Except maybe the robot dude, he seems all right. And the kid."

"You got a soft spot for kids," Gun said. "But that one's weird. I dunno if *any* of them are good guys. Or, hell, bad guys either. We don't know shit about this place, and everybody we met so far either fuckin' tried to kill us or lied to us."

"Or both."

"Or both," Gun agreed. He sighed. He looked out into the big darkness again, as if to find answers there. "But man, I gotta say . . ."

"Yeah. I'm about *this* far away from talking to rocks, man. If these fuckers can stop trying to murder us long enough for me to have a decent conversation . . ."

"Yeah. And maybe, you know, even if they *are* the bad guys, we can just ditch 'em once we meet the *good* guys."

"True!" Jackie said, brightly. "And . . ."

"Yeah?"

"Well, the dream. The fucking *Giant*. That was the whole point of all this, right? Why you went searching for your sword. Why *all this happened*. I mean, that's where they're going, right? To kill the fuckin' big bad ol' Giant?"

"Yeah," Gun said. "Maybe we can finally get this goddamn adventure started."

Jackie looked at her friend, an impish grin growing on her face. Gun tried to stay stern, but he failed. He grinned back.

"So we're doing it?" Jackie asked.

"*Fuck* yeah we're doing it," Gun said. "Ain't like they can really hurt us, right?"

"Indestructible badasses," Jackie agreed. She elbowed him in the shoulder, companionably. "Besides, it's like we said. Comes down to it, it's just you and me, man."

"Against the world," Gun promised. He looked at Jackie. Jackie looked at Gun. She grinned.

"Here's to adventure, Gun."

"Fuck yeah, Jacks. Here's to *adventure*."

A ROUND OF APPLAUSE,
A ROUND OF SHOTS

Good artists borrow, great artists steal . . . but hacks write homage.

To that end, I have to acknowledge the giants that came before, and who I shamelessly stole from: King, certainly, and his supremely strange Dark Tower, Swanwick with the incomparable *Stations of the Tide*. Simmons, of course—*Endymion* over *Hyperion* (leave your angry comments below), and Williams with the imaginative masterclass that was Otherland. Cook, with the lumbering dread of the Black Company, and Bujold, who reminded me that heavy themes can *also* be fun. I aped Stephenson's style, borrowed a sense of scale from Nihei's *Blame!*, and bombed rails of Coheed and Cambria while I was doing it. I got my last name from Le Guin. I stole the name 'The Deader' from a Two Gallants song. I read Miéville's Bas-Lag novels every time I started running dry on ideas, and McCaffrey showed me that it's okay to mix science and dragons. I've never been brave enough to attempt footnotes, but I tried as hard as I could to channel Clarke's dry humor. To Farmer, whose *To Your Scattered Bodies Go* is probably the backbone of this world, I can only say this: *I'm sorry*. And to Donaldson, whose Thomas Covenant, Terisa, and Morn taught me to love frustrating and flawed heroes, I can only say this: *Thanks*.

This book is my homage to all of you. I stole with good intentions.

I started writing—not this book, exactly, but exploring the place that I would eventually name The Wanderlands—over thirty years ago. To make a list of all the folks who helped, supported, and inebriated me during that time would be impossible and not a little silly; hopefully you know who you are and I will thank you in person. There are some, however, that must be named lest I am hounded into many cold hells: Phia, for one, who got me through one of the toughest years and will always prefer Original Flavor Sophie; my cousins James and Derek, to whom the Lost Boys owe no small amount of inspiration and who relentlessly forced me to get out of the house and actually live this life. Diana, who was an ardent cheerleader of the book and Len, who read almost as many versions as he bought me beers during the lean times. Sian, who has kept me sane and offered safe harbor for nearly fifteen years now. Dan, my writing partner-in-crime, who might be the most encouraging person that has ever lived and who taught me the meaning of perseverance. Jenna, who believed in this book from the first and has not only read every version (we're talking scores here) but also listened to me ramble drunkenly about twistcraft and offered sage advice too many times to count. And Shawn; my oldest friend, who would park his car outside of a diner and listen as I fumblingly tried to describe this place that was growing in my head, who has never failed to have my back and who has gotten me into and back out of some of the most outrageous shit you can possibly imagine.

I'll see you all at the yacht party.

A book like this doesn't get on the page without some blood and sweat—and not just mine. I am incredibly lucky to have found my agent, Matt Bialer, who was the first and best champion of this book and instrumental in it finding its true shape, and my editor Betsy Wollheim, a legend and for good reason; if you were able to make sense of this tangled monstrosity of a story, you can thank her. I must also thank the brilliant editorial work of Christine Herman, Leah Spann, Bailey Tamayo, Daniel Cohen, and Jenna Fournier. Much debt to the teams at DAW, Astra, and Sanford Greenburger (whom I'm still getting to know and love). Two special mentions are needed, however; Marylou Capes-Platt, who must have risked her own sanity trying to line edit this spiky behemoth of a book, and Christine, who found me in the slush and was the very first professional person in my life that said . . . Hey! Maybe there's something interesting here. This book might EXIST without all of their hard work and care, but it wouldn't be very good.

But also, thanks to you, who is reading this right now, hopefully in Mr. Turpentine's bellows-and-pump voice, that reedy, creepy waver—the one that promises dark adventures in even darker places. I made this place hoping you'd see it someday, and I hope you had fun exploring the Wanderlands.

I sure as fuck did.